N. S. Sinder

# Deadly Pleasures

# Deadly Pleasures

## Three Masterly Detective Novels by

P. D. James

Book-of-the-Month Club
New York

Printed in the United States of America

# CONTENTS

# AUTHOR'S FOREWORD

IT IS A PARTICULAR pleasure to me that the Book-of-the-Month Club is publishing an omnibus of three of my novels. The three chosen, widely different in theme and mood, have one thing in common: in each of them it was the setting which sparked off my creative imagination and gave rise to the novel. One of the questions most often asked of a novelist is, where do you get your ideas? Does the inspiration come from a real-life crime, from an incident you have seen on television or radio or in a newspaper, from a new and original method of murder, or from a character? For me it is nearly always my response to a particular place which excites and inspires me and which sets in motion the long process of creative plotting and planning which results at last in a novel. After the setting the characters begin to take shape in my mind, followed by the dramatic and often bloody events in which they are caught up.

The actual process of creativity is for me mysterious, as I suspect it is for many novelists. The novel must be meticulously plotted and planned and the characters must come alive for me as breathing, vulnerable human beings before I begin the actual writing. This process of getting in touch with my characters usually takes many months. It is as if the people and their story already exist in some limbo of my imagination and my task as a writer is to get their story down in black and white, a process of revelation rather than of creation.

*The Black Tower* had its genesis when I visited the Purbeck coast of Dorset in Southern England and stood beneath the high cliffs of black shale looking out over a boulder-strewn beach to the turbulent sea. *The Black Tower* is among the most sombre of my novels in setting and plot. The scene of the action—Toynton Grange, a cliff-top home for the young permanently disabled—presents any novelist with themes of loss, regret and despair which are essentially tragic. In the book Adam Dalgliesh, recovering from a serious illness, receives a call for advice from his godfather, Father Baddeley, an elderly priest who is acting as chaplain to Toynton Grange. Dalgliesh travels to Dorset to see him but on his arrival discovers that his friend has died and that his body has been cremated. But this isn't the only death. A patient at Toynton Grange has suffered a violent end, apparently by his own hand, and this tragedy and an uneasy sense of impending disaster loom over the isolated community. Three more deaths are to follow before Dalgliesh is able to unravel the mystery of Toynton Grange.

The setting for *Death of an Expert Witness* is very different: the flat fens of East Anglia stretching unbroken to the cold North Sea. This is a part of England with which I have been familiar from my childhood years in Cambridge. The novel is centred on a forensic science laboratory staffed by scientific experts whose job it is to examine exhibits from scenes of crime. But now murder comes closer to home. The unpopular senior forensic pathologist, Dr. Edwin Lorrimer, is found murdered in his laboratory and Commander Dalgliesh is called from London to the lonely and sinister fens to investigate one of the most unusual and puzzling cases of his career.

*The Skull Beneath the Skin* features my girl private eye, Cordelia Gray, who made her first appearance in *An Unsuitable Job for a Woman*. The setting which inspired the novel is Brownsea Island in Poole Harbour on the South Coast of England. The island is small but very beautiful with a castle originally built in the reign of Henry VIII. Cordelia is engaged for an assignment which is intriguing but not particularly arduous. The actress Clarissa Lisle has been receiving poison-pen messages threatening her death and her husband is anxious that these should be deflected until after her appearance as Duchess of Malfi in a small private theatre on Courcy Island. No one, including the police, believes that Clarissa Lisle is in real danger. But once on the island it soon becomes apparent that her secret enemy is one of the company, and Cordelia finds herself involved in a case as dangerous as it is mysterious. The history of the island and its castle are stained with treachery and death and the horrors of the past impinge on the present. Clarissa's fears turn out to be justified and of the group of people who spend the night before the play in Courcy Castle, three are destined never to leave the island alive.

In all these three novels the setting is a closed community: a home for the disabled, a forensic science laboratory, a castle on an island. A closed community has a particular attraction for the mystery writer. Apart from its fascination as a microcosm of the wider world outside, the closed community helps limit the stain of suspicion which cannot be allowed to spread too far if each suspect is to be a living, credible human being, rather than a cardboard stereotype to be perfunctorily knocked down in the final chapter. The closed community can be a hotbed of intrigue, jealousy or dislike, emotions which can erupt into the ultimate crime. All three of these stories are written within the well-known conventions of the traditional mystery: a mysterious death, a closed circle of suspects, a detective, either amateur or professional, who comes in rather like an avenging deity to solve the crime, and a solution at the end of the novel which the reader should have been able to arrive at by logical deduction from clues which may be deceptive but should also be essentially fair.

One of the criticisms of the mystery is that it is mere formula writing. But what I find continually fascinating is the extraordinary variety of books and talents which this so-called formula is able to accommodate, and how many writers have found the conventions of the mystery liberating rather than inhibiting of their creative imagination. For over thirty years it has been my aim as a novelist to work within these conventions and to use them to say something true about men and women and the society in which they live. I hope that in these three very different novels I have succeeded and that my readers will find them as enjoyable to read as they were for me to write.

—P. D. James
1996

# The Black Tower

# BOOK ONE

•

# Sentence of Life

It was to be the consultant physician's last visit and Dalgliesh suspected that neither of them regretted it, arrogance and patronage on one side and weakness, gratitude and dependence on the other being no foundation for a satisfactory adult relationship however transitory. He came into Dalgliesh's small hospital room preceded by Sister, attended by his acolytes, already dressed for the fashionable wedding which he was to grace as a guest later that morning. He could have been the bridegroom except that he sported a red rose instead of the customary carnation. Both he and the flower looked as if they had been brought and burnished to a peak of artificial perfection, gift wrapped in invisible foil, and immune to the chance winds, frosts and ungentle fingers which could mar more vulnerable perfections. As a final touch, he and the flower had both been lightly sprayed with an expensive scent, presumably an aftershave lotion. Dalgliesh could detect it above the hospital smell of cabbage and ether to which his nose had become so inured during the past weeks that it now hardly registered on the senses. The attendant medical students grouped themselves round the bed. With their long hair and short white coats they looked like a gaggle of slightly disreputable bridesmaids.

Dalgliesh was stripped by Sister's skilled impersonal hands for yet another examination. The stethoscope moved, a cold disc, over his chest and back. This last examination was a formality but the physician was, as always, thorough; nothing he did was perfunctory. If, on this occasion, his original diagnosis had been wrong his self-esteem was too secure for him to feel the need for more than a token excuse. He straightened up and said:

"We've had the most recent path. report and I think we can be certain now that we've got it right. The cytology was always obscure, of course, and the diagnosis was complicated by the pneumonia. But it isn't acute leukemia, it isn't any type of leukemia. What you're recovering from—happily—is an atypical mononucleosis. I congratulate you, Commander. You had us worried."

"I had you interested; you had me worried. When can I leave here?"

The great man laughed and smiled at his retinue, inviting them to share his indulgence at yet one more example of the ingratitude of convalescence. Dalgliesh said quickly:

"I expect you'll be wanting the bed."

"We always want more beds than we can get. But there's no great hurry. You've a long way to go yet. Still, we'll see. We'll see."

When they had left him he lay flat on his back and let his eyes range round the two cubic feet of anaesthetized space, as if seeing the room for the first time. The wash basin with its elbow-operated taps; the neat functional bedside table with its covered water jug; the two vinyl-covered visitors' chairs; the earphones curled above his head; the window curtains with their inoffensive flowered pattern, the lowest denominator of taste. They were the last objects he had expected to see in life. It had seemed a meagre, impersonal place in which to die. Like a hotel room, it was designed for transients. Whether its occupants left on their own feet or sheeted on a mortuary trolley, they left nothing behind them, not even the memory of their fear, suffering and hope.

The sentence of death had been communicated, as he suspected such sentences usually were, by grave looks, a certain false heartiness, whispered consultations, a superfluity of clinical tests, and, until he had insisted, a reluctance to pronounce a diagnosis or prognosis. The sentence of life, pronounced with less sophistry when the worst days of his illness were over, had certainly produced the greater outrage. It was, he had thought, uncommonly inconsiderate if not negligent of his doctors to reconcile him so thoroughly to death and then change their minds. It was embarrassing now to recall with what little regret he had let slip his pleasures and preoccupations, the imminence of loss revealing them for what they were, at best only a solace, at worst a trivial squandering of time and energy. Now he had to lay hold of them again and believe that they were important, at least to himself. He doubted whether he would ever again believe them important to other people. No doubt, with returning strength, all that would look after itself. The physical life would re-assert itself given time. He would reconcile himself to living since there was no alternative and, this perverse fit of resentment and accidie conveniently put down to weakness, would come to believe that he had had a lucky escape. His colleagues, relieved of embarrassment, would congratulate him. Now that death had replaced sex as the great unmentionable it had acquired its own pudency; to die when you had not yet become a nuisance and before your friends could reasonably raise the ritual chant of "happy release" was in the worst of taste.

But, at present, he wasn't sure that he could reconcile himself to his job. Resigned as he had become to the role of spectator—and soon not even to be that—he felt ill-equipped to return to the noisy playground of the world and, if it had to be, was minded to find for himself a less violent corner of it. It wasn't something he had thought about deeply during his periods of consciousness; there hadn't been time. It was more a conviction than a decision. The time had come to change direction. Judges' Rules, rigor mortis, interrogation, the contemplation of decomposing flesh and smashed bone, the whole bloody business of manhunting, he was finished with it. There were other things to do with his time. He wasn't yet sure which things but he would find them. He had over two weeks of convalescence ahead, time to formulate decision, rationalize it, justify it to himself and, more difficult, find the words with which he would attempt to justify it to the Commissioner. It was a bad time to leave the Yard. They would see it as desertion. But then, it would always be a bad time.

He wasn't sure whether this disenchantment with his job was caused solely by his illness, the salutory reminder of inevitable death, or whether it was the symptom of a more fundamental malaise, that latitude in middle-life of alternate doldrums and uncertain winds when one realizes that hopes deferred are no longer realizable, that ports not visited will now never be seen, that this journey and others before it may have been a mistake, that one has no longer even confidence in charts and compass. More than his job now seemed to him trivial and unsatisfactory. Lying sleepless as so many patients must have done before him in that bleak impersonal room, watching the headlamps of passing cars sweep across the ceiling, listening to the secretive and muted noises of the hospital's nocturnal life, he took the dispiriting inventory of his life. His grief for his dead wife, so genuine, so heartbreaking at the time—how conveniently personal tragedy had excused him from further emotional involvement. His love affairs, like the one which at present spasmodically occupied a little of his time and somewhat more of his energy, had been detached, civilized, agreeable, undemanding. It was understood that his time was never completely his own but that his heart most certainly was. The women were liberated. They had interesting jobs, agreeable flats, they were adept at settling for what they could get. Certainly they were liberated from the messy, clogging, disruptive emotions which embroiled other female lives. What, he wondered, had those carefully spaced encounters, both participants groomed for pleasure like a couple of sleek cats, to do with love, with untidy bedrooms, unwashed dishes, babies' nappies, the warm, close, claustrophobic life of marriage and commitment. His bereavement, his job, his poetry, all had been used to justify self-sufficiency. His women had been more amenable to the claims of his poetry than of his dead wife. They had small regard for sentiment, but an exaggerated respect for art. And the worst of it—or perhaps the best—was that he couldn't now change even if he wanted and that none of it mattered. It was absolutely of no importance. In the last fifteen years he hadn't deliberately hurt a single human being. It struck him now that nothing more damning could be said about anyone.

Well, if none of that could be changed, his job could. But first there was one personal commitment to fulfill, one from which perversely he had been relieved that death would so conveniently excuse him. It wasn't going to excuse him now. Propping himself on his elbow he reached out and took Father Baddeley's letter from his locker drawer and read it carefully for the first time. The old man must be nearly eighty now; he hadn't been young when, thirty years ago, he had first come to the Norfolk village as curate to Dalgliesh's father, timid, ineffective, maddeningly inefficient, muddled in everything but the essentials, but never less than his uncompromising self. This was only the third letter which Dalgliesh had received from him. It was dated 11th September and was addressed from Toynton:

> My dear Adam,
>
> I know that you must be very busy but I would very much welcome a visit from you as there is a matter on which I would be glad of your professional advice. It isn't really urgent, except that my heart seems to be wearing out before the rest of me so that I ought not to rest too confidently on the thought of tomorrow. I am here every day, but perhaps a weekend would suit you best. I ought to tell you so that you will know what to expect, that I am Chaplain to Toynton Grange, a private home for the young disabled, and that I live here in Hope Cottage on the estate through the kindness of the Warden, Wilfred Anstey. Usually I eat my midday and evening meal at the Grange but this may not be agreeable to you and it would, of course, lessen our time together. So I shall take the opportunity of my next visit to Wareham to lay in a store of provisions. I have a small spare room in to which I can move so that there will be a room for you here.
>
> Could you send me a card to let me know when you will arrive? I have no car but if you come by train William Deakin, who has a car hire service about five minutes from the station (the station staff will direct you), is very reliable and not expensive. The buses from Wareham are infrequent and don't come beyond Toynton Village. There is then a mile and a half to walk which is quite pleasant if the weather is good but which you may wish to avoid at the end of a long journey. If not, I have drawn a map on the back of this letter.

The map could be guaranteed to confuse anyone accustomed to depend on the orthodox publications of the National Survey rather than on early seventeenth-century charts. The wavy lines presumably represented the sea. Dalgliesh felt the omission of a spouting whale. The Toynton bus station was clearly marked, but the tremulous line thereafter meandered uncertainly past a diversity of fields, gates, pubs and copses of triangular, serrated firs, sometimes retreating upon itself as Father Baddeley realized that metaphorically he had lost his way. One tiny phallic symbol on the coast, and seemingly included as a landmark, since it was nowhere near the marked path, bore the legend "the black tower."

The map affected Dalgliesh much as a child's first drawing might affect an indulgent father. He wondered to what depth of weakness and apathy he must have sunk to reject its appeal. He fumbled in the drawer for a postcard and wrote briefly that he would arrive by car early in the afternoon of Monday 1st October. That should give him plenty of time to get out of hospital and return to his Queenhythe flat for the first few days of convalescence. He signed the card with his initials only, stamped it for first-class delivery and propped it against his water jug so that he shouldn't forget to ask one of the nurses to post it.

There was one other small obligation and one he felt less competent to handle. But it could wait. He must see or write to Cordelia Gray and thank her for her flowers. He didn't know how she discovered that he was ill except perhaps through police friends. Running Bernie Pryde's Detective Agency—if it hadn't by now collapsed as it should have done by all the laws of justice and economics—probably meant that she was in touch with one or two policemen. He believed too, that there had been a casual mention of his inconvenient illness in the London evening papers when they had commented on recent losses in the higher echelons of the Yard.

It had been a small, carefully arranged, personally picked bouquet, as individual as Cordelia herself, a charming contrast to his other offerings of hothouse roses, over-large chrysanthemums shaggy as dust mops, forced spring flowers and artificial-looking gladioli, pink plastic flowers smelling of anaesthetic rigid on their fibrous stems. She must have been recently in a country garden; he wondered where. He wondered too, illogically, whether she was getting enough to eat, but immediately put this ridiculous thought from him. There had, he remembered clearly, been silver discs of honesty, three sprigs of winter heather, four rosebuds, not the starved tight buds of winter but furls of orange and yellow, gentle as the first buds of summer, delicate sprigs of outdoor chrysanthemums, orange-red berries, one bright dahlia like a jewel in the center, the whole bouquet surrounded by the grey furry leaves he remembered from his childhood as rabbits' ears. It had been a touching, very young gesture, one he knew that an older or more sophisticated woman would never have made. It had arrived with only a brief note to say that she had heard of his illness and had sent the flowers to wish him well again. He must see or write to her and thank her personally. The telephone call which one of the nurses had made on his behalf to the Agency was not enough.

But that, and other more fundamental decisions, could wait. First he must see Father Baddeley. The obligation was not merely pious or even filial. He discovered that, despite certain foreseen difficulties and embarrassments, he was looking forward to seeing the old priest again. He had no intention of letting Father Baddeley, however unwittingly, entice him back to his job. If this were really police work, which he doubted, then the Dorset Constabulary could take it over. And, if this pleasant early autumn sunshine continued unbroken, Dorset would be as agreeable a place as any in which to convalesce.

But the stark oblong of white, propped against his water jug, was oddly intrusive. He felt his eyes constantly drawn towards it as if it were a potent symbol, a written sentence of life. He was glad when the staff nurse came in to say that she was now going off duty, and took it away to post.

# BOOK TWO

·

# Death of a Priest

# I

Eleven days later, still weak and with his hospital pallor but euphoric with the deceptive well-being of convalescence, Dalgliesh left his flat high above the Thames at Queenhythe just before the first light and drove southwest out of London. He had finally and reluctantly parted with his ancient Cooper Bristol two months before the onset of his illness and was now driving a Jensen Healey. He was glad that the car had been run in and that he was already almost reconciled to the change. To embark symbolically on a new life with a totally new car would have been irritatingly banal. He put his one case and a few picnic essentials including a corkscrew in the boot and, in the pocket, a copy of Hardy's poems, *The Return of the Native* and Newman and Pevsner's guide to the buildings of Dorset. This was to be a convalescent's holiday: familiar books; a brief visit to an old friend to provide an object for the journey; a route left to each day's whim and including country both familiar and new; even the salutary irritant of a personal problem to justify solitude and self-indulgent idleness. He was disconcerted when, taking his final look round the flat, he found his hand reaching for his scene-of-crime kit. He couldn't remember when last he had travelled without it, even on holiday. But now to leave it behind was the first confirmation of a decision which he would dutifully ponder from time to time during the next fortnight but which he knew in his heart was already made.

He reached Winchester in time for late breakfast at a hotel in the shadow of the Cathedral, then spent the next two hours rediscovering the city before finally driving into Dorset via Wimborne Minster. Now he sensed in himself a reluctance to reach journey's end. He meandered gently, almost aimlessly, north-west to Blandford Forum, bought there a bottle of wine, buttered rolls, cheese and fruit for his lunch and a couple of bottles of Amontillado for Father Baddeley, then wandered southeast through the Winterbourne villages through Wareham to Corfe Castle.

The magnificent stones, symbols of courage, cruelty and betrayal, stood sentinel at the one cleft in the ridge of the Purbeck Hills as they had for a thousand years. As he ate his solitary picnic, Dalgliesh found his eyes constantly drawn to those stark embattled slabs of mutilated ashlar silhouetted high against the gentle sky. As though reluctant to drive under their shadow and unwilling to end the solitude of this peaceful undemanding day he spent some time searching unsuccessfully for marsh gentians in the swampy scrubland before setting off on the last five miles of his journey.

Toynton Village; a thread of terraced cottages, their undulating grey stone roofs glittering in the afternoon sun; a not too picturesque pub at the village end; the glimpse of an uninteresting church tower. Now the road, bordered with a low stone wall, rose gently between sparse plantations of fir and he began to recognize the landmarks on Father Baddeley's map. Soon the road would branch, one narrow route turning westward to skirt the headland, the other leading through a barrier gate to Toynton Grange and the sea. And here, predictably, it was, a heavy iron gate set into a wall of flat, uncemented stones. The wall was up to three feet thick, the stones intricately and skilfully fitted together, bound with lichen and moss and crowned with waving grasses, and it formed a barrier as old and permanent as the headland from which it seemed to have grown. On each side of the gate was a notice painted on board. The one on the left was the newer; it read:

OF YOUR CHARITY PLEASE RESPECT OUR PRIVACY

The one on the right was more didactic, the lettering faded but more professional.

KEEP OUT
THIS LAND IS STRICTLY PRIVATE
DANGEROUS CLIFFS NO ACCESS TO BEACH
CARS AND CARAVANS PARKED HERE WILL BE MOVED

Under the notice was fixed a large postbox.

Dalgliesh thought that any motorist unmoved by this nicely judged mixture of appeal, warning and threats would hesitate before risking his car springs. The track deteriorated sharply beyond the gate and the contrast between the comparative smoothness of the approach road and the boulder edged and stony way ahead was an almost symbolic deterrent. The gate, too, although unlocked, had a heavy latch of intricate design, the manipulation of which gave an intruder ample time in which to repent of his rashness. In his still weakened state, Dalgliesh swung back the gate with some difficulty. When he had driven through and finally closed it behind him it was with a sense of having committed himself to an enterprise as yet imperfectly understood and probably unwise. The problem would probably be embarrassingly unrelated to any of his skills, something that only an unworldly old man—and he perhaps getting senile—could have imagined that a police officer could solve. But at least he had an immediate objective. He was moving, even if reluctantly, back into a world in which human beings had problems, worked, loved, hated, schemed for happiness, and since the job he had determined to relinquish would go on despite his defection, killed and were killed.

Before he turned again to the car his eye was caught by a small clump of unknown flowers. The pale pinkish white heads rose from a mossy pad on top of the wall and trembled delicately in the light breeze. Dalgliesh walked over and stood stock still, regarding in silence their unpretentious beauty. He smelt for the first time the clean half-illusory salt tang of the sea. The air moved warm and gentle against his skin. He was suddenly suffused with happiness and, as always in these rare transitory moments, intrigued by the purely physical nature of his joy. It moved along his veins, a gentle effervescence. Even to analyse its nature was to lose hold of it. But he recognized it for what it was, the first clear intimation since his illness that life could be good.

The car bumped gently over the rising track. When some two hundred yards further on he came to the summit of the rise he expected to see the English Channel spread blue and wrinkled before him to the far horizon and experienced all the remembered disappointment of childhood holidays when after so many false hopes, the eagerly awaited sea still wasn't in sight. Before him was a shallow rock-strewn valley, criss-crossed with rough paths, and to his right what was obviously Toynton Grange.

It was a powerfully built square stone house dating, he guessed, from the first half of the eighteenth century. But the owner had been unlucky in his architect. The house was an aberration, unworthy of the name of Georgian. It faced inland, north-east he estimated, thus offending against some personal and obscure canon of architectural taste which, to Dalgliesh, decreed that a house on the coast should face the sea. There were two rows of windows above the porch, the main ones with gigantic keystones, the row above unadorned and mean in size as if there had been difficulty in fitting them beneath the most remarkable feature of the house, a huge Ionic pediment topped by a statue, a clumsy and, at this distance, unidentifiable lump of stone. In the centre was one round window, a sinister cyclops eye glinting in the sun. The pediment debased the insignificant porch and gave a lowering and cumbersome appearance to the whole façade. Dalgliesh thought that the design would have been more successful if the façade had been balanced by extended bays, but either inspiration or money had run out and the house looked curiously unfinished. There was no sign of life behind the intimidating frontage. Perhaps the inmates—if that was the right word for them—lived at the back. And it was only just three-thirty, the dead part of the day as he remembered from hospital. Probably they were all resting.

He could see three cottages, a pair about a hundred yards from the Grange and a third standing alone higher on the foreland. He thought there was a fourth roof just visible to seaward, but couldn't be sure. It might be only an excrescence of rock. Not knowing which was Hope Cottage it seemed sensible to make first for the nearer pair. He had briefly turned off his car engine while deciding what next to do and now, for the first time, he heard the sea, that gentle continuous rhythmic grunt which is one of the most nostalgic and evocative of sounds. There was still no sign that his approach was observed; the headland was silent, birdless. He sensed something strange and almost sinister in its emptiness and loneliness which even the mellow afternoon sunlight couldn't dispel.

His arrival at the cottages produced no face at the window, no cassock-clad figure framed in the front porch. They were a pair of old, limestone single-storeyed buildings, whose heavy stone roofs, typical of Dorset, were patterned with bright cushions of emerald moss. Hope Cottage was on the right, Faith Cottage on the left, the names comparatively recently painted. The third more distant cottage was presumably Charity, but he doubted whether Father Baddeley had had any hand in this eponymous naming. He didn't need to read the name on the gate to know which cottage housed Father Baddeley. It was impossible to associate his remembered almost total uninterest in his surroundings with those chintzy curtains, that hanging basket of trailing ivy and fuchsia over the door of Faith Cottage or the two brightly painted yellow tubs still garish with summer flowers which had been artfully placed one each side of the porch. Two mushrooms, looking mass-produced in concrete, stood each side of the gate seeming so cosily suburban that Dalgliesh was surprised that they weren't crowned with squatting gnomes. Hope Cottage, in contrast, was starkly austere. There was a solid oak bench in front of the window serving as a seat in the sun, and a conglomeration of sticks and an old umbrella littered the front porch. The curtains, apparently of some heavy material in a dull red, were drawn across the windows.

No one answered to his knock. He had expected no one. Both cottages were obviously empty. There was a simple latch on the door and no lock. After a second's pause he lifted it and stepped into the gloom inside to be met with a smell, warm, bookish, a little musty, which immediately took him back thirty years. He drew back the curtains and light streamed into the cottage. And now his eyes recognized familiar objects: the round single-pedestal rosewood table, dull with dust, set in the middle of the room; the roll-top desk against one wall; the high-backed and winged armchair, so old now that the stuffing was pushing through the frayed cover and the dented seat was worn down to the wood. Surely it couldn't be the same chair? This stab of memory must be a nostalgic delusion. But there was another object, equally familiar, equally old. Behind the door hung Father Baddeley's black cloak with, above it, the battered and limp beret.

It was the sight of the cloak that first alerted Dalgliesh to the possibility that something was wrong. It was odd that his host wasn't here to greet him, but he could think of a number of explanations. His postcard might have gone astray, there might have been an urgent call to the Grange, Father Baddeley might have gone into Wareham to shop and missed the return bus. It was even possible that he had completely forgotten the expected arrival of his guest. But if he were out, why wasn't he wearing his cloak? It was impossible to think of him in summer or winter wearing any other garment.

It was then that Dalgliesh noticed what his eye must have already seen but disregarded, the little stack of service sheets on top of the bureau printed with a black cross. He took the top one over to the window as if hoping that a clearer light would show him mistaken. But there was, of course, no mistake. He read:

Michael Francis Baddeley, Priest
Born 29th October 1896 Died 21st September 1974
R.I.P. Buried at St. Michael & All Angels,
Toynton, Dorset
26th September 1974

He had been dead eleven days and buried five. But he would have known that Father Baddeley had died recently. How else could one account for that sense of his personality still lingering in the cottage, the feeling that he was so close that one strong call could bring his hand to the latch? Looking at the familiar faded cloak with its heavy clasp—had the old man really not changed it in thirty years?—he felt a pang of regret, of grief even, which surprised him by its intensity. An old man was dead. It must have been a natural death; they had buried him quickly enough. His death and burial had been unpublicized. But there had been something on his mind and he had died without confiding it. It was suddenly very important that he should be reassured that Father Baddeley had received his postcard, that he hadn't died believing that his call for help had gone unregarded.

The obvious place to look was in the early Victorian bureau which had belonged to Father Baddeley's mother. Father Baddeley, he remembered, had kept this locked. He had been the least secretive of men, but any priest had to have at least one drawer or desk private from the prying eyes of cleaning women or overcurious parishioners. Dalgliesh could remember Father Baddeley fumbling in the deep pockets of his cloak for the small antique key, secured by string to an old-fashioned clothes peg for easier handling and identification, which opened the lock. It was probably in one of the cloak pockets still.

He dug his hand into both pockets with a guilty feeling of raiding the dead. The key wasn't there. He went over to the bureau and tried the lid. It opened easily. Bending down he examined the lock, then fetched his torch from the car and looked again. The signs were unmistakable: the lock had been forced. It had been quite a neat job and one requiring little strength. The lock was decorative but unsubstantial, intended as a defense against the idly curious but not against determined assault. A chisel or knife, probably the blade of a penknife, had been forced between the desk and the lid and used to pry the lock apart. It had done surprisingly little damage, but the scratch marks and the broken lock itself told their story.

But not who had been responsible. It could have been Father Baddeley himself. If he had lost the key there would have been no chance of replacing it, and how in this remote spot would he have found a locksmith? A physical assault on the desk lid was an unlikely expedient for the man, Dalgliesh remembered; but it wasn't impossible. Or it might have been done after Father Baddeley's death. If the key couldn't be found, someone at Toynton Grange would have had to break open the lock. There might have been documents or papers which they needed; a health insurance card; names of friends to be notified; a will. He shook himself free from conjecture, irritated to find that he had actually considered putting on his gloves before looking further, and made a rapid examination of the contents of the desk drawers.

There was nothing of interest there. Father Baddeley's concern with the world had apparently been minimal. But one thing immediately recognizable caught his eye. It was a neatly stacked row of quarto-size child's exercise books bound in pale green. These, he knew, contained Father Baddeley's diary. So the same books were still being sold, the ubiquitous pale green exercise books, the back cover printed with arithmetical tables, as evocative of primary school as an ink-stained ruler or india rubber. Father Baddeley had always used these books for his diary, one book for each quarter of the year. Now, with the old black cloak hanging limply on the door, its musty ecclesiastical smell in his nose, Dalgliesh recalled the conversation as clearly as if he were still that ten-year-old boy and Father Baddeley, middle-aged then but already seeming ageless, sitting here at his desk.

"It's just an ordinary diary then, Father? It isn't about your spiritual life?"

"This is the spiritual life; the ordinary things one does from hour to hour."

Adam had asked with the egotism of the young.

"Only what you do? Aren't I in it?"

"No. Just what I do. Do you remember what time the Mothers' Union met this afternoon? It was your mother's drawing-room this week. The time was different, I think."

"It was 2:45 P.M. instead of 3:00 P.M., Father. The Archdeacon wanted to get away early. But do you have to be accurate?"

Father Baddeley had seemed to ponder this question, briefly but seriously as if it were new to him and unexpectedly interesting.

"Oh, yes, I think so. I think so. Otherwise it would lose its point."

The young Dalgliesh, to whom the point was already lost beyond ken, had wandered away to pursue his own more interesting and immediate concerns. The spiritual life. It was a phrase he had often heard on the lips of his father's more ultra mundane parishioners although never on the Canon's own. He had occasionally tried to visualize this mysterious other existence. Was it lived at the same time as the ordinary regulated life of getting up, meal times, school, holidays; or was it an existence on some other plane to which he and the uninitiated had no access but into which Father Baddeley could retreat at will? Either way it had surely little to do with this careful recording of daily trivia.

He picked up the last book and looked through it. Father Baddeley's system had not been changed. It was all here, two days to the page, neatly ruled off. The times at which he had daily said morning prayer and evensong; where he had walked and how long it had taken; the monthly trip by bus into Dorchester; the weekly trip to Wareham; his hours spent helping at Toynton Grange; odd treats badly recorded; the methodical account of how he had disposed of every hour of his working day year after unremarkable year, documented with the meticulousness of a book-keeper. "But this is the spiritual life; the ordinary things that one does from day to day." Surely it couldn't be as simple as that?

But where was the current diary, the book for the third quarter of 1974? It had been Father Baddeley's habit to keep old copies of his diary covering the last three years. There should have been fifteen books here; there were only fourteen. The diary stopped at the end of June 1974. Dalgliesh found himself searching almost feverishly through the desk drawers. The diary wasn't there. But he did find something. Pushed beneath three receipted bills for coal, paraffin and electricity was a sheet of cheap rather thin paper with Toynton Grange printed inexpertly and lopsidedly at the top. Underneath someone had typed:

"Why don't you get out of the cottage you silly old hypocrite and let someone have it who would really be some use here? Don't think we don't know what you and Grace Willison get up to when you're supposed to be hearing her confession. Don't you wish you could really do it? And what about that choir boy? Don't think we don't know."

Dalgliesh's first reaction was to be more irritated by the note's silliness than angered by its malice. It was a childish piece of gratuitous spite but without even the dubious merit of verisimilitude. Poor old seventy-seven-year-old Father Baddeley, accused simultaneously of fornication, sodomy and impotence! Could any reasonable man have taken this puerile nonsense seriously enough even to be hurt by it? Dalgliesh had seen plenty of poison pen letters in his professional life. This was a comparatively mild effort; he could almost suppose that the writer's heart hadn't been in it. "Don't you wish you could really do it?" Most poison pen writers could find a more graphic description of that implied activity. And the belated reference to the choir boy, no name, no date. That hadn't been dredged from any real knowledge. Could Father Baddeley really have been concerned enough to have sent for a professional detective and one he hadn't seen for nearly thirty years just to advise on or investigate this petty nastiness? Perhaps. This might not be the only letter. If the trouble were endemic at Toynton Grange, then it was more serious. A poison pen at work in a closed community could cause real trouble and distress, occasionally he or she could literally be a killer. If Father Baddeley suspected that others had received similar letters he might well have looked around for professional help. Or, and this was more interesting, had someone intended Dalgliesh to believe precisely that? Had the note been deliberately planted for him to find? It was odd, surely, that no one had discovered and destroyed it after Father Baddeley's death. Someone from Toynton Grange must have looked through his papers. This was hardly a note one would leave for others to read.

He folded it away in his wallet and began to wander around the cottage. Father Baddeley's bedroom was much as he had expected. A mean window with a dingy cretonne curtain, a single bed still made-up with sheets and blankets but with the counterpane pulled taut over the single lumpy pillow; books lining two walls; a small bedside table with a shoddy lamp; a Bible; a cumbersome and gaudily decorated china ashtray bearing an advertisement for beer. Father Baddeley's pipe still rested in its bowl and beside it Dalgliesh saw a half-used booklet of cardboard matches, the kind given away in restaurants and bars. This bore an advertisement for Ye Olde Tudor Barn near Wareham. One single used match was in the ashtray; it had been shredded down to the burnt-out tip. Dalgliesh smiled. So this small personal habit, too, had survived over thirty years. He could recall Father Baddeley's small squirrel-like fingers delicately shredding the sliver of thin cardboard as if attempting to beat some previous personal record. Dalgliesh picked up the match and smiled; six segments. Father Baddeley had excelled himself.

He wandered into the kitchen. It was small, ill-equipped, neat but not very clean. The small gas stove of old-fashioned design looked as if it would soon qualify for a folk museum. The sink under the window was of stone fitted on one side with a scarred and discolored wooden draining board smelling of stale fat and sour soap. The faded cretonne curtains faintly patterned with overblown roses and daffodils unseasonably intertwined were pulled back to show an inland view of the far Purbeck hills. Clouds tenuous as smoke puffs were drifting and dissolving in the limitless blue sky and the sheep lay like white slugs on their distant pasture.

He explored the pantry. Here at least was evidence that he was expected. Father Baddeley had indeed bought extra food and the tins were a dispiriting reminder of what for him had constituted an adequate diet. Pathetically, he had obviously provided for two, one of whom he confidently expected to have a larger appetite. There was one large tin and one small of many of the staple provisions: baked beans, tuna fish, Irish stew, spaghetti, rice pudding.

Dalgliesh went back to the sitting-room. He was aware of weariness, that the journey had tired him more than he had expected. He saw by the heavy oak clock over the fireplace still ticking solidly on, that it was still not four o'clock, but his body protested that this had already been a long hard day. He craved tea. There had been a caddy of tea in the pantry but no milk. He wondered whether the gas was still on.

It was then that he heard the footfall at the door, the clank of the latch. There was a woman's figure framed against the afternoon light. He heard a gravelly deep but very feminine voice with a trace, no more, of an Irish accent.

"For God's sake! A human being and a male at that. What are you doing here?"

She came into the room leaving the door open behind her and he saw her clearly. She was about thirty-five, he guessed, sturdy, long-legged, her mane of yellow hair, visibly darker at the roots, worn in a long sweep to her shoulders. Her eyes were full-lidded and narrow in the square face, her mouth wide. She was wearing brown ill-fitting slacks with a strap under the foot, dirty, grass-stained white plimsoles and a sleeveless white cotton top, low-necked, which showed a brown and mottled triangle of sunburn. She wore no brassiere and the full, heavy breasts swung loose under the thin cotton. Three wooden bangles clanked on her left forearm. The total impression was of a raffish but not unattractive sexuality, so strong that, although she wore no scent, she brought into the room her own female and individual smell.

He said: "My name's Adam Dalgliesh. I came here intending to visit Father Baddeley. It seems that it won't now be possible."

"Well, that's one way of putting it. You're exactly eleven days late. Eleven days too late to see him and five days too late to bury him. Who are you, a chum? We didn't know that he had any. But then, there were quite a number of things we didn't know about our Reverend Michael. He was a secretive little man. He certainly kept you hidden."

"We hadn't met except briefly since I was a boy and I only wrote to tell him I was coming the day before he died."

"Adam. I like that. They call a lot of kids that nowadays. It's getting trendy again. But you must have found it a bit of a drag when you were at school. Still, it suits you. I can't think why. You aren't exactly of the earth, earthy are you? I know about you now. You've come to collect the books."

"Have I?"

"The ones Michael left you in his will. To Adam Dalgliesh, only son of the late Canon Alexander Dalgliesh, all my books to keep or dispose of as he sees fit. I remember it exactly because I thought the names were so unusual. You haven't lost much time, have you? I'm surprised that the solicitors have even got round to writing to you. Bob Loder isn't usually that efficient. But I shouldn't get too excited if I were you. They never looked particularly valuable to me. A lot of dry old theological tomes. By the way, you weren't expecting to be left any of his money were you? If so, I've got news for you."

"I didn't know that Father Baddeley had any money."

"Nor did we. That was another of his little secrets. He left £19,000. Not a great fortune, but useful. He left it all to Wilfred for the benefit of Toynton Grange, and it came just in time from all I hear. Grace Willison is the only other legatee. She got that old bureau. At least she will get it when Wilfred bothers to have it moved."

She had settled down in the fireside chair, her hair thrown back against the headrest, both legs splayed wide. Dalgliesh pulled out one of the wheel-backed chairs and sat facing her.

"Did you know Father Baddeley well?"

"We all know each other well here, that's half our trouble. Are you thinking of staying here?"

"In the district perhaps for a day or two. But it doesn't seem possible now to stay here . . ."

"I don't see why not if you want to. The place is empty, at least until Wilfred finds another victim—tenant, I should say. I shouldn't think that he'd object. Besides you'll have to sort out the books won't you? Wilfred will want them out of the way before the next incumbent moves in."

"Wilfred Anstey owns the cottage then?"

"He owns Toynton Grange and all the cottages except Julius Court's. He's further out on the headland, the only one with a sea view. Wilfred owns all the rest of the property and he owns us."

She looked at him appraisingly.

"You haven't any useful skills, have you? I mean you're not a physiotherapist or a male nurse or a doctor, or even an accountant? Not that you look like one. Anyway, if you are I'd advise you to keep away before Wilfred decides that you're too useful to let go."

"I don't think that he'd find my particular skills of much use."

"Then I should stay on if it suits you. But I'd better put you in the picture. You might then change your mind."

Dalgliesh said:

"Start with yourself. You haven't told me who you are."

"Good God, nor have I! Sorry. I'm Maggie Hewson. My husband is resident medical officer at the Grange. At least, he lives with me in a cottage provided by Wilfred and appropriately named Charity Cottage, but he spends most of his time at Toynton Grange. With only five patients left you'd wonder what he finds to amuse him. Or would you? What do you suppose he finds to amuse him, Adam Dalgliesh?"

"Did your husband attend Father Baddeley?"

"Call him Michael, we all did except Grace Willison. Yes, Eric looked after him when he was alive and signed the death certificate when he died. He couldn't have done that six months ago, but now that they've graciously restored him to the Medical Register he can actually put his name to a piece of paper to say that you're properly and legally dead. God, what a bloody privilege."

She laughed, and fumbling in the pocket of her slacks produced a packet of cigarettes and lit one. She handed the packet to Dalgliesh. He shook his head. She shrugged her shoulders and blew a puff of smoke towards him.

Dalgliesh asked:

"What did Father Baddeley die of?"

"His heart stopped beating. No, I'm not being facetious. He was old, his heart was tired and on 21st September it stopped. Acute myocardic infarction complicated by mild diabetes, if you want the medical jargon."

"Was he alone?"

"I imagine so. He died at night, at least he was last seen alive by Grace Willison at 7:45 P.M. when he heard her confession. I suppose he died of boredom. No, I can see I shouldn't have said that. Bad taste, Maggie. She says he seemed as usual, a bit tired of course, but then he'd only been discharged from hospital that morning. I came in at nine o'clock the next day to see if he wanted anything from Wareham—I was taking the eleven o'clock bus; Wilfred doesn't allow private cars—and there he lay, dead."

"In bed?"

"No, in that chair where you're sitting now, slumped back with his mouth open and his eyes closed. He was wearing his cassock and a purple ribbon thing round his neck. All quite seemly. But very, very dead."

"So it was you who first found the body?"

"Unless Millicent from next door came pussy-footing in earlier, didn't like the look of him and tiptoed home again. She's Wilfred's widowed sister in case you're interested. Actually, it's rather odd that she didn't come in, knowing that he was ill and alone."

"It must have been a shock for you."

"Not really. I was a nurse before I married. I've seen more dead bodies than I can remember. And he was very old. It's the young ones—the kids particularly—who get you down. God, am I glad to be finished with all that messy business."

"Are you? You don't work at Toynton Grange then?"

She got up and moved over to the fireplace before replying. She blew a cloud of smoke against the looking glass over the mantelpiece then moved her face close to the glass as if studying her reflection.

"No, not when I can avoid it. And by God, do I try to avoid it. You may as well know. I am the delinquent member of the community, the non-co-operator, the drop-out, the heretic. I sow not, neither do I reap. I am impervious to the charms of dear Wilfred. I close my ears to the cries of the afflicted. I do not bend the knee at the shrine."

She turned towards him with a look half challenging, half speculative. Dalgliesh thought that the outburst had been less than spontaneous, the protest had been made before. It sounded like a ritual justification and he suspected that someone had helped her with the script. He said:

"Tell me about Wilfred Anstey."

"Didn't Michael warn you? No, I suppose he wouldn't. Well, it's an odd story but I'll try to make it short. Wilfred's great grandfather built Toynton Grange. His grandfather left it in trust jointly to Wilfred and his sister Millicent. Wilfred bought her out when he started the Home. Eight years ago Wilfred developed multiple sclerosis. It progressed very swiftly; within three months he was chairbound. Then he went on a pilgrimage to Lourdes and got himself cured. Apparently he made a bargain with God. You cure me and I'll devote Toynton Grange and all my money to serving the disabled. God obliged, and now Wilfred's busy fulfilling his part of the bargain. I suppose he's afraid to back out of the agreement in case the disease returns. I don't know that I blame him. I'd probably feel the same myself. We're all superstitious at heart, particularly about disease."

"And is he tempted to back out?"

"Oh, I don't think so. This place gives him a sensation of power. Surrounded by grateful patients, regarded as a half-superstitious object of veneration by the women, Dot Moxon—the matron so-called—fussing round him like an old hen. Wilfred's happy enough."

Dalgliesh asked:

"When exactly did the miracle happen?"

"He claims, when they dipped him in the well. As he tells it, he experienced an initial shock of intense cold followed immediately by a tingling warmth which suffused his whole body, and a feeling of great happiness and peace. That's exactly what I get after my third whisky. If Wilfred can produce it in himself by bathing in ice cold germ-laden water, then all I can say is, he's bloody lucky. When he got back to the hospice he stood on his legs for the first time in six months. Three weeks later he was skipping around like a young ram. He never bothered to return to St. Saviour's hospital in London where he was treated, so that they could record the miraculous cure on his medical record. It would have been rather a joke if he had."

She paused as if about to say something further and then merely added:

"Touching, isn't it?"

"It's interesting. How does he find the money to fulfil his part of the bargain?"

"The patients pay according to means and some of them are sent here under contractual arrangements by local authorities. And then, of course, he's used his own capital. But things are getting pretty desperate, or so he claims. Father Baddeley's legacy came just in time.

And, of course, Wilfred gets the staff on the cheap. He doesn't exactly pay Eric the rate for the job. Philby, the odd job man, is an ex-convict and probably otherwise unemployable; and the matron, Dot Moxon, wouldn't exactly find it easy to get another job after that cruelty investigation at her last hospital. She must be grateful to Wilfred for taking her on. But then, we're all terribly, terribly grateful to dear Wilfred."

Dalgliesh said:

"I suppose I'd better go up to the Grange and introduce myself. You say there are only five patients left?"

"You're not supposed to refer to them as patients, although I don't know what else Wilfred thinks you can call them. Inmates sounds too much like a prison although, God knows, it's appropriate enough. But there are only five left. He's not admitting from the waiting list until he's made up his mind about the Home's future. The Ridgewell Trust's angling for it and Wilfred's considering handing the whole place over to them, lock, stock and gratis. Actually, there were six patients a fortnight or so ago, but that was before Victor Holroyd threw himself over Toynton Head and smashed himself on the rocks."

"You mean he killed himself?"

"Well, he was in his wheelchair ten feet from the cliff-edge and either he slipped the brakes and let himself be carried over or Dennis Lerner, the male nurse with him, pushed him. As Dennis hasn't the guts to kill a chicken let alone a man the general feeling is that Victor did it himself. But as that notion is distressing to dear Wilfred's feelings we're all busy pretending that it was an accident. I miss Victor, I liked him. He was about the only person here I could talk to. But the rest hated him. And now, of course, they've all got bad consciences wondering if they may have misjudged him. There's nothing like dying for putting people at a disadvantage. I mean, when a chap keeps on saying that life isn't worth living you take it that he's just stating the obvious. When he backs it up with action you begin to wonder if there wasn't more to him than you thought."

Dalgliesh was spared the need to reply by the sound of a car on the headland. Maggie, whose ears were apparently as keen as his own, sprang from her chair and ran outside. A large black saloon was approaching the junction of the paths.

"Julius," Maggie called back to him in brief explanation and began a boisterous semaphoring.

The car stopped and then turned towards Hope Cottage. Dalgliesh saw that it was a black Mercedes. As soon as it slowed down Maggie ran like an importunate schoolgirl beside it, pouring her explanation through the open window. The car stopped and Julius Court swung himself lightly out.

He was a tall, loose-limbed young man dressed in slacks and a green sweater patched army fashion on the shoulders and elbows. His light brown hair, cut short, was shaped to his head like a pale glinting helmet. It was an authoritative, confident face but with a trace of self-indulgence in the perceptible pouches under the wary eyes and the slight petulance of the small mouth set in a heavy chin. In middle age he would be heavy, even gross. But now he gave an immediate impression of slightly arrogant good looks, enhanced rather than spoilt by the white triangular scar like a colophon above his right eyebrow.

He held out his hand and said:

"Sorry you missed the funeral."

He made it sound as if Dalgliesh had missed a train. Maggie wailed:

"But darling, you don't understand! He hasn't come for the funeral. Mr. Dalgliesh didn't even know that the old man had snuffed out."

Court looked at Dalgliesh with slightly more interest.

"Oh, I'm sorry. Perhaps you'd better come up to the Grange. Wilfred Anstey will be able to tell you more about Father Baddeley than I. I was at my London flat when the old man died so I can't even provide interesting death bed revelations. Hop in both of you. I've got some books in the back for Henry Carwardine from the London Library. I may as well deliver them now."

Maggie Hewson seemed to feel that she had been remiss in not effecting a proper introduction; she said belatedly:

"Julius Court. Adam Dalgliesh. I don't suppose you've come across each other in London. Julius used to be a diplomat, or is it diplomatist?"

As they got into the car Court said easily:

"Neither is appropriate at the comparatively lowly level I reached in the service. And London is a large place. But don't worry, Maggie, like the clever lady in the TV panel game, I think I can guess what Mr. Dalgliesh does for a living."

He held open the car door with elaborate courtesy. The Mercedes moved slowly towards Toynton Grange.

## II

Georgie Allan looked up from the high narrow bed in the sick bay. His mouth began to work grotesquely. The muscles of his throat stood out hard and taut. He tried to raise his head from the pillow.

"I'll be all right for the Lourdes pilgrimage won't I? You don't think I'll be left behind?"

The words came out in a hoarse, discordant wail. Helen Rainer lifted up the edge of the mattress, tucked the sheet neatly back into place in the orthodox hospital approved style and said briskly:

"Of course you won't be left behind. You'll be the most important patient on the pilgrimage. Now stop fretting, that's a good boy, and try to rest before your tea."

She smiled at him, the impersonal, professionally reassuring smile of the trained nurse. Then lifted her eyebrow at Eric Hewson. Together they went over to the window. She said quietly:

"How long can we go on coping with him?"

Hewson replied:

"Another month or two. It would upset him terribly to have to leave now. Wilfred too. In a few months' time both of them will be readier to accept the inevitable. Besides, he's set his heart on his Lourdes trip. Next time we go I doubt whether he will be alive. He certainly won't be here."

"But he's really a hospital case now. We aren't registered as a nursing home. We're only a home for the young chronic sick and disabled. Our contract is with the local authorities not the National Health Service. We don't pretend to offer a full medical nursing service. We aren't even supposed to. It's time Wilfred either gave up or made up his mind what he's trying to do here."

"I know." He did know, they both did. This wasn't a new problem. Why, he wondered, had so much of their conversation become a boring repetition of the obvious, dominated by Helen's high didactic voice.

Together they looked down at the small paved patio, bordered by the two new single-storey wings which contained the bedrooms and dayrooms, where the little group of remaining patients had gathered for the last sit in the sun before tea. The four wheelchairs were carefully placed a little apart and faced away from the house. The two watchers could see only the back of the patients' heads. Unmoving, they sat looking fixedly toward the headland. Grace Willison, her grey untidy hair ruffled by the light breeze: Jennie Pegram, her neck sunk into her shoulders, her aureole of yellow hair streaming over the back of her wheelchair as if bleaching in the sun; Ursula Hollis's small round poll on its thin neck, high and motionless as a decapitated head on a pole; Henry Carwardine's dark head on its twisted neck, slumped sideways like a broken puppet. But then, they were all puppets. Dr. Hewson had a momentary and insane picture of himself rushing on to the patio and setting the four heads nodding and wagging, pulling invisible strings at the back of the necks so that the air was filled with their loud, discordant cries.

"What's the matter with them?" he asked suddenly. "Something's wrong about this place."

"More than usual?"

"Yes. Haven't you noticed?"

"Perhaps they're missing Michael. God knows why. He did little enough. If Wilfred's determined to carry on here he can find a better use for Hope Cottage now. As a matter of fact, I thought about suggesting that he let me live there. It would be easier for us."

The thought appalled him. So that was what she had been planning. The familiar depression fell on him, physical as a lead weight. Two positive, discontented women, both wanting something that he couldn't give. He tried to keep the panic from his voice.

"It wouldn't do. You're needed here. And I couldn't come to you at Hope Cottage, not with Millicent next door."

"She hears nothing once she's switched on the TV. We know that. And there's a back door if you do have to make a quick get-a-way. It's better than nothing."

"But Maggie would suspect."

"She suspects now. And she's got to know some time."

"We'll talk about it later. It's a bad time to worry Wilfred just now. We've all been on edge since Victor died."

Victor's death. He wondered what perverse masochism had made him mention Victor. It reminded him of those early days as a medical student when he would uncover a suppurating wound with relief because the sight of blood, inflamed tissue and pus was so less frightening than the imagination of what lay beneath the smooth gauze. Well, he had got used to blood. He had got used to death. In time he might even get used to being a doctor.

They moved together into the small clinical room at the front of the building. He went to the basin and began methodically sluicing his hands and forearms as if his brief examination of young Georgie had been a messy surgical procedure requiring a thorough cleansing. Behind his back he could hear the clink of instruments. Helen was unnecessarily tidying the surgical cupboard yet once more. With a sinking heart he realized that they were going to have to talk. But not yet. Not yet. And he knew what she would say. He had heard it all before, the old insistent arguments spoken in that confident school prefect's voice. "You're wasted here. You're a doctor, not a dispensing chemist. You've got to break free, free of Maggie and Wilfred. You can't put loyalty to Wilfred before your vocation." His vocation! That was the word his mother had always used. It made him want to break into hysterical laughter.

He switched on the tap to full and the water came gushing out, swirling round the basin, filling his ears like the sound of the incoming tide. What had it been like for Victor, that hurtle into oblivion? Had the clumsy wheelchair, heavy with its own momentum, sailed into space like one of those ridiculous flying contraptions in a James Bond film, the little manikin secure among his gadgets, ready to pull the lever and sport wings? Or had it twisted and tumbled through the air, bouncing off the rock face, with Victor coffined in canvas and metal, flailing impotent arms, adding his screams to the cry of the gulls? Had his heavy body broken free of the strap in mid-air, or had the canvas held until that final annihilating crash against the flat iron rocks, the first sucking wave of the relentless unthinking sea? And what had been in his mind? Exaltation or despair, terror or a blessed nothingness? Had the clean air and the sea wiped it all away, the pain, the bitterness, the malice?

It was only after his death that the full extent of Victor's malice had been known, in the codicil to his will. He had taken trouble to let the other patients know that he had money, that he paid the full fee at Toynton Grange, modest though that was, and wasn't, as were all the others except Henry Carwardine, dependent upon the benevolence of a local authority. He had never told them the source of his wealth—he had, after all, been a schoolmaster and they were hardly well paid—and they still didn't know. He might have told Maggie of course. There were a number of things he might have told Maggie. But on this she had been unaccountably silent.

Eric Hewson didn't believe that Maggie had taken an interest in Victor simply because of the money. They had, after all, had something in common. They had both made no secret that they hated Toynton Grange, that they were there of necessity not of choice, that they despised their companions. Probably Maggie found Victor's rebarbative malice to her liking. They had certainly spent a great deal of time together. Wilfred had seemed almost to welcome it, almost as if he thought Maggie was at last finding her proper place at Toynton. She had taken her turn at wheeling Victor in his heavy chair to his favorite spot. He had found some kind of peace in sight of the sea. Maggie and he had spent hours together, out of sight of the house, high on the edge of the cliff. But it hadn't worried him. He knew, none better, that Maggie could never love a man who couldn't satisfy her physically. He welcomed the friendship. At least it gave her something to occupy her time, kept her quiet.

He couldn't remember exactly when she had begun to become excited about the money. Victor must have said something. Maggie had changed almost overnight. She had become animated, almost gay. There had been a kind of feverish and suppressed excitement about her. And then Victor had suddenly demanded that he be driven to London for an examination at St. Saviour's Hospital and to consult his solicitor. It was then that Maggie had hinted to him about the will. He had caught something of her excitement. He wondered now what either of them had hoped for. Had she seen the money as a release merely from Toynton Grange, or also from him? Either way, surely, it would have brought salvation for them both. And the idea wasn't absurd. It was known that Victor had no relatives except a sister in New Zealand to whom he never wrote. No, he thought, reaching for the towel and beginning to dry his hands, it hadn't been an absurd dream; less absurd than the reality.

He thought of that drive back from London; the warm, enclosed world of the Mercedes; Julius silent, his hands resting lightly on the wheel; the road a silver reel punctuated with stars slipping endlessly under the bonnet; road signs leaping out of darkness to pattern the blue-black sky; small petrified animals, fur erect, briefly glorified in the headlamps; the road verges drained pale gold in their glare. Victor had sat with Maggie in the back, wrapped in his plaid cloak and smiling, always smiling. And the air had been heavy with secrets, shared and unshared.

Victor had indeed altered his will. He had added a codicil to the bequest which left the whole of his fortune to his sister, a final testimony of petty malice. To Grace Willison, a bar of toilet soap; to Henry Carwardine, a mouthwash; to Ursula Hollis, body deodorant; to Jennie Pegram, a toothpick.

Eric reflected that Maggie had taken it very well. Really very well indeed; if you could call that wild, ringing, uncontrolled laughter taking it well. He recalled her now, reeling about their small stone sitting-room, helpless with hysteria, throwing back her head and baying out her laughter so that it echoed harshly back from the walls, like a menagerie, and rang out over the headland so that he was afraid they would hear it as far as Toynton Grange.

Helen was standing by the window. She said, her voice sharp:

"There's a car outside Hope Cottage."

He walked over to her. Together they looked out. Slowly their eyes met. She took his hand, and her voice was suddenly gentle, the voice he had heard when they had first made love.

"You've got nothing to worry about, darling. You know that, don't you? Nothing to worry about at all."

# III

Ursula Hollis closed her library book, shut her eyes against the afternoon sun and entered into her private daydream. To do so now in the brief fifteen minutes before teatime was an indulgence, and quick as always to feel guilt at so ill-disciplined a pleasure, she was at first afraid that the magic wouldn't work. Usually, she made herself wait until she was in bed at night, wait even until Grace Willison's rasping breath, heard through the unsubstantial partition, had gentled into sleep before she allowed herself to think of Steve and the flat in Bell Street. The ritual had become an effort of will. She would lie there hardly daring to breathe because the images, however clearly conjured up, were so sensitive, so easily dispelled. But now it was happening beautifully. She concentrated, seeing the amorphous shapes and the changing patterns of color focus into a picture, clearly as a developing negative, tuning in her ears to the sounds of home.

She saw the brick wall of the nineteenth-century house opposite with the morning sun lighting its dull façade so that each brick was individually distinct, multi-colored, a pattern of light. The pokey two-roomed flat above Mr. Polanski's delicatessen, the street outside, the crowded heterogeneous life of that square mile of London between Edgware Road and Marylebone Station had absorbed and enchanted her. She was back there now, walking again with Steve through Church Street market on Saturday morning, the happiest day of the week. She saw the local women in their flowered overalls and carpet slippers, heavy wedding rings sunk into their bulbous toil-scarred fingers, their eyes bright in amorphous faces, as they sat gossiping beside their prams of second-hand clothes; the young people, joyfully garbed, squatting on the kerbstone behind their stalls of bric-à-brac; the tourists cheerfully impulsive or cautious and discerning by turns, conferring over their dollars or displaying their bizarre treasures. The street smelt of fruit, flowers and spice, of sweating bodies, cheap wine and old books. She saw the black women with their jutting buttocks and high barbaric staccato chatter, heard their sudden deep-throated laughter, as they crowded round the stall of huge unripe bananas and mangoes as large as footballs. In her dreams she moved on, her fingers gently entwined with Steve's like a ghost passing unseen down familiar paths.

The eighteen months of her marriage had been a time of intense but precarious happiness, precarious because she could never feel that it was rooted in reality. It was like becoming another person. Before, she had taught herself contentment and had called it happiness. After, she realized that there was a world of experience, of sensation, of thought even, for which nothing in those first twenty years of life in the Middlesbrough suburb, or the two and a half years in the Y.W.C.A. hostel in London, had prepared her. Only one thing marred it, the fear which she could never quite suppress that it was all happening to the wrong person, that she was an imposture of joy.

She couldn't imagine what it was about her that had so capriciously caught Steve's fancy that first time when he had called at the enquiry desk in the Council offices to ask about his rates. Was it the one feature which she had always thought of as close to a deformity; the fact that she had one blue and one brown eye? Certainly it was an oddity which had intrigued and amused him, had given her, she realized, an added value in his eyes. He had changed her appearance, making her grow her hair shoulder length, bringing home for her long gaudy skirts in Indian cotton found in the street markets or the shops in the back streets of Edgware Road. Sometimes, catching a glimpse of herself in a shop window, so marvellously altered, she would wonder again which strange predilection had led him to choose her, what possibilities undetected by others, unknown to herself, he had seen in her. Some quality in her had caught his eccentric fancy as did the odd items of bric-à-brac on the Bell Street stalls. Some object, unregarded by the passers-by, would catch his eye and he would turn it to the light this way and that in the palm of his hand, suddenly enchanted. She would make a tentative protest.

"But darling, isn't it rather hideous?"

"Oh, no, it's amusing. I like it. And Mogg will love it. Let's buy it for Mogg."

Mogg, his greatest and, she sometimes thought, his only friend, had been christened Morgan Evans but preferred to use his nickname, regarding it as more appropriate to a poet of the people's struggle. It was not that Mogg struggled greatly himself; indeed Ursula had never met anyone who drank and ate so resolutely at other people's expense. He chanted his confused battle cries to anarchy and hatred in local pubs where his hairy and sad-eyed followers listened in silence or spasmodically banged the table with their beer mugs amid grunts of approval. But Mogg's prose style had been more comprehensible. She had read his letter only once before returning it to the pocket in Steve's jeans, but she could recall every word. Sometimes she wondered whether he had intended her to find it, whether it was fortuitous that he had forgotten to clear out the pockets of his jeans on the one evening when she always took their dirty clothes to the washeteria. It was three weeks after the hospital had given her a firm diagnosis.

"I would say I told you so except that this is my week for abjuring platitudes. I prophesized disaster, but not total disaster. My poor bloody Steve! But isn't it possible for you to get a divorce? She must have had some symptoms before you married. You can—or could—get a divorce for V.D. existing at the time of marriage and what's a dose of clap compared with this? It astounds me, the irresponsibility of the so-called establishment about marriage. They bleat about its sanctity, about protecting it as a staple foundation of society, and then let people acquire a wife with less physical check-up than they would give to a second-hand car. Anyway, you do realize that you must break free don't you? It will be the end of you if you don't. And don't take refuge in the cowardice of compassion. Can you really see yourself wheeling her invalid chair and wiping her bottom? Yes, I know some men do it. But you never did get much of a kick out of masochism did you? Besides, the husbands who can do that know something about loving, and even you, my darling Steve, wouldn't presume to claim that. By the way, isn't she an R.C.? As you married in a Registry Office I doubt whether she considers herself properly married at all. That could be a way out for you. Anyway, see you in the Paviours Arms, Wednesday 8:00 P.M. I will celebrate your misfortune with a new poem and a pint of bitter."

She hadn't really expected him to wheel her chair. She hadn't wanted him to perform the simplest, least intimate physical service for her. She had learnt very early in their marriage that any illness, even transitory colds and sickness, disgusted and frightened him. But she had hoped that the disease would spread very slowly, that she could continue to manage on her own at least for a few precious years. She had schemed how it might be possible. She would get up early so that he needn't be offended by her slowness and ungainliness. She could move the furniture just a few inches, he probably wouldn't even notice, to provide unobtrusive supports so that she needn't take too quickly to sticks and callipers. Perhaps they could find an easier flat, one on the ground floor. If she could have a front door ramp she could get out in the daytime to do her shopping. And there would still be the nights together. Surely nothing could change those?

But it had quickly become evident that the disease, moving inexorably along her nerves like a predator, was spreading at its own pace, not hers. The plans she had made, lying stiffly beside him, distanced in the large double bed, willing that no spasm of muscle should disturb him, had become increasingly unrealistic. Watching her pathetic efforts, he had tried to be considerate and kind. He hadn't reproached her except by his withdrawal, hadn't condemned her growing weakness except by demonstrating his own lack of strength. In her nightmares she drowned; thrashing and choking in a limitless sea, she clutched at a floating bough and felt it sink, sponge soft and rotten, beneath her hands. She sensed morbidly that she was acquiring the propitiatory, simperingly pathetic air of the disabled. It was hard to be natural with him, harder still to talk. She remembered how he used to lie full length on the sofa watching her while she read or sewed, the creature of his selection and creation, draped and celebrated with the eccentric clothes which he had chosen for her. Now he was afraid for their eyes to meet.

She remembered how he had broken the news to her that he had spoken to the medical social worker at the hospital and that there might be a vacancy soon at Toynton Grange.

"It's by the sea darling. You've always liked the sea. Quite a small community too, not one of those huge impersonal institutions. The chap who runs it is very highly regarded and it's basically a religious foundation. Anstey isn't a Catholic himself but they do go regularly to Lourdes. That will please you; I mean that you've always been interested in religion. It's one of the subjects that we haven't really seen eye to eye about. I probably wasn't as understanding about your needs as I ought to have been."

He could afford now to be indulgent of that particular foible. He had forgotten that he had taught her to do without God. Her religion had been one of those possessions that, casually, neither understanding them nor valuing them, he had taken from her. They hadn't really been important to her, those consoling substitutes for sex, for love. She couldn't pretend that she had relinquished them with much of a struggle, those comforting illusions taught in St. Matthew's Primary School, assimilated behind the draped terylene curtains of her aunt's front sitting-room in Alma Terrace, Middlesbrough, with its holy pictures, its photograph of Pope John, its framed papal blessing of her aunt and uncle's wedding. All were part of that orphaned, uneventul, not unhappy childhood which was as remote now as a distant, once-visited alien shore. She couldn't return because she no longer knew the way.

In the end she had welcomed the thought of Toynton Grange as a refuge. She had pictured herself with a group of patients sitting in their chairs in the sun and looking at the sea; the sea, constantly changing but eternal, comforting and yet frightening, speaking to her in its ceaseless rhythm that nothing really mattered, that human misery was of small account, that everything passed in time. And it wasn't, after all, to be a permanent arrangement. Steve, with the help of the local authority social services department, planned to move into a new and more suitable flat; this was only to be a temporary separation.

But it had lasted now for eight months; eight months in which she had become increasingly disabled, increasingly unhappy. She had tried to conceal it since unhappiness at Toynton Grange was a sin against the Holy Ghost, a sin against Wilfred. And for most of the time she thought that she had succeeded. She had little in common with the other patients. Grace Willison, dull, middle-aged, pious. Eighteen-year-old George Allan with his boisterous vulgarity; it had been a relief when he became too ill to leave his bed. Henry Carwardine, remote, sarcastic, treating her as if she were a junior clerk. Jennie Pegram, for ever fussing with her hair and smiling her stupid secret smile. And Victor Holroyd, the terrifying Victor, who had hated her as much as he hated everyone at Toynton Grange. Victor who saw no virtue in concealing unhappiness, who frequently proclaimed that if people were dedicated to the practice of charity they might as well have someone to be charitable about.

She had always taken it for granted that it was Victor who had typed the poison pen letter. It was a letter as traumatic in its way as the one she had found from Mogg. She felt for it now, deep in a side pocket in her skirt. It was still there, the cheap paper limp with much handling. But she didn't need to read it. She knew it now by heart, even the first paragraph. She had read that once, and then had turned the paper over at the top so that the words were hidden. Even to think about them burnt her cheek. How could he—it must be a man surely?—know how she and Steve had made love together, that they had done those particular acts and in that way? How could anyone know? Had she, perhaps, cried out in her sleep, moaning her need and her longing? But, if so, only Grace Willison could possibly have heard from the adjoining bedroom, and how could she have understood?

She remembered reading somewhere that obscene letters were usually written by women, particularly by spinsters. Perhaps it hadn't been Victor Holroyd after all. Grace Willison, dull, repressed, religious Grace. But how could she have guessed what Ursula had never admitted to herself?

"You must have known you were ill when you married him. What about those tremors, the weakness in your legs, the clumsiness in the mornings? You knew you were ill, didn't you? You cheated him. No wonder he seldom writes, that he never visits. He's not living alone, you know. You didn't really expect him to stay faithful, did you?"

And there the letter broke off. Somehow she felt that the writer hadn't really come to the end, that some more dramatic and revelationary finish was intended. But perhaps he or she had been interrupted; someone might have come into the office unexpectedly. The note had been typed on Toynton Grange paper, cheap and absorbent and with the old Remington typewriter. Nearly all the patients and staff occasionally typed. She thought she could remember seeing most of them use the Remington at one time or another. Of course, it was really Grace's machine; it was recognized as primarily hers; she used it to type the stencils for the quarterly newsletter. Often she worked alone in the office when the rest of the patients considered that they had finished the working day. And there would be no difficulty in ensuring that it reached the right recipient.

Slipping it into a library book was the surest way of all. They all knew what the others were reading, how could they help it? Books were laid down on tables, on chairs, were easily accessible to anyone. All the staff and patients must have known that she was reading the latest Iris Murdoch. And, oddly enough, the poison letter had been placed at exactly the page which she had reached.

At first she had taken it for granted that this was just a new example of Victor's power to hurt and humiliate. It was only since his death that she had felt these doubts, had glanced surreptitiously at the faces of her fellow inmates, had wondered and feared. But surely this was nonsense? She was tormenting herself unnecessarily. It must have been Victor and, if it were Victor, then there would be no more letters. But how could even he have known about her and Steve; except that Victor did mysteriously know things. She remembered the scene when she and Grace Willison had been sitting with him here in the patients' patio. Grace lifting her face to the sun and wearing that silly, gentle smile had begun to talk of her happiness, about the next Lourdes pilgrimage. Victor had broken in roughly:

"You're cheerful because you're euphoric. It's a feature of your disease, D.S. patients always have this unreasonable happiness and hope. Read the textbooks. It's a recognized symptom. It's certainly no virtue on your part and it's bloody irritating for the rest of us."

She recalled Grace's voice already tremulous with hurt.

"I wasn't claiming happiness as a virtue. But even if it's only a symptom, I can still give thanks for it; it's a kind of grace."

"As long as you don't expect the rest of us to join in, give thanks by all means. Thank God for the privilege of being no bloody use to yourself or anyone else. And while you're about it, thank Him for some of the other blessings of His creation; the millions toiling to get a living out of barren soil swept by flood, burnt by drought; for pot-bellied children; for tortured prisoners; for the whole doomed, bloody, pointless mess."

Grace Willison had protested quietly through the first smart of her tears:

"But Victor, how can you talk like that? Suffering isn't the whole of life; you can't really believe that God doesn't care. You come with us to Lourdes."

"Of course I do. It's the one chance to get out of this boring crack-brained penitentiary. I like movement, I like travel, I like the sight of the sun shining on the Pyrenees, I enjoy the color. I even get some kind of satisfaction from the blatant commercialism of it all, from the sight of thousands of my fellow beings who are more deluded than I."

"But that's blasphemy!"

"Is it? Well, I enjoy that too."

Grace persisted: "If only you would talk to Father Baddeley, Victor. I'm sure that he would help you. Or perhaps to Wilfred. Why not talk to Wilfred?"

He had burst into raucous laughter, jeering but strangely and frighteningly shot through with genuine amusement.

"Talk to Wilfred! My God, I could tell you something about our saintly Wilfred that would give you a laugh, and one day, if he irritates me enough, I probably shall. Talk to Wilfred!"

She thought she could still hear the distant echo of that laughter. "I could tell you something about Wilfred." Only he hadn't told them, and now he never would. She thought about Victor's death. What impulse had led him on that particular afternoon to make his final gesture against fate? It must have been an impulse: Wednesday wasn't his normal day for an outing and Dennis hadn't wanted to take him. She remembered clearly the scene in the patio. Victor, importunate, insistent, exerting every effort of will to get what he wanted. Dennis flushed, sulky, a recalcitrant child, finally giving way but with a poor grace. And so, they had left together for that final walk, and she had never seen Victor again. What was he thinking of when he released those brakes and hurled himself and the chair towards annihilation? Surely it must have been the impulse of a moment. No one could choose to die with such spectacular horror while there were gentler means available. And surely there were gentler means; sometimes she found herself thinking about them, about those two most recent deaths, Victor's and Father Baddeley's. Father Baddeley, gentle, ineffectual, had passed away as if he had never been; his name now was hardly mentioned. It was Victor who seemed to be still among them. It was Victor's bitter uneasy spirit which hung over Toynton Grange. Sometimes, particularly at dusk, she dared not turn her face towards an adjacent wheelchair in case she should see, not the expected occupant, but Victor's heavy figure shrouded in his heavy plaid cloak, his dark sardonic face with its fixed smile like a rictus. Suddenly, despite the warmth of the afternoon sun, Ursula shivered. Releasing the brakes on her chair she turned and wheeled herself towards the house.

# IV

The front door of Toynton Grange was open and Julius Court led the way into a high square hall, oak panelled and with a checkered black and white marble floor. The house struck very warm. It was like passing through an invisible curtain of hot air. The hall smelt oddly; not with the usual institutional smell of bodies, food and furniture polish overlaid with antiseptic, but sweeter and strangely exotic as if someone had been burning incense. The hall was as dimly lit as a church. An impression reinforced by the two front windows of Pre-Raphaelite stained glass one on each side of the main door. To the left was the expulsion from Eden, to the right the sacrifice of Isaac. Dalgliesh wondered what aberrant fancy had conceived that effeminate angel with his curdle of yellow hair under the plumed helmet or the sword embellished with glutinous lozenges in ruby, bright blue and orange with which he was ineffectively barring the two delinquents from an apple orchard Eden. Adam and Eve, their pink limbs tactfully if improbably entwined with laurel, wore expressions respectively of spurious spirituality and petulant remorse. On the right the same angel swooped like a metamorphosized batman over Isaac's bound body, watched from the thicket by an excessively woolly ram whose face, understandably, bore an expression of the liveliest apprehension.

There were three chairs in the hall, bastard contraptions in painted wood covered with vinyl; themselves deformities, one with an unusually high seat, two very low. A folded wheelchair rested against the far wall and a wooden rail was screwed waist high into the panelling. To the right an open door gave a glimpse of what could be a business room or cloakroom. Dalgliesh could see the fold of a plaid cloak hanging on the wall, a pegboard of keys and the edge of a heavy desk. A carved hall table bearing a brass tray of letters and surmounted by a huge fire bell stood to the left of the door.

Julius led the way through a rear door and into a central vestibule from which rose a heavily carved staircase, its banister half cut away to accommodate the metal cage of a large modern lift. They came to a third door. Julius threw it dramatically open and announced:

"A visitor for the dead. Adam Dalgliesh."

The three of them passed into the room together. Dalgliesh, flanked by his two sponsors, had the unfamiliar sensation of being under escort. After the dimness of the front hall and the central vestibule the dining-room was so bright that he blinked. The tall mullioned windows gave little natural light but the room was harshly lit by two tubes of fluorescent lighting incongruously suspended from the moulded ceiling. Images seemed to fuse together and then parted and he saw clearly the inhabitants of Toynton Grange grouped like a tableau round the oak refectory table at tea.

His arrival seemed to have struck them momentarily into silent surprise. Four of them were in wheelchairs, one a man. The two remaining women were obviously staff; one was dressed as a matron except for the customary status symbol of a cap. Without it, she looked curiously incomplete. The other, a fair-haired younger woman, was wearing black slacks and a white smock but succeeded, despite this unorthodox uniform, in giving an immediate impression of slightly intimidating competence. The three able-bodied men all wore dark brown monk's habits. After a second's pause, a figure at the head of the table rose and came with ceremonial slowness towards them with hands held out.

"Welcome to Toynton Grange, Adam Dalgliesh. My name is Wilfred Anstey."

Dalgliesh's first thought was that he looked like a bit-player acting with practised conviction the part of an ascetic bishop. The brown monk's habit suited him so well that it was impossible to imagine him in any other garb. He was tall and very thin, the wrists from which the full woollen sleeves fell away were brown and brittle as autumn sticks. His hair was grey but strong and shaved very short revealing the boyish curve of the skull. Beneath it the thin long face was mottled brown as if the summer tan were fading unevenly; two shining white patches on the left temple had the appearance of diseased skin. It was difficult to guess his age; fifty perhaps. The gentle questioning eyes with their suggestion of other people's suffering meekly borne were young eyes, the blue irises very clear, the whites opaque as milk. He smiled, a singularly sweet lopsided smile spoilt by the display of uneven and discoloured teeth. Dalgliesh wondered why it was that philanthropists so often had a reluctance to visit their dentist.

Dalgliesh held out his hand and felt it imprisoned between Anstey's two palms. It took an effort of will not to flinch from this clammy encounter of moist flesh. He said:

"I had hoped to pay a few days' visit to Father Baddeley. I'm an old friend. I didn't know until I arrived that he was dead."

"Dead and cremated. His ashes were buried last Wednesday in the churchyard of St. Michael's Toynton. We knew that he would wish them to lie in consecrated ground. We didn't announce his death in the papers because we didn't know that he had friends."

"Except us here." It was one of the women patients who added the gentle but firm correction. She was older than the other patients, grey haired and angular as a Dutch doll propped in her chair. She looked at Dalgliesh steadily with kind and interested eyes.

Wilfred Anstey said:

"Of course. Except us here. Grace was, I think, closer to Michael than anyone else and was with him on the night he died."

Dalgliesh said:

"He died alone, Mrs. Hewson tells me."

"Unhappily yes. But so at the last do we all. You'll join us for tea I hope. Julius, you too, and Maggie of course. And did you say that you hoped to stay with Michael? Then you must, of course, spend the night here."

He turned to the matron.

"Victor's room, I think, Dot. Perhaps, after tea, you would prepare it for our guest."

Dalgliesh said:

"That's very kind of you, but I don't want to be a nuisance. Would there be any objection if, after tonight, I spent a few days in the cottage? Mrs. Hewson tells me that Father Baddeley left me his library. It would be helpful if I could sort and pack the books while I'm here."

Was it his imagination that the suggestion wasn't entirely welcome? But Anstey hesitated only for a second before saying:

"Of course, if that is what you prefer. But first let me introduce you to the family."

Dalgliesh followed Anstey in a formal charade of greetings. A succession of hands, dry, cold, moist, reluctant or firm clasped his. Grace Willison, the middle-aged spinster; a study in grey; skin, hair, dress, stockings, all of them slightly dingy so that she looked like an old-fashioned, stiffly jointed doll neglected too long in a dusty cupboard. Ursula Hollis; a tall, spotty-faced girl dressed in a long skirt of Indian cotton who gave him a tentative smile and brief, reluctant handshake. Her left hand lay limply in her lap as if wearied by the weight of the thick wedding ring. He was aware of something odd about her face but had moved on before he realized that she had one blue eye, one brown. Jennie Pegram; the youngest patient but probably older than she looked with a pale, sharp face and mild lemur-like eyes. She was so short necked that she seemed hunched into her wheelchair. Corn gold hair, parted in the middle, hung like a crimped curtain around the dwarfish body. She cringed deprecatingly at his touch, gave him a sickly smile and whispered "hullo" on a gasp of intaken breath.

Henry Carwardine; a handsome, authoritative face but cut with deep lines of strain; a high beaky nose and long mouth. The disease had wrenched his head to one side so that he looked like a supercilious bird of prey. He took no notice of Dalgliesh's proffered hand but said a brief "how do you do" with an uninterest amounting almost to discourtesy. Dorothy Moxon, the matron; sombre, stout and gloomy eyed under the dark fringe. Helen Rainer; large, slightly protruding green eyes under lids as thin as grape skins and a shapely figure which even the loose-fitting smock couldn't wholly disguise. She would, he thought, be attractive were it not for the discontented droop of the slightly marsupial cheeks. She shook hands firmly with Dalgliesh and gave him a minatory glance as if welcoming a new patient from whom she expected trouble. Dr. Eric Hewson; a fair, good-looking man with a boyish vulnerable face, mud-brown eyes fringed with remarkably long lashes. Dennis Lerner; a lean, rather weak face, eyes blinking nervously behind the steel-rimmed spectacles, a moist handshake. Anstey added, almost as if he thought Lerner needed a word of explanation, that Dennis was the male nurse.

"The two remaining members of our family, Albert Philby, our handyman, and my sister Millicent Hammitt you will meet later I hope. But I mustn't, of course, forget Jeoffrey." As if catching his name, a cat, who had been slumbering on a window seat, uncurled himself, dropped ponderously to the floor and stalked towards them, tail erect. Anstey explained:

"He is named after Christopher Smart's cat. I expect you remember the poem.

> For I will consider my cat Jeoffrey.
> For he is the servant of the living God, duly
> and daily serving him,
> For he counteracts the powers of darkness by his
> electric skin and glaring eyes,
> For he counteracts the Devil, who is death, by
> brisking about the life."

Dalgliesh said that he knew the poem. He could have added that if Anstey had destined his cat for this hieratic role, then he had been unlucky in his choice of the litter. Jeoffrey was a barrel-shaped tabby with a tail like a fox's brush who looked as if his life were dedicated less to the service of his creator than to the gratification of feline lusts. He gave Anstey a disagreeable look compounded of long suffering and disgust and leapt with lightness and precision on to Carwardine's lap where he was ill-received. Gratified at Carwardine's obvious reluctance to acquire him, he settled down with much purring and foot padding and permitted his eyes to close.

Julius Court and Maggie Hewson had settled themselves at the far end of the long table. Suddenly Julius called out:

"Be careful what you say to Mr. Dalgliesh, it may be taken down and given in evidence. He chooses to travel incognito but actually he's Commander Adam Dalgliesh of New Scotland Yard. His job is catching murderers."

Henry Carwardine's cup began an agitated rattle in its saucer. He tried ineffectively to steady it with his left hand. No one looked at him. Jennie Pegram gave an apprehensive gasp, then looked complacently round the table as if she had done something clever. Helen Rainer said sharply:

"How do you know?"

"I live in the world, my darlings, and occasionally read the newspapers. There was a notorious case last year which gained the Commander some public notice."

He turned to Dalgliesh:

"Henry will be drinking wine with me after dinner tonight and listening to some music. You may care to join us. You could perhaps wheel him over. Wilfred will excuse you, I know."

The invitation hardly seemed courteous, excluding as it did all but two of the company and peremptorily claiming the new arrival with no more than a token acknowledgement to his host. But no one seemed to mind. Perhaps it was usual for the two men to drink together when Court was at his cottage. After all, there was no reason why the patients should be compelled to share each other's friends, or those friends obliged to issue a general invitation. Besides, Dalgliesh was obviously invited to provide an escort. He said a brief thank you and sat down at the table between Ursula Hollis and Henry Carwardine.

It was a plain, boarding-school tea. There was no cloth. The scarred oak table reamed with scorch marks held two large brown teapots wielded by Dorothy Moxon, two plates of thickly cut brown bread, thinly spread with what Dalgliesh suspected was margarine, a jar of honey and one of marmite, a dish of rock buns, home made and pebbled with an excrescence of bullet black currants. There was also a bowl of apples. They looked like windfalls. Everyone was drinking from brown earthenware mugs. Helen Rainer went over to a cupboard set under the window and brought over three similar mugs and matching plates for the visitors.

It was an odd tea party. Carwardine ignored the guest except to push the plate of bread and butter towards him, and Dalgliesh at first made little headway with Ursula Hollis. Her pale intense face was turned perpetually towards him, the two discordant eyes searched his. He felt uncomfortably that she was making some demand on him, desperately hoping to evoke a response of interest, of affection even, which he could neither recognize nor was competent to give. But, by happy chance, he mentioned London. Her face brightened, she asked him if he knew Marylebone, the Bell Street market? He found himself involved in a lively, almost obsessive discussion about London's street markets. She became animated, almost pretty and, strangely, it seemed to give her some comfort.

Suddenly Jennie Pegram leaned forward across the table and said with a moue of simulated distaste:

"A funny job catching murderers and getting them hanged. I don't see how you fancy it."

"We don't fancy it, and nowadays they don't get hanged."

"Well, shut up for life then. I think that's worse. And I bet some of those you caught when you were younger got hanged."

He detected the anticipatory, almost lascivious gleam in her eyes. It wasn't new to him. He said quietly:

"Five of them. It's interesting that those are the ones people always want to hear about."

Anstey smiled his gentle smile and spoke as one determined to be fair.

"It isn't only a question of punishment though, Jennie, is it? There is the theory of deterrence; the need to mark public abhorrence of violent crime; the hope of reforming and rehabilitating the criminal; and, of course, the importance of trying to ensure that he doesn't do it again."

He reminded Dalgliesh of a school master he had much disliked who was given to initiating frank discussion as a matter of duty but always with the patronizing air of permitting a limited expression of unorthodox opinion provided the class came back within the allotted time to a proper conviction of the rightness of his own views. But now Dalgliesh was neither compelled nor disposed to cooperate. He broke into Jennie's simple, "Well, they can't do it again if they're hanged, can they?" by saying:

"It's an interesting and important subject, I know. But forgive me if I don't personally find it fascinating. I'm on holiday—actually I'm convalescing—and I'm trying to forget about work."

"You've been ill?" Carwardine, with the deliberate care of a child uncertain of its powers, reached across and helped himself to honey. "I hope your call here isn't, even subconsciously, on your own behalf. You aren't looking for a future vacancy? You haven't a progressive incurable disease?"

Anstey said:

"We all suffer from a progressive incurable disease. We call it life."

Carwardine gave a tight self-congratulatory smile, as if he had scored a point in some private game. Dalgliesh, who was beginning to feel himself part of a mad hatter's tea party, wasn't sure whether the remark was spuriously profound or merely silly. What he was sure was that Anstey had made it before. There was a short, embarrassed silence, then Anstey said:

"Michael didn't let us know he was expecting you." He made it sound like a gentle reproof.

"He may not have received my postcard. It should have arrived on the morning of his death. I couldn't find it in his bureau."

Anstey was peeling an apple, the yellow rind curved over his thin fingers. His eyes were intent on his task. He said:

"He was brought home by the ambulance service. It wasn't convenient that morning for me to fetch him. I understand that the ambulance stopped at the postbox to collect any letters, probably at Michael's request. He later handed a letter to me and one to my sister, so he should have received your card. I certainly found no postcard when I looked in the bureau for his will and for any other written instructions he may have left. That was early on the morning after his death. I may, of course, have missed it."

Dalgliesh said easily:

"In which case it would still be there. I expect Father Baddeley threw it away. It's a pity you had to break into the bureau."

"Break into?" Anstey's voice expressed nothing but a polite, unworried query.

"The lock has been forced."

"Indeed. I imagine that Michael must have lost the key and was forced to that extremity. Forgive the pun. I found the bureau open when I looked for his papers. I'm afraid I didn't think to examine the lock. Is it important?"

"Miss Willison may think so. I understood that the bureau is now hers."

"A broken lock does, of course, reduce its value. But you will find that we place little store on material possessions at Toynton Grange."

He smiled again, dismissing a frivolity, and turned to Dorothy Moxon. Miss Willison was concentrating on her plate. She didn't look up. Dalgliesh said:

"It's probably foolish of me, but I wish I could be sure that Father Baddeley knew that I hoped to visit him. I thought he might have slipped my postcard into his diary. But the last volume isn't in his desk."

This time Anstey looked up. The blue eyes met the dark brown, innocent, polite, unworried.

"Yes, I noticed that. He gave up keeping a diary at the end of June apparently. The surprise is that he kept one, not that he gave up the habit. In the end one grows impatient of the egotism which records trivia as if it had a permanent value."

"It's unusual surely after so many years to stop in mid-year."

"He had just returned from hospital after a grave illness and can't have been in much doubt about the prognosis. Knowing that death could not be far off, he may have decided to destroy the diaries."

"Beginning with the last volume?"

"To destroy a diary must be like destroying memory. One would begin with the years one could best endure to lose. Old memories are tenacious. He made a start by burning the last volume."

Grace Willison again spoke her gentle but firm correction:

"Not by burning, Wilfred. Father Baddeley used his electric fire when he got home from hospital. The grate is filled with a jam pot of dried grasses."

Dalgliesh pictured the sitting-room of Hope Cottage. She was, of course, right. He recalled the old-fashioned grey stone jar, the crumpled bunch of dried leaves and grasses filling the narrow fireplace and thrusting their dusty and soot laden stalks between the bars. They probably hadn't been disturbed for the best part of a year.

The animated chatter at the other end of the table died into speculative silence as it does when people suddenly suspect that something interesting is being said which they ought to hear.

Maggie Hewson had seated herself so close to Julius Court that Dalgliesh was surprised that he had room to drink his tea and had been overtly flirting with him during the meal, whether for her husband's discomfiture or Court's gratification it was difficult to say. Eric Hewson, when he glanced towards them, had the shame-faced look of an embarrassed schoolboy. Court, perfectly at his ease, had distributed his attention among all the women present, with the exception of Grace. Now Maggie looked from face to face and said sharply:

"What's the matter? What did she say?"

No one replied. It was Julius who broke the moment of sudden and inexplicable tension:

"I forgot to tell you. You're doubly privileged in your visitor. The Commander doesn't confine his talents to catching murderers, he publishes verse. He's Adam Dalgliesh, the poet."

This announcement was met with a confused congratulatory murmur during which Dalgliesh fastened on Jennie's comment of "how nice" as the most irritatingly inept. Wilfred smiled encouragingly and said:

"Of course. We are certainly privileged. And Adam Dalgliesh comes at an opportune time. We are due to hold our monthly family social evening on Thursday. May we hope that our guest will recite some of his poems for our pleasure?"

There were a number of answers to that question but, in the present disadvantaged company, none of them seemed either kind or possible.

Dalgliesh said:

"I'm sorry but I don't travel with copies of my own books."

Anstey smiled,

"That will present no problem. Henry has your last two volumes. I am sure he will lend them."

Without looking up from his plate, Carwardine said quietly:

"Given the lack of privacy in this place, I've no doubt you could provide a verbal catalogue of my whole library. But, since you've shown a complete lack of interest in Dalgliesh's work until now, I have no intention of lending my books so that you can blackmail a guest into performing for you like a captive monkey!"

Wilfred flushed slightly and bent his head over his plate.

There was nothing further to be said. After a second's silence, the talk flowed on, innocuous, commonplace. Neither Father Baddeley nor his diary were mentioned again.

# V

Anstey was obviously unworried by Dalgliesh's expressed wish after tea to talk to Miss Willison in private. Probably the request struck him as no more than the pious protocol of courtesy and respect. He said that Grace had the task of feeding the hens and collecting the eggs before dusk. Perhaps Adam could help her?

The two larger wheels of the chair were fitted with a second interior wheel in chrome which could be used by the occupant to drive the chair forward. Miss Willison grasped it and began to make slow progress down the asphalt path jerking her frail body like a marionette. Dalgliesh saw that her left hand was deformed and had little power so that the chair tended to swivel, and progress was erratic. He moved to her left and, while walking beside her, he laid his hand unobtrusively on the back of the chair and gently helped it forward. He hoped that he was doing the acceptable thing. Miss Willison might resent his tact as much as she did the implied pity. He thought that she sensed his embarrassment and had resolved not to add to it even by smiling her thanks.

As they walked together he was intensely aware of her, noting the details of her physical presence as keenly as if she were a young and desirable woman and he on the verge of love. He watched the sharp bones of her shoulders jerking rhythmically under the thin grey cotton of her dress; the purple tributaries of the veins standing like cords on her almost transparent left hand, so small and fragile in contrast to its fellow. This, too, looked deformed in its compensating strength and hugeness as she gripped the wheel as powerfully as a man. Her legs, clad in wrinkled woollen stockings, were thin as sticks; her sandalled feet, too large surely for such inadequate supports, were clamped to the footrest of her chair as if glued to the metal. Her grey hair flecked with dandruff had been combed upward in a single heavy plait fixed to the crown of her head with a plastic white comb, not particularly clean. The back of her neck looked dingy either with fading suntan or inadequate washing. Looking down he could see the lines on her forehead contracting into deeper furrows with the effort of moving the chair, the eyes blinking spasmodically behind the thin framed spectacles.

The hen house was a large ramshackle cage bounded by sagging wire and creosoted posts. It had obviously been designed for the disabled. There was a double entry so that Miss Willison could let herself in and fasten the door behind her before opening the second door into the main cage, and the smooth asphalt path, just wide enough for a wheelchair, ran along each side and in front of the nesting boxes. Inside the first door a rough wooden shelf had been nailed waist high to one of the supports. This held a bowl of prepared meal, a plastic can of water and a wooden spoon riveted to a long handle, obviously for the collection of eggs. Miss Willison took them in her lap with some difficulty and reached forward to open the inner door. The hens, who had unaccountably bunched themselves in the far corner of the cage like the nervous virgins, lifted their beady spiteful faces and instantly came squawking and swooping towards her as if determined on a feathered hecatomb. Miss Willison recoiled slightly and began casting handfuls of meal before them with the air of a neophyte propitiating the furies. The hens began an agitated pecking and gulping. Scraping her hand against the rim of the bowl Miss Willison said:

"I wish I could get more fond of them, or they of me. Both sides might get more out of this activity. I thought that animals developed a fondness for the hand that feeds them but it doesn't seem to apply to hens. I don't see why it should really. We exploit them so thoroughly, first take their eggs and when they're past laying wring their necks and consign them to the pot."

"I hope you don't have to do the wringing."

"Oh, no, Albert Philby has that unpleasant job; not that I think he finds it altogether unpleasant. But I eat my share of the boiled fowl."

Dalgliesh said:

"I feel rather the same. I was brought up in a Norfolk vicarage and my mother always had hens. She was fond of them and they seemed fond of her but my father and I thought they were a nuisance. But we liked the fresh eggs."

"Do you know, I'm ashamed to tell you that I can't really tell the difference between these eggs and the ones from the supermarket. Wilfred prefers us not to eat any food which hasn't been naturally produced. He abhors factory farming and, of course, he's right. He would really prefer Toynton Grange to be vegetarian, but that would make the catering even more difficult than it is now. Julius did some sums and proved to him that these eggs cost us two and a half times more than the shop ones, not counting of course for my labour. It was rather discouraging."

Dalgliesh asked:

"Does Julius Court do the book-keeping here then?"

"Oh, no! Not the real accounts, the ones included in the annual report. Wilfred has a professional accountant for those. But Julius is clever with finance and I know Wilfred looks to him for advice. It's usually rather disheartening advice, I'm afraid; we run on a shoestring really. Father Baddeley's legacy was a real blessing. And Julius has been very kind. Last year the van which we hired to drive us back from the port after our return from Lourdes had an accident. We were all very shaken. The wheelchairs were in the back and two of them got broken. The telephone message that reached here was rather alarmist; it wasn't as bad as Wilfred thought. But Julius drove straight to the hospital where we had been taken for a checkup, hired another van, and took care of everything. And then he bought the specially adapted bus which we have now so that we're completely independent. Dennis and Wilfred between them can drive us all the way to Lourdes. Julius never comes with us, of course, but he's always here to arrange a welcome home party for us when we return after the pilgrimage."

This disinterested kindness was unlike the impression that, even after a short acquaintanceship, Dalgliesh had formed of Court. Intrigued he asked carefully:

"Forgive me if I sound crude but what does Julius Court get out of it, this interest in Toynton?"

"Do you know, I've sometimes asked myself that. But it seems an ungracious question when it's so apparent what Toynton Grange gets out of him. He comes back from London like a breath of the outside world. He cheers us all. But I know that you want to talk about your friend. Shall we just collect the eggs and then find somewhere quiet?"

Your friend. The quiet phrase quietly spoken, rebuked him. They filled up the water containers and collected the eggs together, Miss Willison scooping them up in her wooden spoon with the expertise born of long practice. They found only eight. The whole procedure, which an able-bodied person could have completed in ten minutes, had been tedious, time-consuming and not particularly productive. Dalgliesh, who saw no merit in work for the sake of work, wondered what his companion really thought about a job which had obviously been designed in defiance of economics to give her the illusion of being useful.

They made their way back to the little courtyard behind the house. Only Henry Carwardine was sitting there, a book on his lap but his eyes staring towards the invisible sea. Miss Willison gave him a quick worried glance and seemed about to speak. But she said nothing until they had settled themselves some thirty yards from the silent figure; Dalgliesh at the end of one of the wooden benches and she at his side. Then she said:

"I can never get used to being so close to the sea and yet not being able to look at it. One can hear it so plainly sometimes as we can now. We're almost surrounded by it, we can sometimes smell it and listen to it, but we might be a hundred miles away."

She spoke wistfully but without resentment. They sat for a moment in silence. Dalgliesh could indeed hear the sea clearly now, the long withdrawing rasp of the shingled tide borne to him on the onshore breeze. To the inmates of Toynton Grange that ceaseless murmur must evoke the tantilizingly close but unobtainable freedom of wide blue horizons, scudding clouds, white wings falling and swooping through the moving air. He could understand how the need to see it might grow into an obsession. He said deliberately:

"Mr. Holroyd managed to get himself wheeled to where he could watch the sea."

It had been important to see her reaction and he realized at once that to her the remark had been worse than tactless. She was deeply shaken and distressed. The frail left hand, curved in her lap, began an agitated shaking. Her right hand tightened on the arm of the chair. Her face crimsoned in an unlovely wave, and then became very pale. For a moment he almost wished that he hadn't spoken. But the regret was transitory. It was returning despite himself, he thought with sardonic humor, this professional itch to seek out the facts. They were seldom discovered without some cost, however irrelevant or important they finally proved to be, and it wasn't usually he who paid. He heard her speaking so quietly that he had to bend his head to catch the words.

"Victor had a special need to get away by himself. We understood that."

"But it must have been very difficult to push a light wheelchair like this over the rough turf and up to the edge of the cliff."

"He had a chair which belonged to him, like this type but larger and stronger. And it wasn't necessary to push him up the steep part of the headland. There's an inland path which leads, I understand, to a narrow sunken lane. You can get to the cliff edge that way. Even so it was hard on Dennis Lerner. It took him half an hour hard pushing each way. But you wanted to talk about Father Baddeley."

"If it won't distress you too much. It seems that you were the last person to see him alive. He must have died very soon after you left the cottage since he was still wearing his stole when Mrs. Hewson found his body next morning. Normally he would surely have taken it off very soon after hearing a confession."

There was a silence as if she were making up her mind to something. Then she said:

"He did take it off, as usual, immediately after he'd given me absolution. He folded it up and placed it over the arm of his chair."

This, too, was a sensation which in the long dog days in hospital he had thought never to experience again, the frisson of excitement along the blood at the first realization that something important had been said, that although the quarry wasn't yet in sight nor his spore detectable, yet he was there. He tried to reject this unwelcome surge of tension but it was as elemental and involuntary as the touch of fear. He said:

"But that means that Father Baddeley put on his stole again after you had left. Why should he do that?"

Or someone else had put it on for him. But that thought was best unspoken and its implications must wait.

She said quietly:

"I assume that he had another penitent; that is the obvious explanation."

"He wouldn't wear it to say his evening office?"

Dalgliesh tried to remember his father's practice in these matters on the very rare occasions when the rector did not say his Office in church; but memory provided only the unhelpful boyhood picture of them both holed up in a hut in the Cairngorms during a blizzard, himself watching, half bored, half fascinated, the patterns of the swirling snow against the windows, his father in leggings, anorak and woollen cap quietly reading from his small black prayer book. He certainly hadn't worn a stole then.

Miss Willison said:

"Oh no! He would wear it only when administering a sacrament. Besides, he had said evensong. He was just finishing when I arrived and I joined him in a last collect."

"But if someone followed you, then you weren't the last person to see him alive. Did you point that out to anyone when you were told of his death?"

"Should I have done? I don't think so. If the person himself—or herself—didn't choose to speak it wasn't for me to invite conjecture. Of course, if anyone but you had realized the significance of the stole it wouldn't have been possible to avoid speculation. But no one did, or if they did, they said nothing. We gossip too much at Toynton, Mr. Dalgliesh. It's inevitable perhaps, but it isn't—well—healthy morally. If someone other than I went to confession that night, it's nobody's business but theirs and Father Baddeley's."

Dalgliesh said:

"But Father Baddeley was still wearing his stole next morning. That suggests that he might have died while his visitor was actually with him. If that happened surely the first reaction, however private the occasion, would be to summon medical help?"

"The visitor might have had no doubts that Father Baddeley had died and was beyond that kind of help. If so there might be a temptation to leave him there sitting peaceably in his chair and slip away. I don't think Father Baddeley would call that a sin, and I don't think you could call it a crime. It might seem callous but would it necessarily be so? It could argue an indifference to form and decorum perhaps, but that isn't quite the same thing, is it?"

It would argue, too, thought Dalgliesh, that the visitor had been a doctor or a nurse. Was that what Miss Willison was hinting? The first reaction of a lay person would surely be to seek help, or at least confirmation that death had actually occurred. Unless, of course, he knew for the best or worst of reasons that Baddeley was dead. But that sinister possibility seemed not to have occurred to Miss Willison. Why, indeed, should it? Father Baddeley was old, he was sick, he was expected to die and he had died. Why should anyone suspect the natural and the inevitable? He said something about determining the time of death and heard her gentle, inexorable reply.

"I expect that in your job the actual time of death is always important and so you get used to concentrating on that fact. But in real life does it matter? What matters is whether one dies in a state of grace."

Dalgliesh had a momentary and impious picture of his detective sergeant punctiliously attempting to determine and record this essential information about a victim in an official crime report and reflected that Miss Willison's nice distinction between police work and real life was a salutory reminder of how other people saw his job. He looked forward to telling the Commissioner about it. And then he remembered that this wasn't the kind of casual professional gossip which they would exchange in that final slightly formal and inevitably disappointing interview which would mark the end of his police career.

Ruefully, he recognized in Miss Willison the type of unusually honest witness whom he had always found difficult. Paradoxically, this old-fashioned rectitude, this sensitivity of conscience, were more difficult to cope with than the prevarications, evasions, or flamboyant lying which were part of a normal interrogation. He would have liked to have asked her who at Toynton Grange was likely to have visited Father Baddeley for the purpose of confession, but recognized that the question would only prejudice confidence between them and that, in any case, he wouldn't get a reply. But it must have been one of the able bodied. No one else could have come and gone in secret, unless, of course, he or she had an accomplice. He was inclined to dismiss the accomplice. A wheelchair and its occupant, whether pushed from Toynton Grange or brought by car, must surely have been seen at some stage of the journey.

Hoping that he wasn't sounding too much like a detective in the middle of an interrogation he asked:

"So when you left him he was—what?"

"Just sitting there quietly in the fireside chair. I wouldn't let him get up. Wilfred had driven me down to the cottage in the small van. He said that he would visit his sister at Faith Cottage while I was with Father Baddeley and be outside again in half an hour unless I knocked on the wall first."

"So you can hear sounds between the two cottages? I ask because it struck me that if Father Baddeley had felt ill after you'd left, he might have knocked on the wall for Mrs. Hammitt."

"She says that he didn't knock, but she might not have heard if she had the television on very loudly. The cottages are very well built, but you can hear sounds through that interior wall, particularly if voices are raised."

"You mean that you could hear Mr. Anstey talking to his sister?"

Miss Willison seemed to regret that she had gone so far, and she said quickly:

"Well, just now and then. I remember that I had to make an effort of will to prevent it disturbing me. I wished that they would keep their voices lower, and then felt ashamed of myself for being so easily distracted. It was good of Wilfred to drive me to the cottage. Normally, of course, Father Baddeley would come up to the house to see me and we would use what is called the quiet room next to the business room just inside the front door. But Father Baddeley had only been discharged from hospital that morning and it wasn't right that he should leave the cottage. I could have postponed my visit until he was stronger but he wrote to me from hospital to say that he hoped I would come and precisely at what time. He knew how much it meant to me."

"Was he fit to be alone? It seems not."

"Eric and Dot—that's Sister Moxon—wanted him to come here and be looked after at least for the first night, but he insisted on going straight back home. Then Wilfred suggested that someone should sleep in his spare room in case he wanted help in the night. He wouldn't agree to that either. He really was adamant that he should be left alone that night; he had great authority in his quiet way. Afterwards I think Wilfred blamed himself for not having been more firm. But what could he do? He couldn't bring Father Baddeley here by force."

But it would have been simpler for all concerned if Father Baddeley had agreed to spend at least his first night out of hospital at Toynton Grange. It was surely untypically inconsiderate of him to resist the suggestion so strenuously. Was he expecting another visitor? Was there someone he wanted to see, urgently and in private, someone to whom, like Miss Willison, he had written to give a precisely timed appointment? If so, whatever the reason for the visit, that person must have come on his own feet. He asked Miss Willison if Wilfred and Father Baddeley had spoken together before she had left the cottage.

"No. After I'd been with Father Baddeley about thirty minutes he knocked on the wall with the poker and, soon afterwards, Wilfred honked on the horn. I maneuvered my chair to the front door just as Wilfred arrived to open it. Father Baddeley was still in his chair. Wilfred called out goodnight to him, but I don't think he answered. Wilfred seemed in rather a hurry to get home. Millicent came out to help push my chair into the back of the van."

So neither Wilfred nor his sister had spoken to Michael before driving away that evening, neither had seen him closely. Glancing down at Miss Willison's strong right hand Dalgliesh toyed momentarily with the possibility that Michael was already dead. But that notion, apart from its psychological unlikelihood, was of course, nonsense. She couldn't have relied on Wilfred not coming into the cottage. Come to think of it, it was odd that he hadn't done so. Michael had only returned from hospital that morning. Surely it would have been natural to come in and enquire how he was feeling, to spend at least a few minutes in his company. It was interesting that Wilfred Anstey had made so quick a getaway, that no one had admitted visiting Father Baddeley after seven forty-five.

He asked:

"What lighting was there in the cottage when you were with Father Baddeley?" If the question surprised her, she didn't show it.

"Only the small table lamp on the bureau top behind his chair. I was surprised that he could see to say Evensong, but the prayers, of course, would be familiar to him."

"And the lamp was off next morning?"

"Oh yes, Maggie said that she found the cottage in darkness."

Dalgliesh said:

"I find it rather strange that no one looked in later that night to enquire how Father Baddeley was or help him get to bed."

She said quickly:

"Eric Hewson thought that Millicent was going to look in last thing and she had somehow got the impression that Eric and Helen—Nurse Rainer, you know—had agreed to do so. They all blamed themselves very much the next day. But, as Eric told us, medically it could have made no difference. Father Baddeley died quite peaceably soon after I left."

They sat in silence for a minute. Dalgliesh wondered whether this was the right time to ask her about the poison pen letter. Remembering her distress over Victor Holroyd, he was reluctant to embarrass her further. But it was important to know. Looking sideways at the thin face with its look of resolute tranquillity, he said:

"I looked in Father Baddeley's writing bureau very soon after I arrived, just in case there was a note or unposted letter for me. I found a rather unpleasant poison pen letter under some old receipts. I wondered whether he had spoken to anyone about it, whether anyone else at Toynton Grange had received one."

She was even more distressed by the question than he had feared. For a moment she could not speak. He stared straight ahead until he heard her voice. But, when at last she answered, she had herself well in hand.

"I had one, about four days before Victor died. It was . . . it was obscene. I tore it into small fragments and flushed it down the lavatory."

Dalgliesh said with robust cheerfulness:

"Much the best thing to do with it. But, as a policeman, I'm always sorry when the evidence is destroyed."

"Evidence?"

"Well, sending poison pen letters can be an offense; more important, it can cause a great deal of unhappiness. It's probably best always to tell the police and let them find out who's responsible."

"The police! Oh, no! We couldn't do that. It isn't the kind of problem the police can help with."

"We aren't as insensitive as people sometimes imagine. It isn't inevitable that the culprit would be prosecuted. But it is important to put a stop to this kind of nuisance, and the police have the best facilities. They can send the letter to the forensic science laboratory for examination by a skilled document examiner."

"But they would need to have the document. I couldn't have shown the letter to anyone."

So it had been as bad as that. Dalgliesh asked:

"Would you mind telling me what kind of letter it was? Was it handwritten, typed, on what kind of paper?"

"The letter was typed on Toynton Grange paper, in double spacing, on our old Imperial. Most of us here have learned typewriting. It's one of the ways in which we try to be self-supporting. There was nothing wrong with the punctuation or spelling. There were no other clues that I could see. I don't know who typed it, but I think the writer must have been sexually experienced."

So, even in the middle of her distress, she had applied her mind to the problem. He said:

"There are only a limited number of people with access to that machine. The problem wouldn't have been too difficult for the police."

Her gentle voice was stubborn.

"We had the police here over Victor's death. They were very kind, very considerate. But it was terribly upsetting. It was horrible for Wilfred—for all of us. I don't think we could have stood it again. I'm sure that Wilfred couldn't. However tactful the police are, they have to keep on asking questions until they've solved the case, surely? It's no use calling them in and expecting them to put people's sensitivities before their job."

This was undeniably true and Dalgliesh had little to argue against it. He asked her what, if anything, she had done apart from flushing away the offending letter.

"I told Dorothy Moxon about it. That seemed the most sensible thing to do. I couldn't have spoken about it to a man. Dorothy told me that I shouldn't have destroyed it, that no one could do anything without the evidence. But she agreed that we ought to say nothing at present. Wilfred was particularly worried about money at the time and she didn't want him to have anything else on his mind. She knew how much it would distress him. Besides, I think she had an idea who might have been responsible. If she were right, then we shan't be getting any more letters."

So Dorothy Moxon had believed, or had pretended to believe, that Victor Holroyd was responsible. And if the writer now had the sense and self-control to stop, it was a comfortable theory which, in the absence of the evidence, no one could disprove.

He asked whether anyone else had received a letter. As far as she knew, no one had. Dorothy Moxon hadn't been consulted by anyone else. The suggestion seemed to distress her. Dalgliesh realized that she had seen the note as a single piece of gratuitous spite directed against herself. The thought that Father Baddeley had also received one, was distressing her almost as much as the original letter. Knowing only too well from his experience the kind of letter it must have been, he said gently:

"I shouldn't worry too much about Father Baddeley's letter. I don't think it would have distressed him. It was very mild really, just a spiteful little note suggesting that he wasn't of much help to Toynton Grange and that the cottage could be more usefully occupied by someone else. He had too much humility and sense to be bothered by that kind of nonsense. I imagine that he only kept the letter because he wanted to consult me in case he wasn't the only victim. Sensible people put these things down the WC. But we can't always be sensible. Anyway, if you do receive another letter, will you promise to show it to me?"

She shook her head gently but didn't speak. But Dalgliesh saw that she was happier. She put out her withered left hand and placed it momentarily over his, giving it a slight press. The sensation was unpleasant, her hand was dry and cold, the bones felt loose in the skin. But the gesture was both humbling and dignified.

It was getting cold and dark in the courtyard; Henry Carwardine had already gone in. It was time for her to move inside. He thought quickly and then said:

"It isn't important, and please don't think that I take my job with me wherever I go. But if during the next few days you can recall how Father Baddeley spent the last week or so before he went into hospital, it would be helpful to me. Don't ask anyone else about this. Just let me know what he did from your own memory of him, the times he came to Toynton Grange, where else he may have spent his hours. I should like to have a picture in my mind of his last ten days."

She said:

"I know that he went into Wareham on the Wednesday before he was taken ill, he said to do some shopping and to see someone on business. I remember that because he explained on the Tuesday that he wouldn't be visiting the Grange as usual next morning."

So that, thought Dalgliesh, was when he had bought his store of provisions, confident that his letter wouldn't go unanswered. But then he had been right to be confident.

They sat for a minute not speaking. He wondered what she had thought of so odd a request. She hadn't seemed surprised. Perhaps she saw it as perfectly natural, this wish to build up a picture of a friend's last days on earth. But suddenly he had a spasm of apprehension and caution. Ought he perhaps to stress that his request was absolutely private? Surely not. He had told her not to ask anyone else. To make more of it would only arouse suspicion. And what danger could there be? What had he to go on? A broken bureau lock, a missing diary, a stole replaced as if for confession. There was no real evidence here. With an effort of will he reasoned away this inexplicable spasm of apprehension, strong as a premonition. It was too disagreeable a reminder of those long nights in hospital when he had struggled in restless half-consciousness against irrational terrors and half-understood fears. And this was equally irrational, equally to be resisted by sense and reason, the ridiculous conviction that a simple, almost casual and not very hopeful request had sounded so clearly a sentence of death.

# BOOK THREE

·

# A Stranger for the Night

# I

Before dinner Anstey suggested that Dennis Lerner should show Dalgliesh round the house. He apologized for not escorting the guest himself, but he had an urgent letter to write. The post was delivered and collected shortly before nine o'clock each morning from the box on the boundary gate. If Adam had letters to send he had only to leave them on the hall table, and Albert Philby would take them to the box with the Toynton Grange letters. Dalgliesh thanked him. There was one urgent letter he needed to write, to Bill Moriarty at the Yard, but he proposed to post that himself later in the day at Wareham. He had certainly no intention of leaving it exposed to the curiosity or speculation of Anstey and his staff.

The suggestion for a tour of the Grange had the force of a command. Helen Rainer was helping the patients wash before dinner and Dot Moxon had disappeared with Anstey, so that he was taken round only by Lerner accompanied by Julius Court. Dalgliesh wished the tour were over, or better still, that it could have been avoided without giving hurt. He recalled with discomfort a visit he had paid as a boy with his father to a geriatric hospital on Christmas Day; the courtesy with which the patients accepted yet one more invasion of their privacy, the public display of pain and deformity, the pathetic eagerness with which the staff demonstrated their small triumphs. Now, as then, he found himself morbidly sensitive to the least trace of revulsion in his voice and thought that he detected what was more offensive, a note of patronizing heartiness. Dennis Lerner didn't appear to notice it and Julius walked jauntily with them looking round with lively curiosity as if the place were new to him. Dalgliesh wondered whether he had come to keep an eye on Lerner or on Dalgliesh himself.

As they passed from room to room, Lerner lost his first diffidence and became confident, almost voluble. There was something endearing about his naïve pride in what Anstey was trying to do. Anstey had certainly laid out his money with some imagination. The Grange itself, with its large, high rooms and cold marble floors, its oppressively panelled dark oak walls and mullioned windows, was a depressingly unsuitable house for disabled patients. Apart from the dining-room and the rear drawing-room, which had become a TV and communal sitting-room, Anstey had used the house mainly to accommodate himself and his staff and had built on to the rear a one-storey stone extension to provide ten individual patients' bedrooms on the ground floor and a clinical room and additional bedrooms on the floor above. This extension had been joined to the old stables which ran at right angles to it providing a sheltered patio for the patients' wheelchairs. The stables themselves had been adapted to provide garages, a workshop and a patients' activity room for woodwork and modelling. Here, too, the handcream and bath powder which the Home sold to help with finances were made and packed at a workbench behind a transparent plastic screen erected, presumably, to indicate respect for the principle of scientific cleanliness. Dalgliesh could see, hanging on the screen, the white shadows of protective overalls.

Lerner said:

"Victor Holroyd was a chemistry teacher and he gave us the prescription for the handcream and powder. The cream is really only lanolin, almond oil and glycerine but it's very effective and people seem to like it. We do very well with it. And this corner of the workroom is given over to modelling."

Dalgliesh had almost exhausted his repertoire of appreciative comments. But now he was genuinely impressed. In the middle of the workbench and mounted on a low wooden base was a clay head of Wilfred Anstey. The neck, elongated and sinewy, rose tortoise-like from the folds of the hood. The head was thrust forward and held a little to the right. It was almost a parody, and yet it had an extraordinary power. How, Dalgliesh wondered, had the sculptor managed to convey the sweetness and the obstinacy of that individual smile, to model compassion and yet reduce it to self-delusion, to show humility garbed in a monk's habit and yet convey an overriding impression of the puissance of evil. The plastic wrapped lumps and rolls of clay which lay, disorderly, on the workbench only emphasized the force and technical achievement of this one finished work.

Lerner said:

"Henry did the head. Something's gone a little wrong with the mouth, I think. Wilfred doesn't seem to mind it but no one else thinks that it does him justice."

Julius put his head on one side and pursed his lips in a parody of critical assessment.

"Oh, I wouldn't say that. I wouldn't say that. What do you think of it, Dalgliesh?"

"I think it's remarkable. Did Carwardine do much modelling before he came here?"

It was Dennis Lerner who answered:

"I don't think he did any. He was a senior civil servant before his illness. He modelled this about a couple of months ago without Wilfred giving him a sitting. It's quite good for a first effort, isn't it?"

Julius said:

"The question which interests me is did he do it intentionally, in which case he's a great deal too talented to waste himself here, or were his fingers merely obeying his subconscious? If so, it raises interesting speculations about the origin of creativity and even more interesting ones about Henry's subconscious."

"I think it just came out like that," said Dennis Lerner simply. He looked at it with puzzled respect, clearly seeing nothing in it either for wonder or explanation.

Lastly, they went into one of the small rooms at the end of the extension. It had been arranged as an office and was furnished with two wooden ink-stained desks which looked as if they were rejects from a government office. At one Grace Willison was typing names and addresses on a perforated sheet of sticky labels. Dalgliesh saw with some surprise that Carwardine was typing what looked like a private letter at the other desk. Both the typewriters were very old. Henry was using an Imperial; Grace a Remington. Dalgliesh stood over her and glanced at the list of names and addresses. He saw that the newsletter was widely distributed. Apart from local rectories, and other homes for the chronic sick, it went to addresses in London and even to two in the United States and one near Marseilles. Flustered at his interest, Grace jerked her elbow clumsily and the bound list of names and addresses from which she was working fell to the floor. But Dalgliesh had seen enough; the unaligned small e, the smudged o, the faint almost indecipherable capital w. There was no doubt that this was the machine on which Father Baddeley's note had been typed. He picked up the book and handed it to Miss Willison. Without looking at him, she shook her head and said:

"Thank you, but I don't really need to look at it. I can type all the sixty-eight names by heart. I've done it for so long you see. I can imagine what the people are like just from their names and the names they give to their houses. But I've always been good at remembering names and addresses. It was very useful to me when I worked for a charity to help discharged prisoners and there were so many lists to type. This is quite short, of course. May I add your name so that you get our quarterly magazine? It's only ten pence. I'm afraid with postage so expensive we have to charge more than we'd like."

Henry Cardwardine looked up and spoke:

"I believe this quarter we have a poem by Jennie Pegram which begins:

> Autumn is my favorite time,
> I love its glowing tints.

It's worth ten pence to you Dalgliesh, I should have thought, to discover how she tackles that little problem of rhyming."

Grace Willison smiled happily.

"It's only an amateur production I know, but it does keep the

League of Friends in touch with what is going on here, our personal friends too, of course."

Henry said:

"Not mine. They know I've lost the use of my limbs but I've no wish to suggest that I've lost the use of my mind. At best the newsletter reaches the literary level of a parish magazine; at worst, which is three issues out of four, it's embarrassingly puerile."

Grace Willison flushed and her lip trembled. Dalgliesh said quickly:

"Please add my name. Would it be easier if I paid for a year now?"

"How kind! Perhaps six months would be safer. If Wilfred does decide to transfer the Grange to the Ridgewell Trust they may have different plans for the newsletter. I'm afraid the future is very uncertain for all of us at present. Would you write your address here? Queenhythe. That's by the river, isn't it? How pleasant for you. You won't be wanting any of the handcream or bath powder, I suppose, although we do send the powder to one or two gentlemen customers. But this is really Dennis's department. He sees to the distribution and does most of the packing himself. I'm afraid our hands are too shaky to be much use. But I'm sure he could spare you some of the bath powder."

Dalgliesh was saved from the need to reply to this wistful enquiry by the booming of a gong. Julius said:

"The warning gong. One more boom and dinner will be on the table. I shall return home and see what my indispensable Mrs. Reynolds has left for me. By the way, have you warned the Commander that dinner at Toynton Grange is eaten Trappist fashion in silence? We don't want him to break the rule with inconvenient questions about Michael's will or what possible reason a patient in this abode of love could have for hurling himself over the cliff."

He disappeared at some speed as if afraid that any tendency to linger would expose him to the risk of an invitation to dine.

Grace Willison was obviously relieved to see him go but she smiled bravely at Dalgliesh.

"We do have a rule that no one talks during the evening meal. I hope that it won't inconvenience you. We take it in turns to read from any work we choose. Tonight it's Wilfred's turn so we shall have one of Donne's sermons. They're very fine of course—Father Baddeley enjoyed them, I know—but I do find them rather difficult. And I don't really think that they go well with boiled mutton."

# II

Henry Carwardine wheeled his chair to the lift, drew back the steel grill with difficulty, clanged the gate closed and pressed the button to the floor above. He had insisted on having a room in the main building, firmly rejecting the unsubstantial, meanly proportioned cells in the annex, and Wilfred, despite what Henry thought were obsessive, almost paranoid fears that he might be trapped in a fire, had reluctantly agreed. Henry had confirmed his committal to Toynton Grange by moving one or two chosen pieces of furniture from his Westminster flat and virtually all his books. The room was large, high ceilinged and pleasantly proportioned, its two windows giving a wide view southwest across the headland. Next door was a lavatory and shower which he shared only with any patient being nursed in the sickroom. He knew, without the least qualm of guilt, that he had the most comfortable quarters in the house. Increasingly he was retreating into this tidy and private world, closing the heavy carved door against involvement, bribing Philby to bring up occasional meals on a tray, to buy for him in Dorchester special cheeses, wines, pâté and fruit to augment the institutional meals which the staff of the Grange took it in turns to cook. Wilfred had apparently thought it prudent not to comment on this minor insubordination, this trespass against the law of togetherness.

He wondered what had provoked him to that spatter of malice against harmless, pathetic Grace Willison. It wasn't the first time since

Holroyd's death that he had caught himself speaking with Holroyd's voice. The phenomenon interested him. It set him thinking again about that other life, the one he had so prematurely and resolutely renounced. He had noticed it when chairing committees, how the members played their individual roles, almost as if these had been allocated in advance. The hawk; the dove; the compromiser; the magisterial elder statesman; the unpredictable maverick. How swiftly, if one were absent, a colleague modified his views, subtly adapted even his voice and manner to fill the gap. And so, apparently, he had assumed the mantle of Holroyd. The thought was ironic and not unsatisfying. Why not? Who else at Toynton Grange better fitted that rebarbative, non-conforming role?

He had been one of the youngest Under Secretaries of State ever appointed. He was confidently spoken of as the future head of a Department. That was how he saw himself. And then the disease, touching nerves and muscles at first with tentative fingers, had struck at the roots of confidence, at all the carefully laid plans. Dictating sessions with his personal assistant had become mutual embarrassments to be dreaded and deferred. Every telephone conversation was an ordeal; that first insistent, anxiety pitched ring was enough to set his hand trembling. Meetings which he had always enjoyed and chaired with a quiet if abrasive competence had become unpredictable contests between mind and unruly body. He had become unsure where he had been most confident.

He wasn't alone in misfortune. He had seen others, some of them in his own Department, being helped from their grotesquely graceless invalid cars into their wheelchairs, accepting a lower grade and easier work, moving to a division which could afford to carry a passenger. The Department would have balanced expediency and the public interest with proper consideration and compassion. They would have kept him on long after his usefulness justified it. He could have died, as he had watched others die, in official harness, harness lightened and adjusted to his frail shoulders, but nevertheless harness. He accepted that there was a kind of courage in that. But it wasn't his kind.

It had been a joint meeting with another Department, chaired by himself, that had finally decided him. He still couldn't think of the shambles without shame and horror. He saw himself again, feet impotently padding, his stick beating a tattoo on the floor as he strove to take one step towards his chair, the mucus spluttering out with his welcoming words to shower over his neighbor's papers. The ring of eyes around the table, animals' eyes, watchful, predatory, embarrassed, not daring to meet his. Except for one boy, a young good-looking Principal from the Treasury. He had looked fixedly at the Chairman, not with pity but with an almost clinical interest, noting for future reference one more manifestation of human behavior under stress. The words had come out at last, of course. Somehow he had got through the meeting. But for him, it had been the end.

He had heard of Toynton Grange as one did hear of such places, through a colleague whose wife received the Home's quarterly newsletter and contributed to its funds. It had seemed to offer an answer. He was a bachelor without family. He couldn't hope indefinitely to look after himself, nor on a disability pension could he buy a permanent nurse. And he had to get out of London. If he couldn't succeed, then he would opt out completely, retire to oblivion, away from the embarrassed pity of colleagues, from noise and foul air, from the hazards and inconveniences of a world aggressively organized for the healthy and able bodied. He would write the book on decision-making in Government planned for his retirement, catch up on his Greek, re-read the whole of Hardy. If he couldn't cultivate his own garden, at least he could avert fastidious eyes from the lack of cultivation in everyone else's.

And for the first six months it had seemed to work. There were disadvantages which, strangely, he hadn't expected or considered; the unenterprising, predictable meals; the pressures of discordant personalities; the delay in getting books and wine delivered; the lack of good talk; the self-absorption of the sick, their preoccupation with symptoms and bodily functions; the awful childishness and spurious joviality of institutional life. But it had been just supportable and he had been reluctant to admit failure since all alternatives seemed worse. And then Peter had arrived.

He had come to Toynton Grange just over a year ago. He was a polio victim, the seventeen-year-old only child of a haulage contractor's widow from the industrial Midlands who had made three preparatory visits of officious and ill-informed inspection before calculating whether she could afford to accept the vacancy. Henry suspected that, panicked by the loneliness and debased status of the early months of widowhood, she was already looking for a second husband and was beginning to realize that a seventeen-year-old chairbound son was an obstacle to be carefully weighed by likely candidates against her late husband's money, her own ageing and desperate sexuality. Listening to her spate of obstetric and marital intimacies, Henry had realized once again that the disabled were treated as a different breed. They posed no threat, sexual or otherwise, offered no competition. As companions they had the advantage of animals; literally anything could be spoken in front of them without embarrassment.

So Dolores Bonnington had expressed herself satisfied and Peter had arrived. The boy had made little impression on him at first. It was only gradually that he had come to appreciate his qualities of mind. Peter had been nursed at home with the help of district nurses and had been driven, when his health permitted, to the local comprehensive school. There he had been unlucky. No one, least of all his mother, had discovered his intelligence. Henry Carwardine doubted whether she was capable of recognizing it. He was less ready to acquit the school. Even with the problem of understaffing and overlarge classes, the inevitable logistic difficulties of a huge city comprehensive, someone on the staff of that over-equipped and ill-disciplined menagerie, he thought with anger, ought to have been able to recognize a scholar. It was Henry who conceived the idea that they might provide for Peter the education he had lost; that he might in time enter a university and become self-supporting.

To Henry's surprise, preparing Peter for his 'O' levels had provided the common concern, the sense of unity and community at

Toynton Grange which none of Wilfred's experiments had achieved. Even Victor Holroyd helped.

"It seems that the boy isn't a fool. He's almost totally uneducated, of course. The staff, poor sods, were probably too busy teaching race relations, sexual technique and other contemporary additions to the syllabus and preventing the barbarians from pulling the school down around their ears to have time for someone with a mind."

"He ought to have maths and one science, Victor, at least at 'O' level. If you could help . . ."

"Without a lab?"

"There's the clinical room, you could fix something up there. He wouldn't be taking a science as a main subject at 'A' level?"

"Of course not. I realize my disciplines are included merely to provide an illusion of academic balance. But the boy ought to be taught to think scientifically. I know the suppliers of course. I could probably fix something up."

"I shall pay, of course."

"Certainly. I could afford it myself but I'm a great believer in people paying for their own gratifications."

"And Jennie and Ursula might be interested."

Henry had been amazed to find himself making the suggestion. Affection—he had not yet come to use the word love—had made him kind.

"God forbid! I'm not setting up a kindergarten. But I'll take on the boy for maths and general science."

Holroyd had given three sessions a week each of a carefully measured hour. But there had been no doubt about the quality of his teaching.

Father Baddeley had been pressed into service to teach Latin. Henry himself took English literature and history and undertook the general direction of the course. He discovered that Grace Willison spoke French better than anyone else at Toynton Grange and after some initial reluctance, she agreed to take French conversation twice a week. Wilfred had watched the preparations indulgently, taking no active part but raising no objections. Everyone was suddenly busy and happy.

Peter himself was accepting rather than dedicated. But he proved incredibly hardworking, gently amused perhaps by their common enthusiasm but capable of the sustained concentration which is the mark of a scholar. They found it almost impossible to overwork him. He was grateful, biddable, but detached. Sometimes Henry, looking at the calm girlish face, had the frightening feeling that the teachers were all seventeen-year-old children and the boy alone burdened with the sad cynicism of maturity.

Henry knew that he would never forget that moment when, at last, and joyfully, he had acknowledged love. It had been a warm day in early spring; was it really only six months ago? They had been sitting together where he sat now in the early afternoon sunshine, books on their laps ready to begin the two-thirty history lesson. Peter had been wearing a short-sleeve shirt, and he had rolled up his own sleeves to feel the first warmth of the sun prickling the hairs of his forearm. They had been sitting in silence as he was sitting now. And then, without turning to look at him, Peter had lain the length of his soft inner forearm against Henry's and, deliberately, as if every movement were part of a ritual, an affirmation, had twined their fingers together so that their palms too were joined flesh against flesh. Henry's nerves and blood remembered that moment and would do until he died. The shock of ecstasy, the sudden realization of joy, a spring of sheer unalloyed happiness which for all its surging excitement was yet paradoxically rooted in fulfilment and peace. It seemed in that moment as if everything which had happened in life, his job, his illness, coming to Toynton Grange, had led inevitably to this place, this love. Everything—success, failure, pain, frustration—had led to it and was justified by it. Never had he been so aware of another's body; the beat of the pulse in the thin wrist; the labyrinth of blue veins lying against his, blood flowing in concert with his blood; the delicate unbelievably soft flesh of the forearm; the bones of the childish fingers confidently resting between his own. Besides the intimacy of this first touch all previous adventures of the flesh had been counterfeit. And so they had sat silently, for unmeasured unfathomable time, before turning to look, at first gravely and then smilingly, into each other's eyes.

He wondered now how he could have so underestimated Wilfred. Happily secure in the confidence of love acknowledged and returned, he had treated Wilfred's innuendos and expostulations—when they pierced his consciousness—with pitying contempt, seeing them as no more real or threatening than the bleatings of a timid, ineffectual schoolmaster obsessively warning his boys against unnatural vice.

"It's good of you to give up so much time to Peter, but we ought to remember that we are one family at Toynton Grange. Other people would like a share of your interest. It isn't perhaps kind or wise to show too marked a preference for one person. I think that Ursula and Jennie and even poor Georgie sometimes feel neglected."

Henry had hardly heard; had certainly not bothered to reply.

"Henry, Dot tells me that you've taken to locking your door when giving Peter his lesson. I would prefer that you didn't. It is one of our rules that doors are never locked. If either of you needed medical help suddenly, it could be very dangerous."

Henry had continued to lock his door keeping the key always with him. He and Peter might have been the only two people at Toynton Grange. Lying in bed at night he began to plan and to dream, at first tentatively and then with the euphoria of hope. He had given up too early and too easily. There was still some future before him. The boy's mother hardly visited him, seldom wrote. Why shouldn't the two of them leave Toynton Grange and live together? He had his pension and some capital. He could buy a small house, at Oxford or Cambridge perhaps, and get it adapted for their two wheelchairs. When Peter was at university he would need a home. He made calculations, wrote to his bank manager, schemed how it might be organized so that the plan in its ultimate reasonableness and beauty could be presented to Peter. He knew that there were dangers. He would get worse; with luck Peter might even slightly improve. He must never let himself be a burden to the boy. Father Baddeley had only once spoken to him directly of Peter. He had brought over to Toynton

Grange a book from which Henry had planned to set a passage of précis. On leaving he had said gently, as always not baulking the truth.

"Your disease is progressive, Peter's isn't. One day he's going to have to manage without you. Remember that, my son." Well, he would remember.

In early August Mrs. Bonnington arranged for Peter to spend a fortnight with her at home. She called it taking him for a holiday. Henry had said:

"Don't write. I never expect anything good from a letter. I shall see you again in two weeks."

But Peter hadn't come back. The evening before he was due to return Wilfred had announced the news at dinner, eyes carefully avoiding Henry's.

"You'll be glad for Peter's sake to hear that Mrs. Bonnington has found a place for him nearer his home and that he won't be returning to us. She hopes to marry again fairly soon and she and her husband want to visit Peter more frequently and have him home for occasional weekends. The new home will make arrangements for Peter's education to continue. You have all worked so hard with him. I know you'll be glad to hear that it won't be wasted."

It had been very cleverly planned; he had to give Wilfred that credit. There must have been discreet telephone calls and letters to the mother, negotiations with the new home. Peter must have been on the waiting list for weeks, possibly months. Henry could imagine the phrases.

"Unhealthy interests; unnatural affection; driving the boy too hard; mental and psychological pressure."

Hardly anyone at Toynton Grange had spoken to him about the transfer. They had avoided the contamination of his misery. Grace Willison had said, shrinking from his angry eyes:

"We shall all miss him, but his own mother . . . It's natural that she should want him close to her."

"Of course. By all means let us defer to the sacred rights of motherhood."

Within a week they had apparently forgotten Peter and returned to their old pursuits as easily as children discarding new and unwanted Christmas toys. Holroyd had disconnected his apparatus and packed it away.

"Let it be a lesson to you, my dear Henry. Put not your trust in pretty boys. We can hardly expect that he was dragged to the new home by force."

"He may have been."

"Oh, come now! The boy is practically of age. He has the use of brain and speech. He can hold a pen. We have to face it that our company here was less fascinating than we had deluded ourselves. Peter is amenable. He made no objections when he was dumped here and I've no doubt he made none when he was dragged away."

Henry, on impulse, had grasped Father Baddeley's arm as he passed and asked him:

"Did you collude in this triumph for morality and mother-love?"

Father Baddeley had briefly shaken his head, a gesture so slight that it was hardly discernible. He had seemed about to speak and then, with one pressure on Henry's shoulder, had moved on, for once at a loss, offering no comfort. But Henry had felt a spurt of anger and resentment against Michael as he hadn't against anyone else at Toynton Grange. Michael who had the use of his legs and voice, who wasn't reduced by anger into a jibbering, slobbering buffoon. Michael who could surely have prevented this monstrous thing if he hadn't been inhibited by timidity, by his fear and disgust of the flesh. Michael who had no place at Toynton Grange if not to affirm love.

There had been no letter. Henry had been reduced to bribing Philby to collect the post. His paranoia had reached the stage when he believed that Wilfred might be intercepting letters. He didn't write himself. Whether or not to do so was a preoccupation which took most of his waking hours. But, less than six weeks later, Mrs. Bonnington had written to Wilfred to say that Peter was dead of pneumonia. It could, Henry knew, have happened anywhere at any time. It didn't necessarily mean that the medical and nursing care at the new home had been less good than at Toynton Grange. Peter had always been peculiarly at risk. But in his heart Henry knew that he could have kept Peter safe. In scheming his transfer from Toynton Grange Wilfred had killed him.

And Peter's murderer went about his business, smiled his indulgent lopsided smile, ceremoniously drew the folds of his cloak around him to preserve him from the contamination of human emotion, surveyed complacently the flawed objects of his beneficence. Was it his imagination, Henry wondered, that Wilfred had become afraid of him? Now they seldom spoke. Naturally solitary, Henry had become morose since Peter's death. Except for meal times he spent most of his days in his room, looking out over the desolate headland, neither reading nor working, possessed by a profound ennui. He knew that he hated rather than felt hatred. Love, joy, anger, grief even, were emotions too powerful for his diminished personality. He could entertain only their pale shadows. But hatred was like a latent fever dormant in the blood; sometimes it could flare into terrifying delirium. It was during one such a mood that Holroyd had whispered to him, had wheeled his chair across the patio and maneuvered it close to Henry. Holroyd's mouth, pink and precise as a girl's, a neat, suppurating wound in the heavy blue jaw, puckered to discharge its venom. Holroyd's breath sour in his nostrils.

"I have learnt something of interest about our dear Wilfred. I shall share it with you in time but you must forgive me if I savor it alone for a little longer. There will be a right moment for disclosure. One strives always for the maximum dramatic effect." Hatred and boredom had reduced them to this, thought Henry, two schoolboy buddies whispering secrets together, planning their petty stratagems of vengeance and betrayal.

He looked out of the tall, curved window westward over the rising headland. The darkness was falling. Somewhere out there the restless tide was scouring the rocks, rocks washed clean for ever of Holroyd's blood. Not even a twist of torn cloth remained for the barnacles to fasten on. Holroyd's dead hands like floating weeds moving sluggishly in the tide, sand-filled eyes turned upwards to the swooping gulls. What was that poem of Walt Whitman which Holroyd had read at dinner on the night before he died:

> Approach strong deliveress,
> When it is so, when thou hast taken them I joyously
>     sing the dead,
> Lost in the loving floating ocean of thee,
> Laved in the flood of thy bliss O death.
>
> The night in silence under many a star,
> The ocean shore and the husky whispering wave
>     whose voices I know,
> And the soul turning to thee O vast and well-veiled
>     death,
> And the body gratefully nestling close to thee.

Why that poem, in its sentimental resignation, at once so alien to Holroyd's embattled spirit, and yet so prophetically apposite? Was he telling them, even subconsciously, that he knew what must happen, that he embraced and welcomed it? Peter and Holroyd. Holroyd and Baddeley. And now this policeman friend of Baddeley's had arrived out of his past. Why, and for what? He might learn something when they drank together after dinner with Julius. And so, of course, might Dalgliesh. "There is no art to find the mind's construction in the face." But Duncan was wrong. There was a great deal of art and one in which a Commander of the Metropolitan Police would be better practiced than most. Well, if that was what he had come for, he could make a beginning after dinner. Tonight he, Henry, would dine in his room. Philby when summoned would bring up his tray and plonk it unceremoniously and grudgingly in front of him. It wasn't possible to buy civility from Philby but it was possible, he thought with grim exultation, to buy almost anything else.

# III

"My body is my prison; and I would be so obedient to the Law, as not to break prison; I would not hasten my death by starving or macerating this body. But if this prison be burnt down by continual fevers, or blown down with continual vapours, would any man be so in love with the ground upon which that prison stood, as to desire rather to stay there than to go home?"

It wasn't so much, thought Dalgliesh, that the Donne didn't go with the stewed mutton, as that the mutton didn't go with the home-brewed wine. Neither was in itself unpalatable. The mutton, cooked with onions, potatoes and carrots, and flavoured with herbs, was unexpectedly good if a little greasy. The elderberry wine was a nostalgic reminder of duty visits paid with his father to house-bound and hospitable parishioners. Together they tasted lethal. He reached for the water carafe.

Opposite him sat Millicent Hammitt, her square slab of a face softened by the candlelight, her absence during the afternoon explained by the pungent scent of lacquer which was wafted to him from the stiff, corrugated waves of greying hair. Everyone was present except the Hewsons, dining presumably in their own cottage, and Henry Carwardine. At the far end of the table, Albert Philby sat a little apart, a monkish Caliban in a brown habit, half crouching over his food. He ate noisily, tearing his bread into crusts and wiping them vigorously around his plate. All the patients were being helped to eat. Dalgliesh, despising his squeamishness, tried to shut his ears to the muted slobbering, the staccato rattle of spoon against plate, the sudden retching, unobtrusively controlled.

"If thou didst depart from that Table in peace, thou canst depart from this world in peace. And the peace of that Table is to come to it in pace desiderii, with a contended minde. . . ."

Wilfred stood at a reading desk at the head of the table, flanked by two candles in metal holders. Jeoffrey, distended with food, lay ceremoniously curved at his feet. Wilfred had a good voice and knew how to use it. An actor manqué? Or an actor who had found his stage and played on, happily oblivious of the dwindling audience, of the creeping paralysis of his dream? A neurotic driven by obsession? Or a man at peace with himself, secure at the still center of his being?

Suddenly the four table candles flared and hissed. Dalgliesh's ears caught the faint squeak of wheels, the gentle thud of metal against wood. The door was slowly swinging open. Wilfred's voice faltered, and then broke off. A spoon rasped violently against a plate. Out of the shadows came a wheelchair, its occupant, head bent, swaddled in a thick plaid cloak. Miss Willison gave a sad little moan and scratched the sign of the cross on her grey dress. There was a gasp from Ursula Hollis. No one spoke. Suddenly Jennie Pegram screamed, thin and insistent as a tin whistle. The sound was so unreal that Dot Moxon jerked her head round as if uncertain where the sound was coming from. The scream subsided into a giggle. The girl clamped her hand against her mouth. Then she said:

"I thought it was Victor! That's Victor's cloak."

No one else moved or spoke. Glancing along the table, Dalgliesh let his eyes rest speculatively on Dennis Lerner. His face was a mask of terror which slowly disintegrated into relief, the features seeming to droop and crumble, amorphous as a smudged painting. Carwardine wheeled his chair to the table. He had some difficulty in getting out his words. A globule of mucus gleamed like a yellow jewel in the candle light and dribbled from his chin. At last he said in his high distorted voice:

"I thought I might join you for coffee. It seemed discourteous to absent myself on our guest's first night."

Dot Moxon's voice was sharp:

"Did you have to wear that cloak?"

He turned to her:

"It was hanging in the business room and I felt cold. And we hold so much in common. Need we exclude the dead?"

Wilfred said:

"Shall we remember the Rule?"

They turned their faces to him like obedient children. He waited until they had again begun to eat. The hands which gripped the sides of the reading desk were steady, the beautiful voice perfectly controlled.

"That so riding at Anchor, and in that calme, whether God enlarge thy voyage, by enlarging thy life, or put thee into the harbour by the breath, by the breathlessness of Death, either way, East or West, thou maist depart in peace. . . ."

# IV

It was after eight-thirty before Dalgliesh set out to wheel Henry Carwardine to Julius Court's cottage. The task wasn't easy for a man in the first stages of convalescence. Carwardine, despite his leanness, was surprisingly heavy and the stony path wound uphill. Dalgliesh hadn't liked to suggest using his car since to be hoisted through the narrow door might be more painful and humiliating for his companion than the customary wheelchair. Anstey had been passing through the hall as they left. He had held open the door and helped guide the wheelchair down the ramp, but had made no attempt to assist, nor did he offer the use of the patients' bus. Dalgliesh wondered whether it was his imagination that detected a note of disapproval of the enterprise in Anstey's final goodnight.

Neither man spoke for the first part of the journey. Carwardine rested a heavy torch between his knees and tried to steady its beam on the path. The circle of light, reeling and spinning before them with every lurch of the chair, illumined with dazzling clarity a secret circular night world of greenness, movement and scurrying life. Dalgliesh, a little light-headed with tiredness, felt disassociated from his physical surroundings. The two thick rubber handgrips, slippery to the touch, were loose and twisted irritatingly beneath his hands, seeming to have no relation to the rest of the chair. The path ahead was real only because its stones and crevices jarred the wheels. The night was still and very warm for autumn, the air heavy with the smell of grass and the memory of summer flowers. Low clouds had obscured the stars and they moved forwards in almost total darkness towards the strengthening murmur of the sea and the four oblongs of light which marked Toynton Cottage. When they were close enough for the largest oblong to reveal itself as the rear door of the cottage, Dalgliesh said on impulse:

"I found a rather disagreeable poison pen letter in Father Baddeley's bureau. Obviously someone at Toynton Grange didn't like him. I wondered whether this was personal spite or whether anyone else had received one."

Carwardine bent his head upwards. Dalgliesh saw his face intriguingly foreshortened, his sharp nose a spur of bone, the jaw hanging loose as a marionette's below the shapeless void of mouth. He said:

"I had one about ten months ago, placed inside my library book, I haven't had one since, and I don't know of anyone else who has. It's not the kind of thing people talk about, but I think the news would have got around if the trouble had been endemic. Mine was, I suppose, the usual muck. It suggested what methods of somewhat acrobatic sexual self-gratification might be open to me supposing I still had the physical agility to perform them. It took the desire to do so for granted."

"It was obscene, then, rather than merely offensive?"

"Obscene in the sense of calculated to disgust rather than to deprave or corrupt, yes."

"Have you any idea who was responsible?"

"It was typed on Toynton Grange paper and on an old Remington machine used chiefly by Grace Willison to send out the quarterly newsletter. She seemed the most likely candidate. It wasn't Ursula Hollis; she didn't arrive until two months later. And aren't these things usually sent by respectable middle-aged spinsters?"

"In this case I doubt it."

"Oh, well—I defer to your greater experience of obscenity."

"Did you tell anyone?"

"Only Julius. He counselled against telling anyone else and suggested I tear the note up and flush it down the WC. As that advice coincided with my own inclination, I took it. As I said, I haven't had another. I imagine that the sport loses its thrill if the victim shows absolutely no sign of concern."

"Could it have been Holroyd?"

"It didn't really seem his style. Victor was offensive but not, I should have thought, in that particular way. His weapon was the voice, not the pen. Personally I didn't mind him as much as some of the others did. He hit out rather like an unhappy child. There was more personal bitterness than active malice. Admittedly, he added a somewhat childish codicil to his will the week before he died; Philby and Julius's housekeeper, Mrs. Reynolds, witnessed it. But that was probably because he'd made up his mind to die and wanted to relieve us all of any obligation to remember him with kindness."

"So you think he killed himself?"

"Of course. And so does everyone else. How else could it have happened? It seems the most likely hypothesis. It was either suicide or murder."

It was the first time anyone at Toynton Grange had used that portentous word. Spoken in Carwardine's pedantic, rather high voice it sounded as incongruous as blasphemy on the lips of a nun.

Dalgliesh said:

"Or the chair brakes could have been defective."

"Given the circumstances, I count that as murder."

There was silence for a moment. The chair lurched over a small boulder and the torch light swung upwards in a wide arc, a miniature and frail searchlight. Carwardine steadied it and then said:

"Philby oiled and checked the chair brakes at eight-fifty on the night before Holroyd died. I was in the workroom messing about with my modelling clay at the time. I saw him. He left the workroom shortly afterwards and I stayed on until about ten o'clock."

"Did you tell the police that?"

"Since they asked me, yes. They enquired with heavy tact where exactly I had spent the evening and whether I had touched Holroyd's chair after Philby had left. Since I would hardly have admitted the fact if I had, the question was naïve. They questioned Philby, although not in my presence, and I've no doubt that he confirmed my story. I have an ambivalent attitude towards the police; I confine myself strictly to answering their questions, but on the premise that they are, in general, entitled to the truth."

They had arrived. Light streamed from the rear door of the cottage and Julius Court, a dark silhouette, emerged to meet them. He took the wheelchair from Dalgliesh and pushed it along the short stone passage leading into the sitting-room. On the way Dalgliesh just had time to glimpse through an open door the pine-covered walls, red tiled floor and gleaming chrome of Julius's kitchen, a kitchen too like his own where a woman, overpaid and underworked to assuage her employer's guilt for hiring her at all, cooked the occasional meal to gratify one person's over-fastidious taste.

The sitting-room occupied the whole of the front ground floor of what had obviously originally been two cottages. A fire of driftwood crackled on the open hearth but both the long windows were open to the night. The stone walls vibrated with the thudding of the sea. It was disconcerting to feel so close to the cliff edge and yet not know precisely how close. As if reading his thoughts, Julius said:

"We're just six yards from the forty-foot drop to the rocks. There's a stone patio and low wall outside; we might sit there later if it's warm enough. What will you drink, spirits or wine? I know Henry's preference is for claret."

"Claret please."

Dalgliesh didn't repent of his choice when he saw the labels on the three bottles which were standing, two already uncorked, on the low table near the hearth. He was surprised that wine of such quality should be produced for two casual guests. While Julius busied himself with the glasses, Dalgliesh wandered about the room. It contained enviable objects, if one were in a mood to prize personal possessions. His eyes lit on a splendid Sunderland lustreware jug commemorating Trafalgar, three early Staffordshire figures on the stone mantelpiece, a couple of agreeable seascapes on the longest wall. Above the door leading to the cliff edge was a ship's figure-head finely and ornately carved in oak; two cherubs supported a galleon topped with a shield and swathed with heavy seaman's knots. Seeing his interest, Julius called out:

"It was made about 1660 by Grinling Gibbons, reputedly for Jacob Court, a smuggler in these parts. As far as I can discover, he was absolutely no ancestor of mine, worse luck. It's probably the oldest merchant ship figurehead known to exist. Greenwich think they have one earlier, but I'd give mine the benefit of a couple of years."

Set on a pedestal at the far end of the room and faintly gleaming as if luminous was the marble bust of a winged child holding in his chubby hand a posy of rosebuds and lilies of the valley. The marble was the color of pale coffee except over the lids of the closed eyes which were tinged with a faint pink. The unveined hands held the flowers with the upright, unselfconscious grip of a child; the boy's lips were slightly parted in a half-smile, tranquil and secretive. Dalgliesh stretched out a finger and gently stroked the cheek; he could imagine it warm to his touch. Julius came over to him carrying two glasses.

"You like my marble? It's a memorial piece, of course, seventeenth or very early eighteenth century and derived from Bernini. Henry, I suspect, would like it better if it were Bernini."

Henry called out:

"I wouldn't like it better. I did say I'd be prepared to pay more for it."

Dalgliesh and Court moved back to the fireplace and settled down for what was obviously intended to be a night of serious drinking. Dalgliesh found his eyes straying around the room. There was no bravura, no conscious striving after originality or effect. And yet, trouble had been taken; every object was in the right place. They had, he thought, been bought because Julius liked them; they weren't part of a careful scheme of capital appreciation, nor acquired out of an obsessive need to add to his collection. Yet Dalgliesh doubted whether any had been casually discovered or cheaply bought. The furniture too, betrayed wealth. The leather sofa and the two winged and back buttoned leather chairs were perhaps too opulent for the proportions and basic simplicity of the room, but Julius had obviously chosen them for comfort. Dalgliesh reproached himself for the streak of puritanism which compared the room unfavorably with the snug, unindulgent shabbiness of Father Baddeley's sitting-room.

Carwardine, sitting in his wheelchair and staring into the fire above the rim of his glass, asked suddenly:

"Did Baddeley warn you about the more bizarre manifestations of Wilfred's philanthropy, or was your visit here unpremeditated?"

It was a question Dalgliesh had been expecting. He sensed that both men were more than casually interested in his reply.

"Father Baddeley wrote to say that he would be glad to see me. I decided to come on impulse. I've had a spell in hospital and it seemed a good idea to spend a few days of my convalescence with him."

Carwardine said:

"I can think of more suitable places than Hope Cottage for convalescence, if the inside is anything like the exterior. Had you known Baddeley long?"

"Since boyhood; he was my father's curate. But we last met, and only briefly, when I was at university."

"And having been content to know nothing of each other for a decade or so, you're naturally distressed to find him so inconveniently dead."

Unprovoked, Dalgliesh replied equably:

"More than I would have expected. We seldom wrote except to exchange cards at Christmas but he was a man more often in my thoughts, I suppose, than some people I saw almost daily. I don't know why I never bothered to get in touch. One makes the excuse of busyness. But, from what I remember of him, I can't quite see how he fitted in here."

Julius laughed:

"He didn't. He was recruited when Wilfred was going through a more orthodox phase, I suppose to give Toynton Grange a certain religious respectability. But in recent months I sensed a coolness between them, didn't you, Henry? Father Baddeley was probably no longer sure whether Wilfred wanted a priest or a guru. Wilfred picks up any scraps of philosophy, metaphysics and orthodox religion which take his fancy to make his Technicolor dreamcoat. As a result, as you'll probably discover if you stay long enough, this place suffers from the lack of a coherent ethos. There's nothing more fatal to success. Take my London club, dedicated simply to the enjoyment of good food and wine and the exclusion of bores and pederasts. It's unstated of course, but we all know where we stand. The aims are simple and comprehensible and, therefore, realizable. Here the poor dears don't know whether they're in a nursing home, a commune, a hotel, a monastery or a particularly dotty lunatic asylum. They even have meditation sessions from time to time. I'm afraid Wilfred may be getting a touch of the Zens."

Carwardine broke in:

"He's muddled, but which of us isn't? Basically he's kind and well meaning, and at least he's spent his own personal fortune at Toynton Grange. In this age of noisy and self-indulgent commitment when the first principle of private or public protest is that it mustn't relate to anything for which the protestor can be held in the least responsible or involve him in the slightest personal sacrifice that, at least, is in his favor."

"You like him?" asked Dalgliesh.

Henry Carwardine answered with surprising roughness.

"As he's saved me from the ultimate fate of incarceration in a long-stay hospital and gives me a private room at a price I can afford, I'm naturally bound to find him delightful."

There was a short, embarrassed silence. Sensing it, Carwardine added:

"The food is the worst thing about Toynton, but that can be remedied, even if I do occasionally feel like a greedy schoolboy feasting alone in my room. And listening to my fellow inmates read their favorite bleeding chunks from popular theology and the less enterprising anthologies of English verse is a small price to pay for silence at dinner."

Dalgliesh said:

"Staffing must be a difficulty. According to Mrs. Hewson, Anstey chiefly relies on an ex-convict and an otherwise unemployable matron."

Julius Court reached out for the claret and refilled the three glasses. He said:

"Dear Maggie, discreet as always. It's true that Philby, the handyman, has some kind of record. He's not exactly an advertisement for the place, but someone has to sluice the foul linen, slaughter the chickens, clean the lavatories and do the other jobs which Wilfred's sensitive soul cringes at. Besides, he's passionately devoted to Dot Moxon, and I've no doubt that helps to keep her happy. Since Maggie has let slip so much, you may as well know the truth about Dot. Perhaps you remember something of the case—she was that notorious staff nurse at Nettingfield Geriatric Hospital. Four years ago she struck a patient. It was only a light blow but the old woman fell, knocked her head against a bedside locker and nearly died. Reading between the lines at the subsequent enquiry report, she was a selfish, demanding, foul-mouthed virago who would have tempted a saint. Her family would have nothing to do with her—didn't even visit—until they discovered that there was a great deal of agreeable publicity to be made out of righteous indignation. Perfectly proper too, no doubt. Patients, however disagreeable, are sacrosanct and it's in all our ultimate interests to uphold that admirable precept. The incident sparked off a spate of complaints about the hospital. There was a full-dress enquiry covering the administration, medical services, food, nursing care, the lot. Not surprisingly, they found plenty to enquire into. Two male nurses were subsequently dismissed and Dot left of her own accord. The enquiry, while deploring her loss of control, exonerated her from any suspicion of deliberate cruelty. But the damage was done; no other hospital wanted her. Apart from the suspicion that she wasn't exactly reliable under stress, they blamed her for provoking an enquiry which did no one any good and lost two men their jobs. Afterwards, Wilfred tried to get in touch with her; he thought from the accounts of the enquiry that she'd been hard done by. He took some time to trace her, but succeeded in the end and invited her here as a kind of matron. Actually, like the rest of the staff, she does anything that's needed from nursing to cooking. His motives weren't entirely beneficent. It's never easy to find nursing staff for a remote specialized place like this, apart from the unorthodoxy of Wilfred's methods. If he lost Dorothy Moxon he wouldn't easily find a replacement."

Dalgliesh said:

"I remember the case but not her face. It's the young blonde girl—Jennie Pegram, isn't it?—who looks familiar."

Carwardine smiled; indulgent, a little contemptuous.

"I thought you might ask about her. Wilfred ought to find a way of using her for fund raising, she'd love it. I don't know anyone who's better at assuming that expression of wistful, uncomprehending, long-suffering fortitude. She'd make a fortune for the place properly exploited."

Julius laughed:

"Henry, as you have gathered, doesn't like her. If she looks familiar, you may have seen her on television about eighteen months ago. It was the month for the media to lacerate the British conscience on behalf of the young chronic sick, and the producer sent out his underlings to scavenge for a suitable victim. They came up with Jennie. She had been nursed for twelve years, and very well nursed, in a geriatric unit, partly, I gather, because they couldn't find a more suitable place for her, partly because she rather liked being the petted favorite of the patients and visitors, and partly because the hospital had group physiotherapy and occupational therapy facilities of which our Jennie took advantage. But the program, as you can imagine, made the most of her situation—"Unfortunate twenty-five-year-old girl incarcerated among the old and dying; shut away from the community; helpless; hopeless." All the most senile patients were carefully grouped round her for the benefit of the camera with Jennie in the middle doing her stuff magnificently. Shrill accusations against the inhumanity of the Department of Health, the regional hospital board, the hospital managers. Next day, predictably, there was a public outburst of indignation which lasted, I imagine, until the next protest program. The compassionate British public demanded that a more suitable place be found for Jennie. Wilfred wrote offering a vacancy here, Jennie accepted, and fourteen months ago she arrived. No one quite knows what she makes of us. I should give a lot to look into what passes for Jennie's mind."

Dalgliesh was surprised that Julius had such an intimate knowledge of the patients at Toynton Grange, but he asked no more questions. He dropped unobtrusively out of the chatter and sat drinking his wine, half listening to the desultory voices of his companions. It was the quiet, undemanding talk of men who had acquaintances and interests in common, who knew just enough about each other and cared just sufficiently to create an illusion of companionship. He had no particular wish to share it. The wine deserved silence. He realized that this was the first fine wine he had drunk since his illness. It was reassuring that yet another of life's pleasures still held its power to solace. It took him a minute to realize that Julius was talking to him directly.

"I'm sorry about the proposed poetry reading. But I'm not altogether displeased. It illustrates one thing that you'll realize about Toynton. They exploit. They don't mean to, but they can't help it. They say that they want to be treated as ordinary people, and then make demands no ordinary person would dream of making, and naturally one can't refuse. Now, perhaps, you won't think too harshly of those of us who seem less than enthusiastic about Toynton."

"Us?"

"The little group of normals, physically normal anyway, in thrall to the place."

"Are you?"

"Oh, yes! I get away to London or abroad so that the spell never really has a chance to take hold. But think of Millicent, stuck in that cottage because Wilfred lets her have it rent free. All she wants is to get back to the bridge tables and cream cakes of Cheltenham Spa. So why doesn't she? And Maggie. Maggie would say that all she wanted was a bit of life. Well, that's what we all want, a bit of life. Wilfred tried to get her interested in bird watching. I remember her reply. 'If

I have to watch another bloody seagull shitting on Toynton Head I'll run screaming into the sea.' Dear Maggie. I rather take to Maggie when she's sober. And Eric? Well, he could break away if he had the courage. Looking after five patients and medically supervising the production of hand lotion and bath powder is hardly an honorable job for a registered medical practitioner, even one with an unfortunate predilection for little girls. And then there's Helen Rainer. But I rather fancy that our enigmatic Helen's reason for staying is more elemental and understandable. But they're all a prey of boredom. And now I'm boring you. Would you like to hear some music? We usually listen to records when Henry's here."

The claret, unaccompanied by speech or music, would have contented Dalgliesh. But he could see that Henry was as anxious to hear a record as Julius probably was to demonstrate the superiority of his stereo equipment. Invited to choose Dalgliesh asked for Vivaldi. While the record was playing he strolled out into the night. Julius followed him and they stood in silence at the low barricade of stone at the cliff edge. The sea lay before them, faintly luminous, ghostly under a scatter of high, unemphatic stars. He thought that the tide was on the ebb but it still sounded very close, thudding against the rocky beach in great chords of sound, a bass accompaniment to the high, sweet counterpoint of the distant violins. Dalgliesh thought that he could feel the spume light on his forehead, but when he put up his hand he found it was only a trick of the freshening breeze.

So there must have been two poison pen writers, only one genuinely committed to his or her obscene trade. It was obvious from Grace Willison's distress and Carwardine's laconic disgust that they had received a very different type of letter from the one found at Hope Cottage. It was too great a coincidence that two poison pens should be operating at the same time in so small a community. The assumption was that Father Baddeley's note had been planted in the bureau after his death, with small attempt at concealment, for Dalgliesh to find. If this were so, then it must have been put there by someone who knew about at least one of the other letters; had been told that it was typed on a Toynton Grange machine and on Toynton Grange paper, but who hadn't actually seen it. Grace Willison's letter had been typed on the Imperial machine and she had confided only in Dot Moxon. Carwardine's, like Father Baddeley's, had been typed on the Remington, and he had told Julius Court. The inference was obvious. But how could a man as intelligent as Court expect such a childish ruse to deceive a professional detective, or even an enthusiastic amateur? But then, had it been intended to? Dalgliesh had signed his postcard to Father Baddeley only with his initials. If it had been found by someone with a guilty secret as he searched feverishly through the bureau it would have told him nothing except that Father Baddeley was expecting a visitor on the afternoon of 1st October, a visitor who was probably as innocuous as a fellow clergyman or an old parishioner. But, just in case Father Baddeley had confided that something was on his mind, it would have seemed worthwhile to concoct and plant a false clue. Almost certainly, it had been placed in the bureau shortly before his arrival. If Anstey were telling the truth about looking through Father Baddeley's papers on the morning after his death, it was impossible that he should have missed the poison pen note or failed to remove it.

But even if all this were an elaborate and over-sophisticated edifice of conjecture, and Father Baddeley had indeed received the poison pen note, Dalgliesh now felt certain that it wasn't the reason for his summons. Father Baddeley would have felt perfectly competent both to discover the sender and to deal with him. He was unworldly but not naïve. Unlike Dalgliesh, he had probably seldom become involved professionally with the more spectacular sins but that didn't mean they were outside his comprehension or, for that matter, his compassion. It was arguable, anyway, that those were the sins which did least damage. Of the more corrosive, petty, mean-minded delinquencies in all their sad but limited variety he, like any other parish priest, would have had his fill. He had his answer ready, compassionate but inexorable, offered, Dalgliesh remembered wryly with all the gentle arrogance of absolute certainty. No, when Father Baddeley wrote he wanted professional advice he meant just that; advice which he could only get only from a police officer on a matter which he felt unable to deal with himself. And that was unlikely to include the detection of a spiteful but not particularly vicious poison pen writer operating in a small community of which every member must have been known intimately to him.

The prospect of trying to discover the truth filled Dalgliesh with a profound depression. He was at Toynton Grange merely as a private visitor. He had no standing, no facilities, no equipment even. The task of sorting Father Baddeley's books could be stretched to cover a week, perhaps longer. After that, what excuse would he have to remain? And he had discovered nothing which would justify bringing in the local police. What did these vague suspicions, this sense of foreboding amount to? An old man, dying of heart disease, suffering his final and expected attack peacefully in his fireside chair, reaching perhaps in his last conscious moment for the familiar feel of his stole, lifting it over his head for the last time for reasons, probably only half understood, of comfort, of reassurance, of symbolism, of the simple affirmation of his priesthood or his faith. One could think of a dozen explanations, all simple, all more plausible than the secret visit of a murderous mock penitent. The missing diary; who could ever prove that Father Baddeley hadn't himself destroyed it before his admission to hospital? The forced bureau lock; nothing but the diary was missing and, as far as he knew, nothing valuable had been stolen. In the absence of other evidence, how could he possibly justify an official enquiry into a mislaid key and a broken lock?

But Father Baddeley had sent for him. There had been something on his mind. If Dalgliesh, without too great involvement, inconvenience or embarrassment, could discover in the next week or ten days what it had been, then he would do so. He owed that at least to the old man. But there it would end. Tomorrow he would pay a duty visit to the police and to Father Baddeley's solicitor. If anything came to light, then the police could deal with it. He was finished with police work, professional or amateur, and it would take more than the death of one old priest to change that decision.

# V

When they got back to Toynton Grange shortly after midnight Henry Carwardine said roughly:

"They'll be relying on you to help me to bed, I'm afraid. Dennis Lerner usually wheels me to Toynton Cottage and calls for me at midnight, but since you're here . . . As Julius said, we're great exploiters at Toynton Grange. And I'd better shower. Dennis is off duty tomorrow morning and I can't stomach Philby. My room is on the first floor. We take the lift."

Henry knew that he sounded ungracious but that, he guessed, would be more acceptable to his silent companion than humility or self-pity. It struck him that Dalgliesh looked as if he could have done with help himself. Perhaps the man had been more sick than they realized. Dalgliesh said calmly:

"Another half bottle and I suspect we would both have needed help. But I'll do my best. Put down my clumsiness to inexperience and the claret."

But he was surprisingly gentle and competent, getting Henry out of his clothes, supporting him to the lavatory, and finally, wheeling him under the shower. He spent a little time examining the hoist and equipment and then used them intelligently. When he didn't know what was needed, he asked. Apart from these brief and necessary exchanges, neither spoke. Henry thought that he had seldom been put to bed with such imaginative gentleness. But, catching a glimpse in the bathroom mirror of his companion's drawn preoccupied face, of the dark secretive eyes cavernous with fatigue, he wished suddenly that he hadn't asked for help, that he had tumbled unshowered and fully dressed on to his bed, free from the humiliating touch of these competent hands. He sensed that, behind the disciplined calm, every contact with his naked body was a disagreeable duty. And for Henry himself, illogically and surprisingly, the touch of Dalgliesh's cool hands was like the touch of fear. He wanted to cry out:

"What are you doing here? Go away; don't interfere; leave us in peace." The urge was so strong that he could almost believe that he had spoken the words aloud. And when, at last, he was comfortably bedded by his temporary nurse and Dalgliesh said an abrupt goodbye and immediately left him without another word, he knew that it was because he couldn't bear to hear even the most perfunctory and least gracious word of thanks.

# BOOK FOUR

·

# The Dreadful Shore

# I

He awoke sluggishly soon before seven to disagreeably familiar noises; intrusive plumbing, the clang of apparatus, the squeal of chair wheels, sudden hurrying footsteps, determinedly cheerful exhortatory voices. Telling himself that the bathrooms would be needed for the patients, he shut his eyes resolutely on the bleak, impersonal room and willed himself to sleep again. When he woke an hour later after a fitful doze the annex was silent. Someone—he dimly remembered a brown cloaked figure—had placed a mug of tea on his bedside table. It was cold, the greyish surface mottled with milk. He dragged on his dressing gown and went in search of the bathroom.

Breakfast at Toynton Grange was, as he had expected, laid out in the communal dining room. But, at eight-thirty, he was either too early or too late for the majority of the inmates. Only Ursula Hollis was breakfasting when he arrived. She gave him a shy good morning, then returned her eyes to the library book precariously propped against a jar of honey. Dalgliesh saw that the breakfast was simple, but adequate. There was a bowl of stewed apples; homemade muesli consisting mostly of porridge oats, bran and shredded apple; brown bread and margarine, and a row of boiled eggs each in its eggcup and individually named. The two remaining were cold. Presumably they were all cooked together earlier in the morning, and those who wanted their egg warm took the trouble to be on time. Dalgliesh helped himself to the egg pencilled with his name. It was glutinous at the top and very hard at the bottom, a result which he felt must have taken some perverse culinary skill to achieve.

After breakfast he went in search of Anstey to thank him for his overnight hospitality and to ask if there was anything he wanted in Wareham. He had decided that some of the afternoon had better be given over to shopping if he were to make himself comfortable in Michael's cottage. A short search of the seemingly deserted house found Anstey with Dorothy Moxon in the business room. They were seated together at the table with an open ledger before them. As he knocked and entered they looked up simultaneously with something of the air of guilty conspirators. It seemed to take a couple of seconds before they realized who he was. Anstey's smile, when it came, was as sweet as ever but his eyes were preoccupied and his enquiries over his guest's comforts were perfunctory. Dalgliesh sensed that he wouldn't be sorry to see him go. Anstey might see himself in the role of a welcoming medieval abbot, always ready with the bread and ale, but what he really craved were the gratifications of hospitality without the inconvenience of a guest. He said there was nothing he wanted in Wareham and then asked Dalgliesh how long he expected to be in the cottage. There was absolutely no hurry, of course. Their guest wasn't to feel himself at all in the way. When Dalgliesh replied that he would stay only until Father Baddeley's books were sorted and packed, it was difficult for him to conceal his relief. He offered to send Philby to Hope Cottage with some packing cases. Dorothy Moxon said nothing. She continued to stare fixedly at Dalgliesh as if determined not to betray her irritation at his presence and her desire to get back to the ledger by so much as a flicker of her somber eyes.

It was comforting to be back in Hope Cottage, to smell again the familiar faintly ecclesiastical smell and to look forward to a long exploratory walk along the cliff before setting out for Wareham. But he had scarcely had time to unpack his case and change into stout walking shoes when he heard the patients' bus stopping outside and, going to the window, saw Philby unloading the first of the promised packing cases. Swinging it on to his shoulder, he marched up the short path, kicked open the door, bringing with him into the room a powerful smell of stale sweat, and dropped the case at Dalgliesh's feet with a brusque:

"There's a couple more in the back."

It was an obvious invitation to help unload them, and Dalgliesh took the hint. It was the first time he had seen the handyman in the full light, and the sight wasn't agreeable. He had, in fact, seldom encountered a man whose physical appearance so repelled him. Philby was only a little over five feet tall and stockily built with short plump arms and legs as pale and shapeless as peeled tree trunks. His head was round and his skin, despite his outdoor life, was pink and glossy and very smooth as if blown-up with air. His eyes would have been remarkable in a more attractive face. They were slightly slanted and the irises were large and blue-black in color. His black hair was scanty and combed straight back over the domed skull to end in an untidy and greasy fringe. He was wearing sandals, the right one fastened with string; a pair of dirty white shorts, so brief that they were almost indecent; and a grey vest, stained with sweat. Over this he wore, loosely open and held together only by a cord at the waist, his brown monk's habit. Without this incongruous garb he would have looked merely dirty and disreputable. With it he looked positively sinister.

As he made no attempt to go once the cases were unloaded, Dalgliesh deduced that he expected a tip. The proffered coins were slipped into the pocket of the habit with sly expertise but with no thanks. Dalgliesh was interested to learn that, despite the expensive experiment with home-produced eggs, not all the economic laws were defunct in this unworldly abode of brotherly love. Philby gave the three boxes a vicious valedictory kick as if to earn his tip by demonstrating that they were sound. As they disappointingly remained intact, he gave them a final look of sour displeasure and then departed. Dalgliesh wondered where Anstey had recruited this particular member of the staff. To his prejudiced eye the man looked like a category 'A' rapist on license, but perhaps that was going a little too far even for Wilfred Anstey.

His second attempt to set out was frustrated by a second visitor, this time Helen Rainer who had cycled the short distance from Toynton Grange with her bicycle basket piled high with the linen from his bed. She explained that Wilfred was concerned in case the sheets at Hope Cottage were inadequately aired. It surprised Dalgliesh that she hadn't taken the opportunity to come with Philby in the bus. But perhaps, understandably, she found his proximity distasteful. She came in quietly but briskly and without too obviously making Dalgliesh feel he was a nuisance, unmistakably conveyed the impression that this wasn't a social visit, that she hadn't come to chat, and that there were more important duties awaiting her. They made the bed together, Nurse Rainer flicking the sheets into place and neatly mitring each corner with such brisk expertise that Dalgliesh, a second or two behind her, felt himself slow and incompetent. At first they worked in silence. He doubted whether this was the time to ask, however tactfully, how the misunderstanding had arisen over the neglected visit to Father Baddeley on the last night of his life. His stay in hospital must have intimidated him. It took an effort of will to say:

"I'm probably being over-sensitive, but I wish that someone had been with Father Baddeley when he died, or at least had looked in on him later that night to see that all was well."

She could with justice, he thought, reply to this implied criticism by pointing out that it came inappropriately from someone who had shown no concern for the old man for nearly thirty years. But she said without rancor, almost eagerly:

"Yes, that was bad. It couldn't have made any difference medically, but the misunderstanding shouldn't have happened, one of us ought to have looked in. Do you want this third blanket? If not, I'll take it back to Toynton Grange, it's one of ours."

"Two will be enough. What exactly happened?"

"To Father Baddeley? He died of acute myocarditis."

"I mean, how did the misunderstanding arise?"

"I served him a cold lunch of chicken and salad when he arrived back from hospital and then settled him for his afternoon rest. He was ready for it. Dot took him his afternoon tea and helped him to wash. She got him into his pajamas and he insisted on wearing his cassock on top. I cooked scrambled eggs for him in the kitchen here shortly after six-thirty. He was absolutely insistent that he wanted to spend the rest of the evening undisturbed, except, of course, for Grace Willison's visit, but I told him that someone would come in about ten and he seemed perfectly happy with that. He said that he'd rap on the wall with the poker if he were in any distress. Then I went next door to ask Millicent to listen for him and she offered to look in on him last thing. At least, that's what I understood. Apparently she thought that Eric or I would come. As I said, it shouldn't have happened. I blame myself. It wasn't Eric's fault. As his nurse, I should have ensured that he was seen again professionally before he went to bed."

Dalgliesh asked:

"This insistence on being alone; did you get the impression that he was expecting a visitor?"

"What visitor could he be expecting, other than poor Grace? I think he'd had enough of people while he was in hospital and just wanted some peace."

"And you were all here at Toynton Grange that night?"

"All except Henry who hadn't got back from London. Where else could we be?"

"Who unpacked his case for him?"

"I did. He was admitted to hospital as an emergency and had very few things with him, only those which we found by his bed and packed."

"His Bible, prayer book and his diary?"

She looked up at him briefly, her face expressionless, before bending again to tuck in a blanket.

"Yes."

"What did you do with them?"

"I left them on the small table beside his chair. He may have moved them later."

So the diary had been with Father Baddeley in hospital. That meant that the record would have been up to date. And if Anstey were not lying about its being missing next morning, then it had been removed some time within those twelve hours.

He wondered how he could phrase his next question without arousing her suspicions. Keeping his voice light, he said:

"You may have neglected him in life but you looked after him very thoroughly after he died. First cremation and then burial. Wasn't that a little over-conscientious?"

To his surprise she burst out as if he had invited her to share a justified indignation:

"Of course it was! It was ridiculous! But that was Millicent's fault. She told Wilfred that Michael had frequently expressed his strong wish to be cremated. I can't think when or why. Although they were neighbors, she and Michael didn't exactly live in each other's pockets. But that's what she said. Wilfred was equally sure that Michael would want an orthodox Christian burial, so the poor man got both. It meant a lot of extra trouble and expense and Dr. McKeith from Wareham had to sign a medical certificate as well as Eric. All that fuss just because Wilfred had a bad conscience."

"Did he? About what?"

"Oh, nothing. I just got the impression that he felt that Michael had been a bit neglected one way and another, the usual self-indulgent compunction of the bereaved. Is this pillow going to be adequate? It feels very lumpy to me, and you look as if you could do with a good night's rest. Don't forget to come up to the Grange if there's anything you need. The milk is delivered to the boundary gate. I've ordered a pint for you each day. If that's too much, we can always use it. Now, have you everything you need?"

With a sensation of being under firm discipline Dalgliesh said meekly that he had. Nurse Rainer's briskness, her confidence, her concentration on the job in hand, even her reassuring smile of farewell, all relegated him to the status of a patient. As she wheeled her bicycle down the path and remounted, he felt that he had been visited by the district nurse. But he felt an increased respect for her. She hadn't appeared to resent his questions, and she had certainly been remarkably forthcoming. He wondered why.

## II

It was a warm misty morning under a sky of low cloud. As he left the valley and began to trudge up the cliff path a reluctant rain began to fall in slow heavy drops. The sea was a milky blue, sluggish and opaque, its slopping waves pitted with rain and awash with shifting patterns of floating foam. There was a smell of autumn as if someone far off, undetected even by a wisp of smoke, was burning leaves. The narrow path rose higher skirting the cliff edge, now close enough to give him a brief vertiginous illusion of danger, now twisting inland between a tatter of bronzed bracken crumpled with the wind, and low tangles of bramble bushes, their red and black berries tight and meager compared with the luscious fruit of inland hedgerows. The headland was dissected by low broken walls of stone and studded with small limestone rocks. Some, half buried, protruded tipsily from the soil like the relics of a disorderly graveyard.

Dalgliesh walked warily. It was his first country walk since his illness. The demands of his job meant that walking had always been a rare and special pleasure. Now he moved with something of the uncertainty of those first tentative steps of convalescence, muscles and senses rediscovering remembered pleasures, not with keen delight but with the gentle acceptance of familiarity. The brief metallic warble and churling note of stonechats, busy among the brambles; a solitary black-headed gull motionless as a ship's figurehead on a promontory of rock; clumps of rock samphire, their umbels stained with purple; yellow dandelions, pinpoints of brightness on the faded autumnal grass.

After nearly ten minutes of walking the cliff path began to slope gently downhill and was eventually dissected by a narrow lane running inland from the cliff edge. About six yards from the sea it broadened into a gently sloping plateau of bright green turf and moss. Dalgliesh stopped suddenly as if stung by memory. This then, must be the place where Victor Holroyd had chosen to sit, the spot from which he had plunged to his death. For a moment he wished that it hadn't lain so inconveniently in his path. The thought of violent death broke disagreeably into his euphoria. But he could understand the attraction of the spot. The lane was secluded and sheltered from the wind, there was a sense of privacy and peace; a precarious peace for a man captive in a wheelchair and with only the power of its brakes holding the balance between life and death. But that may have been part of the attraction. Perhaps only here, poised above the sea on this secluded patch of bright moss, could Holroyd, frustrated and chair-bound, gain an illusion of freedom, of being in control of his destiny. He might always have intended to make here his final bid for release, insisting month after month on being wheeled to the same spot, biding his time so that no one at Toynton Grange suspected his real purpose. Instinctively, Dalgliesh studied the ground. Over three weeks had passed since Holroyd's death but he thought he could still detect the faint indentation of the soft turf where the wheels had rested and, less plainly, marks where the short grass had been matted with the scuffle of policemen's feet.

He walked to the cliff edge and looked down. The view, spectacular and frightening, made him catch his breath. The cliffs had changed and here the limestone had given place to an almost vertical wall of blackish clay larded with calcareous stone. Almost a hundred and fifty feet below, the cliff tumbled into a broad fissured causeway of boulders, slabs and amorphous chunks of blue-black rock which littered the foreshore as if hurled in wild disorder by a giant hand. The tide was out and the oblique line of foam moved sluggishly among the furthest rocks. As he looked down on this chaotic and awe-inspiring waste of rock and sea and tried to picture what the fall must have done to Holroyd, the sun moved fitfully from behind the clouds and a band of sunlight moved across the headland lying warm as a hand on the back of his neck, gilding the bracken, marbling the strewn rocks at the cliff edge. But it left the foreshore in shadow, sinister and unfriendly. For a moment Dalgliesh believed that he was looking down on a cursed and dreadful shore on which the sun could never shine.

Dalgliesh had been making for the black tower marked on Father Baddeley's map, less from a curiosity to see it than from the need to set an object for his walk. Still musing on Victor Holroyd's death, he came upon the tower almost unexpectedly. It was a squat intimidating folly, circular for about two-thirds of its height but topped with an octagonal cupola like a pepperpot pierced with eight glazed slit windows, compass points of reflected light which gave it something of the look of a lighthouse. The tower intrigued him and he moved round it touching the black walls. He saw that it had been built of limestone blocks but faced with the black shale as if capriciously decorated with pellets of polished jet. In places the shale had flaked away giving the tower a mottled appearance; black nacreous scales littered the base of the walls and gleamed among the grasses. To the north, and sheltered from the sea, was a tangle of plants as if someone had once tried to plant a small garden. Now nothing remained but a dishevelled clump of Michaelmas daisies, patches of self-seeded antirrhinums, marigolds and nasturtiums, and a single etiolated rose with two white, starved buds, its stem bent double against the stone as if resigned to the first frost.

To the east was an ornate stone porch above an iron-bound oak door. Dalgliesh lifted the heavy handle and twisted it with difficulty. But the door was locked. Looking up he saw that there was a rough stone plaque set in the wall of the porch with a carved inscription:

IN THIS TOWER DIED WILFRED MANCROFT ANSTEY
27TH OCTOBER 1887 AGED 69 YEARS
CONCEPTIO CULPA NASCI PENA LABOR VITA NECESSI MORI
ADAM OF ST. VICTOR AD 1129

A strange epitaph for a Victorian landed gentleman and a bizarre place in which to die. The present owner of Toynton Grange had perhaps inherited a degree of eccentricity. CONCEPTIO CULPA: the theology of original sin had been discarded by modern man with other inconvenient dogma; even in 1887 it must have been on the way out. NASCI PENA: anaesthesia had mercifully done something to vitiate that dogmatic assertion. LABOR VITA: not if twentieth-century technological man could help it. NECESSI MORI: ah, there was still the rub. Death. One could ignore it, fear it, even welcome it, but never defeat it. It remained as obtrusive but more durable than these commemorative stones. Death: the same yesterday, today and for ever. Had Wilfred Mancroft Anstey himself chosen and taken comfort from this stark memento mori?

He continued walking along the cliff edge, skirting a small pebbled bay. About twenty yards ahead was a rough path to the beach, steep and probably treacherous in wet weather but obviously partly the result of a felicitous natural arrangement of the rock face and partly the work of man. Immediately beneath him, however, the cliff fell away in an almost vertical face of limestone. He saw with surprise that even at this early hour there were two roped climbers on the rock. The upper and bareheaded figure was instantly recognizable as Julius Court. When the second looked up Dalgliesh glimpsed the face under the red climbing helmet and saw that his companion was Dennis Lerner.

They were climbing slowly but competently, so competently that he felt no temptation to move back in case the unexpected sight of a spectator should break their concentration. They had obviously done this climb before; the route, the techniques were familiar to them. Now they were on the last pitch. Watching Court's smooth unhurrying movements, the splayed limbs leechlike on the rock face, he found himself reliving some of the climbs of his boyhood and making the ascent with them, mentally documenting each stage. Traverse right about fifteen feet with peg protection; step up with difficulty; then on to a small pinnacle block; gain the next ledge by a mantelshelf; climb the groove with the aid of two pegs and one sling to the horizontal crack; follow the groove again to a small ledge in the corner; finally climb with the aid of two pegs to the top.

Ten minutes later Dalgliesh strolled slowly round to where Julius was heaving his shoulders over the edge of the cliff. He drew himself up and stood, slightly panting, beside Dalgliesh. Without speaking he banged a peg into a crack of the rock beside one of the larger boulders, clipped a sling through the peg and into his waistline and started hauling in the rope. There was a cheerful shout from the rock face. Julius settled himself back against the boulder, rope around his waist, shouted "Climb when you're ready," and began inching the rope through careful hands. Less than fifteen minutes later, Dennis Lerner stood beside him and began coiling the rope. Blinking rapidly Dennis took off his steel-rimmed spectacles, rubbed away what could have been spray or rain drops from his face and twisted the ends behind his ears with shaking fingers. Julius looked at his watch:

"One hour twelve minutes, our best so far."

He turned to Dalgliesh.

"There aren't many climbs on this part of the coast because of the shale, so we try to improve our time. Do you climb? I could lend you some gear."

"I haven't done much since I left school and judging from what I've just seen, I'm not in your class."

He didn't bother to explain that he was still too convalescent to climb safely. Once he might have found it necessary to justify his reluctance, but it had been some years now since he bothered how other people judged his physical courage. Julius said:

"Wilfred used to climb with me but about three months ago we discovered that someone had deliberately frayed one of his ropes. We were about to tackle this particular climb, incidentally. He refused to try to discover who was responsible. Someone at the Grange expressing a personal grievance, I suppose. Wilfred must expect these occasional contretemps. It's an occupational hazard for playing God. He was never in real danger. I always insist on checking equipment before we start. But it unnerved him, perhaps gave him the excuse he was looking for to give up climbing. He was never much good. Now I depend on Dennis when he has a day off, as today."

Lerner turned and smiled directly at Dalgliesh. The smile transformed his face, releasing it from strain. He looked suddenly boyish, confiding:

"I'm just as terrified as Wilfred most of the time but I'm learning. It's fascinating; I'm getting to love it. There's a mild climb about half a mile back, guillemot ledge. Julius started me off there. It's really quite gentle. We could tackle that if you'd like to try."

His naïve eagerness to communicate and share his pleasure was endearing.

Dalgliesh said:

"I hardly think I shall be long enough at Toynton to make it worthwhile."

He intercepted their quick glance at each other, an almost imperceptible meeting of eyes in what? Relief? Warning? Satisfaction?

The three men stood silently while Dennis finished coiling the rope. Then Julius nodded towards the black tower.

"Ugly, isn't it? Wilfred's great grandfather built it shortly after he rebuilt the Grange. It replaced—the Grange I mean—a small Elizabethan manor house which originally stood on the site and was destroyed by fire in 1843. A pity. It must have been more agreeable than the present house. Great grandfather had no eye for form. Neither the house nor the folly have quite come off have they?"

Dalgliesh asked:

"How did he die here, by design?"

"You could say that. He was one of those unamiable and obstinate eccentrics which the Victorian age seemed to breed. He invented his own religion, based I understand on the book of Revelation. In the early autumn of 1887 he walled himself up inside the tower and starved himself to death. According to the somewhat confused testament he left, he was waiting for the second coming. I hope it arrived for him."

"And no one stopped him?"

"They didn't know he was here. The old man was crazy but cunning. He made his secret preparations here, stones and mortar and so on, and then pretended to set off to winter in Naples. It was over three months before they found him. Long before that, he'd torn his fingers to the bone trying to claw himself out. But he'd done his brick and mortar work too well, poor devil."

"How horrible!"

"Yes. In the old days before Wilfred closed the headland, the locals tended to avoid the place, and so to be honest do I. Father Baddeley used to come here occasionally. According to Grace Willison, he said some prayers for great grandfather's soul, sprinkled holy water around and that decontaminated the tower as far as he was concerned. Wilfred uses it for meditation, or so he says. Personally I think it's to get away from the Grange. The sinister family association doesn't seem to worry him. But then, it doesn't really touch him personally. He was adopted. But I expect Millicent Hammitt has told you all about that."

"Not yet. I've hardly spoken to her."

"She will, she will."

Dennis Lerner said surprisingly:

"I like the black tower, particularly in summer when the headland is peaceful and golden and the sun glints on the black stone. It's a symbol really, isn't it? It looks magical, unreal, a folly built to amuse a child. And underneath there's horror, pain, madness and death. I said that to Father Baddeley once."

"And what did he reply?" asked Julius.

"He said, 'Oh, no my son. Underneath there's the love of God.' "

Julius said roughly:

"I don't need a phallic symbol erected by a Victorian eccentric to remind me of the skull under the skin. Like any reasonable man I prepare my own defenses."

Dalgliesh asked:

"What are they?"

The quiet question, even in his own ears, sounded stark as a command. Julius smiled:

"Money and the solace it can buy. Leisure, friends, beauty, travel. And when they fail, as your friend Father Baddeley would have reminded me, they inevitably will, and Dennis's four horses of the apocalypse take over, three bullets in a Luger." He looked up once more at the tower.

"In the meantime, I can do without reminders. My half Irish blood makes me superstitious. Let's get down to the beach."

They slid and clambered cautiously down the cliff path. At the foot of the cliff Dennis Lerner's brown monk's habit lay neatly folded, topped by a rock. He corded it round himself, exchanged his climbing boots for sandals taken from the pocket of the cloak and, thus metamorphosed and with his climbing helmet tucked under his arm, joined his companions as they trudged through the shingle.

All three seemed weary and no one spoke until the cliffs changed and they passed under the shadow of the black shale. The shore was even more remarkable seen close-to, a wide shining platform of boulder-strewn clay, fractured and crevassed as if by an earthquake, a bleak uncompromising shore. The pools were blue-black pits festooned with slimy seaweed; surely no northern sea bred such an exotic green? Even the ubiquitous litter of the shore—tarred splinters of wood, cartons in which the foam bubbled like brown scum, bottles, ends of tarred rope, the fragile bleached bones of a sea bird—looked like the sinister debris of catastrophe, the sad sludge of a dead world.

As if by common consent they moved closer together and picked their way cautiously over the viscous rocks towards the sea until the tide was washing the flatter stones and Dennis Lerner had to hitch up his cloak. Suddenly Julius paused and turned towards the rock face. Dalgliesh turned with him, but Dennis still looked steadfastly out to sea.

"The tide was coming in fast. It must have reached to about here. I got down to the beach by the path we used. It took some minutes of hard running but it was the nearer, really the only way. I didn't see either him or the chair as I plunged and scrambled through the shingle. When I reached the black cliff I had to force myself to look at him. At first I could see nothing unusual, only the sea boiling between the rocks. Then I caught sight of one of the wheels of his chair. It was lying in the center of a flat rock, the sun gleaming on the chrome and the metal spokes. It looked so decorative, so precisely placed, it couldn't surely have landed there by chance. I suppose that it bounced off with the shock of impact and finally rolled on to the stone. I remember that I picked it up and hurled it towards the shore, laughing aloud. Shock, I suppose. The sound echoed back from the rock face."

Lerner, without turning, said in a stifled voice:

"I remember. I heard you. I thought it was Victor laughing; it sounded like Victor."

Dalgliesh asked:

"You saw the accident, then?"

"From a distance of about fifty yards. I'd got back to the cottage from London after lunch and decided to have a swim. It was an exceptionally warm day for September. I was just coming over the headland when I saw the chair lurch forward. There was nothing I, or anyone, could do. Dennis was lying on the grass about ten yards from Holroyd. He scrambled to his feet and ran after the chair hooting like a banshee. Then he ran backwards and forwards along the cliff edge, flailing his arms like a great brown demented crow."

Lerner said through tight lips:

"I know that I didn't behave with much courage."

"It wasn't exactly an occasion for courage, dear boy. No one could expect you to hurl yourself over the cliff after him, although, for a second, I thought you were going to."

He turned to Dalgliesh.

"I left Dennis lying prone on the grass in what I suppose was a state of shock, paused long enough to yell at him to get help from Toynton Grange, and made for the cliff path. It took Dennis about ten minutes to pull himself together and get moving. It might have been more sensible if I'd paid more attention to him and then got him down here with me to help with the corpse. I nearly lost it."

Dalgliesh said:

"The chair must have come over the cliff with considerable speed if he landed as far out as here."

"Yes, odd isn't it? I was looking for him further inshore. Then I saw a tangle of metal about twenty feet to the right already being washed by the tide. And lastly I saw Holroyd. He looked like a great stranded fish rolling in the tide. His face was pale and bloated, even when he was alive poor devil; something to do with the steroids Eric was giving him. Now he looked grotesque. He must have parted from the chair before impact; anyway he was some distance from the wreckage. He was wearing only slacks and a cotton shirt when he died, and now the shirt had been torn away by the rocks and the sea so that all I could see was this great white torso turning and rising as the tide washed over him. He had gashed open his head and cut the neck artery. He must have bled copiously, and the sea had done the rest.

By the time I reached him the foam was still stained pink, pretty as a bubble bath. He looked bloodless, as if he had been in the sea for months. A bloodless corpse, half naked, wallowing in the tide."

A bloodless corpse. A bloodless murder.

The phrase fell unbidden into Dalgliesh's mind. He asked, making his voice unemphatic, hardly interested:

"How did you manage to get hold of him?"

"It wasn't easy. As I've said, the tide was coming in fast. I managed to get my bathing towel under his belt and tried to haul him on to one of the higher rocks, an undignified, clumsy business for both of us. He was considerably heavier than I and his waterlogged trousers added to the weight. I was afraid they would come off. I suppose it wouldn't have mattered if they had, but it seemed important at the time to preserve some dignity for him. I took advantage of each onrush of wave to heave him further to shore and managed to get him on to this rock here, as far as I can remember. I was soaking myself and shivering despite the heat. I remember thinking it odd that the sun didn't seem to have the power to dry my clothes."

Dalgliesh had glanced at Lerner's profile during this recital. A pulse in the thin sun-reddened neck was beating like a pump. He said coolly:

"We must hope that Holroyd's death was less distressing for him than it obviously was for you."

Julius Court laughed:

"You must remember that not everyone has your professional predilection for these entertainments. When I'd got him this far I just hung on grimly like a fisherman to his catch until the party from Toynton Grange arrived with a stretcher. They came stumbling along the beach, the quicker way, strung out, falling over the stones, overladen like a disorganized picnic party."

"What about the wheelchair?"

"I only remembered it when we got back to Toynton. It was a write-off, of course. We all knew that. But I thought that the police might want to examine it to see if the brakes were defective. Rather clever of me wasn't it? The idea didn't seem to occur to anyone else.

But when a party from the Grange came back to look they could only find the two wheels and the main part of the body. The two side pieces with the ratchet hand-brakes were missing. The police searched more thoroughly next morning but with no better luck."

Dalgliesh would have liked to have asked who it was from Toynton Grange who had done the searching. But he was determined not to betray real curiosity. He told himself that he had none. Violent death was no longer his concern and, officially, this violent death never would be. But it was odd that the two vital pieces of the wheelchair hadn't been found. And this rocky shore, with its deep crevices, its pools, its numerous hiding places would have been an ideal place in which to conceal them. But the local police would have thought of that. It was, he supposed, one of the questions he would tactfully have to ask them. Father Baddeley had written to ask for his help the day before Holroyd had died, but that didn't mean that the two events were totally unconnected. He asked:

"Was Father Baddeley very distressed about Holroyd's death? I imagine so."

"Very much, when he knew. But that wasn't until a week later. We'd had the inquest by then and Holroyd had been buried. I thought Grace Willison would have told you. Michael and Victor between them gave us quite a day. When Dennis arrived back at the Grange with his news, the rescue party set out without saying anything to the patients. It was understandable but unfortunate. When we all staggered through the front door about forty minutes later, with what remained of Holroyd half slipping off the stretcher, Grace Willison was wheeling herself through the hall. Just to add to the excitement, she collapsed with shock. Anyway, Wilfred thought that Michael might start earning his money, and sent Eric off to Hope Cottage. Eric found Father Baddeley in the throes of his heart attack. So yet another ambulance was summoned—we thought it might finish Michael off if he had to share his journey to the hospital with what remained of Victor—and the old man went off in happy ignorance. The ward sister broke the news about Victor as soon as the doctors thought he was well enough to take it. According to her, he took it quietly, but was obviously upset. He wrote to Wilfred I believe; a letter of condolence. Father Baddeley had the professional knack of taking other people's death in his stride, and he and Holroyd weren't exactly close. It was the idea of suicide which upset his professional susceptibilities, I imagine."

Suddenly Lerner said in a low voice:

"I feel guilty because I feel responsible."

Dalgliesh said:

"Either you pushed Holroyd over the cliff or you didn't. If you didn't, guilt is an indulgence."

"And if I did?"

"Then it's a dangerous indulgence."

Julius laughed:

"Victor committed suicide. You know it, I know it, so does everyone who knew Victor. If you're going to start fantasizing about his death, it's lucky for you that I decided to swim that afternoon and came over the brow of the hill when I did."

The three of them, as if by common consent, began squelching their way along the shingled shore. Looking at Lerner's pale face, the twitch of muscle at the corner of the slack mouth, the perpetually anxious blinking eyes, Dalgliesh felt they'd had enough of Holroyd. He began to ask about the rock. Lerner turned to him eagerly.

"It's fascinating isn't it? I love the variety of this coast. You get the same shale further to the west at Kimmeridge; there it's known as Kimmeridge coal. It's bituminous you know, you can actually burn it. We did try at Toynton Grange; Wilfred liked the idea that we might be self-supporting even for heating. But the stuff smelt so offensive that we had to give it up. It practically stank us out. I believe people have tried to exploit it from the middle of the eighteenth century but no one's managed yet to deodorize it. The blackstone looks a bit dull and uninteresting now, but if it's polished with beeswax it comes up like jet. Well, you saw the effect on the black tower. People used to make ornaments of it as far back as Roman times. I've got a book on the geology of this coast if you're interested and I could show you my collection of fossils. Wilfred thinks that I ought not to take them now that the cliffs are so denuded, so I've given up collecting. But I've got quite an interesting collection. And I've got what I think is part of an Iron Age shale armlet."

Julius Court was grating through the shingle a few feet ahead. He turned and shouted back at them:

"Don't bore him with your enthusiasm for old rocks, Dennis. Remember what he said. He won't be long enough at Toynton to make it worthwhile."

He smiled at Dalgliesh. He made it sound like a challenge.

# III

Before setting out for Wareham, Dalgliesh wrote to Bill Moriarty at the Yard. He gave such brief information as he had about the staff and patients at Toynton Grange and asked whether anything was officially known. He thought that he could imagine Bill's reaction to the letter, just as he could predict the style of his reply. Moriarty was a first-class detective but, except mercifully in official reports, he affected a facetious, spuriously jovial style when talking or writing about his cases as if nervously anxious to decontaminate violence with humor, or to demonstrate his professional sang-froid in the face of death. But if Moriarty's style was suspect, his information was invariably detailed and accurate. What was more, it would come quickly.

Dalgliesh, when stopping in Toynton village to post his letter, had taken the precaution of telephoning the police before calling in at divisional headquarters. His arrival was, therefore, expected and provided for. The Divisional Superintendent, called away unexpectedly to a meeting with his Chief Constable, had left apologies and instructions for the entertainment of the visitor. His final words to Detective Inspector Daniel, deputed to do the honors, had been:

"I'm sorry to miss the Commander. I met him last year when he lectured at Bramshill. At least he tempers the arrogance of the Met. with good manners and a plausible show of humility. It's refreshing to meet someone from the smoke who doesn't treat provincial forces as if we recruit by lurking outside the hill caves with lumps of raw meat on a pole. He may be the Commissioner's blue-eyed boy but he's a good copper."

"Doesn't he write verse, Sir?"

"I shouldn't try to ingratiate yourself by mentioning that. I invent crossword puzzles for a hobby, which probably requires much the same level of intellectual skill, but I don't expect people to compliment me on it. I got his last book from the library. *Invisible Scars.* Do you suppose, given the fact that he's a copper, that the title is ironic?"

"I couldn't say, Sir, not having read the book."

"I only understood one poem in three but I may have been flattering myself. I suppose he didn't say why we're being honored."

"No, Sir, but as he's staying at Toynton Grange he may be interested in the Holroyd case."

"I can't see why; but you'd better arrange for Sergeant Varney to be available."

"I've asked Varney to join us for lunch, Sir. The usual pub, I thought."

"Why not? Let the Commander see how the poor live."

And so Dalgliesh found himself, after the usual polite preliminaries, invited to lunch at the Duke's Arms. It was an unprepossessing pub, not visible from the High Street, but approached down a dark alleyway between a corn merchant and one of those general stores common in country towns where every possible garden implement and an assortment of tin buckets, hip baths, brooms, twine, aluminum tea pots and dogs' leads swing from the ceiling above a pervading smell of paraffin and turpentine. Inspector Daniel and Sergeant Varney were greeted with uneffusive but evident satisfaction by the burly, shirtsleeved landlord who was obviously a publican who could afford to welcome the local police to his bar without the fear of giving it a bad name. The saloon bar was crowded, smoky and loud with the burr of Dorset voices. Daniel led the way down a narrow passage smelling strongly of beer and faintly of urine and out into an unexpected and sun-filled cobbled yard. There was a cherry tree in the center, its trunk encircled by a wooden bench, and half a dozen sturdy tables and slatted wooden chairs set out on the paved stones which surrounded the cobbles. The yard was deserted. The regulars probably spent too much of their working lives in the open air to see it as a desirable alternative to the camaraderie of the snug, smoke-filled bar, while tourists who might have valued it were unlikely to penetrate to the Duke's Arms.

Without being summoned the publican brought out two pints of beer, a plate of cheese-filled rolls, a jar of homemade chutney and a large bowl of tomatoes. Dalgliesh said he would have the same. The beer proved excellent, the cheese was English Cheddar, the bread had obviously been baked locally and was not the gutless pap of some mass-production oven. The butter was unsalted and the tomatoes tasted of the sun. They ate together in companionable silence.

Inspector Daniel was a stolid six-footer, with a jutting comb of strong undisciplined grey hair and a ruddy sun-tanned face. He looked close to retirement age. His black eyes were restless, perpetually moving from face to face with an amused, indulgent, somewhat self-satisfied expression as if he felt himself personally responsible for the conduct of the world and was, on the whole, satisfied that he wasn't making too bad a job of it. The contrast between these glittering unquiet eyes and his unhurried movements and even more deliberate countryman's voice was disconcerting.

Sergeant Varney was two inches shorter with a round, bland, boyish face on which experience had so far, left no trace. He looked very young, the prototype of that officer whose boyish good looks provoke the perennial middle-aged complaint that the policemen get younger each year. His manner to his superiors was easy, respectful, but neither sycophantic nor deferential. Dalgliesh suspected that he enjoyed an immense self-confidence which he was at some pains to conceal. When he talked about his investigation of Holroyd's death, Dalgliesh could understand why. Here was an intelligent and highly competent young officer who knew exactly where he was going and how he proposed to get there.

Dalgliesh carefully understated his business.

"I was ill at the time Father Baddeley wrote and he was dead when I arrived. I don't suppose he wanted to consult me about anything important, but I have something of a conscience about having let him down. It seemed sensible to have a word with you and see whether anything was happening at Toynton Grange which might have worried him. I must say it seems to me highly unlikely. I've been told about Victor Holroyd's death, of course, but that happened the day after Father Baddeley wrote to me. I did wonder, though, whether there was anything leading up to Holroyd's death which might have worried him."

Sergeant Varney said:

"There was no evidence that Holroyd's death concerned anyone but himself. As I expect you know, the verdict at the inquest was accidental death. Dr. Maskell sat with a jury and if you ask me he was relieved at the verdict. Mr. Anstey is greatly respected in the district even if they do keep themselves very much to themselves at Toynton Grange, and no one wanted to add to his distress. But in my opinion, Sir, it was a clear case of suicide. It looks as if Holroyd acted pretty much on impulse. It wasn't his usual day to be wheeled to the cliff top and he seemed to make up his mind to it suddenly. We had the evidence of Miss Grace Willison and Mrs. Ursula Hollis, who were sitting with Holroyd on the patients' patio, that he called Dennis Lerner over to him and more or less nagged him into wheeling him out. Lerner testified that he was in a particularly difficult mood on the journey and when they got to their usual place on the cliff he became so offensive that Lerner took his book and lay some little distance from the chair. That is where Mr. Julius Court saw him when he breasted the hill in time to see the chair jerk forward and hurtle down the slope and over the cliff. When I examined the ground next morning I could see by the broken flowers and pressed grass exactly where Lerner had been lying and his library book, *The Geology of the Dorset Coast,* was still on the grass where he'd dropped it. It looks to me, Sir, as if Holroyd deliberately taunted him into moving some distance away so that he wouldn't be able to get to him in time once he'd slipped the brakes."

"Did Lerner explain in court exactly what it was that Holroyd said to him?"

"He wasn't specific, Sir, but he more or less admitted to me that Holroyd taunted him with being a homosexual, not pulling his weight at Toynton Grange, looking for an easy life, and being an ungentle and incompetent nurse."

"I would hardly describe that as unspecific. How much truth is there in any of it?"

"That's difficult to say, Sir. He may be all of those things including the first; which doesn't mean to say that he'd welcome Holroyd telling him so."

Inspector Daniel broke in:

"He's not an ungentle nurse and that's for certain. My sister Ella is a staff nurse at the Meadowlands Nursing Home outside Swanage. Old Mrs. Lerner—over eighty she is now—is a patient there. Her son visits regularly and isn't above lending a hand when they're busy. It's odd that he doesn't take a post there, but perhaps it's no bad thing to keep your professional and private life separate. Anyway, they may not have a vacancy for a male nurse. And no doubt he feels some loyalty to Wilfred Anstey. But Ella thinks very highly of Dennis Lerner. A good son, is how she describes him. And it must take the best part of his salary to keep Mum at Meadowlands. Like all the really good places, it's not cheap. No, I'd say that Holroyd was a pretty impossible chap. The Grange will be a good deal happier without him."

Dalgliesh said:

"It's an uncertain way of committing suicide, I should have thought. What surprises me is that he managed to move that chair."

Sergeant Varney took a long drink of his beer.

"It surprised me too, Sir. We weren't able to get the chair intact so I couldn't experiment with it. But Holroyd was a heavy chap, about half a stone heavier than I am, I estimate, and I experimented with one of the older chairs at Toynton Grange as close as possible to the model of his. Provided it were on fairly firm ground and the slope was more than one in three, I could get it moving with a sharp jerk. Julius Court testified that he saw Holroyd's body jerk although he couldn't say from that distance whether the chair was being thrust forward or whether it was a spontaneous reaction on Holroyd's part to the shock of finding himself moving. And one has to remember, Sir, that other methods of killing himself weren't readily to hand. He was almost entirely helpless. Drugs would have been the easiest way, but those are kept locked in the clinical room on the upper floor; he hadn't a hope of getting to anything really dangerous without help. He might have tried hanging himself with a towel in the bathroom but there are no locks on the bathroom or lavatory doors. That, of course, is a precaution against patients collapsing and being too ill to summon assistance, but it does mean that there's a lack of privacy about the place."

"What about a possible defect of the chair?"

"I thought about that, Sir, and it was, of course, brought out at the inquest. But we only recovered the seat of the chair and one of the wheels. The two side pieces with the hand-brakes and the crossbar with the ratchets have never been found."

"Exactly the parts of the chair where any defects of the brakes, whether natural or deliberately produced, might have been apparent."

"If we could have found the pieces in time, Sir, and the sea hadn't done too much damage. But we never found them. The body had broken free of the chair in mid-air or on impact and Court naturally concentrated on retrieving the body. It was being tumbled by the surf, the trousers were waterlogged and it was too heavy for him to shift far. But he got his bathing towel into Holroyd's belt and managed to hold on until help, in the persons of Mr. Anstey, Dr. Hewson, Sister Moxon and the handyman Albert Philby arrived with a stretcher. Together they managed to get the body on to it and struggled back along the beach to Toynton Grange. It was only then that they rang us. It occurred to Mr. Court as soon as they reached the Grange that the chair ought to be retrieved for examination and he sent Philby back to look for it. Sister Moxon volunteered to go with him. The tide had gone out about twenty yards by then and they found the main part of the chair, that is the seat and the back, and one of the wheels."

"I'm surprised that Dorothy Moxon went to search, I would have expected her to stay with the patients."

"So should I, Sir. But Anstey refused to leave Toynton Grange and Dr. Hewson apparently thought that his place was with the body. Nurse Rainer was off duty for the afternoon, and there was no one else to send unless you count Mrs. Millicent Hammitt, and I don't think anyone thought of counting Mrs. Hammitt. It did seem important that two pairs of eyes should be looking for the chair before the light faded."

"And what about Julius Court?"

"Mr. Court and Mr. Lerner thought they ought to be at Toynton Grange to meet us when we arrived, Sir."

"A very proper thought. And by the time you did arrive no doubt it was too dark to make an effective search."

"Yes, Sir, it was seven fourteen when we got to Toynton Grange. Apart from taking statements and arranging for the body to be removed to the mortuary, there was very little we could do until the morning. I don't know whether you've seen that store at low tide, Sir. It looks like a great sheet of black treacle toffee which some prodigious giant has amused himself by smashing up with a gigantic hammer. We searched pretty thoroughly over a wide area but if the metal pieces are lodged in the crevasses between any of those rocks it would take a metal detector to find them—and we'd be lucky then—and lifting tackle to retrieve them. It's most likely, I think, that they've been dragged down under the shingle. There's a great deal of turbulence there at high tide."

Dalgliesh said:

"Was there any reason to suppose that Holroyd had suddenly become suicidal, I mean—why choose that particular moment?"

"I asked about that, Sir. A week earlier, that is on the 5th September, Mr. Court with Doctor and Mrs. Hewson had taken him in Court's car up to London to see his solicitors and a consultant at St. Saviour's Hospital. That's Dr. Hewson's own training hospital. I gather that Holroyd wasn't given much hope that anything more could be done for him. Dr. Hewson said that the news didn't seem to depress him unduly. He hadn't expected anything else. Dr. Hewson more or less told me that Holroyd had insisted on the consultation just for the trip to London. He was a restless man and liked an excuse to get away from Toynton Grange occasionally. Mr. Court was travelling up anyway and offered the use of his car. That matron, Mrs. Moxon, and Mr. Anstey were both adamant that Holroyd hadn't come back particularly depressed; but then they've got something of a vested interest in discrediting the suicide theory. The patients told me a rather different story. They noticed a change in Holroyd after his return. They didn't describe him as depressed, but he certainly wasn't any easier to live with. They described him as excited. Miss Willison used the word elated. She said that he seemed to be making up his mind to something. I don't think that she has much doubt that Holroyd killed himself. When I questioned her she was obviously shocked by the idea and distressed on Mr. Anstey's account. She didn't want to believe it. But I think that she did."

"What about Holroyd's visit to his solicitor? Did he learn anything there to distress him I wonder."

"It's an old family firm, Holroyd and Martinson in Bedford Row. Holroyd's elder brother is now the senior partner. I did ring him to ask but I didn't get far. According to him, the visit was almost entirely social and Victor was no more depressed than usual. They were never close but Mr. Martin Holroyd did visit his brother occasionally at Toynton Grange, particularly when he wanted to talk to Mr. Anstey about his affairs."

"You mean that Holroyd and Martinson are Anstey's solicitors?"

"They've acted for the family for over 150 years I understand. It's a very old connection. That's how Victor Holroyd came to hear about the Grange. He was Anstey's first patient."

"What about Holroyd's wheelchair? Could anyone at Toynton Grange have sabotaged that, either on the day Holroyd died or on the evening before?"

"Philby could, of course. He had the best opportunity. But a number of people could have done it. Holroyd's rather heavy chair, the one which was used for these outings, was kept in the workroom at the end of the passage in the southern extension. I don't know whether you know it, Sir, but it's perfectly accessible even to wheelchairs. Basically it's Philby's workshop. He has the usual standard equipment and tools for carpentry and some metal work there. But the patients can use it too and are, in fact, encouraged either to help him or to indulge in their own hobbies. Holroyd used to do some fairly simple carpentry before he got too ill and Mr. Carwardine occasionally models in clay. The women patients don't usually use it but there'd be nothing surprising to seeing one of the men there."

Dalgliesh said:

"Carwardine told me that he was in the workroom when Philby oiled and checked the brakes at eight forty-five."

"That's rather more than he told me. He gave me the impression that he hadn't really seen what Philby was up to. Philby was a bit coy about whether he could actually remember testing the brakes. I wasn't surprised. It was pretty obvious that they all wanted it to look like an accident if that could be done without provoking the coroner into too many strictures about carelessness. I had a bit of luck, however, when I questioned them about the actual morning of Holroyd's death. After breakfast Philby went back to the workroom shortly after eight forty-five. He was there for just an hour and when he left he locked the place up. He was glueing some repairs and didn't want them disturbed. I got the impression that Philby thinks of the workroom as his domain and doesn't exactly welcome the patients being allowed to use it. Anyway, he pocketed the key and didn't unlock the room until Lerner came fussing to ask for the key shortly before four o'clock so that he could get Holroyd's wheelchair. Assuming that Philby was telling the truth, the only people at Toynton Grange without alibis for the time when the workroom was unlocked and unoccupied early on the morning of 12th September are Mr. Anstey, Holroyd himself, Mr. Carwardine, Sister Moxon and Mrs. Hewson. Mr.Court was in London and didn't arrive back at his cottage until just before Lerner and Holroyd set out. Lerner is clear too. He was busy with the patients at all the relevant times."

That was all very well, thought Dalgliesh, but it proved very little. The workroom had been unlocked the previous evening after Carwardine and Philby had left and, presumably, also during the night. He said:

"You were very thorough, Sergeant. Did you manage to discover all this without alarming them too much?"

"I think so, Sir. I don't think they thought for a moment that anyone else could have been responsible. They took it that I was checking-up on what opportunity Holroyd had to muck about with the chair himself. And if it were deliberately damaged, then my bet is he did it. He was a malicious man, from what I hear. It probably amused him to think that, when the chair was recovered from the sea and the damage discovered, then everyone at Toynton Grange would be under suspicion. That's the kind of final thought that would give him quite a kick."

Dalgliesh said:

"I just can't believe that both brakes failed simultaneously and accidentally. I've seen those wheelchairs at the Grange. The brakes system is very simple but it's effective and safe. And it's almost as difficult to imagine that there was deliberate sabotage. How could the murderer possibly rely on the brakes failing at that particular moment? Lerner or Holroyd might easily have tested them before starting out. The defect might be discovered when the chair was braked on the cliff top or even on the journey. Besides, no one apparently knew that Holroyd was going to insist on an outing that afternoon. What did exactly happen on the cliff top, by the way? Who braked the chair?"

"According to Lerner, Holroyd did. Lerner admits that he never looked at the brakes. All he can say is that he noticed nothing wrong with the chair. The brakes weren't used until they reached their usual stopping place."

For a moment there was silence. They had finished eating and Inspector Daniel felt in the pocket of his tweed jacket and produced his pipe. As he stroked its bowl with his thumb before filling it, he said quietly:

"Nothing was worrying you about the old gentleman's death was it, Sir?"

"He was medically diagnosed as a dying man and somewhat inconveniently for me he died. I worry that I didn't visit him in time to hear what was on his mind; but that's a private worry. Speaking as a policeman, I should rather like to know who saw him last before he died. Officially, it was Grace Willison, but I've a feeling he had a later visitor than she; another patient. When he was found dead next morning he was wearing his stole. His diary is missing, and someone broke into his bureau. As I haven't seen Father Baddeley for over twenty years it's probably unreasonable of me to be so sure that it wasn't he."

Sergeant Varney turned to his Inspector.

"What would be the theological position, Sir, if someone confessed to a priest, got absolution and then killed him to make sure that he kept his mouth shut. Would the confession take as it were?"

The young face was prenaturally grave, it was impossible to tell whether the enquiry had been serious, whether this was a private joke directed against the Inspector, or made with some more subtle motive. Daniel took his pipe from his mouth:

"God, you young men are an ignorant lot of heathens! When I was a kid in Sunday School I put pennies in the collection plate for black bambinos not half as ignorant as your lot. Take it from me lad, it would do you no good theologically or otherwise."

He turned to Dalgliesh.

"Wearing his stole, was he? Now that's interesting."

"I thought so."

"And yet, it is so unnatural? He was alone and may have known that he was dying. Maybe he just felt more comfortable with the feel of it round his neck. Wouldn't you say that, Sir?"

"I don't know what he'd do, or what he'd feel. I've been content not to know for the past twenty years."

"And the forced bureau. Maybe he'd decided to make a start with destroying his papers and couldn't remember where he'd put the key."

"It's perfectly possible."

"And he was cremated?"

"Cremated, on the insistence of Mrs. Hammit, and his ashes buried with the appropriate rite of the Church of England."

Inspector Daniel said nothing more. There was, Dalgliesh thought bitterly as they rose to go, nothing else to say.

## IV

Father Baddeley's solicitors, the firm of Loder and Wainwright, occupied a simple but harmonious house of red brick facing directly on to South Street and typical, Dalgliesh thought, of the more agreeable houses which were built after the old town was virtually destroyed by fire in 1762. The door was propped open by a brass doorstop shaped like a miniature cannon, its dazzling muzzle pointing intimidatingly towards the street. Apart from this bellicose symbol the house and its furnishings were reassuringly welcoming, producing an atmosphere of solid affluence, tradition and professional rectitude. The white painted hall was hung with prints of eighteenth-century Dorchester and smelt of furniture polish. To the left, an open door led to a large waiting-room with an immense circular table on a carved pedestal, half a dozen carved mahogany chairs heavy enough to accommodate a robust farmer in upright discomfort, and an oil painting of an unnamed Victorian gentleman, presumably the founder of the firm, bewhiskered and beribboned and displaying the seal of his watch chain between a delicate thumb and finger as if anxious that the painter should not overlook it. It was a house in which any of Hardy's more prosperous characters would have felt themselves at home, could with confidence have discussed the effects of the abolition of the corn laws or the perfidy of the French privateers. Opposite the waiting-room was a partitioned office occupied by a young girl, dressed up to the waist in black boots and a long skirt like a Victorian governess and above the waist like a pregnant milkmaid. She was laboriously typing at a speed which could have explained Maggie Hewson's strictures about the firm's dilatoriness. In response to Dalgliesh's enquiry she glanced up at him through a curtain of lank hair and said that Mr. Robert was out at present but was expected back in ten minutes. Taking his time over lunch, thought Dalgliesh, and resigned himself to a half-hour wait.

Loder returned some twenty minutes later. Dalgliesh heard him galumphing happily into the reception office; there was the murmur of voices and a second later he appeared in the waiting-room and invited his visitor into his office at the rear of the house. Neither the room—poky, stuffy and untidy—nor its owner were quite what Dalgliesh had expected. Neither suited the house. Bob Loder was a swarthy, heavily built, square-faced man with a blotched skin and unhealthy pallor and small, discouraged eyes. His sleek hair was uniformly dark—too dark to be entirely natural—except for a thin line of silver at the brow and sides. His moustache was dapper and trim above lips so red and moist that they looked about to ooze blood. Noting the lines at the corner of the eyes and the sagging muscles of the neck Dalgliesh suspected that he was neither as young nor as vigorous as he was at pains to suggest.

He greeted Dalgliesh with a heartiness and bonhomie which seemed as unsuited to his personality as it was to the occasion. His manner recalled to Dalgliesh something of the desperate heartiness of ex-officers of his acquaintance who hadn't adjusted themselves to civilian life, or perhaps of a car salesman with little confidence that the chassis and engine will hang together long enough to complete the sale.

Dalgliesh briefly explained the ostensible reason for his visit.

"I didn't know that Father Baddeley was dead until I arrived at Toynton and the first I heard about his bequest to me was from Mrs.

Hewson. That isn't important. You probably haven't had a chance to write yet. But Mr. Anstey wants the cottage cleared for the new occupant and I thought that I'd better check with you before removing the books."

Loder put his head outside the door and yelled for the file. It was produced in a surprisingly quick time. After a perfunctory examination he said:

"That's OK. Perfectly. Sorry about the letter. It wasn't so much the lack of time as no address, don't you know. The dear old chap didn't think of that. Name familiar, of course. Ought I to know you?"

"I don't think so. Perhaps Father Baddeley mentioned my name when he visited you. I believe he did call in a day or so before the start of his last illness."

"That's right, on Wednesday the eleventh p.m. That was only the second time we'd met, come to think of it. He first consulted me about three years ago, soon after he arrived at Toynton Grange. That was to make his will. He didn't have much but, then, he hadn't been spending much and it had accumulated into quite a nice little sum."

"How did he hear of you?"

"He didn't. The dear old chap wanted to make his will, knew that he'd need a solicitor and just took the bus into Wareham, and walked into the first solicitors' office he came to. I happened to be here at the time so I got him. I drew up the will there and then since that was what he wanted and two of the staff here signed it. I'll say this for the old dear, he was the easiest client I've ever had."

"I wondered whether his visit on the eleventh was to consult you about anything that was worrying him. From his last letter to me I rather gathered that he had something on his mind. If there's anything I ought to do . . ."

He let his voice trail away in a long interrogation.

Loder said cheerfully:

"The dear old chap came in some perturbation of spirit. He was thinking of changing his will but hadn't quite made up his mind. He seemed to have got the idea that I could somehow put the money into limbo for him while he came to a decision. I said: "My dear Sir, if you die tonight the money goes to Wilfred Anstey and Toynton Grange. If you don't want that to happen, then you'll have to make up your mind what you do want and I'll draw up a new will. But the money exists. It won't just disappear. And if you don't cancel the old will or change it, then it stands."

"Did he strike you as sensible?"

"Oh, yes, muddled perhaps but more in his imagination than his comprehension if you get me. As soon as I pointed out the facts he understood them. Well, he always had understood them. It's just that he wished for a moment that the problem wasn't there. Don't we all know the feeling?"

"And a day later he went into hospital, and less than a fortnight later the problem was solved for him."

"Yes, poor old dear. I suppose he would have said that providence decided it for him. Providence certainly made its views known in no uncertain way."

"Did he give you any idea what was on his mind? I don't want to pry into professional confidences, but I did get a strong impression that he wanted to consult me about something. If he had a commission for me I'd like to try to carry it out. And I suppose I have the policeman's curiosity to find out what he wanted, to clear up unfinished business."

"A policeman?"

Was the flicker of surprise and polite interest in those tired eyes a little too obvious to be natural?

Loder said:

"Did he invite you as a friend or in a professional capacity?"

"Probably a bit of both."

"Well, I don't see what you can do about it now. Even if he'd told me his intentions about the will and I knew whom he wanted to benefit it's too late to do anything about it now."

Dalgliesh wondered whether Loder seriously thought that he had been hoping for the money himself and was enquiring into a possible way of upsetting Father Baddeley's will.

He said:

"I know that. I doubt whether it was anything to do with his will. It's odd, though, that he never wrote to tell me about my legacy, and he left the main beneficiary in the same ignorance apparently." It was entirely a shot in the dark but it found its mark. Loder spoke carefully, a trifle too carefully.

"Did he? I'd rather thought that that particular embarrassment was part of the old chap's dilemma, the reluctance to disappoint when he'd promised."

He hesitated, seeming to think that he had said either too much or too little and added:

"But Wilfred Anstey could confirm that."

He paused again as if disconcerted by some subtle implication in his words and, obviously irritated at the devious paths into which the conversation was leading him, said more strongly:

"I mean if Wilfred Anstey says he didn't know that he was the principal legatee then he didn't know and I'm wrong. Are you staying long in Dorset?"

"Rather less than a week, I imagine. Just long enough to sort out and pack the books."

"Oh, yes, the books, of course; perhaps that's what Father Baddeley meant to consult you about. He may have thought that a library of theological tomes would be more of a liability than an acceptable bequest."

"It's possible." The conversation seemed to have died. There was a brief, somewhat embarrassed pause before Dalgliesh said, rising from his chair:

"So there was nothing else worrying him as far as you know except this problem of the disposal of his money? He didn't consult you about anything else?"

"No, nothing. If he had, it might have been something I wouldn't have felt able to tell you without breaking a professional confidence. But, as he didn't, I don't see why you shouldn't know that. And what would he have to consult me over, poor old gentleman? No wife, no children, no relatives, as far as I know, no family troubles, no car, a blameless life. What would he need a solicitor for except to draw up his will?"

It was a little late to talk about professional confidence, thought Dalgliesh. There was really no need for Loder to have confided that Father Baddeley had been thinking of changing his will. Given the fact that he hadn't in fact done so that was the kind of information which a prudent solicitor would feel was best left undisclosed. As Loder walked with him to the door, Dalgliesh said casually:

"Father Baddeley's will probably gave nothing but satisfaction. One can hardly say as much of Victor Holroyd's."

The dull eyes were suddenly sharp, almost conspiratorial. Loder said:

"So you've heard about that, have you?"

"Yes. But I'm surprised that you have."

"Oh, news gets around, don't you know, in a country district. As a matter of fact I have friends at Toynton. The Hewsons. Well, Maggie really. We met at the Conservative dance here last winter. It's a pretty dull life stuck there on the cliff for a lively girl."

"Yes. It must be."

"She's quite a lass is our Maggie. She told me about Holroyd's will. I gather that he went up to London to see his brother and it was rather taken for granted that he wanted to discuss his will. But it looks as if big brother didn't much like what Victor proposed and suggested that he thought again. In the event, Holroyd drew up the codicil himself. It wouldn't exactly present any problem for him. All that family have been brought up in the law and Holroyd started reading for the Bar himself before he decided to switch to schoolteaching."

"I understand that Holroyd and Martinson act for the Anstey family."

"That's right, and have for four generations. It's a pity grandfather Anstey didn't consult them before drawing up his will. That case was quite a lesson in the unwisdom of trying to act as your own lawyer. Well, good afternoon, Commander. I'm sorry I couldn't be of more help."

As he looked back when turning out of South Street, Dalgliesh could see Loder still watching after him, the brass cannon shining like a toy at his feet. There were a number of things about the solicitor which he found interesting. Not the least was how Loder had learned his rank.

But there was one other task before he turned his mind to his shopping. He called at the early nineteenth-century hospital, Christmas Close. But here he was unlucky. The hospital knew nothing of Father Baddeley; they admitted only chronic cases. If his friend had suffered a heart attack he would almost certainly have been admitted to the acute ward of a district general hospital despite his age. The courteous porter suggested that he should try either Poole General Hospital, Blandford or the Victoria Hospital at Wimborne, and helpfully directed him to the nearest public telephone.

He tried Poole Hospital first as being the nearest. And here he was luckier than he could have hoped. The clerk who answered the telephone was efficient. Given the date of Father Baddeley's discharge he was able to confirm that the Reverend Baddeley had been a patient and to put Dalgliesh through to the right ward. The staff nurse answered. Yes, she remembered Father Baddeley. No, they hadn't heard that he had died. She spoke the conventional words of regret and was able to make them sound sincere. Then she fetched Nurse Breagan to the telephone. Nurse Breagan usually offered to post patients' letters. Perhaps she could help Commander Dalgliesh.

His rank, he knew, had something to do with their helpfulness, but not all. They were kindly women who were disposed to take trouble, even with a stranger. He explained his dilemma to Nurse Breagan.

"So you see, I didn't know that my friend had died until I arrived yesterday at Toynton Grange. He promised to return the papers we were working on to me, but they're not among his things, I wondered whether he posted them back to me from hospital, either to my London address or to the Yard."

"Well now, Commander, the Father wasn't a great one for writing. Reading, yes; but not writing. But I did post two letters for him. They were both local as far as I can remember. I have to look at the addresses, you see, so that I post them in the right box. The date? Well, I couldn't remember that. But he did hand them to me together."

"Would those be the two letters he wrote to Toynton, one to Mr. Anstey and one to Miss Willison?"

"Come to think of it, Commander, I do seem to remember those names. But I couldn't be sure, you understand."

"It's very clever of you to remember so much. And you're quite sure you only posted those two?"

"Oh, quite sure. Mind you, one of the other nurses might have posted a letter for him, but I couldn't find out for you without difficulty. Some of them have changed wards. But I don't think so. It's usually me that takes the letters. And he wasn't one for writing. That's how I remember the two letters he did send."

It could mean something or nothing. But the information had been worth the trouble. If Father Baddeley had made an appointment for the night of his return home, he must have done so either by telephoning from the hospital once he was well enough, or by letter. And only Toynton Grange itself, the Hewsons and Julius Court were on the telephone. But it might have been more convenient for him to write. The letter to Grace Willison would have been the one arranging her appointment for confession. The one to Anstey might have been the letter of condolence on Holroyd's death to which she had referred. But, on the other hand, it might not.

Before ringing off he asked whether Father Baddeley had made any telephone calls from the hospital.

"Well, he made one, that I do know. That was when he was up and about. He went down to make it from the outpatients' waiting-hall and he asked me if there'd be a London directory there. That's how I remember."

"At what time was this?"

"The morning. Just before I went off duty at twelve."

So Father Baddeley had needed to make a London call, to a number he had to look up. And he had made it, not during the evening, but in office hours. There was one obvious enquiry Dalgliesh could make. But not yet. He told himself that as yet he had learned nothing which could justify even his unofficial involvement. And even if he had, where would all the suspicions, all the clues, ultimately lead? Only to a few fistfuls of ground bones in Toynton churchyard.

# V

It wasn't until after an early dinner at an inn near Corfe Castle that Dalgliesh drove back to Hope Cottage and settled down to begin sorting Father Baddeley's books. But first there were small but necessary domestic chores to tackle. He replaced the dim bulb in the table lamp with a higher wattage; cleaned and adjusted the pilot light on the gas boiler over the sink; cleared a space in the food cupboard for his provisions and wine; and discovered in the outside shed by the aid of his torch a pile of driftwood for kindling, and a tin bath. There was no bathroom at Hope Cottage. Father Baddeley had probably taken his baths at Toynton Grange. But Dalgliesh had every intention of stripping and sluicing himself in the kitchen. Austerity was a small price to pay to avoid the bathroom at Toynton with its hospital smell of strong disinfectant, its intrusive reminders of sickness and deformity. He put a match to the dried grasses in the grate and watched them flare instantaneously into black needles in one sweet-smelling flame. Then he lit a small experimental fire and found to his relief that the chimney was clear. With a wood fire, a good light, books, food and a stock of wine he saw no reason to wish himself elsewhere.

He estimated that there were between two hundred and three hundred books on the sitting-room shelves and three times as many in the second bedroom; indeed the books had so taken over the room that it was almost impossible to get to the bed. The books presented very few surprises. Many of the theological tomes might be of interest to one of the London theological libraries; some, he thought, his aunt might be glad to give a home to; some were destined for his own shelves. There was H. B. Swete's *Greek Old Testament* in three volumes, Thomas à Kempis's *Imitation of Christ;* William Law's *Serious Call;* a leather-bound *Life and Letters of Eminent 19th Century Divines* in two volumes; a first edition of Newman's *Parochial and Plain Sermons.* But there was also a representative collection of the major English novelists and poets and, since Father Baddeley had indulged himself by buying an occasional novel, there was a small but interesting collection of first editions.

At a quarter to ten he heard approaching footsteps and the squeak of wheels, there was a peremptory knock on the door, and Millicent Hammitt entered bringing with her an agreeable smell of fresh coffee and wheeling after her a laden trolley. There was a sturdy blue banded jug of coffee, a similar jug of hot milk, a bowl of brown sugar, two blue banded mugs, and a plate of digestive biscuits.

Dalgliesh felt that he could hardly object when Mrs. Hammitt cast an appreciative glance at the wood fire, poured out two mugs of coffee and made it obvious that she was in no hurry to go.

Dalgliesh had been briefly introduced to her before dinner the previous evening, but there had been time for only half a minute's conversation before Wilfred had taken his stance at the reading desk and the ordained silence fell. She had taken the opportunity to discover, by the expedient of a blunt interrogation with no attempt at finesse, that Dalgliesh was holidaying alone because he was a widower and that his wife had died in childbirth with her baby. Her response to this had been, "Very tragic. And unusual, surely, for these days?" spoken with an accusatory glance across the table and in a tone which suggested that someone had been inexcusably careless.

She was wearing carpet slippers and a thick tweed skirt, incongruously topped by an openwork jumper in pink wool, liberally festooned with pearls. Dalgliesh suspected that her cottage was a similar unhappy compromise between utility and fussiness, but had no inclination to find out. To his relief she made no attempt to help with the books but sat squatting on the edge of the chair, coffee mug cradled in her lap, her legs planted firmly apart to reveal twin balloons of milky white and varicosed thigh above the bite of the stockings. Dalgliesh continued with his job, coffee mug on the floor at his side. He shook each volume gently before allocating it to its pile in case some message should drop out. If it did, Mrs. Hammitt's presence would be embarrassing. But he knew that the precaution was merely his professional habit of leaving nothing to chance. This wouldn't be Father Baddeley's way.

Meanwhile Mrs. Hammitt sipped her coffee and talked, encouraged in her volubility and occasional indiscretion by the belief which Dalgliesh had noticed before that a man who is physically working only hears half what is said to him.

"No need to ask you if you had a comfortable night. Those beds of Wilfred's are notorious. A certain amount of hardness is supposed to be good for disabled patients but I like a mattress I can sink into. I'm surprised that Julius didn't invite you to sleep at his cottage, but he never does have visitors. Doesn't want to put Mrs. Reynolds out I suppose. She's the village constable's widow from Toynton Village and she does for Julius whenever he's here. Grossly overpaid, of course. Well, he can afford it. And you'll be sleeping here tonight, I understand. I saw Helen Rainer coming in with the bed linen. I suppose it won't worry you, sleeping in Michael's bed. No, of course it wouldn't, being a policeman. You aren't sensitive or superstitious about things like that. Quite right too; our death is but a sleep and a forgetting. Or do I mean life? Wordsworth anyway. I used to be very fond of poetry when I was a girl but I can't get along with these modern poets. Still, I should have quite looked forward to your reading."

Her tone suggested that it would have been a solitary and eccentric pleasure. But Dalgliesh had momentarily stopped listening to her. He had found a first edition of *Diary of a Nobody* with an inscription written in a boyish hand, on the title page.

> To Father Baddeley for his Birthday with love from Adam. I bought this from Mr. Snelling in Norwich and he let me have it cheap because of the red stain on page twenty. But I've tested it and it isn't blood.

Dalgliesh smiled. So he'd tested it, had he, the arrogant little blighter. What mysterious concoction of acids and crystals from the remembered chemistry set had resulted in that confident scientific pronouncement? The inscription reduced the value of the book rather more than had the stain, but he didn't think that Father Baddeley had thought so. He placed it on the pile reserved for his own shelves and again let Mrs. Hammitt's voice pierce his consciousness.

"And if a poet can't take the trouble to make himself intelligible to the educated reader, then the educated reader had better leave him alone, that's what I always say."

"I'm sure you do, Mrs. Hammitt."

"Call me Millicent, won't you? We're supposed to be one happy family here. If I have to put up with Dennis Lerner and Maggie Hewson and even that appalling Albert Philby calling me by my Christian name—not that I give him much opportunity, I assure you—I don't see why you shouldn't. And I shall try to call you Adam but I don't think it's going to come easily. You aren't a Christian name person."

Dalgliesh carefully dusted the volumes of Maskell's *Monumenta Ritualica Ecclesiae Anglicanae* and said that, from what he had heard, Victor Holroyd hadn't done much towards promoting the concept of all one happy family.

"Oh, you've heard about Victor then? Maggie gossiping, I suppose. He really was an extremely difficult man, inconsiderate in life and in death. I managed to get on with him fairly well. I think he respected me. He was a very clever man and full of useful information. But no one at the Grange could stand him. Even Wilfred more or less gave up in the end and left him alone. Maggie Hewson was the exception. Odd woman; she always has to be different. Do you know, I believe she thought Victor had willed his money to her. Of course we all knew that he had money. He took good care to let us know that he wasn't one of those patients paid for by the local authority. And I suppose she thought that if she played her cards right some of it might come to her. She more or less hinted it to me once. Well, she was half drunk at the time. Poor Eric! I give that marriage another year at the most. Some men might find her physically attractive, I suppose, if you like that dyed blonde, blowzy, over-sexed type. Of course, her affair, if you can call it an affair, with Victor was just indecent. Sex is for the healthy. I know that the disabled are supposed to have feelings like the rest of us but you'd think that they'd put that sort of thing behind them when they get to the wheelchair stage. That book looks interesting. The binding's good anyway. You might get a shilling or two for that."

Placing a first edition of *Tracts for the Times* out of reach of Millicent's nudging foot and among the books selected for himself, Dalgliesh recognized with transitory self-disgust that, however much he deplored Mrs. Hammitt's uninhibited expression, the sentiment wasn't far from his own thoughts. What, he wondered, must it be like to feel desire, love, lust even, and be imprisoned in an unresponsive body? Or worse, a body only too responsive to some of its urges, but uncoordinated, ugly, grotesque. To be sensitive to beauty, but to live always with deformity. He thought that he could begin to understand Victor Holroyd's bitterness. He asked:

"What happened in the end to Holroyd's money?"

"It all went to his sister in New Zealand, all sixty-five thousand of it. Very right too. Money ought to be kept in the family. But I daresay Maggie had her hopes. Probably Victor more or less promised her. It's the sort of thing he would do. He could be very spiteful at times. But at least he left his fortune where it ought to go. I should be very displeased indeed if I thought that Wilfred had bequeathed Toynton Grange to anyone but me."

"But would you want it?"

"Oh, the patients would have to go, of course. I can't see myself running Toynton Grange as it is now. I respect what Wilfred's trying to do, but he has a particular need to do it. I expect you've heard about his visit to Lourdes and the miracle. Well, that's all right by me. But I haven't had a miracle, thank God, and I've no intention of putting myself in the way of one. Besides, I've done quite enough for the chronic sick already. Half the house was left to me by father and I sold out to Wilfred so that he could start the Home. We had a proper valuation made at the time, naturally, but it wasn't very high. At that time large country houses were a drag on the market. Now, of course, it's worth a fortune. It's a beautiful house isn't it?"

"It's certainly interesting architecturally."

"Exactly. Regency houses of character are fetching fantastic prices. Not that I'm set on selling. After all, it was our childhood home and I have an affection for it. But I should probably get rid of the land. As a matter of fact, Victor Holroyd knew someone locally who would be interested in buying, someone who wants to set up another holiday caravan camp."

Dalgliesh said involuntarily:

"What a horrible thought!"

Mrs. Hammitt was unabashed. She said complacently:

"Not at all. A very selfish attitude on your part, if I may say so. The poor need holidays just like the rich. Julius wouldn't like it, but I'm under no obligation to consider Julius. He'd sell his cottage and get out I suppose. He owns that acre and a half of the headland, but I can't see him driving through a caravan park every time he comes here from London. Besides, they'd more or less have to pass his windows to get down to the beach. That's the only spot with a beach at high tide. I can see them, can't you; knobbly-kneed fathers in natty little shorts carrying the picnic bag, mum following with a blaring transistor, squealing kids, yelling babies. No, I can't see Julius staying here."

"Does everyone here know that you stand to inherit Toynton Grange?"

"Of course; it's no secret. Who else should get it? As a matter of fact, the whole estate should belong to me by right. Perhaps you didn't know that Wilfred isn't really an Anstey, that he was adopted?"

Dalgliesh said cautiously that he thought someone had mentioned as much.

"Then you may as well know the whole of it. It's quite interesting if you're concerned with the law."

Mrs. Hammitt refilled her mug and wriggled back into her chair as if settling herself for a complicated dissertation.

"My father was particularly anxious for a son. Some men are like that, daughters don't really count with them. And I can quite see that I was a disappointment. If a man really wants a son, the only thing that reconciles him to a daughter is her beauty. And that I've never had. Luckily, it didn't seem to worry my husband. We suited very well."

As the only possible answer to this announcement was a vague, congratulatory murmur, Dalgliesh made the appropriate sound.

"Thank you," said Mrs. Hammitt, as if acknowledging a compliment. She went happily on:

"Anyway, when the doctors told father that my mother couldn't bear another child, he decided to adopt a son. I believe he got Wilfred from a children's home, but I was only six at the time and I don't think I was ever told how and where they found him. Illegitimate, of course. People minded more about that kind of thing in 1920 and you could take your pick of unwanted babies. I remember how excited I was at the time to have a brother. I was a lonely child and with more than my share of natural affection. At the time, I didn't see Wilfred as a rival. I was very fond of Wilfred when we were young. I still am. People forget that sometimes."

Dalgliesh asked what happened.

"It was my grandfather's will. The old man distrusted lawyers, even Holroyd and Martinson who were the family solicitors, and he drew up his own will. He left a life interest in the estate to my parents and the whole property in equal shares to his grandchildren. The question was, did he intend to include Wilfred? In the end we had to go to law about it. The case made quite a stir at the time and raised the whole question of the rights of adopted children. Perhaps you remember the case?"

Dalgliesh did have a vague memory of it. He asked:

"When was your grandfather's will made, I mean in relation to your brother's adoption?"

"That was the vital part of the evidence. Wilfred was legally adopted on 3rd May 1921, and grandfather signed his will exactly ten days later on 13th May. It was witnessed by two servants, but they were dead by the time the case was fought. The will was perfectly clear and in order, except that he didn't put in the names. But Wilfred's lawyers could prove that grandfather knew about the adoption and was happy about it. And the will did say children, in the plural."

"But he might have had it in mind that your mother would die first and your father remarry."

"How clever of you! I can see that you've a lawyer's devious mind. That's exactly what my counsel argued. But it was no good. Wilfred won. But you can understand my feelings over the Grange. If grandfather had only signed that will before 3rd May things would be very different, I can tell you."

"But you did get half the value of the estate?"

"That didn't last long I'm afraid. My dear husband got through money very quickly. It wasn't women, I'm glad to say. It was horses. They're just as expensive and even more unpredictable but a less humiliating rival for a wife. And, unlike another woman, you can at least be glad when they win. Wilfred always said that Herbert became senile when he retired from the army, but I didn't complain. I rather preferred him that way. But he did get through the money."

Suddenly she glanced round the room, leaned forward and gave Dalgliesh a sly conspiratorial glance.

"I'll tell you something that no one at Toynton Grange knows, except Wilfred. If he does sell out I shall get half the sale price. Not just half the extra profit, fifty per cent of what he gets. I've got an undertaking from Wilfred, properly signed and witnessed by Victor. Actually it was Victor's suggestion. He thought it would stand up in law. And it isn't kept where Wilfred can get his hands on it. It's with Robert Loder, a solicitor in Wareham. I suppose Wilfred was so confident that he'd never need to sell, that he didn't care what he signed or perhaps he was arming himself against temptation. I don't think for one minute that he will sell. He cares too much about the place for that. But if he should change his mind, then I shall do very nicely."

Dalgliesh said, greatly daring:

"When I arrived, Mrs. Hewson said something about the Ridgewell Trust. Hasn't Mr. Anstey got it in mind to transfer the Home?"

Mrs. Hammitt took the suggestion more calmly than he had expected. She retorted robustly:

"Nonsense! I know Wilfred talks about it from time to time, but he'd never just hand over Toynton Grange. Why should he? Money's tight, of course, but money always is tight. He'll just have to put up the fees or get the local authorities to pay more for the patients they send. There's no reason why he should subsidize the local authorities. And if he still can't make the place pay, then he'd do better to sell out, miracle or no miracle."

Dalgliesh suggested that, in all the circumstances, it was surprising that Anstey hadn't become a Roman Catholic. Millicent seized on the thought with vehemence.

"It was quite a spiritual struggle for him at the time." Her voice deepened and throbbed with the echo of cosmic forces linked in mortal struggle. "But I was glad that he decided to remain in our church. Our father"—her voice boomed out in such a sudden access of hortatory fervor that Dalgliesh, startled, half expected that she was about to launch into the Lord's prayer—"would have been so very distressed. He was a great churchman, Commander Dalgliesh. Evangelical of course. No, I was glad that Wilfred didn't go over."

She spoke as if Wilfred, faced with the Jordan river, had neither liked the look of the water nor had confidence in his boat.

Dalgliesh had already asked Julius Court about Anstey's religious allegiance and had received a different and, he suspected, a more accurate explanation. He recalled their conversation on the patio before they had rejoined Henry; Julius's amused voice: "Father O'Malley who was supposed to be instructing Wilfred, made it plain that his church would in future proclaim on a number of matters that Wilfred had seen as coming within his personal jurisdiction. It occurred to dear Wilfred that he was on the point of joining a very large organization and one which thought that, as a convert, he was receiving rather than bestowing benefit. In the end, after what I have no doubt was a gratifying struggle, he decided to remain in a more accommodating fold."

"Despite the miracle?" Dalgliesh had asked.

"Despite the miracle. Father O'Malley is a rationalist. He admits the existence of miracles but prefers the evidence to be submitted to the proper authorities for thorough examination. After a seemly delay the Church in her wisdom will then pronounce. To go about proclaiming that one has been the recipient of special grace smacks to him of presumption. Worse, I suspect he thinks it in poor taste. He's a fastidious man, is Father O'Malley. He and Wilfred don't really get on. I'm afraid that Father O'Malley has lost his church a convert."

"But the pilgrimages to Lourdes still go on?" Dalgliesh had asked.

"Oh, yes. Twice a year regularly. I don't go. I used to when I first came here but it isn't, in the contemporary idiom, exactly my scene. But I usually make it my business to provide a slap-up tea to welcome them all back."

Dalgliesh, his mind recalled to the present, was aware that his back was beginning to ache. He straightened up just as the clock on the mantelshelf struck the three-quarters. A charred log tumbled from the grate shooting up a final cascade of sparks. Mrs. Hammitt took it as a signal that it was time to go. Dalgliesh insisted first on washing up the coffee mugs and she followed him into the little kitchen.

"It has been a pleasant hour, Commander, but I doubt whether we shall repeat it. I'm not one of those neighbors who keep dropping in. Thank God I can stand my own company. Unlike poor Maggie, I have resources. And I'll say one thing for Michael Baddeley, he did keep himself to himself."

"Nurse Rainer tells me that you persuaded him of the advantages of cremation."

"Did she say that? Well, I daresay she's right. I may have mentioned it to Michael. I strongly disapprove of wasting good ground to bury putrifying bodies. As far as I remember, the old man didn't care what happened to him as long as he ended up in consecrated earth with the proper words said over him. Very sensible. My view entirely. And Wilfred certainly didn't object to the cremation. He and Dot Moxon agreed with me absolutely. Helen protested over the extra trouble, but what she didn't like was having to get a second doctor's signature. Thought it cast some kind of aspersion on dear Eric's clinical judgement, I suppose."

"But surely no one was suggesting that Dr. Hewson's diagnosis was wrong?"

"Of course not! Michael died of a heart attack, and even Eric was competent to recognize that, I should hope. No, don't bother to see me home, I've got my torch. And if there's anything you need at any time, just knock on the wall."

"But would you hear? You didn't hear Father Baddeley."

"Naturally not, since he didn't knock. And after about nine-thirty I wasn't really listening for him. You see, I thought someone had already visited to settle him for the night."

The darkness outside was cool and restless, a black mist, sweet-tasting and smelling of the sea, not the mere absence of light but a positive, mysterious force. Dalgliesh maneuvered the trolley over the doorstep. Walking beside Millicent down the short path, and steadying the trolley with one hand, he asked with careful uninterest:

"Did you hear someone, then?"

"Saw, not heard. Or so I thought. I was thinking of making myself a hot drink and I wondered whether Michael would like one. But when I opened my front door to call in and ask, I thought I saw a figure in a cloak disappearing into the darkness. As Michael's light was off—I could see that the cottage was completely dark—naturally I didn't disturb him. I know now that I was mistaken. Either that or I'm going potty. It wouldn't be difficult in this place. Apparently no one did visit him and now they've all got a bad conscience about it. I can see how I was deceived. It was a night like this. Just a slight breeze but the darkness seeming to move and form itself into shapes. And I heard nothing, not even a footfall. Just a glimpse of a bent head, hooded and a cloak swirling into the darkness."

"And this was at about nine-thirty?"

"Or a little later. Perhaps it was about the time he died. A fanciful person could frighten herself imagining that she'd seen his ghost.

That was what Jennie Pegram actually suggested when I told them at Toynton Grange. Ridiculous girl!"

They had almost reached the door of Faith Cottage. She hesitated and then said as if on impulse, and, he thought, with some embarrassment:

"They tell me that you're worried about the broken lock of Michael's bureau. Well, it was all right the night before he came back from hospital. I found I'd run out of envelopes and I had an urgent letter to write. I thought that he wouldn't mind if I took a look in the bureau. It was locked then."

Dalgliesh said:

"And broken when your brother looked for the will shortly after the body was found."

"So he says, Commander. So he says."

"But you have no proof that he broke it?"

"I've no proof that anyone did. The cottage was full of people running in and out. Wilfred, the Hewsons, Helen, Dot, Philby, even Julius when he arrived from London; the place was like a wake. All I know is that the bureau was locked at nine o'clock on the night before Michael died. And I've no doubt that Wilfred was keen to get his eyes on that will and see if Michael really had left Toynton Grange all he possessed. And I do know that Michael didn't break the lock himself."

"How, Mrs. Hammitt?"

"Because I found the key, just after lunch on the day he died. In the place where, presumably, he always kept it—that old tea tin on the second shelf of the food cupboard. I didn't think he'd mind my having any little bits of food he'd left. I slipped it into my pocket in case it got lost when Dot cleared the cottage. After all, that old bureau desk is quite valuable and the lock ought to be repaired. As a matter of fact, if Michael hadn't left it to Grace in his will, I would have moved it into here and looked after it properly."

"So you still have the key?"

"Of course. No one has ever bothered about it but you. But, as you seem so interested you may as well take it."

She dug her hand into the pocket of her skirt and he felt the cold metal pressed into his palm. She had opened the door of her cottage now and had reached for the light switch. In the sudden glare he blinked, and then saw it clearly, a small silver key, delicate as filigree, but tied now with thin string to a red plastic clothes peg, the red so bright that, for a dazzled second, it looked as if his palm were stained with blood.

# BOOK FIVE

•

# Act of Malice

# I

When he looked back on his first weekend in Dorset, Dalgliesh saw it as a series of pictures, so different from the later images of violence and death that he could almost believe that his life at Toynton Head had been lived on two levels and at different periods of time. These early and gentle pictures, unlike the later harsh black and white stills from some crude horror film, were suffused with color and feeling and smell. He saw himself plunging through the sea-washed shingle of Chesil Bank, his ears loud with bird cries and the grating thunder of the tide to where Portland reared its dark rocks against the sky; climbing the great earthworks of Maiden Castle and standing, a solitary windblown figure, where four thousand years of human history were encompassed in numinous contours of molded earth; eating a late tea in Judge Jeffrey's lodgings in Dorchester as the mellow autumn afternoon faded into dusk; driving through the night between a falling tangle of golden bracken and high untrimmed hedgerows to where the stone-walled pub waited with lighted windows on some remote village green.

And then, late at night when there could be small risk of a visitor from Toynton Grange disturbing him, he would drive back to Hope Cottage to the familiar and welcoming smell of books and a wood fire. Somewhat to his surprise, Millicent Hammitt was faithful to her promise not to disturb him after that first visit. He soon guessed why; she was a television addict. As he sat drinking his wine and sorting Father Baddeley's books, he could hear through the chimney breast the faint and not disagreeable sounds of her nightly entertainment; the sudden access of a half familiar advertising jingle; the antiphonal mutter of voices; the bark of gun shots; feminine screams; the blaring fanfare to the late night film.

He had a sense of living in a limbo between the old life and the new, excused by convalescence from the responsibility of immediate decision, from any exertion which he found disagreeable. And he found the thought of Toynton Grange and its inmates disagreeable. He had taken what action he could. Now he was waiting on events. Once, looking at Father Baddeley's empty and shabby chair, he was reminded irreverently of the fabled excuse of the distinguished atheist philosopher, ushered after death to his astonishment into the presence of God.

"But Lord, you didn't provide sufficient evidence."

If Father Baddeley wanted him to act he would have to provide more tangible clues than a missing diary and a broken lock.

He was expecting no letters except Bill Moriarty's reply since he had left instructions that none were to be forwarded. And he intended to collect Bill's letter himself from the postbox. But it arrived on the Monday, at least a day earlier than he had thought possible. He had spent the morning in the cottage and hadn't walked to the postbox until after his lunch at two-thirty when he had taken back his milk bottles for collection.

The postbox contained the one letter, a plain envelope with a W.C. postmark; the address was typed but his rank omitted. Moriarty had been careful. But as he slipped his thumb under the flap, Dalgliesh wondered if he himself had been careful enough. There was no obvious sign that the letter had been opened; the flap was intact. But the glue was suspiciously weak, and the flap slid open a little too easily under the pressure of his thumb. And the postbox was otherwise empty. Someone, probably Philby, must already have collected the Toynton Grange post. It was odd that he hadn't delivered this letter at Hope Cottage. Perhaps he should have used a poste restante in Toynton village or Wareham. The thought that he had been careless irritated him. The truth is, he thought, that I don't know what, if anything, I'm investigating, and I only spasmodically care. I haven't the stomach to do the job properly or the will and courage to leave it alone. He was in the mood to find Bill's prose style more than usually irritating.

"Nice to see your elegant handwriting again. There's general relief here that the reports of your impending decease were exaggerated.

We're keeping the wreath contributions for a celebration party. But what are you doing anyway gum-shoeing in Dorset among such a questionable group of weirdies? If you pine for work there's plenty here. However, here's the gen.

"Two of your little lot have records. You know, apparently, something about Philby. Two convictions for GBH in 1967 and 1969, four for theft in 1970 and a miscellany of earlier misdemeanors. The only extraordinary thing about Philby's criminal history is the leniency with which judges have sentenced him. Looking at his CRO I'm not altogether surprised. They probably felt that it was unjust to punish too harshly a man who was following the only career for which physiognomy and talents had fitted him. I did manage to have a word with 'the open door' about him. They admit his faults, but say that he is capable, given affection, of a ferocious loyalty. Watch out that he doesn't take a fancy to you.

"Millicent Hammitt was convicted twice for shoplifting by the Cheltenham Magistrates in 1966 and 1968. In the first case there was the usual defense of menopausal difficulties, and she was fined. She was lucky to escape so easily the second time. But that was a couple of months after her husband, a retired army major, had died and the court were sympathetic. They were probably influenced too, by Wilfred Anstey's assurances that she was coming to live with him at Toynton Grange and would be under his eye. There's been no trouble since so I assume that Anstey's surveillance has been effective, the local shopkeepers more accommodating, or Mrs. Hammitt more skilful in lifting the goods.

"That's all the official gen. The rest of them are clean, at least as far as the CRO is concerned. But if you're looking for an interesting villain—and I hardly suppose that Adam Dalgliesh is wasting his talents on Albert Philby—then may I recommend Julius Court? I got a line on him from a man I know who works at the FCO. Court is a bright grammar school boy from Southsea who entered the foreign service after university equipped with all the usual elegant appurtenances but rather short on cash. He was at the Paris Embassy in 1970 when he gave evidence in the notorious murder trial when Alain

Michonnet was accused of murdering Poitaud the racing driver. You may remember the case. There was a fair amount of publicity in the English press. It was pretty clear cut, and the French police were salivating happily at the thought of nailing Michonnet. He's the son of Theo d'Estier Michonnet who owns a chemical manufacturing plant near Marseilles and they've had their eyes on père and fils for quite a time. But Court gave his chum an alibi. The odd thing was that they weren't really chums—Michonnet is aggressively heterosexual as the media make only too boringly plain—and the horrid word blackmail was hissed round the Embassy. No one believed Court's story; but no one could shake it. My informant thinks that Court's motive was nothing more sinister than a desire to amuse himself and to get his superiors twisting their knickers. If that was his motive he certainly succeeded. Eight months later his godfather conveniently died leaving him £30,000 and he chucked the service. He's said to have been rather clever with his investments. Anyway, that's all water under the bridge. Nothing is known to his discredit as they say, except, perhaps, a tendency to be a little too accommodating to his friends. But I give you the story for what it's worth."

Dalgliesh folded the letter and stuffed it into his jacket pocket. He wondered how much, if any, of either story was known at Toynton Grange. Julius Court was unlikely to worry. His past was his own affair; he was independent of Wilfred's suffocating hold. But Millicent Hammitt had a double weight of gratitude. Who else except Wilfred knew, he wondered, about those two discreditable and pathetic incidents? How much would she care if the story became generally known at Toynton Grange? He wished again that he had used a poste restante.

A car was approaching. He looked up. The Mercedes, driven very fast, was coming down the coast road. Julius stepped on the brakes and the car rocked to a stop, its front bumper inches from the gate. He wrenched himself out and began tugging at the gate, calling out to Dalgliesh.

"The black tower's on fire! I saw the smoke from the coast road. Have you a rake at Hope Cottage?"

Dalgliesh put his shoulder to the gate.

"I don't think so. There's no garden. But I found a yard broom—a besom—in the shed."

"Better than nothing. D'you mind coming? It may take the two of us."

Dalgliesh slipped quickly into the car. They left the gate open. Julius drove to Hope Cottage with little regard for the car springs or his passenger's comfort. He opened the boot while Dalgliesh ran to the yard shed. There among the paraphernalia of past occupants was the remembered besom, two empty sacks, and, surprisingly, an old shepherd's crook. He threw them into the capacious boot. Julius had already turned the car and the engine was running. Dalgliesh got in beside him and the Mercedes leapt forward.

As they swung on to the coast road Dalgliesh asked:

"Is anyone there do you know? Anstey?"

"Could be. That's the worry. He's the only one who goes there now. And I can't see otherwise how the fire started. We can get closest to the tower this way, but it means foot slogging it over the headland. I didn't try when I first spotted the smoke. It's no use without something to tackle the fire."

His voice was tight, the knuckles on the wheel shone white. In the driving mirror Dalgliesh saw that the irises of his eyes were large and bright. The triangular scar above the right eye, normally almost invisible, had deepened and darkened. Above it he could see the insistent beat of the temple pulse. He glanced at the speedometer; they were doing over a hundred but the Mercedes, beautifully handled, held the narrow road easily. Suddenly the road twisted and rose and they caught a glimpse of the tower. The broken panes in the slitted windows below the cupola were belching puffballs of greyish smoke like miniature cannon fire. They tumbled merrily over the headland until the wind shook them into shredded dusters of cloud. The effect was absurd and picturesque, as innocuous as a child's entertainment. And then the road dipped and the tower was lost to view.

The coast road, wide enough only for a single car, was bounded to the seaward by a drystone wall. Julius was sure of his way. He had swung the car to the left even before Dalgliesh noticed the narrow gap, gateless but still bounded by two rotting posts. The car bumped to a standstill in a deep hollow to the right of the entry. Dalgliesh seized the crook and sacks and Julius the broom. Thus ridiculously lumbered, they began running across the headland.

Julius had been right; this was the quickest way. But they had to do it on foot. Even had he been willing to drive over this rough, rock-strewn ground it wouldn't have been possible. The headland was crossed with fragmented stone walls, low enough to leap over and with plenty of gaps, but none wide enough for a vehicle. The ground was deceptive. At one minute the tower seemed almost to recede, separated from them by interminable barriers of tumbling stone. Then it was upon them.

The smoke, acrid as a damp bonfire, was rolling strongly from the half-open door. Dalgliesh kicked it wide and leapt to one side as the gusts billowed out. There was an immediate roar and the tongue of flame fanged out at him. With the crook he began raking out the burning debris, some still identifiable—long dried grass and hay, rope ends, what looked like the remains of an old chair—the years of accumulated rubbish since the headland had been public land and the black tower, unlocked, used as a shepherd's shelter or a night lodging for tramps. As he raked out the burning, malodorous clumps he could hear Julius behind him frantically beating them out. Little fires started and crawled like red tongues among the grasses.

As soon as the doorway was clear Julius rushed in stamping down the smoldering remnants of grass and hay with the two sacks. Dalgliesh could see his smoke-shrouded figure coughing and reeling. He dragged him unceremoniously out and said:

"Keep back until I've cleared it. I don't want the two of you on my hands."

"But he's there! I know he is. He must be. Oh, God! The bloody fool!"

The last smoldering clump of grass was out now. Julius, pushing Dalgliesh aside, ran up the stone stairway which circled the walls. Dalgliesh followed. A wooden door to a middle chamber was ajar.

Here there was no window, but in the smoke-filled darkness they could see the huddled sack-like figure against the far wall. He had drawn the hood of the monk's cloak over his head and had swathed himself into its folds like a human derelict wrapped against the cold. Julius's feverish hands got lost in its folds. Dalgliesh could hear him cursing. It took seconds before Anstey's arms were freed and, together, they dragged him to the door and, with difficulty, supported and maneuvered the inert body between them down the narrow stairs and into the fresh-smelling air.

They laid him prone on the grass. Dalgliesh had dropped to his knees, ready to turn him and start artificial respiration. Then Anstey slowly stretched out both arms and lay in an attitude both theatrical and vaguely blasphemous. Dalgliesh, relieved that he wouldn't now have to fasten his mouth over Anstey's, got to his feet. Anstey drew up his knees and began to cough convulsively in hoarse whooping gasps. He turned his face to one side, his cheek resting on the headland. The moist mouth coughing out saliva and bile, seemed to be sucking at the grass as if avid for nourishment. Dalgliesh and Court knelt and raised him between them. He said weakly:

"I'm all right. I'm all right."

Dalgliesh asked:

"We've got the car on the coast road. Can you walk?"

"Yes. I'm all right, I tell you. I'm all right."

"There's no hurry. Better rest for a few minutes before we start."

They lowered him against one of the large boulders and he sat there a little apart from them, still coughing spasmodically, and looking out to sea. Julius paced the cliff edge, restlessly as if fretting at the delay. The stench of the fire was blown gently from the blackened headland like the last waves of a fading pestilence.

After five minutes Dalgliesh called:

"Shall we start now?"

Together and without speaking, they raised Anstey and supported him between them across the headland and to the car.

# II

No one spoke on the drive back to Toynton Grange. As usual, the front of the house seemed deserted, the tessellated hall was empty, unnaturally silent. But Dorothy Moxon's sharp ears must have heard the car, perhaps from the clinical room at the front of the house. Almost immediately she appeared at the top of the stairs.

"What is it? What happened?"

Julius waited until she had come swiftly down, then said quietly:

"It's all right. Wilfred managed to set fire to the black tower with himself inside. He isn't hurt, just shocked. And the smoke hasn't done his lungs any good."

She glanced accusingly from Dalgliesh to Julius as if it were their fault, then put both her arms round Anstey in a gesture fiercely maternal and protective and began to urge him gently up the stairs, muttering encouragement and remonstration into his ear in a soft grumbling monotone which, to Dalgliesh, sounded like an endearment. Anstey, he noticed, seemed less capable of supporting himself now than he had been on the headland and they made slow progress. But when Julius came forward to help, a glance from Dorothy Moxon made him draw back. With difficulty she got Anstey into his small white-painted bedroom at the back of the house and helped him on to the narrow bed. Dalgliesh made a swift mental inventory. The room was much as he had expected. One small table and chair set under the window giving a view of the patients' rear courtyard; a well-stocked bookcase; one rug; a crucifix over the bed; a bedside table with a simple lamp and a carafe of water. But the thick mattress bounced gently as Wilfred rolled on to it. The towel hanging beside the wash basin looked luxuriantly soft. The bedside rug, plain in design, was no strip of worn, discarded carpet. The hooded dressing gown in white towelling hanging behind the door had a look of simplicity, almost austerity; but Dalgliesh did not doubt that it was agreeably soft to the skin. This might be a cell, but it lacked none of the essential comforts.

Wilfred opened his eyes and fixed his blue gaze on Dorothy

Moxon. It was interesting, Dalgliesh thought, how he managed to combine humility with authority in one look. He held out a suppliant hand.

"I want to talk to Julius and Adam, Dot dear. Just for a moment. Will you?"

She opened her mouth, clamped it shut again, and stomped out without a word, closing the door firmly behind her. Wilfred closed his eyes again and appeared mentally to withdraw himself from the scene. Julius looked down at his hands. His right palm was red and swollen and a blister had already formed over the bowl of the thumb. He said with a note of surprise:

"Funny! My hand's burnt. I never felt it at the time. Now it's beginning to hurt like hell."

Dalgliesh said:

"You should get Miss Moxon to dress it. And it might be as well to let Hewson have a look at it."

Julius took a folded handkerchief from his pocket, soaked it in cold water at the wash basin and wrapped it inexpertly round his hand.

He said:

"It can wait."

The realization that he was in pain appeared to have soured his temper. He stood over Wilfred and said crossly:

"Now that a definite attack has been made on your life and damn nearly succeeded, I suppose you'll act sensibly for once and send for the police."

Wilfred did not open his eyes, he said weakly:

"I have a policeman here."

Dalgliesh said:

"It isn't for me. I can't undertake an official investigation for you. Court is right, this is a matter for the local police."

Wilfred shook his head.

"There's nothing to tell them. I went to the black tower because there were things I needed to think over in peace. It's the only place where I can be absolutely alone. I was smoking; you know how you all complain about my smelly old pipe. I remember knocking it out against the wall as I went up. It must have been still alight. All that dried grass and straw would have gone up at once."

Julius said grimly:

"It did. And the outside door? I suppose you forgot to lock it after you, despite all the fuss you make about never leaving the black tower open. You're a careless lot at Toynton Grange aren't you? Lerner forgets to check the wheelchair brakes and Holroyd goes over the cliff. You knock out your pipe above a floor strewn with highly combustible dry straw, leave the door open to provide a draught, and bloody nearly immolate yourself."

Anstey said:

"That's how I prefer to believe it happened."

Dalgliesh said quickly:

"Presumably there's a second key to the tower. Where is it kept?"

Wilfred opened his eyes and stared into space as if patiently dissociating himself from this dual interrogation.

"Hanging on a nail on the keyboard in the business room. It was Michael's key, the one I brought back here after his death."

"And everyone knows where it's hung?"

"I imagine so. All the keys are kept there and the one to the tower is distinctive."

"How many people at Toynton Grange knew that you planned to be in the tower this afternoon?"

"All of them. I told them my plans after prayers. I always do. People have to know where to find me in an emergency. Everyone was there except Maggie and Millicent. But what you're suggesting is ridiculous."

"Is it?" asked Dalgliesh.

Before he could move, Julius, who was nearer the door, had slipped out. They waited in silence. It was another two minutes before he returned. He said with grim satisfaction:

"The business room is empty and the key isn't there. That means whoever took it hasn't yet had a chance to put it back. Incidentally, I called in on Dot on my way back. She's lurking in her surgical hell sterilizing enough equipment for a major operation. It's like confronting a harpy through a hiss of steam. Anyway, she claims with bad grace that she was in the business room continually from 2 p.m. until about five minutes before we got back. She can't remember whether the tower key was on the keyboard. She didn't notice it. I'm afraid I've made her suspicious, Wilfred, but it seemed important to establish some facts."

Dalgliesh thought that the facts could have been established without direct questioning. But it was too late now to initiate more discreet enquiries and in any case he had neither the heart nor stomach to undertake them. Certainly, he had no wish to pit the claims of orthodox detection against Julius's enthusiastic amateurism. But he asked:

"Did Miss Moxon say whether anyone had come into the business room while she was there? They may have made an attempt to replace the key."

"According to her, the place was—untypically—like a railway station. Henry wheeled himself in shortly after two, and then went out again. No explanation. Millicent dropped in about half an hour ago looking, so she said, for you, Wilfred. Dennis arrived a few minutes later to look up an unspecified telephone number. Maggie arrived just before we did. Again, no explanation. She didn't stay, but she did ask Dot whether she'd seen Eric. The only safe deduction from all this is that Henry couldn't have been on the headland at the material time. But then, we know he wasn't. Whoever started that fire had the use of a pair of very sound legs."

His own, or someone else's, thought Dalgliesh.

He spoke again directly to the quiet figure on the bed.

"Did you see anyone when you were in the tower, either before or after the fire started?"

Wilfred paused before replying.

"I think so."

Seeing Julius's face, he went on quickly:

"I'm sure I did, but only very briefly. When the fire started I was sitting at the southern window, the one overlooking the sea. I smelt smoke and went down into the middle chamber. I opened the door to the base of the tower and saw the hay smoldering and a sudden tongue of flame. I could have got out then, but I panicked. I'm terrified of fire. It isn't a rational fear. It goes well beyond that. I suppose you'd call it a phobia. Anyway, I scrambled ignominiously back into the top room and began running from window to window looking hopelessly for help. It was then I saw—unless it was an hallucination—a figure in a brown habit slipping between that clump of boulders to the southwest."

Julius said:

"From which he could escape unrecognized by you either to the road or down the cliffs to the beach. That's if he were agile enough for the cliff path. What sort of figure, a man or a woman?"

"Just a figure. I only had a glimpse. I shouted but the wind was against me and he obviously didn't hear. I never thought of it being a woman."

"Well, think now. The hood was up, I suppose?"

"Yes. Yes it was."

"And on a warm afternoon! Think it out for yourself, Wilfred. Incidentally, there are three brown habits hanging in the business room. I felt in the pockets for the key. That's why I noticed. Three habits. How many have you altogether?"

"Eight of the lightweight summer ones. They're always kept hanging in the business room. Mine has rather different buttons, but otherwise we have them in common. We're not really particular which one we take."

"You're wearing yours; presumably Dennis and Philby are wearing theirs. That means two are missing."

"Eric may be wearing one, he does occasionally. And Helen sometimes slips into one if the day is chilly. I seem to remember that one is in the sewing room being mended. And I think one was missing just before Michael died, but I can't be sure. It may have turned up again. We don't really keep a check on them."

Julius said:

"So it's practically impossible to know whether one is missing. I suppose what we ought to be doing, Dalgliesh, is to check up on them now. If she hasn't had a chance to replace the key, presumably she's still got the habit."

Dalgliesh said:

"We've no proof that it was a woman. And why hang on to the habit? It could be discarded anywhere in Toynton Grange without suspicion."

Anstey propped himself up and said with sudden strength:

"No, Julius, I forbid it! I won't have people questioned and cross-examined. It was an accident."

Julius, who seemed to be relishing his role of chief inquisitor, said:

"All right. It was an accident. You forgot to lock the door. You knocked out your pipe before it was dead and started the fire smoldering. The figure you saw was just someone from Toynton Grange taking an innocent stroll on the headland, somewhat overclad for the time of year and so immersed in the beauty of nature that he, or she, neither heard your shout, smelt the fire nor noticed the smoke. What happened then?"

"You mean, after I saw the figure? Nothing. I realized of course that I couldn't get out of the windows and I climbed down again into the middle room. I opened the door to the bottom of the tower. The last thing I remember was a great billow of choking smoke and a sheet of flame. The smoke was suffocating me. The flames seemed to be searing my eyes. I hadn't even time to shut the door again before I was overcome. I suppose I should have kept both doors shut and sat tight. But it isn't easy to make sensible decisions in a state of panic."

Dalgliesh asked:

"How many people here knew that you are abnormally afraid of fire?"

"Most of them suspect, I should think. They may not know just how obsessive and personal a fear it is, but they do know that fire worries me. I insist on all the patients sleeping on the ground floor. I've always worried about the sick room, and I was reluctant to let Henry have an upper room. But someone has to sleep in the main part of the house, and we must have the sick room close to the clinical room and the nurses' bedrooms in case there's an emergency at night. It's sensible and prudent to fear fire in a place like this. But prudence has nothing to do with the terror I feel at the sight of smoke and flame."

He put one hand up to his eyes and they saw that he had begun to tremble. Julius looked down at the shaking figure with almost clinical interest.

Dalgliesh said:

"I'll get Miss Moxon."

He had hardly turned to the door when Anstey shot out a protesting hand. They saw that the trembling had stopped. He said, looking at Julius:

"You do believe that the work I'm doing here is worthwhile?"

Dalgliesh wondered if only he had noticed a fraction of a second's pause before Julius replied evenly:

"Of course."

"You're not just saying that to comfort me, you believe it?"

"I wouldn't say it otherwise."

"Of course not, forgive me. And you agree that the work is more important than the man?"

"That's more difficult. I could argue that the work is the man."

"Not here. This place is established now. It could go on without me if it had to."

"Of course it could, if it's adequately endowed, and if the local authorities continue to send contractual patients. But it won't have to go on without you if you act sensibly instead of like the reluctant hero of a third-rate TV drama. It doesn't suit you, Wilfred."

"I'm trying to be sensible and I'm not being brave. I haven't much physical courage you know. It's the virtue I most regret. You two have it—no, don't argue. I know, and I envy you for it. But I don't really need courage for this situation. You see, I can't believe that someone is really trying to kill me." He turned to Dalgliesh.

"You explain, Adam. You must see what I'm getting at."

Dalgliesh said carefully:

"It could be argued that neither of the two attempts were serious. The frayed climbing rope? It's hardly a very certain method, and most people here must know that you wouldn't start a climb without checking your equipment and that you certainly wouldn't climb alone. This afternoon's little charade? You would probably have been safe enough if you'd closed both the doors and stayed in the top room; uncomfortably hot probably, but in no real danger. The fire would have burnt itself out in time. It was opening the middle door and gasping in a lungful of smoke which nearly did for you."

Julius said:

"But suppose the grass had burnt fiercely and the flames had caught the wood floor of the first storey? The whole of the middle of the tower would have gone up in a matter of seconds; the fire must have reached the top room. If it had, nothing could have saved you." He turned to Dalgliesh:

"Isn't that true?"

"Probably. That's why you ought to tell the police. A practical joker who takes risks like that has to be taken seriously. And the next time there mightn't be someone handy to rescue you."

"I don't think there will be a next time. I think I know who's responsible. I'm not really quite as foolish as I seem. I'll take care, I promise. I have a feeling that the person responsible won't be here with us much longer."

Julius said:

"You're not immortal, Wilfred."

"I know that, too, and I could be wrong. So I think it's time I spoke to the Ridgewell Trust. The Colonel is overseas, visiting his homes in India, but he's due back on the 18th. The trustees would like my answer by the end of October. It's a question of tying-up capital for future developments. I wouldn't hand over to them without a majority agreement from the family. I propose to hold a family council. But, if someone is really trying to frighten me into breaking my vow, then I'll see that my work here is made indestructible, whether I'm alive or dead."

Julius said:

"If you hand the whole property over to the Ridgewell Trust, it isn't going to please Millicent."

Wilfred's face set into a mask of obstinacy. Dalgliesh was interested to see how the features changed. The gentle eyes became stern and glazed as if unwilling to see, the mouth set into an uncompromising line. And yet the whole expression was one of petulant weakness.

"Millicent sold out to me perfectly willingly and at a fair valuation. She can't reasonably complain. If I'm driven out of here, the work goes on. What happens to me isn't important."

He smiled at Julius.

"You aren't a believer, I know, so I'll find another authority for you. How about Shakespeare? 'Be absolute for death, and life and death shall thereby be the sweeter.' "

Julius Court's eyes briefly met Dalgliesh's over Wilfred's head. The message simultaneously passed was simultaneously understood. Julius had some difficulty in controlling his mouth. At last he said dryly:

"Dalgliesh is supposed to be convalescent. He's already practically passed out with the exertion of saving you. I may look healthy enough but I need my strength for the pursuit of my own personal pleasures. So if you are determined to hand over to the Ridgewell Trust by the end of the month, try being absolute for life, at least for the next three weeks, there's a good chap."

## III

When they were outside the room Dalgliesh asked:

"Do you believe he's in real danger?"

"I don't know. It was probably a closer thing this afternoon than someone intended." He added with affectionate scorn:

"Silly old pseud! Absolute for death! I thought we were about to move on to *Hamlet* and be reminded that the readiness is all. One thing is certain though, isn't it? He isn't putting on a show of courage. Either he doesn't believe that someone at Toynton Grange has it in for him, or he thinks he knows his enemy and is confident that he can deal with him, or her. Or, of course, he started the fire himself. Wait until I've had this hand bandaged and then come in for a drink. You look as if you need it."

But there were things Dalgliesh had to do. He left Julius, volubly apprehensive, to the mercies of Dorothy Moxon and walked back to Hope Cottage to collect his torch. He was thirsty, but there was no time for anything but cold water from the kitchen tap. He had left the cottage windows open but the little sitting-room, insulated by thick stone walls, was as warm and stuffy as on the day he had arrived. As he closed the door, Father Baddeley's cassock swung against it and he caught again the musty, faintly ecclesiastical smell. The crochet chair back and arm covers were sleekly in place uncrumpled by Father Baddeley's head and hands. Something of his personality still lingered here, although already Dalgliesh felt its presence less strongly. But there was no communication. If he wanted Father Baddeley's counsel he would have to seek it in paths familiar but unaccustomed and to which he no longer felt that he had any right of way.

He was ridiculously tired. The cool, rather harsh-tasting water only brought him to a clearer realization of just how tired. The thought of the narrow bed upstairs, of throwing himself down upon its hardness, was almost irresistible. It was ridiculous that so comparatively little exertion could so exhaust him. And it seemed to have become insufferably hot. He drew a hand over his brow and felt the sweat, clammy cold on his fingers. Obviously he had a temperature. He had, after all, been warned by the hospital that the fever might recur. He felt a surge of anger against his doctors, against Wilfred Anstey, against himself.

It would be easy now to pack his things and get back to the London flat. It would be cool and unencumbered there high above the Thames at Queenhythe. People would leave him alone supposing him to be still in Dorset. Or he could leave a note for Anstey and drive away now; the whole of the West Country was open to him. There were a hundred better places for convalescence than this claustrophobic, self-regarding community dedicated to love and self-fulfillment through suffering, where people sent each other poison pen letters, played at childish and malicious pranks or got tired of waiting for death and hurled themselves into annihilation. And there was nothing to keep him at Toynton; he told himself so with stubborn insistence, resting his head against the coolness of the small square of glass over the sink which had obviously served Father Baddeley as a shaving mirror. It was probably some freak aftermath of illness that made him at once so indecisive and so stubbornly reluctant to leave. For someone who had made up his mind never to go back to detection, he was giving a good imitation of a man committed to his job.

He saw no one as he left the cottage and began the long trudge up the cliff. It was still a bright day on the headland with that sudden almost momentary intensification of light which comes before the setting of the autumn sun. The cushions of moss on the fragmented walls were an intense green, dazzling the eye. Each individual flower was bright as a gem, its image shimmering in the gently moving air. The tower, when at last he came up to it, glistened like ebony and seemed to shiver in the sun. He felt that if he touched it it would reel and dissolve. Its long shadow lay like a monitory finger across the headland.

Taking advantage of the light, since the torch would be more use inside the tower, he began his search. The burnt straw and blackened debris lay in untidy heaps close to the porch, but the light breeze, never absent from this peak of the headland, had already begun to shift the humps and had strewn odd strands almost to the edge of the cliff. He began by scrutinizing the ground close to the walls, then moved out in widening circles. He found nothing until he reached the clump of boulders about fifty yards to the southwest. They were a curious formation, less a natural outcrop of the headland than an artifact, as if the builder of the tower had transported to the site double the weight of stone needed and had amused himself by arranging the surplus in the form of a miniature mountain range. The stones formed a long semicircle about forty yards long, the peaks, from six to eight feet high, linked by smaller, more rounded uplands. There was adequate cover here for a man to escape undetected either to the cliff path or by way of the rapidly falling ground to the northwest to within a couple of hundred yards of the road.

It was here, behind one of the larger boulders, that Dalgliesh found what he had expected to find, a light-weight brown monk's habit. It was tightly rolled into a bolster and wedged into the crevice between two smaller stones. There was nothing else to be seen, no discernible footprints in the firm dry turf, no tin smelling of paraffin. Somewhere he expected to find a tin. Although the straw and dry grass in the base of the tower would have burned quickly enough once a fire was well established, he doubted whether a thrown match could have been relied upon to start a blaze.

He tucked the habit under his arm. If this were a murder hunt the forensic scientists would examine it for traces of fibre, for dust, for paraffin, for any biological or chemical link with someone at Toynton Grange. But it wasn't a murder hunt; it wasn't even an official investigation. And even if fibres were identified on the habit which matched those from a shirt, a pair of slacks, a jacket, a dress even, of someone at Toynton Grange, what did that prove? Apparently any of the helpers had a right to array themselves in Wilfred's curious idea of a working uniform. The fact that the habit had been abandoned, and at that point, suggested that the wearer had chosen to escape down the cliff rather than by way of the road; otherwise why not continue to rely on its camouflage? Unless, of course, the wearer were a woman and one who didn't normally thus array herself. In that case, to be seen by chance on the headland shortly after the fire would be damning. But no one, man or woman, would choose to wear it on the cliff path. It was the quicker but the more difficult route and the habit would be a dangerously entangling garment. Certainly it would bear telltale traces of sandy earth or green stains from the seaweed-covered rocks on that difficult scramble to the beach. But perhaps that was what he was meant to believe. Had the habit, like Father Baddeley's letter, been planted for him to discover, so neatly, so precisely placed exactly where he might have expected to find it? Why abandon it at all? Thus rolled, it was hardly an impossible burden to manage on that slippery path to the shore.

The door of the tower was still ajar. Inside the smell of the fire still lingered but half pleasantly now in the first cool of the early evening, an evocative autumnal smell of burnt grass. The lower part of the rope banister had burnt away and hung from the iron rings in scorched and tattered fragments.

He switched on his torch and began systematically to search among the blackened threads of burnt straw. He found it within minutes, a battered, soot-covered and lidless tin which could once have held cocoa. He smelt it. It could have been his imagination that a trace of paraffin still lingered.

He made his way up the stone steps carefully hugging the fire-blackened wall. He found nothing in the middle chamber and was glad to climb out of this dark, windowless and claustrophobic cell into the upper room. The contrast with the chamber below was immediate and striking. The little room was filled with light. It was only six feet wide and the domed and ribbed ceiling gave it a charming, feminine and slightly formal air. Four of the eight compass point windows were without their glass and the air streamed in, cool and scented with the sea. Because the room was so small the height of the tower was accentuated. Dalgliesh had the sensation of being suspended in a decorative pepper pot between sky and sea. The quiet was absolute, a positive peace. He could hear nothing but the ticking of his watch and the ceaseless anodyne surge of the sea. Why, he wondered, hadn't that self-tormented Victorian Wilfred Anstey signalled his distress from one of these windows? Perhaps, by the time his will to endure had been broken by the tortures of hunger and thirst, the old man had been too weak to mount the stairs. Certainly nothing of his final terror and despair had penetrated to this miniature light-filled eyrie. Looking out of the southern window Dalgliesh could see the crinkled sea layered in azure and purple with one red triangle of sail stationary on the horizon. The other windows gave a panoramic view of the whole sunlit headland; Toynton Grange and its clutter of cottages could be identified only by the chimney of the house itself since they lay in the valley. Dalgliesh noticed too that the square of mossy turf, where Holroyd's wheelchair had rested before that final convulsive heave towards destruction, and the narrow sunken lane were also invisible. Whatever had happened on that fateful afternoon, no one could have seen it from the black tower.

The room was simply furnished. There was a wooden table and a chair set against the seaward window, a small oak cupboard, a rush mat on the floor, a slatted old-fashioned easy chair with cushions set in the middle of the room; a wooden cross nailed to the wall. He saw that the door of the cupboard was ajar and the key in the lock. Inside he found a small and unedifying collection of paperback pornography. Even allowing for the natural tendency—to which Dalgliesh admitted himself not immune—to be disdainful of the sexual tastes of others, this was not the pornography that he would have chosen. It was a paltry and pathetic little library of flagellation, titillation and salacity, incapable, he thought, of stimulating any emotion beyond ennui and vague disgust. True it contained *Lady Chatterley's Lover*—a novel which Dalgliesh considered overrated as literature and not qualifying as pornography—but the rest was hardly respectable by any standard. Even after a gap of over twenty years, it was difficult to believe that the gentle, aesthetic and fastidious Father Baddeley had developed a taste for this pathetic trivia. And if he had, why leave the cupboard unlocked or the key where Wilfred could find it? The obvious conclusion was that the books were Anstey's and that he had only just had time to unlock the cupboard before he smelt the fire. In the subsequent panic he had forgotten to lock away the evidence of his secret indulgence. He would probably return in some haste and confusion as soon as he was fit enough and got the opportunity. And, if this were true, it proved one thing: Anstey could not have started the fire.

Leaving the cupboard door ajar precisely as he had found it, Dalgliesh then carefully searched the floor. The rough mat of what looked like plaited hemp was torn in places and overlaid with dust. From the drag on its surface and the lie of the torn and minute filaments of fibre he deduced that Anstey had moved the table from the eastern to the southern window. He found too, what looked like traces of two different kinds of tobacco ash, but they were too small to be collected without his magnifying glass and tweezers. But, a little to the right of the eastern window and resting between the interstices of the mat, he found something which could be identified easily with the naked eye. It was a single used yellow match identical with those in the booklet by Father Baddeley's bed, and it had been peeled down in five separate pieces to its blackened head.

## IV

The front door of Toynton Grange was, as usual, open. Dalgliesh walked swiftly and silently up the main staircase to Wilfred's room. As he approached he could hear talking. Dot Moxon's expostulatory and belligerent voice dominating the broken murmur of male voices. Dalgliesh went in without knocking. Three pairs of eyes regarded him with wariness and, he thought, with some resentment. Wilfred was still lying propped up in his bed. Dennis Lerner quickly turned away to look fixedly out of the window, but not before Dalgliesh had seen that his face was blotched, as if he had been crying. Dot was sitting by the side of the bed, stolid and immovable as a mother watching a sick child. Dennis muttered, as if Dalgliesh had asked for an explanation:

"Wilfred has told me what happened. It's unbelievable."

Wilfred spoke with a mulish obstinacy which only emphasized his satisfaction at not being believed.

"It happened, and it was an accident."

Dennis was beginning "How could . . ." when Dalgliesh interrupted by laying the rolled habit on the foot of the bed. He said:

"I found this among the boulders by the black tower. If you hand it over to the police it may tell them something."

"I'm not going to the police and I forbid anyone here—anyone—to go on my behalf."

Dalgliesh said calmly:

"Don't worry; I've no intention of wasting their time. Given your determination to keep them out of it, they'd probably suspect that you lit the fire yourself. Did you?"

Wilfred cut swiftly into Dennis's gasp of incredulity and Dot's outraged protest.

"No, Dot, it's perfectly reasonable that Adam Dalgliesh should think as he does. He has been professionally trained in suspicion and scepticism. As it happens, I didn't attempt to burn myself to death. One family suicide in the black tower is enough. But I think I know who did light the fire and I shall deal with that person in my own time and in my own way. In the meantime nothing is to be said to the family, nothing. Thank God I can be sure of one thing, none of them can have had a hand in this. Now that I'm assured of that I shall know what to do. And now if you would all be kind enough to leave . . ."

Dalgliesh didn't wait to see if the others proposed to obey. He contented himself with one final word from the door.

"If you're thinking of private vengeance, then forget it. If you can't, or daren't, act within the law, then don't act at all."

Anstey smiled his sweet infuriating smile.

"Vengeance, Commander? Vengeance? That word has no place in our philosophy at Toynton Grange."

Dalgliesh saw and heard no one as he passed again through the main hall. The house might have been an empty shell. After a second's thought he walked briskly over the headland to Charity Cottage. The headland was deserted except for a solitary figure making its way down the slope from the cliff; Julius carrying what looked like a bottle in either hand. He held them aloft in a half pugilistic, half celebratory gesture. Dalgliesh lifted his hand in a brief salute and, turning, made his way up the stone path to the Hewson's cottage.

The door was open and at first he heard no sign of life. He knocked, and getting no reply, stepped inside. Charity Cottage, standing on its own, was larger than the other two and the stone sitting room, bathed now in sunshine from its two windows, was agreeably proportioned. But it looked dirty and unkempt, reflecting in its untidiness Maggie's dissatisfied and restless nature. His first impression was that she had proclaimed her intention that their stay would be brief by not bothering to unpack. The few items of furniture looked as if they still stood where the whim of the removal men had first deposited them. A grubby sofa faced the large television screen which dominated the room. Eric's meager medical library was stacked flat on the shelves of the bookcase, which held also a miscellany of crockery, ornaments, records and crushed shoes. A standard lamp of repellent design was without its shade. Two pictures were propped with their faces against the wall, their cords hanging knotted and broken. There was a square table set in the middle of the room bearing what looked like the remains of a late lunch; a torn packet of water biscuits spilling crumbs; a lump of cheese on a chipped plate; butter oozing from its greasy wrapping; a topless bottle of tomato ketchup with the sauce congealed round the lip. Two bloated flies buzzed their intricate convolutions above the debris.

From the kitchen came the rush of water and the roar of a gas boiler. Eric and Maggie were washing up. Suddenly the boiler was turned off and he heard Maggie's voice:

"You're so bloody weak! You let them all use you. If you are poking that supercilious bitch—and don't think I care a damn either way—it's only because you can't say no to her. You don't really want her any more than you want me."

Eric's reply was a low mutter. There was a crash of crockery. Then Maggie's voice rose again:

"For Christ's sake, you can't hide away here for ever! That trip to St. Saviour's, it wasn't as bad as you feared. No one said anything."

This time Eric's reply was perfectly intelligible:

"They didn't need to. Anyway, who did we see? Just the consultant in physical medicine and that medical records officer. She knew all right and she let me see it. That's how it'd be in general practice, if I ever got a job. They'd never let me forget it. The practice delinquent. Every female patient under sixteen tactfully diverted to one of the partners, just in case. At least Wilfred treats me like a human being. I can make a contribution. I can do my job."

Maggie almost yelled at him:

"What kind of a job, for God's sake?" And then both their voices were lost in the roar from the boiler and the rush of water. Then it stopped and Dalgliesh heard Maggie's voice again, high, emphatic.

"All right! All right! All right! I've said I won't tell, and I won't. But if you keep on nagging about it, I may change my mind."

Eric's reply was lost but it sounded like a long expostulatory murmur. Then Maggie spoke again:

"Well, what if I did? He wasn't a fool, you know. He could tell that something was up. And where's the harm? He's dead, isn't he? Dead. Dead. Dead."

Dalgliesh suddenly realized that he was standing stock still, straining his ears to hear as if this were an official case, his case, and every surreptitiously stolen word was a vital clue. Irritated, he almost shook himself into action. He had taken a few steps back to the doorway and had raised his fist to knock again and more loudly when Maggie, carrying a small tin tray, emerged from the kitchen with Eric at her back. She recovered quickly from her surprise and gave a shout of almost genuine laughter.

"Oh God, don't say Wilfred has called in the Yard itself to grill me. The poor little man has got himself into a tizzy. What are you going to do, darling, warn me that anything I say will be taken down and may be given in evidence?"

The door darkened and Julius came in. He must, thought Dalgliesh, have run down the headland to arrive so quickly. Why the hurry, he wondered. Breathing heavily, Julius swung two bottles of whisky on to the table.

"A peace offering."

"So I should think!" Maggie had become flirtatious. Her eyes brightened under the heavy lids and she slewed them from Dalgliesh to Julius as if uncertain where to bestow her favors. She spoke to Dalgliesh:

"Julius has been accusing me of attempting to roast Wilfred alive in the black tower. I know: I realize it isn't funny. But Julius is, when he's trying to be pompous. And honestly, it's a nonsense. If I wanted to get my own back on St. Wilfred I could do it without pussyfooting about the black tower in drag, couldn't I darling?"

She checked her laughter and her glance at Julius was at once minatory and conspiratorial. It provoked no response. Julius said quickly:

"I didn't accuse you. I simply enquired with the utmost tact where you'd been since one o'clock."

"On the beach, darling. I do go there occasionally. I know I can't prove it, but neither can you prove that I wasn't there."

"That's rather a coincidence isn't it, your happening to walk on the beach?"

"No more a coincidence than your happening to drive along the coast road."

"And you didn't see anyone?"

"I told you darling, not a soul. Was I expected to? And now, Adam, it's your turn. Are you going to charm the truth out of me in the best Metropolitan tradition?"

"Not I. This is Court's case. That's one of the first principles of detection, never interfere with another man's conduct of his case."

Julius said:

"Besides, Maggie dear, the Commander isn't interested in our paltry concerns. Strange as it may seem, he just doesn't care. He can't even pretend an interest in whether Dennis hurled Victor over the cliff and I'm covering up for him. Humiliating, isn't it?"

Maggie's laugh was uneasy. She glanced at her husband like an inexperienced hostess who fears that the party is getting out of control.

"Don't be silly, Julius. We know that you aren't covering up. Why should you? What would there be in it for you?"

"How well you know me, Maggie! Nothing. But then, I might have done it out of sheer good nature." He looked at Dalgliesh with a sly smile and added:

"I believe in being accommodating to my friends."

Eric said suddenly and with surprising authority:

"What was it you wanted, Mr. Dalgliesh?"

"Just information. When I arrived at the cottage I found a booklet of matches by Father Baddeley's bed advertising the Olde Tudor Barn near Wareham. I thought I might try it for dinner tonight. Did he go there often, do you know?"

Maggie laughed.

"God, no! Never I should think. It's hardly Michael's scene. I gave him the matches. He liked trifles like that. But the Barn's not bad. Bob Loder took me there for lunch on my birthday and they did us quite well."

Julius said:

"I'll describe it. Ambience: a chain of colored fairy lights strung round an otherwise genuine and agreeable seventeenth-century barn. First course: tinned tomato soup with a slice of tomato to add verisimilitude and color contrast; frozen prawns in bottled sauce on a bed of limp lettuce; half a melon—ripe if you're lucky; or the chef's own homemade pâté fresh from the local supermarket. The rest of the menu you may imagine. It's usually a variety of steak served with frozen vegetables and what they describe as french fried. If you must drink, stick to the red. I don't know whether the owner makes it or merely sticks the labels on the bottles but at least it's wine of a kind. The white is cat's pee."

Maggie laughed indulgently.

"Oh, don't be such a snob darling, it's not as bad as that. Bob and I had quite a decent meal. And, whoever bottled the wine, it had the right effect as far as I was concerned."

Dalgliesh said:

"But it may have deteriorated. You know how it is. The chef leaves and a restaurant changes almost overnight."

Julius laughed:

"That's the advantage of the Olde Barn Menu. The chef can and does change fortnightly but the tinned soup is guaranteed to taste the same."

Maggie said:

"It won't have changed since my birthday. That was only the 11th September. I'm Virgo, darlings. Appropriate, isn't it?"

Julius said:

"There are one or two decent places within driving distance. I can let you have a few names."

He did so and Dalgliesh dutifully noted them at the back of his diary. But as he walked back to Hope Cottage his mind had already registered more important information.

So Maggie was on lunching terms with Bob Loder; the obliging Loder, equally ready to alter Father Baddeley's will—or to dissuade him from altering it?—and to help Millicent cheat her brother out of half his capital from the sale of Toynton Grange. But that little ploy, had, of course, been Holroyd's idea. Had Holroyd and Loder cooked it up between them? Maggie had told them about her luncheon date with sly satisfaction. If her husband neglected her on her birthday she wasn't without consolation. But what of Loder? Was his interest no more than a readiness to avail himself of a complaisant and dissatisfied woman, or had he a more sinister motive for keeping in touch with what happened at Toynton Grange? And the shredded match? Dalgliesh hadn't yet compared it with the stubs in the booklet still by Father Baddeley's bed, but he had no doubt that one of the stubs would match. He couldn't question Maggie further without rousing suspicion, but he didn't need to. She couldn't have given the booklet of matches to Father Baddeley before the afternoon of 11th September, the day before Holroyd's death. And on the afternoon of the eleventh, Father Baddeley had visited his solicitor. He couldn't, then, have received the booklet of matches until that evening at the earliest. And that meant that he must have been in the black tower on either the following morning or afternoon. It would be useful when opportunity offered, to have a word with Miss Willison and ask whether Father Baddeley had been at the Grange on the Wednesday morning. According to the entries in his diary it had certainly been his invariable routine to visit the Grange every morning. And that meant that he had almost certainly been in the black tower on the afternoon of the twelfth, and, possibly, sitting at the eastern window. Those drag marks on the fibre matting had looked very recent. But even from that window, he couldn't have seen Holroyd's chair go over the cliff; couldn't even have watched the distant figures of Lerner and Holroyd making their way along the sunken lane to that patch of green turf. And, even if he could, what would his evidence be worth, an old man sitting alone, reading and probably dozing in the afternoon sun? It was surely ludicrous to search here for a motive for murder. But suppose Father Baddeley had known beyond doubt that he had neither dozed nor read? Then it wasn't a question of what he had seen, but of what he had singularly failed to see.

# BOOK SIX

•

# A Bloodless Murder

# I

The next afternoon, on the last day of her life, Grace Willison sat in the courtyard in the afternoon sun. Its rays were still warm on her face but now they touched her parched skin with a gentler valedictory warmth. From time to time a cloud moved across the face of the sun and she found herself shivering with the first intimation of winter. The air smelt keener, the afternoons were darkening fast. There wouldn't be many more days warm enough for her to sit outside. Even today she was the only patient in the courtyard and she was grateful for the warmth of the rug across her knees.

She found herself thinking about Commander Dalgliesh. She wished that he had come more often to Toynton Grange. He was still at Hope Cottage apparently. Yesterday he had helped Julius rescue Wilfred from the fire in the black tower. Wilfred had bravely made light of his ordeal as one would expect. It had only been a small fire caused entirely by his own carelessness; he had never been in real danger. But, all the same, she thought, it was fortunate that the Commander had been at hand to help.

Would he leave Toynton, she wondered, without coming to say goodbye to her? She hoped not. She had liked him so much in their brief time together. How pleasant it would be if he could be sitting here with her now, talking about Father Baddeley. No one at Toynton Grange now ever mentioned his name. But, of course, the Commander couldn't be expected to give up his time.

The thought was entirely without bitterness or resentment. There really wasn't anything to interest him at Toynton Grange. And it wasn't as if she could issue a personal invitation. She allowed herself for one minute to indulge in regret for the retirement which she had hoped for and planned. Her small pension from the Society, a little cottage, sun filled and bright with chintz and geraniums; her dear mother's possessions, the ones she had sold before she came to

Toynton; the rose-patterned tea service; the rosewood writing table; the series of water colors of English cathedrals; how lovely to be able to invite anyone she liked to her own home to take tea with her. Not a communal institutional tea at a bleak refectory table, but proper afternoon tea. Her table; her tea service; her food; her guest.

She became aware of the weight of the book on her lap. It was a paperback edition of Trollope's *Last Chronicle of Barset.* It had lain there all the afternoon. Why, she wondered, was she so strangely reluctant to read it? And then she remembered. This had been the book she was rereading on that dreadful afternoon when Victor's body had been brought home. She hadn't opened it since. But that was ridiculous. She must put the thought out of her mind. It was stupid, no, it was wrong, to spoil a book she so loved—its leisurely world of cathedral intrigue, its sanity, its delicate moral sensibility—by contaminating it with images of violence, hatred and blood.

She curved her deformed left hand around the book and parted the pages with her right. There was a book mark between the last pages she had read, a single pink antirrhinum pressed between a sheet of tissue. And then she remembered. It was a flower from the small posy Father Baddeley had brought her on the afternoon of Victor's death. Normally he never picked wild flowers except for her. They hadn't lasted long, less than a day. But this single flower she had pressed at once between the leaves of her book. She gazed at it, motionless.

A shadow fell across the page. A voice said:

"Anything wrong?"

She looked up and smiled.

"Nothing. It's just that I've remembered something. Isn't it extraordinary how the mind rejects anything which it associates with horror or great distress? Commander Dalgliesh asked me if I knew what Father Baddeley did on the few days before he went into hospital. And, of course, I do know. I know what he did on the Wednesday afternoon. I don't suppose it's the least important, but it would be nice to tell him. I know that everyone here is terribly busy but do you think that . . . ?"

"Don't worry. I'll find time to drop in at Hope Cottage. It's time he showed his face here if he proposes to stay on much longer. And now, don't you think it would be wise for you to come in? It's getting chilly."

Miss Willison smiled her thanks. She would have preferred to have stayed out a little longer. But she didn't like to insist. It was meant kindly. She closed her book again and her murderer grasped the chair with strong hands and wheeled her in to her death.

# II

Ursula Hollis always asked her nurses to leave her curtains undrawn and tonight in the faint haze of light from her luminous bedside clock, she could still just discern the oblong frame which separated darkness outside from the darkness within. It was nearly midnight. The night was starless and very still. She lay in blackness so thick that it was almost a weight on her chest, a dense curtain descending to stifle breath. Outside, the headland was asleep, except, she supposed, for the small animals of the night scurrying among the rigid grasses. Inside Toynton Grange she could still hear distant sounds; brisk footsteps passing down a passage; the quiet closing of a door; the squeak of unoiled wheels as someone moved a hoist or a wheelchair; the mouselike scrabbling sounds from next door as Grace Willison moved restlessly in her bed; a sudden blare of music, instantly muted, as someone opened and shut the sitting room door. Her bedside clock snatched at the seconds and ticked them into oblivion. She lay rigid, the warm tears flowing in a constant stream over her face to seep, suddenly cold and sticky, into her pillow. Under the pillow was Steve's letter. From time to time she folded her right arm painfully across her chest and insinuated her fingers under the pillow to feel the envelope's knife sharp edge.

Mogg had moved into the flat; they were living together. Steve had written the news almost casually as if it were merely a temporary and mutually convenient arrangement for sharing the rent and the chores. Mogg was doing the cooking; Mogg had redecorated the sitting room and put up more shelves; Mogg had found him a clerical job with his publishers which might lead to a permanent and better post. Mogg's new book of poems were due out in the spring. There was only a perfunctory enquiry after Ursula's health. He hadn't even made the usual vague and insincere promises to visit. He had written no word about her return home, the planned new flat, his negotiations with the local authority. There was no need. She never would return. They both knew it. Mogg knew it.

She hadn't received the letter until teatime. Albert Philby had been unaccountably late in fetching the post and it was after four o'clock before it was placed in her hand. She was grateful that she had been alone in the sitting-room, that Grace Willison hadn't yet come in from the courtyard to get ready for tea. There had been no one to watch her face as she read it, no one to make tactful enquiries, or, more tactfully, to refrain. And anger and shock had carried her through until now. She had held on to anger, feeding it with memory and imagination, willing herself to eat her usual two slices of bread, to drink her tea, to contribute her sentences of platitude and small talk to the party. Only now, when Grace Willison's heavy breathing had settled into a gentle snoring, when there was no longer a risk that Helen or Dot might pay a last visit, when Toynton Grange was finally wrapping itself in silence for the night, could she give way to desolation and loss and indulge in what she knew was self-pity. And the tears, when once they started, would not stop. The grief once indulged was unassuageable. She had no control over her crying. It no longer even distressed her; it had nothing to do with grief or longing. It was a physical manifestation, involuntary as a hiccup, but silent and almost consoling; an interminable stream.

She knew what she had to do. She listened through the rhythm of her tears. There was no sound from next door except Grace Willison's snoring which was now regular. She put out her hand and switched on the light. The bulb had the lowest wattage which Wilfred could buy but the brightness was still blinding. She imagined it, a dazzling oblong of light shining out to signal her intention to all the world. She knew that there was no one to see it, but in imagination the headland was suddenly full of running feet and loud with calling voices. She had stopped crying now but her swollen eyes saw the room as if it were a half-developed photograph, an image of bleared and distorted shapes, shifting and dissolving and seen through a stinging curtain pierced with needles of light.

She waited. Nothing happened. There was still no sound from next door but Grace's harsh and regular breathing. The next step was easy; she had done it twice before. She dropped both her pillows on the floor and, maneuvering her body to the edge of the bed, let herself drop gently on top of their soft cushion. Even with the pillows to break her weight it seemed that the room shook. Again she waited. But there were no quick footsteps hurrying down the passage. She raised herself upwards on the pillows against the bed and began propelling herself towards its foot. It was an easy matter to stretch out her hand and withdraw the cord from her dressing gown. Then she began her painful progress towards the door.

Her legs were powerless; what strength she had was in her arms. Her dead feet lay white and flabby as fish on the cold floor, the toes splayed like obscene excrescences vainly scrabbling for a grip. The linoleum was unpolished but smooth and she slid along with surprising speed. She remembered with what joy she had discovered that she could do this; that, ridiculous and humiliating as the trick might be, she could actually move around her room without the use of her chair.

But now she was going farther afield. It was lucky that the modern insubstantial doors of the annex rooms were opened by depressing a handle and not turning a knob. She made the dressing gown cord into a loop and, at the second attempt, managed to throw it over the handle. She tugged and the door quietly opened. Discarding one of the pillows, she edged her way into the silent passage. Her heart was thudding with such power it must surely betray her. Again she slipped the cord over the handle and, maneuvering herself a few feet down the passage, heard the door click shut.

One single light-bulb, heavily shaded, was always kept burning at the far end of the corridor and she could see without difficulty where the short staircase led to the upper floor. This was her objective. Reaching it proved astonishingly easy. The linoleum in the passage, although never polished, seemed smoother than that in her room; or perhaps she had gained the knack of progress. She slid forward with almost exhilarating ease.

But the staircase was more difficult. She was relying on pulling herself up by the banister, step by step. But it was necessary to take the pillow with her. She would need it on the floor above. And the pillow seemed to have swollen into a gigantic, soft, white encumbrance. The stairs were narrow and it was difficult to prop it safely. Twice it tumbled down and she had to slide after it to retrieve it. But after four steps had been painfully negotiated she worked out the best method of progress. She tied one end of the dressing gown cord around her waist and the other tightly round the middle of the pillow. She wished she had put on the dressing gown. It would have hampered her progress, but she was already shivering.

And so, step by step, gasping and sweating despite the cold, she pulled herself up, grasping the banisters with both hands. The stairs creaked alarmingly. She expected any minute to hear the faint summons of a bedside bell and hear from the distance Dot or Helen's hurrying footsteps.

She had no idea how long it took to reach the top of the stairs. But at last she was sitting crouched and shivering on the final step, grasping the banisters with both hands so convulsively that the wood shook, and peering down at the hall below. It was then that the cloaked figure appeared. There were no warning footsteps, no cough, no sound of human breath. One second the passage was empty. In the next a brown cloaked figure—head bent, hood drawn well over the face—had moved silently and swiftly beneath her, and disappeared down the passage. She waited terrified, hardly daring to breathe, huddling herself as far as possible out of view. It would come back. She knew that it would come back. Like the dreadful figure of death which she had seen in old books, carved on monumental tombs, it would pause beneath her and throw back the concealing hood to reveal the grinning skull, the eyeless sockets, would poke at her through the banister its fleshless fingers. Her heart, beating in icy terror against the rib cage, seemed to have grown too large for her body. Surely its frantic thudding must betray her! It seemed an eternity, but she realized that it could only have been less than a minute before the figure reappeared and passed, beneath her terrified eyes, silently and swiftly into the main house.

Ursula realized then that she wasn't going to kill herself. It had only been Dot, or Helen, or Wilfred. Who else could it have been? But the shock of that silent figure, passing like a shadow, had restored in her the will to live. If she had really wanted to die, what was she doing here crouched in cold discomfort at the top of the stairs? She had her dressing gown cord. Even now she could tie it round her neck and let herself slip unresisting down the stairs. But she wouldn't. The very thought of that last fall, the strangling cord biting into her neck, made her moan in agonized protest. No, she had never meant to kill herself. No one, not even Steve, was worth an eternity of damnation. Steve might not believe in Hell, but what did Steve really know about anything that mattered? But she had to complete her journey now. She had to get hold of that bottle of aspirin which she knew must be somewhere in the clinical room. She wouldn't use it, but she would keep it always within reach. She would know that, if life became intolerable, the means to end it was at hand. And perhaps, if she just took a handful, and left the bottle by the bed they would realize at last that she was unhappy. That was all she intended; all she had ever intended. They would send for Steve. They would take some notice of her misery. Perhaps they might even force Steve to take her back to London. Having come so far at such cost, she had to get to the clinical room.

The door presented no problem. But when she had sidled through, she realized that this was the end. She couldn't switch on the light. The low bulb in the corridor gave a faint diffused glow but, even with the door of the clinical room ajar, it was inadequate to show her the position of the light. And if she were to succeed in switching it on with the dressing gown cord, she had to know accurately at what spot to aim. She stretched out her hand and felt along the wall. Nothing. She held the cord in a loop and flung it softly and repeatedly where she thought the switch might be. But it fell away uselessly. She began to cry again, defeated, desperately cold, suddenly realizing that she had the whole painful journey to do again in reverse, and that dragging herself back into bed would be the most difficult and painful of all.

And then, suddenly, a hand stretched out of the darkness and the light was switched on. Ursula gave a little scream of fright. She looked up. Framed in the doorway, wearing a brown habit open down the front and with the hood flung back was Helen Rainer. The two women, petrified, stared at each other speechlessly. And Ursula saw that the eyes bent on hers were as full of terror as her own.

# III

Grace Willison's body jerked into wakefulness and immediately began to tremble uncontrollably as if a strong hand were shaking her into full consciousness. She listened in the darkness, raising her head with difficulty from the pillow; but she could hear nothing. Whatever noise, real or imagined, had woken her was now stilled. She switched on her bedside lamp; nearly midnight. She reached for her book. It was a pity that the paperback Trollope was so heavy. It meant that it had to be propped up on the coverlet and since, once stretched into her conventional attitude for sleep she couldn't easily bend her knees, the effort of slightly raising her head and peering down at the small print was tiring both to her eyes and to the muscles of her neck. The discomfort sometimes made her wonder whether reading in bed was the pleasant indulgence she had always believed it to be since those childhood days when her father's parsimony over the electricity bill and her mother's anxiety about eye strain and eight hours good sleep each night, had denied her a bedside lamp.

Her left leg was jerking uncontrollably and she watched, detached and interested the erratic jump of the coverlet as if an animal were loose among the bed clothes. To wake suddenly like this once she had first fallen asleep was always a bad sign. She was in for a restless night. She dreaded sleeplessness and for a moment was tempted to pray that she might be spared it just for tonight. But she had finished her prayers and it seemed pointless to pray again for a mercy which experience had taught her she wasn't going to receive. Pleading to God for something which he had already made it perfectly plain he wasn't disposed to give you was to behave like a peevish, importunate child. She watched her limb's antics with interest, vaguely comforted by the sensation which was now almost self-induced of being detached from her unruly body.

She lay down her book and decided instead to think about the pilgrimage to Lourdes in fourteen days' time. She pictured the happy bustle of departure—she had a new coat saved for the occasion—the drive across France with the party gay as a picnic; the first glimpse of the mists swirling around the foothills of the Pyrenees; the snow-capped peaks; Lourdes itself with its concentrated business, its air of being always *en fête*. The Toynton Grange party, except for the two Roman Catholics, Ursula Hollis and Georgie Allan, were not part of an official English pilgrimage, did not take Mass, grouped themselves with becoming humility at the back of the crowd when the bishops in their crimson robes made their slow way round Rosary Square, the golden monstrance held high before them. But how inspiring, how colorful, how splendid it all was! The candles weaving their patterns of light, the colors, the singing, the sense of belonging again to the outside world but a world in which sickness was honored, no longer regarded as an alienation, a deformity of the spirit as well as the body. Only thirteen more days now. She wondered what her father, implacably Protestant, would have said about this keenly awaited pleasure. But she had consulted Father Baddeley about the propriety of going on pilgrimage and his advice had been very clear. "My dear child, you enjoy the change and the journey, and why not? And surely no one could believe themselves harmed by a visit to Lourdes. By all means help Wilfred to celebrate his bargain with the Almighty."

She thought about Father Baddeley. It was still difficult to accept that she wouldn't ever again be talking with him in the patients' courtyard or praying with him in the quiet room. Dead; an inert, neutral, unattractive word. Short, uncompromising, a lump of a word. The same word, come to think of it, for a plant, an animal or a man. That was an interesting thought. One would have expected a distinctive, more impressive or momentous word for the death of a man. But why? He was only part of the same creation, sharing its universal life, dependent on the same air. Dead. She had hoped to be able to feel that Father Baddeley was close to her; but it hadn't happened, it just wasn't true. They are all gone into the world of light. Well, gone away, not interested any more in the living.

She ought to put out her light; electricity was expensive; if she didn't intend to read it was her duty to lie in the darkness. Lighten our darkness; her mother had always liked that collect; and by Thy great mercy defend us from all the perils and dangers of this night. Only there was no peril here, only sleeplessness and pain; the familiar pain to be tolerated, almost welcomed as an old acquaintance because she knew that she could cope with the worst it could do; and this new frightening pain which, sometime soon, she would have to worry someone about.

The curtain trembled in the breeze. She heard a sudden click, unnaturally loud, so that for a second her heart thudded. There was a rasp of metal on wood. Maggie hadn't checked the window fastening before bedding her down for the night. It was too late now. Her chair was at the side of the bed but she couldn't get into it without help. But all would be well unless it were a stormy night. And she was perfectly safe, no one would climb in. There was nothing at

Toynton Grange to steal. And beyond that fluttering curtain of white, nothing; nothing but a black void, dark cliffs stretching to the unsleeping sea.

The curtain billowed, bursting into a white sail, a curve of light. She exclaimed at the beauty of it. Cool air streamed across her face. She turned her eyes to the door and smiled a welcome. She began to say:

"The window—would you be good enough . . . ?"

But she didn't finish. There were three seconds only left to her of earthly time. She saw the cloaked figure, hood well down obscuring the face, moving swiftly towards her on silent feet like an apparition, familiar but horribly different, ministering hands that held death, blackness bearing down on her. Unresisting, since that was her nature and how could she resist, she did not die ungently, feeling at the last through the thin veil of plastic only the strong, warm, oddly comforting lineaments of a human hand. Then the hand reached out and delicately, without touching the wooden stand, switched off the bedside lamp. Two seconds later the light was switched on again, and, as if by afterthought, the cloaked figure stretched out a hand for the Trollope, gently rustled the pages, found the pressed flower between the fold of tissue, and crumpled them both with strong fingers. Then the hand reached out for the lamp again and the light went out for the last time.

## IV

At last they were back in Ursula's room. Helen Rainer closed the door with quiet firmness and leaned back momentarily against it as if exhausted. Then she went quickly over to the window and swept the curtains across in two swift gestures. Her heavy breathing filled the little room. It had been a difficult journey. Helen had left her in the clinical room briefly while she positioned Ursula's wheelchair at the foot of the stairs. Once they reached it all would be well. Even if they were seen together in the ground-floor corridor it would be assumed that Ursula had rung her night bell and was being helped to the bathroom. The stairs were the problem and the descent, with Helen half-supporting, half-carrying her, had been exhausting and noisy, five long minutes of labored breathing, creaking banisters, hissed instructions, of Ursula's half-stifled moans of pain. It seemed now like a miracle that no one had appeared in the hall. It would have been quicker and easier to have moved into the main part of the Grange and used the lift, but the clanging metal grill and the noisy engine would have woken half the house.

But at last they were safely back and Helen, white faced but calm, pulled herself together and moved away from the door and began with professional competence to put Ursula to bed. Neither spoke until the task was completed and Ursula lay in rigid half-fearful silence.

Helen bent her face close to Ursula's, unpleasantly close. In the glare of the bedside lamp she could see the features magnified, coarsened, pores like miniature craters, two unplucked hairs standing like bristles at the corner of the mouth. Her breath smelt slightly sour. Odd, thought Ursula, that she hadn't noticed it before. The green eyes seemed to grow and protrude as she hissed her instructions, her dreadful warning.

"When the next patient goes, he'll have to start admitting from the waiting list or give in. He can't run this place on less than six patients. I've taken a look at the books when he's left them about in the business room and I know. He'll either sell out completely or hand over to the Ridgewell Trust. If you want to get out of here there are better ways than killing yourself. Help me to ensure that he sells out, and get back to London."

"But how?"

Ursula found herself whispering back like a conspirator.

"He'll hold what he calls a family council. He always does when there's something important affecting all the household to decide. We all give our views. Then we go away to meditate in silence for one hour. Then we all vote. Don't let anyone persuade you to vote for the Ridgewell Trust. That way you'll be trapped here for life. It's hard enough for local authorities to find a place for the young chronic sick. Once they know you're being looked after, they'll never transfer you."

"But if the Grange does close down, will they really send me home?"

"They'll have to, back to London anyway. That's still your permanent address. You're the responsibility of your own local authority, not of Dorset. And once back, at least you'll see him. He could visit you, take you out, you could go home for weekend leaves. Besides, the disease isn't really advanced yet. I don't see why you shouldn't manage together in one of those flats for disabled couples. After all he is married to you. He's got responsibilities, duties."

Ursula tried to explain:

"I don't mind about responsibilities and duties. I want him to love me."

Helen had laughed, a coarse, uncomfortable sound.

"Love. Is that all? Isn't that what we all want? Well, he can't stay in love with someone he never sees, can he? It doesn't work like that with men. You've got to get back to him."

"And you won't tell?"

"Not if you promise."

"To vote your way?"

"And to keep your mouth shut about trying to kill yourself, about everything that's happened here tonight. If anyone mentions hearing a noise in the night, you rang for me and I was taking you to the lavatory. If Wilfred discovers the truth he'll send you to a mental hospital. You wouldn't want that, would you?"

No, she wouldn't want that. Helen was right. She had to get home. How simple it all was. She felt suddenly filled with gratitude, and struggled to hold out her arms towards Helen. But Helen had moved away. Firm hands were tucking in the bed clothes, rocking the mattress. The sheets were drawn taut. She felt imprisoned, but secure, a baby swaddled for the night. Helen stretched out her hand to the light. In the darkness a white blur moved towards the door. Ursula heard the soft click of the latch.

Lying there alone exhausted but strangely comforted she remembered that she hadn't told Helen about the cloaked figure. But it could be of no importance. It was probably Helen herself answering Grace's bell. Was that what Helen had meant when she warned, say nothing about anything that happened here tonight? Surely not. But she would say nothing. How could she speak without betraying that she had been crouching there on the stairs. And everything was going to be all right. She could sleep now. How lucky that Helen had gone to the clinical room to get a couple of aspirin for a headache and had found her! The house was blessedly unnaturally quiet. There was something strange, something different, about the silence. And then, smiling into the darkness she remembered. It was Grace. No sound, no rasp of snoring breath came through the thin partition to disturb her. Tonight even Grace Willison was sleeping in peace.

## V

Usually Julius Court fell asleep within minutes of turning out his bedside light. But tonight he turned in restless wakefulness, mind and nerves fidgety, his legs as cold and heavy as if it were winter. He rubbed them together, considering whether to dig out his electric blanket. But the bother of re-making the bed discouraged him. Alcohol seemed a better and quicker remedy both for sleeplessness and the cold.

He walked over to the window and looked out over the headland. The waning moon was obscured by scudding clouds; the darkness inland pierced only by a single oblong of yellow light. But as he watched, blackness was drawn like a shutter over the far window. Instantaneously the oblong became a square; then that, too, was extinguished. Toynton Grange lay, a faintly discerned shape etched in darkness on the silent headland. Curious, he looked at his watch. The time was eighteen minutes past midnight.

# VI

Dalgliesh awoke at first light, to the cold, quiet morning, and dragging on his dressing gown, went downstairs to make tea. He wondered if Millicent was still at the Grange. Her television had been silent all the previous evening and now, although she was neither an early nor a noisy riser, Hope Cottage was wrapped in the slightly clandestine and unmistakable calm of complete isolation. He lit the lamp in the sitting room, carried his cup to the table, and spread out his map. Today he would explore the northeast of the county aiming to arrive at Sherborne for lunch. But first it would be courteous to call at Toynton Grange and enquire after Wilfred. He felt no real concern; it was difficult to think of yesterday's charade without irritation. But it might be worth making one more attempt to persuade Wilfred to call in the police, or at least to take the attack on himself more seriously. And it was time that he paid some rent for the use of Hope Cottage. Toynton Grange could hardly be so prosperous that a tactful contribution wouldn't be welcome. Neither chore need keep him at the Grange for longer than ten minutes.

There was a knock on the door and Julius came in. He was fully dressed and, even at this early hour, gave his usual impression of slightly elegant informality. He said, calmly, and as if the news were hardly worth the trouble of telling.

"I'm glad you're up. I'm on my way to Toynton Grange. Wilfred has just rung. Apparently Grace Willison has died in her sleep and Eric is in a tizzy about the death certificate. I don't know what Wilfred thinks I can do about it. Restoring Eric to the medical register seems to have restored him also to the customary arrogance of his profession. Grace Willison wasn't due, in his opinion, to die for at least another eighteen months, possibly two years. That being so he's at a loss to put a name to this insubordination. As usual, they're all extracting the maximum drama from the situation. I shouldn't miss it if I were you."

Dalgliesh glanced towards the adjacent cottage without speaking. Julius said cheerfully:

"Oh, you needn't worry about disturbing Millicent; I'm afraid she's there already. Apparently her television broke down last night so she went up to Toynton Grange to see a late program and decided, for some unaccountable reason, to stay the night. Probably saw an opportunity of saving her own bed linen and bath water."

Dalgliesh said:

"You go on, I'll follow you later."

He drank his tea without haste and spent three minutes shaving. He wondered why he had been so reluctant to accompany Julius, why, if he had to go to Toynton Grange, he preferred to walk there on his own. He wondered, too, why he felt so keen a regret. He had no wish to involve himself in the controversy at Toynton. He had no particular curiosity about Grace Willison's death. He was aware of feeling nothing except an inexplicable unease amounting almost to grief for a woman he had barely known and a vague distaste that the start of a beautiful day should have been spoilt by the intimations of decay. And there was something else; a sense of guilt. It seemed to him both unreasonable and unfair. By dying she seemed to have allied herself with Father Baddeley. There were two accusing ghosts, not one. This was to be a double failure. It was by an effort of will that he set out for Toynton Grange.

He could be in no doubt which room was Grace Willison's, he could hear the raised voices even as he entered the annex. When he opened the door he saw that Wilfred, Eric, Millicent, Dot and Julius were grouped around the bed with the desultory, uneasy air of strangers meeting fortuitously at the scene of an accident with which they would much prefer not to become involved but which they hardly like to leave.

Dorothy Moxon stood at the end of the bed, her heavy hands, red as hams, clasped to the rail. She was wearing her matron's cap. The effect, so far from providing a touch of professional reassurance, was grotesque. The high frilled pie crust of muslin looked like a morbid and bizarre celebration of death. Millicent was still in her dressing gown, an enveloping plaid in heavy wool frogged like a ceremonial uniform which must once have belonged to her husband. In contrast, her slippers were insubstantial fripperies in pink fur. Wilfred and Eric were wearing their brown habits. They glanced briefly at the door when he entered, then immediately turned their attention back to the bed. Julius was saying:

"There was a light in one of the annex rooms shortly after midnight. Isn't that when you say she died, Eric?"

"It could have been about then. I'm only going by the cooling of the body and the beginning of rigor mortis. I'm not an expert in these things."

"How odd! I thought that death was the one thing you were expert at."

Wilfred said quietly:

"The light was from Ursula's room. She rang shortly after midnight to be taken to the lavatory. Helen looked after her, but she didn't go into Grace. There was no need. She didn't ring. No one saw her after Dot put her to bed. She made no complaint then."

Julius turned again to Eric Hewson:

"You haven't any option, have you? If you can't say what she died of, you can't write a certificate. Anyway, I should play for safety if I were you. After all, you've only recently been permitted to sign a death certificate. Better not take any chances of getting it wrong."

Eric Hewson said:

"You keep out of it, Julius, I don't need your advice. I don't know why Wilfred rang you."

But he spoke without conviction, like an insecure and frightened child, his eyes flicking to the door as if hoping for the arrival of an ally. Julius was unabashed:

"It seems to me that you need any advice that's going. What's worrying you anyway? Do you suspect foul play? What a ridiculous phrase that is, come to think of it, so delightfully British, compounded of the public school ethos and the boxing ring."

Eric exerted himself to make a show of authority.

"Don't be ridiculous! Obviously it's a natural death. The difficulty is that I'm puzzled why it should have happened now. I know D.S. patients can go off quickly like that, but in her case I didn't expect it. And Dot says that she seemed just as usual when she put her to bed at ten o'clock. I'm wondering whether there was some other organic disease present which I missed."

Julius went on happily:

"The police do not suspect foul play. Well, you've got a representative of them here if you want professional advice. Ask the Commander if he suspects foul play."

They turned and looked at Dalgliesh as if fully aware of his presence for the first time. The window latch was rattling with irritating insistence. He went across to the window and glanced out. The ground close to the stone wall had been dug for a width of about four feet as if someone had intended to plant a border. The sandy earth was smooth and undisturbed. But of course it was! If a secret visitor had wanted to get into Grace's room unseen, why climb in at the window when the door of Toynton Grange was never locked?

He fastened the catch and, moving back to the bed, looked down at the body. The dead face looked not exactly peaceful, but slightly disapproving, the mouth a little open, the front teeth, more rabbity than in life, pressing against the lower lip. The eyelids had contracted showing a glimpse of the irises of the eye so that she seemed to be peering at her own two hands disposed so neatly over the taut coverlet. The strong right hand, blotched with the brown stigmata of age, was curved over the withered left as if instinctively protecting it from his pitying gaze. She was shrouded for her last sleep in an old-fashioned white nightdress of creased cotton with a child's bow in narrow blue ribbon tied incongruously under her chin. The long sleeves were gathered into frilled wrists. There was a fine darn about two inches from her elbow. His eyes fixed obsessively on it. Who today, he wondered, would take such trouble? Certainly her diseased tormented hands couldn't have woven that intricate pattern of repair. Why should he find that darn more pathetic, more heart shaking, than the concentrated calm of the dead face?

He was aware that the company had stopped arguing, that they were looking at him in a half-wary silence. He picked up the two books on Miss Willison's bedside table, her prayer book and a paperback copy of *The Last Chronicle of Barset.* There was a book mark in the prayer book. She had, he saw, been reading the collect and gospel for the day. The place was marked by one of those sentimental cards favored by the pious, a colored picture of a haloed St. Francis surrounded by birds and apparently preaching to a motley and incongruous congregation of animals remote from their habitat and drawn with finicky precision. He wondered, irrelevantly, why there was no bookmark in the Trollope. She was not a woman to turn down the pages, and surely of the two volumes this was the one in which she would more easily lose her place. The omission vaguely worried him.

"Is there a next of kin?" he asked, and Anstey answered:

"No. She told me that her parents were only children. They were both over forty when she was born and they died within months of each other about fifteen years ago. She had an older brother but he was killed in the war in North Africa. El Alamein, I believe."

"What about her estate?"

"Oh, nothing, nothing at all. After her parents' death she worked for several years for Open Door, the discharged prisoners charity, and had a small disability pension from them, a pittance merely. That, of course, dies with her. Her fees here were paid by the local authority."

Julius Court said with sudden interest:

"The Open Door. Did she know Philby before you took him on?"

Anstey looked as if he found this irrelevant question in poor taste.

"She may have done; she certainly never said so. It was Grace who suggested that The Open Door might find us a handyman, that this was a way in which Toynton Grange could help the work of the charity. We have been very glad of Albert Philby. He's one of the family. I haven't repented my decision to take him on."

Millicent broke in:

"And you got him cheap, of course. Besides it was Philby or no one wasn't it? You didn't have much luck with the labor exchange when the applicants found that you were offering £5 a week and all found. I sometimes wonder why Philby stays."

Discussion of this point was prevented by the entrance of Philby himself. He must have been told of Miss Willison's death for he showed no surprise to find her room full of people and gave no explanation of his presence. Instead he stationed himself beside the door like an embarrassing and unpredictable guard dog. The company behaved as if they had decided that it would be prudent not to notice him. Wilfred turned to Eric Hewson:

"Can't you reach a diagnosis, without a postmortem? I hate the idea of her being cut up, the indignity, the impersonality. She was so sensitive about her body, so modest in a way we don't understand nowadays. An autopsy is the last thing she herself would have wanted."

Julius said coarsely:

"Well, it's the last thing she's going to get, isn't it?"

Dot Moxon spoke for the first time. She swung round on him in sudden anger, her heavy face blotched, hands clenched.

"How dare you! What has it to do with you? You didn't care about her dead or alive, her or any of the patients. You only use this place for your own purpose."

"Use?" The grey eyes flickered and then widened; Dalgliesh could almost see the irises growing. Julius stared at Dot with incredulous anger.

"Yes, use! Exploit, if you like. It gives you a kick, doesn't it, to come visiting Toynton Grange when London begins to bore you, patronizing Wilfred, pretending to advise him, handing out treats to the inmates like Father Christmas? It makes you feel good, reinforces your ego to contrast your health with their deformity. But you take damned good care not to put yourself out. The kindness doesn't really cost you anything. No one but Henry gets invited to your cottage. But then Henry was quite important in his time wasn't he? He and you have things to gossip about. You're the only one here with a view of the sea, but we don't find you inviting us to wheel the chairs on to your patio. No bloody fear! That's one thing you could have done for Grace, take her to your place occasionally, let her sit quietly and look at the sea. She wasn't stupid, you know. You might even have enjoyed her conversation. But that would have spoilt the appearance of your elegant patio wouldn't it, an ugly middle-aged woman in a wheelchair? And now she's dead you come here pretending to advise Eric. Well, for God's sake, cut it out!"

Julius laughed uneasily. He seemed to have himself in hand but his voice was high and brittle.

"I don't know what I've done to deserve that outburst. I didn't realize that by buying a cottage from Wilfred I'd made myself responsible for Grace Willison or for anyone else at Toynton Grange for that matter. I've no doubt it's a shock for you, Dot, losing another patient so soon after Victor, but why take it out on me? We all know that you're in love with Wilfred and I've no doubt that's pretty unrewarding for you, but it's hardly my fault. I may be a little ambivalent in my sexual tastes but I'm not competing for him, I assure you."

Suddenly she blundered up to him and threw back her arm to slap his face in a gesture at once theatrical and absurd. But before she could strike, Julius had caught her wrist. Dalgliesh was surprised at the quickness and effectiveness of his reaction. The taut hand, white and trembling with effort, held hers high in a muscled vice so that they looked like two ill-matched contestants locked in a tableau of conflict. Suddenly he laughed and dropped her hand. He lowered his hand more slowly, his eyes still on her face, and began massaging and twisting her wrist. Then he laughed again, a dangerous sound, and said softly:

"Careful! Careful! I'm not a helpless geriatric patient, you know."

She gave a gasp and, bursting into tears, blundered sobbing from the room, an ungainly and pathetic but not a ridiculous figure. Philby slipped out after her. His departure caused as little interest as his arrival. Wilfred said softly:

"You shouldn't have said that, Julius, any of it."

"I know. It was unforgivable. I'm sorry. I'll tell Dot so when we are feeling calmer."

The brevity, the absence of self-justification and the apparent sincerity of the apology silenced them. Dalgliesh said quietly:

"I imagine that Miss Willison would have found this quarrelling over her body a great deal more shocking than anything that could happen to her on the mortuary slab."

His words recalled Wilfred to the matter in hand; he turned to Eric Hewson:

"But we didn't have all this trouble with Michael, you gave a certificate without difficulty then."

Dalgliesh could detect the first trace of peevishness in his voice.

Eric explained:

"I knew why Michael had died, I had seen him only that morning. It was only a matter of time for Michael after that last heart attack. He was a dying man."

"As we all are," said Wilfred. "As we all are."

The pious platitudes seemed to irritate his sister. She spoke for the first time.

"Don't be ridiculous, Wilfred. I'm certainly not dying and you would be very disconcerted to be told that you were. And as for Grace, she always looked to me a great deal sicker than anyone here seemed to understand. Now perhaps you will realize that it isn't always the ones who make the most fuss who need the most attention."

She turned to Dalgliesh:

"What exactly will happen if Eric doesn't give a certificate? Does it mean that we'll have the police here again?"

"A policeman will probably come, yes; just an ordinary policeman. He'll be the coroner's officer and he will take charge of the body."

"And then?"

"The coroner will arrange for a postmortem. According to the result he will either issue a certificate for the registrar or he'll conduct an inquest."

Wilfred said:

"It's all so horrible, so unnecessary."

"It's the law and Dr. Hewson knows that it is the law."

"But what do you mean, it's the law? Grace died of D.S., we all know that. What if there was some other disease present? Eric can't treat her or do anything to help her now. What law are you talking about?"

Dalgliesh patiently explained:

"The doctor who attends a dead person during his last illness is required to sign and deliver to the registrar a certificate in a prescribed form stating the cause of death to the best of his knowledge and belief. At the same time he is required to deliver to a qualified informant, and that could be the occupant of the house where the death occurred, a notice to the effect that he has signed such a certificate. There is no statutory duty on a doctor to report any death to the coroner, but it's usual to do so where there is any doubt. When the doctor reports a death to a coroner he's not relieved of his duty to issue a certificate of the cause of death but there is provision for him to state on the form that he has reported the death so that the registrar will know that he must defer registration until he hears from the coroner. Under Section 3 of the Coroners Act 1887 a coroner has a duty to make enquiries whenever he is informed that there is lying within his jurisdiction the body of a person who there is reason to believe may have died a violent or unnatural death or a sudden death, the cause of which is unknown, or who has died in prison or in any place or circumstances which under another Act require an inquest to be held. That, since you have enquired—and in somewhat tedious detail—is the law. Grace Willison has died suddenly and in Dr. Hewson's opinion the cause is at present unknown. His best course is to report the death to the coroner. It will mean a postmortem, but not necessarily an inquest."

"But I hate the thought of her lying mangled on an autopsy slab." Wilfred was beginning to sound like an obstinate child. Dalgliesh said coolly:

"Mangled isn't exactly the word. A postmortem is an organized and perfectly tidy procedure. And now if you will excuse me I'll get back to my breakfast."

Suddenly Wilfred made an almost physical effort to pull himself together. He straightened up, and crossed his hands into the wide sleeves of his habit and stood for a moment in silent meditation. Eric Hewson looked at him, puzzled, then glanced from Dalgliesh to Julius as if seeking guidance. Then Wilfred spoke:

"Eric, you had better ring the coroner's officer now. Normally Dot would lay out the body but that had better wait until we get instructions. After you have telephoned, please let everyone know that I want to talk to all the family immediately after breakfast. Helen and Dennis are with them at present. Millicent, perhaps you could find Dot and see that she is all right. And now I should like to speak to you Julius, and to Adam Dalgliesh."

He stood for a moment, eyes closed, at the foot of Grace's bed. Dalgliesh wondered whether he were praying.Then he led the way out. As they followed, Julius whispered with hardly a movement of his lips:

"Unpleasantly reminiscent of those summonses to the headmaster's study. We should have fortified ourselves with breakfast."

In the business room Wilfred wasted no time.

"Grace's death means that I have to make my decision sooner than I'd hoped. We can't carry on with only four patients. On the other hand, I can hardly start admitting from the waiting list if the Grange isn't going to continue. I shall hold a family council on the afternoon Grace is buried. I think it would be right to wait until then. If there are no complications, that should be in less than a week's time. I should like you both to take part and help us to our decision."

Julius said quickly:

"That's impossible, Wilfred. I've absolutely no interest; interest, I mean in the legal or insurance sense. It just isn't my business."

"You live here. I've always thought of you as one of the family."

"Sweet of you, and I'm honored. But it isn't true. I'm not one of the family and I have absolutely no right to vote on a decision that can't really affect me one way or the other. If you decide to sell out, and I wouldn't blame you, I probably shall too. I don't fancy living on Toynton Head once it's a caravan site. But it won't matter to me. I'll get a good price from some bright young executive from the Midlands who won't give a damn about peace and quiet but who will build a natty cocktail bar in the sitting room and run up a flagpole on the patio. I shall probably look for my next cottage in the Dordogne after careful enquiries about any bargains which the owner may have made with God or the devil. Sorry, but it's a definite no."

"And you, Adam?"

"I've even less right to an opinion than Court. This place is home to the patients. Why on earth should their future be decided, at least in part, by the vote of a casual visitor?"

"Because I greatly trust your judgement."

"There's no reason why you should. In this matter, better trust your accountant."

Julius asked:

"Are you inviting Millicent to the family council?"

"Of course. She may not have always given me the support I hoped for from her, but she is one of the family."

"And Maggie Hewson?"

Wilfred said curtly:

"No."

"She's not going to like that. And isn't it a little hurtful to Eric?"

Wilfred said magisterially:

"As you have just made it plain that you don't consider yourself in any way concerned, why not leave me to decide what's hurtful to Eric. And now, if you will both excuse me, I shall join the family for breakfast."

# VII

As they left Wilfred's room, Julius said roughly and as if on impulse:

"Come up to the cottage and have breakfast. Have a drink anyway. Or if it's too early for alcohol, have coffee. Anyway, please come. I've started the day in a mood of self-disgust and I'm bad company for myself."

It was too close to an appeal to be easily disregarded. Dalgliesh said:

"If you can give me about five minutes. There's someone I want to see. I'll meet you in the hall."

He remembered from his first conducted tour of the Grange which was Jennie Pegram's room. There might, he thought, be a better time for this encounter but he couldn't wait for it. He knocked and heard the note of surprise in her answering "come in." She was sitting in her wheelchair in front of her dressing table, her yellow hair flowing over her shoulders. Taking the poison pen letter from his wallet he walked up behind her and laid it in front of her. In the mirror their eyes met.

"Did you type that?"

She let her glance travel over it without picking it up. Her eyes flickered; a red stain began to travel like a wave over her neck. He heard the hiss of indrawn breath, but her voice was calm.

"Why should I?"

"I can suggest reasons. But did you?"

"Of course not! I've never seen it before."

She glanced at it again dismissively, contemptuously.

"It's . . . it's stupid, childish."

"Yes, a poor effort. Done in a hurry, I imagine. I thought you might take rather a poor view of it. Not quite as exciting or imaginative as the others."

"What others?"

"Come now, let's start with the one to Grace Willison. That did you credit. An imaginative effort, cleverly composed to spoil her pleasure in the only real friend she had made here, and nasty enough to ensure that she would be ashamed to show it to anyone. Except, of course, to a policeman. Even Miss Willison didn't mind showing it to a policeman. Where obscenity is concerned, we enjoy an almost medical dispensation."

"She wouldn't dare! And I don't know what you're talking about."

"Wouldn't she? It's a pity you can't ask her. You know that she's dead?"

"That's nothing to do with me."

"Luckily for you, I don't think it is. She wasn't the suicidal type. I wonder if you were as lucky—or unlucky—with your other victims, with Victor Holroyd for example."

There was no mistaking her terror now. The thin hands were twisting the handle of her hairbrush in a desperate pantomime.

"That wasn't my fault! I never wrote to Victor! I never wrote to anyone."

"You aren't as clever as you think are you. You forget about fingerprints. Perhaps you didn't realize that forensic laboratories can detect them on writing paper. And then there's the timing. All the letters have been received since you arrived at Toynton Grange. The first was received before Ursula Hollis was admitted and I think we can rule out Henry Carwardine. I know that they've stopped since Mr. Holroyd's death. Was that because you realized just how far you'd gone? Or did you hope that Mr. Holroyd would be held responsible? But the police will know that those letters weren't written by a man. And then there's the saliva test. All except fifteen per cent of the population excrete their blood group in their saliva. It's a pity you didn't know that before you licked the envelope flaps."

"The envelopes . . . but they weren't . . ."

She gasped at Dalgliesh. Her eyes widened with terror. The flush receded leaving her very pale.

"No, there weren't any envelopes. The notes were folded and placed in the victim's library book. But no one knows that except the recipients and you."

She said, not looking at him:

"What are you going to do?"

"I don't know yet."

And he didn't know. He felt a mixture, strange to him, of embarrassment, anger and some shame. It had been so easy to trick her, so easy and so contemptible. He saw himself as clearly as if he were an onlooker, healthy and able, sitting magisterially in judgement on her weakness, delivering the customary admonition from the bench, deferring sentence. The picture was distasteful. She had caused Grace Willison pain. But at least she could claim some psychological excuse. How much of his own anger and disgust had its roots in guilt? What had he done to make Grace Willison's last days happier? Yet something would have to be done about her. She was unlikely at present to make more mischief at Toynton Grange, but what of the future? And Henry Carwardine presumably had a right to know. So, one could argue, had Wilfred and the Ridgewell Trustees if they took over. Some people, too, would argue that she needed help. They would produce the orthodox contemporary solution, referral to a psychiatrist. He just didn't know. It wasn't a remedy in which he had much confidence. It would gratify her vanity, perhaps, and minister to her urge for self-importance to be taken seriously. But if the victims had resolved to keep silent, if only to protect Wilfred from worry, what right had he to deride their motive or break their confidence? He had been used in his job to working to rules. Even when he had taken an unorthodox decision, which wasn't seldom, the moral issues—if one could use that word and he never had—had been clear and unambiguous. His illness must have sapped his will and judgement as well as his physical strength for this paltry problem to defeat him. Ought he to leave a sealed note for Anstey or his successor to open in case of further trouble? Really it was ridiculous to be driven to such a weak and histrionic expedient. For God's sake, why couldn't he make a straight decision? He wished that Father Baddeley were alive, knowing on whose frail shoulders he could safely have lain this particular burden.

He said:

"I shall leave it to you to tell the victims, all of them, that you were responsible and that it won't happen again. You had better see that it doesn't. I leave it to your ingenuity to think out an excuse. I know that you must miss all the fuss and attention you had at your last hospital. But why compensate by making other people unhappy?"

"They hate me."

"Of course they don't. You hate yourself. Did you write these notes to anyone else except Miss Willison and Mr. Carwardine?"

She looked up at him slyly from under her eyelids.

"No. Only those two."

It was probably a lie, he thought wearily. Ursula Hollis had probably had a letter. Would it do more harm or less if he asked her?

He heard Jennie Pegram's voice, stronger now, more confident. She lifted her left hand and began stroking her hair, drawing the strands across her face. She said:

"No one here cares about me. They all despise me. They never wanted me to come here. I didn't want it either. You could help me but you don't really care. You don't even want to listen."

"Get Dr. Hewson to refer you to a psychiatrist and confide in him. He's paid to listen to neurotics talking about themselves. I'm not."

He regretted the unkindness as soon as the door was closed. He knew what had prompted it; the sudden remembrance of Grace Willison's shrunken, ugly body in its cheap nightdress. It was well, he thought, in a mood of self-disgust, that he was giving up his job if pity and anger could so destroy his detachment. Or was it Toynton Grange? This place, he thought, is getting on my nerves.

As he walked quickly down the passage the door next to Grace Willison's room opened and he saw Ursula Hollis. She beckoned him in, swivelling her wheelchair to clear the doorway."

"They've told us to wait in our rooms. Grace is dead."

"Yes, I know."

"What is it? What happened?"

"No one really knows yet. Dr. Hewson is arranging for a post-mortem."

"She didn't kill herself—or anything."

"I'm sure not. It looked as if she died quietly in her sleep."

"You mean like Father Baddeley?"

"Yes, just like Father Baddeley."

They paused, staring at each other. Dalgliesh asked:

"You didn't hear anything last night?"

"Oh, no! Nothing! I slept very well that is, after Helen had been in to me."

"Would you have heard if she called out or if anyone went in to her?"

"Oh yes, if I wasn't asleep. Sometimes she kept me awake with her snoring. But I didn't hear her call out, and she went to sleep before I did. My light was out before twelve-thirty and I thought then how quiet she was."

He moved towards the door and then paused, feeling that she was reluctant to see him go. He asked:

"Is anything worrying you?"

"Oh, no! Nothing. It was just the uncertainty about Grace, not knowing, everyone being so mysterious. But if they're going to do a postmortem . . . I mean the postmortem will tell us how she died."

"Yes," he said without conviction, as if reassuring himself as well as her, "the postmortem will tell us."

# VIII

Julius was waiting alone in the front hall and they left the Grange together walking through the bright morning air, abstracted, a little apart, their eyes fixed on the path. Neither spoke. As if yoked by an invisible cord, they paced, carefully distanced, towards the sea. Dalgliesh was glad of his companion's silence. He was thinking about Grace Willison, trying to understand and analyze the root of his concern and unrest, emotions which seemed to him illogical to the point of perversity. There had been no visible marks on the body; no lividity; no petechiae on face or forehead; no sign of disturbance in her room; nothing unusual except an unlatched window. She had lain there stiffening in the quietus of natural death. Why then this irrational suspicion? He was a professional policeman, not a clairvoyant. He worked by evidence not by intuition. How many postmortems were carried out in a year? Over 170,000 wasn't it? 170,000 deaths which required at least some preliminary investigation. Most of them could provide an obvious motive, at least for one person. Only the pathetic derelicts of society had nothing to leave, however meager, however uncoveted to sophisticated eyes. Every death benefited someone, enfranchised someone, lifted a burden from someone's shoulders, whether of responsibility, the pain of vicarious suffering or the tyranny of love. Every death was a suspicious death if one looked only at motive, just as every death, at the last, was a natural death. Old Dr. Blessington, one of the first and greatest of the forensic pathologists, had taught him that. It had, he remembered, been Blessington's last postmortem, the young Detective Constable Dalgliesh's first. The hands of both had been shaking, but for very different reasons, although the old man had been as steady as a surgeon once the first incision was made. The body of a forty-two-year-old, red-haired prostitute was on the slab. The postmortem assistant had with two strokes of his gloved hand wiped from her face the blood, the dirt, the pancake of paint and matted powder, leaving it pale, vulnerable, anonymous. His strong living hand, not death, had erased from it all personality. Old Blessington had demonstrated the cunning of his craft.

"You see, lad, the first blow, warded off by her hand, slipped down the neck and throat towards the right shoulder. A lot of blood, a lot of mess, but no great harm done. With the second, directed upwards and across, he severed the trachea. She died of shock, blood loss and asphyxia, probably in that order from the look of the thymus. When we get them on the slab, lad, there's no such thing as unnatural death."

Natural or unnatural, he was through with it now. It was irritating that with a will so strong, his mind apparently needed this constant reassurance, that it was so obstinately reluctant to leave the problems alone. What possible justification, anyway, had he for going to the local police with a complaint that death was becoming a little too common at Toynton? An old priest dying of heart disease, without enemies, without possessions, except a modest fortune unexceptionally willed for charitable purposes to the man who had befriended him, a notable philanthropist whose character and reputation were beyond reproach. And Victor Holroyd? What could the police do about that death other than they had already most competently done. The facts had been investigated, the inquest jury had pronounced their finding. Holroyd had been buried, Father Baddeley cremated. All that remained was a coffin of broken bones and decaying flesh and a fistful of grey, gritty dust in Toynton churchyard; two more secrets added to the store of secrets buried in that consecrated earth. All of them were beyond human solving now.

And now this third death, the one for which everyone at Toynton Grange had probably been superstitiously waiting, in thrall to the theurgy that death comes in threes. They could all relax now. He could relax. The coroner would order a postmortem, and Dalgliesh had little doubt of the result. If Michael and Grace Willison had both been murdered, their killer was too clever to leave signs. And why should he? With a frail, sick, disease-ridden woman, it would have been only too easy, as simple and quick as a firm hand placed over nose and mouth. And there would be nothing to justify his interference. He couldn't say: I, Adam Dalgliesh, have had one of my famous hunches—I disagree with the coroner, with the pathologist, with the local police, with all the facts. I demand in the light of this new death that Father Baddeley's incinerated bones be resurrected and forced to yield up their secret.

They had reached Toynton Cottage. Dalgliesh followed Julius round to the seaward porch which led directly from the stone patio into the sitting-room. Julius had left the door unlocked. He pushed it open and stood a little aside so that Dalgliesh could go in first. Then they both stood stock still, stricken into immobility. Someone had been there before them. The marble bust of the smiling child had been smashed to pieces.

Still without speaking they moved together warily over the carpet. The head, hacked into anonymity lay among a holocaust of marble fragments. The dark grey carpet was bejewelled with gleaming grits of stone. Broad ribbons of light from the windows and open door lay across the room and, in their rays, the jagged slivers twinkled like a myriad of infinitesimal stars. It looked as if the destruction had at first been systematic. Both ears had been cleanly severed, and lay together, obscene objects oozing invisible blood, while the bouquet of flowers, so delicately carved that the lilies of the valley had seemed to tremble with life, lay a little distance from the hand as if tossed lightly aside. A miniature dagger of marble had lodged upright in the sofa, a microcosm of violence.

The room was very still; its ordered comfort, the measured ticking of the carriage clock on the mantelshelf, the insistent thudding of the sea, all heightened the sense of outrage, the crudity of destruction and hate.

Julius dropped to his knees and picked up a shapeless lump which had once been the child's head. After a second he let it drop from his loosened grasp. It rolled clumsily, obliquely, across the floor and came to rest against the foot of the sofa. Still without speaking, he reached over and picked up the posy of flowers cradling it gently in his hands. Dalgliesh saw that his body was shaking; he was very pale and his forehead, bent over the carving, glistened with sweat. He looked like a man in shock.

Dalgliesh went over to the side table which held a decanter and poured out a generous measure of whisky. Silently he handed the glass to Julius. The man's silence and the dreadful shaking worried him. Anything, he thought, violence, a storm of rage, a spate of obscenity would be better than this unnatural silence. But when Julius did speak his voice was perfectly steady. He shook his head at the offered glass.

"No, thank you. I don't need a drink. I want to know what I'm feeling, know it here in my belly not just in my head. I don't want my anger dulled, and by God, I don't need it stimulated! Think of it, Dalgliesh. He died three hundred years ago, this gentle boy. The marble must have been carved very shortly afterwards. It was of absolutely no practical use to anyone for three hundred years except to give comfort and pleasure and remind us that we are dust. Three hundred years. Three hundred years of war, revolution, violence, greed. But it survived. It survived until this year of grace. Drink that whisky yourself, Dalgliesh. Raise the glass and toast the age of the despoiler. He didn't know that this was here, unless he peers and pries when I am away. Anything of mine would have served. He could have destroyed anything. But when he saw this, he couldn't resist it. Nothing else could have given him quite such an exaltation of destruction. This isn't just hatred of me you know. Who ever did it, hated this too. Because it gave pleasure, was made with an intention, not just a lump of clay thrown against a wall, paint stamped into a canvas, a piece of stone smoothed into innocuous curves. It had gravity and integrity. It grew out of privilege and tradition, and contributed to it. God, I should have known better than to bring it here among these barbarians!"

Dalgliesh knelt beside him. He picked up two portions of a smashed forearm and fitted them together like a puzzle. He said:

"We know probably to within a few minutes when it was done. We know that it needed strength and that he—or she—probably used a hammer. There ought to be marks on that. And he couldn't have walked here and back in the time. Either he escaped down your path here to the shore, or he came by van and then went on to collect the post. It shouldn't be difficult to find out who is responsible."

"My God, Dalgliesh, you have a policeman's soul haven't you? Is that thought supposed to comfort me?"

"It would me; but then, as you say, it's probably a matter of soul."

"I'm not calling in the police if that's what you're suggesting. I don't need the local fuzz to tell me who did this. I know, and so do you, don't you?"

"No. I could give you a short list of suspects in order of probability, but that's not the same thing."

"Spare yourself the trouble. I know and I'll deal with him in my own way."

"And give him the added satisfaction of seeing you brought up on a charge of assault or G.B.H. I suppose."

"I wouldn't get much sympathy from you would I, or from the local bench? Vengeance is mine saith Her Majesty's Commission of the Peace. Naughty, destructive boy, underprivileged lad! Five pounds fine and put him on probation. Oh! don't worry! I shan't do anything rash. I'll take my time, but I'll deal with it. You can keep your local pals out of it. They weren't exactly a flaming success when they investigated Holroyd's death were they? They can keep their clumsy fingers out of my mess."

Getting to his feet he added with sulky obstinacy, almost as an afterthought.

"Besides, I don't want any more fuss here at present, not just after Grace Willison's death. Wilfred's got enough on his plate. I'll clear this mess away and tell Henry that I have taken the marble back to London. No one else from the Grange comes here, thank God, so I shall be spared the usual insincere condolences."

Dalgliesh said:

"I find it interesting, this concern for Wilfred's peace of mind."

"I thought you might. In your book I am a selfish bastard. You've got an identikit to selfish bastards, and I don't precisely fit. Ergo, find a reason. There has to be a first cause."

"There's always a cause."

"Well, what is it? Am I somehow in Wilfred's pay? Am I fiddling the books? Has he some hold over me? Is there, perhaps some truth in Moxon's suspicions? Or perhaps I'm Wilfred's illegitimate son."

"Even a legitimate son might reasonably feel that it was worth causing Wilfred some distress to discover who did this. Aren't you being too scrupulous? Wilfred must know that someone at Toynton Grange, probably one of his disciples, nearly killed him, intentionally or otherwise. My guess is that he'd take the loss of your marble fairly philosophically."

"He doesn't have to take it. He's not going to know. I can't explain to you what I don't understand myself. But I am committed to Wilfred. He is so vulnerable and pathetic. And it is all so hopeless! If you must know, he reminds me in some way of my parents. They had a small general store in Southsea. Then when I was about fourteen, a large chain store opened next door. That was the end for them. They tried everything; they wouldn't give in. Extended credit when they weren't getting their money anyway; special offers when their profit margins were practically nil; hours spent after closing time rearranging the window; balloons given free to the local kids. It didn't matter, you see. It was all utterly pointless and futile. They couldn't succeed. I thought I could have borne their failure. What I couldn't bear was their hope."

Dalgliesh thought that, in part, he did see. He knew what Julius was saying. Here am I, young, rich, healthy. I know how to be happy. I could be happy, if only the world were really as I want it to be. If only other people wouldn't persist in being sick, deformed, in pain, helpless, defeated, deluded. Or if only I could be just that bit more selfish so that I didn't care. If only there weren't the black tower. He heard Julius speaking:

"Don't worry about me. Remember I am bereaved. Don't they say that the bereaved always have to work through their grief? The appropriate treatment is a detached sympathy and plenty of good plain nourishment. We'd better get some breakfast."

Dalgliesh said quietly:

"If you're not going to ring the police, then we might as well clear up this mess."

"I'll get a dustbin. I can't bear the noise of the vacuum cleaner."

He disappeared into his immaculate, fashionably over-equipped kitchen, and came back with a dustpan and two brushes. In an odd companionship they knelt together to their task. But the brushes were too soft to dislodge the slivers of marble, and in the end they had to pick them up laboriously one by one.

# IX

The forensic pathologist was a locum tenens senior registrar, and if he had expected this three-week stint of duty in the agreeable West Country to be less arduous than his London job, he was disappointed. When the telephone rang for the tenth time that morning he peeled off his gloves, tried not to think about the fifteen naked cadavers still waiting on their refrigerated shelves and lifted the receiver philosophically. The confident masculine voice, except for its pleasant country burr, could have been the voice of any Metropolitan police officer, and the words, too, he had heard before.

"That you, Doc? We've got a body in a field three miles north of Blandford which we don't like the look of. Could you come to the scene?"

The summons seldom differed. They always had a body they didn't like the look of, in a ditch, a field, a gutter, in the tangled steel of a smashed car. He took up his message pad and asked the usual questions, heard the expected replies. He said to the mortuary assistant:

"OK Bert, you can sew her up now. She's no twelve-guinea special. Tell the Coroner's officer that he can issue the disposal order. I'm off to a scene. Get the next two ready for me, will you?"

He glanced for the last time at the emaciated body on the table. There had been nothing difficult about Grace Miriam Willison, spinster, aged 57. No external signs of violence, no internal evidence to justify sending the viscera for analysis. He had muttered to his assistant with some bitterness that if the local GPs were going to look to an over-stretched forensic pathology service to settle their differential diagnoses the service might as well pack up. But her doctor's hunch had been right. There was something he'd missed, the advanced neoplasm in the upper stomach. And much good that knowledge now would do him or her. That, or the D.S. or the heart condition had killed her. He wasn't God and he'd taken his choice. Or maybe she'd just decided that she had had enough and turned her face to the wall.

In her state it was the mystery of continuing life not the fact of death that needed explaining. He was beginning to think that most patients died when they decided that it was their time to die. But you couldn't put that on a certificate.

He scribbled a final note on Grace Willison's record, called out a final instruction to his assistant, then pushed his way through the swing doors towards another death, another body, towards, he thought, with something like relief, his proper job.

# BOOK SEVEN

•

# Mist on the Headland

# I

The church of St. Michael's at Toynton was an uninteresting Victorian reconstruction of an earlier building, the churchyard a triangular patch of swathed grass between the west wall, the road and a row of rather dull cottages. Victor Holroyd's grave, pointed out by Julius, was an oblong mound crudely patched with squares of weedy turf. Beside it, a simple wooden cross marked the spot where Father Baddeley's ashes had been buried. Grace Willison was to lie next to him. Everyone at Toynton Grange was at the funeral except Helen Rainer who had been left to nurse Georgie Allan, and Maggie Hewson whose absence, unremarked, was apparently taken for granted. But Dalgliesh, when he arrived alone, had been surprised to see Julius's Mercedes parked opposite the lych gate beside the Toynton Grange bus.

The churchyard was encumbered and the path between the headstones narrow and overgrown so that it took some time to maneuver the three wheelchairs round the open grave.

The local vicar was taking a belated holiday and his substitute, who apparently knew nothing of Toynton Grange, was obviously surprised to see four of the mourners garbed in brown monk's habits. He asked if they were Anglican Franciscans, an enquiry which provoked a fit of nervous giggling from Jennie Pegram. Anstey's answer, unheard by Dalgliesh, apparently failed to reassure and the priest, puzzled and disapproving, took the service with carefully controlled speed as if anxious to free the churchyard as soon as possible from the risk of contamination by the imposters. The little party sang, at Wilfred's suggestion, Grace's favorite hymn "Ye Holy Angels Bright." It was, thought Dalgliesh, a hymn peculiarly unsuited for amateur unaccompanied singing and their uncertain and discordant voices rose reed thin in the crisp autumnal air.

There were no flowers. Their absence, the rich smell of newly turned earth, the mellow autumn sunlight, the ubiquitous scent of burning wood, even the sense of unseen but inquisitive eyes peering morbidly from behind the hedges, brought back with stabbing pain the memory of another funeral.

He had been a fourteen-year-old schoolboy, at home for his half term. His parents were in Italy and Father Baddeley was in charge of the parish. A local farmer's son, a shy, gentle, over-conscientious eighteen-year-old, home for the weekend from his first term at university, had taken his father's gun and shot dead both parents, his fifteen-year-old sister and, finally, himself. They were a devoted family, he a loving son. For the young Dalgliesh, who was beginning to imagine himself in love with the girl, it had been a horror eclipsing all subsequent horrors. The tragedy, unexplained, appalling, had at first stunned the village. But grief had quickly given way to a wave of superstitious anger, terror and repulsion. It was unthinkable that the boy should be buried in consecrated ground and Father Baddeley's gentle but inexorable insistence that all the family should lie together in one grave had made him temporarily an outcast. The funeral, boycotted by the village, had been held on such a day as this. The family had no close relatives. Only Father Baddeley, the sexton and Adam Dalgliesh had been there. The fourteen-year-old boy, rigid with uncomprehended grief, had concentrated on the responses willing himself to divorce the unbearably poignant words from their sense, to see them merely as black unmeaning symbols on the prayer book page, and to speak them with firmness, even with nonchalance, across the open grave. Now, when this unknown priest raised his hand to speak the final blessing over Grace Willison's body, Dalgliesh saw instead the frail upright figure of Father Baddeley, the wind ruffling his hair. As the first sods fell on the coffin and he turned away he felt like a traitor. The memory of one occasion on which Father Baddeley had not relied on him in vain only reinforced his present nagging sense of failure.

It was probably this which made him reply tartly to Wilfred when he walked up to him and said:

"We are going back for luncheon now. We shall start the family council at half past two and the second session at about four. Are you quite sure you won't help us?"

Dalgliesh opened the door of his car.

"Can you give me one reason why it would be right that I should?" Wilfred turned away; for once he looked almost disconcerted. Dalgliesh heard Julius's low laugh.

"Silly old dear! Does he really think that we don't know that he wouldn't be holding a family council if he weren't confident that the decision would go his way? What are your plans for the day?"

Dalgliesh said that they were still uncertain. In fact he had decided to exercise away his self-disgust by walking along the cliff path as far as Weymouth and back. But he wasn't anxious to invite Julius's company.

He stopped at a nearby pub for a luncheon of cheese and beer, drove quickly back to Hope Cottage, changed into slacks and windcheater and set off eastwards along the cliff path. It was very different from that first early morning walk the day after his arrival when all his newly awakened senses had been alive to sound and color and smell. Now he strode strongly forward, deep in thought, eyes on the path, hardly aware even of the labored, sibilant breath of the sea. He would soon have to make a decision about his job; but that could wait for another couple of weeks. There were more immediate if less onerous decisions. How much longer should he stay at Toynton? He had little excuse to linger. The books had been sorted, the boxes were almost ready for cording. And he was making no progress with the problem which had kept him in Hope Cottage. There was small hope now of solving the mystery of Father Baddeley's summons. It was as if, living in Father Baddeley's cottage, sleeping in his bed, Dalgliesh had absorbed something of his personality. He could almost believe that he smelt the presence of evil. It was an alien faculty which he half resented and almost wholly distrusted. And yet it was increasingly strong. He was sure now that Father Baddeley had been murdered. And yet, when as a policeman he looked hard at the evidence, the case dissolved like smoke in his hand.

Perhaps because he was deep in unproductive thought the mist took him by surprise. It rode in from the sea, a sudden physical invasion of white obliterating clamminess. At one moment he was striding in the mellow afternoon sunlight with the breeze prickling the hairs on his neck and arms. The next, sun, color and smell were blotted out and he stood stock still pushing at the mist as if it were an alien force. It hung on his hair, caught at his throat and swirled in grotesque patterns over the headland. He watched it, a writhing transparent veil passing over and through the brambles and bracken, magnifying and altering form, obscuring the path. With the mist came a sudden silence. He was only aware that the headland had been alive with birds now that their cries were mute. The silence was uncanny. In contrast, the sound of the sea swelled and became all pervasive, disorganized, menacing, seeming to advance on him from all sides. It was like a chained animal, now moaning in sullen captivity, now breaking free to hurl itself with roars of impotent rage against the high shingles.

He turned back towards Toynton, uncertain of how far he had walked. The return journey was going to be difficult. He had no sense of direction except for the thread of trodden earth under his feet. But he thought that the danger would be slight if he went slowly. The path was barely visible but for most of the route it was fringed with brambles, a welcome if prickly barrier when, momentarily disorientated, he lost his way. Once the mist lifted slightly and he strode forward more confidently. But it was a mistake. Only just in time he realized that he was teetering on the edge of a wide crevice splitting the path and that what he had thought was a rising bank of moving mist was foam dying on the cliff face fifty feet below.

The black tower reared out of the mist so suddenly that his first realization of its presence was to scrape his palms—instinctively flung forward—against its cold infrangible scales. Then, suddenly, the mist rose and thinned and he saw the top of the tower. The base was still shrouded in swirls of white clamminess but the octagonal cupola with its three visible slits seemed to float gently from behind the last sinuous threads of mist to hang motionless in space, dramatic, menacingly solid, and yet unsubstantial as a dream. It moved with the mist, a fugitive vision, now descending so low that he could almost believe it within his reach, now rising, numinous and unobtainable, high over the thudding sea. It could surely have no contact with the cold stones on which his palms rested or the firm earth beneath his feet. To steady his balance he rested his head against the tower and felt reality hard and sharp against his forehead. Here at least was a landmark. From here he thought he could remember the main twists and turns of the path.

It was then that he heard it; the spine-chilling scrape, unmistakable, of bone ends clawing against the stone. It came from inside the tower. Reason asserted itself over superstition so quickly that his mind hardly had time to recognize its terror. Only the painful thudding of his heart against the rib cage, the sudden ice in the blood, told him that for one second he had crossed the border into the unknowable world. For one second, perhaps less, childish nightmares long suppressed rose to confront him. And then the terror passed. He listened more carefully, and then explored. The sound was quickly identified. To the seaward side of the tower and hidden in the corner between the porch and the round wall was a sturdy bramble. The wind had snapped one of the branches and two sharp unleashed ends were scraping against the stone. Through some trick of acoustics the sound, distorted, seemed to come from within the tower. From such coincidences, he thought, smiling grimly, were ghosts and legends born.

Less than twenty minutes later he stood above the valley and looked down on Toynton Grange. The mist was thinning now and he could just discern the Grange itself—a substantial, dark shadow marked by blurs of lights from the windows. His watch showed that it was eight minutes past three. So they would all be closeted now in solitary meditation waiting for the four o'clock summons to announce their final votes. He wondered how, in fact, they were passing their time. But the result was hardly in doubt. Like Julius he thought it unlikely that Wilfred would have called a council unless he were sure of getting his way. And that, presumably, would mean handing over to the Ridgewell Trust. Dalgliesh assessed how the votes might go. Wilfred would no doubt have received an undertaking that all jobs would be safe. Given that assurance Dot Moxon, Eric Hewson and Dennis Lerner would probably vote for the take-over. Poor Georgie Allan would have little choice. The views of the other patients were less certain but he had the feeling that Carwardine would be content enough to stay, particularly with the increased comfort and professional skill which the Trust would bring. Millicent, of course, would want to sell out and she would have had an ally in Maggie Hewson, if Maggie had been allowed to participate.

Looking down on the valley he saw the twin squares of light from the windows of Charity Cottage where, excluded, Maggie waited alone for the return of Eric. There was a stronger and brighter haze from the edge of the cliff. Julius, when at home, was extravagant with electricity.

The lights, although temporarily obscured as the mist shifted and re-formed, were a useful beacon. He found himself almost running down the slope of the headland. And then, curiously, the light in the Hewson cottage windows went off and on again three times, deliberate as a signal.

He had such a strong impression of an individual call for help that he had to remind himself of reality. She couldn't know that he, or anyone, was on the headland. It could only be by chance if the signal were seen by anyone at Toynton Grange, preoccupied as they were with meditation and decision. Besides, most of the patients' rooms were at the back of the house. It had probably been no more than a fortuitous flickering of the lights; she had been uncertain, perhaps, whether to watch television in the dark.

But the twin smudges of yellow light, now shining more strongly as the mist thinned, drew him towards the Hewson cottage. It was only about three hundred yards out of his way. She was there alone. He might as well look in, even at the risk of becoming involved in an alcoholic recital of grievances and resentment.

The front door was unlocked. When no voice responded to his knock he pushed it open and went in. The sitting-room, dirty, untidy, with its grubby air of temporary occupation, was empty. All three bars of the portable electric fire were glowing red and the room struck very warm. The television screen was a blank. The single unshaded lightbulb in the middle of the ceiling shone down garishly on the square table, the opened and almost empty bottle of whisky, the upturned glass, the sheet of writing paper with its scrawl of black biro, at first relatively firm, then erratic as an insect trail across the white surface. The telephone had been moved from its usual place on the top of the bookcase and stood now, cord taut, on the table, the receiver hanging loosely over the edge.

He didn't wait to read the message. The door into the back hall was ajar and he pushed it open. He knew with the sick and certain premonition of disaster, what he would find. The hall was very narrow and the door swung against her legs. The body twisted so that the flushed face slowly turned and looked down at him with what seemed a deprecating, half melancholy, half rueful surprise at finding herself at such a disadvantage. The light in the hall, from a single bulb, was garish, and she hung elongated like a bizarre and gaudily painted doll strung up for sale. The scarlet tight-fitting slacks, the white satin overblouse, the painted toe and finger nails and the matching gash of mouth looked horrible but unreal. One thrust of a knife and the sawdust would surely spill out from the stuffed veins to pyramid at his feet.

The climber's rope, a smooth twist of red and fawn, gay as a bell rope, was made to take the weight of a man. It hadn't failed Maggie. She had used it simply. The rope had been doubled and the two ends passed through the loop to form a noose, before being fastened, clumsily but effectively, to the top banister. The surplus yards lay tangled on the upper landing.

A high kitchen stool fitted with two steps had fallen on its side obstructing the hallway as if she had kicked it from under her. Dalgliesh placed it beneath the body and, resting her knees on its cushioned plastic, mounted the steps and slipped the noose over her head. The whole weight of her inert body sagged against him. He let it slip through his arms to the floor and half carried it into the sitting-room. Laying her on the mat in front of the fireplace he forced his mouth over hers and began artificial respiration.

Her mouth was fumed with whisky. He could taste her lipstick, a sickly ointment on his tongue. His shirt, wet with sweat, stuck to her blouse, gumming together his thudding chest and her soft, still warm but silent body. He pumped his breath into her, fighting an atavistic repugnance. It was too like raping the dead. He felt the absence of her heart beat as keenly as an ache in his chest.

He was aware that the door had opened only by the sudden chill of flowing air. A pair of feet stood beside the body. He heard Julius's voice.

"Oh, my God! Is she dead? What happened?"

The note of terror surprised Dalgliesh. He glanced up for one second into Court's stricken face. It hung over him like a disembodied mask, the features bleached and distorted with fear. The man was fighting for control. His whole body was shaking. Dalgliesh, intent on the desperate rhythm of resuscitation, jerked out his commands in a series of harsh disjointed phrases.

"Get Hewson. Hurry."

Julius's voice was a high, monotonous mutter.

"I can't! Don't ask me. I'm no good at that sort of thing. He doesn't even like me. We've never been close. You go. I'd rather stay here with her than face Eric."

"Then ring him. Then the police. Wrap the receiver in your handkerchief. May be prints."

"But they won't answer! They never do when they are meditating."

"Then for God's sake fetch him!"

"But her face! It's covered with blood!"

"Lipstick. Smudged. Phone Hewson."

Julius stood unmoving. Then he said:

"I'll try. They will have finished meditating by now. It's just four. They may answer."

He turned to the telephone. From the corner of his eye Dalgliesh glimpsed the lifted receiver shaking in his hands, and the flash of white handkerchief which Julius had wrapped around the instrument as awkwardly as if trying to bandage a self-inflicted wound. After two long minutes the telephone was answered. He couldn't guess by whom. Nor did he afterwards remember what Julius had said.

"I've told them. They're coming."

"Now the police."

"What shall I tell them?"

"The facts. They'll know what to do."

"But oughtn't we to wait? Suppose she comes round?"

Dalgliesh straightened himself up. He knew that for the last five minutes he had been working on a dead body. He said:

"I don't think she's going to come round."

Immediately he bent again to his task, his mouth clamped over hers, feeling with his right palm for the first pulse of life in the silent heart. The pendant lightbulb swung gently in the movement of air from the open door so that a shadow moved like a drawn curtain over the dead face. He was aware of the contrast between the inert flesh, the cool unresponsive lips bruised by his own, and her look of flushed intentness, a woman preoccupied in the act of love. The crimson stigmata of the rope was like a double-corded bracelet clasping the heavy throat. Remnants of cold mist stole in the door to twine themselves round the dust-encrusted legs of table and chairs. The mist stung his nostrils like an anaesthetic; his mouth tasted sour with the whisky-tainted breath.

Suddenly there was a rush of feet; the room was full of people and voices. Eric Hewson was edging him aside to kneel beside his wife; behind him Helen Rainer flicked open a medical bag. She handed him a stethoscope. He tore open his wife's blouse. Delicately, unemotionally, she lifted Maggie's left breast so that he could listen to the heart. He pulled off the stethoscope and threw it aside holding out his hand. This time, still without speaking, she handed him a syringe.

"What are you going to do?" It was Julius Court's hysterical voice.

Hewson looked up at Dalgliesh. His face was deathly white. The irises of his eyes were huge. He said:

"It's only digitalis."

His voice, very low, was a plea for reassurance, for hope. But it sounded, too, like a plea for permission, a small abdication of responsibility. Dalgliesh nodded. If the stuff were digitalis it might work. And surely the man wouldn't be fool enough to inject anything lethal? To stop him now might be to kill her. Would it have been better to carry on with the artificial respiration? Probably not; in any case that was a decision for a doctor. And a doctor was here. But in his heart Dalgliesh knew that the argument was academic. She was as beyond harm as she was beyond help.

Helen Rainer now had a torch in her hand and was shining it on Maggie's breast. The pores of the skin between the pendulous breasts looked huge, miniature craters clogged with powder and sweat. Hewson's hand began to shake. Suddenly she said:

"Here, let me do it."

He handed over the syringe. Dalgliesh heard Julius Court's incredulous "Oh, no! No!" and then watched the needle go in as cleanly and surely as a *coup de grâce.*

The slim hands didn't tremble as she withdrew the syringe, held a pad of cotton wool over the puncture mark and, without speaking, handed the syringe to Dalgliesh.

Suddenly Julius Court stumbled out of the room. He came back almost immediately holding a glass. Before anyone could stop him he had grasped the whisky bottle by the top of its neck and had poured out the last half inch. Jerking one of the chairs out from the table he sat down and slumped forward, his arms half circling the bottle.

Wilfred said:

"But Julius . . . nothing should be touched until the police arrive!"

Julius took out his handkerchief and wiped it over his face.

"I needed that. And what the hell! I haven't interfered with her prints. And she's had a rope round her neck, or haven't you noticed? What d'you think she died of—alcoholism?"

The rest of them stood in a tableau round the body. Hewson still knelt at his wife's side; Helen cradled her head. Wilfred and Dennis stood one on each side, the folds of their habits hanging motionless in the still air. They looked, thought Dalgliesh, like a motley collection of actors posing for a contemporary diptych, their eyes fixed with wary anticipation on the bright body of the martyred saint.

Five minutes later Hewson stood up. He said dully:

"No response. Move her to the sofa. We can't leave her there on the floor."

Julius Court rose from his chair and he and Dalgliesh together lifted the sagging body and placed it on the sofa. It was too short, and the scarlet-tipped feet, looking at once grotesque and pathetically vulnerable, stuck out stiffly over the end. Dalgliesh heard the company sigh gently, as if they had satisfied some obscure need to make the body comfortable. Julius looked round, apparently at a loss, searching for something with which to cover the corpse. It was Dennis Lerner who, surprisingly, produced a large white handkerchief, shook it free of its folds and placed it with ritual precision over Maggie's face. They all looked at it intently as if watching for the linen to stir with the first tentative breath.

Wilfred said:

"I find it a strange tradition that we cover the faces of the dead. Is it because we feel that they are at a disadvantage, exposed defenceless to our critical gaze? Or is it because we fear them? I think the latter."

Ignoring him, Eric Hewson turned to Dalgliesh.

"Where . . . ?"

"Out there in the hall."

Hewson went to the door and stood silently surveying the dangling rope, the bright chrome and yellow kitchen stool. He turned towards the circle of watchful, compassionate faces.

"How did she get the rope?"

"It may be mine." Wilfred's voice sounded interested, confident. He turned to Dalgliesh.

"It's newer looking than Julius's rope. I bought it shortly after the old one was found frayed. I keep it on a hook in the business room. You may have noticed it. It was certainly hanging there when we left for Grace's funeral this morning. You remember, Dot?"

Dorothy Moxon moved forward from her shadowed refuge against the far wall. She spoke for the first time. They looked round as if surprised to find her in the company. Her voice sounded unnatural, high, truculent, uncertain.

"Yes, I noticed. I mean, I'm sure I would have noticed if it hadn't been there. Yes, I remember. The rope was there."

"And when you got back from the funeral?" asked Dalgliesh.

"I went alone into the business room to hang up my cloak. I don't think it was there then. I'm almost sure not."

"Didn't that worry you?" asked Julius.

"No, why should it? I'm not sure that I consciously noticed that the rope was missing at the time. It's only now, looking back, that I am fairly confident that it wasn't there. Its absence wouldn't have particularly concerned me even had I registered it. I should have assumed that Albert had borrowed it for some purpose. He couldn't have done so, of course. He came with us to the funeral, and got into the bus before me."

Lerner said suddenly:

"The police have been telephoned?"

"Of course," said Julius, "I rang them."

"What were you doing here?" Dorothy Moxon's didactic question sounded like an accusation, but Julius who seemed to have taken control of himself, answered calmly enough:

"She switched the light off and on three times before she died. I happened to see it through the mist from my bathroom window. I didn't come at once. I didn't think it was important or that she was really in trouble. Then I felt uneasy and decided to walk over. Dalgliesh was already here."

Dalgliesh said:

"I saw the signal from the headland. Like Julius, I didn't feel more than slightly uneasy, but it seemed right to look in."

Lerner had moved over to the table. He said:

"She's left a note."

Dalgliesh said sharply:

"Don't touch it!"

Lerner withdrew his hand as if it had been stung. They moved round the table. The note was written in black biro on the top sheet of a quarto-size pad of white writing paper. They read silently:

> "Dear Eric, I've told you often
> enough that I couldn't stick it out
> in this lousy hole any longer. You
> thought it was just talk. You've been
> so busy fussing over your precious
> patients I could die of boredom and you
> wouldn't notice. Sorry if I've mucked
> up your little plans. I don't kid
> myself you'll miss me. You can have her
> now and by God you're welcome to each
> other. We had some good times. Remember
> them. Try to miss me. Better dead. Sorry
> Wilfred. The black tower."

The first eight lines were plainly and strongly written, the last five were an almost illegible scrawl.

"Her handwriting?" asked Anstey.

Eric Hewson replied in a voice so low that they could barely hear him.

"Oh, yes. Her handwriting."

Julius turned to Eric and said with sudden energy:

"Look, it's perfectly plain how it happened. Maggie never intended to kill herself. She wouldn't. She's not the type. For God's sake, why should she? She's young enough, healthy, if she didn't like it here she could walk out. She's an SRN. She's not unemployable. This was all meant to frighten you. She tried to telephone Toynton Grange and get you over here—just in time, of course. When no one replied, she signalled with the lights. But by that time she was too drunk to know exactly what she was doing and the whole thing became horribly real. Take that note, does it read like a suicide note?"

"It does to me," said Anstey. "And I suspect it will to the coroner."

"Well, it doesn't to me. It could just as well be the note of a woman planning to go away."

Helen Rainer said calmly:

"Only she wasn't. She wouldn't be leaving Toynton wearing just a shirt and slacks. And where is her case? No woman plans to leave home without taking her makeup and nightwear."

There was a capacious black shoulder bag beside a leg of the table. Julius picked it up and began rummaging in it. He said:

"There's nothing here. No nightdress or toilet bag."

He continued his inspection. Then he glanced suddenly from Eric to Dalgliesh. An extraordinary succession of emotions crossed his face; surprise, embarrassment, interest. He closed the bag and placed it on the table.

"Wilfred's right. Nothing should be touched until the police arrive."

They stood in silence. Then Anstey said:

"The police will want to know where we all were this afternoon, no doubt. Even in an obvious case of suicide these questions have to be asked. She must have died when we were nearly at the end of our meditation hour. That means, of course, that none of us has an alibi. Given the circumstances it is perhaps fortunate that Maggie chose to leave a suicide note."

Helen Rainer said calmly:

"Eric and I were together in my room for the whole of the hour."

Wilfred stared at her, disconcerted. For the first time since he had entered the cottage he seemed at a loss. He said:

"But we were holding a family council! The rules are that we meditate in silence and alone."

"We didn't meditate and we weren't precisely silent. But we were alone—alone together." She stared past him, defiant, almost triumphant, into the eyes of Eric Hewson. He gazed at her appalled.

Dennis Lerner, as if to dissociate himself from controversy, had moved over to stand by Dot Moxon by the door. Now he said quietly:

"I think I can hear cars. It must be the police."

The mist had muffled the sound of their approach. Even as Lerner spoke Dalgliesh heard the dual slam of car doors. Eric's first reaction was to kneel by the sofa, shielding Maggie's body from the door. Then he scrambled clumsily to his feet as if afraid to be discovered in a compromising position. Dot, without looking round, moved her solid body away from the door.

The little room was suddenly as overcrowded as a bus shelter on a wet night, smelling of mist and damp raincoats. But there was no confusion. The new arrivals moved solidly and calmly in, bringing with them their equipment, moving as purposefully as encumbered members of an orchestra taking their appointed places. The group from Toynton Grange fell back and regarded them warily. No one spoke. Then Inspector Daniel's slow voice broke the silence.

"Well, now, and who found the poor lady?"

"I did," said Dalgliesh. "Court arrived about twelve minutes later."

"Then I'll just have Mr. Dalgliesh, Mr. Court and Dr. Hewson. That'll do to start with."

Wilfred said:

"I should prefer to stay, if you please."

"Well, Sir, I daresay. Mr. Anstey isn't it? But we can't always have what we'd prefer. Now if you'll all go back to the Grange, Detective Constable Burroughs will accompany you and anything that's on your minds you can say to him. I'll be with you later."

Without a further word, Wilfred led the way.

Inspector Daniel looked at Dalgliesh:

"Well, Sir, seemingly for you there's no convalescence from death at Toynton Head."

# II

When he had handed over the syringe and given his account of the finding of the body Dalgliesh didn't wait to watch the investigation. He had no wish to give the impression that he was keeping a critical eye on Inspector Daniel's handling of the case; he disliked the role of spectator, and he felt uncomfortably that he was getting in their way. None of the men present were getting in each other's. They moved confidently in the cramped space, each a specialist, yet giving the impression of a team. The photographer maneuvered his portable lights into the narrow hall; the plainclothes fingerprint expert, his case open to display the neatly arranged tools of his craft, settled down at the table, brush poised, to begin his methodical dusting of the whisky bottle; the police surgeon knelt, absorbed and judicial, beside the body and plucked at Maggie's mottled skin as if hoping to stimulate it into life. Inspector Daniel leaned over him and they conferred together. They looked, thought Dalgliesh, like two poulterers expertly assessing the qualities of a dead chicken. He was interested that Daniel had brought the police surgeon and not a forensic pathologist. But why not? A Home Office pathologist, given the huge areas which most of them had to cover, could seldom arrive promptly on the scene. And the initial medical examination here presented no obvious problems. There was no sense in committing more resources than were needed for the job. He wondered whether Daniel would have come himself if it hadn't been for the presence at Toynton Grange of a Metropolitan Police Commander.

Dalgliesh formally asked Daniel's permission to return to Hope Cottage. Eric Hewson had already left. Daniel had asked him only a few necessary brief and gentle questions before suggesting that he should join the others at Toynton Grange. Dalgliesh sensed the relief at his departure. Even these imperturbable experts moved more freely released from the inhibiting restraints of public grief.

Now the Inspector exerted himself to do more than nod a curt dismissal. He said:

"Thank you, Sir. I'll call in for a word with you before I leave if I may," and bent again to his contemplation of the body.

Whatever Dalgliesh had expected to find at Toynton Head it wasn't this; the old familiar routine commemoration of unnatural death. For a moment he saw it with Julius Court's eyes, an esoteric necromantic rite, carried out by its drab practitioners in silence or between grunts and muttered words as brief as incantations, a secret ministration to the dead. Certainly Julius seemed engrossed by the procedure. He made no move to leave but stood to one side of the door and, without taking his fascinated eyes from Inspector Daniel, held it open for Dalgliesh. Daniel didn't suggest that he, too, might now leave but Dalgliesh thought it unlikely that this was because the Inspector had forgotten his presence.

It was nearly three hours later before Inspector Daniel's car drove up to Hope Cottage. The inspector was alone; Sergeant Varney and the others, he explained, had already left. He came in bringing with him remnants of mist like ectoplasm and a rush of cold damp air. His hair was jewelled with moisture and his long ruddy face glowed as if he had come in from a walk in the sun. At Dalgliesh's invitation he took off his trench coat and settled himself in the wheel-backed chair in front of the wood fire. His black lively eyes roamed over the cottage, taking in the scruffed rug, the meager grate, the shabbiness of the wallpaper. He said:

"So this is where the old gentleman lived."

"And died. You'll take whisky? Or there's coffee if you prefer it."

"Whisky, thank you, Mr. Dalgliesh. Mr. Anstey didn't exactly make him comfortable, did he? But I daresay all the money goes on the patients, and very rightly no doubt."

Some went on Anstey himself, thought Dalgliesh, remembering the sybaritic cell which was Wilfred's bedroom. He said:

"It's better than it looks. My packing cases don't exactly add to the cosiness. But I doubt whether Father Baddeley noticed the shabbiness or if he did, that he cared."

"Well, it's warm enough anyway. This sea mist seems to seep into your bones. It's clearer inland, though, once you get beyond Toynton village. That's why we made good time."

He sipped his whisky gratefully. After a minute's silence he said:

"This business tonight, Mr. Dalgliesh. It looks straightforward enough. Her prints and Court's on the whisky bottle, and hers and Hewson's on the telephone. There's no hope of getting any dabs from the electric light switch, of course, and those on the biro don't amount to anything. We found a couple of samples of her handwriting. The document chappies at the lab can take a look at them but it's clear enough to me—and Dr. Hewson incidentally—that she wrote that suicide note. It's a strong distinctive scrawl for a woman."

"Except for the last three lines."

"The reference to the black tower? She was pretty far gone when she added that. Incidentally, Mr. Anstey takes it as an admission that it was she who started the fire which nearly killed him. And that wasn't the first attempt according to him. You've heard, no doubt, about the frayed climbing rope? He gave me a full account of the incident in the black tower including your finding the brown habit."

"Did he? He was anxious enough at the time to keep it from the police. So now it's to be laid very neatly at Maggie Hewson's door."

"It always surprises me—although it shouldn't by now—how violent death unlooses tongues. He says that she was the one he suspected from the start; that she made no secret of her hatred of Toynton Grange or her resentment of him in particular."

Dalgliesh said:

"Nor did she. I would be surprised if a woman who expressed her feelings with such uninhibited relish should feel the need for any other release. The fire; the frayed climbing rope; they strike me as being either part of a deliberate stratagem or the manifestations of frustrated hatred. Maggie Hewson was nothing if not candid about her dislike of Anstey."

"Mr. Anstey sees the fire as part of a deliberate stratagem. According to him she was trying to frighten him into selling out. She was desperate to get her husband away from Toynton Grange."

"Then she'd misjudged her man. My guess is that Anstey isn't selling out. By tomorrow he'll have made up his mind to pass Toynton Grange to the Ridgewell Trust."

"He's making up his mind now, Mr. Dalgliesh. Apparently Mrs. Hewson's death interrupted their final decision. He was anxious for me to interview all the inmates as quickly as possible so that they could get down to it. Not that it took much time, to get the basic facts, anyway. No one was seen leaving Toynton Grange after the party arrived back after the funeral. Apart from Dr. Hewson and Nurse Rainer, who admit to having spent the meditation hour together in her room, all the others claim that they were alone. The patients' quarters, as you no doubt know, are at the back. Anyone, anyone not disabled that is, could have left the house. But there's no evidence that anyone did."

Dalgliesh said:

"And even if someone did, this mist would have been an effective shield. Anyone could have walked about the headland unseen. Were you convinced, by the way, that Maggie Hewson did start the fire?"

"I'm not investigating arson or attempted murder, Mr. Dalgliesh. Mr. Anstey told me what he did in confidence and said that he wanted the whole subject dropped. She could have done it, but there is no real evidence. He could have done it himself."

"I doubt that. But I did wonder if Henry Carwardine might have had a hand in it. He couldn't have started the fire himself, of course, but he might have paid an accomplice. I don't think he likes Anstey. But that's hardly a motive. He doesn't have to stay at Toynton Grange. But he's highly intelligent and, I should have thought, fastidious. It's difficult to imagine him embroiling himself with such childish mischief."

"Ah, but he isn't using his intelligence is he, Mr. Dalgliesh? That's his trouble. He gave up too easily and too early, that one. And who can know the truth about motive? Sometimes I think not even the villain himself. I daresay it isn't easy for a man like that, living in such a restricted community, dependent always on others, having always to be grateful to Mr. Anstey. Well, no doubt he is grateful to Mr. Anstey; they all are. But gratitude can be the very devil sometimes, particularly if you have to be grateful for services you'd rather be without."

"You're probably right. I know little of Carwardine's feelings, or of anyone else's at Toynton Grange. I've taken very good care not to know. Did the proximity of violent death induce any of the others to reveal their little secrets?"

"Mrs. Hollis had a contribution. I don't know what she thought it proved, or why she thought it worth telling for that matter. But she may have wanted her little moment of importance. That blonde patient was the same—Miss Pegram isn't it? Kept hinting that she knew Dr. Hewson and Nurse Rainer were lovers. No real evidence, of course, just spite and self-importance. I may have my ideas about those two, but I'd want more evidence than I heard tonight before I started thinking about conspiracy to murder. Mrs. Hollis's story wasn't even particularly relevant to Maggie Hewson's death. She said that the night Grace Willison died she glimpsed Mrs. Hewson passing along the dormitory corridor wearing a brown habit and with the hood drawn over her face. Apparently Mrs. Hollis is in the habit of slipping out of bed at night and propelling herself round the room on her pillow. She says that its a form of exercise, that she's trying to be more mobile and independent. Anyway on the night in question, she managed to get her door ajar—no doubt the idea of taking a skid down the passage—and saw this cloaked figure. She thought afterwards that it must have been Maggie Hewson. Anyone with proper business—any of the staff—would have worn the hood down."

"If they were about their proper business. When exactly was this?"

"A little after midnight she says. She closed the door again and got back into bed with some difficulty. She heard and saw nothing more."

Dalgliesh said consideringly:

"I'm surprised from the little I've seen of her that she could manage to get back to bed unaided. Getting out is one thing, pulling herself back would be a great deal more difficult. Hardly worth the exercise, I should have thought."

There was a short silence. Then Inspector Daniel asked, his black eyes full on Dalgliesh's face:

"Why did Dr. Hewson refer that death to the coroner, Sir? If he had doubts about his medical diagnosis, why not ask the hospital pathologist, or one of his local chums to open her up for him?"

"Because I forced his hand and gave him no choice. He couldn't refuse to refer it without looking suspicious. And I don't think he has any local chums. He's not on those terms with his medical colleagues. How did you hear about it?"

"From Hewson. After hearing the girl's story I had another word with him. But Miss Willison's death was apparently straightforward."

"Oh, yes. Just like this suicide. Just like Father Baddeley's death. All apparently straightforward. She died of cancer of the stomach. But this business tonight. Did you find out anything about the rope?"

"I forgot to mention that, Mr. Dalgliesh. It's the rope which has clinched it. Nurse Rainer saw Mrs. Hewson taking it from the business room at about half past eleven this morning. Nurse Rainer had been left behind to look after that bed-bound patient—Georgie Allan isn't it?—but everyone else was at Miss Willison's funeral. She was writing up the patient's medical record and needed a fresh sheet. All the stationery is kept in a filing cabinet in the business room. It's expensive and Mr. Anstey doesn't like to issue it wholesale. He's afraid that people will use it as scribbling pads. When she reached the hall Nurse Rainer saw Mrs. Hewson slipping out of the business room with the rope over her arm."

"What explanation did Maggie give?"

"According to Nurse Rainer all she said was: 'Don't worry, I'm not going to fray it. Quite the reverse. You'll get it back practically as good as new, if not from me.' "

Dalgliesh said:

"Helen Rainer wasn't in any particular hurry to provide that information when we first found the body. But, assuming she isn't lying, it certainly completes your case."

"I don't think she is lying, Mr. Dalgliesh. But I did look at the boy's medical record. Nurse Rainer began a fresh sheet this afternoon. And there seems little doubt that the rope was hanging in the business room when Mr. Anstey and Sister Moxon left for the funeral.

Who else could have taken it? They were all at the funeral except Nurse Rainer, that very sick boy and Mrs. Hammitt."

Dalgliesh said:

"I'd forgotten about Mrs. Hammitt. I noticed that almost everyone from Toynton Grange was at the cemetery. It didn't occur to me that she wasn't."

"She says she disapproves of funerals. People ought to be cremated in what she calls decent privacy. She says that she spent the morning cleaning her gas stove. For what it's worth, the stove has certainly been cleaned."

"And this evening?"

"Meditating at Toynton Grange with the others. They were all supposed to be separate and alone. Mr. Anstey placed the small interviewing room at her disposal. According to Mrs. Hammitt, she never left it until her brother rang the bell to summon them together just before four o'clock. Mr. Court telephoned shortly afterwards. She died sometime during the meditation hour, no doubt about that. And the police surgeon reckons nearer four than three."

Was Millicent strong enough, Dalgliesh wondered, to have strung up Maggie's heavy body? Probably, with the help of the kitchen stool. And the strangling itself would have been easy enough once Maggie was drunk. A silent movement behind her chair, the noose dropped by gloved hands over the drooping head, the sudden upward jerk as the rope bit into the flesh. Any one of them could have done it, could have crept out unnoticed into the concealing mist towards the smudge of light marking the Hewson cottage. Helen Rainer was the slightest; but Helen was a nurse, skilful in lifting heavy bodies. And Helen Rainer might not have been alone. He heard Daniel speaking:

"We'll get that stuff in the syringe analyzed and we had better ask the lab to take a look at the whisky. But those two little jobs shouldn't hold up the inquest. Mr. Anstey is anxious to get that over as soon as possible so that it doesn't interfere with the pilgrimage to Lourdes on the twenty-third. None of them seems worried about the funeral. That can wait until they get back. I don't see why they shouldn't get away, if the lab can do the analysis quickly. And we know that the whisky's all right; Court still seems healthy enough. I was wondering, Mr. Dalgliesh, just why he took that swig. Incidentally, he'd given her the whisky; half a dozen bottles for her birthday on 11th September. A generous gentleman."

Dalgliesh said:

"I thought he might have been feeding her whisky. But I don't think Court took that drink to save the forensic boys trouble. He needed it."

Daniel gazed consideringly into his half-empty glass:

"Court's been pressing his theory that she never intended killing herself, that the whole setup was play-acting, a desperate plea for attention. She might well have chosen that moment. They were all at the Grange making an important decision which affected her future, and yet she'd been excluded. He could be right; the jury may buy it. But it won't provide much consolation for the husband."

Hewson, thought Dalgliesh, might be looking elsewhere for consolation. He said:

"It seems out of character. I can see her making some dramatic *démarche* if only to relieve the monotony. What I can't see is her wanting to stay on at Toynton as a failed suicide, attracting the slightly pitying contempt that people feel for someone who can't even succeed in killing herself. My problem is that I find a genuine suicide attempt even less in character."

Daniel said:

"Maybe she didn't expect to have to stay at Toynton. Maybe that was the idea, to convince her husband that she'd kill herself unless he found another job. I can't see many men taking that risk. But she did kill herself, Mr. Dalgliesh, whether she intended to or not. This case rests on two bits of evidence: Nurse Rainer's story about the rope, and the suicide note. If Rainer convinces the jury, and the document examiner confirms that Mrs. Hewson wrote that note, then I'll be taking no bets on the verdict. In character or not, you can't get away from the evidence."

But there was other evidence, thought Dalgliesh, less strong but not uninteresting. He said:

"She looked as if she were going somewhere, or perhaps expecting a visitor. She'd recently had a bath, her pores were clogged with powder. Her face was made up and she'd painted her nails. And she wasn't dressed for a solitary evening at home."

"So her husband said. I thought myself that it looked as if she'd dolled herself up. That could support the theory of a faked suicide attempt. If you're planning to be the center of attraction you may as well dress for the show. There's no evidence that she did have a visitor, although it's true enough that no one would have seen him in the mist. I doubt whether he could have found his way once he'd left the road. And if she was planning to leave Toynton, then someone would have had to fetch her. The Hewsons have no car, Mr. Anstey doesn't allow private transport; there's no bus today; and we've checked the car hire firms."

"You've wasted no time."

"A matter of a few telephone calls, Mr. Dalgliesh. I like to get these details out of the way while they're in my mind."

"I can't see Maggie sitting quietly at home while the rest of them settled her future. She was friendly with a solicitor in Wareham, Robert Loder. I suppose he wasn't calling for her?"

Daniel shifted his heavy weight forward and threw another plank of driftwood on the fire. The fire was burning sluggishly as if the chimney were blocked with mist. He said:

"The local boy friend. You aren't the only one to suggest that, Mr. Dalgliesh. I thought it as well to ring the gentleman's home and have a word. Mr. Loder's in Poole General Hospital having his piles operated on. He was admitted yesterday and they gave him a week's notice. A nasty painful complaint. Hardly a comfortable time, you might say, to plan to run away with another man's wife."

Dalgliesh asked:

"What about the one person at Toynton who did have his own car? Court?"

"It was an idea I had put to him, Mr. Dalgliesh. I got a definite reply if not a very gentlemanlike one. What it amounted to was that he'd do a great deal for dear Maggie but that self-preservation was the first law of nature and it just happens that his tastes don't run in that direction. Not that he was against the idea that she planned to leave Toynton. As a matter of fact, he suggested it, although I don't know how he thought it tied up with his previous view that Mrs. Hewson faked a suicide attempt. Both theories can't be true."

Dalgliesh asked:

"What was it that he found in her bag, a contraceptive?"

"Ah, you noticed that, did you? Yes, her Dutch cap. She wasn't on the pill seemingly. Court tried to be tactful about it, but as I told him, you can't be tactful about violent death. That's the one social catastrophe that the etiquette books can't help with. It's the strongest indication that she might have been planning to leave, that and her passport. They were both in the bag. You could say she was equipped for any eventuality."

Dalgliesh said:

"She was equipped with the two items which she couldn't replace by a brief visit to the nearest chemist. I suppose you could argue that it's reasonable to keep the passport in her handbag. But the other?"

"Who's to know how long it was there. And women do keep things in odd places. No point in getting fanciful. And there's no reason to suppose that the two of them were set for a flit, she and Hewson. If you ask me he's as tied to Anstey and the Grange as any of the patients, poor devil. You know his story, I suppose?"

"Not really. I told you. I've taken good care not to become involved."

"I had a sergeant like him once. The women couldn't leave him alone. It's that vulnerable, lost small boy look they have, I suppose. Name of Purkiss. Poor devil. He couldn't cope with the women and he couldn't cope without them. It did for his career. He runs a garage now, somewhere near Market Harborough, they tell me. And it's worse for Hewson. He doesn't even like his job. Forced into it, I gather, by one of those strong-minded mothers, a widow, determined to make her ewe lamb into a doctor. Appropriate enough, I suppose.

It's the modern equivalent of the priesthood isn't it? He told me that the training wasn't so bad. He's got a phenomenal memory and can learn almost any facts. It's the responsibility he can't take. Well, there's not much of that at Toynton Grange. The patients are incurable and there's not much that they or anyone else expect him to do about it. Mr. Anstey wrote to him and took him on, I gather, after he'd had his name removed from the Register by the GMC. He'd been having an affair with a patient, a girl of sixteen. There was a suggestion that it had started a year or so earlier, but he was lucky. The girl stuck to her story. He couldn't write prescriptions for dangerous drugs at Toynton Grange or sign death certificates, of course. Not until they restored his name to the Register six months ago. But they couldn't take away his medical knowledge and I've no doubt that Mr. Anstey found him useful."

"And cheap."

"Well, there's that, of course. And now he doesn't want to leave. I suppose he might have killed his wife to stop her nagging him to go, but personally I don't believe it and neither will a jury. He's the sort of man who gets a woman to do his dirty work."

"Helen Rainer?"

"That'd be daft, wouldn't it, Mr. Dalgliesh? And where's the evidence?"

Dalgliesh wondered briefly whether to tell Daniel about the conversation between Maggie and her husband which he had overheard after the fire. But he put the thought from him. Hewson would either deny it or be able to explain it. There were probably a dozen petty secrets in a place like Toynton Grange. Daniel would feel bound to question him, of course. But he would see it as an irritating duty forced on him by an over suspicious and officious intruder from the Met. determined to twist plain facts into a tangle of complicated conjecture. And what possible difference could it make? Daniel was right. If Helen stuck to her story about seeing Maggie collect the rope; if the document examiner confirmed that Maggie had written the suicide note; then the case was closed. He knew now what the inquest verdict would be, just as he had known that the postmortem on Grace Willison would reveal nothing suspicious. Once again he saw himself, as if in a nightmare, watching impotently as the bizarre charabanc of facts and conjecture hurtled on its predestined course. He couldn't stop it because he had forgotten how. His illness seemed to have sapped his intelligence as well as his will.

The spar of driftwood, charred now into a blackened spear, jewelled with sparks, slowly toppled and died. Dalgliesh was aware that the room was very cold and that he was hungry. Perhaps because of the occluding mist smudging the twilight hour between day and night, the evening seemed to have lasted for ever. He wondered whether he ought to offer Daniel a meal. Presumably the man could eat an omelette. But even the effort of cooking seemed beyond him.

Suddenly the problem solved itself. Daniel got slowly to his feet and reached for his coat. He said:

"Thank you for the whisky, Mr. Dalgliesh. And now I'd best be on my way. I'll see you at the inquest, of course. It'll mean your staying on here. But we'll get on with the case as quickly as we can."

They shook hands. Dalgliesh almost winced at the grip. At the doorway Daniel paused, tugging on his coat.

"I saw Dr. Hewson alone in that small interviewing room which they tell me Father Baddeley used to use. And if you ask me, he'd have been better off with a priest. No difficulty in getting him to talk. Trouble was to stop him. And then he began crying and it all came out. How could he go on living without her? He'd never stopped loving her, longing for her. Funny, the more they're feeling, the less sincere they sound. But you'll have noticed that, of course. And then he looked up at me, his face blubbered with tears and said,

'She didn't lie for me because she cared. It was only a game to her. She never pretended to love me. It was just that she thought the GMC committee were a set of pompous old bores who despised her and she wasn't going to give them the satisfaction of seeing me go to prison. And so she lied.'

"Do you know, Mr. Dalgliesh, it was only then that I realized that he wasn't speaking about his wife. He wasn't even thinking of her. Or of Nurse Rainer for that matter. Poor devil! Ah, well, it's an odd job we have, you and I."

He shook hands again as if he had already forgotten that last crushing grip, and with a final keen-eyed survey of the sitting-room as if to reassure himself that everything was still in place, slipped out into the mist.

## III

In the business room Dot Moxon stood with Anstey at the window and looked out of the curtain of misty darkness. She said bitterly:

"The Trust won't want either of us, you realize that? They may name the home after you, but they won't let you stay on as Warden, and they'll get rid of me."

He laid his hand on her shoulder. She wondered how she could ever have longed for that touch or been comforted by it. He said with the controlled patience of a parent comforting a wilfully obtuse child:

"They've given me an undertaking. No one's job will be lost. And everyone will get a rise. From now on you'll all be paid National Health Service rates. And they have a contributory pension scheme, that's a big advantage. I've never been able to provide that."

"And what about Albert Philby? You're not telling me that they've promised to keep Albert on, an established, respectable national charity like the Ridgewell Trust."

"Philby does present a problem. But he'll be dealt with sympathetically."

"Dealt with sympathetically! We all know what that means. That's what they said to me in my last job, before they forced me out! And this is his home! He trusts us. We've taught him to trust us! And we have a responsibility for him."

"Not any longer, Dot."

"So we betray Albert and exchange what you've tried to build up here for Health Service rates of pay and a pension scheme! And my position? Oh, they won't sack me, I know that. But it won't be the same. They'll make Helen matron. She knows that too. Why else did she vote for the take-over?"

He said quietly:

"Because she knew that Maggie was dead." Dot laughed bitterly: "It's worked out very nicely for her hasn't it? For both of them."

He said:

"Dot dear, you and I have to accept that we cannot always choose the way in which we are called to serve."

She wondered how she had never noticed it before, that irritating note of unctuous reproof in his voice. She turned abruptly away. The hand, thus rejected, slipped heavily from her shoulders. She remembered suddenly what he reminded her of: the sugar Father Christmas on her first Christmas tree, so desirable, so passionately desired. And you bit into nothingness; a trace of sweetness on the tongue and then an empty cavity grained with white sand.

# IV

Ursula Hollis and Jennie Pegram sat together in Jennie's room, the two wheelchairs side by side in front of the dressing table. Ursula was leaning across and brushing Jennie's hair. She wasn't sure how she came to be here, so oddly employed. Jennie had never asked her before. But tonight, waiting for Helen to put them to bed, Helen, who had never before been so late, it was comforting not to be alone with her thoughts, comforting even to watch the corn gold hair rise with each brush stroke, to fall slowly, a delicate shining mist, over the hunched shoulders. The two women found themselves whispering, cosily, like conspiring schoolgirls. Ursula said:

"What do you think will happen now?"

"To Toynton Grange? The Trust will take over and Wilfred will go, I expect. I don't mind. At least there'll be more patients. It's boring here now with so few of us. And Wilfred told me that they plan to build a sun-lounge out on the cliff. I'll like that. And we're bound to get more treats, trips and so on. We haven't had many recently. As a matter of fact, I was thinking of leaving. They keep writing from my old hospital wanting me back."

Ursula knew that they hadn't written. But it didn't matter. She contributed her own morsel of fantasy.

"So was I. Steve is keen for me to move nearer London so that he can visit. Just until he's found us a more suitable flat of course."

"Well, the Ridgewell Trust have a home in London haven't they? You could be transferred there."

How strange that Helen hadn't told her that! Ursula whispered:

"It's odd that Helen voted for the takeover. I thought she wanted Wilfred to sell out."

"Probably she did until she knew that Maggie was dead. Now that she's got rid of Maggie, I suppose she feels she may as well stay on. I mean the field's clear now, isn't it?"

Got rid of Maggie. But surely no one had got rid of Maggie but Maggie herself? And Helen couldn't have known that Maggie was going to die. Only six days ago she had been urging Ursula to vote for the sell out. She couldn't have known then. Even at the preliminary family council, before they all parted for their meditation hour, she had made it plain where her interests lay. And then during that meditation hour, she had changed her mind. No, Helen couldn't have known that Maggie was going to die. Ursula found the thought comforting. Everything was going to be all right. She had told Inspector Daniel about the hooded figure she had seen on the night of Grace's death, not the whole truth, of course, but enough to lift a weight of nagging and irrational worry from her mind. He hadn't thought it important. She had sensed that from the way he had listened, his few brief questions. And he was right, of course. It wasn't important. She wondered now how she could ever have lain awake fretted by inexplicable anxieties, haunted by images of evil and death, cloaked and hooded, stalking the silent corridors. And it must have been Maggie. With the news of Maggie's death she had suddenly become sure of it. It was difficult to know why, except that the figure had looked at once theatrical and surreptitious, so much a stranger, wearing the monk's robe with none of the slovenly familiarity of the Toynton Grange staff. But she had told the Inspector about it. There was no need to worry any more. Everything was going to be all right. Toynton Grange wouldn't close down after all. But it didn't matter. She would get a transfer to the London home, perhaps on exchange. Someone there was sure to want to come to the seaside. She heard Jennie's high childish voice.

"I'll let you into a secret about Maggie if you swear not to tell. Swear."

"I swear."

"She wrote poison pen letters. She sent one to me."

Ursula's heart seemed to lurch. She said quickly:

"How do you know?"

"Because mine was typed on Grace Willison's typewriter and I actually saw Maggie typing it the evening before. The office door was ajar. She didn't know that I was watching."

"What did she say?"

"It was all about a man who is in love with me. One of the television producers actually. He wanted to divorce his wife and take me away with him. It made a great deal of fuss and jealousy at the hospital at the time. That's partly why I had to leave. As a matter of fact I could still go to him if I chose."

"But how did Maggie know?"

"She was a nurse, wasn't she? I think she knew one of the staff nurses at my old hospital. Maggie was clever at finding out things. I think she knew something about Victor Holroyd, too, but she didn't say what. I'm glad that she's dead. And if you had one of the letters, then you won't have any more now. Maggie's dead and the letters will stop. Brush a little harder and to the right Ursula. That's lovely, lovely. We ought to be friends, you and me. When the new patients start arriving we must stick together. That's if I decide to stay, of course."

Brush poised in midair, Ursula saw in the mirror the reflection of Jennie's sly, self-satisfied smile.

# V

Shortly after ten o'clock, his supper eaten, Dalgliesh walked out into the night. The mist had lifted as mysteriously as it had appeared and the cool air, smelling of rain-washed grass, moved gently against his hot face. Standing in the absolute silence he could just hear the sibilant whisper of the sea.

A torch light, erratic as a will-o'-the-wisp, was weaving towards him from the direction of the Grange. Out of the darkness a bulky shadow emerged and took form. Millicent Hammitt had returned home. At the door of Faith Cottage she paused and called out to him.

"Goodnight, Commander. Your friends have left, then?"

Her voice was high, almost belligerent.

"The inspector has gone, yes."

"You may have noticed that I didn't join the rush to participate in Maggie's ill-considered charade. I have no taste for these excitements. Eric has decided to sleep tonight at Toynton Grange. Much the best thing for him, no doubt. But, as I understand that the police have taken away the body, he needn't pretend to oversensitivity. Incidentally, we've voted for the Ridgewell Trust takeover. What with one thing and another, quite an eventful evening."

She turned to open the door. Then she paused and called out again. "They tell me that her nails were painted red."

"Yes, Mrs. Hammitt."

"Her toe nails, too."

He didn't reply. She said with sudden anger.

"Extraordinary woman!"

He heard the door close. A second later her light shone through the curtains. He went inside. Almost too weary to climb the stairs to bed, he stretched himself in Father Baddeley's chair staring into the dead fire. As he watched, the white ash shifted gently, a blackened spar of driftwood glowed momentarily into life, and he heard for the first time that night the familiar and comforting moan of the wind in the chimney. And then there followed another familiar sound. Faintly through the wall came a merry syncopated jingle. Millicent Hammitt had turned on the television.

# BOOK EIGHT

# The Black Tower

# I

Next day Dalgliesh walked up to the Grange to explain to Wilfred that he must now stay on at Hope Cottage until after the inquest, and to pay his token rent. He found Wilfred alone in the business room. Surprisingly, there was no sign of Dot Moxon. Wilfred was studying a map of France spread out on the desk. A bundle of passports in a rubber band weighed down one corner. He seemed hardly to hear what his guest said. He replied "The inquest. Yes, of course," as if it were a forgotten luncheon engagement, then bent again over the map. He made no mention of Maggie's death and Dalgliesh's formal condolences were coldly received as if they were in poor taste. It was as if by divesting himself of Toynton Grange, he had detached himself from further responsibility, even from concern. Now nothing remained but his twin obsessions, his miracle and the pilgrimage to Lourdes.

Inspector Daniel and the forensic laboratory worked quickly. The inquest was held exactly one week after Maggie's death, a week in which the inhabitants of Toynton Grange seemed as resolutely determined to keep out of Dalgliesh's way as he was to avoid them. No one, not even Julius, showed any inclination to chat over Maggie's death. It was as if they saw him now merely as a police officer, an unwelcome intruder of uncertain allegiance, a potential spy. He drove away from Toynton Head early every morning and returned late each night to darkness and silence. Neither the police activities nor the life at Toynton Grange touched him. He continued his daily, compulsive exploration of Dorset like a prisoner on licence and looked forward to the inquest as the final day of release.

It came at last. None of the patients from Toynton Grange attended except Henry Carwardine, surprisingly since he was not required to give evidence. As the company stood in whispering reverential groups outside the courthouse in the usual disorganized hiatus which follows attendance at the more somber public rituals, he wheeled his chair with vigorous thrusts of the arms to where Dalgliesh stood. He looked and sounded euphoric.

"I realize that these ceremonial tidying up of legal loose ends aren't exactly a novelty to you as they are to me. But this one wasn't without interest, I thought. Less fascinating technically and forensically than Holroyd's, but with more human interest."

"You sound like a connoisseur of inquests."

"If we go on like this at Toynton Grange I soon shall be. Helen Rainer was the star turn today, I thought. That extraordinary suit and hat in which she chose to appear were, I take it, the dress uniform of a state registered nurse. A very wise choice. Hair up; the merest trace of make-up; a general air of dedicated professionalism. 'Mrs. Hewson may have believed that there was a relationship between me and her husband. She had too much free time to brood. Naturally Dr. Hewson and I have to work closely together. I have a high opinion of his kindness and competence but there has never been anything improper between us. Dr. Hewson was devoted to his wife.' Nothing improper! I never believed that people actually used that expression."

Dalgliesh said:

"At inquests they do. Did the jury believe her, do you suppose?"

"Oh, I think so, don't you? Difficult to imagine our lady with the lamp garbed as she was this afternoon in grey samite—gabardine anyway—mystic, wonderful, romping between the sheets. She was wise I think to admit that she and Hewson had spent the meditation hour together in her room. But that, as she explained, was because both had already come to their decision and couldn't afford to waste sixty minutes mulling it over when they had so much to discuss professionally together."

"They had to choose between their alibi for what it was worth, and the risk to reputation. On the whole they chose wisely."

Henry swung round his wheelchair with aggressive exuberance.

"It rather foxed the honest jurymen of Dorset, though. You could see the way their minds were working. If they aren't lovers why were they closeted together? But if they were together, then Hewson couldn't have killed his wife. But unless they were lovers he wouldn't have had a motive for murdering his wife. But if he had such a motive, why admit that they were together? Obviously to give him an alibi. But he wouldn't need an alibi if he hadn't the usual motive. And if he had such a motive, then he and the girl would have been together. Very puzzling."

Mildly amused, Dalgliesh asked:

"What did you think about Hewson's performance?"

"He did well too. Not quite the professional competence and detachment of yourself, my dear Commander, but quiet, sincere, some natural grief bravely under control. Sensible of him to admit that Maggie desperately wanted him to leave Toynton Grange but that he felt an obligation to Wilfred, 'who took me on when I wasn't finding it easy to get a job'. No mention, of course, of being struck off the Medical Register and no one tactless enough to bring it up."

Dalgliesh said:

"And no one tactless enough to suggest that he and Helen may have been lying about their relationship."

"What else do you expect? What people know and what they can legally prove—or care to state in a court of law—are two very different things. Besides, we must at all costs protect dear Wilfred from the contamination of truth. No, I thought it went very well. Suicide while the balance of her mind, etc., etc. Poor Maggie! Stigmatized as a selfish, pleasure-seeking slut addicted to the bottle, out of sympathy with her husband's dedication to his noble profession and not even competent to make a comfortable home for him. Court's suggestion that it might have been an accidental death, play-acting which got out of hand, received no credence from the jury, did it? They took the view that a woman who drank the best part of a bottle of whisky, borrowed a rope and wrote a farewell letter was carrying play-acting a little far and did Maggie the compliment of believing that she intended what she did. I thought that the forensic scientist was extraordinarily definite in his opinion, given the basically subjective nature of document examination. There seems no doubt that Maggie did write the suicide note."

"The first four lines of it, which were all he felt competent to pronounce on. What did you think of the verdict?"

"Oh, I agree with Julius. She was planning to be cut down just in time amidst general hullabaloo. But with the best part of a bottle of whisky inside her she wasn't even competent to stage-manage her own resurrection. Incidentally, Julius gave me a graphic description of the drama in Charity Cottage, including Helen's impressive debut in the role of Lady Macbeth:

> Give me the syringe. The sleeping and the dead,
> Are but as pictures; 'tis the eye of childhood
> That fears a painted devil."

There was no expression on Dalgliesh's face or in his voice. He said:

"How entertaining for you both. It's a pity Court wasn't as detached at the time. He might have made himself useful instead of behaving like a hysterical queer."

Henry smiled, gratified to have provoked the response he wanted. He said:

"So you don't like him? Neither, I suspect, did your friend in holy orders."

Dalgliesh spoke on impulse:

"I know that this is nothing to do with me, but isn't it time that you got away from Toynton Grange?"

"Got away? To where do you suggest?"

"There must be other places."

"The world is full of places. But what do you suppose I could do, or be, or hope for in any of them? As a matter of fact, I did once plan to leave. It was a particularly foolish dream. No, I shall stay on at the Grange. The Ridgewell Trust have the professionalism and experience which Anstey lacks. I could do worse. Besides, Wilfred himself is to stay; and I still have a debt to pay Wilfred. In the meantime, this formality over, we can all relax and set off tomorrow to Lourdes in peace. You ought to come with us, Dalgliesh. You've hung around here so long that I suspect you rather enjoy our company. Besides, I don't think your convalescence has really done you a great deal of good. Why not come to Lourdes and see what the odor of incense and a change of scene can do for you?"

The Toynton Grange bus, driven by Philby, had drawn level with them now and the back ramp was being lowered. Dalgliesh watched in silence as Eric and Helen detached themselves from Wilfred, laid their hands simultaneously on the handle bars and wheeled Henry briskly into the bus. The ramp was raised, Wilfred took his seat in the front beside Philby, and the Toynton Grange bus disappeared from view.

Colonel Ridgewell and the trustees arrived after lunch. Dalgliesh watched as the car drew up and the somber-suited party disappeared into the house. Later they emerged and walked with Wilfred over the headland towards the sea. Dalgliesh was a little surprised to see that Eric and Helen were with them but not Dorothy Moxon. He could see the Colonel's grey hair lifting in the breeze as he paused to swing his walking stick in wide explanatory sweeps or stood suddenly still conferring with the little group who quickly closed round him. No doubt, thought Dalgliesh, they would want to inspect the cottages. Well, Hope Cottage was ready for them. The book shelves were empty and dusted, the packing cases corded and labelled for the carrier, his suitcase packed except for the few things he needed on this his last night. But he had no wish to get involved in introductions or to stand making small talk.

When the party finally turned back and made their way towards Charity Cottage, he got into his car and drove off, with no clear direction in mind, no particular aim, no intention except to keep driving long into the night.

# II

The next morning was airless and sultry, inducing headache, the sky a tent of stained calico ponderous with unspilt rain. The pilgrimage party was due to set out at nine o'clock and at half past eight Millicent Hammitt barged in, without a preliminary knock, to say goodbye. She was wearing a blue-grey tweed suit badly seated, with a short double-breasted jacket; a blouse in a harsher and discordant blue adorned with a garish brooch at the neck; brogues; and a grey felt hat pulled down to cover the ears. She dumped a bulging airline bag and her shoulder bag at her feet, drew on a pair of fawn cotton gloves and held out her hand. Dalgliesh put down his coffee cup. His right hand was grasped in a crushing grip.

"Goodbye then, Commander. Odd, but I've never really got used to using your Christian name. You'll be gone, I understand, by the time we return?"

"I plan to drive back to London later this morning."

"I hope you've enjoyed your stay. At least it has been eventful. One suicide, one natural death and the end of Toynton Grange as an independent institution. You can't have been bored."

"And one attempted murder."

"Wilfred in the burning tower? It sounds like the title of an *avant-garde* play. I've always had my doubts about that particular excitement. If you ask me, Wilfred set it up himself to justify handing over his responsibilities. No doubt that explanation occurred to you."

"Several explanations occurred to me but none of them made much sense."

"Little at Toynton Grange ever does. Well, the old order changeth yielding place to new and God fulfils Himself in many ways. We must hope that He will."

Dalgliesh asked if Millicent had any plans.

"I shall stay on in the cottage. Wilfred's agreement with the Trust stipulates that I may live there for life, and I assure you, I've every intention of dying at my own convenience. It won't be the same, of course, knowing that the place belongs to strangers."

Dalgliesh asked:

"How does your brother feel about the hand-over?"

"Relieved. Well, it's what he schemed for isn't it? He doesn't know what he's let himself in for, of course. Incidentally, he hasn't given this cottage to the Trust. This will continue to belong to him and he plans to move in after the place has been converted into something more civilized and comfortable. He's also offered to help at Toynton Grange in any capacity in which the Trust feel he can be of use. If he imagines that they'll let him stay on as warden he's in for a shock. They've got their own plans for the Grange and I doubt whether they include Wilfred, even if they have agreed to pander to his vanity by naming the home after him. I suppose Wilfred imagines that everyone will defer to him as their benefactor and the original owner. I can assure you they won't. Now that the deed of gift—or whatever it is—is signed and the Trust are the legal owners. Wilfred counts for as little as Philby, less probably. It's his own fault. He should have sold out completely."

"Wouldn't that have broken faith?"

"Superstitious nonsense! If Wilfred wanted to dress up in monk's garb and behave like a medieval abbot he should have applied for entry to a monastery. An Anglican one would have been perfectly respectable. The twice yearly pilgrimage will go on, of course. That's one of Wilfred's stipulations. It's a pity you aren't coming with us Commander. We stay at an agreeable little pension, really quite cheap and the food is excellent; and Lourdes is a cheerful little place. Quite an atmosphere. I don't say I wouldn't have preferred Wilfred to have had his miracle in Cannes, but it might have been worse. He could have got cured at Blackpool."

She paused at the door to turn and say:

"I expect the bus will stop here so that the others can take leave of you." She made it sound as if they would be conferring a privilege. Dalgliesh said that he would walk up with her and say goodbye at

Toynton Grange. He had discovered one of Henry Carwardine's books on Father Baddeley's shelf and wanted to return it. There was also his bed linen to take back and some leftover tins of food which Toynton Grange could probably use.

"I'll take the tins later. Just leave them here. And you can return the linen any time. The Grange is never locked. Philby will be back later anyway. He only drives us to the port and sees us on the boat and then comes back to caretake and feed Jeoffrey and, of course, the hens. They're rather missing Grace's help with the hens although no one thought that she did anything very useful when she was alive. And it's not only the hens. They can't lay their hands on her list of the Friends. Actually, Wilfred wanted Dennis to stay at home this time. He's got one of his migraines and looks like death. But no one can make Dennis miss a pilgrimage."

Dalgliesh walked up to the Grange with her. The bus was drawn up outside the front door and the patients were already loaded. The pathetically depleted party had a bizarre air of slightly spurious joviality. Dalgliesh's first impression from their varied garb was that they proposed to pursue quite different and unrelated activities. Henry Carwardine, in a belted tweed coat and deerstalker hat, looked like an Edwardian gentleman on his way to the grouse moors. Philby, incongruously formal in a dark suit with high collar and black tie, was an undertaker's man loading a hearse. Ursula Hollis had dressed like a Pakistani immigrant in full fig whose only concession to the English climate was an ill-cut jacket in mock fur. Jennie Pegram, wearing a long blue headscarf, had apparently made an attempt to impersonate Saint Bernadette. Helen Rainer, dressed as she had been at the inquest, was a prison matron in charge of a group of unpredictable delinquents. She had already taken her seat at the head of Georgie Allan's stretcher. The boy's eyes were feverishly bright and Dalgliesh could hear his high frenetic chatter. He was wearing a blue and white striped woollen scarf and clutching an immense teddy bear, its neck adorned with pale blue ribbon and what, to Dalgliesh's astounded eyes, looked like a pilgrimage medal. The party could have been an oddly assorted party of team supporters on their way to a football match, but one, Dalgliesh thought, that hardly expected the home side to win.

Wilfred was gently fussing over the remainder of the luggage. He, Eric Hewson and Dennis Lerner were wearing their monk's habits. Dennis looked desperately ill, his face was taut with pain and his eyes half closed as if even the dull morning light were intolerable. Dalgliesh heard Eric whisper to him:

"For God's sake, Dennis, give up and stay at home! With two wheelchairs less we can perfectly well manage."

Lerner's high voice held a tinge of hysteria.

"I'll be all right. You know it never lasts more than twenty-four hours. For God's sake leave me alone!"

At last the medical paraphernalia, decently shrouded, was loaded, the ramp was raised, the rear door finally slammed and they were off. Dalgliesh waved in response to the frantically signalling hands and watched as the brightly painted bus lurched slowly over the headland looking, as it receded, as vulnerable and insubstantial as a child's toy. He was surprised, and a little saddened, that he could feel such pity and regret for people with whom he had taken such care not to become involved. He remained watching until the bus bumped slowly up the slope of the valley and finally tipped over the headland out of sight.

Now the headland was deserted, Toynton Grange and its cottages stood unlit and unpeopled under the heavy sky. It had grown darker in the last half hour. There would be a storm before midday. Already his head ached with the premonition of thunder. The headland lay in the sinister anticipatory calm of a chosen battlefield. He could just hear the thudding of the sea, less a noise than a vibration on the dense air like the sullen menace of distant guns.

Restless and perversely reluctant to leave now that he was at last free to go, he walked up to the gate to collect his paper and any letters. The bus had obviously stopped for the Toynton Grange post and there was nothing in the box but the day's copy of *The Times,* an official-looking buff envelope for Julius Court and a square white one addressed to Father Baddeley. Tucking the newspaper under his arm he split open the stout linen-backed envelope and began to walk back, reading on his way. The letter was written in a firm, strong masculine hand; the printed address was a Midlands deanery. The writer was sorry not to have replied earlier to Father Baddeley's letter but it had been posted on to him in Italy, where he had taken a locum post for the summer. At the end of the conventional enquiries, the methodical recording of family and diocesan concerns, the perfunctory and predictable comments on public affairs, came the answer to the mystery of Father Baddeley's summons:

"I went at once to visit your young friend, Peter Bonnington, but he had, of course, been dead for some months. I am so very sorry. In the circumstances there seemed little point in enquiring whether he had been happy at the new home or had really wanted to move from Dorset. I hope that his friend at Toynton Grange managed to visit before he died. On your other problem, I don't think I can offer much guidance. Our experience in the diocese where, as you know, we are particularly interested in young offenders, is that providing residential care for ex-prisoners whether in a home or in the kind of self-supporting hostel you envisage requires a great deal more capital than you have available. You could probably buy a small house even at today's prices, but at least two experienced staff would be needed initially and you would have to support the venture until it became established. But there are a number of existing hostels and organizations who would very much welcome your help. There certainly couldn't be a better use for your money, if you have decided, as you obviously have, that it ought not now to go to Toynton Grange. I think that you were wise to call in your policeman friend. I'm sure that he will be best able to advise you."

Dalgliesh almost laughed aloud. Here was an ironical, and fitting end to failure. So that was how it had begun! There had been nothing sinister behind Father Baddeley's letter, no suspected crime, no conspiracy, no hidden homicide. He had simply wanted, poor, innocent, unworldly old man, some professional advice on how to buy, equip, staff and endow a hostel for young ex-offenders for the sum of £19,000. Given the present state of the property market and the level of inflation, what he had needed was a financial genius. But he had written to a policeman, probably the only one he knew. He had written to an expert in violent death. And why not? To Father Baddeley all policemen were fundamentally alike, experienced in crime and familiar with criminals, dedicated to prevention as well as detection. And I, thought Dalgliesh bitterly, have done neither. Father Baddeley had wanted professional advice, not advice on how to deal with evil. There he had his own infallible guidelines; there he was at home. For some reason, almost certainly connected with the transfer of that young, unknown patient, Peter Bonnington, he had become disenchanted with Toynton Grange. He had wanted advice on how else to use his money. How typical of my arrogance, thought Dalgliesh, to suppose that he wanted me for anything more.

He stuffed the letter into his jacket pocket and strolled on, letting his eyes glance over the folded newspaper. An advertisement stood out as clearly as if it had been marked, familiar words leaping to the eye.

> Toynton Grange. All our friends will wish to know that from the day of our return from the October Pilgrimage we shall be part of the larger family of the Ridgewell Trust. Please continue to remember us in your prayers at this time of change. As our list of friends has unfortunately been mislaid will all those who wish to keep in touch please write to me urgently.
>
> Wilfred Anstey, Warden.

Of course! The list of Toynton Grange Friends, unaccountably mislaid since Grace Willison's death, those sixty-eight names which Grace had known by heart. He stood stock still under the menacing sky and read the notice again. Excitement gripped him, as violently physical as a twist of the stomach, a surge of the blood. He knew with immediate, with heart-lifting certainty that here at last was the end of the tangled skein. Pull gently on this one fact and the thread would begin, miraculously, to run free.

If Grace Willison had been murdered, as he obstinately believed, postmortem result notwithstanding, it had been because of something she knew. But it must have been vital information, knowledge which she alone possessed. One did not kill merely to silence intriguing but evidentially useless suspicions about where Father Baddeley had been on the afternoon of Holroyd's death. He had been in the black tower. Dalgliesh knew it and could prove it; Grace Willison might have known it too. But the shredded match and Grace's testimony taken together could prove nothing. With Father Baddeley dead, the worst anyone could do would be to point out that it was strange that the old priest hadn't mentioned seeing Julius Court walking over the headland. And Dalgliesh could imagine Julius's contemptuous, sardonic smile. A sick, tired old man, sitting with his book at the eastern window. Who could say now that he hadn't slept the hours away before making his way back to Toynton Grange across the headland while, on the beach unseen below, the rescue party toiled with their burden? With Father Baddeley dead, his testimony silenced, no police force in the world would reopen the case on that secondhand evidence. The worst harm Grace could have done to herself might have been to betray that Dalgliesh wasn't just convalescing at Toynton, that he too was suspicious. That betrayal might just have tipped the scales for her from life to death. Then she might have become too dangerous to let live. Not because she knew that Father Baddeley had been in the black tower on the afternoon of the 12th September, but because she possessed more specific, more valuable information. There was only one distribution list of the Friends of Toynton Grange and she could type it by heart. Julius had been present when she made that claim. The list could be torn up, burnt, utterly destroyed. But there was only one way in which those sixty-eight names could be erased from one frail woman's consciousness.

Dalgliesh quickened his pace. He found himself almost running down the headland. His headache seemed surprisingly to have lifted despite the lowering sky, the dense, storm-laden air. Change the metaphor, still trite but well proved. In this job it wasn't the last piece of jigsaw, the easiest of all, that was important. No, it was the neglected, uninteresting small segment which, slotted into place, suddenly made sense of so many other discarded pieces. Delusive colors, amorphous and ambiguous shapes came together as now to reveal the first recognizable outline of the finished picture.

And now, that piece in place, it was time to move the others speculatively over the board. For the present, forget proof, forget autopsy reports and the formal legal certainty of inquest verdicts; forget pride, the fear of ridicule, the reluctance to become involved. Get back to the first principle applied by any divisional detective constable when he smelt villainy on his patch. *Cui bono?* Who was living above his means? Who was in possession of more money than could reasonably be explained? There were two such people at Toynton Grange, and they were linked by Holroyd's death. Julius Court and Dennis Lerner. Julius who had said that his answer to the black tower was money and the solace it could buy; beauty, leisure, friends, travel. How could a legacy of £30,000, however cleverly invested, enable him to live as he lived now? Julius, who helped Wilfred with the accounts and knew better than anyone how precarious were the finances of Toynton Grange. Julius who never went to Lourdes because it wasn't his scene, but who took care to be at his cottage to give a welcome home party for the pilgrims. Julius who had been so untypically helpful when the pilgrimage bus had had an accident, driving immediately to the scene, taking charge, buying a new and specially adapted bus so that the pilgrimages could be independent. Julius, who had provided the evidence to clear Dennis Lerner from any suspicion of Holroyd's murder.

Dot had accused Julius of using Toynton Grange. Dalgliesh recalled the scene at Grace's death bed; Dot's outburst, the man's first incredulous look, the quick reactive spite. But what if he were using the place for a more specific purpose than to gratify the insidious pleasure of patronage and easy generosity. Using Toynton Grange. Using the pilgrimage. Scheming to preserve them both because both were essential to him.

And what of Dennis Lerner? Dennis, who stayed on at Toynton

Grange being paid less than the normal wages and who could yet support his mother in an expensive nursing home. Dennis who resolutely overcame his fear so that he could go climbing with Julius. What better opportunity to meet and talk in absolute privacy without exciting suspicion? And how convenient that Wilfred had been frightened by the frayed rope into giving up rock climbing. Dennis, who could never bear to miss a pilgrimage even when as today, he could hardly stand with migraine. Dennis who was in charge of distributing the handcream and bath powder, who did most of the packing himself.

And it explained Father Baddeley's death. Dalgliesh had never been able to believe that his friend had been killed to prevent him disclosing that he hadn't glimpsed Julius walking over the headland on the afternoon of Holroyd's death. In the absence of clear proof that the old man hadn't, even momentarily, slumbered at his window, an allegation that Julius had lied, based on that evidence, would have been embarrassing perhaps but hardly dangerous. But what if Holroyd's death had been part of a larger and more sinister conspiracy? Then it might well have seemed necessary to snuff out—and how simply!—an obstinate, intelligent and ever-present watcher who could have been silenced in no other way once he smelt out the presence of evil. Father Baddeley had been taken to hospital before he learnt of Holroyd's death. But when he did learn, the significance of what he had so singularly failed to see must have struck him. He would have taken some action. And he had taken action. He had made a telephone call to London, to a number he had needed to look up. He had made an appointment with his murderer.

Dalgliesh walked quickly on, past Hope Cottage and, almost without conscious decision, to Toynton Grange. The heavy front door opened to his touch. He smelt again the slightly intimidating spicy smell, masking more sinister, less agreeable odors. It was so dark that he had at once to switch on the light. The hall blazed like an empty film set. The black and white checkered floor was dazzling to the eyes, a gigantic chess board, waiting for the pieces to move into place.

He paced through the empty rooms switching on the lights as he went. Room after room burst into brilliance. He found himself touching tables and chairs as he passed as if the wood were a talisman, looking intently around with the wary eye of a traveller returning unwelcomed to a deserted home. And his mind continued to shuffle the pieces of jigsaw. The attack on Anstey, the final and most dangerous attempt in the black tower. Anstey himself assumed that it was a final attempt to frighten him into selling out. But suppose it had had another purpose, not to close Toynton Grange but to make its future secure? And there was no other way, given Anstey's dwindling resources, than to pass it over to an organization financially sound and already well established. And Anstey hadn't sold out. Satisfied by the last, the most dangerous attack on him, that it couldn't have been the work of a patient and that his dream was still intact, he had given his inheritance away. Toynton Grange would go on. The pilgrimages would continue. Was that what someone—someone who knew only too well how financially precarious the home was—had always schemed for and intended?

Holroyd's visit to London. It was obvious that he had learnt something on that visit, had somehow acquired knowledge which had sent him back to Toynton Grange restless and elated. Was it also knowledge which had made him too dangerous to live? Dalgliesh had assumed that he had been told something by his solicitor, something perhaps about his own financial concerns for those of the Anstey family. But the visit to the solicitor hadn't been the main purpose of the trip. Holroyd and the Hewsons had also been to St. Saviour's hospital, the hospital where Anstey had been treated. And there, in addition to seeing the consultant in physical medicine with Holroyd, they had visited the medical records department. Hadn't Maggie said when she and Dalgliesh first met? "He never went back to St. Saviour's hospital so that they could record the miraculous cure on his medical record. It would have been rather a joke if he had." Suppose Holroyd had gained some knowledge in London but gained it, not directly, but through a confidence from Maggie Hewson given, perhaps, during one of their lonely periods together on the cliff edge. He remembered Maggie Hewson's words:

"I've said I won't tell. But if you keep on nagging about it I may change my mind." And then: "What if I did? He wasn't a fool you know. He could tell that something was up. And he's dead, dead, dead!" Father Baddeley was dead. But so was Holroyd. And so was Maggie. Was there any reason why Maggie had to die, and at that particular time?

But this was to go too fast. It was still all conjecture, all speculation. True, it was the only theory which fitted all the facts. But that wasn't evidence. He had still no proof that any of the deaths at Toynton Head had been murder. One fact was certain. If Maggie had been killed, then somehow she had been persuaded unwittingly to connive in her own death.

He became aware of a faint bubbling sound and detected the pungent smell of grease and hot soap from the direction of the kitchen. The kitchen itself stank like a Victorian workhouse laundry. A pail of teacloths was simmering on the old-fashioned gas stove. In the bustle of departure Dot Moxon must have forgotten to turn off the gas. The grey linen was billowing above the dark evil-smelling scum, the gas plate was splattered with sponges of dried foam. He turned off the gas and the teacloths subsided into their murky bath. With the extinguishing plop of the flame the silence was suddenly intensified; it was as if he had turned off the last evidence of human life.

He moved on into the activity room. The work tops were shrouded with dust sheets. He could see the outline of the row of polythene bottles and the tins of bath powder waiting to be sieved and packed. Henry Carwardine's bust of Anstey still stood on its wooden plinth. It had been covered by a white plastic bag tied at the throat with what looked like one of Carwardine's old ties. The effect was peculiarly sinister; the nebulous features under the transparent shroud, the empty eye sockets, the sharp nose pointing the thin plastic made it as potent an image as a severed head.

In the office at the end of the annex Grace Willison's desk still stood squarely under the north window, the typewriter under its grey cover. He pulled open the desk drawers. They were as he expected, immaculately tidy and ordered, banks of writing paper with Toynton Grange heading; envelopes carefully graded by size; typewriter ribbons; pencils; erasers; carbon paper still in its box; the sheets of perforated sticky labels on which she had typed the names and addresses of the Friends. Only the bound list of names was missing, the list of sixty-eight addresses; one of them in Marseilles. And here typed in that book and imprinted on Miss Willison's mind had been the vital link in the chain of greed and death.

The heroin had travelled far before it was finally packed at the bottom of a tin of bath powder in Toynton Grange. Dalgliesh could picture each stage of that journey as clearly as if he had travelled it himself. The fields of opium poppies on the high Anatolian plateau, the bulging pods oozing their milky sap. The secret rendering down of the raw opium into base morphine even before it left the hills. The long journey by mule train, rail, road or air towards Marseilles, one of the main distribution ports of the world. The refinement into pure heroin in one of a dozen clandestine laboratories. And then, the arranged rendezvous among the crowds at Lourdes, perhaps at Mass, the package slipped quickly into the waiting hand. He remembered wheeling Henry Carwardine across the headland on his first evening at Toynton, the thick rubber handgrips twisting beneath his hand. How simple to wrench one off, to insert a small plastic bag into the hollow strut, its drawstring taped to the metal. The whole operation would take less than a minute. And there would be plenty of opportunity. Philby didn't go on the pilgrimages. It would be Dennis Lerner who would have charge of the wheelchairs. What safer way for a drug smuggler to pass through customs than as the member of a recognized and respected pilgrimage. And the subsequent arrangements had been equally foolproof. The suppliers would need to know in advance the date of each pilgrimage, just as the customers and distributors would need to be told when the next consignment would come in. How more easily than by means of an innocuous newsletter from a respectable charity, a newsletter despatched so conscientiously and so innocently each quarter by Grace Willison.

And Julius's testimony in a French court, the alibi for a murderer. Had that been, not a reluctant yielding to blackmail, not a payment for services rendered, but payment in advance for services to come?

Or had Julius, as Bill Moriarty's informant suggested, given Michonnet his alibi with no other motive than a perverse pleasure in thwarting the French police, gratuitously obliging a powerful family and causing his superiors the maximum of embarrassment? Possibly. He might neither have expected nor wanted any other reward. But if one were offered? If it were tactfully made known to him that a certain commodity could be supplied in strictly limited quantities if he could find a way to smuggle it into England? Would he later have been able to resist the temptation of Toynton Grange and its six-monthly pilgrimage?

And it was so easy, so simple, so foolproof. And so incredibly profitable. What was illegal heroin fetching now? Something like £4,000 an ounce. Julius had no need to deal in bulk or complicate his distribution arrangements beyond the one or two trusted agents to make himself secure for life. Ten ounces brought in each time would buy all the leisure and beauty that any man could desire. And with the Ridgewell Trust takeover the future was secure. Dennis Lerner would keep his job. The pilgrimages would continue. There would be other homes open to his exploitation, other pilgrimages. And Lerner was completely in his power. Even if the newsletter was discontinued and the home no longer needed to pack and sell its handcream and powder, the heroin would still come in. The arrangements for notification and distribution were a minor matter of logistics compared with the fundamental problem of getting the drug safely, reliably and regularly through the port.

There was as yet no proof. But with luck, and if he were right, there would be in three days' time. He could telephone the local police now and safely leave it to them to contact the central drug control branch. Better still, he could telephone Inspector Daniel and arrange to call in to see him on his way back to London. Secrecy was essential. There must be no risk of suspicion. It would take only one telephone call to Lourdes to cancel this consignment and leave him again with nothing but a hotchpotch of half-formulated suspicions, coincidences, unsubstantiated allegations.

The nearest telephone, he remembered, was in the dining room.

It had an external line, and he saw that this had been switched through to the exchange. But when he lifted the receiver, the line was dead. He felt the usual momentary irritation that an instrument, taken for granted, should be reduced to a ridiculous and useless lump of plastic and metal, and reflected that a house with a dead telephone seemed always so much more isolated than one with no telephone at all. It was interesting, perhaps even significant, that the line was silent. But it didn't matter. He would get on his way and hope to find Inspector Daniel at police headquarters. At this stage when his theory was still little more than conjecture he was reluctant to talk to anyone else. He replaced the receiver. A voice from the doorway said:

"Having difficulty, Commander?"

Julius Court must have stepped through the house as delicately as a cat. He stood now, one shoulder resting lightly against the door post, both hands deep in his jacket pockets. The assumption of ease was deceptive. His body, poised on the balls of his feet as if to spring, was rigid with tension. The face above the high rolled collar of his sweater was as skeletal and defined as a carving, the muscles taut under the flush skin. His eyes unblinking, unnaturally bright, were fixed on Dalgliesh with the speculative intentness of a gambler watching the spinning balls.

Dalgliesh said calmly:

"It's out of order apparently. It doesn't matter. My housekeeper will expect me when she sees me."

"Do you usually roam about other people's houses to make your private calls? The main telephone is in the business room. Didn't you know?"

"I doubt whether I should have been any luckier."

They looked at each other, silent in the greater silence. Across the length of the room Dalgliesh could recognize and follow the process of his adversary's thought as plainly as if it were registering visibly on a graph, the black needle tracing the pattern of decision. There was no struggle. It was the simple weighing of probabilities.

When Julius at last drew his hand slowly out of his pocket it was almost with relief that Dalgliesh saw the muzzle of the Luger. The die was cast. Now there was no going back, no more pretense, no more uncertainty.

Julius said quietly:

"Don't move, I'm an excellent shot. Sit down at the table. Hands on the top. Now, tell me how you found me out. I'm assuming that you have found me out. If not, then I've miscalculated. You will die and I shall be put to a great deal of trouble and inconvenience and we'll both be aggrieved to know that it wasn't after all necessary."

With his left hand Dalgliesh took Father Baddeley's letter from his jacket pocket and slid it across the table.

"This will interest you. It came this morning addressed to Father Baddeley."

The grey eyes did not move from his.

"Sorry. I'm sure it's fascinating but I have my mind on other matters. You read it to me."

"It explains why he wanted to see me. You needn't have worried to concoct the poison pen letter or destroy his diary. His problem had nothing to do with you. Why kill him anyway? He was in the tower when Holroyd died; he knew perfectly well that he hadn't slept, that you hadn't come over the headland. But was that knowledge dangerous enough to snuff him out?"

"It was, in Baddeley's hands. The old man had a deep-rooted instinct for what he would describe as evil. That meant he had a deep-rooted suspicion of me, particularly of what he saw as my influence over Dennis. We were playing out our private comedy on a level which I don't think the procedures of the Metropolitan Police would recognize. It could only have one end. He telephoned me at my London flat from the hospital three days before he was discharged and asked me to come to see him on 26th September after nine o'clock. I went prepared. I drove down from London and left the Mercedes in that hollow behind the stone wall off the coast road. I took one of the habits from the business room while they were all at dinner. Then I walked to Hope Cottage. If anyone had seen me, then I should have had to change my plan. But no one did. He was sitting alone by the dying fire waiting for me. I think he knew about two minutes after I entered that I would kill him. There wasn't even a flicker of surprise when I pressed the plastic against his face. Plastic, you note. It wouldn't leave any telltale threads in the nostrils or windpipe. Not that Hewson would have noticed, poor fool. Baddeley's diary was on the table and I took it away with me just in case he'd made any incriminating entries. Just as well. He had, I discovered, a tedious habit of recording precisely where he'd been and when. But I didn't break into the bureau. I didn't need to. You can put that little peccadillo down to Wilfred. He must have been frantic to get his eyes on the old man's will. Incidentally, I never found your postcard and I suspect Wilfred looked no further once he'd found the will. Probably the old man tore it up. He disliked keeping trifles. Afterwards I went back and slept in some discomfort in the car. Next morning I rejoined the London road and arrived here when all the excitement was over. I saw in the diary that he had invited an A.D. to stay and that the visitor was expected on the first of October. It struck me as a bit odd. The old man didn't have visitors. So I planted the poison pen letter the evening before, just in case Baddeley had confided that something was on his mind. I must say, it was a bit disconcerting to discover that the mysterious A.D. was you, my dear Commander. Had I known, I might have tried for a little more subtlety."

"And the stole? He was wearing his stole."

"I should have removed it, but one can't remember everything. You see, he didn't believe I was protecting Dennis to save Wilfred grief or out of kindness to Dennis. He knew me too well. When he accused me of corrupting Dennis, of using Toynton for some purpose of my own, I said that I would tell him the truth, that I wanted to make my confession. He must have known in his heart that this was death, that I was only amusing myself. But he couldn't take the risk. If he refused to take me seriously, then all his life would have been a lie. He hesitated for just two seconds, then he put the stole round his neck."

"Didn't he even give you the gratification of a flicker of fear?"

"Oh, no! Why should he? We were alike in one thing. Neither of us feared death. I don't know where Baddeley thought he was going as he just had time to make that last archaic sign of his allegiance, but wherever it was he apparently saw nothing to fear. Neither do I. I know just as certainly as he did what will follow my death. Annihilation. It would be unreasonable to fear that. I'm not so unreasonable. Once you have lost the fear of death—absolutely lost it—then all other fears are meaningless. Nothing can touch you. All that is necessary is to keep the means of death to hand. Then one is invulnerable. I apologize for the fact that, in my case, it has to be a gun. I do realize that at the moment I look melodramatic, ridiculous. But I can't fancy killing myself any other way. Drowning? That onrush of suffocating water? Drugs? Some interfering fool might drag me back. Besides, I do fear that shadow land between life and death. A knife? Messy and uncertain. There are three bullets here, Dalgliesh. One for you, and two, in case they should be needed, for me."

"If you trade in death as you do, it's as well no doubt to come to terms with it."

"Everyone who takes hard drugs wants to die. You know that as well as I do. There is no other way they can do it with so little inconvenience and so much profit to others, and with such pleasure to themselves, at least initially."

"And Lerner? I suppose you paid his mother's nursing home fees. What are they, about £200 a month? You got him cheap. Even so, he must have known what he was bringing in."

"Will be bringing in, three days from now. Will go on bringing in. I told him that it was cannabis, a perfectly harmless drug; one which an over-sensitive government have chosen to make illegal but which my London friends happen to fancy and are prepared to pay highly for. He chooses to believe me. He knows the truth, but he won't admit to himself that he knows. That's reasonable, sensible, a necessary self-deception. It's how we all manage to go on living. You must know that your job is a dirty job, crooks catching crooks, and that you waste your intelligence by doing it. But it wouldn't exactly add to your peace of mind to admit the fact. And if you ever chuck it, you won't give that as your reason. Are you going to chuck it, by the way? Somehow I've gained the impression that you might be."

"That shows some discernment. I did have it in mind. But not now."

The decision to go on, arrived at when and why Dalgliesh didn't know, seemed to him as irrational as the decision to give up. It wasn't a victory. A kind of defeat even. But there would be time enough, if he lived, to analyze the vicissitudes of that personal conflict. Like Father Baddeley, a man lived and died as he had to. He heard Julius's amused voice.

"A pity. But as this seems likely to be your last job, why not tell me how you found me out."

"Is there time? I don't relish spending my last five minutes in a recital of professional incompetence. It won't give me any satisfaction and I don't see why I should gratify your curiosity."

"No. But it's more in your interests than mine. Oughtn't you to be playing for time? Besides, if it's fascinating enough I might relax my guard, might give you a chance to pounce or fling a chair at me or whatever they train you to do in this kind of situation. Or somebody may come, or I may even change my mind."

"Will you?"

"No."

"Then gratify my curiosity. I can guess about Grace Willison. You killed her in the same way you killed Father Baddeley once you decided that I was getting dangerously suspicious, because she could type by heart the list of Friends, the list which included your distributors. But Maggie Hewson, why did she have to die?"

"Because of something she knew. Haven't you guessed that? I've over-estimated you. She knew that Wilfred's miracle was a delusion. I drove the Hewsons and Victor to London for his appointment at St. Saviour's hospital. Eric and Maggie went to the medical records department to have a look at Wilfred's folder. I suppose they wanted to gratify a natural professional curiosity while they were there. They discovered that he'd never had disseminated sclerosis, that his latest tests had shown that it was a wrong diagnosis. All he'd suffered from was hysterical paralysis. But I must be shocking you, my dear Commander. You're a pseudo-scientist, aren't you? It must be hard for you to accept that medical technology can err."

"No. I believe in the possibility of a wrong diagnosis."

"Wilfred, apparently, doesn't share your healthy scepticism. He never returned to the hospital for his next checkup, so no one bothered to write to him about their little mistake. Why should they? But it was knowledge that the two Hewsons couldn't keep to themselves. They told me, and subsequently Maggie must have told Holroyd. He probably guessed on the drive back to Toynton that something was up. I tried to bribe her with whisky to keep the knowledge to herself—she actually believed in my solicitude for dear Wilfred—and it worked until Wilfred excluded her from the decision on the future of the home. She was furious. She told me that she planned to burst into the last session at the end of the meditation and publicly proclaim the truth. I couldn't risk that. It was the one fact, the only fact, that could have made him sell out. It would have stopped the hand-over to the Ridgewell Trust. Toynton Grange and the pilgrimage had to go on.

"She wasn't really looking forward to the fracas that would follow breaking the news and it was easy enough to persuade her to leave the party at Toynton Grange to indulge their various reactions to her news and escape up to town with me immediately afterwards. I suggested that she should leave a deliberately ambiguous note, one which could be read as a threat of suicide. Then she could return to Toynton if and when she felt like it and see how Eric was reacting as a presumptive widower. It was the kind of histrionic gesture which appealed to dear Maggie. It got her out of an awkward situation here, provided the maximum of worry and inconvenience to Wilfred and Eric, and provided her with a free holiday in my London flat and the prospect of plenty of excitement if and when she chose to return. She even volunteered to fetch the rope herself. We sat there drinking together until she was too fuddled to suspect me but still sober enough to write the note. The last scrawled lines, the reference to the black tower, were, of course, added by me."

"So that was why she was bathed and dressed."

"Of course. Tarted up to make an effective entrance at Toynton Grange, and also I flatter myself, to impress me. I was gratified that I ranked clean underclothes and painted toe nails. I don't know what precisely she thought I had in mind for us when we reached London. Dear Maggie was never quite in touch with reality. To pack her contraceptive was perhaps more optimistic than discreet. But she may have had her plans. The dear girl was certainly delirious at the thought of leaving Toynton. She died happy I assure you."

"And, before leaving the cottage, you gave the signal with the light."

"I had to have some excuse for turning up and finding the body. It seemed prudent to add verisimilitude. Someone might have looked out of a window and been able to confirm my story. I didn't bargain for it being you. Finding you here busily doing your boy scout turn gave me a bad moment. And you were remarkably obstinate about not leaving the body."

It must have been almost as bad a moment, thought Dalgliesh, as finding Wilfred so nearly choked to death. There had been nothing faked about Julius's terror either then or after Maggie's death. He asked:

"And was Holroyd pushed over the cliff for the same reason, to stop him talking?"

Julius laughed:

"Now this will amuse you; a delicious irony. I didn't even know that Maggie had confided in Holroyd until I challenged her with it after his death. And Dennis never knew. Holroyd began taunting Dennis as he usually did. Dennis was more or less inured to it and merely moved with his book a little way apart. Then Holroyd began on a more sinister line of torment. He began shouting at Dennis. He wondered what Wilfred would say when he learned that his precious pilgrimages were a fraud, that Toynton Grange itself was founded on a lie. He told Dennis to make the most of the next pilgrimage; it would certainly be the last. Dennis panicked; he thought that Holroyd had discovered about the drug smuggling. He didn't pause to ask himself how in the hell Holroyd could have found out. He told me afterwards that he couldn't even remember scrambling to his feet, releasing the brakes and hurling the chair forward. But he did, of course. There was no one else to do it. It couldn't have landed where it did if it hadn't gone over the cliff with considerable force. I was on the beach beneath them when Holroyd came over. One of the irritating things about that murder was that I've never received any sympathy for the traumatic experience of having Holroyd smashed to death only twenty yards from me. I hope you will give it to me now."

Dalgliesh reflected that the murder must have been doubly convenient for Julius. It removed Holroyd and his dangerous knowledge; it put Dennis Lerner finally in his power. He said:

"And you disposed of the two side pieces of the wheelchair while Lerner was fetching help."

"About fifty yards away, down a deep cleft between two rocks. It seemed, at the time, a sensible way of complicating the case. Without the brakes no one could be sure that it wasn't an accident. On reflection I should have left well alone and let it be assumed that Holroyd killed himself. Essentially he did. That's what I've persuaded Dennis."

Dalgliesh asked:

"What are you going to do now?"

"Put a bullet in your head, conceal your body in your own car and get rid of both together. It's a trite method of murder I know, but I understand that it works."

Dalgliesh laughed. He was surprised that the sound could be so spontaneous.

"You propose to drive about sixty miles, I take it, in an easily identifiable car with the murdered body of a Commander of the Metropolitan Police in the boot—his own boot incidentally. A number of men of my acquaintance in the maximum security wings of Parkhurst and Durham would admire your nerve even while not exactly relishing the prospect of welcoming you to their company. They're a quarrelsome, uncivilized bunch. I don't think you're going to have a lot in common."

"I shall be at risk. But you'll be dead."

"Of course. So in effect will you from the moment the bullet enters my body, unless you count a life sentence as living. Even if you try to fake finger prints on the trigger, they'll know that I was murdered. I'm not the type to kill myself or to drive my car into remote woods and quarries to put a bullet in my brain. And the forensic evidence will give the lab a field day."

"If they find your body. How long before they even begin looking? Three weeks?"

"They'll be looking hard. If you can think of a suitable spot to dump me and the car, so can they. Don't assume that the police can't read an ordnance survey. And how do you propose to get back here? By picking up a train at Bournemouth or Winchester? By hitchhiking, hiring a bicycle, walking through the night? You can hardly travel on to London by train, and pretend that you joined the train at Wareham. It's a small station and you're known there. Going or returning, you'll be remembered."

Julius said consideringly:

"You're right, of course. Then it means the cliffs. They must fish you out of the sea."

"With a bullet in my head? Or are you expecting me to walk over the cliff edge to suit your convenience? You could try physical force, of course, but then you'll have to come dangerously close, close enough for a fight. We're fairly evenly matched. I take it you don't intend to be dragged over with me? Once they find my body and that bullet, then you're finished. The trail begins here remember. I was last seen alive when the Toynton Grange bus left, and there's no one here but we two."

It was then that, simultaneously, they heard the distant slam of the front door. The sound, sharp as a gunshot, was followed by the thud of footsteps, heavy and firm, crossing the front hall.

# III

Julius said quickly:

"Call out, and I kill you both. Stand to the left of the door."

The footsteps were crossing the central hall now unnaturally loud in the eerie silence. Both men held their breath. Philboy stood in the doorway.

He saw the gun immediately. His eyes widened and then blinked rapidly. He looked from one man to the other. When he spoke he sounded hoarse, apologetic. He spoke directly to Dalgliesh like a child explaining a misdemeanor:

"Wilfred sent me back early. Dot thought she'd left the gas on."

His eyes turned again to Julius. This time the terror was unmistakable. He said "Oh, no!" Almost instantaneously, Julius fired. The crack of the revolver, although expected, was still shattering, still unbelievable. Philby's body stiffened, rocked, then fell backward like an axed tree with a crash which shook the room. The bullet had gone in precisely between the eyes. Dalgliesh knew that this was where Julius had intended it to go; that he had used this necessary killing to demonstrate that he knew how to use his gun. This had been target practice. He said calmly, his gun now turned on Dalgliesh again:

"Go over to him."

Dalgliesh bent by the dead man. The eyes still seemed to hold their last look of wild surprise. The wound was a neat grumous slit in the low heavy forehead, so unremarkable that it could have been used for a forensic ballistics demonstration of the effect of discharge at six feet. There were no powder marks, as yet little blood, only the soiling of the skin by the spin of the bullet. It was a precise, almost decorative stigma giving no clue to the destructive tumult within.

Julius said:

"That settles the score for my smashed marble. Is there an exit wound?"

Gently Dalgliesh turned the heavy head.

"No. You must have hit a bone."

"That's what I intended. Two bullets left. But this is a bonus, Commander. You were wrong about my being the last person to see you alive. I shall drive away to establish my alibi and, in the eyes of the police, the last person to see you alive will have been Philby, a criminal with a propensity to violence. Two bodies in the sea with bullet wounds. A pistol, licensed, I may say, stolen from my bedside drawer. Let the police concoct a theory to explain that. It shouldn't be difficult. Is there any blood?"

"Not yet. There will be. But not much."

"I'll remember that. It will be easy enough to wipe it from this linoleum. Get that plastic hood from Carwardine's bust of Wilfred and tie it over his head. Use his own tie. And hurry. I shall be just six paces behind you. And if I get impatient I might feel it worthwhile doing my own work."

Hooded with white plastic, his wound a third eye, Philby was transformed into an inert guy, its bulging body grotesquely stuffed into a dapper undersized suit, its tie askew under the clownish fea tures. Julius said:

"Now get one of the lighter wheelchairs."

He motioned Dalgliesh once again towards the workroom and followed, always a careful six feet behind. Three folded chairs were standing against the wall. Dalgliesh prized one open and wheeled it in beside the body. There would be finger prints to find here. But what did they prove? This might even be the chair in which he had wheeled Grace Willison.

"Now get him into it."

As Dalgliesh hesitated he said, allowing his voice a trace of controlled impatience:

"I don't want to have to manage two bodies alone. But I can if I need to. There's a hoist in the bathroom. If you can't lift him unaided, then get it. But I thought they taught policemen useful little knacks like this."

Dalgliesh managed without the hoist. But it wasn't easy. The wheel brakes slid on the linoleum and it took more than two minutes before the heavy, unresponsive body slumped back against the canvas. Dalgliesh had succeeded in gaining some time but at a cost; he had lost strength. He knew that he would stay alive just as long as his mind with its store of dreadfully appropriate experience, and his physical strength could be used by Julius. It would be inconvenient for Julius to have to carry two bodies to the cliff edge, but it could be done. Toynton Grange had facilities for moving inert bodies. At present Dalgliesh was less of an encumbrance alive than dead, but the margin was dangerously narrow; there was no sense in reducing it further. The optimum moment for action would come, and it would come for both of them. Both of them were waiting for it, Dalgliesh to attack, Julius to shoot. Both knew the cost of a mistake in recognizing that moment. Two bullets left and he had to ensure that neither of them ended in his body. And as long as Julius kept his distance and held the gun he was inviolable. Somehow Dalgliesh had to draw him close enough for physical contact. Somehow he had to divert that concentration if only for a fraction of a second.

Julius said:

"And now we'll take a walk together to Toynton Cottage."

He still kept his careful distance behind as Dalgliesh wheeled the chair with its grotesque burden down the ramp of the front door and across the headland. The sky was a grey suffocating blanket pressing down on them. The close air was harsh and metallic on the tongue and smelt as strong as rotting seaweed. In the half-light the pebbles on the path glittered like semi-precious stones. Half way across the headland Dalgliesh heard a high querulous wail and, looking back, saw that Jeoffrey was following them, tail erect. The cat padded behind Julius for another fifty yards and then, as unpredictably as he had appeared, turned tail and made off for home. Julius, his unblinking eyes on Dalgliesh's back, seemed to notice neither his arrival nor his departure. They walked on in silence. Philby's head had fallen back, his neck collared by the canvas of the chair. His cyclops wound, gummed to the plastic, stared into Dalgliesh's face in what seemed mute reproach. The path was dry. Looking down Dalgliesh saw that the wheels made only an imperceptible thread on the patches of dry turf and the dusty, gritty path. And behind him he could hear Julius's shoes scuffing the marks into oblivion. There would be no useful evidence left here.

And now they stood on the stone patio. It seemed to shake under their feet with the thunder of the waves as if earth and sea anticipated the coming storm. But the tide was ebbing. No curtain of spray rose between them and the cliff edge. Dalgliesh knew that it was the moment of great danger. He made himself laugh aloud, and wondered whether the sound rang as false to Julius's ears as it did to his own.

"Why so amused?"

"It's easy to see that your killing is normally done at a distance, a commercial transaction merely. You propose to hurl us into the sea at your own back door, a broad enough hint for even the stupidest detective constable. And they won't be putting stupid officers on this crime. Your cleaning woman is expected this morning isn't she? And this is one part of the coast with a beach, even at high tide. I thought you wanted to delay discovery of the bodies."

"She won't come out here. She never does."

"How do you know what she does when you aren't here? She may shake the dusters over the cliff. It may even be her habit to paddle. But have it your own way. I'm merely pointing out that your only hope of success—and I don't rate it high—is to delay discovery of our bodies. No one will start looking for Philby until the pilgrimage returns in three days' time. If you get rid of my car it will be even longer before they start looking for me. That gives you opportunity to dispose of this consignment of heroin before the hunt is up, assuming you still intend to let Lerner bring it in. But don't let me interfere."

Julius's hand on the gun did not waver. As if considering a proposition for a picnic site, he said:

"You're right, of course. You ought to go into deep water and further along the coast. The best place is the black tower. The sea will be still washing the cliffs there. We've got to get him to the tower."

"How? He must weigh over twelve stone. I can't push him unaided up the cliff edge. You'll hardly be much help if you walk behind with a gun in my back. And what about wheel marks?"

"The rain will finish those. And we shan't go up the headland.

We'll drive along the coast road and approach the tower over the cliff as we did when we rescued Anstey. Once the couple of you are in the boot of the car I'll watch for Mrs. Reynolds through my glasses. She cycles in from Toynton village, and she's always exactly on time. We ought to plan to meet her just outside the boundary gate. I'll stop and let her know that I shan't be back for dinner. That pleasant minute of ordinary conversation should impress the coroner if they ever get your bodies to an inquest. And eventually, the tedious business over, I'll drive off to Dorchester for an early luncheon."

"With the wheelchair and the plastic hood in the boot?"

"With the chair and the hood locked in the boot. I shall establish an alibi for the whole of today and return to Toynton Grange this evening. And I shan't forget to wash the plastic hood before replacing it, dust the chair to remove your prints and examine the floor for bloodstains. And, of course, retrieve the cartridge case. Were you hoping I would overlook that? Don't worry, Commander. I do realize that, by then, I'll be planning without your valuable assistance, but thanks to you, I shall have a day or two to work out the details. One of two sophistications attract me. I'm wondering if I could make use of the smashed marble. Couldn't that be worked in to provide the motive for Philby's murderous attack on you?"

"I should keep it simple."

"Perhaps you're right. My first two murders were models of simplicity and none the worse for it. Now get him into the boot of the Mercedes. It's parked at the back. But first through into the scullery. You'll find two sheets in the washing machine. Take the one from the top. I don't want fibres and shoe dust in the car."

"Won't Mrs. Reynolds notice that one is missing?"

"She washes and irons tomorrow. A woman of strict routine. By this evening I shall have replaced it. Don't waste time."

Julius's mind must be registering every second, thought Dalgliesh, yet his voice betrayed no anxiety. Not once did he glance at his watch, or even at the clock on the kitchen wall. He kept his eyes and the muzzle of the Luger on his victim. Somehow that concentration had to be broken. And the time was running out.

The Mercedes was parked outside the stone garage. Under Julius's direction Dalgliesh raised the unlocked lid of the boot and spread the creased sheet over the floor. It was an easy matter to tumble Philby's body from the wheelchair. Dalgliesh folded the chair and placed it on top of the body. Julius said:

"Now get in beside him."

Could this be the best opportunity, the last opportunity even, to act; here outside Julius's own cottage with the murdered man in his car and the evidence plain? But plain to whom? Dalgliesh knew that if he sprang on Julius now he would gain nothing but a second's release from frustration and anger before the bullet hit him. Two bodies instead of one would be driven to the black tower and tumbled into deep water. In his mind's eye he could see Julius poised in solitary triumph on the edge of the cliff, the gun curving through the air like a falling bird to cleave the tumbling waves, beneath which two bodies were being torn and tugged by the ebbing tide. The plan would go ahead. A little more tedious, taking longer since there would be two bodies to wheel unaided across the headland. But who was there to prevent it? Certainly not Mrs. Reynolds even now cycling along the road from Toynton village. And if she suspected, if she even mentioned casually when she dismounted to greet Julius on the road that she had heard what sounded like a shot? Then there were still two bullets left in the gun. And he was no longer sure that Julius was sane.

But there was at least something he could do at this moment, something he had planned to do. But it wasn't going to be easy. He had hoped that, for a couple of seconds at least, the raised lid of the boot would have partly screened him from Julius's view. But Julius was standing immediately behind the car; Dalgliesh was in full view. But there was one advantage. The grey eyes never flickered, dared not flicker from his face. If he were quick and cunning, if he were lucky, he might bring it off. He placed his hands as if casually on his hips. He could feel the slight weight of his thin leather wallet in his back trouser pocket lying curved against his buttock. Julius said with dangerous quietness:

"I said get in on top of him. I'm not risking driving with you any closer."

Dalgliesh's right thumb and forefinger twisted at the pocket button. Thank God the button hole was reasonably loose. He said:

"Then you'd better drive fast unless you want to have a corpse dead of suffocation to explain."

"A night or two in the sea and your lungs will be too waterlogged for that kind of diagnosis."

The button was undone now. He insinuated his right forefinger and thumb gently into the top of the pocket and grasped the wallet. Everything now depended on its sliding out easily, on his being able to drop it unseen behind the wheel of the car. He said:

"They won't, you know. The PM will show perfectly clearly that I was dead before I hit the water."

"And so you will be, with a bullet in your body. Given that, I doubt whether they'll look for signs of suffocation. But thank you for the warning. I'll drive fast. Now get in."

Dalgliesh shrugged his shoulders and bent with sudden energy to get into the boot as if momentarily relinquishing hope. He rested his left hand on the bumper. Here, at least, there would be a palm mark which would be difficult to explain. But then he remembered. He had rested his palm on the bumper when loading the shepherd's crook, the sacks and the besom into the boot. It was only a small discouragement but it depressed him. He let his right hand dangle and the leather slipped from his finger and thumb to fall under the right wheel. No dangerously quiet word of command followed. Julius neither spoke nor moved, and he was still alive. With luck he would stay alive now until they reached the black tower. He smiled at the irony that his heart should now rejoice at a gift which a short month ago he had so grudgingly welcomed.

The boot lid slammed down. He was cramped in total blackness, total silence. He felt a second of claustrophobic panic, the irresistible urge to stretch his curled body and batter his clenched hands against the metal. The car did not move. Julius would be free now to check his timing. Philby's body lay heavily against him. He could smell the dead man as if he still breathed, an amalgam of grease, mothballs and sweat, the air of the boot was hot with his presence. He felt a moment of guilt that Philby was dead; he alive. Could he have saved him by calling out a warning? It could only have resulted, he knew, in both their deaths. Philby would have come on; must have come on. And even if he had turned and run, Julius would have followed and disposed of him. But now the feel of the cold moist flesh pressing against him, the hairs on the limp wrist sharp as bristles, pricked him like a reproach. The car rocked gently and began to move.

He had no means of knowing if Julius had seen the wallet and removed it; he thought it unlikely. But would Mrs. Reynolds find it? It was lying in her path. She would almost certainly dismount from her bicycle outside the garage. If she did find it, then he guessed she would have no rest until it was returned. He thought of his own Mrs. Mack, a Metropolitan police constable's widow who cleaned and occasionally cooked for him; of her almost obsessive honesty, her meticulous concern for her employer's belongings, the perpetual explanatory notes about missing laundry, the increased cost of shopping, a mislaid cuff link. No, Mrs. Reynolds wouldn't rest with the wallet in her possession. He had cashed a check on his last visit to Dorchester; the three ten pound notes, the bundle of credit cards, his police warrant, all would particularly worry her. She would probably waste some time going to Hope Cottage. Not finding him there, what then? His guess was that she would ring the local police, terrified that he might discover his loss before she had reported it. And the police? If he were lucky they would see the incongruity of a wallet dropped so conveniently in her path. Suspicious or not, they would be courteous enough to get in touch with him at once. They might find it worthwhile ringing Toynton Grange since the cottage was not on the telephone. They would discover that the telephone was inexplicably out of order. It was at least an even chance that they would think it worthwhile sending a patrol car, and if one were reasonably close it could come quickly. Logically, one action must follow another. And he had one piece of luck. Mrs. Reynolds, he remembered, was the village constable's widow. At least she wouldn't be afraid of using the telephone, would know whom to ring. His life depended on her seeing the wallet. A few square inches of brown leather on the paved courtyard. And the light was darkening under the stormladen sky.

Julius was driving very fast even over the bumpy ground of the headland. The car stopped. Now he would be opening the boundary gate. Another few seconds of driving and the car stopped again. Now he must have met Mrs. Reynolds and was exchanging that half-minute of conversation. Now they were off again, this time with smooth road under their wheels.

There was something else he could do. He moved his hand under his cheek and bit into his left thumb. The blood tasted warm and sweet. He smeared it across the roof of the boot and, scuffling aside the sheet, pressed his thumb into the carpet. Group AB rhesus negative. It was a rare enough group. And with any luck Julius would miss these minute telltale smears. He hoped the police searcher would be more perspicacious.

He began to feel stifled, his head thudded. He told himself that there was plenty of air, that this pressure on his chest was no more than psychological trauma. And then the car rocked gently and he knew that Julius was driving off the road and into the hollow behind the stone wall which divided the headland from the road. It was a convenient stopping place. Even if another car passed, and this was unlikely, the Mercedes wouldn't be visible. They had arrived. The final part of the journey was about to begin.

There were only about one hundred and fifty yards of rock-strewn and lumpy turf to where the black tower stood squat and malignant under the menacing sky. Dalgliesh knew that Julius would prefer to make a single journey. He would want to get as quickly as possible out of all sight of the road. He would want the business over so that he could get on his way. More important, he needed to make no physical contact with either victim. Their clothes would yield nothing when their bloated bodies were finally fished from the sea; but Julius would know how difficult to eradicate, without telltale cleaning, would be the infinitesimally small traces of hair, fibre or blood on his own clothes. So far he was absolutely clean. It would be one of his strongest cards. Dalgliesh would be allowed to live at least until they reached the shelter of the tower. He felt confident enough of this to take his time in getting Philby's body strapped into the chair. Afterwards he leaned for a moment over the handlebars breathing heavily, simulating more exhaustion than he felt. Somehow, despite the hard pushing ahead, he must conserve his strength. Julius slammed down the boot lid and said:

"Get a move on. The storm is almost on us."

But he didn't shift his fixed gaze to glance at the sky, nor had he need. They could almost smell the rain in the freshening breeze.

Although the wheels of the chair were well oiled the going was hard. Dalgliesh's hands slid on the rubber handgrips. Philby's body, strapped like a recalcitrant child, jerked and rolled as the wheels struck stones or clumps of grass. Dalgliesh felt the sweat rolling into his eyes. It gave him the opportunity he needed to get rid of his jacket. When it came to the last physical struggle the man least encumbered would have an advantage. He stopped pushing and stood gasping. The feet behind him stopped too.

It might happen now. There was nothing he could do if it did. He comforted himself with the thought that he would know nothing. One press of Julius's finger on the trigger and his busy fearful mind would be stilled. He remembered Julius's words. "I know what will happen to me when I die; annihilation. It would be unreasonable to fear that." If only it were that simple! But Julius did not press. The dangerously quiet voice behind him said:

"Well?"

"I'm hot. May I take off my jacket?"

"Why not? Drape it over Philby's knees. I'll chuck it in the sea after you. It would be torn off your body by the tide anyway."

Dalgliesh slid his arms from his jacket and placed it folded over Philby's knees. Without looking round he said:

"You'd be unwise to shoot me in the back. Philby was killed instantly. It has to look as if he shot me first but only to wound, before

I wrenched the gun from him and finished him off. No fight with only one gun could reasonably result in two instantaneous killings, and one in the small of the back."

"I know. Unlike you, I may be inexperienced in the cruder manifestations of violence but I'm not a fool and I do understand about firearms. Get on."

They moved forward, carefully distanced, Dalgliesh pushing his macabre passenger and hearing behind him the soft rustle of the following feet. He found himself thinking about Peter Bonnington. It was because an unknown boy, now dead, had been moved from Toynton Grange that he, Adam Dalgliesh, was now walking across Toynton Head with a gun at his back. Father Baddeley would have discerned a pattern. But then Father Baddeley had believed that there was a great underlying pattern. Given that assurance, all human perplexities were no more than exercises in spiritual geometry. Suddenly Julius began speaking. Dalgliesh could almost imagine that he felt the need to entertain his victim on this last tedious walk, that he was making some attempt at justification.

"I can't be poor again. I need money as I need oxygen. Not just enough; more than enough. Much more. Poverty kills. I don't fear death but I fear that particular slow and corrosive process of dying. You didn't believe me, did you—that story about my parents?"

"Not altogether. Was I expected to?"

"Yet that at least was true. I could take you to pubs in Westminster—Christ, you probably know them—and bring you face to face with what I fear; the pathetic elderly queens managing on their pensions. Or not managing. And they, poor sods, haven't even been used to having money. I have. I'm not ashamed of my nature. But if I'm to live at all, I have to be rich. Did you really expect me to let one sick old fool and a dying woman stand in my way?"

Dalgliesh didn't reply. Instead he asked:

"I suppose you came this way when you set fire to the tower."

"Of course. I did as we've done now, drove to the hollow and came on foot. I knew when Wilfred, a creature of habit, was likely to be in the tower and I watched him walk over the headland through my binoculars. If it wasn't that day, it would be another. There was no difficulty in helping myself to the key and a habit. I saw to that a day in advance. Anyone who knows Toynton Grange can move about it undetected. Even if I were seen, I don't have to explain my presence there. As Wilfred says, I'm one of the family. That's why killing Grace Willison was so easy. I was home and in bed soon after midnight and with no worse effects than cold legs and a little difficulty in getting to sleep. By the way, I ought to say, in case you harbor any doubts, that Wilfred knows nothing of the smuggling. If I were about to die and you to live instead of the other way round you could look forward to the pleasure of breaking the news. Both pieces of news. His miracle a delusion and his abode of love a staging post for death. I should give a great deal to see his face."

They were within feet now of the black tower. Without overtly changing direction Dalgliesh steered the wheelchair as close as he dared to the porch. The wind was gently rising in short moaning crescendos. But then, there would always be a breeze on this wind-scoured promontory of grass and rock. Suddenly he stopped. He held the chair with his left hand and half turned towards Julius, carefully balancing his weight. It was now. It had to be now.

Julius said sharply:

"Well, what is it?"

Time stopped. A second was stilled into infinity. In that brief, timeless lacuna, Dalgliesh's mind was drained free of tension and fear. It was as if he were detached from the past and the future, aware simultaneously of himself, of his adversary, of the sound, scent and color of sky, cliff and sea. The pent up anger at Father Baddeley's death, the frustration and indecision of the last few weeks, the controlled suspense of the past hour; all were calmed in this moment before their final release. He spoke, his voice, high and cracked, simulating terror. But, even to his own ears, the terror sounded horribly real.

"The tower! There's someone inside!"

It came again as he had prayed it would, the bone ends, piercing the torn flesh, scrabbling frantically against unyielding stone. He sensed rather than heard the sharp hiss of Julius's intake of breath. Then time moved on, and in that second, Dalgliesh sprang.

As they fell, Julius's body beneath him, Dalgliesh felt the hammer blow on his right shoulder, the sudden numbness, the sticky warmth, soothing as a balm, flowing into his shirt. The shot echoed back from the black tower, and the headland came alive. A cloud of gulls rose screaming from the rock face. Sky and cliff were a tumult of wildly beating wings. And then as if the laden clouds had waited for this signal, the sky was ripped open with the sound of tearing canvas, and the rain fell.

They fought like famished animals clawing at their prey, without skill, eyes stung and blinded by rain, locked in a rigor of hate.

Dalgliesh, even with the weight of Julius's body beneath him, felt his strength ebbing. It had to be now, now while he was on top. And he still had the use of his good left shoulder. He twisted Julius's wrist into the clammy earth and pressed with all his strength on the beat of the pulse. He could feel Julius's breath like a hot blast on his face. They lay cheek to cheek in a horrible parody of exhausted love. And still the gun did not drop from those rigid fingers. Slowly, in painful spasms, Julius bent his right arm towards Dalgliesh's head. And then the gun went off. Dalgliesh felt the bullet pass over his hair to spend itself harmlessly in the sheeting rain.

And now they were rolling towards the cliff edge. Dalgliesh, weakening, felt himself clutching Julius as if for support. The rain was a stinging lance on his eyeballs. His nose was pressed suffocatingly into the sodden earth. Humus. A comforting and familiar last smell. His fingers clawed impotently at the turf as he rolled. It came apart in moist clumps in his hands. And suddenly Julius was kneeling over him, hands at his throat, forcing his head back over the cliff edge. The sky, the sea and the sheeting rain were one turbulent whiteness, one immense roaring in his ears. Julius's streaming face was out of his reach, the rigid arms pressing down the cruel encircling hands. He had to bring that face closer. Deliberately he slackened his muscles and loosened his already weakening hold on Julius's shoulders. It worked. Julius relaxed his grasp and instinctively bent his head forward to look into Dalgliesh's face. Then he screamed as Dalgliesh's thumbs gouged into his eyes. Their bodies fell apart. And Dalgliesh was on his feet and scrambling up the headland to fling himself behind the wheelchair.

He crouched behind it, heaving against the sagging canvas for support, watching Julius advance, hair streaming, eyes wild, the strong arms stretching forward, eager for that final clutch. Behind him the tower streamed black blood. The rain slashed like hail against the boulders, sending up a fine mist to mingle with his hoarse breath. Its painful rhythm tore at his chest and filled his ears like the death throes of some great animal. Suddenly he released the brakes and with his last strength hurled the chair forward. He saw his murderer's astonished and desperate eyes. For one second he thought that Julius would fling himself against the chair. But at the last moment he leapt aside, and the chair and its dreadful burden sailed over the cliff.

"Explain that when they fish it out!" Dalgliesh never knew whether he spoke to himself or shouted the words aloud. And then Julius was on him.

This was the end. He wasn't fighting now, only letting himself be rolled downwards towards death. He could hope for nothing except to carry Julius over with him. Hoarse, discordant cries were hurting his ears. The crowd were shouting for Julius. All the world was shouting. The headland was full of voices, of shapes. Suddenly the weight on his chest lifted. He was free. He heard Julius whisper "Oh, no!" Dalgliesh heard the sad despairing protest as clearly as if the voice had been his own. It wasn't the last horrified cry of a desperate man. The words were quiet, rueful, almost amused. Then the air was darkened by a shape, black as a great bird, passing spread-eagled over his head in what seemed slow motion. Earth and sky turned slowly together. A solitary seagull screamed. The earth thudded. A white ring of amorphous blobs was bending over him. But the ground was soft, irresistibly soft. He let his consciousness bleed away into it.

# IV

The surgical registrar came out of Dalgliesh's room to where a group of large men were obstructing the corridor. He said:

"He'll be OK for questioning in about half an hour or so. We've extracted the bullet. I've handed it over to your chap. We've put up a drip but don't let that worry you. He's lost a fair amount of blood but there's no real damage. There's no harm now in your going in."

Daniel asked:

"Is he conscious?"

"Barely. Your chap in there says he's been quoting King Lear. Something about Cordelia anyway. And he's fretting because he hasn't said thank you for the flowers."

Daniel said:

"He won't be needing flowers this time, thank God. He can thank Mrs. Reynolds's sharp eyes and common sense for that. And the storm helped. But it was a close thing. Court would have carried him over the cliff if we hadn't come up on them before he noticed us. Well, we may as well go in if you think it's OK."

A uniformed constable appeared, helmet under his arm.

"Well?"

"The Chief Constable's on his way, Sir. And they've pulled out Philby's body half strapped to a wheelchair."

"And Court's?"

"Not yet, Sir. They reckon he'll be washed in further down the coast."

Dalgliesh opened his eyes. His bed was ringed with black and white figures advancing and receding in a ritual dance. Nurses' caps floated like disembodied wings above the smudged faces as if uncertain where to settle. Then the picture cleared and he saw the circle of half familiar faces. Sister was here, of course. And the consultant had got back early from his wedding. He wasn't wearing his rose any more. The faces broke simultaneously into wary smiles. He made himself smile back. So it wasn't acute leukemia; it wasn't any kind of leukemia.

He was going to get better. And once they'd removed this heavy contraption which for some reason they'd fixed to his right arm he could get out of here and back to his job. Wrong diagnosis or not, it was nice of them, he thought sleepily, looking up into the ring of smiling eyes, to look so pleased that he wasn't going to die after all.

# Death of an Expert Witness

# CONTENTS

# AUTHOR'S NOTE

There is no official forensic science laboratory in East Anglia and, even if there were, it is in the highest degree improbable that it would have anything in common with Hoggatt's Laboratory, whose staff, like all other characters in this story—even the most unpleasant—are purely imaginary and bear no resemblance to any person living or dead.

# BOOK ONE

·

# A Call to Murder

# I

The call had come at 6:12 precisely. It was second nature to him now to note the time by the illuminated dial of his electric bedside clock before he had switched on his lamp, a second after he had felt for and silenced the raucous insistence of the telephone. It seldom had to ring more than once, but every time he dreaded that the peal might have woken Nell. The caller was familiar, the summons expected. It was Detective-Inspector Doyle. The voice, with its softly intimidating suggestion of Irish burr, came to him strong and confident, as if Doyle's great bulk loomed over the bed.

"Doc Kerrison?" The interrogation was surely unnecessary. Who else in this half-empty, echoing house would be answering at 6:12 in the morning? He made no reply and the voice went on.

"We've got a body. On the wasteland—a clunch field—a mile northeast of Muddington. A girl. Strangulation by the look of it. It's probably pretty straightforward but as it's close . . ."

"All right. I'll come."

The voice expressed neither relief nor gratitude. Why should it? Didn't he always come when summoned? He was paid well enough for his availability, but that wasn't the only reason why he was so obsessively conscientious. Doyle, he suspected, would have respected him more if he had occasionally been less accommodating. He would have respected himself more.

"It's the first turn off the A142 after you leave Gibbet's Cross. I'll have a man posted."

He replaced the receiver, swung his legs out of bed, and, reaching for his pencil and pad, noted the details while they were still fresh in his mind. In a clunch field. That probably meant mud, particularly after yesterday's rain. The window was slightly open at the bottom. He pushed it open, wincing at the rasp of the wood, and put out his head. The rich, loamy smell of the fen autumn night washed over his face, strong, yet fresh. The rain had stopped and the sky was a tumult of gray clouds through which the moon, now almost full, reeled like a pale, demented ghost. His mind stretched out over the deserted fields and the desolate dikes to the wide, moon-bleached sands of the Wash and the creeping fringes of the North Sea. He could fancy that he smelled its medicinal tang in the rain-washed air. Somewhere out there in the darkness, surrounded by all the paraphernalia of violent death, was a body. His mind recalled the familiar ambience of his trade: men moving like black shadows behind the glare of the arc lights, the police cars tidily parked; the flap of the screens, desultory voices conferring as they watched for the first lights of his approaching car. Already they would be consulting their watches, calculating how long it would be before he could make it.

Shutting the window with careful hands, he tugged trousers over his pajamas and pulled a polo-necked sweater over his head. Then he picked up his flashlight, switched off the bedside light, and made his way downstairs, treading warily and keeping close to the wall to avoid the creaking treads. But there was no sound from Eleanor's room. He let his mind wander down the twenty yards of landing and the three stairs to the back bedroom where his sixteen-year-old daughter lay. She was always a light sleeper, uncannily sensitive even in sleep to the ring of the telephone. But she couldn't possibly have heard. He had no need to worry about three-year-old William. Once asleep, he never woke before morning.

Actions as well as thought were patterned. His routine never varied. He went first to the small washroom near the back door where his wellington boots, the thick red socks protruding like a pair of amputated feet, stood ready at the door. Pushing up his sleeves over the elbow, he swilled cold water over his hands and arms, then bent down and sluiced the whole of his head. He performed this act of almost ceremonial cleansing before and after every case. He had long ago ceased to ask himself why. It had become as comforting and necessary as a religious ritual, the brief preliminary washing which was like a dedication, the final ablution which was both a necessary chore and an absolution, as if by wiping the smell of his job from his body he could cleanse it from his mind. The water splashed heavily against the glass, and rising to fumble for a towel, he saw his face distorted, the mouth hanging, the heavily lidded eyes half hidden by glistening weeds of black hair like the surfacing visage of a drowned man. The melancholy of the early hours took hold of him. He thought:

"I'm forty-five next week and what have I achieved? This house, two children, a failed marriage, and a job that I'm frightened of losing because it's the only thing I've made a success of." The Old Rectory, inherited from his father, was unmortgaged, unencumbered. This wasn't true, he thought, of anything else in his anxiety-ridden life. Love, the lack of it, the growing need, the sudden terrifying hope of it, was only a burden. Even his job, the territory where he moved with most assurance, was hedged with anxiety.

As he dried his hands carefully, finger by finger, the old familiar worry returned, heavy as a morbid growth. He hadn't yet been appointed as Home Office Pathologist in succession to old Dr. Stoddard and he very much wanted to be. The official appointment wouldn't give him more money. The police already employed him on an item of service basis and paid generously enough for each case. That and the fees for coroner's postmortems provided an income that was one of the reasons why his professional colleagues in the Pathology Department of the district general hospital both envied and resented his unpredictable absences on police work, the long days in court, the inevitable publicity.

Yes, the appointment was important to him. If the Home Office looked elsewhere it would be difficult to justify to the Area Health Authority a continuing private arrangement with the local Force. He wasn't even sure that they would want him. He knew himself to be a good forensic pathologist, reliable, more than competent professionally, almost obsessively thorough and painstaking, a convincing and unflappable witness. The Force knew that their meticulously erected edifices of proof wouldn't fall to pieces under cross-examination when he was in the witness box, although he sometimes suspected that they found him too scrupulous for complete comfort. But he hadn't the easy masculine camaraderie, the blend of cynicism and *machismo* which had bound old Doc Stoddard so strongly to the Force. If they had to do without him he wouldn't be greatly missed, and he doubted whether they would put themselves out to keep him.

The garage light was blinding. The overhead door swung up easily to his touch and the light splayed out over the gravel of the drive and the unkempt verges of silvered grass. But at least the light wouldn't wake Nell. Her bedroom was at the back of the house. Before switching on the engine he studied his maps. Muddington. It was a town on the edge of his area, about seventeen miles to the northwest, less than half an hour's drive each way if he were lucky. If the laboratory scientists were there already—and Lorrimer, the Senior Biologist, never missed a homicide if he could help it—then there mightn't be much for him to do. Allow, say, an hour at the scene, and with luck he would be home again before Nell woke and she need never know that he had been away. He switched off the garage light. Carefully, as if the gentleness of his touch could somehow silence the engine, he turned on the ignition. The Rover moved slowly into the night.

## II

Standing motionless behind the curtains on the front landing, her right hand cupped around the pale flicker of her night-light, Eleanor Kerrison watched the sudden red blaze of the Rover's rear lights as the car stopped at the gate before turning left and accelerating out of sight. She waited until the glare of the headlights had finally faded from view. Then she turned and made her way along the corridor to William's room. She knew that he wouldn't have woken. His sleep was a sensuous gluttony of oblivion. And while he slept she knew that he was safe, that she could be free of anxiety. To watch him then was such a mingled sensation of yearning and pity that sometimes, frightened of her waking thoughts but more afraid of the nightmares of sleep, she would carry her night-light into his bedroom and crouch by the cot for an hour or more, her eyes fixed on his sleeping face, her restlessness soothed by his peace.

Although she knew that he wouldn't wake, she turned the handle of the door as carefully as if expecting it to explode. The night-light, burning steadily in its saucer, was unnecessary, its yellow gleam extinguished by the moonlight that streamed through the uncurtained windows. William, bagged in his grubby sleeping suit, lay as always on his back, both arms flung above his head. His head had flopped to one side and the thin neck, stretched so still that she could see the pulse beat, looked too fragile to bear the weight of his head. His lips were slightly parted, and she could neither see nor hear the thin whisper of breath. As she watched he suddenly opened sightless eyes, rolled them upward, then closed them with a sigh and fell again into his little semblance of death.

She closed the door softly behind her and went back to her own room next door. Dragging the eiderdown from her bed, she wrapped it around her shoulders and shuffled her way down the landing to the top of the stairs. The heavily studded oak banister curved down into the darkness of the hall from which the tick of the grandfather clock sounded as unnaturally loud and ominous as a time bomb. The atmosphere of the house came up to her nostrils, sour as a stale thermos flask, redolent with the sad effluent of stodgy clerical dinners. Placing the night-light against the wall, she sat down on the top stair, humping the eiderdown high over her shoulders and gazing into the darkness. The stair carpet was gritty to her bare soles. Miss Willard never vacuumed it, pleading that her heart couldn't stand the strain of lugging the cleaner from step to step, and her father never appeared to notice the drabness or dirtiness of his house. He was, after all, so seldom there. Sitting rigid in the darkness, she thought of her father. Perhaps he was already at the scene of the crime. It depended how far he had to drive. If it were on the very fringe of his area he might not be back until lunchtime.

But what she hoped was that he would return before breakfast so that he would find her here, crouched lonely and exhausted on the top stair, waiting for him, frightened because he had left her alone. He would put away the car quietly, leaving the garage open in case the thud of the door woke her, then sneak in like a thief at the back door. She would hear the swirl of water from the downstairs washroom, his footsteps on the tessellated floor of the hall. Then he would look up and see her. He would come running up the stairs, torn between anxiety for her and fear of disturbing Miss Willard, his face suddenly old with weariness and concern as he put his arms around her trembling shoulders.

"Nell, darling, how long have you been here? You shouldn't be out of bed. You'll get cold. Come on, old girl, there's nothing to be frightened of now. I'm back. Look, I'll take you back to bed again and you try to get some sleep. I'll see to the breakfast. Suppose I bring it up on a tray in about half an hour. How would you like that?"

And he would guide her back to her room, cajoling, murmuring reassurance, trying to pretend that he wasn't frightened, frightened that she would start to cry for her mother, that Miss Willard would appear, censorious and whining, complaining that she had to get her sleep, that the precarious little household would fall apart and he would be parted from William. It was William he loved, William he couldn't bear to lose. And he could keep William and stop the court from giving Mummy custody only if she were at home to help care for her brother.

She thought about the day ahead. It was Wednesday, a gray day. Not a black day when she wouldn't see her father at all, but not a yellow day like Sunday when, unless on call, he might be there most of the time. In the morning, immediately after breakfast, he would be at the public mortuary doing the postmortem. There would be other autopsies too, patients who had died in the hospital, the old, the suicides, the accident victims. But the body he was probably examining now would be first on the mortuary table. Murder has priority. Wasn't that what they always said at the lab? She mused, but without real curiosity, on what he might be doing at this very moment to that unknown cadaver, young or old, male or female. Whatever he was doing, the body wouldn't feel it, wouldn't know about it. The dead had nothing to be frightened of any more, and there was nothing to fear from them. It was the living who held the power to hurt. And suddenly two shadows moved in the darkness of the hall, and she heard her mother's voice, pitched high, frighteningly unfamiliar, a strained, cracked, alien voice.

"Always your job! Your bloody job! And my God, no wonder you're good at it. You haven't the guts to be a real doctor. You made one wrong diagnosis early on and that was the end, wasn't it? You couldn't take responsibility for living bodies, blood that can flow, nerves that can actually feel. All you're fit for is messing about with the dead. It makes you feel good, doesn't it, the way they defer to you? The phone calls at all hours of the day and night, the police escort. Never mind that I'm buried alive here in this bloody fen with your children. You don't even see me any more. I'd be more interesting to you if I were dead and laid out on your slab. At least you'd be forced to take some notice of me."

Then the low defensive mumble of her father's voice, dispirited, abject. She had listened in the darkness and wanted to call out to him:

"Don't answer her like that! Don't sound so defeated! Can't you understand that it only makes her despise you more?"

His words had come to her in snatches, barely audible.

"It's my job. It's what I do best. It's all that I can do." And then, more clearly: "It's what keeps us."

"Not me. Not any longer."

And then the slam of the door.

The memory was so vivid that for a second she thought she heard the echo of that slam. She stumbled to her feet, clutching the eiderdown around her, and opened her mouth to call to them. But then she saw that the hall was empty. There was nothing but the faint image of the stained glass in the front door where the moonlight streamed through, the ticking of the clock, the bundle of coats hanging from the hall stand. She sank back again onto the stair.

And then she remembered. There was something she had to do. Slipping her hand into her dressing-gown pocket she felt the cold, slippery plasticine of her model of Dr. Lorrimer. Carefully she drew it out through the folds of the eiderdown and held it close to the flame of the night-light. The model was a little misshapen, the face furred with fluff from her pocket, but it was still intact. She straightened the long limbs and pressed the strands of black cotton she had used for hair more firmly into the scalp. The white coat, cut from an old handkerchief, was particularly successful, she thought. It was a pity that she hadn't been able to use one of his handkerchiefs, a strand of his hair. The model represented more than Dr. Lorrimer who had been unkind to her and William, who had practically thrown them out of the laboratory. It stood for the whole of Hoggatt's Lab.

And now to kill it. Gently she knocked the head against the baluster. But the plasticine merely flattened, the head lost its identity. She remodeled it with careful fingers, then held it close to the flame. But the smell was disagreeable and she was afraid that the white linen would burst into flame. She dug the nail of her little finger deeply in behind the left ear. The cut was clean and sharp, right through to the brain. That was better. She sighed, satisfied. Holding the dead creature in her right palm, she squeezed the pink plasticine, the white coat, the cotton hair into one amorphous lump. Then, huddling deep into the eiderdown, she sat and waited for the dawn.

# III

The car, a green Morris Minor, had been toppled over the edge of a shallow depression in the wasteland and had lurched to rest on a grassy plateau about ten feet from the ridge like a clumsy animal going to earth. It must have been there for years, abandoned to the plunderers, an illicit plaything for the local children, a welcome shelter for the occasional vagrant like the seventy-year-old alcoholic who had stumbled on the body. The two front wheels had been removed, and the rusted back wheels with their rotting tires were firmly embedded in the chalky earth. The paintwork was battered and scratched, the interior stripped of instruments and steering wheel. Two mounted arc lights, one directed downward from the top of the bank and the other precariously planted on the edge of the plateau, illumined its stark decrepitude. Thus brightly lit it looked, thought Kerrison, like some grotesque and pretentious modern sculpture, symbolically poised on the brink of chaos. The back seat, its padding springing from the slashed plastic, had been ripped out and hurled to one side.

In the front seat rested the body of the girl. Her legs were decorously planted together, the glazed eyes were slyly half-open, the mouth, devoid of lipstick, was fixed in a drool elongated by two small trickles of blood. They gave a face that must have been pretty, or at least childishly vulnerable, the vacuous look of an adult clown. The thin coat, too thin surely for a night in early November, was pulled waist high. She was wearing stockings, and the suspender clips bit into plump white thighs.

Drawing close to the body, under the watchful eyes of Lorrimer and Doyle, he thought, as he often did at such a scene, that it looked unreal, an anomaly, so singularly and ridiculously out of place that he had to stifle a nervous impulse to laugh. He didn't feel this so strongly when a corpse was far advanced in decay. It was then as if the rotting, maggot-infested flesh, or the tags of matted clothing, had already become part of the earth that clung to and enclosed them, no more unnatural or frightening than a clump of compost or a drift of decaying leaves. But here, colors and outlines intensified in the glare, the body, still outwardly so human, looked an absurd burlesque, the skin of the pallid cheek as artificial as the stained plastic of the car against which it rested. It seemed ridiculous that she should be beyond help. As always he had to fight the impulse to fasten his mouth over hers and begin resuscitation, to plunge a needle into the still-warm heart.

He had been surprised to find Maxim Howarth, newly appointed Director of the Forensic Science Laboratory, at the scene, until he remembered that Howarth had said something about following through the next murder case. He supposed that he was expected to instruct. Withdrawing his head from the open door he said:

"It's almost certainly a case of manual throttling. The slight bleeding from the mouth is caused by the tongue being caught between the teeth. Manual strangulation is invariably homicidal. She couldn't have done this herself."

Howarth's voice was carefully controlled.

"I should have expected more bruising of the neck."

"That's usual, certainly. There's always some damage to the tissues, although the extent of the bruised area depends on the position of the assailant and victim, the way in which the neck is grasped as well as the degree of pressure. I'd expect to find deep-seated internal bruising, but it's possible to get this without many superficial signs. This happens when the murderer has maintained pressure until death; the vessels have been emptied of blood and the heart stops beating before the hands are removed. The cause of death is asphyxia, and one expects to find the usual signs of this. What is so interesting here is the cadaveric spasm. You'll see that she's clutching the bamboo handle of her bag. The muscles are absolutely rigid, proof that the grasp occurred at or about the moment of death. I've never before seen cadaveric spasm in a case of homicidal manual throttling, and it's interesting. She must have died extraordinarily quickly. But you'll get a clearer idea of what exactly happened when you watch the postmortem."

Of course, thought Howarth, the postmortem. He wondered how early Kerrison would expect to get down to that job. He wasn't afraid that his nerve would fail him, only his stomach, but he wished he hadn't said he would be there. There was no privacy for the dead; the most one could hope for was a certain reverence. It now seemed to him monstrous that tomorrow he, a stranger, would be looking unrebuked at her nakedness. But for the present he had seen enough. He could step aside now without loss of face. Turning up the collar of his Burberry against the chill morning air, he climbed up the slope to the rim of the hollow and stood looking down at the car. This must be what shooting a film was like: the brightly lit scene, the ennui of waiting for the chief actors to appear, the brief moments of activity, the concentrated attention to detail. The body could easily be that of an actress simulating death. He half expected one of the police to dart forward and rearrange her hair.

The night was nearly over. Behind him the eastern sky was already brightening, and the wasteland, which had been a formless void of darkness above the lumpy earth, was assuming an identity and a shape. To the west he could see the outline of houses, probably a council estate, a trim row of identical roofs and square slabs of darkness broken by patterned squares of yellow as the early risers switched on their lights. The track along which his car had bumped, rock-strewn and silver, alien as a moonscape in the glare of the headlights, took shape and direction, became ordinary. Nothing was left mysterious. The place was an arid scrubland between the two ends of the town, litter-strewn and edged with sparse trees above a ditch. He knew that the ditch would be dank with nettles and sour with rotting rubbish, the trees wounded by vandals, the trunks carved with initials, the low branches hanging torn from the boughs. Here was an urban no-man's-land, fit territory for murder.

It was a mistake to have come, of course; he should have realized that the role of voyeur was always ignoble. Few things were more demoralizing than to stand uselessly by while other men demonstrated their professional competence. Kerrison, that connoisseur of death, literally sniffing at the body. The photographers, taciturn, preoccupied with lighting and angles. Inspector Doyle, in charge of a murder case at last, impresario of death, tense with the suppressed excitement of a child at Christmas gloating over a new toy. Once, while waiting for Kerrison to arrive, Doyle had actually laughed, a hearty guffaw, filling the hollow. And Lorrimer? Before touching the body he had briefly crossed himself. It was so small and precise a gesture that Howarth could have missed it, except that nothing that Lorrimer did escaped him. The others seemed unsurprised at the eccentricity. Perhaps they were used to it. Domenica hadn't told him that Lorrimer was religious. But then his sister hadn't told him anything about her lover. She hadn't even told him that the affair was over. But he had needed only to look at Lorrimer's face during the past month to know that. Lorrimer's face, Lorrimer's hands. Odd that he hadn't noticed before how long the fingers were. With what apparent gentleness they had taped the plastic bags over the girl's hands to preserve, as he had tonelessly explained, conscientious in his role of instructor, any evidence under the fingernails. He had taken a sample of blood from the plump, flaccid arm, feeling for the vein as carefully as if she could still flinch at the needle's prick.

Lorrimer's hands. Howarth thrust the tormenting, brutally explicit images out of his mind. He had never before resented one of Domenica's lovers. He hadn't even been jealous of her dead husband. It had seemed to him perfectly reasonable that she should eventually wish to marry, just as she might choose, in a fit of boredom or acquisitiveness, to buy herself a fur coat or a new item of jewelry. He had even quite liked Charles Schofield. Why was it then that, even from the first moment, the thought of Lorrimer in his sister's bed had been intolerable? Not that he could ever have been in her bed, at least not at Leamings. He wondered yet again where they had managed to meet, how Domenica had contrived to take a new lover without the whole laboratory and the whole village knowing. How could they have met and where?

It had begun, of course, at that disastrous dinner party twelve months ago. At the time it had seemed both natural and civilized to celebrate the taking up of his directorship with a small private party at his house for the senior staff. They had, he remembered, eaten melon, followed by *boeuf stroganoff* and a salad. He and Domenica liked good food and, occasionally, she enjoyed cooking it. He had opened the 1961 claret for them because that was the wine he and Dom had chosen to drink and it hadn't occurred to him to offer his guests less. He and Dom had changed because that was their habit. It amused them to dine in some style, formally separating the working day from their evenings together. It hadn't been his fault that Bill Morgan, the Vehicle Examiner, had chosen to come in open-necked shirt and corduroys; neither he nor Dom had cared a damn what their guests chose to wear. If Bill Morgan felt awkward about these unimportant shibboleths of taste, he should learn either to change his clothes or to develop more social confidence in his sartorial eccentricities.

It had never occurred to Howarth that the six senior staff sitting awkwardly around his table in the candlelight, unmellowed even by the wine, would see the whole occasion as an elaborate gastronomic charade designed to demonstrate his social and intellectual superiority. At least Paul Middlemass, the Principal Scientific Officer Document Examiner, had appreciated the wine, drawing the bottle across the table toward him and refilling his glass, his lazy, ironic eyes watching his host. And Lorrimer? Lorrimer had eaten practically nothing, had drunk less, pushing his glass almost petulantly aside and fixing his great smoldering eyes on Domenica as if he had never before seen a woman. And that, presumably, had been the beginning of it. How it had progressed, when and how they had continued to meet, how it had ended, Domenica hadn't confided.

The dinner party had been a private and public fiasco. But what, he wondered, had the senior staff expected? An evening of solid drinking in the private snug in the Moonraker? A free-for-all jollification in the village hall for the whole laboratory including the cleaner, Mrs. Bidwell, and old Scobie, the laboratory attendant? "Knees Up Mother Brown" in the public bar? Perhaps they had thought that the first move should have come from their side. But that was to admit that there were two sides. The conventional sophistry was that the laboratory worked as a team harnessed by a common purpose, reins lightly but firmly in the Director's hands. That had worked well enough at Bruche. But there he had directed a research laboratory with a common discipline. How could you direct a team when your staff practiced half a dozen different scientific disciplines, used their own methods, were responsible for their own results, stood finally alone to justify and defend them in the only place where the quality of a forensic scientist's work could properly be judged, the witness box of a court of law? It was one of the loneliest places on earth, and he had never stood there.

Old Dr. Mac, his predecessor, had, he knew, taken the occasional case, to keep his hand in as he would say, trotting out to a scene of crime like an old bloodhound happily sniffing after half-forgotten scents, doing the analysis himself, and finally appearing, like a resurrected Old Testament prophet, in the witness box, greeted by the judge with dry judicial compliments, and boisterously welcomed in the bar by counsel like a long-missed old reprobate drinking comrade happily restored to them. But that could never be his way. He had been appointed to manage the laboratory and he would manage it in his own style. He wondered, morbidly introspective in the cold light of dawn, whether his decision to see the next murder case through from the call to the scene of crime to the trial had really arisen from a desire to learn or merely from a craven wish to impress or, worse, to propitiate, his staff, to show them that he valued their skills, that he wanted to be one of the team. If so, it had been one more error of judgment to add to the bleak arithmetic of failure since he had taken up his new job.

It looked as if they had nearly finished. The girl's rigid fingers had been prised from her handbag and Doyle's hands, gloved, were spreading out its few contents on a plastic sheet laid on the hood of the car. Howarth could just make out the shape of what looked like a small purse, a lipstick, a folded sheet of paper. A love letter probably, poor little wretch. Had Lorrimer written letters to Domenica? he wondered. He was always first at the door when the mail arrived and usually brought his sister her letters. Perhaps Lorrimer had known that. But he must have written. There must have been assignations. Lorrimer would hardly have risked telephoning from the laboratory or from home in the evenings when he, Howarth, might have taken the call.

They were moving the body now. The mortuary van had moved closer to the rim of the hollow and the stretcher was being maneuvered into place. The police were dragging out the screens from their van, ready to enclose the scene of crime. Soon there would be the little clutch of spectators, the curious children shooed away by the adults, the press photographers. He could see Lorrimer and Kerrison conferring together a little way apart, their backs turned, the two dark heads close together. Doyle was closing his notebook and supervising the removal of the body as if it were a precious exhibit that he was frightened someone would break. The light was strengthening.

He waited while Kerrison climbed up beside him and together they walked toward the parked cars. Howarth's foot struck a beer can. It clattered across the path and bounced against what looked like the battered frame of an old pram, with a bang like a pistol shot. The noise startled him. He said pettishly:

"What a place to die! Where in God's name are we exactly? I just followed the police cars."

"It's called the clunch field. That's the local name for the soft chalk they mined here from the Middle Ages onward. There isn't any hard building stone hereabouts, so they used clunch for most domestic building and even for some church interiors. There's an example in the Lady Chapel at Ely. Most villages had their clunch pits. They're overgrown now. Some are quite pretty in the spring and summer, little oases of wild flowers."

He gave the information almost tonelessly, like a dutiful guide repeating by rote the official spiel. Suddenly he swayed and reached for the support of his car door. Howarth wondered if he were ill or whether this was the extremity of tiredness. Then the pathologist straightened himself and said, with an attempt at briskness:

"I'll do the P.M. at nine o'clock tomorrow at St. Luke's. The hall porter will direct you. I'll leave a message."

He nodded a goodbye, forced a smile, then eased himself into his car and slammed the door. The Rover bumped slowly toward the road.

Howarth was aware that Doyle and Lorrimer were beside him. Doyle's excitement was almost palpable. He turned to look across the clunch field to the distant row of houses, their yellow brick walls and mean square windows now plainly visible.

"He's over there somewhere. In bed probably. That is, if he doesn't live alone. It wouldn't do to be up and about too early, would it? No, he'll be lying there wondering how to act ordinary, waiting for the anonymous car, the ring at the door. If he's on his own, it'll be different, of course. He'll be creeping about in the half-dark, wondering if he ought to burn his suit, scraping the mud off his shoes. Only he won't be able to get it all off. Not every trace. And he won't have a boiler big enough for the suit. And even if he had, what will he say when we ask for it? So maybe he'll be doing nothing. Just lying there and waiting. He won't be asleep. He didn't sleep last night. And he won't be sleeping again for quite a time."

Howarth felt slightly sick. He had eaten a small and early dinner and knew himself to be hungry. The sensation of nausea on an empty stomach was peculiarly unpleasant. He controlled his voice, betraying nothing but a casual interest.

"You think it's relatively straightforward then?"

"Domestic murder usually is. And I reckon that this is a domestic murder. Married kid, torn stump of a ticket for the local Oddfellows' hop, letter in her bag threatening her if she doesn't leave another bloke alone. A stranger wouldn't have known about this place. And she wouldn't have come here with him even if he had. By the look of her, they were sitting there cozily together before he got his hands on her throat. It's just a question of whether the two of them set off home together or whether he left early and waited for her."

"Do you know yet who she is?"

"Not yet. There's no diary in the bag. That kind don't keep diaries. But I shall know in about half an hour."

He turned to Lorrimer.

"The exhibits should be at the lab by nine or thereabouts. You'll give this priority?"

Lorrimer's voice was harsh.

"Murder gets priority. You know that."

Doyle's exultant, self-satisfied bellow jangled Howarth's nerves.

"Thank God something does! You're taking your time over the Gutteridge case. I was in the Biology Department yesterday and Bradley said the report wasn't ready; he was working on a case for the defense. We all know the great fiction that the lab is independent of the police and I'm happy to go along with it most of the time. But old Hoggatt founded the place as a police lab, and when the chips are down that's what it's all about. So do me a favor. Get moving with this one for me. I want to get chummy and get him quickly."

He was rocking gently on his heels, his smiling face uplifted to the dawn like a happy dog sniffing at the air, euphoric with the exhilaration of the hunt. It was odd, thought Howarth, that he didn't recognize the cold menace in Lorrimer's voice.

"Hoggatt's does an occasional examination for the defense if they ask us and if the exhibit is packed and submitted in the approved way. That's departmental policy. We're not yet a police lab even if you do walk in and out of the place as if it's your own kitchen. And I decide priorities in my laboratory. You'll get your report as soon as it's ready. In the meantime, if you want to ask questions, come to me, not to my junior staff. And, unless you're invited, keep out of my laboratory."

Without waiting for an answer, he walked over to his car. Doyle looked after him in a kind of angry bewilderment.

"Bloody hell! His lab! What's wrong with him? Lately he's been as touchy as a bitch in heat. He'll find himself on a brain shrinker's couch or in the bin if he doesn't get hold of himself."

Howarth said coldly:

"He's right, of course. Any inquiry about the work should be made to him, not to a member of his staff. And it's usual to ask permission before walking into a laboratory."

The rebuke stung. Doyle frowned. His face hardened. Howarth had a disconcerting glimpse of the barely controlled aggression beneath the mask of casual good humor. Doyle said:

"Old Dr. Mac used to welcome the police in his lab. He had this odd idea, you see, that helping the police was what it was all about. But if we're not wanted, you'd better talk to the chief. No doubt he'll issue his instructions."

He turned on his heel and made off toward his car without waiting for a reply. Howarth thought:

"Damn Lorrimer! Everything he touches goes wrong for me." He felt a spasm of hatred so intense, so physical, that it made him retch. If only Lorrimer's body were sprawled at the bottom of the clunch pit. If only it were Lorrimer's cadaver that would be cradled in porcelain on the postmortem table next day, laid out for ritual evisceration. He knew what was wrong with him. The diagnosis was as simple as it was humiliating: that self-infecting fever of the blood which could lie deceptively dormant, then flare, as now, into torment. Jealousy, he thought, was as physical as fear; the same dryness of the mouth, the thudding heart, the restlessness that destroyed appetite and peace. And he knew now that, this time, the sickness was incurable. It made no difference that the affair was over, that Lorrimer, too, was suffering. Reason couldn't cure it, nor, he suspected, could distance, nor time. It could be ended only by death; Lorrimer's or his own.

## IV

At half past six, in the front bedroom of 2 Acacia Close, Chevisham, Susan Bradley, wife of the Higher Scientific Officer in the Biology Department of Hoggatt's Laboratory, was welcomed by the faint, plaintive wail of her two-month-old baby, hungry for her first feed of the day. Susan switched on the bedside lamp, a pink glow under its frilled shade, and reaching for her dressing gown, shuffled sleepily to the bathroom next door, and then to the nursery. It was a small room at the back of the house, little more than a box, but when she pressed down the switch of the low-voltage nursery light she felt again a glow of maternal, proprietorial pride. Even in her sleepy morning daze the first sight of the nursery lifted her heart: the nursing chair with its back decorated with rabbits; the matching changing table fitted with drawers for the baby's things; the wicker cot in its stand which she had lined with a pink, blue, and white flowered cotton to match the curtains; the bright fringe of nursery-rhyme characters which Clifford had pasted around the wall.

With the sound of her footsteps the cries became stronger. She picked up the warm, milky-smelling cocoon and crooned reassurance. Immediately the cries ceased and Debbie's moist mouth, opening and shutting like a fish, sought her breast, the small, wrinkled fists, freed from the blanket, unfurled to clutch against her crumpled nightdress. The books said to change baby first, but she could never bear to make Debbie wait. And there was another reason. The walls of the modern house were thin, and she didn't want the sound of crying to wake Cliff.

But suddenly he was at the door, swaying slightly, his pajama jacket gaping open. Her heart sank. She made her voice sound bright, matter-of-fact.

"I hoped she hadn't woken you, darling. But it's after half past six. She slept over seven hours. Getting better."

"I was awake already."

"Go back to bed, Cliff. You can get in another hour's sleep."

"I can't sleep."

He looked around the little nursery with a puzzled frown, as if disconcerted not to find a chair. Susan said:

"Bring in the stool from the bathroom. And put on your dressing gown. You'll catch cold."

He placed the stool against the wall and crouched there in sullen misery. Susan raised her cheek from resting against the soft furriness of the baby's head. The small, snub-nosed leech latched onto her breast, fingers splayed in an ecstasy of content. Susan told herself that she must keep calm, mustn't let nerves and muscles knot themselves into the familiar ache of worry. Everyone said that it was bad for the milk. She said quietly:

"What's wrong, darling?"

But she knew what was wrong. She knew what he would say. She felt a new and frightening sense of resentment that she couldn't even feed Debbie in peace. And she wished he would do up his pajamas. Sitting like that, slumped and half-naked, he looked almost dissolute. She wondered what was happening to her. She had never felt like this about Cliff before Debbie was born.

"I can't go on. I can't go in to the lab today."

"Are you ill?"

But she knew that he wasn't ill, at least not yet. But he would be ill if something wasn't done about Edwin Lorrimer. The old misery descended on her. People wrote in books about a black weight of worry, and they were right, that was just how it felt, a perpetual physical burden that dragged at the shoulders and the heart, denying joy, even destroying, she thought bitterly, their pleasure in Debbie. Perhaps in the end it would destroy even love. She didn't speak but settled her small, warm burden more comfortably against her arm.

"I've got to give up the job. It's no use, Sue. I can't go on. He's got me in such a state that I'm as useless as he says I am."

"But Cliff, you know that isn't true. You're a good worker. There were never complaints about you at your last lab."

"I wasn't an H.S.O. then. Lorrimer thinks I ought never to have been promoted. He's right."

"He isn't right. Darling, you mustn't let him sap your confidence. That's fatal. You're a conscientious, reliable forensic biologist. You mustn't worry if you're not as quick as the others. That isn't important. Dr. Mac always said it's accuracy that counts. What does it matter if you take your time? You get the answer right in the end."

"Not any longer. I can't even do a simple peroxidase test now without fumbling. If he comes within two feet of me my hands start shaking. And he's begun checking all my results. I've just finished examining the stains on the mallet from the suspected Pascoe murder. But he'll work late tonight doing it again. And he'll make sure that the whole Biology Department knows why."

Cliff couldn't, she knew, stand up to bullying or sarcasm. Perhaps it was because of his father. The old man was paralyzed now after a stroke and she supposed that she ought to feel sorry for him lying there in his hospital bed, useless as a felled tree, mouth slavering, only the angry eyes moving in impotent fury from face to watching face. But from what Cliff had let slip he had been a poor father, an unpopular and unsuccessful schoolmaster yet with unreasonable ambitions for his only son. Cliff had been terrified of him. What Cliff needed was encouragement and affection. Who cared if he never rose any higher than H.S.O.? He was kind and loving. He looked after her and Debbie. He was her husband and she loved him. But he mustn't resign. What other job could he get? What else was he suited for? Unemployment was as bad in East Anglia as it was elsewhere. There was the mortgage to pay and the electricity bill for the central heating—they couldn't economize there because of Debbie needing warmth—and the hire purchase on the bedroom suite to find. Even the nursery furniture wasn't paid for yet. She had wanted everything nice and new for Debbie, but it had taken all their remaining savings. She said:

"Couldn't you apply to Establishment Department for a transfer?"

The despair in his voice tore at her heart.

"No one will want me if Lorrimer says I'm no good. He's probably the best forensic biologist in the service. If he thinks I'm useless, then I'm useless."

It was this, too, that she was beginning to find irritating, the obsequious respect of the victim for his oppressor. Sometimes, appalled by her disloyalty, she could begin to understand Dr. Lorrimer's contempt. She said:

"Why not have a word with the Director?"

"I might have if Dr. Mac was still there. But Howarth wouldn't care. He's new. He doesn't want any trouble with the senior staff, particularly now when we're getting ready to move into the new lab."

And then she thought of Mr. Middlemass. He was the Principal Scientific Officer Document Examiner, and she had worked for him as a young S.O. before her marriage. It was at Hoggatt's Laboratory that she had met Cliff. Perhaps he could do something, could speak to Howarth for them, could use his influence with Estabs. She wasn't sure how she expected him to help, but the need to confide in someone was overwhelming. They couldn't go on like this. Cliff would have a breakdown. And how would she manage with the baby and Cliff ill and the future uncertain? But surely Mr. Middlemass could do something. She believed in him because she needed to believe. She looked across at Cliff.

"Don't worry, darling, it's going to be all right. We're going to think of something. You go in today and we'll talk about it in the evening."

"How can we? Your mother's coming to supper."

"After supper then. She'll be catching the quarter-to-eight bus. We'll talk then."

"I can't go on like this, Sue."

"You won't have to. I'll think of something. It's going to be all right. I promise you, darling. It's going to be all right."

## V

"Mum, did you know that every human being is unique?"

"Of course I did. It stands to reason, doesn't it? There's only one of every person. You're you. I'm me. Pass your dad the marmalade and keep your sleeve out of that butter."

Brenda Pridmore, the recently appointed Clerical Officer/Receptionist at Hoggatt's Laboratory, pushed the marmalade jar across the breakfast table and began methodically slicing thin strips from the white of her fried egg, postponing, as she had from early childhood, that cataclysmic moment when she would plunge the fork into the glistening yellow dome. But indulgence in this small personal ritual was almost automatic. Her mind was preoccupied with the excitements and discoveries of her wonderful first job.

"I mean biologically unique. Inspector Blakelock, he's the Assistant Police Liaison Officer, told me that every human being has a unique fingerprint and no two types of blood are exactly the same. If the scientists had enough systems they could distinguish them all, the blood types I mean. He thinks that day may come in time. The forensic serologist will be able to say with certainty where the blood came from, even with a dried stain. It's dried blood that's difficult. If the blood is fresh we can do far more with it."

"Funny job you've got yourself." Mrs. Pridmore refilled the teapot from the kettle on the Aga hob and eased herself back into her chair. The farmhouse kitchen, its flowered cretonne curtains still undrawn, was warm and cozily domestic, smelling of toast, fried bacon, and hot, strong tea.

"I don't know that I like the idea of you checking in bits of body and bloodstained clothes. I hope you wash your hands properly before you come home."

"Oh Mum, it's not like that! The exhibits all arrive in plastic bags with identifying tags. We have to be ever so particular that all of them are labeled and properly entered in the book. It's a question of continuity of evidence, what Inspector Blakelock calls the integrity of the sample. And we don't get bits of body."

Remembering suddenly the sealed bottles of stomach contents, the carefully dissected pieces of liver and intestines, looking, when you came to think of it, no more frightening than exhibits in the science laboratory at school, she said quickly:

"Well, not in the way you mean. Dr. Kerrison does all the cutting up. He's a forensic pathologist attached to the laboratory. Of course, some of the organs come to us for analysis."

Inspector Blakelock, she remembered, had told her that the laboratory refrigerator had once held a whole head. But that wasn't the kind of thing to tell Mum. She rather wished that the Inspector hadn't told her. The refrigerator, squat and gleaming like a surgical sarcophagus, had held a sinister fascination for her ever since. But Mrs. Pridmore had seized gratefully on a familiar name.

"I know who Dr. Kerrison is, I should hope. Lives at the Old Rectory at Chevisham alongside the church, doesn't he? His wife ran off with one of the doctors at the hospital, left him and the two kids, that odd-looking daughter and the small boy, poor little fellow. You remember all the talk there was at the time, Arthur?"

Her husband didn't reply, nor did she expect him to. It was an understood convention that Arthur Pridmore left breakfast conversation to his women. Brenda went happily on:

"Forensic science isn't just helping the police to discover who's guilty. We help clear the innocent too. People sometimes forget that. We had a case last month—of course, I can't mention names—when a sixteen-year-old choir girl accused her vicar of rape. Well, he was innocent."

"So I should hope! Rape indeed!"

"But it looked very black against him. Only he was lucky. He was a secreter."

"A what, for goodness' sake?"

"He secreted his blood group in all his body fluids. Not everyone does. So the biologist was able to examine his saliva and compare his blood group with the stains on the victim's . . ."

"Not at breakfast time, Brenda, if you don't mind."

Brenda, her eyes suddenly alighting on a round milk stain on the tablecloth, herself thought that breakfast wasn't perhaps the most suitable time for a display of her recently acquired information about the investigation of rape. She went on to a safer subject.

"Dr. Lorrimer—he's the Principal Scientific Officer in charge of the Biology Department—says that I ought to work for an A-level subject and try for a job as an Assistant Scientific Officer. He thinks that I could do better than just a clerical job. And once I got my A.S.O. I'd be on a scientific grade and could work myself up. Some of the most famous forensic scientists have started that way, he said. He's offered to give me a reading list, and he says he doesn't see why I shouldn't use some of the laboratory equipment for my practical work."

"I didn't know that you worked in the Biology Department."

"I don't. I'm mainly on Reception with Inspector Blakelock, and sometimes I help out in the general office. But we got talking when I had to spend an afternoon in his laboratory checking reports for courts with his staff, and he was ever so nice. A lot of people don't like him. They say he's too strict; but I think he's just shy. He might have been Director if the Home Office hadn't passed him over and appointed Dr. Howarth."

"He seems to be taking quite an interest in you, this Mr. Lorrimer."

"Dr. Lorrimer, Mum."

"Dr. Lorrimer, then. Though why he wants to call himself a doctor beats me. You don't have any patients at the lab."

"He's a Ph.D., Mum. Doctor of Philosophy."

"Oh, is he? I thought he was supposed to be a scientist. Anyway, you'd better watch your step."

"Oh Mum, don't be daft. He's old. He must be forty or more. Mum, did you know that our lab is the oldest forensic science lab in the country? There are regional labs covering the whole country but ours was the first. Colonel Hoggatt started it in Chevisham Manor when he was Chief Constable in 1898, then left the manor house to his Force when he died. Forensic science was in its infancy then, Inspector Blakelock says, and Colonel Hoggatt was one of the first Chief Constables to see its possibilities. We've got his portrait in the hall. We're the only lab with its founder's name. That's why the Home Office has agreed that the new laboratory will still be called Hoggatt's. Other police forces send their exhibits to their regional laboratory, North-East or the Metropolitan and so on. But in East Anglia they say, 'Better send it to Hoggatt's.' "

"You'd better send yourself to Hoggatt's if you want to get there by eight-thirty. And I don't want you taking any shortcuts through the new lab. It isn't safe, only half-built, especially these dark mornings. Like as not you'd fall into the foundations or get a brick down on your head. They're not safe, building sites aren't. Look what happened to your Uncle Will."

"All right, Mum. We're not supposed to go through the new lab anyway. Besides, I'm going by bike. Are these my sandwiches or Dad's?"

"Yours, of course. You know your dad's home to dinner on Wednesdays. Cheese and tomato this morning, and I've put you in a boiled egg."

When Brenda had waved goodbye, Mrs. Pridmore sat down for her second cup of tea and looked across at her husband.

"I suppose it's all right, this job she's found for herself."

Arthur Pridmore, when he did condescend to talk at breakfast, talked with the magisterial authority of head of his family, Mr. Bowlem's bailiff, and Peoples' warden at the village church. He laid down his fork.

"It's a good job, and she was lucky to get it. Plenty of girls from the grammar school after it, weren't they? An established civil servant, isn't she? And look what they're paying her. More than the pigman gets at the farm. Pensionable too. She's a sensible girl and she'll be all right. There aren't many opportunities left locally for girls with good O-levels. And you didn't want her to take a job in London."

No indeed, Mrs. Pridmore hadn't wanted Brenda to go to London, a prey to muggers, I.R.A. terrorists, and what the press mysteriously called "the drug scene." None of her infrequent, but uneventful and pleasant, visits to the capital on Women's Institute theater excursions or rare shopping trips had failed to shake her conviction that Liverpool Street Station was the cavernous entry to an urban jungle, where predators armed with bombs and syringes lurked in every Underground station, and seducers laid their snares for innocent provincials in every office. Brenda, thought her mother, was a very pretty girl. Well, no point in denying it, she took after her mother's side of the family for looks even if she had her dad's brains, and Mrs. Pridmore had no intention of exposing her to the temptations of London. Brenda was walking out with Gerald Bowlem, younger son of her father's boss, and if that came off there's no denying it would be a very satisfactory marriage. He wouldn't get the main farm, of course, but there was a very nice little property over at Wisbech that would come to him. Mrs. Pridmore couldn't see the sense of more examinations and all this talking about a career. This job at the lab would do Brenda very well until she married. But it was a pity that there was all this emphasis on blood.

As if reading her thoughts, her husband said:

"Of course it's exciting for her. It's all new. But I daresay it's no different from other jobs, pretty dull most of the time. I don't reckon anything really frightening will happen to our Brenda at Hoggatt's Lab."

This conversation about their only child's first job was one they'd had before, a comforting reiteration of mutual reassurance. In imagination Mrs. Pridmore followed her daughter as she pedaled vigorously on her way; bumping down the rough farm track between Mr. Bowlem's flat fields to Tenpenny Road, past old Mrs. Button's cottage where, as a child, she had been given rice cake and homemade lemonade, by Tenpenny Dike where she still picked cowslips in summer, then a right turn into Chevisham Road and the straight two miles skirting Captain Massey's land and into Chevisham village. Every yard of it was familiar, reassuring, unmenacing. And even Hoggatt's Laboratory, blood or no blood, had been part of the village for over seventy years, while Chevisham Manor had stood for nearly three times as long. Arthur was right. Nothing frightening could happen to their Brenda at Hoggatt's. Mrs. Pridmore, comforted, drew back the curtains and settled down to enjoy her third cup of tea.

## VI

At ten minutes to nine the mail van stopped outside Sprogg's Cottage on the outskirts of Chevisham to deliver a single letter. It was addressed to Miss Stella Mawson, Lavender Cottage, Chevisham, but the postman was a local man and the difference in name caused him no confusion. There had been Sproggs living in the cottage for four generations, and the small triangle of green in front of the gate had been Sprogg's Green for almost as long. The present owner, having improved the cottage by the addition of a small brick garage and a modern bathroom and kitchen, had decided to celebrate the metamorphosis by planting a lavender hedge and renaming the property.

But the villagers regarded the new name as no more than a foreigner's eccentric fancy which they were under no obligation either to use or to recognize. The lavender hedge, as if in sympathy with their views, failed to survive the first fen winter and Sprogg's Cottage remained Sprogg's.

Angela Foley, the twenty-seven-year-old personal secretary to the Director of Hoggatt's Laboratory, picked up the envelope and guessed at once by the quality of the paper, the expertly typed address, and the London postmark what it must be. It was a letter they had been expecting. She took it through to the kitchen where she and her friend were breakfasting and handed it over without speaking, then watched Stella's face as she read. After a minute she asked:

"Well?"

"It's what we feared. He can't wait any longer. He wants a quick sale, and there's a friend of his who thinks he might like it for a week-end cottage. As sitting tenants we get first refusal, but he must know by next Monday whether we're interested."

She tossed the letter across the table. Angela said bitterly:

"Interested! Of course we're interested! He knows we are. We told him weeks ago that we were writing around trying to get a mortgage."

"That's just lawyer's jargon. What his solicitor is asking is whether we're able to go ahead. And the answer is that we can't."

The arithmetic was plain. Neither of them needed to discuss it. The owner wanted sixteen thousand pounds. None of the mortgage societies they had approached would advance them more than ten. Together they had a little over two thousand saved. Four thousand short. And, with no time left, it might just as well be forty.

Angela said:

"I suppose he wouldn't take less?"

"No. We've tried that. And why should he? It's a fully converted, reed-thatched seventeenth-century cottage. And we've improved it. We've made the garden. He'd be a fool to let it go for under sixteen even to a sitting tenant."

"But, Star, we are sitting tenants! He's got to get us out first."

"That's the only reason why he's given us as long as he has. He knows we could make it difficult for him. But I'm not prepared to stay on here under sufferance, knowing that we'd have to go in the end. I couldn't write under those conditions."

"But we can't find four thousand in a week! And, with things as they are, we couldn't hope for a bank loan even if . . ."

"Even if I had a book coming out this year, which I haven't. And what I make from writing barely pays my part of the housekeeping. It was tactful of you not to say so."

She hadn't been going to say it. Stella wasn't a conveyorbelt writer. You couldn't expect her novels to make money. What was it that last reviewer had said? "Fastidious observation wedded to elegantly sensitive and oblique prose." Not surprisingly, Angela could quote all the reviews even if she sometimes wondered what exactly they were trying to say. Wasn't it she who pasted them with meticulous care into the clippings-book which Stella so affected to despise? She watched while her friend began what they both called her tiger prowl, that compulsive pacing up and down, head lowered, hands sunk in her dressing-gown pockets. Then Stella said:

"It's a pity that cousin of yours is so disagreeable. Otherwise one might not have minded asking him for a loan. He wouldn't miss it."

"But I've already asked him. Not about the cottage, of course. But I've asked him to lend me some money."

It was ridiculous that this should be so difficult to say. After all, Edwin was her cousin. She had a right to ask him. And it was her grandmother's money after all. There was really no reason why Star should be cross. There were times when she didn't mind Star's anger, times even when she deliberately provoked it, waiting with half-shameful excitement for the extraordinary outburst of bitterness and despair of which she herself was less a victim than a privileged spectator, relishing even more the inevitable remorse and self-incrimination, the sweetness of reconciliation. But now for the first time she recognized the chill of fear.

"When?"

There was nothing for it now but to go on.

"Last Tuesday evening. It was after you decided that we'd have to cancel our bookings for Venice next March because of the exchange rate. I wanted it to be a birthday present, Venice I mean."

She had pictured the scene. Herself handing over the tickets and the hotel reservations tucked into one of those extra-large birthday cards. Star trying to hide her surprise and pleasure. Both of them poring over maps and guidebooks, planning the itinerary of every marvelous day. To see for the first time and together that incomparable view of San Marco from the western end of the Piazza. Star had read to her Ruskin's description: "A multitude of pillars and white domes, clustered into a long low pyramid of colored light." To stand together on the Piazzetta in the early morning and look across the shimmering water to San Giorgio Maggiore. It was a dream, as insubstantial as the crumbling city. But the hope of it had been worth steeling herself to ask Edwin for that loan.

"And what did he say?"

There was no chance now of softening that brutal negative, of erasing the whole humiliating episode from her memory.

"He said no."

"I suppose you told him why you wanted it. It didn't occur to you that we go away from here to be private, that our holidays are our own affair, that it might humiliate me to have Edwin Lorrimer know that I can't afford to take you to Venice, even on a ten-day package tour."

"I didn't." She cried out in vehement protest, horrified to hear the crack in her voice and feel the first hot, gritty tears. It was odd, she thought, that it was she who could cry. Star was the emotional, the vehement one. And yet Star never cried.

"I didn't tell him anything, except that I needed the money."

"How much?"

She hesitated, wondering whether to lie. But she never lied to Star.

"Five hundred pounds. I thought we might as well do it properly. I just told him that I badly needed five hundred pounds."

"So, not surprisingly, faced with that irrefutable argument, he declined to hand out. What exactly did he say?"

"Only that grandmother had made her intentions perfectly plain in her will and that he had no intention of upsetting them. Then I said that most of the money would come to me after his death, anyway—I mean, that's what he told me when the will was read—and it would be too late then. I'd be an old lady. I might die first. It was now that was important. But I didn't tell him why I wanted it. I swear that."

"Swear? Don't be dramatic. You're not in a court of law. And then what did he say?"

If only Star would stop that agitated pacing, would only turn and looked at her instead of questioning her in that cold, inquisitorial voice. And the new bit was even harder to tell. She couldn't explain to herself why it should be, but it was something that she had tried to put out of her mind, for the present anyway. One day she would tell Star, the moment when it was right to tell. She had never imagined being forced into confidence with such brutal suddenness.

"He said that I shouldn't rely on getting anything in his will. He said that he might acquire new obligations. *Obligations* was the word he used. And if he did, the will would no longer stand."

And now Star swung around and faced her.

"New obligations. Marriage! No, that's too ridiculous. Marriage, that desiccated, pedantic, self-satisfied prude. I doubt whether he ever deliberately touches a human body except his own. Solitary, masochistic, surreptitious vice, that's all he understands. No, not vice, the word's too strong. But marriage! Wouldn't you have thought . . ."

She broke off. Angela said:

"He didn't mention marriage."

"Why should he? But what else would automatically set aside an existing will unless he made a new one? Marriage cancels a will. Didn't you know that?"

"You mean that as soon as he married I should be disinherited?"

"Yes."

"But that isn't fair!"

"Since when has life been noted for its fairness? It wasn't fair that your grandmother left her fortune to him instead of sharing it with you just because he's a man and she had an old-fashioned prejudice that women shouldn't own money. It isn't fair that you're only a secretary at Hoggatt's because no one bothered to educate you for anything else. It isn't fair, come to that, that you should have to support me."

"I don't support you. In every way except the unimportant one, you support me."

"It's humiliating to be worth more dead than alive. If my heart gave out tonight, then you'd be all right. You could use the life insurance money to buy the place and stay on. The bank would advance the money once they knew you were my legatee."

"Without you I shouldn't want to stay on."

"Well, if you do have to leave here, at least it will give you an excuse to live on your own, if that's what you want."

Angela cried out in vehement protest:

"I shall never live with anyone else but you. I don't want to live anywhere but here, in this cottage. You know that. It's our home."

It was their home. It was the only real home she'd ever known. She didn't need to look around her to fix with startling clarity each familiar loved possession. She could lie in bed at night and in imagination move confidently around the cottage touching them in a happy exploration of shared memories and reassurance. The two Victorian luster plant pots on their matching pedestals, found in The Lanes at Brighton one summer weekend. The eighteenth-century oil of Wicken Fen by an artist whose indecipherable signature, peered at through a microscope, had provided so many shared moments of happy conjecture. The French sword in its decorated scabbard, found in a country sale room and now hanging above their fireplace. It wasn't just that their possessions, wood and porcelain, paint and linen, symbolized their joint life. The cottage, their belongings, were their joint life, adorned and gave reality to it just as the bushes and flowers they had planted in the garden staked out their territory of trust.

She had a sudden and terrifying memory of a recurrent nightmare. They were standing facing each other in an empty attic room, bare walls squared with the pale imprints of discarded pictures, floorboards harsh to the feet, two naked strangers in a void, herself trying to reach out her hands to touch Stella's fingers, but unable to lift the heavy monstrous bolsters of flesh that had become her arms. She shivered and then was recalled to the reality of the cold autumn morning by the sound of her friend's voice.

"How much did your grandmother leave? You did tell me, but I've forgotten."

"About thirty thousand, I think."

"And he can't have spent any of it, living with his old father in that poky cottage. He hasn't even renovated the windmill. His salary alone must be more than enough for the two of them, apart from the old man's pension. Lorrimer's a senior scientist, isn't he? What does he get?"

"He's a Principal Scientific Officer. The scale goes up to eight thousand."

"God! More in a year than I could earn from four novels. I suppose if he jibbed at five hundred he'd hardly part with four thousand, not at a rate of interest we could afford. But it wouldn't hurt him. I've a good mind to ask him for it after all."

Stella was only teasing, of course; but she recognized this too late to control the panic in her voice.

"No, please, Star! No, you mustn't!"

"You really hate him, don't you?"

"Not hate. Indifference. I just don't want to be under an obligation to him."

"Nor, come to that, do I. And you shan't be."

Angela went out to the hall and came back pulling on her coat. She said:

"I'll be late at the lab if I don't hurry. The casserole is in the oven. Try to remember to switch on at half past five. And don't touch the regulator. I'll turn down the heat when I get back."

"I think I can just about manage that."

"I'm taking sandwiches for lunch, so I shan't be back. There's the cold ham and salad in the fridge. Will that be enough, Star?"

"No doubt I'll survive."

"Yesterday evening's typing is in the folder, but I haven't read it through."

"How remiss of you."

Stella followed her friend out to the hall. At the door she said:

"I expect they think at the lab that I exploit you."

"They know nothing about you at the lab. And I don't care what they think."

"Is that what Edwin Lorrimer thinks, too, that I exploit you? Or what does he think?"

"I don't want to talk about him."

She folded her scarf over her blond hair. In the antique mirror with its frame of carved shells she saw both their faces distorted by a defect in the glass: the brown and green of Stella's huge, luminous eyes smeared like wet paint into the deep clefts between nostrils and mouth; her own wide brow bulging like that of a hydrocephalic child. She said:

"I wonder what I'd feel if Edwin died this week; a heart attack, a car accident, a brain hemorrhage."

"Life isn't as convenient as that."

"Death isn't. Star, shall you reply today to that solicitor?"

"He doesn't expect an answer until Monday. I can phone him at the London office on Monday morning. That's another five days. Anything can happen in five days."

# VII

"But they're just like mine! The panties I mean. I've got a pair like that! I bought them from Marks and Spencer's in Cambridge with my first salary check."

It was 10:35 and Brenda Pridmore, at the reception desk at the rear of the main hall of Hoggatt's Laboratory, watched wide-eyed while Inspector Blakelock drew toward him the first labeled bag of exhibits from the clunch pit murder. She put out a finger and tentatively slid it over the thin plastic through which the knickers, crumpled and stained around the crotch, were clearly visible. The detective-constable who had brought in the exhibits had said that the girl had been to a dance. Funny, thought Brenda, that she hadn't bothered to put on clean underclothes. Perhaps she wasn't fastidious. Or perhaps she had been in too much of a hurry to change. And now the intimate clothes which she had put on so unthinkingly on the day of her death would be smoothed out by strange hands, scrutinized under ultraviolet light, perhaps be handed up, neatly docketed, to the judge and jury in the Crown Court.

Brenda knew that she would never again be able to wear her own panties, their prettiness contaminated forever by the memory of this dead unknown girl. Perhaps they had even bought them together in the same store, on the same day. She could recall the excitement of spending for the first time money she had actually earned. It had been a Saturday afternoon and there had been a crush around the lingerie counter, eager hands rummaging among the panties. She had liked the pair with the sprays of pink machine-embroidered flowers across the front. So, too, had this unknown girl. Perhaps their hands had touched. She cried:

"Inspector. Isn't death terrible?"

"Murder is. Death isn't; at least, no more than birth is. You couldn't have one without the other or there'd be no room for us all. I reckon I won't worry overmuch when my time comes."

"But that policeman who brought in the exhibits said that she was only eighteen. That's my age."

He was making out the folder for the new case, meticulously transferring details from the police form to the file. And his head, with the cropped dry hair which reminded her so of corn stubble, was bent low over the page so that she could not see his face. Suddenly she remembered being told that he had lost an only daughter, killed by a hit-and-run driver, and she wished the words unsaid. Her face flared and she turned her eyes away. But when he replied his voice was perfectly steady.

"Aye, poor lass. Led him on, I daresay. They never learn. What's that you've got?"

"It's the bag of male clothes, suit, shoes, and underwear. Do you think these belong to the chief suspect?"

"They'll be the husband's, likely as not."

"But what can they prove? She was strangled, wasn't she?"

"No telling for certain until we get Dr. Kerrison's report. But they usually examine the chief suspect's clothes. There might be a trace of blood, a grain of sand or earth, paint, minute fibers from the victim's clothes, a trace of her saliva even. Or she could have been raped. All that bundle will go into the Biology Search Room with the victim's clothes."

"But the policeman didn't say anything about rape! I thought you said this bundle belongs to the husband."

"You don't want to let it worry you. You have to learn to be like a doctor or a nurse, detached, isn't it?"

"Is that how forensic scientists feel?"

"Likely as not. It's their job. They don't think about victims or suspects. That's for the police. They're only concerned with scientific facts."

He was right, thought Brenda. She remembered the time only three days previously when the Senior Scientific Officer of the Instrument Section had let her look into the giant scanning electron microscope and watch the image of a minute pill of putty burst instantaneously into an exotic incandescent flower. He had explained:

"It's a coccolith, magnified six thousand times."

"A what?"

"The skeleton of a microorganism that lived in the ancient seas from which the chalk in the putty was deposited. They're different, depending on where the chalk was quarried. That's how you can differentiate one sample of putty from another."

She had exclaimed:

"But it's so lovely!"

He had taken her place at the eyepiece of the instrument.

"Yes, nice, isn't it?"

But she had known that, while she looked back in wonder across a million years, his mind was on the minute scrape of putty from the heel of the suspect's shoe, the trace that might prove a man was a rapist or a murderer. And yet, she had thought, he doesn't really mind. All he cares about is getting the answer right. It would have been no use asking him whether he thought there was a unifying purpose in life, whether it could really be chance that an animal so small that it couldn't be seen by the naked eye could die millions of years ago in the depths of the sea and be resurrected by science to prove a man innocent or guilty. It was odd, she thought, that scientists so often weren't religious when their work revealed a world so variously marvelous and yet so mysteriously unified and at one. Dr. Lorrimer seemed to be the only member of Hoggatt's who was known to go regularly to church. She wondered if she dared ask him about the coccolith and God. He had been very kind this morning about the murder. He had arrived at the laboratory over an hour late, at ten o'clock, looking terribly tired because he had been up that night at the scene of crime, and had come over to the reception desk to collect his personal mail. He had said:

"You'll be getting exhibits from your first murder case this morning. Don't let them worry you, Brenda. There's only one death we need to be frightened of, and that's our own."

It was a strange thing to have said, an odd way to reassure her. But he was right. She was suddenly glad that Inspector Blakelock had done the documentation on the clunch pit murder. Now, with care, the owner of those stained panties would remain, for her, unknown, anonymous, a number in the biology series on a manila folder. Inspector Blakelock's voice broke into her thoughts:

"Have you got those court reports we checked yesterday ready for the mail?"

"Yes, they've been entered in the book. I meant to ask you. Why do all the court statements have 'Criminal Justice Act 1967 sections 2 and 9' printed on them?"

"That's the statutory authority for written evidence to be tendered at committal proceedings and the Crown Court. You can look up the sections in the library. Before the 1967 act the labs had a hard time of it, I can tell you, when all scientific evidence had to be given orally. Mind you, the court-going officers still have to spend a fair amount of time attending trials. The defense doesn't always accept the scientific findings. That's the difficult part of the job, not the analysis but standing alone in the witness box to defend it under cross-examination. If a man's no good in the box, then all the careful work he does here goes for nothing."

Brenda suddenly remembered something else that Mrs. Mallett had told her, that the motorist who had killed his daughter had been acquitted because the scientist had crumbled under the cross-examination; something to do with the analysis of chips of paint found on the road that matched the suspect's car. It must be terrible to lose an only child; to lose any child. Perhaps that was the worst thing that could happen to a human being. No wonder Inspector Blakelock was often so quiet; that when the police officers came in with their hearty banter he answered only with that slow, gentle smile.

She glanced across at the laboratory clock. Ten-forty-five. Any minute now the Scene of Crime course would be arriving for their lecture on the collection and preservation of scientific evidence, and this brief spell of quiet would be over. She wondered what Colonel Hoggatt would think if he could visit his laboratory now. Her eyes were drawn, as they so often were, to his portrait hanging just outside the Director's office. Even from her place at the desk she could read the gold lettering on the frame.

Colonel William Makepeace Hoggatt V.C.
Chief Constable 1894–1912
Founder of Hoggatt's Forensic Science Laboratory

He was standing in the room that was still used as a library, his ruddy face stern and bewhiskered under the sprouting plumes of his hat, his braided, bemedaled tunic fastened with a row of gilt buttons. One proprietorial hand was laid, light as a priestly blessing, on an old-fashioned microscope in gleaming brass. But the minatory eyes weren't fixed on this latest scientific wonder; they were fixed on Brenda. Under his accusing gaze, recalled to duty, she bent again to her work.

# VIII

By twelve o'clock the meeting of senior scientists in the Director's office to discuss the furniture and equipment for the new laboratory was over, and Howarth rang for his secretary to clear the conference table. He watched her as she emptied and polished the ashtray (he didn't smoke and the smell of ash offended him), collected together the copies of the laboratory plans, and gathered up the strewn discarded papers. Even from his desk Howarth could see Middlemass's complex geometrical doodles and the crumpled agenda, ringed with coffee stains, of the Senior Vehicle Examiner, Bill Morgan.

He watched the girl as she moved with quiet competence about the table wondering, as always, what, if anything, was going on behind that extraordinarily wide brow, those slanted, enigmatic eyes. He missed his old personal assistant, Marjory Faraker, more than he had expected. It had, he thought ruefully, been good for his self-conceit to find that her devotion didn't, after all, extend to leaving London where, surprisingly, she had been discovered to have a life of her own, to join him in the fens. Like all good secretaries she had acquired, or at least known how to simulate, some of the idealized attributes of wife, mother, mistress, confidante, servant, and friend without being, or indeed expecting to be, any of these. She had flattered his self-esteem, protected him from the minor irritations of life, preserved his privacy with maternal pugnacity; had ensured, with infinite tact, that he knew all he needed to know about what was going on in his laboratory.

He couldn't complain about Angela Foley. She was a more than competent shorthand typist and an efficient secretary. Nothing was left undone. It was just that for her, he felt that he hardly existed, that his authority, meekly deferred to, was nevertheless a charade. The fact that she was Lorrimer's cousin was irrelevant. He had never heard her mention his name. He wondered from time to time what sort of a life she led in that remote cottage with her writer friend, how far it had satisfied her. But she told him nothing, not even about the laboratory. He knew that Hoggatt's had a heartbeat—all institutions did—but the pulse eluded him. He said:

"The Foreign and Commonwealth Office wants us to take a Danish biologist for two or three days next month. He's visiting England to look at the Service. Fit him in, will you, when I'm free to give him some time. You'd better consult Dr. Lorrimer about his diary commitments. Then let the F.C.O. know what days we can offer."

"Yes, Dr. Howarth."

At least the autopsy was over. It had been worse than he had expected, but he had seen it through and without disgrace. He hadn't expected that the colors of the human body would be so vivid, so exotically beautiful. Now he saw again Kerrison's gloved fingers, sleek as eels, busying themselves at the body's orifices. Explaining, demonstrating, discarding. Presumably he had become as immune to disgust as he obviously was to the sweet-sour smell of his mortuary. And to all the experts in violent death, faced daily with the final disintegration of the personality, pity would be as irrelevant as disgust.

Miss Foley was ready to go now and had come up to the desk to clear his "Out" tray. He said:

"Has Inspector Blakelock worked out last month's average turnaround figures yet?"

"Yes, sir. The average for all exhibits is down to twelve days, and the blood alcohol has fallen to 1.2 days. But the figure for crimes against the person is up again. I'm just typing the figures now."

"Let me have them as soon as they're ready, please."

There were memories which, he suspected, would be even more insistent than Kerrison marking out with his cartilage knife on the milk-white body the long line of the primary incision. Doyle, that great black bull, grinning at him in the washroom afterward as, side by side, they washed their hands. And why, he wondered, had he felt it necessary to wash. His hands hadn't been contaminated.

"The performance was well up to standard. Neat, quick, and thorough, that's Doc Kerrison. Sorry we shan't be able to call for you when we're ready to make the arrest. Not allowed. You'll have to imagine that bit. But there'll be the trial to attend, with any luck."

Angela Foley was standing in front of the desk, looking at him strangely, he thought.

"Yes?"

"Scobie has had to go home, Dr. Howarth. He's not at all well. He thinks it may be this two-day flu that's going about. And he says that the incinerator has broken down."

"Presumably he telephoned for the mechanic before he left."

"Yes, sir. He says it was all right yesterday morning when Inspector Doyle came with the court orders authorizing the destruction of the cannabis exhibits. It was working then."

Howarth was irritated. This was one of those minor administrative details which Miss Faraker would never have dreamed of troubling him with. Miss Foley was, he guessed, expecting him to say something sympathetic about Scobie, to inquire whether the old man had been fit to cycle home. Dr. MacIntyre had, no doubt, bleated like an anxious sheep when any of the staff were ill. He bent his head over his papers.

But Miss Foley was at the door. It had to be now. He made himself say:

"Ask Dr. Lorrimer to come down for a few minutes, will you please?"

He could, perfectly casually, have asked Lorrimer to stay on after the meeting. Why hadn't he? Probably because there might have been an echo of the headmaster in so public a request. Perhaps because this was an interview he had been glad to postpone, even temporarily.

Lorrimer came in and stood in front of the desk. Howarth took out Bradley's personal file from his right-hand drawer and said:

"Sit down, will you, please. This annual report on Bradley. You've given him an adverse marking. Have you told him?"

Lorrimer remained standing. He said:

"I'm required by the reporting rules to tell him. I saw him in my office at ten-thirty, as soon as I got back from the P.M."

"It seems a bit hard. According to his file, it's the first adverse report he's had. We took him on probation eighteen months ago. Why hasn't he made out?"

"I should have thought that was obvious from my detailed markings. He's been promoted above his capacity."

"In other words, the Board made a mistake?"

"That's not so unusual. Boards occasionally do. And not only when it comes to promotions."

The allusion was blatant, a deliberate provocation, yet Howarth decided to ignore it. With an effort he kept his voice level.

"I'm not prepared to countersign this report as it stands. It's too early to judge him fairly."

"I made that excuse for him last year when he'd been with us six months. But if you disagree with my assessment you'll presumably say so. There's a space provided."

"I intend to use it. And I suggest that you try the effect of giving the boy some support and encouragement. There are two reasons for an inadequate performance. Some people are capable of doing better and will if judiciously kicked into it. Others aren't. To kick them is not only pointless, it destroys what confidence they have. You run an efficient department. But it might be more efficient and happier if you learned how to understand people. Management is largely a matter of personal relationships."

He made himself look up. Lorrimer said through lips so stiff that the words sounded cracked:

"I hadn't realized that your family were noted for success in their personal relationships."

"The fact that you can't take criticism without becoming as personal and spiteful as a neurotic girl is an example of what I mean."

He never knew what Lorrimer was about to reply. The door opened and his sister came in. She was dressed in slacks and a sheepskin jacket, her blond hair bound with a scarf. She looked at them both without embarrassment and said easily:

"Sorry, I didn't realize you were engaged. I ought to have asked Inspector Blakelock to ring."

Without a word, Lorrimer, deathly pale, turned on his heels, walked past her, and was gone. Domenica looked after him, smiled, and shrugged. She said:

"Sorry if I interrupted something. It's just to say that I'm going to Norwich for a couple of hours to buy some materials. Is there anything you want?"

"Nothing, thank you."

"I'll be back before dinner, but I think I'll give the village concert a miss. Without Claire Easterbook the Mozart will be pretty insupportable. Oh, and I'm thinking of going up to London for the best part of next week."

Her brother didn't reply. She looked at him and said:

"What's wrong?"

"How did Lorrimer know about Gina?"

He didn't need to ask her if it was she who had told him. Whatever else she may have confided, it would not have been that. She went across, ostensibly to study the Stanley Spencer set in the overmantel of the fireplace, and asked lightly:

"Why? He didn't mention your divorce, did he?"

"Not directly, but the allusion was intended."

She turned to face him.

"He probably took the trouble to find out as much as possible about you when he knew that you were a candidate for the job here. It isn't such a large Service after all."

"But I came from outside it."

"Even so, there would be contacts, gossip. A failed marriage is one of those unconsidered trifles he might expect to sniff out. And what of it? After all, it's not unusual. I thought forensic scientists were particularly at risk. All those late hours at scenes of crime and the unpredictable court attendances. They ought to be used to marital breakups."

He said, knowing that he sounded as petulant as an obstinate child:

"I don't want him in my lab."

"Your lab? It isn't quite as simple as that, is it? I don't think the Stanley Spencer is right over the fireplace. It looks incongruous. It's strange that Father bought it. Not at all his kind of picture, I should have said. Did you put it here to shock?"

Miraculously, his anger and misery were assuaged. But then she had always been able to do that for him.

"Merely to disconcert and confuse. It's intended to suggest that I may be a more complex character than they assume."

"Oh, but you are! I've never needed *Assumption at Cookham* to prove it. Why not the Greuze? It would look good with that carved overmantel."

"Too pretty."

She laughed and was gone. He picked up Clifford Bradley's report and, in the space provided, wrote:

"Mr. Bradley's performance has been disappointing, but not all the difficulties are of his making. He lacks confidence and would benefit from more active encouragement and support than he has received. I have corrected the final marking to what I consider a more just assessment and have spoken to the Senior Biologist about the personnel management in his department."

If he did finally decide that, after all, this wasn't the job for him, that snide comment should go some way to ensure that Lorrimer stood no chance of succeeding him as Director of Hoggatt's.

# IX

At one-forty-eight precisely Paul Middlemass, the Document Examiner, opened his file on the clunch pit murder. The Document Examination Room, which occupied the whole of the front of the building immediately under the roof, smelled like a stationer's shop, a pungent amalgam of paper and ink, sharpened by the tang of chemicals. Middlemass breathed it as his native air. He was a tall, rangy, large-featured man with a mobile, wide-mouthed face of agreeable ugliness and iron-gray hair that fell in heavy swathes over parchment-colored skin. Easygoing and seemingly indolent, he was in fact a prodigious worker with an obsession for his job. Paper in all its manifestations was his passion. Few men, in or outside the Forensic Science Service, knew so much about it. He handled it with joy and with a kind of reverence, gloated over it, knew its provenance almost by its smell. Identification of the sizing and loading of a specimen by spectrographic or X-ray crystallography merely confirmed what touch and sight had already pronounced. The satisfaction of watching the emergence of an obscure watermark under soft X-rays never palled, and the final pattern was as fascinating to his unsurprised eyes as the expected potter's mark to a collector of porcelain.

His father, long dead, had been a dentist, and his son had taken for his own use the old man's inordinately large store of self-designed surgical white coats. They were old-fashioned in cut, waisted and full-skirted as the coat of a Regency buck, and with crested metal buttons fastening high to the side of the throat. Although they were too short in the arm so that his lean wrists protruded like those of an overgrown schoolboy, he wore them with a certain panache, as if this unorthodox working garb, so different from the regulation white coats of the rest of the laboratory staff, symbolized that unique blend of scientific skill, experience, and flair which distinguishes the good Document Examiner.

He had just finished telephoning his wife, having remembered rather belatedly that he was due to help out that evening with the village concert. He liked women and before his marriage had enjoyed a succession of casual, satisfactory, and uncommitted affairs. He had married late, a buxom research scientist from Cambridge twenty years his junior, and drove back to their modern flat on the outskirts of the city each night in his Jaguar—his chief extravagance—frequently late, but seldom too late to bear her off to their local pub. Secure in his job, with a growing international reputation, and uxoriously contented with his comely Sophie, he knew himself to be successful and suspected himself to be happy.

The Document Examination Laboratory with its cabinets and range of monorail cameras took up what some of his colleagues, notably Edwin Lorrimer, regarded as more than its share of room. But the laboratory, lit by rows of fluorescent lights and with its low ceiling, was stuffy and ill-ventilated, and this afternoon the central heating, unreliable at the best of times, had concentrated all its efforts on the top of the building. Usually he was oblivious of his working conditions, but a subtropical temperature was difficult to ignore. He opened the door to the passage. Opposite and a little to the right were the male and female lavatories, and he could hear the occasional feet, light or heavy, hurried or dilatory, of passing members of staff and hear the swing of the two doors. The sounds didn't worry him. He applied himself to his task.

But the specimen he was now poring over held little mystery. If the crime had been other than murder he would have left it to his Scientific Officer assistant, not yet returned from a belated lunch. But murder invariably meant a court appearance and cross-examination—the defense seldom let the scientific evidence go unchallenged in this, the gravest of charges—and a court appearance put document examination in general, and Hoggatt's Laboratory in particular, on public trial. He made it a matter of principle always to take the murder cases himself. They were seldom the most interesting. What he most enjoyed were the historical investigations, the satisfaction of demonstrating, as he had only last month, that a document dated 1872 was printed on paper containing chemical wood pulp that was first used in 1874, a discovery that had initiated a fascinating unraveling of complicated documentary fraud. There was nothing complicated and little of interest about the present job. Yet, only a few years ago, a man's neck could have depended upon his opinion. He seldom thought of the half-dozen men who had been hanged during the twenty years of his forensic experience, primarily because of his evidence, and when he did, it was not the strained but oddly anonymous faces in the dock which he remembered, or their names, but paper and ink, the thickened downward stroke, the peculiar formation of a letter. Now he spread out on his table the note taken from the dead girl's handbag, placing on each side the two specimens of the husband's handwriting which the police had been able to obtain. One was a letter to the suspect's mother written on holiday at Southend—how, he wondered, had they managed to extract that from her? The other was a brief telephoned message about a football match. The note taken from the victim's purse was even briefer.

"You've got your own chap so lay off Barry Taylor or you'll be sorry. It would be a pity to spoil a nice face like yours. Acid isn't pretty. Watch it. A Wellwisher."

The style, he decided, was derived from a recent television thriller; the writing was obviously disguised. It was possible that the police would be able to provide him with some more samples of the suspect's handwriting when they visited the lad's place of work, but he didn't really need them. The similarities between the threatening note and the samples were unmistakable. The writer had tried to alter the slant of his hand and had changed the shape of the small *r*. But the lifts of the pen came regularly at every fourth letter—Middlemass had never yet found a forger who remembered to vary the interval at which he lifted pen from paper—and the dot above the *i*, high and slightly to the left, and the overemphatic apostrophe were almost a trademark. He would analyze the paper sample, photograph and enlarge each individual letter, and then mount them on a comparison chart, and the jury would pass it solemnly from hand to hand and wonder why it needed a highly paid expert to come and explain what anyone could see with his own eyes.

The telephone rang. Middlemass stretched out a long arm and held the instrument to his left ear. Susan Bradley's voice, at first apologetic, then conspiratorial, and finally close to tears, squeaked into his ear in a long monologue of complaint and desperation. He listened, made soft encouraging noises, held the receiver an inch or two from his ear, and meanwhile noted that the writer, poor bastard, hadn't even thought of altering the distinctive crossbar of his small letter *t*. Not that it would have done him any good. And he couldn't have known, poor devil, that his effort would feature as an exhibit in his trial for murder.

"All right," he said. "Don't worry. Leave it to me."

"And you won't let him know that I phoned you?"

"Of course not, Susan. Relax. I'll settle it."

The voice crackled on.

"Then tell him not to be a fool, for God's sake. Hasn't he noticed that we've got one and a half million unemployed? Lorrimer can't sack him. Tell Clifford to hang on to his job and stop being a bloody fool. I'll deal with Lorrimer."

He replaced the receiver. He had liked Susan Moffat who, for two years, had worked for him as his S.O. She had both more brains and more guts than her husband, and he had wondered, without greatly caring, why she had married Bradley. Pity, probably, and an overdeveloped maternal instinct. There were some women who simply had to take the unfortunate literally to their breast. Or perhaps it was just lack of choice, the need for a home of her own and a child. Well, it was too late to try and stop the marriage now, and it certainly hadn't occurred to him to try at the time. And at least she had the home and the kid. She had brought the baby to the lab to see him only a fortnight ago. The visit of the prune-faced yelling bundle had done nothing to change his own resolution not to produce a child, but certainly Susan herself had seemed happy enough. And she would probably be happy again if something could be done about Lorrimer.

He thought that the time had perhaps come to do something about Lorrimer. And he had, after all, his own private reason for taking on the job. It was a small personal obligation, and to date it hadn't particularly fretted what he supposed other people called conscience. But Susan Bradley's call had reminded him. He listened. The footsteps were familiar. Well, it was a coincidence, but better now than later. Moving to the door he called at the retreating back:

"Lorrimer, I want a word with you."

Lorrimer came and stood inside the door, tall, unsmiling in his carefully buttoned white coat, and regarded Middlemass with his dark, wary eyes. Middlemass made himself look into them, and then turned his glance away. The irises had seemed to dilate into black pools of despair. It was not an emotion he felt competent to deal with, and he felt discomforted. What on earth was eating the poor devil? He said, carefully casual:

"Look, Lorrimer, lay off Bradley, will you? I know he's not exactly God's gift to forensic science, but he's a conscientious plodder and you're not going to stimulate either his brain or his speed by bullying the poor little beast. So cut it out."

"Are you telling me how to manage my staff?"

Lorrimer's voice was perfectly controlled, but the pulse at the side of his temple had begun to beat visibly. Middlemass found it difficult not to fix his eyes on it.

"That's right, mate. This member of your staff anyway. I know damn well what you're up to and I don't like it. So stow it."

"Is this meant to be some kind of a threat?"

"More a friendly warning, reasonably friendly anyway. I don't pretend to like you, and I wouldn't have served under you if the Home Office had been daft enough to appoint you Director of this lab. But I admit that what you do in your own department isn't normally my business, only this happens to be an exception. I know what's going on, I don't like it, and I'm making it my business to see that it stops."

"I didn't realize that you had this tender regard for Bradley. But of course, Susan Bradley must have phoned you. He wouldn't have the guts to speak for himself. Did she telephone you, Middlemass?"

Middlemass ignored the question. He said:

"I haven't any particular regard for Bradley. But I did have a certain regard for Peter Ennalls, if you can remember him."

"Ennalls drowned himself because his fiancée threw him over and he'd had a mental breakdown. He left a note explaining his action and it was read out at the inquest. Both things happened months after he'd left the Southern Laboratory; neither had anything to do with me."

"What happened while he was at the lab had a hell of a lot to do with you. He was a pleasant, rather ordinary lad with two good A-levels and an unaccountable wish to become a forensic biologist when he had the bad luck to begin work under you. As it happens, he was my wife's cousin. I was the one who recommended him to try for the job. So I have a certain interest, you could say a certain responsibility."

Lorrimer said:

"He never said that he was related to your wife. But I can't see what difference it makes. He was totally unsuited for the job. A forensic biologist who can't work accurately under pressure is no use to me or the Service and he'd better get out. We've no room for passengers. That's what I propose to tell Bradley."

"Then you'd better have second thoughts."

"And how are you going to make me?"

It was extraordinary that lips so tight could produce any sound, that Lorrimer's voice, high and distorted, could have forced itself through the vocal cords without splitting them.

"I shall make it plain to Howarth that you and I can't serve in the same lab. He won't exactly welcome that. Trouble between senior staff is the last complication he wants just now. So he'll suggest to Establishment Department that one of us gets a transfer before we have the added complication of moving into a new lab. I'm banking on Howarth—and Estabs, come to that—concluding that it's easier to find a forensic biologist than a Document Examiner."

Middlemass surprised himself. None of this rigmarole had occurred to him before he spoke. Not that it was unreasonable. There wasn't another Document Examiner of his caliber in the Service and Howarth knew it. If he categorically refused to work in the same laboratory as Lorrimer, one of them would have to go. The quarrel wouldn't do either of them any good with the Establishment

Department, but he thought he knew which one it would harm most.

Lorrimer said:

"You helped stop me getting the directorship, now you want to drive me out of the lab."

"Personally I don't care a damn whether you're here or not. But just lay off bullying Bradley."

"If I were prepared to take advice about the way I run my department from anyone, it wouldn't be a third-rate paper fetishist with a second-rate degree, who doesn't know the difference between scientific proof and intuition."

The taunt was too absurd to puncture Middlemass's secure self-esteem. But at least it warranted a retort. He found that he was getting angry. And suddenly he saw light. He said:

"Look, mate, if you can't make it in bed, if she isn't finding you quite up to the mark, don't take your frustration out on the rest of us. Remember Chesterfield's advice. The expense is exorbitant, the position ridiculous, and the pleasure transitory."

The result astounded him. Lorrimer gave a strangled cry and lunged out. Middlemass's reaction was both instinctive and deeply satisfying. He shot out his right arm and landed a punch on Lorrimer's nose. There was a second's astonished silence in which the two men regarded each other. Then the blood spurted and Lorrimer tottered and fell forward. Middlemass caught him by the shoulders and felt the weight of his head against his chest. He thought: "My God, he's going to faint." He was aware of a tangle of emotion: surprise at himself, boyish gratification, pity, and an impulse to laugh. He said:

"Are you all right?"

Lorrimer tore himself from his grasp and stood upright. He fumbled for his handkerchief and held it to his nose. The red stain grew. Looking down, Middlemass saw Lorrimer's blood spreading on his white coat, decorative as a rose. He said:

"Since we're engaging in histrionics, I believe your response ought now to be, 'By God, you swine, you'll pay for this.' "

He was astounded by the sudden blaze of hate in the black eyes. Lorrimer's voice came to him muffled by the handkerchief.

"You will pay for it." And then he was gone.

Middlemass was suddenly aware of Mrs. Bidwell, the laboratory cleaner, standing by the door, eyes large and excited behind her ridiculous upswept diamanté spectacles.

"Nice goings-on, I don't think. Senior staff fighting each other. You ought to be ashamed of yourselves."

"Oh we are, Mrs. Bidwell. We are." Slowly Middlemass eased his long arms from his coat. He handed it to her.

"Drop this in the soiled linen, will you."

"Now you know very well, Mr. Middlemass, that I don't go into the gents' cloakroom, not in working hours. You put it in the basket yourself. And if you want a clean one now, you know where to find it. I'm putting out no more clean linen until tomorrow. Fighting, indeed. I might have known that Dr. Lorrimer would be mixed up in it. But he's not a gentleman you'd expect to find using his fists. Wouldn't have the guts, that would be my view. But he's been odd in his manner these last few weeks, no doubt about that. You heard about that spot of bother in the front hall yesterday, I suppose? He practically pushed those kids of Dr. Kerrison's out of the door. All they were doing was waiting for their dad. No harm in that, I suppose. There's a very nasty atmosphere in this lab recently, and if a certain gentleman doesn't take hold of himself there'll be mischief done, you mark my words."

# X

It was nearly five o'clock and dark before Detective-Inspector Doyle got back to his home in the village four miles to the north of Cambridge. He had tried to telephone his wife once, but without success: the line was engaged. Another of her interminable, secretive, and expensive telephone calls to one of her old nursing friends, he thought, and, duty satisfied, made no further attempt. The wrought-iron gate, as usual, was open and he parked in front of the house. It wasn't worth garaging the car for a couple of hours, which was all the time he could allow himself.

Scoope House hardly looked its best in the late afternoon of a dark November evening. No wonder that the agents hadn't recently sent anyone to view. It was a bad time of the year. The house was, he thought, a monument to miscalculation. He had bought it for less than seventeen thousand and had spent five thousand on it to date, expecting to sell it for at least forty. But that was before the recession had upset the calculations of more expert speculators than he. Now, with the property market sluggish, there was nothing to do but wait. He could afford to hang onto the house until the market quickened. He wasn't sure that he would be given a chance to hold onto his wife. He wasn't even sure that he wanted to. The marriage, too, had been a miscalculation, but given the circumstances of the time, an understandable one. He wasted no time on regrets.

The two tall oblongs of light from the first-floor drawing-room window should have been a welcoming promise of warmth and comfort. Instead they were vaguely menacing; Maureen was at home. But where else, she would have argued, was there for her to go in this dreary East Anglian village on a dull November evening?

She had finished tea, and the tray was still at her side. The milk bottle, with its crushed top pressed back, a single mug, sliced bread spilling out of its wrapper, a slab of butter on a greasy dish, a bought fruitcake in its unopened carton. He felt the customary surge of irritation, but said nothing. Once when he had remonstrated at her sluttishness she had shrugged:

"Who sees, who cares?"

He saw and he cared, but it had been many months since he had counted with her. He said:

"I'm taking a couple of hours' nap. Wake me at seven, will you?"

"You mean we aren't going to the Chevisham concert?"

"For God's sake, Maureen, you were yelling yesterday that you couldn't be bothered with it. Kid's stuff. Remember?"

"It's not exactly the Talk of the Town, but at least we were going out. Out! Out of this dump. Together for a change. It was something to dress up for. And you said we'd have dinner afterwards at the Chinese restaurant at Ely."

"Sorry. I couldn't know I'd be on a murder case."

"When will you be back? If there's any point in asking."

"God knows. I'm picking up Sergeant Beale. There are still one or two people we've got to see who were at the Muddington dance, notably a lad called Barry Taylor who has some explaining to do. Depending on what we get out of him, I may want to drop in on the husband again."

"That'll please you, won't it, keeping him in a muck sweat. Is that why you became a cop—because you like frightening people?"

"That's about as stupid as saying you became a nurse because you get a kick out of emptying bedpans."

He flung himself in a chair and closed his eyes, giving way to sleep. He saw again the boy's terrified face, smelled again the sweat of fear. But he'd stood up well to that first interview, hindered rather than helped by the presence of his solicitor, who had never seen his client before and had made it painfully apparent that he would prefer never to see him again. He had stuck to his story, that they'd quarreled at the dance and he had left early. That she hadn't arrived home by one o'clock. That he'd gone out to look for her on the road and across the clunch pit field, returning alone half an hour later. That he'd seen no one and hadn't been anywhere near the clunch pit or the derelict car. It was a good story, simple, unelaborated, possibly even true except in that one essential. But, with luck, the lab report on her blood and the stain on his jacket cuff, the minute traces of sandy soil and dust from the car on his shoes, would be ready by Friday. If Lorrimer worked late tonight—and he usually did—the blood analysis might even be available by tomorrow. And then would come the elaborations, the inconsistencies, and finally the truth. She said:

"Who else was at the scene?"

It was something, he thought, that she had bothered to ask. He said sleepily:

"Lorrimer, of course. He never misses a murder scene. Doesn't trust any of us to know our jobs, I suppose. We had the usual half-hour hanging about for Kerrison. That maddened Lorrimer, of course. He's done all the work at the scene—all anyone can do—and then he has to cool his heels with the rest of us, waiting for God's gift to forensic pathology to come screaming up with a police escort and break the news to us that what we all thought was a corpse is—surprise, surprise—indeed a corpse, and that we can safely move the body."

"The forensic pathologist does more than that."

"Of course he does. But not all that much more, not at the actual scene. His job comes later."

He added:

"Sorry I couldn't call. I did try but you were engaged."

"I expect that was Daddy. His offer still stands, the job of Security Officer in the Organization. But he can't wait much longer. If you don't accept by the end of the month, then he'll advertise."

Oh God, he thought, not that again.

"I wish your dear Daddy wouldn't talk about the Organization. It makes the family business sound like the Mafia. If it were, I might be tempted to join. What Daddy's got are three cheap, shabby shops selling cheap, shabby suits to cheap, shabby fools who wouldn't recognize a decent cloth if it were shoved down their throats. I might've considered coming into the business if dear Daddy hadn't already got Big Brother as a co-director, ready to take over from him, and if he didn't make it so plain that he only tolerates me because I'm your husband. But I'm damned if I'm going to fart around like a pansy floor-walker watching that no poor sod nicks the Y-fronts, even if I am dignified with the name Security Officer. I'm staying here."

"Where you've got such useful contacts."

And what exactly, he wondered, did she mean by that? He'd been careful not to tell her anything, but she wasn't altogether a fool. She could have guessed. He said:

"Where I've got a job. You knew what you were taking on when you married me."

But no one ever does know that, he thought. Not really.

"Don't expect me to be here when you get back."

That was an old threat. He said easily:

"Suit yourself. But if you're thinking of driving, forget it. I'm taking the Cortina, the clutch is playing up on the Renault. So if you're planning on running home to Mummy before tomorrow morning, you'll have to phone Daddy to call for you, or take a taxi."

She was speaking, but her voice, peevishly insistent, was coming from far away, no longer coherent words but waves of sound beating against his brain. Two hours. Whether or not she bothered to rouse him, he knew that he would wake almost to the minute. He closed his eyes and slept.

# BOOK TWO

·

# Death in a White Coat

# I

It was very peaceful in the front hall of Hoggatt's at eight-forty in the morning. Brenda often thought that this was the part of the working day she liked best, the hour before the staff arrived and the work of the lab got really under way, when she and Inspector Blakelock worked together in the quiet emptiness of the hall, still and solemn as a church, making up a supply of manila folders ready to register the day's new cases, repacking exhibits for collection by the police, making a final check of the laboratory reports to courts to ensure that the examination was complete, that no relevant detail had been omitted. Immediately on arrival she would put on her white coat, and at once she felt different, no longer young and uncertain, but a professional woman, almost like a scientist, a recognized member of the lab staff. Then she would go into the kitchen at the back of the house and make tea. After the dignification of the white coat this domestic chore was something of a letdown, and she didn't really need a drink so soon after breakfast. But Inspector Blakelock, who motored from Ely every day, was always ready for his tea, and she didn't mind making it.

"That's the stuff to give the troops," he would invariably say, curving back moist lips to the mug's brim and gulping the hot liquid down as if his throat were asbestos. "You make a nice cup of tea, Brenda, I'll say that for you." And she would reply:

"Mum says the secret is always to warm the pot and let the tea brew for just five minutes."

This small ritual exchange, so invariable that she could silently mouth his words and had to resist an impulse to giggle, the familiar domestic aroma of the tea, the gradual warmth as she curved her hands around the thick mug, constituted a reassuring and comforting beginning to the working day.

She liked Inspector Blakelock. He spoke seldom, but he was never impatient with her, always kind, a companionable father figure. Even her mother, when she visited the lab before Brenda took up her post, had been happy about her working alone with him. Brenda's cheeks still burned with shame when she remembered her mother's insistence that she should visit Hoggatt's to see where her daughter was going to work, although Chief Inspector Martin, the Senior Police Liaison Officer, had apparently thought it perfectly reasonable. He had explained to her mother how it was an innovation for Hoggatt's to have a clerical officer on the desk instead of a junior police officer. If she made a success of the job it would mean a permanent saving in police manpower as well as useful training for her. As Chief Inspector Martin had told her mother, "The reception desk is the heart of the laboratory." At present he was with a party of police officers visiting the United States and Inspector Blakelock was totally in charge doing the two jobs, not only receiving the exhibits, making out the register of court attendances, and preparing the statistics, but discussing the cases with the detective in charge, explaining what the laboratory could hope to do, rejecting those cases where the scientists couldn't help, and checking that the final statements for the court were complete. Brenda guessed that it was a big responsibility for him and was determined not to let him down.

Already, when she had been making the tea, the first exhibit of the day had arrived, brought in no doubt by a detective-constable working on the case. It was another plastic bag of clothes from the clunch pit murder. As Inspector Blakelock turned it over in his large hands, she glimpsed through the plastic a pair of dark blue trousers with a greasy waistband, a wide-lapeled striped jacket, and a pair of black shoes with pointed toes and ornate buckles. Inspector Blakelock was studying the police report. He said:

"These belong to the boyfriend she was messing about with at the dance. You'll need a new file for the report, but register it to Biology under the Muddington reference with a subgroup number. Then attach one of the red Immediate slips. Murder gets priority."

"But we might have two or three murders at the same time. Who decides the priority then?"

"The head of the department concerned. It's his job to allocate the work to his staff. After murder and rape, it's usual to give priority to those cases where the accused hasn't been bailed."

Brenda said:

"I hope you don't mind my asking so many questions. Only I do want to learn. Dr. Lorrimer told me that I ought to find out all I can and not just look on this job as routine."

"You ask away, lass, I don't mind. Only you don't want to listen too much to Dr. Lorrimer. He isn't the Director here, even if he thinks he is. When you've registered that clobber, the bundle goes on the Biology shelf."

Brenda entered the exhibit number carefully in the daybook and moved the plastic-shrouded bundle to the shelf of exhibits waiting to go into the Biology Search Room. It was good to be up to date with the entering. She glanced up at the clock. It was nearly eight-fifty. Soon the day's mail would be delivered and the desk would be heaped with padded envelopes containing yesterday's blood samples from the drunk-and-driving cases. Then the police cars would start arriving. Uniformed or plainclothes policemen would bring in large envelopes of documents for Mr. Middlemass, the Document Examiner; specially prepared kits issued by the laboratory for the collection of saliva, blood, and semen stains; unwieldy bags of stained and dirty bed linen and blankets; the ubiquitous blunt instruments; bloodstained knives carefully taped into their boxes.

And at any moment now the first members of staff would be arriving. Mrs. Bidwell, the cleaner, should have been with them twenty minutes ago. Perhaps she had caught Scobie's influenza. The first of the scientific staff to arrive would probably be Clifford Bradley, the Higher Scientific Officer in the Biology Department, scurrying through the hall as if he had no right to be there, with his anxious, hunted eyes and that stupid, drooping moustache, so preoccupied that he hardly noticed their greeting. Then Miss Foley, the Director's secretary, calm and self-possessed, wearing always that secret smile. Miss Foley reminded Brenda of Mona Rigby at school, who was always chosen to play the Madonna in the Christmas nativity play. She had never liked Mona Rigby—who wouldn't have been chosen twice for the coveted role if the staff had known as much about her as did Brenda—and she wasn't sure that she really liked Miss Foley. Then someone she did like, Mr. Middlemass, the Document Examiner, with his jacket slung over his shoulders, leaping up the stairs three steps at a time and calling out a greeting to the desk. After that they would come in almost any order. The hall would become alive with people, rather like a railway terminus, and at the heart of the seeming chaos, controlling and directing, helping and explaining, were the staff of the reception desk.

As if to signal that the working day was about to begin, the telephone rang. Inspector Blakelock's hand enveloped the receiver. He listened in silence for what seemed a longer period than normal, then she heard him speak.

"I don't think he's here, Mr. Lorrimer. You say he never came home last night?"

Another silence. Inspector Blakelock half turned away from her and bent his head conspiratorially over the mouthpiece as if listening to a confidence. Then he rested the receiver on the counter and turned to Brenda:

"It's Dr. Lorrimer's old dad. He's worried. Apparently Dr. Lorrimer didn't take him his early tea this morning and it looks as if he didn't come home last night. His bed hasn't been slept in."

"Well, he can't be here. I mean, we found the front door locked when we arrived."

There could be no doubt about that. As she had come around the corner of the house from putting her bicycle in the old stable block, Inspector Blakelock had been standing at the front door almost as if he were waiting for her. Then, when she had joined him, he had shone his flashlight on the locks and inserted the three keys, first the Yale, and then the Ingersoll, and lastly the security lock which disconnected the electronic warning system from Guy's Marsh police station. Then they had stepped together into the unlighted hall. She had gone to the cloakroom at the back of the building to put on her white coat and he had gone to the box in Chief Inspector Martin's office to switch off the system that protected the inner doors of the main laboratory rooms.

She giggled and said:

"Mrs. Bidwell hasn't turned up to start the cleaning and now Dr. Lorrimer's missing. Perhaps they've run away together. The great Hoggatt scandal."

It wasn't a very funny joke, and she wasn't surprised when Inspector Blakelock didn't laugh. He said:

"The locked door doesn't necessarily signify. Dr. Lorrimer has his own keys. And if he did make his bed and then come in extra early this morning, like as not he'd have relocked the door and set the internal alarms."

"But how would he have got into the Biology Lab, then?"

"He'd have had to have opened the door and then left it open when he reset the alarms. It doesn't seem likely. When he's here alone he usually relies on the Yale."

He put the receiver again to his ear and said:

"Hold on a moment, will you, Mr. Lorrimer. I don't think he's here, but I'll just check."

"I'll go," said Brenda, anxious to demonstrate helpfulness. Without waiting to lift the hatch she slipped under the counter. As she turned she saw him with startling clarity, brightly instantaneous as a camera flash. Inspector Blakelock, with his mouth half-open in remonstrance, his arm flung out toward her in a gesture, stiff and histrionic, of protection or restraint. But now, uncomprehending, she laughed and ran up the wide stairs. The Biology Laboratory was at the back of the second floor, running with its adjoining search room almost the whole length of the building. The door was shut. She turned the knob and pushed it open, feeling along the wall for the light switch. Her fingers found it and she pressed it down. The two long fluorescent tubes suspended from the ceiling blinked, then glimmered, then glowed into steady light.

She saw the body immediately. He was lying in the space between the two large central examination tables, face downward, his left hand seeming to claw at the floor, his right arm hunched beneath him. His legs were straight. She gave a curious little sound between a cry and a moan and knelt beside him. The hair above his left ear was matted and spiked like her kitten's fur after he had washed, and she couldn't see the blood against the dark hair. But she knew that it was blood. Already it had blackened on the collar of his white coat and a small pool had separated and congealed on the lab floor. Only his left eye was visible, fixed and dull and retracted, like the eye of a dead calf. Tentatively she felt his cheek. It was cold. But she had known as soon as she had seen that glazed eye that this was death.

She had no memory of closing the lab door or coming down the stairs. Inspector Blakelock was still behind the counter, rigid as a statue, the telephone receiver in his hand. She wanted to laugh at the sight of his face, he looked so funny. She tried to speak to him, but the words wouldn't come. Her jaw jabbered uncontrollably and her teeth clattered together. She made some kind of gesture. He said something that she couldn't catch, dropped the receiver on the counter, and raced upstairs.

She staggered to the heavy Victorian armchair against the wall outside Chief Inspector Martin's office, Colonel Hoggatt's chair. The portrait looked down at her. As she watched, the left eye seemed to grow larger, the lips twisted to a leer.

Her whole body was seized with a terrible cold. Her heart seemed to have grown immense, thudding against the rib cage. She was breathing in great gulps, but still there wasn't enough air. Then she became aware of the crackling from the telephone. Rising slowly like an automaton, she made her way over to the counter and picked up the receiver. Mr. Lorrimer's voice, frail and querulous, was bleating at the other end. She tried to say the accustomed words "Hoggatt's Laboratory here. Reception speaking." But the words wouldn't come. She replaced the receiver in its cradle and walked back to her chair.

She had no memory of hearing the long peal of the doorbell, of moving stiffly across the hall to answer it. Suddenly the door crashed open and the hall was full of people, loud with voices. The light seemed to have brightened, which was odd, and she saw them all like actors on a stage, brightly lit, faces made grotesque and heightened by makeup, every word clear and comprehensible as if she were in the front row of the stalls. Mrs. Bidwell, the cleaner, in her mackintosh with the imitation fur collar, her eyes bright with indignation, her voice pitched high.

"What the hell's going on here! Some bloody fool phoned my old man and told him that I needn't come in today, that Mrs. Schofield wanted me. Who's playing silly buggers?"

Inspector Blakelock was coming down the stairs, slowly and deliberately, the chief protagonist making his entrance. They stood in a small circle and looked up at him, Dr. Howarth, Clifford Bradley, Miss Foley, Mrs. Bidwell. The Director stepped forward. He looked as if he were going to faint. He said:

"Well, Blakelock?"

"It's Dr. Lorrimer, sir. He's dead. Murdered."

Surely they couldn't all have repeated that word in unison, turning their faces toward each other, like a Greek chorus. But it seemed to echo in the quiet of the hall, becoming meaningless, a sonorous groan of a word. *Murder. Murder. Murder.*

She saw Dr. Howarth run toward the stairs. Inspector Blakelock turned to accompany him, but the Director said:

"No, you stay here. See that no one gets any farther than the hall. Phone the Chief Constable and Dr. Kerrison. Then get me the Home Office."

Suddenly they seemed to notice Brenda for the first time. Mrs. Bidwell came toward her. She said:

"Did you find him then? You poor little bugger!"

And suddenly it wasn't a play any more. The lights went out. The faces became amorphous, ordinary. Brenda gave a little gasp. She felt Mrs. Bidwell's arms go around her shoulders. The smell of the mackintosh was pressed into her face. The fur was as soft as her kitten's paw. And, blessedly, Brenda began to cry.

# II

In a London teaching hospital close by the river, from which he could in his more masochistic moments glimpse the window of his own office, Dr. Charles Freeborn, Controller of the Forensic Science Service, all six foot four of him, lay rigidly in his narrow bed, his nose peaked high above the methodical fold of the sheet, his white hair a haze against the whiter pillow. The bed was too short for him, an inconvenience to which he had accommodated himself by neatly sticking out his toes over the foot board. His bedside locker held the conglomerate of offerings, necessities, and minor diversions considered indispensable to a brief spell in the hospital. They included a vase of official-looking roses, scentless but florid, through whose funereal and unnatural blooms Commander Adam Dalgliesh glimpsed a face so immobile, upturned eyes fixed on the ceiling, that he was momentarily startled by the illusion that he was visiting the dead. Recalling that Freeborn was recovering from nothing more serious than a successful operation for varicose veins, he approached the bed and said tentatively:

"Hello!"

Freeborn, galvanized from his torpor, sprang up like a jack-in-the-box, scattering from his bedside locker a packet of tissues, two copies of the *Journal of the Forensic Science Society,* and an open box of chocolates. He shot out a lean, speckled arm encircled by the hospital identity bracelet and crushed Dalgliesh's hand.

"Adam! Don't creep up on me like that, damn you! God, am I glad to see you! The only good news I've had this morning is that you'll be in charge. I thought that you might have already left. How long can you spare? How are you getting there?"

Dalgliesh answered the questions in order.

"Ten minutes. By chopper from the Battersea heliport. I'm on my way now. How are you, Charles? Am I being a nuisance?"

"I'm the nuisance. This couldn't have happened at a worse time. And the maddening part of it is that it's my own fault. The op could have waited. Only the pain was getting rather tedious and Meg insisted that I have it done now before I retire, on the theory, I suppose, that better in the government's time than my own."

Recalling what he knew of the ardors and achievements of Freeborn's forty-odd years in the Forensic Science Service, the difficult war years, the delayed retirement, the last five years when he had exchanged his directorship for the frustrations of bureaucracy, Dalgliesh said:

"Sensible of her. And there's nothing you could have done at Chevisham."

"I know. It's ridiculous, this feeling of responsibility because one isn't actually at one's post when disaster strikes. They phoned from the duty office to break the news to me just after nine. Better that than learning it from my visitors or this evening's paper, I suppose they thought. Decent of them. The Chief Constable must have called in the Yard within a few minutes of getting the news. How much do you know?"

"About as much as you, I imagine. I've spoken to the C.C. and to Howarth. They've given me the main facts. The skull smashed, apparently by a heavy mallet which Lorrimer had been examining. The lab found properly locked when the Assistant Police Liaison Officer and the young C.O. arrived at eight-thirty this morning. Lorrimer's keys in his pocket. He often worked late and most of the lab staff knew that he proposed to do so last night. No sign of a break-in. Four sets of keys. Lorrimer had one set as the Senior P.S.O. and Deputy Security Officer. The Assistant Police Liaison Officer has the second. Lorrimer or one of the Police Liaison Officers were the only people authorized to lock and open up the building. The Director keeps the third set of keys in his security cupboard, and the fourth is in a safe at Guy's Marsh police station in case the alarm rings in the night."

Freeborn said:

"So either Lorrimer let in his murderer or the murderer had a key."

There were, thought Dalgliesh, other possibilities, but now was not the time to discuss them. He asked:

"Lorrimer would have let in anyone from the lab, I suppose?"

"Why not? He'd probably have admitted any of the local police whom he personally knew, particularly if it were a detective concerned with a recent case. Otherwise, I'm not so sure. He may have admitted a friend or relative, although that's even more doubtful. He was a punctilious blighter and I can't see him using the lab as a convenient place for a rendezvous. And, of course, he would have let in the forensic pathologist."

"That's a local man, Henry Kerrison, they tell me. The C.C. said that they called him in to look at the body. Well, they could hardly do anything else. I didn't know you'd found a successor to Death-House Donald."

"Nor have we. Kerrison is doing it on an item of service basis. He's well thought of and we'll probably appoint him if we can get the Area Health Authority to agree. There's the usual difficulty about his hospital responsibilities. I wish to hell we could get the Forensic Pathology Service sorted out before I go. But that's one headache I'll have to leave to my successor."

Dalgliesh thought without affection of Death-House Donald, with his ghoulish schoolboy humor—"Not that cake knife, my dear lady. I used it this morning on one of Slash Harry's victims and the edge is rather blunted"—his mania for self-advertisement, and his intolerable bucolic laugh, and was grateful that at least he wouldn't be interrogating that redoubtable old phony. He said:

"Tell me about Lorrimer. What was he like?"

This was the question that lay at the heart of every murder investigation; and yet he knew its absurdity before he asked it. It was the strangest part of a detective's job, this building up of a relationship with the dead, seen only as a crumpled corpse at the scene of crime or naked on the mortuary table. The victim was central to the mystery of his own death. He died because of what he was. Before the case was finished Dalgliesh would have received a dozen pictures of Lorrimer's personality, transferred like prints from other men's minds. From these amorphous and uncertain images he would create his own imaginings, superimposed and dominant, but essentially just as incomplete, just as distorted—as were the others—by his own preconceptions, his own personality. But the question had to be asked. And at least he could rely on Freeborn to answer it without initiating a philosophical discussion about the basis of the self. But their minds must for a moment have flowed together, for Freeborn said:

"It's odd how you always have to ask that question, that you'll only see him through other men's eyes. Aged about forty. Looks like John the Baptist without his beard and is about as uncompromising. Single. Lives with an elderly father in a cottage just outside the village. He is—was—an extremely competent forensic biologist, but I doubt whether he would have gone any higher. Obsessional, edgy, uncomfortable to be with. He applied for the job at Hoggatt's, of course, and was runner-up to Howarth."

"How did he and the lab take the new appointment?"

"Lorrimer took it pretty hard, I believe. The lab wouldn't have welcomed his appointment. He was pretty unpopular with most of the senior staff. But there are always one or two who would have preferred a colleague to a stranger even if they hated his guts. And the Union made the expected noises about not appointing a forensic scientist."

"Why did you appoint Howarth? I take it you were on the Board."

"Oh yes. I accept a share of the responsibility. That's not to say that I think we made a mistake. Old Doc Mac was one of the really great forensic scientists—we started together—but there's no denying that he'd let the reins slip a bit in recent years. Howarth has already increased the work turnover by ten percent. And then there's the commissioning of the new lab. It was a calculated risk to take a man without forensic experience, but we were looking for a manager primarily. At least, most of the Board were and the rest of us were persuaded that it would be no bad thing, without, I confess, being precisely clear what we meant by that blessed word. Management. The new science. We all make obeisance to it. In the old days we got on with the job, jollied staff along if they needed it, kicked the sluggards in the backside, encouraged the unconfident, and persuaded a reluctant and skeptical police force to use us. Oh, and sent in an occasional statistical return to the Home Office just to remind them that we were there. It seemed to work all right. The Service didn't collapse. Have you ever considered what exactly is the difference between administration and management, Adam?"

"Keep it as a question to confound the candidate at your next Board. Howarth was at the Bruche Research Institute, wasn't he? Why did he want to leave? He must have taken a cut in pay."

"Not more than about six hundred a year, and that wouldn't worry him. His father was rich, and it all came to him and his half sister."

"But it's a bigger place surely? And he can't be getting the research at Hoggatt's."

"He gets some, but essentially, of course, it's a service laboratory. That worried us a bit on the Board. But you can hardly set out to persuade your most promising applicant that he's downgrading himself. Scientifically and academically—he's a pure physicist—he was well ahead of the rest of the field. Actually we did press him a bit and he gave the usual reasons. He was getting stale, wanted a new sphere of activity, was anxious to get away from London. Gossip has it that his wife had recently left him and he wanted to make a clean break. That was probably the reason. Thank God he didn't use that blasted word *challenge*. If I have to listen to one more candidate telling me he sees the job as a challenge I'll throw up over the boardroom table. Adam, I'm getting old."

He nodded his head toward the window.

"They're in a bit of a twitch over there, I need hardly say."

"I know. I've had an exceedingly brief but tactful interview. They're brilliant at implying more than they actually say. But obviously it's important to get it solved quickly. Apart from confidence in the Service, you'll all want to get the lab back to work."

"What's happening now? To the staff, I mean."

"The local C.I.D. have locked all the interior doors and they're keeping the staff in the library and the reception area until I arrive. They're occupying themselves writing out an account of their movements since Lorrimer was last seen alive and the local force are getting on with the preliminary checking of alibis. That should save some time. I'm taking one officer, John Massingham, with me. The Met Lab will take on any of the forensic work. They're sending a chap down from Public Relations Branch to handle the publicity, so I won't have that on my plate. It's obliging of that pop group to break up so spectacularly. That and the government's troubles should keep us off the front page for a day or two."

Freeborn was looking down at his big toes with mild distaste as if they were errant members whose deficiencies had only now become apparent to him. From time to time he wriggled them, whether in obedience to some medical instruction or for his own private satisfaction, it was impossible to say. After a moment he spoke.

"I started my career at Hoggatt's, you know. That was before the war. All any of us had then was wet chemistry, test tubes, beakers, solutions. And girls weren't employed because it wasn't decent for them to be concerned with sex cases. Hoggatt's was old-fashioned even for the 1930 Service. Not scientifically, though. We had a spectrograph when it was still the new wonder toy. The fens threw up some odd crimes. Do you remember the Mulligan case, old man who chopped up his brother and tied the remains to the Leamings sluice gates? There was some nice forensic evidence there."

"Some fifty bloodstains on the pigsty wall, weren't there? And Mulligan swore it was sow's blood."

Freeborn's voice grew reminiscent.

"I liked that old villain. And they still drag out those photographs I took of the splashes and use them to illustrate lectures on bloodstains. Odd, the attraction Hoggatt's had—still has, for that matter. An unsuitable Palladian mansion in an unexciting East Anglian village on the edge of the black fens. Ten miles to Ely, and that's hardly a center of riotous activity for the young. Winters to freeze your marrow and a spring wind—the fen blow they call it—that whips up the peat and chokes your lungs like smog. And yet the staff, if they didn't leave after the first month, stayed forever. Did you know that Hoggatt's has got a small Wren chapel on the lab grounds? Architecturally it's much superior to the house because old Hoggatt never messed with it. He was almost entirely without esthetic taste, I believe. He used it as a chemical store once it had been deconsecrated or whatever it is they do to unused churches. Howarth has got a string quartet going at the lab and they gave a concert there. Apparently he's a noted amateur violinist. At the moment he's probably wishing that he'd stuck to music. This isn't a propitious start for him, poor devil. And it was always such a happy lab. I suppose it was the isolation that gave us such a feeling of camaraderie."

Dalgliesh said grimly:

"I doubt whether that will survive an hour of my arrival."

"No. You chaps usually bring as much trouble with you as you solve. You can't help it. Murder is like that, a contaminating crime. Oh, you'll solve it, I know. You always do. But I'm wondering at what cost."

Dalgliesh did not answer. He was both too honest and too fond of Freeborn to make comforting and platitudinous promises. Of course, he would be tactful. That didn't need saying. But he would be at Hoggatt's to solve a murder, and all other considerations would go down before that overriding task. Murder was always solved at a cost, sometimes to himself, more often to others. And Freeborn was right. It was a crime that contaminated everyone whom it touched, innocent and guilty alike. He didn't grudge the ten minutes he had spent with Freeborn. The old man believed, with simple patriotism, that the Service to which he had given the whole of his working life was the best in the world. He had helped to shape it, and he was probably right. Dalgliesh had learned what he had come to learn. But as he shook hands and said goodbye he knew that he left no comfort behind him.

# III

The library at Hoggatt's was at the rear of the ground floor. Its three tall windows gave a view of the stone terrace and the double flight of steps going down to what had once been a lawn and formal gardens, but which was now a half-acre of neglected grass, bounded to the west by the brick annex of the Vehicle Examination Department, and to the east by the old stable block, now converted into garages. The room was one of the few in the house spared by its former owner's transforming zeal. The original bookcases of carved oak still lined the walls, although they now housed the laboratory's not inconsiderable scientific library, while extra shelf room for bound copies of national and international journals had been provided by two movable steel units which divided the room into three bays. Under each of the three windows was a working table with four chairs; one table was almost completely covered by a model of the new laboratory.

It was in this somewhat inadequate space that the staff were congregated. A detective-sergeant from the local C.I.D. sat impassively near the door, a reminder of why they were so inconveniently incarcerated. They were allowed out to the ground-floor cloakroom under tactful escort and had been told they could telephone home from the library. But the rest of the laboratory was at present out of bounds.

They had all, on arrival, been asked to write a brief account of where they had been, and with whom, the previous evening and night. Patiently, they waited their turn at one of the three tables. The statements had been collected by the sergeant and handed out to his colleague on the reception desk, presumably so that the preliminary checking could begin. Those of the junior staff who could provide a satisfactory alibi were allowed home as soon as it had been checked; one by one and with some reluctance at missing the excitements to come they went their way. The less fortunate, together with those who had arrived first at the laboratory that morning and all the senior scientists, had been told that they must await the arrival of the team from

Scotland Yard. The Director had put in only one brief appearance in the library. Earlier he had gone with Angela Foley to break the news of Lorrimer's death to his father. Since his return he had stayed in his own office with Detective-Superintendent Mercer of the local C.I.D. It was rumored that Dr. Kerrison was with them.

The minutes dragged while they listened for the first hum of the approaching helicopter. Inhibited by the presence of the police, by prudence, delicacy, or embarrassment from talking about the subject foremost in their minds, they spoke to each other with the wary politeness of uncongenial strangers stranded in an airport lounge. The women were, on the whole, better equipped for the tedium of the wait. Mrs. Mallett, the typist from the general office, had brought her knitting to work and, fortified by an unshakable alibi—she had sat between the postmistress and Mr. Mason from the general store at the village concert—and with something to occupy her hands, sat clicking away with understandable if irritating complacency until given the order of release. Mrs. Bidwell, the laboratory cleaner, had insisted on visiting her broom cupboard, under escort, and had provided herself with a feather duster and a couple of rags with which she had made a vigorous onslaught on the bookshelves. She was unusually silent, but the group of scientists at the tables could hear her muttering to herself as she punished the books at the end of one of the bays.

Brenda Pridmore had been allowed to collect the exhibits-received book from the counter and, white-faced but outwardly composed, was checking the previous month's figures. The book took more than its share of the available table space; but at least she had a legitimate job. Claire Easterbrook, Senior Scientific Officer in the Biology Department and, with Lorrimer's death, the Senior Biologist, had taken from her briefcase a scientific paper she had prepared on recent advances in blood grouping and had settled down to revise it with as little apparent concern as if murder at Hoggatt's were a routine inconvenience for which, prudently, she was always provided.

The rest of the staff passed the time each in his own way. Those who preferred the pretense of business immersed themselves in a book and, from time to time, made an ostentatious note. The two Vehicle Examiners, who were reputed to have no conversation except about cars, squatted side by side, their backs against the steel book racks, and talked cars together with desperate eagerness. Middlemass had finished *The Times* crossword by quarter to ten and had made the rest of the paper last as long as possible. But now even the deaths column was exhausted. He folded the paper and tossed it across the table to eagerly waiting hands.

It was a relief when Stephen Copley, the Senior Chemist, arrived just before ten, bustling in as usual, his rubicund face with its tonsure and fringe of black curly hair glistening as if he had come in from the sun. Nothing was known to disconcert him, certainly not the death of a man he had disliked. But he was secure in his alibi, having spent the whole of the previous day in the Crown Court and the evening and night with friends at Norwich, only getting back to Chevisham in time for a late start that morning. His colleagues, relieved to find something to talk about, began questioning him about the case. They spoke rather too loudly to be natural. The rest of the company listened with simulated interest as if the conversation were a dramatic dialogue provided for their entertainment.

"Who did they call for the defense?" asked Middlemass.

"Charlie Pollard. He hung his great belly over the box and explained confidentially to the jury that they needn't be frightened of the so-called scientific expert witnesses because none of us, including himself, of course, really know what we're talking about. They were immensely reassured, I need hardly say."

"Juries hate scientific evidence."

"They think they won't be able to understand it so naturally they can't understand it. As soon as you step into the box you see a curtain of obstinate incomprehension clanging down over their minds. What they want is certainty. Did this paint particle come from this car body? Answer yes or no. None of those nasty mathematical probabilities we're so fond of."

"If they hate scientific evidence they certainly hate arithmetic more. Give them a scientific opinion that depends on the ability to divide a factor by two-thirds and what do you get from counsel? 'I'm afraid you'll have to explain yourself more simply, Mr. Middlemass. The jury and I haven't got a higher degree in mathematics, you know.' Inference: You're an arrogant bastard and the jury would be well advised not to believe a word you say."

It was the old argument. Brenda had heard it all before when she ate her lunchtime sandwiches in the room, halfway between a kitchen and a sitting room, which was still called the Junior Mess. But now it seemed terrible that they should be able to talk so naturally while Dr. Lorrimer lay there dead upstairs. Suddenly she had a need to speak his name. She looked up and made herself say:

"Dr. Lorrimer thought that the Service would end up with about three immense laboratories doing the work for the whole country with exhibits coming in by air. He said that he thought all the scientific evidence ought to be agreed by both sides before the trial."

Middlemass said easily:

"That's an old argument. The police want a local lab nice and handy, and who's to blame them? Besides, three-quarters of forensic scientific work doesn't require all this sophisticated instrumentation. There's more of a case for highly equipped regional laboratories with local out-stations. But who'd want to work in the small labs if the more exciting stuff went elsewhere?"

Miss Easterbrook had apparently finished her revision. She said:

"Lorrimer knew that this idea of the lab as a scientific arbiter wouldn't work, not with the British accusatorial system. Anyway, scientific evidence ought to be tested like any other evidence."

"But how?" asked Middlemass. "By an ordinary jury? Suppose you're an expert Document Examiner outside the Service and they call you for the defense. You and I disagree. How can the jury judge between us? They'll probably choose to believe you because you're better-looking."

"Or you, more likely, because you're a man."

"Or one of them—the crucial one—will reject me because I remind him of Uncle Ben and all the family know that Ben was the world's champion liar."

"All right. All right." Copley spread plump hands in a benediction of appeasement. "It's the same as democracy. A fallible system but the best we've got."

Middlemass said:

"It's extraordinary, though, how well it works. You look at the jury, sitting there politely attentive, like children on their best behavior because they're visitors in an alien country and don't want to make fools of themselves or offend the natives. Yet how often do they come up with a verdict that's manifestly perverse having regard to the evidence?"

Claire Easterbrook said dryly:

"Whether it's manifestly perverse having regard to the truth is another matter."

"A criminal trial isn't a tribunal for eliciting the truth. At least we deal in facts. What about the emotions? Did you love your husband, Mrs. B.? How can the poor woman explain that, probably like the majority of wives, she loved him most of the time, when he didn't snore in her ear all night or shout at the kids or keep her short of Bingo money."

Copley said:

"She can't. If she's got any sense and if her counsel has briefed her properly, she'll get out her handkerchief and sob, 'Oh yes, sir. A better husband never lived, as God's my witness.' It's a game, isn't it? You win if you play by the rules."

Claire Easterbrook shrugged:

"If you know them. Too often it's a game where the rules are known only to one side. Natural enough when that's the side that makes them up."

Copley and Middlemass laughed.

Clifford Bradley had half hidden himself from the rest of the company behind the table holding the model of the new laboratory. He had taken a book from the shelves at random but, for the last ten minutes, hadn't even bothered to turn the page.

They were laughing! They were actually laughing! Getting up from the table he groped his way down the farthest bay and replaced his book in the rack, leaning his forehead against the cold steel. Unobtrusively Middlemass strolled up beside him and, back to the company, reached up to take a book from the shelf. He said:

"Are you all right?"

"I wish to God they'd come."

"So do we all. But the chopper should be here any minute now."

"How can they laugh like that? Don't they care?"

"Of course they care. Murder is beastly, embarrassing, and inconvenient. But I doubt whether anyone is feeling a purely personal grief. And other people's tragedies, other people's danger, always provoke a certain euphoria as long as one is safe oneself." He looked at Bradley and said softly:

"There's always manslaughter, you know. Or even justified homicide. Though, come to think of it, one could hardly plead that."

"You think I killed him, don't you?"

"I don't think anything. Anyway, you've got an alibi. Wasn't your mother-in-law with you yesterday evening?"

"Not all the evening. She caught the seven-forty-five bus."

"Well, with luck, there'll be evidence that he was dead by then." And why, thought Middlemass, should Bradley assume that he wasn't? Bradley's dark and anxious eyes narrowed with suspicion.

"How did you know that Sue's mother was with us last night?"

"Susan told me. Actually, she telephoned me at the lab just before two. It was about Lorrimer." He thought and then said easily, "She was wondering whether there was a chance he might ask for a transfer now that Howarth has been in the post a year. She thought I might have heard something. When you get home, tell her that I don't propose to tell the police about the call unless she does first. Oh, and you'd better reassure her that I didn't bash in his head for him. I'd do a lot for Sue, but a man has to draw the line somewhere."

Bradley said with a note of resentment:

"Why should you worry? There's nothing wrong with your alibi. Weren't you at the village concert?"

"Not all the evening. And there's a certain slight embarrassment about my alibi even when I was ostensibly there."

Bradley turned to him and said with sudden vehemence:

"I didn't do it! Oh God, I can't stand this waiting!"

"You've got to stand it. Pull yourself together, Cliff! You won't help yourself or Susan by going to pieces. They're English policemen, remember. We're not expecting the K.G.B."

It was then that they heard the long-awaited sound, a distant grinding hum like that of an angry wasp. The desultory voices at the tables fell silent, heads were raised and, together, the company moved toward the windows. Mrs. Bidwell rushed for a place of vantage. The red and white helicopter rattled into sight over the top of the trees and hovered, a noisy gadfly, above the terrace. No one spoke. Then Middlemass said:

"The Yard's wonder boy, appropriately, descends from the clouds. Well, let's hope that he works quickly. I want to get into my lab. Someone should tell him that he's not the only one with a murder on his hands."

# IV

Detective-Inspector the Honorable John Massingham disliked helicopters, which he regarded as noisy, cramped, and frighteningly unsafe. Since his physical courage was beyond question by either himself or anyone else, he would normally have had no objection to saying so. But he knew his chief's dislike of unnecessary chat and, strapped as they were side by side in uncomfortably close proximity in the Enstrom F28, he decided that the Chevisham case would get off to the most propitious start by a policy of disciplined silence. He noted with interest that the cockpit instrument panel was remarkably similar to a car dashboard; even the airspeed was shown in miles per hour instead of knots. He was only sorry that there the resemblance ended. He adjusted his earphones more comfortably and settled down to soothe his nerves by a concentrated study of his maps.

The red-brown tentacles of London's suburbs had at last been shaken off, and the checkered autumn landscape, multi-textured as a cloth collage, unrolled before them in a changing pattern of brown, green, and gold, leading them on to Cambridge. The fitful sunshine moved in broad swathes across the neat, segmented villages, the trim municipal parks and open fields. Miniature tin cars, beetle-bright in the sun, pursued each other busily along the roads.

Dalgliesh glanced at his companion, at the strong, pale face, the spatter of freckles over the craggy nose and wide forehead, and the thatch of red hair springing under the headphones, and thought how like the boy was to his father, that redoubtable, thrice-decorated peer, whose courage was equaled only by his obstinacy and naiveté. The marvel of the Massinghams was that a lineage going back five hundred years could have produced so many generations of amiable nonentities. He remembered when he had last seen Lord Dungannon. It had been a debate in the House of Lords on juvenile delinquency, a subject on which His Lordship considered himself an expert since he had, indubitably, once been a boy and had, briefly, helped organize a youth club on his grandfather's estate. His thoughts, when they finally came, had been uttered in all their simplistic banality, in no particular order of logic or relevance, and in a curiously gentle voice punctuated by long pauses in which he had gazed thoughtfully at the throne and appeared to commune happily with some inner presence. Meanwhile, like lemmings who have smelled the sea, the noble lords streamed out of their chamber in a body to appear, as if summoned by telepathy, when Dungannon's speech drew to its close. But if the family had contributed nothing to statesmanship and little to the arts, they had died with spectacular gallantry for orthodox causes in every generation.

And now Dungannon's heir had chosen this far from orthodox job. It would be interesting to see if, for the first time and in so unusual a field, the family achieved distinction. What had led Massingham to choose the police service instead of his family's usual career of the army as an outlet for his natural combativeness and unfashionable patriotism Dalgliesh had not inquired, partly because he was a respecter of other men's privacy, and partly because he wasn't sure that he wanted to hear the answer. So far Massingham had done exceptionally well. The police were a tolerant body and took the view that a man couldn't help who his father was. They accepted that Massingham had gained his promotion on merit, although they were not so naive as to suppose that being the elder son of a peer did any man harm. They called Massingham the Honjohn behind his back, and occasionally to his face, and bore no malice.

Although the family was now impoverished and the estate sold—Lord Dungannon was bringing up his considerable family in a modest villa in Bayswater—the boy had still gone to his father's school. No doubt, thought Dalgliesh, the old warrior was unaware that other schools existed; like every other class, the aristocracy, however poor, could always find the money for the things they really wanted. But he was an odd product of that establishment, having none of the slightly *dégagé* elegance and ironic detachment which characterized its alumni. Dalgliesh, if he hadn't known his history, would have guessed that Massingham was the product of a sound, upper-middle-class family—a doctor or a solicitor, perhaps—and of an old established grammar school. It was only the second time they had worked together. The first time, Dalgliesh had been impressed by Massingham's intelligence and enormous capacity for work, and by his admirable ability to keep his mouth shut and to sense when his chief wanted to be alone. He had also been struck by a streak of ruthlessness in the boy which, he thought, ought not to have surprised him since he knew that, as with all good detectives, it must be present.

And now the Enstrom was rattling above the towers and spires of Cambridge, and they could see the shining curve of the river, the bright autumnal avenues leading down through green lawns to miniature hump-backed bridges, King's College Chapel upturned and slowly rotating beside its great striped square of green. And, almost immediately, the city was behind them and they saw, like a crinkled ebony sea, the black earth of the fens. Below them were straight roads ridged above the fields, with villages strung along them as if clinging to the security of high ground; isolated farms with their roofs so low that they looked half submerged in the peat; an occasional church tower standing majestically apart from its village with the gravestones planted around it like crooked teeth. They must be getting close now; already Dalgliesh could see the soaring west tower and pinnacles of Ely Cathedral to the east.

Massingham looked up from his map-reading and peered down. His voice crackled through Dalgliesh's earphones:

"This is it, sir."

Chevisham was spread beneath them. It lay on a narrow plateau above the fens, the houses strung along the northerly of two converging roads. The tower of the impressive cruciform church was immediately identifiable, as were Chevisham Manor and, behind it, sprawling over the scarred field and linking the two roads, the brick and concrete of the new laboratory building. They rattled along the main street of what looked like a typical East Anglian village. Dalgliesh glimpsed the ornate red brick front of the local chapel, one or two prosperous-looking houses with Dutch gables, a small close of recently built semidetached boxes with the developer's board still in place, and what looked like the village general store and post office. There were few people about, but the noise of the engines brought figures from shops and houses and pale faces, their eyes shielded, strained up at them.

And now they were turning toward Hoggatt's Laboratory, coming in low over what must be the Wren chapel. It stood about a quarter of a mile from the house in a triple circle of beech trees, an isolated building so small and perfect that it looked like an architect's model precisely set in a fabricated landscape, or an elegant ecclesiastical folly, justifying itself only by its classical purity, as distanced from religion as it was from life. It was odd that it lay so far from the house. Dalgliesh thought that it had probably been built later, perhaps because the original owner of the mansion had quarreled with the local parson and, in defiance, had decided to make his own arrangements for spiritual ministrations. Certainly the house hardly looked large enough to support a private chapel. For a few seconds as they descended, he had an unimpeded view through a gap in the trees of the west front of the chapel. He saw a single high arched window with two balancing niches, the four Corinthian pilasters separating the bays, the whole crowned with a large decorated pediment and topped with a hexagonal lantern. The helicopter seemed almost to be brushing the trees. The brittle autumn leaves, shaken by the rush of air, flurried down like a shower of charred paper over the roof and the bright green of the grass.

And then, sickeningly, the helicopter soared, the chapel lurched out of sight, and they were poised, engines rattling, ready to land on the wide terrace behind the house. Over its roof he could see the forecourt patterned with parking lots, the police cars tidily aligned, and what looked like a mortuary van. A broad drive, bordered with straggling bushes and a few trees, led down to what the map showed as Stoney Piggott Road. There was no gate to the driveway. Beyond it he could see the bright flag of a bus stop and the bus shelter. Then the helicopter began to descend and only the rear of the house was in view. From a ground-floor window he could see the smudges of watching faces.

There was a reception committee of three, their figures oddly foreshortened, the necks straining upward. The thrash of the rotor blades had tugged their hair into grotesque shapes, flurried the legs of their trousers, and flattened their jackets against their chests. Now, with the stilling of the engines, the sudden silence was so absolute that he saw the three motionless figures as if they were a tableau of dummies in a silent world. He and Massingham unclasped their seat belts and clambered to earth. For about five seconds the two groups stood regarding each other. Then, with a single gesture, the three waiting figures smoothed back their hair and advanced warily to meet him. Simultaneously his ears unblocked and the world again became audible. He turned to thank and speak briefly to the pilot. Then he and Massingham walked forward.

Dalgliesh already knew Superintendent Mercer of the local C.I.D.; they had met at a number of police conferences. Even at sixty feet his oxlike shoulders, the round comedian's face with the wide, upturned mouth, and the button-bright eyes had been instantly recognizable. Dalgliesh felt his hand crushed, and then Mercer made the introductions. Dr. Howarth: a tall, fair man, almost as tall as Dalgliesh himself, with widely spaced eyes of a remarkably deep blue and the lashes so long that they might have looked effeminate on any face less arrogantly male. He could, Dalgliesh thought, have been judged an outstandingly handsome man were it not for a certain incongruity of feature, perhaps the contrast between the fineness of the skin stretched over the flat cheekbones and the strong, jutting jaw and uncompromising mouth. Dalgliesh would have known that he was rich. The blue eyes regarded the world with the slightly cynical assurance of a man accustomed to getting what he wanted when he wanted it by the simplest of expedients, that of paying for it. Beside him, Dr. Henry Kerrison, although as tall, looked diminished. His creased, anxious face was bleached with weariness and there was a look in the dark, heavily lidded eyes that was uncomfortably close to defeat. He grasped Dalgliesh's hand with a firm, cool grip but didn't speak. Howarth said:

"There's no entrance now to the back of the house; we have to go around to the front. This is the easiest way."

Carrying their scene-of-crime cases, Dalgliesh and Massingham followed him around the side of the house. The faces at the ground-floor window had disappeared and it was extraordinarily quiet. Trudging through the leaves that had drifted over the path, sniffing the keen autumnal air with its hint of smokiness, and feeling the sun on his face, Massingham felt a surge of animal well-being. It was good to be out of London. This promised to be the kind of job he most liked. The little group turned the corner of the house and Dalgliesh and Massingham had their first clear view of the facade of Hoggatt's Laboratory.

# V

The house was an excellent example of late seventeenth-century domestic architecture, a three-story brick mansion with a hipped roof and four dormer windows, the center three-bay projection surmounted by a pediment with a richly carved cornice and medallions. A flight of four wide, curved stone steps led to the doorway, imposing on its pilasters but solidly, unostentatiously right. Dalgliesh paused momentarily to study the facade. Howarth said:

"Agreeable, isn't it? But wait till you see what the old man did to some of the interior."

The front door, with its elegant but restrained brass door handle and knocker, was fitted with two security locks, a Chubb and an Ingersoll, in addition to the Yale. At a superficial glance there was no sign of forcing. It was opened almost before Howarth had lifted his hand to ring. The man who stood aside, unsmiling, for them to enter, although not in uniform, was immediately recognizable to Dalgliesh as a police officer. Howarth introduced him briefly as Inspector Blakelock, Assistant Police Liaison Officer. He added:

"All three locks were in order when Blakelock arrived this morning. The Chubb connects the electronic warning system to Guy's Marsh police station. The internal protection system is controlled from a panel in the Police Liaison Officer's room."

Dalgliesh turned to Blakelock.

"And that was in order?"

"Yes, sir."

"There is no other exit?"

It was Howarth who answered.

"No. My predecessor had the back door and one side door permanently barred. It was too complicated coping with a system of security locks for three doors. Everyone comes in and goes out by the front."

Except possibly one person last night, thought Dalgliesh.

They passed through the entrance hall which ran almost the whole length of the house, their feet suddenly loud on the marble tessellated floor. Dalgliesh was used to receiving impressions at a glance. The party did not pause on their way to the stairs, but he had a clear impression of the room, the high molded ceiling, the two elegant pedimented doors to right and left, an oil painting of the laboratory founder on the right-hand wall, the gleaming wood of the reception counter at the rear. A police officer with a sheaf of papers before him was using the desk telephone, presumably still checking alibis. He went on with his conversation without glancing up.

The staircase was remarkable. The balustrades were carved oak panels decorated with scrolls of acanthus foliage, each newel surmounted by a heavy oak pineapple. There was no carpet and the unpolished wood was heavily scarred. Dr. Kerrison and Superintendent Mercer mounted behind Dalgliesh in silence. Howarth, leading the way, seemed to feel the need to talk:

"The ground floor is occupied with Reception and the Exhibits Store, my office, my secretary's room, the general office, and the Police Liaison Officer's room. That's all, apart from the domestic quarters at the rear. Chief Inspector Martin is the chief P.L.O. but he's in the U.S.A. at the moment and we only have Blakelock on duty. On this floor we have Biology at the back, Criminalistics at the front, and the Instrument Section at the end of the corridor. But I've put a plan of the lab in my office for you. I thought you might like to take that over if it's convenient. But I haven't moved any of my things until you've examined the room. This is the Biology Lab."

He glanced at Superintendent Mercer, who took the key from his pocket and unlocked the door. It was a long room obviously converted from two smaller ones, possibly a sitting room or small drawing room. The ceiling carvings had been removed, perhaps because Colonel Hoggatt had thought them inappropriate to a working laboratory, but the scars of the desecration remained. The original windows had been replaced by two long windows occupying almost the whole of the end wall. There was a range of benches and sinks under the windows, and two islands of workbenches in the middle of the room, one fitted with sinks, the other with a number of microscopes. To the left was a small glass-partitioned office; to the right, a darkroom. Beside the door was an immense refrigerator.

But the most bizarre objects in the room were a pair of unclothed window-dressers' dummies, one male and one female, standing between the windows. They were unclothed and denuded of their wigs. The pose of the bald, egg-shaped heads, the jointed arms stiffly flexed in a parody of benediction, the staring eyes and curved, arrowlike lips gave them the hieratic look of a couple of painted deities. And at their feet, a white-clad sacrificial victim, was the body.

Howarth stared at the two dummies as if he had never seen them before. He seemed to think that they required explanation. For the first time he had lost some of his assurance. He said:

"That's Liz and Burton. The staff dress them in a suspect's clothes so that they can match up bloodstains or slashes." He added: "Do you want me here?"

"For the moment, yes," answered Dalgliesh.

He knelt by the body. Kerrison moved to stand beside him. Howarth and Mercer stayed one each side of the door.

After two minutes Dalgliesh said:

"Cause of death obvious. It looks as if he was struck by a single blow and died where he fell. There's surprisingly little bleeding."

Kerrison said:

"That's not unusual. As you know, you can get serious intercranial injury from a simple fracture, particularly if there's extradural or subdural hemorrhage or actual laceration of the brain substance. I agree that he was probably killed by a single blow and that wooden mallet on the table seems the likely weapon. But Blain-Thompson will be able to tell you more when he gets him on the table. He'll be doing the P.M. this afternoon."

"Rigor is almost complete. What sort of estimate did you make of the time of death?"

"I saw him just before nine and I thought then that he'd been dead about twelve hours, perhaps a little longer. Say between eight and nine P.M. The window is closed and the temperature pretty steady at sixty-five Fahrenheit. I usually estimate a fall in body temperature in these circumstances of about one and a half degrees Fahrenheit an hour. I took it when I examined the body and, taken with the rigor which was almost fully established then, I'd say it was unlikely that he was alive much after nine P.M. But you know how unreliable these estimates can be. Better say between eight-thirty and midnight."

Howarth said from the door:

"His father says that Lorrimer rang him at a quarter to nine. I went to see the old man this morning with Angela Foley to break the news to him. She's my secretary. Lorrimer was her cousin. But you'll be seeing the old man, of course. He seemed pretty confident about the time."

Dalgliesh said to Kerrison:

"It looks as if the blood flowed fairly steadily, but without any preliminary splashing. Would you expect the assailant to be blood-stained?"

"Not necessarily, particularly if I'm right about the mallet being the weapon. It was probably a single swinging blow delivered when Lorrimer had turned his back. The fact that the murderer struck above the left ear doesn't seem particularly significant. He could have been left-handed, but there's no reason to suppose he was."

"And it wouldn't have required particular force. A child could probably have done it."

Kerrison hesitated, disconcerted.

"Well, a woman, certainly."

There was one question that Dalgliesh had formally to ask, although, from the position of the body and the flow of the blood, the answer was in little doubt.

"Did he die almost immediately, or is there any possibility that he could have walked about for a time, even locked the door and set the alarms?"

"That's not altogether unknown, of course, but in this case I'd say it was highly unlikely, virtually impossible. I did have a man only a month ago with an ax injury, a seven-inch depressed fracture of the parietal bone and extensive extradural hemorrhage. He went off to a pub, spent half an hour with his mates, and then reported to the casualty department and was dead within a quarter of an hour. Head injuries can be unpredictable, but not this one, I think."

Dalgliesh turned to Howarth.

"Who found him?"

"Our Clerical Officer, Brenda Pridmore. She starts work at eight-thirty with Blakelock. Old Mr. Lorrimer phoned to say that his son hadn't slept in his bed, so she went up to see if Lorrimer were here. I arrived almost immediately with the cleaner, Mrs. Bidwell. Some woman had telephoned her husband early this morning to ask her to come to my house to help my sister, instead of to the lab. It was a false call. I thought that it was probably some stupid village prank, but that I'd better get in as soon as possible in case something odd was happening. So I put her bicycle in the trunk of my car and got here just after nine. My secretary, Angela Foley, and Clifford Bradley, the Higher Scientific Officer in the Biology Department, arrived at about the same time."

"Who at any time has been alone with the body?"

"Brenda Pridmore, of course, but very briefly, I imagine. Then Inspector Blakelock came up on his own. Then I was here alone for no more than a few seconds. Then I locked the laboratory door, kept all the staff in the main hall, and waited there until Dr. Kerrison arrived. He was here within five minutes and examined the body. I stood by the door. Superintendent Mercer arrived shortly afterwards and I handed over the key of the Biology Lab to him."

Mercer said:

"Dr. Kerrison suggested that I call in Dr. Greene—he's the local police surgeon—to confirm his preliminary findings. Dr. Greene wasn't alone with the body. After he'd made a quick and fairly superficial examination I locked the door. It wasn't opened again until the photographers and the fingerprint officers arrived. They've taken his dabs and examined the mallet, but we left it at that when we knew the Yard had been called in and you were on the way. The print boys are still here, in the Police Liaison Officer's room, but I let the photographers go."

Putting on his search gloves, Dalgliesh ran his hands over the body. Under his white coat Lorrimer was wearing gray slacks and a tweed jacket. In the inside pocket was a thin leather wallet containing six pound notes, his driver's license, a book of stamps, and two credit cards. The right outer pocket held a pouch with his car keys and three others, two Yale and a smaller intricate key, probably to a desk top or drawer. There were a couple of ballpoint pens clipped to the top left-hand pocket of his white coat. In the bottom right-hand pocket was a handkerchief, his bunch of laboratory keys, and, not on the bunch, a single heavy key which looked fairly new. There was nothing else on the body.

He went over to study two exhibits lying on the central workbench, the mallet and a man's jacket. The mallet was an unusual weapon, obviously handmade. The handle of crudely carved oak was about eighteen inches long and might, he thought, have once been part of a heavy walking stick. The head, which he judged to weigh just over two pounds, was blackened on one side with congealed blood from which one or two coarse gray hairs sprouted like whiskers. It was impossible to detect in the dried slough a darker hair which might have come from Lorrimer's head, or with the naked eye to distinguish his blood. That would be a job for the Metropolitan Police Laboratory when the mallet, carefully packed and with two identifying exhibit tags instead of one, reached the Biology Department later in the day.

He said to the Superintendent:

"No prints?"

"None, except for old Pascoe's. He's the owner of the mallet. They weren't wiped away, so it looks as if this chap wore gloves."

That, thought Dalgliesh, would point to premeditation, or to the instinctive precaution of a knowledgeable expert. But if he came prepared to kill it was odd that he had relied on seizing the first convenient weapon; unless, of course, he knew that the mallet would be ready to hand.

He bent low to study the jacket. It was the top half of a cheap mass-produced suit in a harsh shade of blue with a paler pinstripe, and with wide lapels. The sleeve had been carefully spread out and the cuff bore a trace of what could have been blood. It was apparent that Lorrimer had already begun the analysis. On the bench was the electrophoresis apparatus plugged into its power pack and with two columns of six paired small circles punched in the sheet of agar gel. Beside it was a test-tube holder with a series of blood samples. To the right lay a couple of buff-colored laboratory files with biology registrations and, beside them, flat open on the bench, a quarto-sized loose-leaf notebook with a ring binding. The left-hand page, dated the previous day, was closely covered in hieroglyphics and formulas in a thin, black, upright hand. Although most of the scientific jottings meant little to him, Dalgliesh could see that the time at which Lorrimer had started and finished each analysis had been carefully noted. The right-hand page was blank.

He said to Howarth:

"Who is the Senior Biologist now that Lorrimer's dead?"

"Claire Easterbrook. Miss Easterbrook, but it's advisable to call her Ms."

"Is she here?"

"With the others in the library. I believe she has a firm alibi for the whole of yesterday evening, but as she's a senior scientist she was asked to stay. And, of course, she'll want to get back to work as soon as the staff are allowed into the laboratory. There was a murder two nights ago in a clunch pit at Muddington—that jacket is an exhibit—and she'll want to get on with that as well as coping with the usual heavy load."

"I'd like to see her first, please, and here. Then Mrs. Bidwell. Is there a sheet we could use to cover him?"

Howarth said:

"I imagine there's a dust sheet or something of the kind in the linen cupboard. That's on the next floor."

"I'd be grateful if you'd go with Inspector Massingham and show him. Then if you'd wait in the library or your own office I'll be down to have a word when I've finished here."

For a second he thought that Howarth was about to demur. He frowned, and the handsome face clouded momentarily, petulant as a child's. But he left with Massingham without a word. Kerrison was still standing by the body, rigid as a guard of honor. He gave a little start as if recalling himself to reality and said:

"If you don't want me any longer I ought to be on my way to the hospital. You can contact me at St. Luke's at Ely or here at the Old Rectory. I've given the sergeant an account of my movements last night. I was at home all the evening. At nine o'clock by arrangement, I rang one of my colleagues at the hospital, Dr. J. D. Underwood, about a matter which is coming up at the next medical committee. I think he's already confirmed that we did speak. He hadn't got the information I was waiting for but he rang me back at about a quarter to ten."

There was as little reason to delay Kerrison as there was at present to suspect him. After he had left, Mercer said:

"I thought of leaving two sergeants, Reynolds and Underhill, and a couple of constables, Cox and Warren, if that will suit you. They're all sound, experienced officers. The chief said to ask for anyone and anything you need. He's at a meeting in London this morning, but he'll be back tonight. I'll send up the chaps from the mortuary van if you're ready for them to take him away."

"Yes, I've finished with him. I'll have a word with your men as soon as I've seen Miss Easterbrook. But ask one of the sergeants to come up in ten minutes to pack up the mallet for the Yard lab, will you? The chopper pilot will want to get back."

They spoke a few more words about the liaison arrangements with the local force, then Mercer left to supervise the removal of the body. He would wait to introduce Dalgliesh to his seconded officers; after that, his responsibility would end. The case was in Dalgliesh's hands.

# VI

Two minutes later Claire Easterbrook was shown into the laboratory. She entered with an assurance that a less experienced investigator than Dalgliesh might have mistaken for arrogance or insensitivity. She was a thin, long-waisted girl of about thirty, with a bony, intelligent face and a cap of dark, curling hair which had been layered by an obviously expert, and no doubt expensive, hand to lie in swathes across the forehead and to curl into the nape of her high-arched neck. She was wearing a chestnut-brown sweater in fine wool belted into a black skirt which swung calf length above high-heeled boots. Her hands, with the nails cut very short, were ringless, and her only ornament was a necklace of large wooden beads strung on a silver chain. Even without her white coat the impression she gave—and no doubt intended—was of a slightly intimidating professional competence. Before Dalgliesh had a chance to speak she said, with a trace of belligerence:

"I'm afraid you'll be wasting your time with me. My lover and I dined last night in Cambridge at the Master's Lodge of his college. I was with five other people from eight-thirty until nearly midnight. I've already given their names to the constable in the library."

Dalgliesh said mildly:

"I'm sorry, Ms. Easterbrook, that I had to ask you to come up before we were able to remove Dr. Lorrimer's body. And as it seems impertinent to invite you to sit down in your own laboratory, I won't. But this isn't going to take long."

She flushed, as if he had caught her out in a social solecism. Glancing with reluctant distaste at the shrouded, lumpen shape on the floor, at the stiff, protruding ankles, she said:

"He'd look more dignified if you'd left him uncovered. Like this he could be a sack of rubbish. It's a curious superstition, the universal instinct to cover up the recently dead. After all, we're the ones at a disadvantage."

Massingham said lightly:

"Not, surely, with the Master and his wife to vouch for your alibi?"

Their eyes met, his coolly amused, hers dark with dislike.

Dalgliesh said:

"Dr. Howarth tells me you're the Senior Biologist now. Could you explain to me, please, what Dr. Lorrimer was doing here last night? Don't touch anything."

She went at once over to the table and regarded the two exhibits, the files, and the scientific paraphernalia. She said:

"Would you open this file, please?"

Dalgliesh's gloved hands slipped between the covers and flipped it open.

"He rechecked Clifford Bradley's result on the Pascoe case. The mallet belongs to a sixty-four-year-old fen farm laborer called Pascoe whose wife has disappeared. His story is that she's walked out on him, but there are one or two suspicious circumstances. The police sent in the mallet to see if the stains on it are human blood. They aren't. Pascoe says that he used it to put an injured dog out of his misery. Bradley found that the blood reacted to anti-dog serum and Dr. Lorrimer has duplicated his result. So the dog it was that died."

Too mean to waste a bullet or send for a vet, thought Massingham savagely. It struck him as odd that the death of this unknown mongrel should, for a moment, anger him more than the killing of Lorrimer.

Miss Easterbrook moved over to the open notebook. The two men waited. Then she frowned and said, obviously puzzled:

"That's odd. Edwin always noted the time he began and finished an analysis and the procedure he adopted. He's initialed Bradley's result on the Pascoe file, but there's nothing in the book. And it's obvious that he's made a start with the clunch pit murder, but that isn't noted either. The last reference is five-forty-five and the final note is unfinished. Someone must have torn out the right-hand page."

"Why do you suppose anyone should do that?"

She looked straight into Dalgliesh's eyes and said calmly:

"To destroy the evidence of what he'd been doing, or the result of his analysis, or the time he'd spent on it. The first and second would be rather pointless. It's obvious from the apparatus what he's been doing, and any competent biologist could duplicate the work. So it's probably the last."

So the appearance of intelligence wasn't misleading. Dalgliesh asked:

"How long would he take checking the Pascoe result?"

"Not long. Actually, he'd started on that before six and I think he'd finished when I left at six-fifteen. I was the last to leave. The junior staff had gone. It isn't usual for them to work after six. I usually stay later, but I had to dress for the dinner party."

"And the work he's done on the clunch pit case—how long would that have taken?"

"Difficult to say. I should have thought it would have kept him busy until nine or later. He was grouping a sample of the victim's blood and the blood from the dried stain by the ABO blood group system, and using electrophoresis to identify the haptoglobins and PGM, the enzyme phosphoglucomutase. Electrophoresis is a technique for identifying the protein and enzyme constituents of the blood by placing the samples in a gel of starch or agar and applying an electric current. As you can see, he'd actually started the run."

Dalgliesh was aware of the scientific principle of electrophoresis but didn't think it necessary to mention the fact. He opened the clunch pit file and said:

"There's nothing on the file."

"He would write up the result on the file later. But he wouldn't have started the analysis without noting the details in his book."

There were two pedal-bins against the wall. Massingham opened them. One, plastic-lined, was obviously for laboratory waste and broken glass. The other was for wastepaper. He stirred the contents: paper tissues, a few torn envelopes, a discarded newspaper. There was nothing that resembled the missing page.

Dalgliesh said:

"Tell me about Lorrimer."

"What do you want to know?"

"Anything that could throw light on why someone disliked him enough to smash in his skull."

"I can't help you there, I'm afraid. I've no idea."

"You liked him?"

"Not particularly. It's not a question I've given much thought to. I got on all right with him. He was a perfectionist who didn't suffer fools gladly. But he was all right to work with if you knew your job. I do."

"So he wouldn't need to check your work. What about those who don't know their jobs?"

"You'd better ask them, Commander."

"Was he popular with his staff?"

"What has popularity to do with it? I don't suppose I'm popular, but I don't go in fear of my life."

She was silent for a moment, then said in a more conciliatory tone:

"I probably sound obstructive. I don't mean to be. It's just that I can't help. I've no idea who could have killed him or why. I only know that I didn't."

"Had you noticed any change in him recently?"

"Change? You mean, in his mood or behavior? Not really. He gave the impression of a man under strain; but then, he was that kind of man, solitary, obsessional, overworked. One rather odd thing. He's been interesting himself in the new C.O., Brenda Pridmore. She's a pretty child, but hardly his intellectual level, I should have thought. I don't think there was anything serious, but it caused a certain amount of amusement in the lab. I think he was probably trying to prove something to someone, or, perhaps, to himself."

"You've heard about the telephone call to Mrs. Bidwell, of course?"

"I imagine the whole lab knows. It wasn't I who rang her, if that's what you're thinking. In any case, I should have known that it wouldn't work."

"How do you mean, it wouldn't work?"

"It depended, surely, on old Lorrimer not being at home yesterday. After all, the caller couldn't rely on his not noticing that Edwin hadn't come home last night until he didn't get his early tea brought to him. As it happens, he went off to bed quite happily. But the hoaxer couldn't have known that. Normally, Edwin would have been missed much earlier."

"Was there any reason to suppose that old Mr. Lorrimer wouldn't be at the cottage yesterday?"

"He was supposed to be admitted to Addenbrooke's hospital in the afternoon for treatment of a skin complaint. I think the whole Biology Lab knew. He used to telephone often enough, fretting about the arrangements and whether Edwin would get time off to drive him there. Yesterday, just after ten, he rang to say that the bed wouldn't be available for him after all."

"Who took the call?"

"I did. It rang in his private office and I took it there. Edwin hadn't returned from the clunch pit autopsy. I told him as soon as he arrived."

"Whom else did you tell?"

"When I came out of the office I think I said something casually about old Mr. Lorrimer not having to go into the hospital after all. I'm not sure of the actual words. I don't think anyone made a comment or took much apparent notice."

"And all the biology staff were in the lab at the time and heard you?"

Suddenly she lost her composure. She flushed and hesitated, as if realizing for the first time where all this was leading. The two men waited. Then, angry with herself, she burst out, clumsily defensive:

"I'm sorry, but I can't remember. You'll have to ask them. It didn't seem important at the time and I was busy. We were all busy. I think everyone was there, but I can't be certain."

"Thank you," said Dalgliesh coolly. "You've been remarkably helpful."

# VII

Mrs. Bidwell arrived at the door as the two attendants from the mortuary van were carrying out the body. She seemed to regret its disappearance and looked at the chalk outline marked by Massingham on the floor as if this were a poor substitute for the real thing. Gazing after the covered metal container, she said:

"Poor devil! I never thought to see him carried out of his lab feet first. He were never popular, you know. Still, I don't suppose that's worrying him where he is now. Is that one of my dust sheets you've had over him?"

She peered suspiciously at the sheet, now folded neatly at the end of one of the benches.

"It came from the laboratory linen cupboard, yes."

"Well, as long as it's put back where you found it. Come to that, it had better go straight into the soiled linen. But I don't want any of your chaps taking it away. Laundry disappears fast enough as it is."

"Why wasn't he popular, Mrs. Bidwell?"

"Too particular by half. Mind you, you've got to be these days if you want to get any work done. But from what I hear he was too fussy for his own good. And he'd been getting worse, no doubt about that. And very odd he'd been lately, too. Nervy. You heard about the unpleasantness in the reception hall the day before yesterday, I suppose? Oh well, you will. Ask Inspector Blakelock. Just before lunch it was. Dr. Lorrimer had a real old tussle with that barmy daughter of Dr. Kerrison's. Nearly pushed her out of the door. Screeching like a banshee, she was. I came into the hall just in time to see it. Her dad isn't going to like that, I said to Inspector Blakelock. He's crazy about those kids. Mark my words, I said, if Dr. Lorrimer doesn't take a hold of himself there'll be murder done in this lab. I said the same to Mr. Middlemass."

"I want you to tell me about the telephone call this morning, Mrs. Bidwell. What time was it?"

"It was near enough seven o'clock. We was eating breakfast and

I just filled the teapot for second cups. Had the kettle in me hand when it rang."

"And who answered it?"

"Bidwell. Phone's in the hall and he got up and went out to it. Cursin' he was 'cos he'd just settled down to his kipper. He hates cold kipper, does Bidwell. We always has kippers on Thursday on account of Marshall's fish van coming from Ely Wednesday afternoons."

"Does your husband usually answer the phone?"

"He always answers the phone. And if he's not in I lets it ring. I can't abide the dratted things. Never could. Wouldn't have it in the house if our Shirley hadn't paid to get it put in. She's married now and lives Mildenhall way and she likes to think we can ring her if we want her. Fat lot of use that is. I can't never hear what anyone says. And the ring is enough to put the fear of God in a soul. Telegrams and phone rings. I hate 'em both."

"Who at the lab would know that your husband always answered the phone?"

"Best part of them, more than likely. They knows I won't touch the thing. There's no secret about that. We're all as the good Lord made us and some of us a sight worse. Nothing to be ashamed of."

"Of course not. Your husband's at work now, I expect?"

"That's right. Yeoman's Farm, Captain Massey's place. Tractor work mostly. Been there twenty years, near enough."

Dalgliesh nodded almost imperceptibly to Massingham and the Inspector slipped out to have a quiet word with Sergeant Underhill. It would be as well to check with Mr. Bidwell while his memory of the call was fresh. Dalgliesh went on:

"What happened then?"

"Bidwell came back. Said that I wasn't to go to the lab this morning because Mrs. Schofield wanted me over at Leamings particular. I was to bike there and she'd run me and the bike home afterwards. Sticking out of the back of that red Jaguar she's got, I suppose. I thought it was a bit of a cheek seeing as I'm due here mornings, but I've nothing against Mrs. Schofield and if she wanted me I wasn't above obliging. The lab would just have to wait, I said to Bidwell. I can't be in two places at once, I said. What don't get done today will get done tomorrow."

"You work here every morning?"

"Except weekends, that's right. Gets here as near eight-thirty as makes no odds, and works till about ten. Then back at twelve in case any of the gentlemen wants their lunch cooking. The girls mostly manage for themselves. Afterwards I washes up for them. I reckons to get away by two-thirty most days. Mind you, it's light work. Scobie—he's the lab attendant—and I sees to the working labs but all the heavy cleaning is supposed to be done by the contractors. They comes on Mondays and Fridays only, from seven until nine, a whole van full of them from Ely, and does the main hall, the stairs, and all the heavy polishing. Inspector Blakelock gets here early those mornings to let them in and Scobie keeps an eye on them. Not that you'd know they'd been most days. No personal interest, you see. Not like the old days when me and two women from the village did the lot."

"So what would you normally have done as soon as you arrived if this had been an ordinary Thursday? I want you to think carefully, Mrs. Bidwell. This may be very important."

"No need to think. I'd do the same as I does every day."

"Which is?"

"Take off me hat and coat in the downstairs cloakroom. Put on me overalls. Get cleaning bucket and powder and disinfectant from the broom cupboard. Clean the toilets, male and female. Then check dirty laundry and get it bagged up. Put out clean white coats where wanted. Then dust and tidy Director's office and general office."

"Right," said Dalgliesh. "Let's do the rounds then, shall we?"

Three minutes later a curious little procession made its way up the stairs. Mrs. Bidwell, clad now in a navy-blue working overall and carrying a plastic bucket in one hand and a mop in the other, led the way. Dalgliesh and Massingham followed. The two lavatories were on the top floor at the rear opposite the Document Examination Laboratory. They had obviously been converted from what had once been an elegant bedroom. But now a narrow passage leading to the single barred window had been constructed down the middle of the room. A mean-looking door gave entry to the women's cloakroom on the left, and, a few yards down, a similar door led to the men's washroom on the right. Mrs. Bidwell led the way into the left-hand room. It was larger than Dalgliesh had expected, but poorly lit from a single round window with pivoting opaque glass set about four feet from the floor. The window was open. There were three cubicles. The outer room contained two lavatory hand basins with a paper towel dispenser and, to the left of the door, a long Formica-covered counter with a glass above it which apparently served as a dressing table. To the right was a wall-mounted gas-fired incinerator, a row of clothes hooks, a large wicker laundry basket, and two rather battered cane chairs.

Dalgliesh said to Mrs. Bidwell:

"Is this how you would expect to find it?"

Mrs. Bidwell's sharp little eyes peered round. The doors to the three lavatories were open and she gave them a quick inspection.

"No better nor no worse. They're pretty good about the toilets, I'll say that for them."

"And the window is usually kept open?"

"Winter and summer, except it's bitter cold. That's the only ventilation, you see."

"The incinerator is off. Is that usual?"

"That's right. Last girl to leave turns it off at night, then I puts it on next morning."

Dalgliesh looked inside. The incinerator was empty except for a trace of carbon ash. He went over to the window. Rain had obviously driven in sometime during the night and the dried splashes were clearly visible on the tiled floor. But even the inside pane, where no rain could have splashed, was remarkably clean and there was no discernible dust around the sill. He said:

"Did you clean the window yesterday, Mrs. Bidwell?"

"Of course I did. It's like I told you. I cleans the lavatories every morning. And when I cleans, I cleans. Shall I get on with it now?"

"I'm afraid there'll be no cleaning done today. We'll pretend that you've finished in here. Now what happens? What about the laundry?"

The laundry basket contained only one coat, marked with the initials C.M.E. Mrs. Bidwell said:

"I wouldn't expect many dirty coats, not on a Thursday. They usually manages to make them last a week and drop them in here on Friday before they go home. Monday's the busy day for laundry and putting out the new coats. Looks as though Miss Easterbrook spilled her tea yesterday. That's not like her. But she's particular, is Miss Easterbrook. You wouldn't find her going around with a dirty coat, no matter what day of the week."

So there was at least one member of the Biology Department, thought Dalgliesh, who knew that Mrs. Bidwell would make an early visit to the lab to put out a clean white coat. It would be interesting to learn who had been present when the fastidious Miss Easterbrook had had her accident with the tea.

The male washroom, apart from the urinal stalls, differed very little from the women's. There was the same round open window, the same absence of any marks on the panes or sill. Dalgliesh carried over one of the chairs and, carefully avoiding any contact with the window or the sill, looked out. There was a drop of about six feet to the top of the window beneath, and an equal drop to that on the first floor. Below them both a paved terrace ran right up to the wall. The absence of soft earth, the rain in the night, and Mrs. Bidwell's efficient cleaning meant that they would be lucky to find any evidence of a climb. But a reasonably slim and sure-footed man or woman with enough nerve and a head for heights could certainly have got out this way. But if the murderer were a member of the lab staff, why should he risk his neck when he must have known that the keys were on Lorrimer? And if the murderer were an outsider, then how account for the locked front door, the intact alarm system, and the fact that Lorrimer must have let him in?

He turned his attention to the washbasins. None was particularly dirty, but near the rim of the one nearest the door there was a smear of porridgelike mucus. He bent his head over the basin and sniffed. His sense of smell was extremely acute and, from the plug hole, he detected the faint but unmistakably disagreeable smell of human vomit.

Mrs. Bidwell, meanwhile, had thrown open the lid of the laundry basket. She gave an exclamation.

"That's funny. It's empty."

Dalgliesh and Massingham turned. Dalgliesh asked:

"What were you expecting to find, Mrs. Bidwell?"

"Mr. Middlemass's white coat, that's what."

She darted out of the room. Dalgliesh and Massingham followed. She flung open the door of the Document Examination Room and glanced inside. Then she closed the door again and stood with her back against it. She said:

"It's gone! It's not hanging on the peg. So where is it? Where's Mr. Middlemass's white coat?"

Dalgliesh asked:

"Why did you expect to find it in the laundry basket?"

Mrs. Bidwell's black eyes grew immense. She slewed her eyes furtively from side to side and then said with awed relish:

"Because it had blood on it, that's why. Lorrimer's blood!"

# VIII

Lastly, they went down the main staircase to the Director's office. From the library there was a broken murmur of voices, subdued and spasmodic as a funeral gathering. A detective-constable was standing at the front door with the detached watchfulness of a man paid to endure boredom but ready to leap into action should, unaccountably, the boredom end.

Howarth had left his office unlocked and the key in the door. Dalgliesh was interested that the Director had chosen to wait with the rest of the staff in the library and wondered whether this was intended to demonstrate solidarity with his colleagues, or was a tactful admission that his office was one of the rooms that had been due to receive Mrs. Bidwell's early morning attention and must, therefore, be of special interest to Dalgliesh. But that reasoning was surely too subtle. It was difficult to believe that Howarth hadn't entered his room since the discovery of the body. If there were anything to remove, he best of all must have had the chance to do it.

Dalgliesh had expected the room to be impressive, but it still surprised him. The plasterwork of the coved ceiling was splendid, a joyous riot of wreaths, shells, ribbons, and trailing vines, ornate and yet disciplined. The fireplace was of white and mottled marble with a finely carved frieze of nymphs and piping shepherds and a classical overmantel with open pediment. He guessed that the agreeably proportioned salon, too small to be partitioned and not large enough for a working laboratory, had escaped the fate of so much of the house more for administrative and scientific convenience than from any sensitivity on Colonel Hoggatt's part to its innate perfection. It was newly furnished in a style guaranteed not to offend, a nice compromise of bureaucratic orthodoxy and modern functionalism. There was a large glass-fronted bookcase to the left of the fireplace, and a personal locker and a coat stand to the right. A rectangular conference table and four chairs, of a type provided for senior public servants, stood between the tall windows. Next to it was a steel security cupboard fitted with a combination lock. Howarth's desk, a plain contraption in the same wood as the conference table, faced the door. Apart from an inkstained blotter and a pen stand it held a small wooden bookshelf containing the *Shorter Oxford Dictionary,* a dictionary of quotations, *Roget's Thesaurus,* and *Fowler's Modern English Usage.* The choice seemed curious for a scientist. There were three metal trays marked "In," "Pending," and "Out." The "Out" tray held two manila files, the top labeled "Chapel—Proposals for transfer to Department of the Environment," and the second, a large, old, and unwieldy file which had been much mended, was marked "New Laboratory—Commissioning."

Dalgliesh was struck by the emptiness and impersonality of the whole room. It had obviously been recently decorated for Howarth's arrival; the pale gray-green carpet, with its matching square under the desk, was as yet unmarked, and the curtains hung in pristine folds of dark green. There was only one picture, positioned in the overmantel, but this was an original, an early Stanley Spencer showing the Assumption of the Virgin. Plump, foreshortened, varicosed thighs in red bloomers floated upward from a circle of clutching workworn hands to a reception committee of gaping cherubim. It was, he thought, an eccentric choice for the room, discordant both in date and in style. It was the only object, apart from the books, that reflected a personal taste; Dalgliesh hardly supposed that it had been provided by a government agency. Otherwise the office had the underfurnished, expectant atmosphere of a room refurbished to receive an unknown occupant and still awaiting the imprint of his taste and personality. It was hard to believe that Howarth had worked here for almost a year. Mrs. Bidwell, her tight little mouth pursed and eyes narrowed, regarded it with obvious disapproval. Dalgliesh asked:

"Is this how you would have expected to find it?"

"That's right. Every bloody morning. Nothing for me to do here really, is there? Mind you, I dusts and polishes around and runs the Hoover over the carpet. But he's neat and tidy, there's no denying it. Not like old Dr. MacIntyre. Oh, he was a lovely man! But messy! You should have seen his desk of a morning. And smoke! You couldn't hardly see across the room sometimes. He had this lovely skull on his desk to keep his pipes in. They dug it up when they was making the trench for the pipes to the new Vehicle Examination extension. Been in the ground more than two hundred years, Dr. Mac said, and he showed me the crack—just like a cracked cup—where his skull had been bashed in. That's one murder they never solved. I miss that skull. Real lovely that used to look. And he had all these pictures of himself and his friends at university with oars crossed above them, and a colored one of the Highlands with hairy cattle paddling in a lake, and one of his father with his dogs, and such a lovely picture of his wife—dead she was, poor soul—and another big picture of Venice with gondolas and a lot of foreigners in fancy dress, and a cartoon of Dr. Mac done by one of his friends, showing the friend lying dead, and Dr. Mac in his deerstalker hat looking for clues with his magnifying glass. That was a real laugh, that was. Oh, I loved Dr. Mac's pictures!" She looked at the Spencer with a marked lack of enthusiasm.

"And there's nothing unusual about the room this morning?"

"I told you, same as usual. Well, look for yourself. Clean as a new pin. It looks different in the day, mind you, when he's working here. But he always leaves it as if he isn't expecting to come back in the morning."

There was nothing else to be learned from Mrs. Bidwell. Dalgliesh thanked her and told her that she could go home as soon as she had checked with Detective-Sergeant Reynolds in the library that he had all the necessary information about where she had spent the previous evening. He explained this with his usual tact, but tact was wasted on Mrs. Bidwell. She said cheerfully and without rancor:

"No use trying to pin this on me, or Bidwell come to that. We was together at the village concert. Sat five rows back between Joe Machin—he's the sexton—and Willie Barnes—he's the rector's warden—and we stayed there until the end of the show. No sneaking out at halftime like some I could mention."

"Who sneaked out, Mrs. Bidwell?"

"Ask him yourself. Sat at the end of the row in front of us, a gentleman whose office we might or might not be standing in at this very moment. Do you want to talk to him? Shall I ask him to step in?" She spoke hopefully and looked toward the door like an eager gun dog, ears pricked for the command to retrieve.

"We'll see to that, thank you, Mrs. Bidwell. And if we want to talk to you again we'll get in touch. You've been very helpful."

"I thought I might make coffee for them all before I go. No harm in that, I suppose?"

There was no point in warning her not to talk to the lab staff, or, come to that, to the whole village. Dalgliesh had no doubt that his search of the cloakrooms and the missing bloodstained coat would soon be common knowledge. But no great harm would be done. The murderer must know that the police would be immediately alive to the possible significance of that false early morning call to Mrs. Bidwell. He was dealing with intelligent men and women, experienced, even if vicariously, in criminal investigation, knowledgeable about police procedure, aware of the rules that governed his every move. He had no doubt that, mentally, most of the group now waiting in the library to be interviewed were following his actions almost to the minute.

And among them, or known to them, was a murderer.

# IX

Superintendent Mercer had selected his two sergeants with an eye to contrast, or, perhaps, with a view to satisfying any prejudices that Dalgliesh might harbor about the age and experience of his subordinates. Sergeant Reynolds was near the end of his service, a stolid, broad-shouldered, slow-speaking officer of the old school and a native of the fens. Sergeant Underhill, recently promoted, looked young enough to be his son. His boyish, open face with its look of disciplined idealism was vaguely familiar to Massingham, who suspected that he might have seen it in a police recruitment pamphlet, but decided in the interest of harmonious cooperation to give Underhill the benefit of the doubt.

The four police officers were sitting at the conference table in the Director's office. Dalgliesh was briefing his team before he started on the preliminary interviews. He was, as always, restlessly aware of time passing. It was already after eleven and he was anxious to finish at the laboratory and see old Mr. Lorrimer. The physical clues to his son's murder might lie in the laboratory; the clue to the man himself lay elsewhere. But neither his words nor his tone betrayed impatience.

"We start by assuming that the telephone call to Mrs. Bidwell and Lorrimer's death are connected. That means the call was made by the murderer or an accomplice. We'll keep an open mind about the caller's sex until we get confirmation from Bidwell, but it was probably a woman, probably also someone who knew that old Mr. Lorrimer was expected to be in the hospital yesterday and who didn't know that the appointment had been cancelled. If the old man had been home, the ruse could hardly hope to succeed. As Miss Easterbrook has pointed out, no one could rely on his going early to bed last night and not realizing until after the lab opened this morning that his son hadn't come home."

Massingham said:

"The killer would have made it his business to get here early this morning, assuming that he didn't know that his plan had misfired. And, assuming, of course, the call wasn't a double bluff. It would be a neat ploy, wasting our time, confusing the investigation, and diverting suspicion from everyone except the early arrivals."

But for one of the suspects, it could have been an even neater ploy, thought Dalgliesh. It had been Mrs. Bidwell's arrival at Howarth's house in obedience to the call which had given the Director himself the excuse for arriving so early. He wondered what time Howarth usually put in an appearance. That would be one of the questions to be asked. He said:

"We'll start by assuming that it wasn't a bluff, that the murderer, or his accomplice, made the call to delay Mrs. Bidwell's arrival and the discovery of the body. So what was he hoping to do? Plant evidence or destroy it? Tidy up something that he'd overlooked; wipe the mallet clean; clear up the evidence of whatever it was he was doing here last night; replace the keys on the body? But Blakelock had the best opportunity to do that, and he wouldn't need to have taken them in the first place. The call could have given someone the chance to replace the spare set in the security cupboard here. But that would be perfectly possible without delaying Mrs. Bidwell's arrival. And, of course, it may have been done."

Underhill said:

"But is it really likely, sir, that the call was intended to delay the finding of the body and to give the killer time to replace the keys? Admittedly Mrs. Bidwell could be expected to be first in the Biology Department this morning when she put out the clean coats. But the murderer couldn't rely on that. Inspector Blakelock or Brenda Pridmore could easily have had occasion to go there."

Dalgliesh thought it a risk that the murderer might well have thought worth taking. In his experience the early-morning routine in an institution seldom varied. Unless Blakelock had the early-morning job of checking on lab security—and this was yet another of the questions to be asked—he and Brenda Pridmore would probably have got on with their normal work at the reception desk. In the ordinary course of events Mrs. Bidwell would have been the one to find the body. Any member of staff who went into the Biology Lab before her would have needed a good excuse to explain his presence there, unless, of course, he was a member of the Biology Department.

Massingham said:

"It's odd about the missing white coat, sir. It can hardly have been removed or destroyed to prevent us learning about the fight between Middlemass and Lorrimer. That unedifying but intriguing little episode must have been around the lab within minutes of its happening. Mrs. Bidwell would see to that."

Both Dalgliesh and Massingham wondered how far Mrs. Bidwell's description of the quarrel, given with the maximum dramatic effect, had been accurate. It was obvious that she had come into the laboratory after the blow had been struck and had in fact seen very little. Dalgliesh had recognized, with foreboding, a familiar phenomenon: the desire of a witness, aware of the paucity of her evidence, to make the most of it lest the police be disappointed, while remaining as far as possible within the confines of truth. Stripped of Mrs. Bidwell's embellishments, the core of hard fact had been disappointingly small.

"What they was quarreling about I couldn't take it on myself to say, except that it was about a lady, and that Dr. Lorrimer was upset because she'd telephoned Mr. Middlemass. The door was open and I did hear that much when I passed to go into the ladies' toilet. I daresay she rang him to arrange a date and Dr. Lorrimer didn't like it. I never saw a man more white. Like death he looked, with a handkerchief held up against his face all bloodied, and his black eyes glaring over the top of it. And Mr. Middlemass was turkey red. Embarrassed, I daresay. Well, it's not what we're used to at Hoggatt's, senior staff knocking each other about. When proper gentlemen start in with the fists there's usually a woman at the bottom of it. Same with this murder if you ask me."

Dalgliesh said:

"We'll be getting Middlemass's version of the affair. I'd like now to have a word with all the lab staff in the library and then Inspector Massingham and I will start the preliminary interviews: Howarth, the two women, Angela Foley and Brenda Pridmore, Blakelock, Middlemass, and any of the others without a firm alibi. I'd like you, Sergeant, to get on with organizing the usual routine. I shall want one of the senior staff in each department while the search is going on. They're the only ones who can tell whether anything in their lab has changed since yesterday. You'll be looking—admittedly without much hope—for the missing page of Lorrimer's notebook, any evidence of what he was doing here last night apart from working on the clunch pit murder, any sign of what happened to the missing coat. I want a thorough search of the whole building, particularly possible means of access and exit. The rain last night is a nuisance. You'll probably find the walls washed clean, but there may be some evidence that he got out through one of the lavatory windows.

"You'll need a couple of men on the grounds. The earth is fairly soft after the rain and if the murderer came by car or motorcycle there could be tire marks. Any we find can be checked against the tire index here; we needn't waste time going to the Met Lab for that. There's a bus stop immediately opposite the laboratory entrance. Find out what time the buses pass. There's always the possibility that one of the passengers or crew noticed something. I'd like the laboratory building checked first, and as quickly as possible so that the staff can get back to work. They've a new murder on their hands and we can't keep the place closed longer than is absolutely necessary. I'd like to give them access by tomorrow morning.

"Then there's the smear of what looks like vomit on the first basin in the men's washroom. The smell from the pipe is still fairly distinct. I want a sample of that to go to the Met Lab urgently. You'll probably have to unscrew the joint to get at the base of the U-bend. We shall need to find out who used the room last yesterday evening and whether he noticed the smear on the basin. If no one admits to having been sick during the day, or can't produce a witness that he was, we shall want to know what they all ate for the evening meal. It could be Lorrimer's vomit, so we'll need some information on his stomach contents. I'd also like a sample of his blood and hair to be left here at the lab. But Dr. Blain-Thomson will be seeing to that."

Reynolds said:

"We take it that the crucial time is from six-fifteen, when he was last seen alive in his lab, until midnight?"

"For the present. When I've seen his father and confirmed that he made that call at eight-forty-five we may be able to narrow it down. And we shall get a clearer idea of the time of death when Dr. Blain-Thomson has done the P.M. But judging from the state of rigor, Dr. Kerrison wasn't far out."

But Kerrison didn't need to be far out, if he were the murderer. Rigor mortis was notoriously unreliable, and if he wanted an alibi for himself, Kerrison could shift the time of death by up to an hour without suspicion. If the timing were tight he might not need even an hour. It had been prudent of him to call in the police surgeon to confirm his estimate of the time of death. But how likely was Dr. Greene, experienced as he might be in viewing bodies, to disagree with the opinion of a consultant forensic pathologist unless the latter's judgment was manifestly perverse? If Kerrison were guilty, he had run little risk by calling in Greene.

Dalgliesh got to his feet.

"Right," he said. "Let's get on with it, shall we?"

# X

Dalgliesh disliked having more than one other officer present with him at his preliminary and informal interview, so Massingham was taking the notes. They were hardly necessary; Dalgliesh, he knew, had almost total recall. But he still found the practice useful. They were sitting together at the conference table in the Director's office, but Howarth, perhaps because he objected to sitting in his own room other than at his desk, preferred to stand. He was leaning casually against the fireplace. From time to time Massingham lifted an unobtrusive eyebrow to glance at the clear-cut, dominant profile outlined against the classical frieze. There were three bunches of keys on the table: the bunch taken from Lorrimer's body, that handed over by Inspector Blakelock, and the set that Dr. Howarth, manipulating the security lock, had taken from its box in the cupboard. Each set of keys was identical, one Yale key and two security keys to the front door, and one smaller key on a plain metal ring. None was named, presumably for security reasons. Dalgliesh said:

"And these are the only three sets in existence?"

"Except for the set at Guy's Marsh police station, yes. Naturally, I checked earlier this morning that the police still have their set. The keys are kept in the safe under the control of the station officer, and they haven't been touched. They need a set at the police station in case the alarm goes off. There was no alarm last night."

Dalgliesh already knew from Mercer that the station keys had been checked. He said:

"And the smallest key?"

"That's the one to the Exhibits Store. The system is for all incoming exhibits, after they've been registered, to be stored there until they're issued to the head of the appropriate department. It's his responsibility to allocate them to a specific officer. In addition, we store the exhibits that have been examined and are awaiting collection by the police, and those that have been presented to the court during the case and are returned to us for destruction. Those are mainly drugs. They're destroyed here in the incinerator and the destruction witnessed by one of the laboratory staff and the officer in charge of the case. The Exhibits Store is also protected by the electronic alarm system, but, obviously, we need a key for internal security when the system hasn't been set."

"And all the laboratory internal doors and your office were protected last night once the internal alarm system was set? That means that an intruder could only have got out undetected through the top floor lavatory windows. All the others are either barred or fitted with the electronic alarm?"

"That's right. He could have got in that way too, of course, which was what concerned us most. But it wouldn't have been an easy climb, and the alarm would have gone off as soon as he tried to gain access to any of the main rooms in the laboratory. We did consider extending the alarm system to the lavatory suite soon after I arrived, but it seemed unnecessary. We haven't had a break-in in the seventy-odd years of the lab's existence."

"What are the precise arrangements about locking the laboratory?"

"Only the two Police Liaison Officers and Lorrimer as the Deputy Security Officer were authorized to lock up. He or the Police Liaison Officer on duty was responsible for ensuring that no staff were left on the premises and that all the internal doors were shut before the alarm was set, and the front door finally locked for the night. The alarm system to Guy's Marsh police station is set whether the door is locked on the inside or the out."

"And these other keys found on the body, the three in this leather pouch and the single key. Do you recognize any of those?"

"Not the three in the pouch. One is obviously his car key, and I take it that the other two are house keys. But the single one looks very like the key to the Wren chapel. If it is, I didn't know that Lorrimer had it. Not that it's important. But as far as I know, there's only one key to the chapel in existence and that's hanging on the board in the Chief Liaison Officer's room. It isn't a security lock and we're not particularly worried about the chapel. There's nothing left there of real value. But occasionally architects and archaeological societies want to view it, so we let them borrow the key and they sign for it in a book in the office. We don't allow them through the laboratory grounds to get at it. They have to use the back entrance in Guy's Marsh Road. The contract cleaners take it once every two months to clean and check the heating—we have to keep it reasonably warm in winter because the ceiling and carving are rather fine—and Miss Willard goes there from time to time, to do some dusting. When her father was rector of Chevisham, he used occasionally to hold services in the chapel, and I think she has a sentimental regard for the place."

Massingham went out to Chief Inspector Martin's office and brought in the chapel key. The two matched. The small notebook which he had found hanging with the key showed that it had last been collected by Miss Willard on Monday the twenty-fifth of October. Howarth said:

"We're thinking of transferring the chapel to the Department of the Environment once we occupy the new laboratory. It's a constant irritation to the Treasury that our funds are used to heat and maintain it. I've set up a string quartet here, and we held a concert on August the twenty-sixth in the chapel, but otherwise it's completely unused. I expect you will want to take a look at it, and it's worth seeing in its own right. It's a very fine specimen of late seventeenth-century church architecture, although, in fact, it isn't by Wren but by Alexander Fort, who was strongly influenced by him."

Dalgliesh asked suddenly:

"How well did you get on with Lorrimer?"

Howarth replied calmly:

"Not particularly well. I respected him as a biologist, and I certainly had no complaints either about his work or about his cooperation with me as Director. He wasn't an easy man to know, and I didn't find him particularly sympathetic. But he was probably one of the most respected serologists in the Service, and we shall miss him. If he had a fault, it was a reluctance to delegate. He has two scientific officer serologists in his department for the grouping of liquid blood and stains, saliva, and semen samples, but he invariably took the murder cases himself. Apart from his casework and attendance at trials and at scenes of crime, he did a considerable amount of lecturing to detective training courses and police familiarization courses."

Lorrimer's rough notebook was on the desk. Dalgliesh pushed it toward Howarth and said:

"Have you seen this before?"

"His rough notebook? Yes, I think I've noticed it in his department, or when he was carrying it with him. He was obsessively tidy and had a dislike of odd scraps of paper. Anything of importance was noted in that book and subsequently transferred to the files. Claire Easterbrook tells me that the last page is missing."

"That's why we're particularly anxious to know what he was doing here last night, apart from working on the clunch pit murder. He could have got into any of the other laboratories, of course?"

"If he'd switched off the internal alarm, yes. I believe it was his usual practice, when he was last on the premises, to rely on the Yale lock and the bolt on the front door and only check the internal doors and set the security alarm before he finally left. Obviously it's important not to set off the alarm accidentally."

"Would he have been competent to undertake an examination in another department?"

"It depends on what he was trying to do. Essentially, of course, he was concerned with the identification and grouping of biological material, blood, body stains, and the examination of fibers and animal and plant tissues. But he was a competent general scientist and his interests were wide—his scientific interests. Forensic biologists, particularly in the smaller laboratories, which this has been up to now, become pretty versatile. But he wouldn't attempt to use the more sophisticated instruments in the Instrument Section, the mass spectrometer, for example."

"And you personally have no idea what he could have been doing?"

"None. I do know that he came into this office. I had to look up the name of a consultant surgeon who was giving evidence for the defense in one of our old cases, and I had the medical directory on my desk when I left last night. This morning it was back in its place in the library. Few things irritated Lorrimer more than people removing books from the library. But if he was in this office last night, I hardly imagine it was merely to check on my carelessness with the reference books."

Lastly, Dalgliesh asked him about his movements the previous night.

"I played the fiddle at the village concert. The rector had five minutes or so to fill in and asked me if the string quartet would play something which he described as short and cheerful. The players were myself, a junior chemist, one of the scientific officers from the Document Examination Department, and a typist from the general office. Miss Easterbrook should have been the first cello, but she had a dinner engagement which she regarded as important and couldn't make it. We played the Mozart Divertimento in D major and came third on the program."

"And you stayed for the rest of the concert?"

"I intended to. Actually, the hall was incredibly stuffy and just before the interval at eight-thirty I slipped out. I stayed out."

Dalgliesh asked what precisely he'd done.

"Nothing. I sat on one of those flat tombstones for about twenty minutes, then I left."

"Did you see anyone, or did anyone see you?"

"I saw a hobbyhorse—I know now that it must have been Middlemass deputizing for Chief Inspector Martin—come out of the male dressing room. He pranced around rather happily, I thought, and snapped his jaws at an angel on one of the graves. Then he was joined by the troupe of morris-dancers coming through the graveyard from the Moonraker. It was an extraordinary sight. There was the racing moon and these extraordinary figures with their bells jingling and their hats decked with evergreens moving through the swirl of ground mist out of the darkness toward me. It was like an outré film or a ballet. All it needed was second-rate background music, preferably Stravinsky. I was sitting motionless on the gravestone, some distance away, and I don't think they saw me. I certainly didn't make myself known.

The hobbyhorse joined them, and they went into the hall. Then I heard the fiddle start up. I suppose I stayed sitting there for about another ten minutes, and then I left. I walked for the rest of the evening along Leamings Dike and got home about ten o'clock. My half sister, Domenica, will be able to confirm the time."

They spent a little time discussing the administrative arrangements for the investigation. Dr. Howarth said that he would move into Miss Foley's room and make his office available to the police. There would be no chance of the lab opening for the rest of the day, but Dalgliesh said that he hoped it would be possible for work to start again the next morning. Before Howarth left, Dalgliesh said:

"Everyone I've spoken to respected Dr. Lorrimer as a forensic biologist. But what was he like as a man? What, for example, did you know about him except that he was a forensic biologist?"

Dr. Howarth said coldly:

"Nothing. I wasn't aware there was anything to know, except that he was a forensic biologist. And now, if you've no more immediate questions, I must telephone Establishment Department and make sure that, in the excitement of his somewhat spectacular exit, they're not forgetting to send me a replacement."

# XI

With the resilience of youth, Brenda Pridmore had recovered quickly from the shock of finding Lorrimer's body. She had resolutely refused to be taken home; by the time Dalgliesh was ready to see her, she was perfectly calm and, indeed, anxious to tell her story. With her cloud of rich auburn hair and her freckled, wind-tanned face she looked the picture of bucolic health. But the gray eyes were intelligent, the mouth sensitive and gentle. She gazed across the desk at Dalgliesh as intently as a docile child and totally without fear. He guessed that all her young life she had been used to receiving an avuncular kindness from men and never doubted that she would receive it, too, from these unknown officers of police. In response to Dalgliesh's questioning, she described exactly what had happened from the moment of her arrival at the laboratory that morning to the discovery of the body. Dalgliesh asked:

"Did you touch him?"

"Oh no! I knelt down and I think I did put out my hand to feel his cheek. But that was all. I knew that he was dead, you see."

"And then?"

"I don't remember. I know I rushed downstairs and Inspector Blakelock was standing at the bottom looking up at me. I couldn't speak, but I suppose he saw by my face that something was wrong. Then I remember sitting on the chair outside Chief Inspector Martin's office and looking at Colonel Hoggatt's portrait. Then I don't remember anything until Dr. Howarth and Mrs. Bidwell arrived."

"Do you think anyone could have got out of the building past you while you were sitting there?"

"The murderer, you mean? I don't see how he could have. I know I wasn't very alert, but I hadn't fainted or anything silly like that. I'm sure I would have noticed if anyone had come across the hall. And even if he did manage to slip past me, he would have bumped into Dr. Howarth, wouldn't he?"

Dalgliesh asked her about her job at Hoggatt's, how well she had known Dr. Lorrimer. She prattled away with artless confidence about her life, her colleagues, her fascinating job, Inspector Blakelock who was so good to her and who had lost his own only daughter, telling with every sentence more than she knew. It wasn't that she was stupid, thought Massingham, only honest and ingenuous. For the first time they heard Lorrimer spoken of with affection.

"He was always terribly kind to me, although I didn't work in the Biology Department. Of course, he was a very serious man. He had so many responsibilities. The Biology Department is terribly overworked and he used to work late nearly every night, checking results, catching up with the backlog. I think he was disappointed at not being chosen to succeed Dr. Mac. Not that he ever said so to me—well he wouldn't, would he?—I'm far too junior and he was far too loyal."

Dalgliesh asked:

"Do you think anyone could have misunderstood his interest in you, might have been a little jealous?"

"Jealous of Dr. Lorrimer because he stopped sometimes at the desk to talk to me about my work and was kind to me? But he was old! That's just silly!"

Suppressing a grin as he bent over his notebook and penned a few staccato outlines, Massingham thought that it probably was.

Dalgliesh asked:

"It seems there was some trouble the day before he died when Dr. Kerrison's children called at the laboratory. Were you in the hall then?"

"You mean when he pushed Miss Kerrison out of the front hall? Well, he didn't actually push her, but he did speak very sharply. She had come with her small brother and they wanted to wait for Dr. Kerrison. Dr. Lorrimer looked at them, well, really as if he hated them. It wasn't at all like him. I think he's been under some terrible strain. Perhaps he had a premonition of his death. Do you know what he said to me after the clunch pit exhibits came in? He said that the only death we have to fear is our own. Don't you think that was an extraordinary remark?"

"Very strange," agreed Dalgliesh.

"And that reminds me of another thing. You did say that anything might be important. Well, there was a funny kind of letter arrived for Dr. Lorrimer yesterday morning. That's why he stopped at the desk, so that I could hand over any personal mail. There was just this thin brown envelope with the address printed, printed by hand in capital letters, I mean. And it was just his name, no qualifications after it. Odd, wasn't it?"

"Did he receive many private letters here?"

"Oh no, none really. The lab writing paper says that all communications have to be addressed to the Director. We deal at the desk with the exhibits received, but all the correspondence goes to the general office for sorting. We only hand over the personal letters, but there aren't many of those."

In the quick preliminary examination that he and Massingham had made of Lorrimer's meticulously tidy office, Dalgliesh had found no personal correspondence. He asked whether Miss Pridmore knew if Dr. Lorrimer had gone home for lunch. She said that he had. So it was possible that he had taken the letter home. It could mean anything, or nothing. It was just one more small fact that would have to be investigated.

He thanked Brenda Pridmore and reminded her again to come back to him if she remembered anything that could be of importance, however small. Brenda was not used to dissembling. It was obvious that something had occurred to her. She blushed and dropped her eyes. The metamorphosis from happy confidante to guilty schoolgirl was pathetically comic. Dalgliesh said gently:

"Yes?"

She didn't speak, but made herself meet his eyes and shook her head. He waited for a moment, then said:

"The investigation of murder is never agreeable. Like most unpleasant things in life, it sometimes seems easier not to get involved, to keep oneself uncontaminated. But that isn't possible. In a murder investigation, to suppress a truth is sometimes to tell a lie."

"But suppose one passes on information, something private, perhaps, which one hasn't any real right to know—and it throws suspicion on the wrong person?"

Dalgliesh said gently:

"You have to trust us. Will you try to do that?"

She nodded, and whispered, "Yes," but she said nothing further. He judged that this was not the time to press her. He let her go and sent for Angela Foley.

# XII

In contrast to Brenda Pridmore's artless confiding, Angela Foley presented a bland, inscrutable gaze. She was an unusual-looking girl with a heart-shaped face and a wide, exceedingly high forehead from which hair, baby fine, the color of ripe grain, was strained back and plaited into a tight coil on top of her head. Her eyes were narrow, slanted, and so deeply set that Dalgliesh found it hard to guess their color. Her mouth was small, pursed, and uncommunicative above the pointed chin. She wore a dress in fine fawn wool, topped with an elaborately patterned short-sleeved tabard, and short laced boots, a sophisticated and exotic contrast to Brenda's orthodox prettiness and neat, hand-knitted twinset.

If she was distressed by her cousin's violent death, she concealed it admirably. She said that she had worked as the Director's secretary for five years, first with Dr. MacIntyre and now with Dr. Howarth. Before that, she had been a shorthand typist in the general office of the laboratory, having joined Hoggatt's straight from school. She was twenty-seven. Until two years ago she had lived in a bed-sitting room in Ely, but now shared Sprogg's Cottage with a woman friend. They had spent the whole of the previous evening in each other's company. Edwin Lorrimer and his father had been her only living relatives, but they had seen very little of each other. The family, she explained, as if this were the most natural thing in the world, had never been close.

"So you know very little of his private affairs, his will, for example?"

"No, nothing. When my grandmother left him all her money, and we were at the solicitor's office, he said that he would make me his heir. But I think he just felt guilty at the time that I wasn't named in the will. I don't suppose it meant anything. And, of course, he may have changed his mind."

"Do you remember how much your grandmother left?"

She paused for a moment. Almost, he thought, as if calculating whether ignorance would sound more suspicious than knowledge. Then she said:

"I think it was about thirty thousand. I don't know how much it is now."

He took her briefly but carefully through the events of the early morning. She and her friend had a car, a Mini, but she usually cycled to work. She had done so that morning, arriving at the laboratory at her usual time, just before nine o'clock, and had been surprised to see Dr. Howarth with Mrs. Bidwell in his car, driving in before her. Brenda Pridmore had opened the door. Inspector Blakelock was coming downstairs and he had broken the news of the murder. They had all stayed in the hall together while Dr. Howarth went up to the Biology Lab. Inspector Blakelock had telephoned for the police and for Dr. Kerrison. When Dr. Howarth returned to the hall he had asked her to go with Inspector Blakelock and check on the keys. She and the Director were the only two members of the staff who knew the combination of his security cupboard. He had stayed in the hall, she thought talking to Brenda Pridmore. The keys had been in their box in the cupboard, and she and Inspector Blakelock had left them there. She had reset the combination lock and returned to the hall. Dr. Howarth had gone into his office to talk to the Home Office, telling the rest of the staff to wait in the hall. Later, after the police and Dr. Kerrison had arrived, Dr. Howarth had driven her in his car to break the news to old Mr. Lorrimer. Then he had left her with the old man to return to the laboratory, and she had telephoned for her friend. She and Miss Mawson had been there together until Mrs. Swaffield, the rector's wife, and a constable arrived, about an hour later.

"What did you do at Postmill Cottage?"

"I made tea and took it in to my uncle. Miss Mawson stayed in the kitchen most of the time doing the washing-up for him. The kitchen was in a bit of a mess, mostly dirty crockery from the previous day."

"How did your uncle seem?"

"Worried, and rather cross about having been left alone. I don't think he quite realized Edwin was dead."

There seemed little else to be learned from her. As far as she knew, her cousin had had no enemies. She had no idea who could have killed him. Her voice, high, rather monotonous, the voice of a small girl, suggested that it was not a matter of much concern to her. She expressed no regret, advanced no theories, answered all his questions composedly in her high, unemphatic voice. He might have been a casual and unimportant visitor gratifying a curiosity about the routine of the working of the laboratory. He felt an instinctive antipathy toward her. He had no difficulty in concealing it, but it interested him since it was a long time since a murder suspect had provoked in him so immediate and physical a reaction. But he wondered whether it was prejudice that glimpsed in those deep and secretive eyes a flash of disdain, of contempt even, and he would have given a great deal to know what was going on behind that high, rather bumpy forehead.

When she had left, Massingham said:

"It's odd that Dr. Howarth sent her and Blakelock to check on the keys. He must have immediately realized their importance. Access to the lab is fundamental to this case. So why didn't he check on them himself? He knew the combination."

"Too proud to take a witness, and too intelligent to go without one. And he may have thought it more important to supervise things in the hall. But at least he was careful to protect Angela Foley. He didn't send her alone. Well, let's see what Blakelock has to say about it."

## XIII

Like Dr. Howarth, Inspector Blakelock chose not to sit. He stood at attention, facing Dalgliesh across Howarth's desk like a man on a disciplinary charge. Dalgliesh knew better than to try to get him to relax. Blakelock had first learned the technique of replying to questions in his detective-constable days in the witness box. He gave the information he was asked for, no more and no less, his eyes fixed on some spot a foot above Dalgliesh's right shoulder. When he gave his name in a firm, expressionless voice, Dalgliesh half expected him to reach out his right hand for the Book and take the oath.

In reply to Dalgliesh's questioning he described his movements since leaving his house in Ely to come to the laboratory. His account of the finding of the body tallied with that of Brenda Pridmore. As soon as he had seen her face as she came down the stairs he had realized that something was wrong and had dashed up to the Biology Lab without waiting for her to speak. The door had been open and the light on. He described the position of the body as precisely as if its rigid contours were imprinted on the mind's retina. He had known at once that Lorrimer was dead. He hadn't touched the body except, instinctively, to slip his hand into the pocket of the white coat and feel that the keys were there.

Dalgliesh asked:

"When you arrived at the laboratory this morning you waited for Miss Pridmore to catch you up before coming in. Why was that?"

"I saw her coming around the side of the building after having put her bicycle away, and it seemed courteous to wait, sir. And it saved me having to reopen the door to her."

"And you found the three locks and the internal security system in good order?"

"Yes, sir."

"Do you make a routine check of the laboratory as soon as you arrive?"

"No, sir. Of course, if I found that any of the locks or the security panel had been tampered with I should check at once. But everything was in order."

"You said earlier that the telephone call from Mr. Lorrimer senior was a surprise to you. Didn't you notice Dr. Lorrimer's car when you arrived this morning?"

"No, sir. The senior scientific staff use the end garage."

"Why did you send Miss Pridmore to see if Dr. Lorrimer was here?"

"I didn't, sir. She slipped under the counter before I could stop her."

"So you sensed that something was wrong?"

"Not really, sir. I didn't expect her to find him. But I think it did briefly occur to me that he might have been taken ill."

"What sort of a man was Dr. Lorrimer, Inspector?"

"He was the Senior Biologist, sir."

"I know. I'm asking you what he was like as a man and a colleague."

"I didn't really know him well, sir. He wasn't one for lingering at the reception desk to chat. But I got on all right with him. He was a good forensic scientist."

"I've been told that he took an interest in Brenda Pridmore. Didn't that mean that he occasionally lingered at the desk?"

"Not for more than a few minutes, sir. He liked to have a word with the girl from time to time. Everyone does. It's nice to have a young thing about the lab. She's pretty and hardworking and enthusiastic, and I think Dr. Lorrimer wanted to encourage her."

"No more than that, Inspector?"

Blakelock said stolidly:

"No, sir."

Dalgliesh then asked him about his movements on the previous evening. He said that he and his wife had bought tickets for the village concert, although his wife was reluctant to go because of a bad headache. She suffered from sinus headaches which were occasionally disabling. But they had attended for the first half of the program and, because her headache was worse, had left at the interval. He had driven back to Ely, arriving home about a quarter to nine. He and his wife lived in a modern bungalow on the outskirts of the city with no near neighbors and he thought it unlikely that anyone would have noticed their return. Dalgliesh said:

"There seems to have been a general reluctance on the part of everyone to stay for the second part of the program. Why did you bother to go when you knew your wife was unwell?"

"Dr. MacIntyre—he's the former Director, sir—liked the laboratory staff to take part in village activities, and Chief Inspector Martin feels the same. So I'd got the tickets and my wife thought we might as well use them. She hoped that the concert might help her to forget her headache. But the first half was rather rowdy and, in fact, it got worse."

"Did you go home and fetch her, or did she meet you here?"

"She came out earlier in the afternoon by the bus, sir, and spent the afternoon with Mrs. Dean, wife of the minister at the chapel. She's an old friend. I went around to collect my wife when I left work at six o'clock. We had a fish-and-chip supper there before the concert."

"That's your normal time for leaving?"

"Yes, sir."

"And who locks up the laboratory if the scientists are working after your time for leaving?"

"I always check who's left, sir. If there are junior staff working then I have to stay until they've finished. But that isn't usual. Dr. Howarth has a set of keys and would check the alarm system and lock up if he worked late."

"Did Dr. Lorrimer normally work after you had left?"

"About three or four evenings a week, sir. But I had no anxiety about Dr. Lorrimer locking up. He was very conscientious."

"Would he let anyone into the laboratory if he were here alone?"

"No, sir, not unless they were members of the staff, or of the police force, maybe. But it would have to be an officer he knew. He wouldn't let anyone in who hadn't got proper business here. Dr. Lorrimer was very particular about unauthorized people coming into the laboratory."

"Was that why he tried forcibly to remove Miss Kerrison the day before yesterday?"

Inspector Blakelock did not lose his composure. He said:

"I wouldn't describe it as a forcible removal, sir. He didn't lay hands on the girl."

"Would you describe to me exactly what did happen, Inspector?"

"Miss Kerrison and her small brother came to meet their father. Dr. Kerrison was lecturing that morning to the inspectors' training course. I suggested to Miss Kerrison that she sit down on the chair and wait, but Dr. Lorrimer came down the stairs at that moment to see if the mallet had arrived for examination. He saw the children and asked rather peremptorily what they were doing there. He said that a forensic science lab wasn't a place for children. Miss Kerrison said that she didn't intend to leave, so he walked toward her as if he intended to put her out. He looked very white, very strange, I thought. He didn't lay a hand on her but I think she was frightened that he was going to. I believe she's very highly strung, sir. She started screeching and screaming, 'I hate you. I hate you.' Dr. Lorrimer turned and went back up the stairs and Brenda tried to comfort the girl."

"And Miss Kerrison and her small brother left without waiting for their father?"

"Yes, sir. Dr. Kerrison came down about fifteen minutes later and I told him that the children had come for him but had left."

"You said nothing about the incident?"

"No, sir."

"Was this typical of Dr. Lorrimer's behavior?"

"No, sir. But he hadn't been looking well in recent weeks. I think he's been under some strain."

"And you've no idea what kind of strain?"

"No, sir."

"Had he enemies?"

"Not to my knowledge, sir."

"So you've no idea who might have wanted him dead?"

"No, sir."

"After the discovery of Dr. Lorrimer's body, Dr. Howarth sent you with Miss Foley to check that his bunch of keys were in the security cupboard. Will you describe exactly what you and she did?"

"Miss Foley opened the cupboard. She and the Director are the only two people who know the combination."

"And you watched?"

"Yes, sir, but I can't remember the figures. I watched her twisting and setting the dial."

"And then?"

"She took out the metal cash box and opened it. It wasn't locked. The keys were inside."

"You were watching her closely all the time, Inspector? Are you absolutely sure that Miss Foley couldn't have replaced the keys in the box without your seeing?"

"No, sir. That would have been quite impossible."

"One last thing, Inspector. When you went up to the body Miss Pridmore was here alone. She told me that she's virtually certain that no one could have slipped out of the laboratory during that time. Have you considered that possibility?"

"That he might have been here all night, sir? Yes. But he wasn't hiding in the Chief Liaison Officer's room because I would have seen him when I went to turn off the internal alarm. That's the room closest to the front door. I suppose he could have been in the Director's office, but I don't see how he could have crossed the hall and opened the door without Miss Pridmore noticing even if she were in a state of shock. It isn't as if the door were ajar. He'd have had to turn the Yale lock."

"And you are absolutely certain that your own set of keys never left your possession last night?"

"I'm certain, sir."

"Thank you, Inspector. That's all for the present. Would you please ask Mr. Middlemass to come in?"

# XIV

The Document Examiner strolled into the office with easy assurance, arranged his long body without invitation in Howarth's armchair, crossed his right ankle over his left knee, and raised an interrogatory eyebrow at Dalgliesh like a visitor expecting nothing from his host but boredom, but politely determined not to show it.

He was wearing dark brown corduroy slacks, a fawn turtleneck sweater in fine wool, and bright purple socks with leather slip-on shoes. The effect was of a *dégagé* informality, but Dalgliesh noticed that the slacks were tailored, the sweater cashmere, and the shoes handmade. He glanced down at Middlemass's statement of his movements since seven o'clock the previous evening. Unlike the efforts of his colleagues, it was written with a regular pen, not a ballpoint, in a fine, high, italic script, which succeeded in being both decorative and virtually illegible. It was not the kind of hand he had expected. He said:

"Before we get down to this, could you tell me about your quarrel with Lorrimer?"

"My version of it, you mean, as opposed to Mrs. Bidwell's?"

"The truth, as opposed to speculation."

"It wasn't a particularly edifying episode, and I can't say I'm proud of it. But it wasn't important. I'd just started on the clunch pit murder case when I heard Lorrimer coming out of the washroom. I had a private matter I wanted a word about so I called him in. We talked, quarreled, he struck out at me, and I reacted with a punch to his nose. It bled spectacularly over my coat. I apologized. He left."

"What was the quarrel about? A woman?"

"Well hardly, Commander, not with Lorrimer. I think Lorrimer knew that there were two sexes but I doubt whether he approved of the arrangement. It was a small private matter, something that happened a couple of years ago. Nothing to do with this lab."

"So we have the picture of your settling down to work on an exhibit from a murder case, an important exhibit since you chose to examine it yourself. You are not, however, so absorbed in this task that you can't listen to footsteps passing the door and identify those of Lorrimer. It seems to you a convenient moment to call him in and discuss something that happened two years ago, something you've apparently been content to forget in the interim, but which now so incenses you both that you end by trying to knock each other down."

"Put like that, it sounds eccentric."

"Put like that, it sounds absurd."

"I suppose it was absurd in a way. It was about a cousin of my wife's, Peter Ennalls. He left school with two A-levels in science and seemed keen on coming into the Service. He came to me for advice and I told him how to go about it. He ended up as an S.O. under Lorrimer in the Southern Lab. It wasn't a success. I don't suppose it was entirely Lorrimer's fault, but he hasn't got the gift of managing young staff. Ennalls ended up with a failed career, a broken engagement, and what is euphemistically described as a nervous breakdown. He drowned himself. We heard rumors about what had happened at the Southern. It's a small Service and these things get around. I didn't really know the boy; my wife was fond of him.

"I'm not blaming Lorrimer for Peter's death. A suicide is always ultimately responsible for his own destruction. But my wife believes that Lorrimer could have done more to help him. I telephoned her after lunch yesterday to explain that I'd be home later and our conversation reminded me that I'd always meant to speak to Lorrimer about Peter. By coincidence I heard his footsteps. So I called him in with the result that Mrs. Bidwell has no doubt graphically described. Mrs. Bidwell, I don't doubt, detects a woman at the bottom of any male quarrel. And if she did talk about a woman or a telephone call, then the woman was my wife and the telephone call was the one I've told you about."

It sounded plausible, thought Dalgliesh. It might even be the truth. The Peter Ennalls story would have to be checked. It was just another chore when they were already hard-pressed and the truth of it was hardly in doubt. But Middlemass had spoken in the present tense: "Lorrimer hasn't the gift of managing junior staff." Were there, perhaps, junior staff closer to home who had suffered at his hands? But he decided to leave it for now. Paul Middlemass was an intelligent man. Before he made a more formal statement he would have time to ponder about the effect on his career of putting his signature to a lie. Dalgliesh said:

"According to this statement you were playing the part of a hobbyhorse for the morris-dancers at yesterday evening's village concert. Despite this, you say you can't give the name of anyone who could vouch for you. Presumably both the dancers and the audience could see the hobbyhorse galumphing around, but not you inside it. But wasn't anyone there when you arrived at the hall, or when you left?"

"No one who saw me to recognize me. It's a nuisance but it can't be helped. It happened rather oddly. I'm not a morris-dancer. I don't normally go in for these rustic rites and village concerts aren't my idea of entertainment. It was the Senior Liaison Officer's show, Chief Inspector Martin, but he had the chance of this U.S.A. visit unexpectedly and asked me to deputize. We're about the same size and I suppose he thought that the outfit would fit me. He needed someone fairly broad in the shoulders and strong enough to take the weight of the head. I owed him a favor—he had a tactful word with one of his mates on highway patrol when I was caught speeding a month ago—so I couldn't very well not oblige.

"I went to a rehearsal last week and all it amounted to was, as you say, galumphing around the dancers after they've done their stuff, snapping my jaws at the audience, frisking my tail, and generally making a fool of myself. That hardly seemed to matter since no one could recognize me. I'd no intention of spending the whole evening at the concert, so I asked Bob Gotobed, he's the leader of the troupe, to give me a ring from the hall about fifteen minutes before we were due to go on. We were scheduled to appear after the intermission and they reckoned that that would be about eight-thirty. The concert, as you've probably been told, started at seven-thirty."

"And you stayed working in your lab until the call came?"

"That's right. My S.O. went out and got me a couple of beef and chutney sandwiches and I ate them at my desk. Bob phoned at eight-fifteen to say that they were running a bit ahead of time and that I'd better come over. The lads were dressed and were proposing to have a beer in the Moonraker. The hall hasn't a license, so all the audience get in the intermission is coffee or tea served by the Mothers' Union. I left the lab at, I suppose, about eight-twenty."

"You say here that Lorrimer was alive then as far as you know?"

"We know that he was alive twenty-five minutes later, if his dad is right about the telephone call. But actually I think I saw him. I went out of the front door because that's the only exit but I had to go around the back to the garages to get my car. The light was on then in the Biology Department and I saw a figure in a white coat move briefly across the window. I can't swear that it was Lorrimer. I can only say that it never occurred to me at the time that it wasn't. And I knew, of course, that he must be in the building. He was responsible for locking up and he was excessively tedious about security. He wouldn't have left without checking on all the departments, including Document Examination."

"How was the front door locked?"

"Only with the Yale and a single bolt. That's what I expected. I let myself out."

"What happened when you got to the hall?"

"To explain that I'll have to describe the architectural oddities of the place. It was put up cheaply five years ago by the village builder and the committee thought they'd save money by not employing an architect. They merely told the chap that they wanted a rectangular hall with a stage and two dressing rooms and lavatories at one end, and a reception hall, cloakroom, and a room for refreshments at the other. It was built by Harry Gotobed and his sons. Harry is a pillar of the chapel and a model of Nonconformist rectitude. He doesn't hold with the theater, amateur or otherwise, and I think they had some difficulty in persuading him even to build a stage. But he certainly didn't intend to have any communicating door between the male and female dressing rooms. As a result what we've got is a stage with two rooms behind, each with its separate lavatory. There's an exit at each side into the graveyard, and two doors onto the stage, but there's literally no common space behind the stage. As a result the men dress in the right-hand dressing room and come onto the stage from the prompt side, and the women from the left. Anyone who wants to enter from the opposite side has to leave the dressing room, scurry in their costume and probably in the rain through the graveyard, and, if they don't trip over a gravestone, break their ankle, or fall into an open grave, finally make a triumphant, if damp, appearance on the proper side."

Suddenly he threw back his head and gave a shout of laughter, then recovered himself and said:

"Sorry, poor taste. It's just that I was remembering last year's performance by the dramatic society. They'd chosen one of those dated domestic comedies where the characters spend most of their time in evening dress making snappy small talk. Young Birdie Corrigan from the general store played the maid. Scurrying through the churchyard she thought she saw old Maggie Gotobed's ghost. She made her entrance screaming, cap awry, but remembered her part sufficiently to gasp: 'Holy Mother of God, dinner is served!' Whereat the cast trooped dutifully off stage, the men to one side and the women to the other. Our hall adds considerably to the interest of the performances, I can tell you."

"So you went into the right-hand dressing room?"

"That's right. It was a complete shambles. The cast have to hang up their outdoor coats as well as keep the costumes there. There's a row of coat hooks and a bench down the middle of the room, one rather small mirror, and space for two people only to make up simultaneously. The single hand basin is in the lavatory. Well, no doubt you'll be looking at the place for yourself. Last night it was chaotic with outdoor coats, costumes, boxes, and props piled on the bench and overflowing onto the floor. The hobbyhorse costume was hanging on one of the pegs, so I put it on."

"There was no one there when you arrived?"

"No one in the room, but I could hear someone in the lavatory. I knew that most of the troupe were over at the Moonraker. When I had got myself into the costume the lavatory door opened and Harry Sprogg, he's a member of the troupe, came out. He was wearing his costume."

Massingham made a note of the name: Harry Sprogg. Dalgliesh asked:

"Did you speak?"

"I didn't. He said something about being glad I'd made it and that the chaps were over at the Moonraker. He said he was just going to dig them out. He's the only teetotaler of the party so I suppose that's why he didn't go over with them. He left and I followed him out into the cemetery."

"Without having spoken to him?"

"I can't remember that I said anything. We were only together for about a couple of seconds. I followed him out because the dressing room was stuffy—actually it stank—and the costume was extraordinarily heavy and hot. I thought I'd wait outside where I could join the boys when they came across from the pub. And that's what I did."

"Did you see anyone else?"

"No, but that doesn't mean there was no one there. Vision's a bit restricted through the headpiece. If someone had been standing motionless in the graveyard, I could easily have missed him. I wasn't expecting to see anyone."

"How long were you there?"

"Less than five minutes. I galumphed around a bit and tried a few trial snaps of the jaw and whisks of the tail. It must have looked daft if anyone was watching. There's a particularly repulsive memorial there, a marble angel with an expression of nauseating piety and a hand pointed upward. I pranced around that once or twice and snapped my jaws at its asinine face. God knows why! Perhaps it was the joint effect of moonlight and the place itself. Then I saw the chaps coming across the graveyard from the Moonraker and I joined up with them."

"Did you say anything then?"

"I may have said good evening or hello, but I don't think so. They wouldn't have recognized my voice through the headpiece anyway. I raised the front right-hand hoof and made a mock obeisance and then tagged on behind. We went in to the dressing room together. We could hear the audience settling into their seats, and then the stage manager put his head in and said, 'Right, boys.' Then the six dancers went on, and I could hear the violin strike up, the stamping of feet, and the jangling of bells. Then the music changed, and that was the signal for me to join them and do my bit. Part of the act was to go down the steps from the stage and frolic among the audience. It seemed to go down well enough to judge by the girlish shrieks, but if you're thinking of asking whether anyone recognized me, I shouldn't bother. I don't see how they could have."

"But after the performance?"

"No one saw me after the performance. We came tumbling down the steps from the stage into the dressing room, but the applause went on. Then I realized with considerable horror that some fools in the audience were calling out 'Encore.' The lads in green needed no second invitation and they were up the stairs again like a troop of parched navvies who'd just been told that the bar's open. I took the view that my agreement with Bill Martin covered one performance, not including an encore, and that I'd made enough of a fool of myself for one evening. So when the fiddle struck up and the stamping began I got out of the costume, hung it back on the nail, and made off. As far as I know no one saw me leave and there was no one in the parking lot when I unlocked my car. I was at home before ten and my wife can vouch for that if you're interested. But I don't suppose you are."

"It would be more helpful if you could find someone to vouch for you between eight-forty-five and midnight."

"I know. Maddening, isn't it? If I'd known someone was proposing to murder Lorrimer during the evening I'd have taken good care not to put the headpiece on until the second before we went on stage. It's a pity the beast's head is so large. It's supported, as you'll discover, from the wearer's shoulders and doesn't actually touch the head or face. If it did you might find a hair or some biological evidence that I'd actually worn the thing. And prints are no good. I handled it at the rehearsal and so did a dozen other people. The whole incident is an example to me of the folly of indulging in good nature. If I'd only told old Bill just what he could do with his blasted hobbyhorse I should have been home and, quite literally, dry before eight o'clock with a nice cozy alibi at the Panton Arms for the rest of the evening."

Dalgliesh ended the interview by asking about the missing white coat.

"It's a fairly distinctive design. Actually I've got half a dozen of them, all inherited from my father. The other five are in the linen cupboard here, if you want to have a look at them. They're waisted, in very heavy white linen, buttoning high to the neck with crested Royal Army Dental Corps buttons. Oh, and they've got no pockets. The old man thought pockets were unhygienic."

Massingham thought that a coat already stained with Lorrimer's blood might be seen by a murderer as a particularly useful protective garment. Echoing his thought, Middlemass said:

"If it is found again I don't think I could say with certainty exactly what bloodstains resulted from our punch-up. There was one patch about four inches by two on the right shoulder, but there may have been other splashes. But presumably the serologists would be able to give you some idea of the comparative age of the stains."

If the coat were ever found, thought Dalgliesh. It wouldn't be an easy thing to destroy completely. But the murderer, if he had taken it, would have had all night to dispose of the evidence. He asked:

"And you dropped this particular coat in the soiled-linen basket in the men's washroom immediately after the quarrel?"

"I meant to, but then I thought better of it. The stain wasn't large and the sleeves were perfectly clean. I put it on again and dropped it in the soiled-linen basket when I washed before leaving the lab."

"Do you remember what washbasin you used?"

"The first one, nearest the door."

"Was the basin clean?"

If Middlemass were surprised by the question, he concealed it.

"As clean as it ever is after a day's use. I wash fairly vigorously so it was clean enough when I left it. And so was I."

The picture came into Massingham's mind with startling clarity: Middlemass in his blood-spattered coat bending low over the washbasin, both taps running full on, the water swirling and gurgling down the waste pipe, water stained pink with Lorrimer's blood. But what about the timing? If old Lorrimer really had spoken to his son at eight-forty-five then Middlemass must be in the clear, at least for the first part of the evening. And then he pictured another scene: Lorrimer's sprawled body, the raucous ring of the telephone, Middlemass's gloved hand slowly lifting the receiver. But could old Lorrimer really mistake another voice for that of his son?

When the Document Examiner had left, Massingham said:

"At least he has one person to corroborate his story. Dr. Howarth saw the hobbyhorse prancing around the angel memorial in the churchyard. They've hardly had opportunity this morning to concoct that story together. And I don't see how else Howarth could have known about it."

Dalgliesh said:

"Unless they concocted the story in the graveyard last night. Or unless it was Howarth, not Middlemass, who was inside that hobbyhorse."

# XV

"I didn't like him, and I was frightened of him, but I didn't kill him. I know everyone will think that I did, but it's not true. I couldn't kill anyone or anything; not an animal, let alone a man."

Clifford Bradley had stood up fairly well to the long wait for questioning. He wasn't incoherent. He had tried to behave with dignity. But he had brought into the room with him the sour contagion of fear, that most difficult of all emotions to hide. His whole body twitched with it: the restless hands clasping and unclasping in his lap, the shuddering mouth, the anxious, blinking eyes. He was not an impressive figure, and fear had made him pitiable. He would make an ineffective murderer, thought Massingham. Watching him, he felt some of the instinctive shame of the healthy in the presence of the diseased. It was easy to imagine him retching over that washbasin, vomiting up his guilt and terror. It was less easy to envisage him tearing out the page of the notebook, destroying the white coat, organizing that early-morning telephone call to Mrs. Bidwell. Dalgliesh said mildly:

"No one is accusing you. You're familiar enough with Judge's Rules to know that we wouldn't be talking like this if I were about to caution you. You say that you didn't kill him. Have you any idea who did?"

"No. Why should I have? I didn't know anything about him. All I know is that I was at home with my wife last night. My mother-in-law came to supper and I saw her off on the seven-forty-five bus to Ely. Then I went straight home, and I was home all evening. My mother-in-law telephoned about nine o'clock to say that she'd reached home safely. She didn't speak to me because I was having a bath. My wife told her that. But Sue can confirm that, except for taking her mother to the bus, I was home all evening."

Bradley admitted that he hadn't known that old Mr. Lorrimer's hospital admission had been postponed. He thought that he had been out of the laboratory in the washroom when the old man's call came through. He knew nothing of the early telephone call to Mrs. Bidwell, the missing page from Lorrimer's notebook, or Paul Middlemass's missing white coat. Asked about his supper on Wednesday night, he said that they had eaten curry made with tinned beef, together with rice and tinned peas. Afterward there had been a trifle which, he explained defensively, had been made with stale cake and custard. Massingham suppressed a shudder as he made a careful note of these details. He was glad when Dalgliesh said that Bradley could go. There seemed nothing else of importance to be learned from him in his present state; nothing more to be learned, indeed, from anyone at the laboratory. He was fretting to see Lorrimer's house, Lorrimer's next of kin.

But before they left, Sergeant Reynolds had something to report. He was finding it difficult to keep the excitement from his voice.

"We've found some tire marks, sir, about halfway up the drive among the bushes. They look pretty fresh to me. We've got them protected until the photographer arrives and then we'll get a plaster cast made. It's difficult to be sure until we compare them with a tire index, but it looks to me as if the two back tires were a Dunlop and a Semperit. That's a pretty odd combination. It should help us to get the car."

It was a pity, thought Dalgliesh, that Superintendent Mercer had told the photographers they could go. But it wasn't surprising. Given the present pressure of work on the Force, it was difficult to justify keeping men hanging about indefinitely. And at least the fingerprint officers were still here. He said:

"Have you been able to get in touch with Mr. Bidwell yet?"

"Captain Massey says he's up on the five-acre raising sugar beet. He'll tell him you want to see him when he comes in for his dockey."

"His what?"

"His dockey, sir. That's the meal break which we have in these parts at about half past ten or eleven."

"I'm relieved that Captain Massey has a proper sense of priority between agriculture and murder."

"They're a good bit behind with the five-acre, sir, but Captain Massey will see that he calls in at Guy's Marsh station as soon as they've finished work this afternoon."

"If he doesn't, you'd better dig him out, even if you have to borrow Captain Massey's tractor to do it. That telephone call is important. I'll have a word with the senior scientists in the library now and explain to them that I want them present in the departments when you do the internal search. The rest of them can go home. I'll tell them that we hope to have finished searching by the end of the day. It should be possible for the lab to open again tomorrow morning. Inspector Massingham and I will be seeing Dr. Lorrimer's father at Postmill Cottage. If anything breaks, you can contact us there or through the car radio control from Guy's Marsh."

Less than ten minutes later, with Massingham at the wheel of the police Rover, they were on their way.

# BOOK THREE

# An Experimental Man

# I

Postmill Cottage lay two miles to the north of the village at the junction of Stoney Piggott Road and Tenpenny Lane, where the road curved gently upward, but so imperceptibly that it was difficult for Dalgliesh to believe that he was on slightly higher ground until the car was parked on the grass verge, and turning to close the door he saw the village strung out along the road below him. Under the turbulent painter's sky, with its changing clusters of white, gray, and purple cumulus clouds massing against the pale azure blue of the upper air, and the sunlight moving fitfully across the fields and glittering on roofs and windows, it looked like an isolated frontier outpost, but welcoming, prosperous, and secure. Violent death might lurk eastward in the dark fenlands, but surely not under these neat domestic roofs. Hoggatt's Laboratory was hidden by its belt of trees, but the new building was immediately identifiable, its concrete stumps, ditches, and half-built walls looking like the orderly excavation of some long-buried city.

The cottage, a low building of brick with a white wood-clad front and with the rounded top and sails of the windmill visible behind, was separated from the road by a wide ditch. A wooden plank bridge and white-painted gate led to the front path and the latched door. The first impression of melancholy neglect, induced perhaps by the cottage's isolation and the bareness of outer walls and windows, proved on second glance illusory. The front garden had the disheveled, overgrown look of autumn, but the roses in the two circular beds, one each side of the path, had been properly tended. The gravel path was clear of weeds, the paintwork on door and windows was shining. Twenty feet farther on, two wide and sturdy planks bridged the ditch and led to a flagstoned yard and a brick garage.

There was an old and grubby red Mini already parked next to a police car. Dalgliesh deduced from the bundle of parish magazines, a smaller one of what looked like concert programs, and the bunch of shaggy chrysanthemums and autumn foliage on the back seat that the rector, or more probably his wife, was already at the cottage, probably on her way to help with the church decorations, although Thursday was an unusual day, surely, for this ecclesiastical chore. He had scarcely turned from this scrutiny of the rectory car when the door of the cottage opened and a woman bustled down the path toward them. No one who had been born and bred in a rectory could be in any doubt that here was Mrs. Swaffield. She looked indeed like a prototype of a country rector's wife, large-bosomed, cheerful, and energetic, exuding the slightly intimidating assurance of a woman adept at recognizing authority and competence at a glance, and making immediate use of them. She was wearing a tweed skirt covered with a flowered cotton apron, a hand-knitted twinset, thick brogues, and openwork woollen stockings. A felt hat, shaped like a porkpie, its crown stabbed with a steel hatpin, was jammed uncompromisingly over a broad forehead.

"Good morning. Good morning. You're Commander Dalgliesh and Inspector Massingham. Winifred Swaffield. Come in, won't you. The old gentleman is upstairs changing. He insisted on putting on his suit when he heard you were on the way, although I assured him that it wasn't at all necessary. He'll be down in a minute. In the front parlor would be best I think, don't you? This is Constable Davis, but of course you know all about him. He tells me that he's been sent here to see that no one goes into Dr. Lorrimer's room and to stop any visitors from bothering the old gentleman. Well, we haven't had any so far except one reporter and I soon got rid of him, so that's all right. But the constable has really been very helpful to me in the kitchen. I've just been getting some lunch for Mr. Lorrimer. It'll only be soup and an omelette, I'm afraid, but there doesn't seem to be much else in the larder except tins and he might be glad of those in the future. One doesn't like to come laden from the rectory like a Victorian do-gooder.

"Simon and I wanted him to come back to the rectory at once but he doesn't seem anxious to leave, and really one mustn't badger people, especially the old. And perhaps it's just as well. Simon's down with this two-day flu—that's why he can't be here—and we don't want the old gentleman to catch it. But we can't let him stay here alone tonight. I thought that he might like to have his niece here, Angela Foley, but he says no. So I'm hoping that Millie Gotobed from the Moonraker will be able to sleep here tonight, and we'll have to think again tomorrow. But I mustn't take up your time with my worries."

At the end of this speech, Dalgliesh and Massingham found themselves ushered into the front living room. At the sound of their footsteps in the narrow hall Constable Davis had emerged from what was presumably the kitchen, had sprung to attention, saluted, blushed, and given Dalgliesh a glance of mingled appeal and slight desperation before disappearing again. The smell of homemade soup had wafted appetizingly through the door.

The sitting room, which was stuffy and smelled strongly of tobacco, was adequately furnished, yet gave an impression of cheerless discomfort, a cluttered repository of the mementoes of aging and its sad solaces. The chimney breast had been boarded up and an old-fashioned gas fire hissed out an uncomfortably fierce heat over a sofa in cut moquette with two greasy circles marking where innumerable heads had once rested. There was a square oak table with bulbous carved legs and four matching chairs with vinyl seats, and a large dresser set against the wall opposite the window, hung with the cracked remnants of long-smashed tea sets. On the dresser were two bottles of Guinness and an unwashed glass. To the right of the fire was a high winged armchair and beside it a wicker table with a ramshackle lamp, a tobacco pouch, an ashtray bearing a picture of Brighton pier, and an open checkerboard with the pieces set out, crusted with dried food and accumulated grime. The alcove to the left of the fire was filled with a large television set. Above it were a couple of shelves holding a collection of popular novels in identical sizes and bindings, issued by a book club to which Mr. Lorrimer had once apparently briefly belonged. They looked as if they had been gummed together unopened and unread.

Dalgliesh and Massingham sat on the sofa. Mrs. Swaffield perched upright on the edge of the armchair and smiled across at them encouragingly, bringing into the room's cheerlessness a reassuring ambience of homemade jam, well-conducted Sunday schools, and massed women's choirs singing Blake's "Jerusalem." Both men felt immediately at home with her. Both in their different lives had met her kind before. It was not, thought Dalgliesh, that she was unaware of the frayed and ragged edges of life. She would merely iron them out with a firm hand and neatly hem them down.

Dalgliesh asked:

"How is he, Mrs. Swaffield?"

"Surprisingly well. He keeps talking about his son in the present tense, which is a little disconcerting, but I think he realizes all right that Edwin is dead. I don't mean to imply that the old gentleman is senile. Not in the least. But it's difficult to know what the very old are feeling sometimes. It must have been a terrible shock, naturally. Appalling, isn't it? I suppose a criminal from one of those London gangs broke in to get his hands on an exhibit. They're saying in the village that there were no signs of a break-in, but a really determined burglar can get in anywhere, I've always been told. I know Father Gregory has had terrible trouble with break-ins at St. Mary's at Guy's Marsh. The poor box has been rifled twice and two pews of kneelers stolen, the ones the Mothers' Union had specially embroidered to celebrate their fiftieth anniversary. Goodness knows why anyone should want to take those. Luckily we've had no trouble of that kind here. Simon would hate to have to lock the church. Chevisham has always been a most law-abiding village, which is why this murder is so shocking."

Dalgliesh wasn't surprised that the village already knew that there had been no break-in at the lab. Presumably one of the staff, on the excuse of needing to telephone home and say that he wouldn't be back for luncheon and avid to break the exciting news, had been less than discreet. But it would be pointless to try to trace the culprit. In his experience news percolated through a village community by a process of verbal osmosis, and it would be a bold man who tried to control or stem that mysterious diffusion. Mrs. Swaffield, like any proper rector's wife, had undoubtedly been one of the first to know. Dalgliesh said:

"It's a pity that Miss Foley and her uncle don't seem to get on. If he could go to stay temporarily with her that would at least solve your immediate problem. She and her friend were here when you arrived this morning, I take it?"

"Yes, both of them. Dr. Howarth came himself with Angela to break the news, which I think was thoughtful of him, then left her here when he went back to the lab. He wouldn't want to be away for more than a short time, naturally. I think Angela phoned her friend and she came at once. Then the constable arrived and I was here shortly afterwards. There was no point in Angela and Miss Mawson staying on once I'd come, and Dr. Howarth was anxious for most of the staff to be actually in the lab when you arrived."

"And there are no other relatives and no close friends, as far as you know?"

"None, I think. They kept very much to themselves. Old Mr. Lorrimer doesn't come to church or take any part in village affairs, so Simon and I never really got to know him. I know that people expect the clergy to come around knocking at doors and rooting people out, but Simon doesn't really believe it does much good, and I must say I think he's right. Dr. Lorrimer, of course, went to St. Mary's at Guy's Marsh. Father Gregory might be able to tell you something about him, although I don't think he took a very active part in church life. He used to pick up Miss Willard from the Old Rectory and drive her over. She might be worth having a word with, although it seems unlikely that they were close. I imagine that he drove her to church because Father Gregory suggested it rather than from inclination. She's an odd woman, not really suitable to look after children, I should have thought. But here comes the one you really want to talk to."

Death, thought Dalgliesh, obliterates family resemblance as it does personality; there is no affinity between the living and the dead. The man who came into the room, shuffling a little but still upright, had once been as tall as his son; the sparse gray hair brushed back from a high forehead still showed streaks of the black it had once been; the watery eyes, sunken under the creased lids, were as dark. But there was no kinship with that rigid body on the laboratory floor. Death, in separating them forever, had robbed them even of their likeness.

Mrs. Swaffield made the introductions in a voice of determined encouragement as if they had all suddenly gone deaf. Then she melted tactfully away, murmuring something about soup in the kitchen. Massingham sprang to help the old man to a chair, but Mr. Lorrimer, with a stiff chopping motion of the hand, gestured him aside. Eventually, after some hesitation, as if the sitting room were unfamiliar to him, he lowered himself into what was obviously his usual place, the shabby, high-backed armchair to the right of the fire, from which he regarded Dalgliesh steadily.

Sitting there, bolt upright, in his old-fashioned and badly cut dark blue suit, which smelled strongly of mothballs and now hung loosely on his diminished bones, he looked pathetic, almost grotesque, but not without dignity. Dalgliesh wondered why he had troubled to change. Was it a gesture of respect for his son, the need to formalize grief, a restless urge to find something to do? Or was it some atavistic belief that authority was on its way and should be propitiated by an outward show of deference? Dalgliesh was reminded of the funeral of a young detective-constable killed on duty. What he had found almost unbearably pathetic had not been the sonorous beauty of the burial service, or even the young children walking hand in hand with careful solemnity behind their father's coffin. It had been the reception afterward in the small police house, the carefully planned home-cooked food and the drink, ill-afforded, which the widow had prepared for the refreshment of her husband's colleagues and friends. Perhaps it had comforted her at the time, or solaced her in memory. Perhaps old Mr. Lorrimer, too, felt happier because he had taken trouble.

Settling himself some distance from Dalgliesh on the extraordinarily lumpy sofa, Massingham opened his notebook. Thank God the old man was calm anyway. You could never tell how the relatives were going to take it. Dalgliesh, as he knew, had the reputation of being good with the bereaved. His condolences might be short, almost formal, but at least they sounded sincere. He took it for granted that the family would wish to cooperate with the police, but as a matter of justice, not of retribution. He didn't connive at the extraordinary psychological interdependence by which the detective and the bereaved were often supported, and which it was so fatally easy to exploit. He made no specious promises, never bullied the weak or indulged the sentimental. And yet they seem to like him, thought Massingham. God knows why. At times he's cold enough to be barely human.

He watched Dalgliesh stand up as old Mr. Lorrimer came into the room; but he made no move to help the old man to his chair. Massingham had glanced briefly at his chief's face and seen the familiar look of speculative detached interest. What, if anything, he wondered, would move Dalgliesh to spontaneous pity? He remembered the other case they had worked on together a year previously, when he had been a detective-sergeant: the death of a child. Dalgliesh had regarded the parents with just such a look of calm appraisal. But he had worked eighteen hours a day for a month until the case was solved. And his next book of poems had contained that extraordinary one about a murdered child which no one at the Yard, even those who professed to understand it, had had the temerity even to mention to its author. He said now:

"As Mrs. Swaffield explained, my name is Dalgliesh and this is Inspector Massingham. I expect Dr. Howarth told you that we would be coming. I'm very sorry about your son. Do you feel able to answer some questions?"

Mr. Lorrimer nodded toward the kitchen.

"What's she doing in there?"

His voice was surprising, high-timbered and with a trace of the querulousness of age, but extraordinarily strong for an old man.

"Mrs. Swaffield? Making soup, I think."

"I suppose she's used the onions and carrots we had in the vegetable rack. I thought I could smell carrots. Edwin knows I don't like carrots in soup."

"Did he usually cook for you?"

"He does all the cooking if he isn't away at a scene of crime. I don't eat much dinner at midday, but he leaves me something to heat up, a stew from the night before or a bit of fish in sauce, maybe. He didn't leave anything this morning because he wasn't home last night. I had to get my own breakfast. I fancied bacon, but I thought I'd better leave that in case he wants it for tonight. He usually cooks bacon and eggs if he's home late."

Dalgliesh asked:

"Mr. Lorrimer, have you any idea why anyone should want to murder your son? Had he any enemies?"

"Why should he have enemies? He didn't know anyone except at the lab. Everyone had a great respect for him at the lab. He told me so himself. Why would anyone want to harm him? Edwin lived for his work."

He brought out the last sentence as if it were an original expression of which he was rather proud.

"You telephoned him last night at the laboratory, didn't you? What time was that?"

"It was a quarter to nine. The telly went blank. It didn't blink and go zigzag like it sometimes does. Edwin showed me how to adjust the knob at the back for that. It went blank with just one little circle of light and then that failed. I couldn't see the nine o'clock news, so I rang Edwin and asked him to send for the TV man. We rent the set, and they're supposed to come at any hour, but there's always some excuse. Last month when I telephoned they didn't come for two days."

"Can you remember what your son said?"

"He said that it wasn't any use telephoning late at night. He'd do it first thing in the morning before he went to work. But, of course, he hasn't. He didn't come home. It's still broken. I don't like to telephone myself. Edwin always sees to everything like that. Do you think Mrs. Swaffield would ring?"

"I'm sure that she would. When you telephoned him did he say anything about expecting a visitor?"

"No. He seemed in a hurry, as if he didn't like it because I phoned. But he always said to ring the lab up if I was in trouble."

"And he said nothing else at all except that he'd ring the TV mechanic this morning?"

"What else would he say? He wasn't one for chatting over the telephone."

"Did you ring him at the laboratory yesterday about your hospital appointment?"

"That's right. I was supposed to go in to Addenbrooke's yesterday afternoon. Edwin was going to drive me in. It's my leg, you see. It's psoriasis. They're going to try a new treatment."

He made as if to roll up his trouser leg. Dalgliesh said quickly:

"That's all right, Mr. Lorrimer. When did you know that the bed wasn't available after all?"

"About nine o'clock they rang. He'd only just left home. So I phoned the lab. I know the number of the Biology Department, of course. That's where he works—the Biology Department. Miss Easterbrook answered the phone and said that Edwin was at the hospital attending a postmortem but she would give him the message when he got in. Addenbrooke's said they'd probably send for me next Tuesday. Who's going to take me now?"

"I expect Mrs. Swaffield will arrange something, or perhaps your niece could help. Wouldn't you like her to be with you?"

"No. What can she do? She was here this morning with that friend of hers, the writing woman. Edwin doesn't like either of them. The friend—Miss Mawson, isn't it?—was rummaging around upstairs. I've got very good ears. I could hear her all right. I went out of the door and there she was coming down. She said she'd been to the bathroom. Why was she wearing the washing-up gloves if she was going to the bathroom?"

Why indeed? thought Dalgliesh. He felt a spasm of irritation that Constable Davis hadn't arrived sooner. It was perfectly natural that Howarth should come with Angela Foley to break the news and should leave her with her uncle. Someone had to stay with him, and who more suitable than his only remaining relative? It was probably natural, too, that Angela Foley should send for the support of her friend. Probably both of them were interested in Lorrimer's will. Well, that too was natural enough. Massingham shifted on the sofa. Dalgliesh could sense his anxiety to get upstairs into Lorrimer's room. He shared it. But books and papers, the sad detritus of a dead life, could wait. The living witness might not again be so communicative. He asked:

"What did your son do with himself, Mr. Lorrimer?"

"After work, do you mean? He stays in his room mostly. Reading, I suppose. He's got quite a library of books up there. He's a scholar, is Edwin. He doesn't care much about the television, so I sit down here. Sometimes I can hear the record player. Then there's the garden most weekends, cleaning the car, cooking, and shopping. He has quite a full life. And he doesn't get much time. He's at the lab until seven o'clock most nights, sometimes later."

"And friends?"

"No. He doesn't go in for friends. We keep ourselves to ourselves."

"No weekends away?"

"Where would he want to go? And what would happen to me? Besides, there's the shopping. If he isn't on call for a scene-of-crime visit he drives me into Ely Saturday morning, and we go to the supermarket. Then we have lunch in the city. I enjoy that."

"What telephone calls did he have?"

"From the lab? Only when the Police Liaison Officer rings up to say that he's wanted at a murder scene. Sometimes that's in the middle of the night. But he never wakes me. There's a telephone extension in his room. He just leaves me a note and he's usually back in time to bring me a cup of tea at seven o'clock. He didn't do that this morning, of course. That's why I rang the lab. I rang his number first but there wasn't any reply. So then I rang the reception desk. He gave me both numbers in case I couldn't get through to him in an emergency."

"And no one else has telephoned him recently, no one has come to see him?"

"Who would want to come and see him? And no one has telephoned except that woman."

Dalgliesh said, very quietly:

"What woman, Mr. Lorrimer?"

"I don't know what woman. I only know she rang. Monday of last week it was. Edwin was having a bath and the phone kept on ringing so I thought I'd better answer it."

"Can you remember exactly what happened and what was said, Mr. Lorrimer, from the time you lifted the receiver? Take your time, there's no hurry. This may be very important."

"There wasn't much to remember. I was going to say our number and ask her to hang on, but she didn't give me any time. She started speaking as soon as I lifted the receiver. She said: 'We're right, there is something going on.' Then she said something about the can being burned and that she'd got the numbers."

"That the can had been burned and she'd got the numbers?"

"That's right. It doesn't sound sense now, but it was something like that. Then she gave me the numbers."

"Can you remember them, Mr. Lorrimer?"

"Only the last one, which was 1840. Or it may have been two numbers, 18 and 40. I remembered those because the first house we had after I was married was number 18 and the second was 40. It was quite a coincidence, really. Anyway, those numbers stuck in my mind. But I can't remember the others."

"How many numbers altogether?"

"Three or four altogether, I think. There were two, and then the 18 and the 40."

"What did the numbers sound like, Mr. Lorrimer? Did you think she was giving you a telephone number or a car registration, for example? Can you remember what impression they made on you at the time?"

"No impression. Why should they? More like a telephone number, I suppose. I don't think it was a car registration. There weren't any letters, you see. It sounded like a date: 1840."

"Have you any idea who was telephoning?"

"No. I don't think it was anyone at the lab. It didn't sound like one of the lab staff."

"How do you mean, Mr. Lorrimer? How did the voice seem?"

The old man sat there, staring straight ahead. His hands, with the long fingers like those of his son, but with their skin dry and stained as withered leaves, hung heavily between his knees, grotesquely large for the brittle wrists. After a moment he spoke. He said:

"Excited." There was another silence. Both detectives looked at him. Massingham thought that here again was an example of his chief's skill. He would have gone charging upstairs in search of the will and papers. But this evidence, so carefully elicited, was vital. After a moment the old man spoke again. The word, when it came, was surprising. He said:

"Conspiratorial. That's what she sounded. Conspiratorial."

They sat, still patiently waiting, but he said nothing else. Then they saw that he was crying. His face didn't change, but a single tear, bright as a pearl, dropped onto the parched hands. He looked at it as if wondering what it could be. Then he said:

"He was a good son to me. Time was, when he first went to college up in London, that we lost touch. He wrote to his mother and me, but he didn't come home. But these last years, since I've been alone, he's taken care of me. I'm not complaining. I daresay he's left me a bit of money, and I've got my pension. But it's hard when the young go first. And who will look after me now?"

Dalgliesh said quietly:

"We need to look at his room, examine his papers. Is the room locked?"

"Locked? Why should it be locked? No one went into it but Edwin."

Dalgliesh nodded to Massingham, who went out to call Mrs. Swaffield. Then they made their way upstairs.

# II

It was a long, low-ceilinged room with white walls and a casement window that gave a view of a rectangle of unmown grass, a couple of gnarled apple trees heavy with fruit burnished green and gold in the autumn sun, a straggling hedge beaded with berries, and beyond it the windmill. Even in the genial light of afternoon the mill looked a melancholy wreck of its former puissance. The paint was peeling from the walls and the great sails, from which the slats had fallen like rotten teeth, hung heavy with inertia in the restless air. Behind the windmill, the acres of black fenland, newly sliced by the autumn plowing, stretched in glistening clumps between the dikes.

Dalgliesh turned away from this picture of melancholy peace to examine the room. Massingham was already busy at the desk. Finding the lid unlocked, he rolled it back for a few inches, then let it drop again. Then he tried the drawers. Only the top left-hand one was locked. If he were impatient for Dalgliesh to take Lorrimer's keys from his pocket and open it, he concealed his eagerness. It was known that the older man, who could work faster than any of his colleagues, still liked occasionally to take his time. He was taking it now, regarding the room with his dark, somber eyes, standing very still as if he were picking up invisible waves.

The place held a curious peace. The proportions were right and the furniture fitted where it had been placed. A man might have space to think in this uncluttered sanctum. A single bed, neatly covered with a red and brown blanket, stood against the opposite wall. A long wall shelf above the bed held an adjustable reading lamp, a radio, a record player, a clock, a carafe of water, and the Book of Common Prayer. In front of the window stood an oak working table with a wheelback chair. On the table were a blotter and a brown and blue pottery mug stacked with pencils and ballpoint pens. The only other items of furniture were a shabby winged armchair with a low table beside it, a double wardrobe in oak to the left of the door, and to the right an old-fashioned desk with a rolltop. The telephone was fitted to the wall.

There were no pictures and no mirror, no masculine impedimenta, no trivia on desk top or table ledge. Everything was functional, well-used, unadorned. It was a room a man could be at home in.

Dalgliesh walked over to look at the books. He estimated that there must be about four hundred of them, completely covering the wall. There was little fiction, although the nineteenth-century English and Russian novelists were represented. Most of the books were histories or biographies, but there was a shelf of philosophy: Teilhard de Chardin's *Science and Christ,* Jean-Paul Sartre's *Being and Nothingness: A Humanist Outlook,* Simone Weil's *First and Last,* Plato's *Republic,* the *Cambridge History of Late Greek and Early Mediaeval Philosophy.* It looked as if Lorrimer had at one time been trying to teach himself ancient Greek. The shelf held a Greek primer and a dictionary.

Massingham had taken down a book on comparative religion. He said:

"It looks as if he was one of those men who torment themselves trying to discover the meaning of existence."

Dalgliesh replaced the Sartre he had been studying.

"You find that reprehensible?"

"I find it futile. Metaphysical speculation is about as pointless as a discussion on the meaning of one's lungs. They're for breathing."

"And life is for living. You find that an adequate personal credo?"

"To maximize one's pleasures and minimize one's pain, yes, sir, I do. And, I suppose, to bear with stoicism those miseries I can't avoid. To be human is to ensure enough of those without inventing them. Anyway, I don't believe you can hope to understand what you can't see or touch or measure."

"A logical positivist. You're in respectable company. But he spent his life examining what he could see or touch or measure. It doesn't seem to have satisfied him. Well, let's see what his personal papers have to tell."

He turned his attention to the desk, leaving the locked drawer to the last. He rolled back the top to reveal two small drawers and a number of pigeonholes. And here, neatly docketed and compartmentalized, were the minutiae of Lorrimer's solitary life. A drawer with three bills waiting to be paid, and one for receipts. A labeled envelope containing his parents' marriage lines, his own birth and baptismal certificates. His passport, an anonymous face but with the eyes staring as if hypnotized, the neck muscles taut. The lens of the camera might have been the barrel of a gun. A life insurance certificate. Receipted bills for fuel, electricity, and gas. The maintenance agreement for the central heating. The rental agreement for the television. A wallet with his bank statement. His portfolio of investments, sound, unexciting, orthodox.

There was nothing about his work. Obviously he kept his life as carefully compartmentalized as his filing system. Everything to do with his profession, the journals, the drafts of his scientific papers, were kept in his office at the lab. They were probably written there. That might account for some of the late hours. It would certainly have been impossible to guess from the contents of his desk what his job had been.

His will was in a separate labeled envelope together with a brief letter from a firm of Ely solicitors, Messrs. Pargeter, Coleby, and Hunt. The will was very short and had been made five years earlier. Lorrimer had left Postmill Cottage and £10,000 to his father, and the rest of his estate absolutely to his cousin, Angela Maud Foley. To judge from the portfolio of investments, Miss Foley would inherit a useful capital sum.

Lastly, Dalgliesh took Lorrimer's bunch of keys from his pocket and unlocked the top left-hand drawer. The lock worked very easily. The drawer was crammed with papers covered with Lorrimer's handwriting. Dalgliesh took them over to the table in front of the window and motioned Massingham to draw up the armchair. They sat there together. There were twenty-eight letters in all and they read them through without speaking. Massingham was aware of Dalgliesh's long fingers picking up each sheet, dropping it from his hand, then shifting it across the desk toward him, then picking up the next. The clock seemed to him to be ticking unnaturally loudly and his own breathing to have become embarrassingly obtrusive. The letters were a liturgy of the bitter exfoliation of love. It was all here: the inability to accept that desire was no longer returned, the demand for explanations which, if attempted, could only increase the hurt, the excoriating self-pity, the spasms of irrational renewed hope, the petulant outbursts at the obtuseness of the lover unable to see where her happiness lay, the humiliating self-abasement.

"I realize that you won't want to live in the fens. But that needn't be a difficulty, darling. I could get a transfer to the Metropolitan Lab if you prefer London. Or we could find a house in Cambridge or Norwich, a choice of two civilized cities. You once said that you liked to live among the spires. Or if you wished, I could stay on here and we could have a flat in London for you, and I'd join you whenever I could. I ought to be able to make it most Sundays. The week without you would be an eternity, but anything would be bearable if I knew that you belonged to me. You do belong to me. All the books, all the seeking and the reading, what does it come to in the end? Until you taught me that the answer was so simple."

Some of the letters were highly erotic. They were probably the most difficult of all love letters to write successfully, thought Massingham. Didn't the poor devil know that, once desire was dead, they could only disgust? Perhaps those lovers who used a private nursery talk for their most secret acts were the wisest. At least the eroticism was personal. Here the sexual descriptions were either embarrassingly Lawrencian in their intensity, or coldly clinical. He recognized with surprise an emotion that could only be shame. It wasn't just that some of the outpourings were brutally explicit. He was accustomed to perusing the private pornography of murdered lives; but these letters, with their mixture of crude desire and elevated sentiment, were outside his experience. The naked suffering they expressed seemed to him neurotic, irrational. Sex no longer had any power to shock him; love, he decided, obviously could.

He was struck by the contrast between the tranquillity of the man's room and the turbulence of his mind. He thought: at least this job teaches one not to hoard personal debris. Police work was as effective as religion in teaching a man to live each day as if it were his last. And it wasn't only murder that violated privacy. Any sudden death could do as much. If the helicopter had crashed on landing, what sort of a picture would his leavings present to the world? A conformist, right-wing philistine, obsessed with his physical fitness? *Homme moyen sensuel,* and *moyen* everything else for that matter? He thought of Emma, with whom he slept whenever they got the opportunity, and who, he supposed, would eventually become Lady Dungannon unless, as seemed increasingly likely, she found an elder son with better prospects and more time to devote to her. He wondered what Emma, cheerful hedonist with her frank enjoyment of bed, would have made of these self-indulgent, masturbatory fantasies, this humiliating chronicle of the miseries of defeated love.

One half-sheet was covered with a single name. Domenica, Domenica, Domenica. And then Domenica Lorrimer, a clumsy, uneuphonic linking. Perhaps its infelicity had struck him, for he had written it only once. The letters looked labored, tentative, like those of a young girl practicing in secret the hoped-for married name. All the letters were undated, all without superscription and signature. A number were obviously first drafts, a painful seeking after the elusive word, the holograph scored with deletions.

But now Dalgliesh was pushing toward him the final letter. Here there were no alterations, no uncertainties, and if there had been a previous draft, Lorrimer had destroyed it. This was as clear as an affirmation. The words, strongly written in Lorrimer's black upright script, were set out in even lines, neatly as an exercise in calligraphy. Perhaps this was one he had intended to post after all.

"I have been seeking for the words to explain what has happened to me, what you have made happen. You know how difficult this is for me. There have been so many years of writing official reports, the same phrases, the same bleak conclusions. My mind was a computer programmed to death. I was like a man born in darkness, living in a deep cave, crouching for comfort by my small inadequate fire, watching the shadows flickering over the cave drawings and trying to find in their crude outlines some significance, a meaning to existence to help me endure the dark. And then you came and took me by the hand and led me out into the sunlight. And there was the real world, dazzling my eyes with its color and its beauty. And it needed only your hand and the courage to take a few small steps out of the shadows and imaginings into the light. *Ex umbris et imaginibus in veritatem.*"

Dalgliesh laid the letter down. He said:

" 'Lord, let me know mine end, and the number of my days: that I may be certified how long I have to live.' Given the choice, Lorrimer would probably have preferred his murder to go unavenged than for any eyes but his to have seen these letters. What do you think of them?"

Massingham was uncertain whether he was expected to comment on their subject matter or their style. He said cautiously:

"The passage about the cave is effective. It looks as if he worked over that one."

"But not entirely original. An echo of Plato's *Republic.* And like Plato's caveman, the brightness dazzled and the light hurt his eyes. George Orwell wrote somewhere that murder, the unique crime, should result only from strong emotions. Well, here is the strong emotion. But we seem to have the wrong body."

"Do you think Dr. Howarth knew, sir?"

"Almost certainly. The wonder is that no one at the lab apparently did. It's not the kind of information that Mrs. Bidwell, for one, would keep to herself. First, I think, we check with the solicitors that this will still stands, and then we see the lady."

But this program was to be changed. The wall telephone rang, shattering the peace of the room. Massingham answered. It was Sergeant Underhill trying, but with small success, to keep the excitement out of his voice.

"There's a Major Hunt of Messrs. Pargeter, Coleby, and Hunt of Ely wants to see Mr. Dalgliesh. He'd prefer not to talk over the telephone. He says could you ring and say when it would be convenient for Mr. Dalgliesh to call. And, sir, we've got a witness! He's over at Guy's Marsh police station now. The name's Alfred Goddard. He was a passenger last night passing the lab in the nine-ten bus."

# III

"Running down drive he were like the devil out of hell."

"Can you describe him, Mr. Goddard?"

"Naw. He weren't old."

"How young?"

"I never said 'e were young. I never seed 'im near enough to tell. But he didn't run like an old 'un."

"Running for the bus, perhaps."

"If 'e were 'e never catched it."

"He wasn't waving?"

" 'Course he weren't. Driver couldn't see 'im. No point in waving at back of bloody bus."

Guy's Marsh police station was a red brick Victorian building with a white wooden pediment, which looked so like an early railway station that Dalgliesh suspected that the nineteenth-century police authority had economized by making use of the same architect and the same set of plans.

Mr. Alfred Goddard, waiting comfortably in the interview room with a huge mug of steaming tea before him, looked perfectly at home, neither gratified nor impressed to find himself a key witness in a murder investigation. He was a nut-brown, wrinkled, undersized countryman who smelled of strong tobacco, alcohol, and cow dung. Dalgliesh recalled that the early fen settlers had been called "yellow-bellies" by their highland neighbors because they crawled froglike over their marshy fields, or "slodgers" splashing web-footed through the mud. Either would have suited Mr. Goddard. Dalgliesh noticed with interest that he was wearing what looked like a leather thong bound around his left wrist and guessed that this was dried eel skin, the ancient charm to ward off rheumatism. The misshapen fingers stiffly cradling the mug of tea suggested that the talisman had been less than efficacious.

Dalgliesh doubted whether he would have troubled to come forward if Bill Carney, the conductor of the bus, hadn't known him as a regular on the Wednesday evening service traveling from Ely to Stoney Piggott via Chevisham and had directed the inquiring police to his remote cottage. Having been summarily dug out of his lair, however, he displayed no particular resentment against Bill Carney or the police and announced that he was prepared to answer questions if, as he explained, they were put to him "civil-like." His main grievance in life was the Stoney Piggott bus: its lateness, infrequency, rising fares, and, in particular, the stupidity of the recent experiment of using double-deckers on the Stoney Piggott route, and his own subsequent banishment each Wednesday to the upper deck because of his pipe.

"But how fortunate for us that you were there," Massingham had pointed out. Mr. Goddard had merely snorted into his tea.

Dalgliesh continued with the questioning:

"Is there anything at all you can remember about him, Mr. Goddard? His height, his hair, how he was dressed?"

"Naw. Middling tall and wearing a shortish coat, or mac maybe. Flapping open, maybe."

"Can you remember the color?"

"Darkish, maybe. I never seed 'im for more'n a second, see. Then trees got in the way. Bus were moving off when I first set eyes on him."

Massingham interposed:

"The driver didn't see him, nor did the conductor."

"More than likely. They was on lower deck. Isn't likely they'd notice. And driver were driving bloody bus."

Dalgliesh said:

"Mr. Goddard, this is very important. Can you remember whether there were any lights on in the lab?"

"What do you mean, lab?"

"The house the figure was running from."

"Lights in the house? If you mean house why not say house?"

Mr. Goddard pantomimed the ardors of intensive thought, pursing his lips into a grimace and half closing his eyes. They waited. After a nicely judged interval he announced:

"Faint lights, maybe. Not blazing out, mind you. I reckon I seed some lights from bottom windows."

Massingham asked:

"You're quite sure it was a man?"

Mr. Goddard bestowed on him the glance of mingled reproof and chagrin of a viva-voce candidate faced with what he obviously regards as an unfair question.

"Wearing trousers, wasn't he? If he weren't a man then he ought to have been."

"But you can't be absolutely sure?"

"Can't be sure of nothing these days. Time was when folk dressed in a decent, God-fearing manner. Man or woman, it were human and it were running. That's all I seed."

"So it could have been a woman in slacks?"

"Never run like a woman. Daft runners women be, keeping their knees tight together and kicking out ankles like bloody ducks. Pity they don't keep their knees together when they ain't running, I say."

The deduction was fair enough, thought Dalgliesh. No woman ran precisely like a man. Goddard's first impression had been that of a youngish man running, and that was probably exactly what he had seen. Too much questioning now might only confuse him.

The driver and conductor, summoned from the bus depot and still in uniform, were unable to confirm Goddard's story, but what they were able to add was useful. It was not surprising that neither of them had seen the runner, since the six-foot wall and its overhanging trees cut off a view of the laboratory from the bottom deck and they could only have glimpsed the house when the bus was passing the open drive and slowing down at the stop. But if Mr. Goddard were right and the figure had only appeared when the bus was moving off, they still wouldn't have seen him.

It was helpful that they were both able to confirm that the bus, on that Wednesday evening at least, was running on time. Bill Carney had actually looked at his watch as they moved away. It had shown nine-eleven. The bus had halted at the stop for a couple of seconds. None of the three passengers had made any preliminary moves to get off, but both the driver and the conductor had noticed a woman waiting in the shadow of the bus shelter and had assumed that she would board. However, she hadn't done so, but had turned away and moved back farther into the shadow of the shelter as the bus drew up. The conductor had thought it strange that she was waiting there, since there wasn't another bus that night. But it had been raining slightly and he had assumed, without thinking about it very deeply, that she had been sheltering. It wasn't his job, as he reasonably pointed out, to drag passengers on the bus if they didn't want a ride.

Dalgliesh questioned them both closely about the woman, but there was little firm information they could give. Both agreed that she had been wearing a headscarf and that the collar of her coat had been turned up at her ears. The driver thought that she had been wearing slacks and a belted mackintosh. Bill Carney agreed about the slacks but thought that she had been wearing a duffle coat. Their only reason for assuming that the figure was a woman was the headscarf. Neither of them could describe it. They thought it unlikely that any of the three passengers on the lower deck would be able to help. Two of them were elderly regulars, both apparently asleep. The third was unknown to them.

Dalgliesh knew that all three would have to be traced. This was one of those time-consuming jobs which were necessary but which seldom produced any worthwhile information. But it was astonishing how much the most unlikely people did notice. The sleepers might have been jogged awake by the slowing down of the bus and have had a clearer look at the waiting woman than either the conductor or driver. Mr. Goddard, not surprisingly, hadn't noticed her. He inquired caustically how a chap was expected to see through the roof of a bloody bus shelter and, in any case, he'd been looking the other way, hadn't he, and a good job for them that he had. Dalgliesh hastened to propitiate him and, when his statement was at last completed to the old man's satisfaction, watched him driven back to his cottage, sitting in some style, like a tiny upright manikin, in the back of the police car.

But it was another ten minutes before Dalgliesh and Massingham could set out for Ely. Albert Bidwell had presented himself conveniently if belatedly at the police station, bringing with him a hefty sample of the mud from the five-acre field and an air of sullen grievance. Massingham wondered how he and his wife had originally met and what had brought together two such dissimilar personalities. She, he felt sure, was born a cockney; he, a fenman. He was taciturn where she was garrulous, slow-thinking where she was sharp, and as incurious as she was avid for gossip and excitement.

He admitted to taking the telephone call. It was a woman and the message was that Mrs. Bidwell was to go to Leamings to give Mrs. Schofield a hand instead of to the lab. He couldn't remember if the caller had given her name but didn't think so. He had taken calls from Mrs. Schofield once or twice before when she had rung to ask his wife to help with dinner parties or suchlike. Women's business. He couldn't say whether the voice sounded the same. Asked whether he had assumed that the caller was Mrs. Schofield, he said that he hadn't assumed anything.

Dalgliesh asked:

"Can you remember whether the caller said that your wife was to come to Leamings or go to Leamings?"

The significance of this question obviously escaped him but he received it with surly suspicion and, after a long pause, said he didn't know. When Massingham asked whether it was possible that the caller hadn't been a woman but a man disguising his voice, he gave him a look of concentrated disgust as if deploring a mind that could imagine such sophisticated villainy. But the answer provoked his longest response. He said, in a tone of finality, that he didn't know whether it was a woman, or a man pretending to be a woman, or, maybe, a lass. All he knew was that he'd been asked to give his wife a message, and he'd given it to her. And if he'd known it would cause all this botheration he wouldn't have answered the phone.

And with that they had to be content.

# IV

In Dalgliesh's experience, solicitors who practiced in cathedral cities were invariably agreeably housed, and the office of Messrs. Pargeter, Coleby, and Hunt was no exception. It was a well-preserved and maintained Regency house with a view of the cathedral green, an imposing front door whose ebony-black paint gleamed as if it were still wet, and whose brass knocker in the shape of a lion's head had been polished almost to whiteness. The door was opened by an elderly and very thin clerk, Dickensian in his old-fashioned black suit and stiff collar, whose appearance of lugubrious resignation brightened somewhat at seeing them, as if cheered by the prospect of trouble. He bowed slightly when Dalgliesh introduced himself and said:

"Major Hunt is, of course, expecting you, sir. He is just concluding his interview with a client. If you will step this way he won't keep you waiting more than a couple of minutes."

The waiting room into which they were shown resembled the sitting room of a men's club in its comfort and air of controlled disorder. The chairs were leather and so wide and deep that it was difficult to imagine anyone over sixty rising from them without difficulty. Despite the heat from two old-fashioned radiators there was a coke fire burning in the grate. The large, circular mahogany table was spread with magazines devoted to the interests of the landed gentry, most of which looked very old. There was a glass-fronted bookcase packed with bound histories of the county and illustrated volumes on architecture and painting. The oil over the mantelpiece of a phaeton with horses and attendant grooms looked very like a Stubbs and, thought Dalgliesh, probably was.

He only had time briefly to inspect the room and had walked over to the window to look out toward the Lady Chapel of the cathedral when the door opened and the clerk reappeared to usher them into Major Hunt's office. The man who rose from behind his desk to receive them was in appearance the opposite of his clerk. He was a stocky, upright man in late middle age, dressed in a shabby but well-tailored tweed suit, ruddy-faced and balding, his eyes keen under the spiky, restless eyebrows. He gave Dalgliesh a frankly appraising glance as he shook hands, as if deciding where exactly to place him in some private scheme of things, then nodded as if satisfied. He still looked more like a soldier than a solicitor, and Dalgliesh guessed that the voice with which he greeted them had acquired its loud, authoritative bark across the parade grounds and in the messes of the Second World War.

"Good morning, good morning. Please sit down, Commander. You come on tragic business. I don't think we have ever lost one of our clients by murder before."

The clerk coughed. It was just such a cough as Dalgliesh would have expected, inoffensive but discreetly minatory and not to be ignored.

"There was Sir James Cummins, sir in 1923. He was shot by his neighbor, Captain Cartwright, because of the seduction of Mrs. Cartwright by Sir James, a grievance aggravated by some unpleasantness over fishing rights."

"Quite right, Mitching. But that was in my father's time. They hanged poor Cartwright. A pity, my father always thought. He had a good war record—survived the Somme and Arras and ended on the scaffold. Battle-scarred, poor devil. The jury would probably have made a recommendation of mercy if he hadn't cut up the body. He did cut up the body, didn't he, Mitching?"

"Quite right, sir. They found the head buried in the orchard."

"That's what did it for Cartwright. English juries won't stand for cutting up the body. Crippen would be alive today if he'd buried Belle Elmore in one piece."

"Hardly, sir. Crippen was born in 1860."

"Well he wouldn't have been long dead. It wouldn't surprise me if he'd reached his century. Only three years older than your father, Mitching, and much the same build, small, pop-eyed, and wiry. They live forever, that type. Ah well, to our muttons. You'll both take coffee, I hope. I can promise you it will be drinkable. Mitching has installed one of those glass retort affairs and we grind our own fresh beans. Coffee then, please, Mitching."

"Miss Makepeace is preparing it now, sir."

Major Hunt exuded postprandial well being, and Massingham guessed, with some envy, that his business with his last client had been chiefly done over a good lunch. He and Dalgliesh had snatched a hurried sandwich and beer at a pub between Chevisham and Guy's Marsh. Dalgliesh, known to enjoy food and wine, had an inconvenient habit of ignoring mealtimes when in the middle of a case. Massingham wasn't fussy about the quality; it was the quantity he deplored. But, at least, they were to get coffee.

Mitching had stationed himself near the door and showed no inclination to leave. This was apparently perfectly acceptable. Dalgliesh thought that he and the Major were like a couple of comedians in the process of perfecting their antiphonal patter and reluctant to lose any opportunity of practicing it. Major Hunt said:

"You want to know about Lorrimer's will, of course."

"And anything else you can tell us about him."

"That won't be much, I'm afraid. I've only seen him twice since I dealt with his grandmother's estate. But of course I'll do what I can. When murder comes in the window, privacy goes out the door. That's so, isn't it, Mitching?"

"There are no secrets, sir, in the fierce light that beats upon the scaffold."

"I'm not sure that you've got that one right, Mitching. And we don't have scaffolds now. Are you an abolitionist, Commander?"

Dalgliesh said:

"I'm bound to be until the day comes when we can be absolutely sure that we could never under any circumstances make a mistake."

"That's the orthodox answer, but it begs quite a lot of questions, doesn't it? Still you're not here to discuss capital punishment. Mustn't waste time. Now the will. Where did I put Mr. Lorrimer's box, Mitching?"

"It's here, sir."

"Then bring it over, man. Bring it over."

The clerk carried the black tin box from a side table and placed it in front of Major Hunt. The Major opened it with some ceremony and took out the will. Dalgliesh said:

"We've found one will in his desk. It's dated the third of May 1971. It looks like the original."

"So he didn't destroy it? That's interesting. It suggests that he hadn't finally made up his mind."

"So there's a later will?"

"Oh indeed there is, Commander. Indeed there is. That's what I wanted to talk to you about. Signed by him only last Friday and both the original and the only copy left here with me. I have them here. Perhaps you'd like to read it yourself."

He handed over the will. It was very short. Lorrimer, in the accepted form, revoked all previous wills, proclaimed himself to be of sound mind, and disposed of all his property in less than a dozen lines. Postmill Cottage was left to his father together with a sum of ten thousand pounds. One thousand pounds was left to Brenda Pridmore "to enable her to buy any books required to further her scientific education." All the rest of his estate was left to the Academy of Forensic Science to provide an annual cash prize of such amount as the Academy should see fit for an original essay on any aspect of the scientific investigation of crime, the essay to be judged by three judges, selected annually by the Academy. There was no mention of Angela Foley.

Dalgliesh said:

"Did he give you any explanation why he left his cousin, Angela Foley, out of the will?"

"As a matter of fact he did. I thought it right to point out that in the event of his death his cousin, as his only surviving relative apart from his father, might wish to contest the will. If she did, a legal battle would cost money and might seriously deplete the estate. I didn't feel any obligation to press him to alter his decision. I merely thought it right to point out the possible consequences. You heard what he replied, didn't you, Mitching?"

"Yes indeed, sir. The late Mr. Lorrimer expressed his disapprobation of the way in which his cousin chose to live; in particular he deplored the relationship which, he alleged, subsisted between his cousin and the lady with whom I understand she makes her home and said that he did not wish the said companion to benefit from his estate. If his cousin chose to contest the will, he was prepared to leave the matter to the courts. It would no longer be of any concern to himself. He would have made his wishes clear. He also pointed out, if I remember rightly, sir, that the will was intended to be transitional in its nature. He had it in mind to marry and if he did so the will would, of course, become void. In the meantime he wished to guard against what he saw as the remote contingency of his cousin inheriting absolutely should he die unexpectedly before his personal affairs became clearer."

"That's right, Mitching, that in effect is what he said. I must say that it reconciled me somewhat to the new will. If he were proposing to get married obviously it would no longer stand and he could think again. Not that I thought it necessarily an unjust or unfair will. A man has the right to dispose of his property as he sees fit, if the state leaves him anything to dispose of. It struck me as a bit odd that, if he were engaged to be married, he didn't mention the lady in the interim will. But I suppose the principle's sound enough. If he'd left her a paltry sum she'd hardly have thanked him, and if he'd left her the lot, she'd probably promptly have married another chap and it would all pass to him."

Dalgliesh asked:

"He didn't tell you anything about the proposed marriage?"

"Not even the lady's name. And naturally I didn't ask. I'm not even sure that he had anyone particular in mind. It could have been only a general intention, or, perhaps, an excuse for altering the will. I merely congratulated him and pointed out that the new will would be void as soon as the marriage took place. He said that he understood that and would be coming to make a new will in due course. In the meantime this was what he wanted and this was what I drew up. Mitching signed it, with my secretary as a second witness. Ah, here she is with the coffee. You remember signing Mr. Lorrimer's will, eh?"

The thin, nervous-looking girl who had brought in the coffee gave a terrified nod in response to the Major's bark and hastened out of the room. Major Hunt said with satisfaction:

"She remembers. She was so terrified that she could hardly sign. But she did sign. It's all there. All correct and in order. I hope we can draw up a valid will, eh, Mitching? But it will be interesting to see if the little woman makes a fight for it."

Dalgliesh asked how much Angela Foley would be making a fight for.

"The best part of fifty thousand pounds, I daresay. Not a fortune these days but useful, useful. The original capital was left to him absolutely by old Annie Lorrimer, his paternal grandmother. An extraordinary old woman. Born and bred in the fens. Kept a village store with her husband over at Low Willow. Tom Lorrimer drank himself into a comparatively early grave—couldn't stand the fen winters—and she carried on alone. Not all the money came from the shop, of course, although she sold out at a good time. No, she had a nose for the horses. Extraordinary thing. God knows where she got it from. Never mounted a horse in her life to my knowledge. Shut up the shop and went to Newmarket three times a year. Never lost a penny, so I've heard, and saved every pound she won."

"What family had she? Was Lorrimer's father her only son?"

"That's right. She had one son and one daughter, Angela Foley's mother. Couldn't bear the sight of either of them, as far as I can see. The daughter got herself in the family way by the village sexton and the old woman cast her off in approved Victorian style. The marriage turned out badly and I don't think Maud Foley saw her mother again. She died of cancer about five years after the girl was born. The old woman wouldn't have her granddaughter back, so she ended up in local authority care. Most of her life's been spent in foster homes, I believe."

"And the son?"

"Oh, he married the local schoolmistress, and that turned out reasonably well as far as I know. But the family were never close. The old lady wouldn't leave her money to her son because, she said, it would mean two lots of death duties. She was well over forty when he was born. But I think the real reason was simply that she didn't much like him. I don't think she saw much of the grandson, Edwin, either, but she had to leave the money somewhere and hers was a generation which believes that blood is thicker than charitable soup and male blood thicker than female. Apart from the fact she'd cast off her daughter and never taken any interest in her granddaughter, her generation didn't believe in leaving money outright to women. It only encourages seducers and fortune hunters. So she left it absolutely to her grandson, Edwin Lorrimer. At the time of her death I think he had qualms of conscience about his cousin. As you know, the first will made her his legatee."

Dalgliesh said:

"Do you know if Lorrimer told her that he intended to change his will?"

The solicitor looked at him sharply.

"He didn't say. In the circumstances it would be convenient for her if she could prove that he did."

So convenient, thought Dalgliesh, that she would certainly have mentioned the fact when first interviewed. But even if she had believed herself to be her cousin's heir, that didn't necessarily make her a murderess. If she had wanted a share of her grandmother's money, why wait until now to kill for it?

The telephone rang. Major Hunt muttered an apology and reached for the receiver. Holding his palm over the mouthpiece, he said to Dalgliesh:

"It's Miss Foley ringing from Postmill Cottage. Old Mr. Lorrimer wants to have a word with me about the will. She says he's anxious to know whether the cottage now belongs to him. Do you want me to tell him?"

"That is for you. But he's the next of kin; he may as well know the terms of the will now as later. And so may she."

Major Hunt hesitated. Then he spoke into the receiver.

"All right, Betty. Put Miss Foley on the line."

He looked up again at Dalgliesh.

"This piece of news is going to put the cat among the pigeons in Chevisham."

Dalgliesh had a sudden picture of Brenda Pridmore's eager young face shining across Howarth's desk at him.

"Yes," he said grimly. "Yes, I'm afraid it is."

# V

Howarth's house, Leamings, was three miles outside Chevisham village on the Cambridge road, a modern building of concrete, wood, and glass cantilevered above the flat fenlands, with two white wings like folded sails. Even in the fading light it was impressive. The house stood in uncompromising and splendid isolation, depending for its effect on nothing but perfection of line and artful simplicity. No other building was in sight except a solitary black wooden cottage on stilts, desolate as an execution shed, and, dramatically, an intricate mirage hung above the eastern skyline, the marvelous single tower and octagon of Ely Cathedral. From the rooms at the back one would see an immensity of sky and look out over vast, unhedged fields dissected by Leamings Dike, changing with the seasons from black scarred earth, through the spring sowing to the harvest; would hear nothing but the wind and, in summer, the ceaseless susurration of the grain.

The site had been small and the architect had needed ingenuity. There was no garden, nothing but a short drive leading to a paved courtyard and the double garage. Outside the garage, a red Jaguar XJS stood beside Howarth's Triumph. Massingham cast envious eyes on the Jaguar and wondered how Mrs. Schofield had managed to get such quick delivery. They drove in and parked beside it. Even before Dalgliesh had switched off the engine, Howarth had strolled out and was quietly waiting for them. He was wearing a butcher's long blue and white striped apron in which he seemed perfectly at ease, evidently seeing no need either to explain or remove it. As they made their way up the open-tread, carved wooden stairs Dalgliesh complimented him on the house. Howarth said:

"It was designed by a Swedish architect who did some of the modern additions at Cambridge. Actually it belongs to a university friend. He and his wife are spending a couple of years' sabbatical at Harvard. If they decide to stay on in the States, they may sell. Anyway, we're settled for the next eighteen months and can then look around if we have to."

They were mounting a wide circular wooden staircase rising from the well of the house. Upstairs someone was playing, very loudly, a record of the finale of the third Brandenburg Concerto. The glorious contrapuntal sound beat against the walls and surged through the house; Massingham could almost imagine it taking off on its white wings and rollicking joyously over the fens. Dalgliesh said, above the music:

"Mrs. Schofield likes it here?"

Howarth's voice, carefully casual, came down to them. "Oh, she may have moved on by then. Domenica likes variety. My half sister suffers from Baudelaire's *horreur de domicile*—she usually prefers to be elsewhere. Her natural habitat is London, but she's with me now because she's illustrating a new limited edition of Crabbe for the Paradine Press."

The record came to an end. Howarth paused and said with a kind of roughness, as if regretting an impulse to confide:

"I think I ought to tell you that my sister was widowed just over eighteen months ago. Her husband was killed in a car crash. She was driving at the time but she was lucky. At least, I suppose she was lucky. She was scarcely scratched. Charles Schofield died three days later."

"I'm sorry," said Dalgliesh. The cynic in him wondered why he had been told. Howarth had struck him as essentially a private man, one not lightly to confide a personal or family tragedy. Was it an appeal to chivalry, a covert plea for him to treat her with special consideration? Or was Howarth warning him that she was still distraught with grief, unpredictable, unbalanced even? He could hardly be implying that, since the tragedy, she had indulged an irresistible impulse to kill her lovers.

They had reached the top of the stairs and were standing on a wide wooden balcony seemingly hung in space. Howarth pushed open a door and said:

"I'll leave you to it. I'm making an early start on cooking dinner tonight. She's in here." He called:

"This is Commander Dalgliesh and Detective-Inspector Massingham of the Met. The men about the murder. My sister, Domenica Schofield."

The room was immense, with a triangular window from roof to floor jutting out over the fields like a ship's prow, and a high curved ceiling of pale pine. The furniture was scant and very modern. The room looked, in fact, more like a musician's studio than a sitting room. Against the wall was a jangle of music stands and violin cases and, mounted above them, a bank of modern and obviously expensive stereo equipment. There was only one picture, a Sidney Nolan oil of Ned Kelly. The faceless metallic mask, with the two anonymous eyes gleaming through the slit, was appropriate to the austerity of the room, the stark blackness of the darkening fens. It was easy to imagine him, a grim latter-day Hereward, striding over the clogging acres.

Domenica Schofield was standing at a drawing desk placed in the middle of the room. She turned, unsmilingly, to look at them with her brother's eyes, and Dalgliesh encountered again those disconcerting pools of blue under the thick, curved brows. As always, in those increasingly rare moments when, unexpectedly, he came face to face with a beautiful woman, his heart jerked. It was a pleasure more sensual than sexual and he was glad that he could still feel it, even in the middle of a murder investigation.

But he wondered how studied was that smooth, deliberate turn, that first gaze, remote yet speculative, from the remarkable eyes. In this light, the irises, like those of her brother, were almost purple, the whites stained with a paler blue. She had pale, honey-colored skin, with flaxen hair drawn back from the forehead and tied in a clump at the base of her neck. Her blue jeans were pulled tightly over the strong thighs and were topped with an open-necked shirt of checkered blue and green. Dalgliesh judged her to be about ten years younger than her half brother. When she spoke, her voice was curiously low for a woman, with a hint of gruffness.

"Sit down." She waved her right hand vaguely toward one of the chrome and leather chairs. "You don't mind if I go on working?"

"Not if you don't mind being talked to while you do, and if you don't object to my sitting while you stand."

He swung the chair closer to her easel, from where he could see both her face and her work, and settled himself. The chair was remarkably comfortable. He sensed that already she was regretting her lack of civility. In any confrontation the one standing has a psychological advantage, but not if the adversary is sitting very obviously at his ease in a spot he has himself selected. Massingham, with an almost ostentatious quietness, had lifted a second chair for himself and placed it against the wall to the left of the door. She must have been aware of his presence at her back, but she gave no sign. She could hardly object to a situation she had herself contrived, but, as if sensing that the interview had started unpropitiously, she said:

"I'm sorry to seem so obsessively busy, but I have a deadline to meet. My brother probably told you that I'm illustrating a new edition of Crabbe's poems for the Paradine Press. This drawing is for 'Procrastination'—Dinah among her curious trifles."

Dalgliesh had known that she must be a competent professional artist to have gained the commission, but he was impressed by the sensitivity and assurance of the line drawing before him. It was remarkably detailed but unfinicky, a highly decorative and beautifully composed balance of the girl's slender figure and Crabbe's carefully enumerated objects of desire. They were all there, meticulously drawn: the figured wallpaper, the rose carpet, the mounted stag's head, and the jeweled, enameled clock. It was, he thought, a very English illustration of the most English of poets. She was taking trouble with the period details. On the right-hand wall was mounted a cork board on which were pinned what were obviously preliminary sketches: a tree, half-finished interiors, articles of furniture, small impressions of landscape. She said:

"It's as well one doesn't have to like a poet's work to illustrate him competently. Who was it called Crabbe 'Pope in worsted stockings'? After twenty lines my brain begins to thud in rhymed couplets. But perhaps you're an Augustan. You write verse, don't you?"

She made it sound as if he collected cigarette cards for a hobby.

Dalgliesh said:

"I've respected Crabbe ever since I read as a boy that Jane Austen said she could have fancied being Mrs. Crabbe. When he went to London for the first time he was so poor that he had to pawn all his clothes, and then he spent the money on an edition of Dryden's poems."

"And you approve of that?"

"I find it appealing." He quoted:

> "Miseries there were, and woes the world around,
> But these had not her pleasant dwelling found;
> She knew that mothers grieved and widows wept
> And she was sorry, said her prayers and slept:
> For she indulged, nor was her heart so small
> That one strong passion should engross it all."

She gave him a swift elliptical glance.

"In this case there is happily no mother to grieve nor widow to weep. And I gave up saying my prayers when I was nine. Or were you only proving that you could quote Crabbe?"

"That, of course," replied Dalgliesh. "Actually I came to talk to you about these."

He took a bundle of the letters out of his coat pocket, opened one of the pages, and held it out toward her. He asked:

"This is Lorrimer's handwriting?"

She glanced dismissively at the page.

"Of course. It's a pity he didn't send them. I should have liked to have read them, but not now, perhaps."

"I don't suppose they're so very different from the ones he did send."

For a moment he thought that she was about to deny receiving any. He thought: "She's remembered that we can easily check with the postman." He watched the blue eyes grow wary. She said:

"That's how love ends, not with a bang, but a whimper."

"Less a whimper than a cry of pain."

She wasn't working, but stood still, scrutinizing the drawing. She said:

"It's extraordinary how unattractive misery is. He'd have done better to have tried honesty. 'It means a lot to me, it doesn't mean very much to you. So why not be generous? It won't cost you anything except an occasional half-hour of your time.' I'd have respected him more."

"But he wasn't asking for a commercial arrangement," said Dalgliesh. "He was asking for love."

"That's something I didn't have to give, and he had no right to expect."

None of us, thought Dalgliesh, have a right to expect it. But we do. Irrelevantly a phrase of Plutarch fell into his mind. "Boys throw stones at frogs in sport. But the frogs do not die in sport, they die in earnest."

"When did you break it off?" he asked.

She looked surprised for a moment.

"I was going to ask how you knew that I'd done the breaking. But, of course, you've got the letters. I suppose he was whining. I told him that I didn't want to see him again about two months ago. I haven't spoken to him since."

"Did you give him a reason?"

"No. I'm not sure that there was a reason. Does there have to be? There wasn't another man, if that's what you have in mind. What a beautifully simple view you must have of life. I suppose police work produces a card-index mentality. Victim—Edwin Lorrimer. Crime—Murder. Accused—Domenica Schofield. Motive—Sex. Verdict—

Guilty. What a pity that you can't any longer finish it off neatly with Sentence—Death. Let's say I was tired of him."

"When you'd exhausted his possibilities, sexual and emotional?"

"Say intellectual, rather, if you'll forgive the arrogance. I find that one exhausts the physical possibilities fairly soon, don't you? But if a man has wit, intelligence, and his own peculiar enthusiasms, then there's some kind of purpose in the relationship. I knew a man once who was an authority on seventeenth-century church architecture. We used to drive for miles looking at churches. It was fascinating while it lasted, and I now know quite a lot about the late seventeenth century. That's something on the credit side."

"Whereas Lorrimer's only intellectual enthusiasms were popular philosophy and forensic science."

"Forensic biology. He was curiously inhibited about discussing it. The Official Secrets Act was probably engraved on what he would have described as his soul. Besides, he could be boring even about his job. Scientists invariably are, I've discovered. My brother is the only scientist I've ever met who doesn't bore me after the first ten minutes of his company."

"Where did you make love?"

"That's impertinent. And is it relevant?"

"It could be—to the number of people who knew that you were lovers."

"No one knew. I don't relish my private affairs being giggled over in the women's toilet at Hoggatt's."

"So no one knew except your brother and yourself?"

They must have decided in advance that it would be stupid and dangerous to deny that Howarth had known. She said:

"I hope you're not going to ask whether he approved."

"No. I took it for granted that he disapproved."

"Why the hell should you?" The tone was intended to be light, almost bantering, but Dalgliesh could detect the sharp edge of defensive anger. He said mildly:

"I am merely putting myself in his place. If I had just started a new job, and one of some difficulty, my half sister's affair with a member of my own staff, and one who probably thought he'd been supplanted, would be a complication I'd prefer to do without."

"Perhaps you lack my brother's confidence. He didn't need Edwin Lorrimer's support to run his lab effectively."

"You brought him here?"

"Seducing a member of my brother's staff here in his own house? Had I disliked my brother, it might have given the affair extra piquancy. Toward the end I admit it could have done with it. But as I don't, it would merely have been in poor taste. We both have cars, and his is particularly roomy."

"I thought that was the expedient of randy adolescents. It must have been uncomfortable and cold."

"Very cold. Which was another reason for deciding to stop it." She turned to him with sudden vehemence.

"Look, I'm not trying to shock you. I'm trying to be truthful. I hate death and waste and violence. Who doesn't? But I'm not grieving, in case you thought of offering condolences. There's only one man whose death has grieved me, and it isn't Edwin Lorrimer. And I don't feel responsible. Why should I? I'm not responsible. Even if he killed himself I shouldn't feel that it was my fault. As it is, I don't believe his death had anything to do with me. He might, I suppose, have felt like murdering me. I never had the slightest motive for murdering him."

"Have you any idea who did?"

"A stranger, I imagine. Someone who broke into the lab either to plant or to destroy some forensic evidence. Perhaps a drunken driver hoping to get his hands on his blood sample. Edwin surprised him and the intruder killed him."

"The blood alcohol analysis isn't done in the Biology Department."

"Then it could have been an enemy, someone with a grudge. Someone he'd given evidence against in the past. After all, he's probably well known in the witness box. Death of an expert witness."

Dalgliesh said:

"There's the difficulty of how his killer got in and out of the lab."

"He probably gained entrance during the day and hid after the place was locked up for the night. I leave it to you to discover how he got away. Perhaps he slipped out after the lab had been opened for the morning during the kerfuffle after that girl—Brenda Pridmore, isn't it?—discovered the body. I don't suppose that anyone was keeping an eye on the front door."

"And the false telephone call to Mrs. Bidwell?"

"Probably no connection, I'd say. Just someone trying to be funny. She's probably too scared now to admit what happened. I should question the junior female staff of the lab if I were you. It's the kind of joke a rather unintelligent adolescent might find amusing."

Dalgliesh went on to ask her about her movements on the previous evening. She said that she hadn't accompanied her brother to the concert, having a dislike of rustic junketing, no wish to hear the Mozart indifferently played, and a couple of drawings to complete. They'd had an early supper at about six-forty-five, and Howarth had left home at seven-twenty. She had continued working uninterrupted either by a telephone call or a visitor until her brother returned shortly after ten, when he had told her about his evening over a shared nightcap of hot whisky. Both of them had then gone early to bed.

She volunteered without being asked that her brother had seemed perfectly normal on his return, although both of them had been tired. He had attended a murder scene the night before and had lost some hours' sleep. She did occasionally make use of Mrs. Bidwell, for example before and after a dinner party she and Howarth had given soon after their arrival, but certainly wouldn't call on her on a day when she was due at the lab.

Dalgliesh asked:

"Did your brother tell you that he left the concert for a time after the interval?"

"He told me that he sat on a tombstone for about half an hour contemplating mortality. I imagine that, at that stage of the proceedings, he found the dead more entertaining than the living."

Dalgliesh looked up at the immense curved wooden ceiling. He said:

"This place must be expensive to keep warm in winter. How is it heated?"

Again there was that swift elliptical flash of blue.

"By gas central heating. There isn't an open fire. That's one of the things we miss. So we couldn't have burned Paul Middlemass's white coat. Actually, we'd have been fools to try. The most sensible plan would be to weigh it down with stones in the pockets and sling it into Leamings Sluice. You'd probably dredge it up in the end, but I don't see how that would help you to discover who put it there. That's what I would have done."

"No you wouldn't," said Dalgliesh mildly. "There weren't any pockets."

She didn't offer to see them out, but Howarth was waiting for them at the foot of the stairs. Dalgliesh said:

"You didn't tell me that your sister was Lorrimer's mistress. Did you really convince yourself that it wasn't relevant?"

"To his death? Why should it be? It may have been relevant to his life. I very much doubt whether it was to hers. And I'm not my sister's keeper. She's capable of speaking for herself, as you've probably discovered."

He walked with them out to the car, punctilious as a host speeding on a couple of unwelcome guests. Dalgliesh said, his hand on the car door:

"Does the number 1840 mean anything to you?"

"In what context?"

"Any you choose."

Howarth said calmly:

"Whewell published *Philosophy of the Inductive Sciences;* Tchaikovsky was born; Berlioz composed the *Symphonie Funèbre et Triomphale.* I think that's the limit of my knowledge of an unremarkable year. Or if you want a different context, the ratio of the mass of the proton to the mass of the electron."

Massingham called from the other side of the Rover:

"I thought that was 1836, unless you're not fussy about rounding up. Good night, sir."

As they turned out of the drive, Dalgliesh asked:

"How do you come to remember that remarkably irrelevant piece of information?"

"From school. We may have been disadvantaged when it came to social mix, but the teaching wasn't bad. It's a figure that sticks in the mind."

"Not in mine. What did you think of Mrs. Schofield?"

"I didn't expect her to be like that."

"As attractive, as talented, or as arrogant?"

"All three. Her face reminds me of someone, an actress. French, I think."

"Simone Signoret when she was young. I'm surprised that you're old enough to remember."

"I saw a revival last year of *Casque d'Or.*"

Dalgliesh said: "She told us at least one small lie."

Apart, thought Massingham, from the one major lie which she may or may not have told. He was experienced enough to know that it was that central lie, the affirmation of innocence, which was the most difficult to detect; and the small, ingenious fabrications, so often unnecessary, which in the end confused and betrayed.

"Sir?"

"About where she and Lorrimer made love, in the back of his car. I don't believe that. Do you?"

It was rare for Dalgliesh to question a subordinate so directly. Massingham disconcertingly felt himself under test. He gave careful thought before replying.

"Psychologically it could be wrong. She's a fastidious, comfort-loving woman with a high opinion of her own dignity. And she must have watched the body of her husband being pulled from the wreckage of their car after that accident when she'd been driving. Somehow I don't think she'd fancy sex in the back of anyone's car. Unless, of course, she's trying to exorcise the memory. It could be that."

Dalgliesh smiled. "Actually I was thinking on less esoteric lines. A scarlet Jaguar, and the latest model, is hardly the most inconspicuous vehicle for driving around the country with a lover. And old Mr.

Lorrimer said that his son hardly left home in the evenings or at night, unless to a murder scene. These are unpredictable. On the other hand he was frequently late at the lab. Not all the lateness could have been work. I think that he and Mrs. Schofield had a rendezvous somewhere fairly close."

"You think it important, sir?"

"Important enough to cause her to lie. Why should she care if we know where they chose to disport themselves? I could understand it if she told us to mind our own business. But why bother to lie? There was another moment, too, when very briefly she lost composure. It was when she talked about seventeenth-century church architecture. I got the impression that there was a small, almost undetectable moment of confusion when she realized that she'd stumbled into saying something indiscreet, or at least something she wished unsaid. When the interviews are out of the way tomorrow, I think we'll take a look at the chapel at Hoggatt's."

"But Sergeant Reynolds had a look at it this morning, sir, after he'd searched the grounds. It's just a locked, empty chapel. He found nothing."

"Probably because there's nothing to find. It's just a hunch. Now we'd better get back to Guy's Marsh for that press conference and then I must have a word with the Chief Constable if he's back. After that I'd like to see Brenda Pridmore again; and I want to call later at the Old Rectory for a word with Dr. Kerrison. But that can wait until we've seen what Mrs. Gotobed at the Moonraker can do about dinner."

## VI

Twenty minutes later, in the kitchen at Leamings, an incongruous compromise between a laboratory and rustic domesticity, Howarth was mixing *sauce vinaigrette*. The sickly, pungent smell of the olive oil, curving in a thin golden stream from the bottle, brought back, as always, memories of Italy and of his father, that dilettante collector of trivia, who had spent most of each year in Tuscany or Venice, and whose self-indulgent, hypochondriacal, solitary life had ended, appropriately enough since he affected to dread old age, on his fiftieth birthday. He had been less a stranger to his two motherless children than an enigma, seldom with them in person, always present mysteriously to their minds.

Maxim recalled a memory of his dressing-gowned figure, patterned in mauve and gold, standing at the foot of his bed on that extraordinary night of muted voices, sudden running footsteps, inexplicable silences, in which his stepmother had died. He had been home from prep school for the holidays, eight years old, ignored in the crisis of the illness, frightened and alone. He remembered clearly his father's thin, rather weary voice, already assuming the languors of grief.

"Your stepmother died ten minutes ago, Maxim. Evidently fate does not intend me to be a husband. I shall not again risk such grief. You, my boy, must look after your stepsister. I rely on you." And then a cold hand casually laid on his shoulder as if conferring a burden. He had accepted it, literally, at eight years old, and had never laid it down. At first the immensity of the trust had appalled him. He remembered how he had lain there, terrified, staring into the darkness. Look after your sister. Domenica was three months old. How could he look after her? What ought he to feed her on? How dress her? What about his prep school? They wouldn't let him stay at home to look after his sister. He smiled wryly, remembering his relief at discovering next morning that her nurse was, after all, to remain. He recalled his first efforts to assume responsibility, resolutely seizing the pram handles and straining to push it up the Broad Walk, struggling to lift Domenica into her high chair.

"Give over, Master Maxim, do. You're more of a hindrance than a help."

But afterward the nurse had begun to realize that he was becoming more of a help than a nuisance, that the child could safely be left with him while she and the only other servant pursued their own unsupervised devices. Most of his school holidays had been spent helping to look after Domenica. From Rome, Verona, Florence, and Venice his father, through his solicitor, sent instructions about allowances and schools. It was he who helped buy the clothes, took her to school, comforted, and advised. He had attempted to support her through the agonies and uncertainties of adolescence, even before he had outgrown his own. He had been her champion against the world. He smiled, remembering the telephone call to Cambridge from her boarding school, asking him to fetch her that very night "outside the hockey pavilion—gruesome torture house—at midnight. I'll climb down the fire escape. Promise." And then their private code of defiance and allegiance: *"Contra mundum."*

*"Contra mundum."*

His father arrived from Italy, so little perturbed by the Reverend Mother's insistent summons that it was obvious that he had, in any case, been planning to return.

"Your sister's departure was unnecessarily eccentric, surely. Midnight assignation. Dramatic car drive across half England. Mother Superior seemed particularly pained that she had left her trunk behind, although I can appreciate that it would have been an encumbrance on the fire escape. And you must have been out of college all night. Your tutor can't have liked that."

"I'm postgraduate now, Father. I took my degree eighteen months ago."

"Indeed. Time passes so quickly at my age. Physics, wasn't it? A curious choice. Couldn't you have called for her after school in the orthodox way?"

"We wanted to get as far away from the place as possible before they noticed she'd gone and started looking."

"A reasonable strategy, so far as it goes."

"Dom hates school, Father. She's utterly miserable there."

"So was I at school, but it never occurred to me to expect otherwise. Reverend Mother seems a charming woman. A tendency to halitosis when under stress, but I shouldn't have thought that would have troubled your sister. They can hardly have come into intimate contact. She isn't prepared to have Domenica back, by the way."

"Need Dom go anywhere, Father? She's nearly fifteen. She doesn't have to go to school. And she wants to be a painter."

"I suppose she could stay at home until she's old enough for art college, if that's what you advise. But it's hardly worth opening the London house just for one. I shall return to Venice next week. I'm only here to consult Dr. Mavers-Brown."

"Perhaps she could go back to Italy with you for a month or so. She'd love to see the Accademia. And she ought to see Florence."

"Oh, I don't think that would do, my boy. Quite out of the question. She had much better take a room at Cambridge and you can keep an eye on her. They have some quite agreeable pictures in the Fitzwilliam Museum. Oh dear, what a responsibility children are! It's quite wrong that I should be troubled like this in my state of health. Mavers-Brown was insistent that I avoid anxiety."

And now he lay, coffined in his final self-sufficiency, in that most beautiful of burial grounds, the British Cemetery at Rome. He would have liked that, thought Maxim, if he could have borne the thought of his death at all, as much as he would have resented the overaggressive Italian driver whose ill-judged acceleration at the junction of the Via Vittoria and the Corso had placed him there.

He heard his sister's steps on the stairs.

"So they've gone."

"Twenty minutes ago. We had a brief valedictory skirmish. Was Dalgliesh offensive?"

"No more offensive than I to him. Honors even, I should have said. I don't think he liked me."

"I don't think he likes anyone much. But he's considered highly intelligent. Did you find him attractive?"

She answered the unspoken question.

"It would be like making love to a public hangman."

She dipped her finger in the vinaigrette dressing.

"Too much vinegar. What have you been doing?"

"Apart from cooking? Thinking about father. Do you know,

Dom, when I was eleven I became absolutely convinced that he'd murdered our mothers."

"Both of them? I mean yours and mine? What an odd idea. How could he have? Yours died of cancer and mine of pneumonia. He couldn't have fixed that."

"I know. It's just that he seemed such a natural widower. I thought at the time that he'd done it to stop them having any more babies."

"Well, it would do that, all right. Were you wondering whether a tendency to murder is inherited?"

"Not really. But so much is. Father's total inability to make relationships, for example. That incredible self-absorption. Do you know, he'd actually put me down for Stonyhurst before he remembered that it was your mother, not mine, who'd been R.C."

"A pity he did find out. I should like to have seen what the Jesuits made of you. The trouble with a religious education, if you're a pagan like me, is that you're left all your life feeling that you've lost something, not that it isn't there."

She walked over to the table and stirred a bowl of mushrooms with her finger.

"I can make relationships. The trouble is that I get bored and they don't last. And I only seem to know one way to be kind. It's as well that we last, isn't it? You'll last for me until the day I die. Shall I change now, or do you want me to see to the wine?"

"You'll last for me until the day I die." *Contra mundum.* It was too late now to sever that cord even if he wanted to. He remembered Charles Schofield's gauze-cocooned head, the dying eyes still malicious behind two slits in the bandages, the swollen lips painfully moving.

"Congratulations, Giovanni. Remember me in your garden in Parma."

What had been so astounding was not the lie itself, or that Schofield had believed it, or pretended to believe it, but that he had hated his brother-in-law enough to die with that taunt on his lips. Or had he taken it for granted that a physicist, poor philistine, wouldn't know his Jacobean dramatists? Even his wife, that indefatigable sexual sophisticate, had known better.

"I suppose you'd sleep together if Domenica happened to want it. A spot of incest wouldn't worry her. But you don't need to, do you? You don't need anything as normal as sex to be more to each other than you are. Neither of you wants anyone else. That's why I'm leaving. I'm getting out now while there's still something left of me to get out."

"Max, what is it?"

Domenica's voice, sharpened with anxiety, recalled him to the present. His mind spun back through a kaleidoscope of spinning years, through superimposed whirling images of childhood and youth, to that last unforgettable image, still, perfectly in focus, patterned forever in his memory, Lorrimer's dead fingers clawing at the floor of his laboratory, Lorrimer's dull, half-open eye, Lorrimer's blood. He said:

"You get changed. I'll see to the wine."

# VII

"What will people say?"

"That's all you ever think of, Mum, what will people say. What does it matter what they say? I haven't done anything to be ashamed of."

"Of course not. If anyone says different your dad'll soon put them right. But you know what tongues they have in this village. A thousand pounds. I couldn't hardly believe it when that solicitor rang. It's a tidy sum. And by the time Lillie Pearce has passed the news around in the Stars and Plough it'll be ten thousand, more than likely."

"Who cares about Lillie Pearce, silly old cow."

"Brenda! I won't have that language. And we have to live in this village."

"You may have to. I don't. And if that's the kind of minds they've got the sooner I move away the better. Oh, Mum, don't look like that! He only wanted to help me, he wanted to be kind. And he probably did it on impulse."

"Not very considerate of him, though, was it? He might have talked it over with your dad or me."

"But he didn't know that he was going to die."

Brenda and her mother were alone in the farmhouse, Arthur Pridmore having left after supper for the monthly meeting of the Parochial Church Council. The washing-up was finished and the long evening stretched before them. Too restless to settle to the television and too preoccupied with the extraordinary events of the day to take up a book, they sat in the firelight, edgy, half excited and half afraid, missing Arthur Pridmore's reassuring bulk in his high-backed chair. Then Mrs. Pridmore shook herself into normality and reached for her sewing basket.

"Well, at least it will help toward a nice wedding. If you have to take it, better put it in the Post Office. Then it'll add interest and be there when you want it."

"I want it now. For books and a microscope like Dr. Lorrimer intended. That's why he left it to me and that's what I'm going to do with it. Besides, if people leave money for a special purpose you can't use it for something else. And I don't want to. I'm going to ask Dad to put up a shelf and a workbench in my bedroom and I'll start working for my science A-levels straightaway."

"He ought not to have thought of you. What about Angela Foley? She's had a terrible life, that girl. She never got a penny from her grandmother's will, and now this."

"That's not our concern, Mum. It was up to him. Maybe he might have left it to her if they hadn't rowed."

"How do you mean, rowed? When?"

"Last week sometime. Tuesday it was, I think. It was just before I came home and most of the staff had left. Inspector Blakelock sent me up to Biology with a query on one of the court reports. They were together in Dr. Lorrimer's room and I heard them quarreling. She was asking him for money and he said he wouldn't give her any and then he said something about changing his will."

"You mean you stood there listening?"

"Well, I couldn't help it, could I? They were talking quite loudly. He was saying terrible things about Stella Mawson, you know, that writer Angela Foley lives with. I wasn't eavesdropping on purpose. I didn't want to hear."

"You could have gone away."

"And come up again all the way from the front hall? Anyway, I had to ask him about the report for the Munnings case. I couldn't go back and tell Inspector Blakelock that I hadn't got the answer because Dr. Lorrimer was having a row with his cousin. Besides, we always listened to secrets at school."

"You're not at school now. Really, Brenda, you worry me sometimes. One moment you behave like a sensible adult, and the next anyone would think you were back in the fourth form. You're eighteen now, an adult. What has school to do with it?"

"I don't know why you're getting so het-up. I didn't tell anyone."

"Well, you'll have to tell that detective from Scotland Yard."

"Mum! I can't! It hasn't got anything to do with the murder."

"Who's to say? You're supposed to tell the police anything that's important. Didn't he tell you that?"

He had told her exactly that. Brenda remembered his look, her own guilty blush. He had known that she was keeping something back. She said, with stubborn defiance:

"Well, I can't accuse Angela Foley of murder, or as good as accuse her, anyway. Besides," she proclaimed triumphantly, remembering something Inspector Blakelock had told her, "it would be hearsay, not proper evidence. He couldn't take any notice of it. And, Mum, there's another thing. Suppose she didn't really expect him to alter the will so soon? That solicitor told you that Dr. Lorrimer made the new will last Friday, didn't he? Well, that was probably because he had to go to a scene of crime in Ely on Friday morning. The police call only came through at ten o'clock. He must have gone into his solicitors then."

"What do you mean?"

"Nothing. Only if people think that I had a motive, then so did she."

"Of course you didn't have a motive! That's ridiculous. It's wicked! Oh, Brenda, if only you'd come to the concert with Dad and me."

"No thank you. Miss Spencer singing 'Pale Hands I Loved,' and the Sunday School kids doing their boring old Maypole dance, and the W.I. with their handbells, and old Mr. Matthews bashing away with the acoustic spoons. I've seen it all before."

"But you'd have had an alibi."

"So I would if you and Dad had stayed here at home with me."

"It wouldn't have mattered where you'd been if it weren't for that thousand pounds. Well, let's hope Gerald Bowlem understands."

"If he doesn't, he knows what he can do! I don't see what it's got to do with Gerald. I'm not married to him, nor engaged for that matter. He'd better not interfere."

She looked across at her mother and was suddenly appalled. She had only seen her look like this once before, the night when she had had her second miscarriage and had been told by old Dr. Greene that there could never now be another baby. Brenda had been only twelve at the time. But her mother's face, suddenly remembered, had looked exactly as it did now, as if an obliterating hand had passed over it, wiping off brightness, blunting the contours of cheek and brow, dulling the eyes, leaving an amorphous mask of desolation.

She remembered and understood what before she had only felt, the anger and resentment that her mother, indestructible and comforting as a great rock in a weary land, should herself be vulnerable to pain. She was there to soothe Brenda's miseries, not to suffer herself, to comfort, not to seek comfort. But now Brenda was older and she was able to understand. She saw her mother clearly, like a stranger newly met. The cheap dress, spotlessly clean as always, with the brooch Brenda had given her for her last birthday pinned to the lapel. The ankles thickening above the sensible low-heeled shoes, the pudgy hands speckled with the brown stains of age, the wedding ring of dull gold biting into the flesh, the curly hair that had once been red-gold like her own, still brushed plainly to one side and held in a tortoise-shell slide, the fresh, almost unlined skin. She put her arms around her mother's shoulders.

"Oh, Mum, don't worry. It'll be all right. Commander Dalgliesh will find out who did it and then everything will be back to normal. Look. I'll make you some cocoa. Don't let's wait till Dad's back from the P.C.C. We'll have it now. Mum, it's all right. Really it is. It's all right."

Simultaneously their ears caught the hum of the approaching car. They gazed at each other, speechless, guilty as conspirators. This wasn't their ancient Morris. And how could it be? The Parochial Church Council never finished their business before half past eight.

Brenda went to the window and peered out. The car stopped. She turned to her mother, white-faced.

"It's the police! It's Commander Dalgliesh!"

Without a word, Mrs. Pridmore got resolutely to her feet. She placed a hand briefly on her daughter's shoulder, then went out into the passage and opened the door before Massingham had lifted his hand to knock. She said through stiff lips:

"Come in, please. I'm glad that you're here. Brenda has something to tell you, something that I think you ought to know."

## VIII

The day was nearly over. Sitting in his dressing gown at the small table in front of the window in his bedroom at the Moonraker, Dalgliesh heard the church clock strike half past eleven. He liked his room. It was the larger of the two that Mrs. Gotobed had been able to offer. The single window looked out over the churchyard toward the village hall and beyond it to the clerestory and square flint tower of St.

Nicholas's Church. There were only three rooms for guests at the inn. The smallest and noisiest, since it was over the public bar, had fallen to Massingham. The main guest room had already been taken by an American couple touring East Angelia, perhaps in search of family records. They had sat at their table in the dining parlor, happily occupied with maps and guidebooks, and if they had been told that their newly arrived fellow guests were police officers investigating a murder, they were too well-bred to betray interest. After a brief smile and a good evening in their soft transatlantic voices they had turned their attention again to Mrs. Gotobed's excellent casserole of hare in cider.

It was very quiet. The muted voices from the bar had long since been silent. It was over an hour since he had heard the last shouted goodbyes. Massingham, he knew, had spent the evening in the public bar hoping, presumably, to pick up scraps of useful information. Dalgliesh hoped that the beer had been good. He had been born close enough to the fens to know that, otherwise, Massingham would have found it a frustrating evening.

He got up to stretch his legs and shoulders, looking around with approval at the room. The floorboards were of ancient oak, black and stout as ships' timbers. A fire of wood and turf burned in the iron Victorian grate, the pungent smoke curtsying under a decorated hood of wheat ears and flower posies tied with ribbons. The large double bed was of brass, high and ornate with four great knobs, large as polished cannonballs, at the corners. Mrs. Gotobed had earlier folded back the crocheted cover to reveal a feather mattress shaken to an inviting plumpness. In any four-star hotel he might have enjoyed greater luxury, but hardly such comfort.

He returned to his work. It had been a crowded day of interrogation and renewed interrogation, telephone calls to London, a hurriedly arranged and unsatisfactory press conference, two consultations with the Chief Constable, the gathering of those odd-shaped pieces of information and conjecture which, in the end, would click together to form the completed picture. It might be a trite analogy, this comparison of detection with fitting together a jigsaw. But it was remarkably apt, not least because it was so often that tantalizing, elusive piece with the vital segment of a human face that made the picture complete.

He turned the page to the last interview of the day, with Henry Kerrison at the Old Rectory. The smell of the house was still in his nostrils, an evocative smell of stale cooking and furniture polish, reminding him of childhood visits with his parents to overlarge, ill-heated country vicarages. Kerrison's housekeeper and children had long been in bed and the house had held a melancholy, brooding silence as if all the tragedies and disappointments of its numerous incumbents still hung in the air.

Kerrison had answered the door himself and had shown him and Massingham into his study where he was occupied in sorting colored slides of postmortem injuries to illustrate a lecture he was to give the following week to the detection training school. On the desk was a framed photograph of himself as a boy with an older man, obviously his father. They were standing on a crag, climbing ropes slung around their shoulders. What interested Dalglicsh as much as the photograph itself was the fact that Kerrison hadn't bothered to remove it.

He hadn't appeared to resent his visitors' late arrival. It was possible to believe that he welcomed their company. He had worked on in the light of his desk lamp, fitting each slide into his viewer, then sorting it into the appropriate heap, intent as a schoolboy with a hobby. He had answered their questions quietly and precisely, but as if his mind were elsewhere. Dalgliesh asked him whether his daughter had talked to him about the incident with Lorrimer.

"Yes, she did tell me. When I got home for lunch from my lecture I found her crying in her room. It seems that Lorrimer was unnecessarily harsh. But Nell is a sensitive child and it's not always possible to know the precise truth of the matter."

"You didn't talk to him about it?"

"I didn't talk to anyone. I did wonder whether I ought to, but it would have meant questioning Inspector Blakelock and Miss Pridmore, and I didn't wish to involve them. They had to work with Lorrimer. So, for that matter, did I. The effectiveness of an isolated institution like Hoggatt's largely depends on good relationships among the staff. I thought it was best not to take the matter further. That may have been prudence, or it may have been cowardice. I don't know."

He had smiled sadly, and added:

"I only know that it wasn't a motive for murder."

A motive for murder. Dalgliesh had discovered enough motives in this first crowded but not very satisfactory day. But motive was the least important factor in a murder investigation. He would gladly have exchanged the psychological subtleties of motive for a single, solid, incontrovertible piece of physical evidence linking a suspect with the crime. And, so far, there was none. He still awaited the report from the Metropolitan Laboratory on the mallet and the vomit. The mysterious figure seen by old Goddard fleeing from Hoggatt's remained mysterious; no other person had yet been traced or had come forward to suggest that he wasn't a figment of the old man's imagination. The tire marks near the gate, now definitely identified from the tire index at the laboratory, still hadn't been linked to a car. Not surprisingly, no trace had been found of Middlemass's white coat and no indication whether or how it had been disposed of. An examination of the village hall and the hobbyhorse costume had produced nothing to disprove Middlemass's account of his evening, and it was apparent that the horse, a heavy, all-enveloping contraption of canvas and serge, ensured that its wearer would be unidentifiable even, in Middlemass's case, to his elegant handmade shoes.

The central mysteries of the case remained. Who was it who had telephoned the message to Lorrimer about the can being burned and the number 1840? Was it the same woman who had rung Mrs. Bidwell? What had been written on the missing sheet from Lorrimer's rough notebook? What had prompted Lorrimer to make that extraordinary will?

Lifting his head from the files, he listened. There was a noise, faintly discernible, like the creeping of myriad insects. He remembered it from his childhood nights, lying awake in the nursery of his father's Norfolk vicarage, a sound he had never heard in the noise of cities, the first, gentle, sibilant whisper of the night rain. Soon it was followed by a spatter of drops against the window and the rising moan of the wind in the chimney. The fire spluttered and then flared into sudden brightness. There was a violent flurry of rain against the pane and then, as quickly as it had begun, the brief storm was over. He opened the window to savor the smell of the damp night air and gazed out into a blanket of darkness, black fen earth merging with the paler sky.

As his eyes became accustomed to the night, he could discern the low rectangle of the village hall and, beyond it, the great medieval tower of the church. Then the moon sailed out from behind the clouds and the churchyard became visible, the obelisks and gravestones gleaming pale as if they exuded their own mysterious light. Below him, faintly luminous, lay the gravel path along which, the previous night, the morris-dancers, bells jangling, had made their way through the rising mist. Staring out over the churchyard he pictured the hobbyhorse pawing the ground to meet them, rearing its grotesque head among the gravestones, and snapping the air with its great jaws. And he wondered again who had been inside its skin.

The door beneath his window opened and Mrs. Gotobed appeared and crooned into the darkness, enticing in her cat: "Snowball! Snowball! Good boy now." There was a flash of white, and the door was closed. Dalgliesh latched his window and decided that he, too, would call it a day.

# BOOK FOUR

·

# Hanged by the Neck

# I

Sprogg's Cottage, low-built and top-heavy under its low, occluding roof of thatch, wire-netted, strong against the fen winter gales, was almost invisible from the road. It lay about three-quarters of a mile northeast from the village and was fronted by Sprogg's Green, a wide, triangular grass verge planted with willows. Pushing open the white wicker gate on which someone had optimistically but fruitlessly substituted the word *Lavender* for *Sprogg's*, Dalgliesh and Massingham stepped into a front garden as brightly ordered and conventional as that of a suburban villa. An acacia tree in the middle of the lawn flaunted its autumn glory of red and gold; the yellow climbing roses trained over the door still gleamed with a faint illusion of summer; and a massed bed of geraniums, fuchsia, and dahlias, supported by stakes and carefully tended, flared in discordant glory against the bronze of the beech hedge. There was a hanging basket of pink geraniums beside the door, now past their best but still bright with a few tattered blooms. The knocker was a highly polished brass fish, every scale gleaming.

The door was opened by a slight, almost fragile, woman, barefooted and wearing a cotton overblouse, patterned in greens and brown, above her corduroy slacks. She had coarse dark hair strongly streaked with gray and worn in a short bob, with a heavy fringe that curved low to meet her eyebrows. Her eyes were her most remarkable feature, immense, the irises brown speckled with green, translucently clear under the strongly curved brows. Her face was pale and taut, deeply etched with lines across the forehead and running from the widely springing nostrils to the corners of the mouth. It was the face, thought Dalgliesh, of a tortured masochist in a medieval triptych, the muscles bulging and knotted as if they had been racked. But no one coming under the gaze of those remarkable eyes could call it plain or ordinary. Dalgliesh said:

"Miss Mawson? I'm Adam Dalgliesh. This is Inspector Massingham."

She gave him a direct, impersonal gaze and said without smiling:

"Come through into the study, will you? We don't light the sitting-room fire until the evening. If you want to speak to Angela, I'm afraid she's not here at present. She's over at Postmill Cottage with Mrs. Swaffield meeting the Social Security people. They're trying to persuade old Lorrimer to go into an old people's home. Apparently he's being obstinately resistant to the blandishments of bureaucracy. Good luck to him."

The front door opened directly into a sitting room with a low, oak-beamed ceiling. The room surprised him. To enter it was like walking into an antique shop, but one where the proprietor had arranged his oddly assorted wares with an eye to the general effect. The mantelshelf and every ledge bore an ornament; three hanging cupboards held a variety of mugs, teapots, painted jugs, and Staffordshire figures; and the walls were almost covered with prints, framed old maps, small oil paintings, and Victorian silhouettes in oval frames. Above the fireplace was the most spectacular object, a curved sword with a finely wrought scabbard. He wondered whether the room reflected merely an indiscriminate acquisitiveness, or whether these carefully disposed objects served as comforting talismans against the alien, undomesticated spirits of the encroaching fens. A wood fire was laid but not lit in the open hearth. Under the window a polished gate-legged table was already laid for two.

Miss Mawson led the way through to her study. It was a smaller, less cluttered room at the back with a latticed window giving a view of a stone terrace, a lawn with a sundial in the middle, and a wide field of sugar beet, still unharvested. He saw with interest that she wrote by hand. There was a typewriter, but it stood on a table by itself. The working desk under the window held only a pad of unlined paper, covered with a black upright holograph in an elegant italic. The lines were carefully patterned on the paper, and even the marginal alterations were aligned.

Dalgliesh said:

"I'm sorry if we're interrupting your work."

"You aren't. Sit down, won't you both. It isn't going well this morning. If it were I should have hung a 'Don't Disturb' notice on the knocker and you wouldn't have got in. Still, it's nearly finished; only one chapter to do now. I suppose you want me to give Angela an alibi. Helping the police, isn't it called? What were we doing on Wednesday night; and when, and why, and where, and with whom?"

"We would like to ask you some questions, certainly."

"But that one first, presumably. There's no difficulty. We spent the evening and night together from six-fifteen, which was the time she arrived home."

"Doing what, Miss Mawson?"

"What we normally do. We separated the day from the evening, me with whisky, Angela with sherry. I asked about her day and she inquired about mine. Then she lit the fire and cooked the meal. We had avocado pear with *sauce vinaigrette*, chicken casserole, and cheese and biscuits. We washed up together and then Angela typed my manuscript for me until nine. At nine we turned on the television and watched the news, followed by the play. That brought us to ten-forty-five, cocoa for Angela, whisky for me, and bed."

"Neither of you left the cottage?"

"No."

Dalgliesh asked how long she had lived in the village.

"Me? Eight years. I was born in the fens—at Soham actually—and spent most of my childhood here. But I went up to London University when I was eighteen, took a second-class degree, and then worked, not particularly successfully, at various jobs in journalism and publishing. I came here eight years ago when I heard that the cottage was to let. That's when I first decided to give up my job and become a full-time writer."

"And Miss Foley?"

"She came to live here two years ago. I advertised locally for a part-time typist and she replied. She was living in lodgings at Ely then and wasn't particularly happy there, so I suggested that she move in. She had to depend on the bus to get to work. Living here is obviously much more convenient for the lab."

"So you've lived long enough in the village to get to know people?"

"As much as one ever does in the fens. But not well enough to point the finger at a murderer for you."

"How well did you know Dr. Lorrimer?"

"By sight. I wasn't told that Angela was his cousin until she came to live with me. They're not close and he never came here. I've met most of the lab staff, of course. Dr. Howarth started a string quartet soon after he arrived, and last August they gave a concert in the Wren chapel. Afterwards there was wine and cheese in the vestry. I met a number of the staff then. Actually, I already knew them by sight and name, as one does in a village. We use the same post office and the same pub. But if you're hoping for village and lab gossip, it's no use coming to me."

Dalgliesh said:

"Was the concert in the chapel successful?"

"Not particularly. Howarth is a very fine amateur violinist and Claire Easterbrook is a competent cellist, but the other two weren't up to much. He hasn't repeated the experiment. I gather that there was a certain amount of unkind comment about a new arrival who saw it as his duty to civilize the underprivileged natives, and it may have got to his ears. He does rather give the impression that he sees himself as bridging single-handed the culture gap between the scientist and the artist. Or perhaps he wasn't satisfied with the acoustics. My own view is that the other three didn't want to go on playing with him. As a leader of a quartet he probably behaved with much the same arrogance as he does as Director. The lab is certainly more efficient; the work output is up twenty percent. Whether the staff are happy is another matter."

So she wasn't altogether immune to lab and village gossip, thought Dalgliesh. He wondered why she was being so frank. Equally frank, he asked bluntly:

"When you were at Postmill Cottage yesterday, did you go upstairs?"

"Fancy the old man telling you that! What did he think I was after, I wonder? I went up to the bathroom to see if there was a tin of scouring powder there to clean the sink. There wasn't."

"You know about Dr. Lorrimer's will, of course?"

"I imagine the whole village does. Actually I was probably the first to know. The old man was getting agitated to know whether there was any money coming, so Angela rang the solicitor. She'd met him at the time her grandmother's will was read. He told her that the cottage was to go to the old man with ten thousand pounds, so she was able to put his mind at rest."

"And Miss Foley herself gets nothing?"

"That's right. And that new Clerical Officer at the lab, whom Edwin had apparently taken a fancy to, gets a thousand pounds."

"A not particularly just will."

"Have you ever known beneficiaries who thought a will was just? His grandmother's will was worse. Angela lost the money then, when it could have made a difference to her life. Now she doesn't need it. We manage perfectly well here."

"Presumably it wasn't a shock to her. Didn't he tell her of his intentions?"

"If that's meant to be a tactful way of finding out whether she had a motive for murder, you can ask her yourself. Here she is."

Angela Foley came through the sitting room, tugging off her headscarf. Her face darkened at the sight of the visitors, and she said with quick, defensive annoyance:

"Miss Mawson likes to work in the mornings. You didn't say that you were coming."

Her friend laughed.

"They haven't worried me. I've been getting a useful insight into police methods. They're effective without being crude. You're back early."

"The Social Work Department rang to say that they can't get over until after lunch. Uncle doesn't want to see them, but he wants to see me even less. He's having lunch with the Swaffields at the rectory, so I thought I might as well come home."

Stella Mawson lit a cigarette.

"You've arrived at an opportune time. Mr. Dalgliesh was inquiring tactfully whether you had a motive for murdering your cousin; in other words, did Edwin tell you that he was about to alter his will?"

Angela Foley looked at Dalgliesh and said calmly:

"No. He never discussed his affairs with me and I didn't discuss mine with him. I don't think I've spoken to him during the last two years except about lab business."

Dalgliesh said:

"It's surprising, surely, that he should want to change a long-standing will without talking to you about it?"

She shrugged, and then explained:

"It had nothing to do with me. He was only my cousin, not my brother. He transferred to Hoggatt's from the Southern Laboratory five years ago to live with his father, not because I was here. He didn't really know me. If he had, I doubt whether he would have liked me. He owed me nothing, not even justice."

"Did you like him?"

She paused and thought, as if the question were one to which she herself wanted an answer. Stella Mawson, eyes narrowed, regarded her through the cigarette smoke. Then Miss Foley spoke:

"No, I didn't like him. I think I was even a little afraid of him. He was like a man psychologically burdened, unsure of his place in life. Lately the tension and unhappiness were almost palpable. I found it embarrassing and, well, somehow menacing. People who were really secure in their own personalities didn't seem to notice or be bothered by it. But the less secure felt threatened. I think that's why Clifford Bradley was so afraid of him."

Stella Mawson said:

"Bradley probably reminded Edwin of himself when he was young. He was painfully insecure, even in his job, when he first started. D'you remember how he used to practice his evidence on the night before he went into the box; writing down all the possible questions the opposing counsel might ask, making sure that he was word-perfect with the answers, learning all the scientific formulas by heart to impress the jury? He made a mess of one of his first cases and never forgave himself."

There was a strange little silence. Angela Foley seemed about to speak, then changed her mind. Her enigmatic gaze was fixed on her friend. Stella Mawson's eyes shifted. She walked over to her desk and stubbed out her cigarette. She said:

"Your aunt told you. She used to have to read out the questions for him over and over again; an evening of tension and incomprehensible boredom. Don't you remember?"

"Yes," said Angela in her high, dispassionate voice. "Yes, I remember." She turned to Dalgliesh.

"If there's nothing else you want to ask me, there are things I need to get on with. Dr. Howarth isn't expecting me at the lab until this afternoon. And Stella will want to work."

Both women showed them out, standing together in the doorway as if politely speeding departing guests. Dalgliesh almost expected them to wave goodbye. He hadn't questioned Miss Foley about the quarrel with her cousin. The time might come for that, but it wasn't yet. It had interested but not surprised him that she had lied. But what had interested him more was Stella Mawson's story of Lorrimer rehearsing his evidence on the night before a trial. Whoever had told her this, he was fairly certain that it hadn't been Angela Foley.

As they drove away, Massingham said:

"Fifty thousand pounds could change her whole life, give her some independence, get her away from here. What sort of life is it for a young woman, just the two of them, stuck here in this isolated swamp? And she seems little more than a drudge."

Dalgliesh, unusually, was driving. Massingham glanced at the somber eyes in the mirror, the long hands laid lightly on the wheel. Dalgliesh said:

"I'm remembering what old George Greenall, the first detective-sergeant I worked under, told me. He'd had twenty-five years in the C.I.D. Nothing about people surprised him, nothing shocked him. He said: 'They'll tell you that the most destructive force in the world is hate. Don't you believe it, lad. It's love. And if you want to make a detective you'd better learn to recognize it when you meet it.' "

## II

Brenda was over an hour late at the laboratory on Thursday morning. After the excitement of the previous day she had overslept and her mother had deliberately not called her. She had wanted to go without her breakfast, but Mrs. Pridmore had placed the usual plate of bacon and egg before her and had said firmly that Brenda wouldn't leave the house until it was eaten. Brenda, only too aware that both her parents would be happier if she never set foot in Hoggatt's again, knew better than to argue.

She arrived, breathless and apologetic, to find Inspector Blakelock trying to cope with two days' intake of exhibits, a steady stream of arrivals, and a constantly ringing telephone. She wondered how he would greet her, whether he had learned about the thousand pounds, and, if so, whether it would make any difference. But he seemed his usual stolid self. He said:

"As soon as you've taken off your things, you're to go to the Director. He's in Miss Foley's office. The police are using his. Don't bother about making tea. Miss Foley will be out until after lunch. She has to see someone from the local authority social services about her uncle."

Brenda was glad that she wouldn't have to face Angela Foley yet. Last night's admission to Commander Dalgliesh was too like betrayal to be comfortable. She said:

"Everyone else is in, then?"

"Clifford Bradley hasn't made it. His wife telephoned to say that he's not well. The police have been here since half past eight. They've been checking all the exhibits, especially the drugs, and they've made another search of the whole lab. Apparently they've got the idea that there's something odd going on."

It was unusual for Inspector Blakelock to be so communicative. Brenda asked:

"What do you mean, something odd?"

"They didn't say. But now they want to see every file in the lab with a number 18 or 40 or 1840 in the registration."

Brenda's eyes widened.

"Do you mean for this year only, or do we have to go back to those on microfilm?"

"I've got out this year's and last year's to begin with, and Sergeant Underhill and the constable are working on them now. I don't know what they hope to find, and by the look of them, neither do they. Better look nippy. Dr. Howarth said that you were to go into him as soon as you arrive."

"But I can't do shorthand and typing! What do you think he wants me for?"

"He didn't say. Mostly getting out files, I imagine. And I daresay there'll be a bit of telephoning and fetching and carrying."

"Where's Commander Dalgliesh? Isn't he here?"

"He and Inspector Massingham left about ten minutes ago. Off to interview someone, I daresay. Never mind about them. Our job's here, helping to keep this lab working smoothly."

It was as close as Inspector Blakelock ever got to a rebuke. Brenda hurried to Miss Foley's office. It was known that the Director didn't like people to knock on his door, so Brenda entered with what confidence she could muster. She thought, I can only do my best. If that's not good enough, he'll have to lump it. He was sitting at the desk apparently studying a file. He looked up without smiling in response to her good morning, and said:

"Inspector Blakelock has explained to you that I want some help this morning while Miss Foley's away? You can work with Mrs. Mallett in the general office."

"Yes, sir."

"The police will be needing some more files. They're interested in particular numbers only. But I expect Inspector Blakelock has explained that."

"Yes, sir."

"They're working on the 1976 and '75 registrations now, so you'd better start getting out the 1974 series and any earlier years they want."

He took his eyes from the files and looked directly at her for the first time.

"Dr. Lorrimer left you some money, didn't he?"

"Yes, sir. One thousand pounds for books and apparatus."

"You don't need to call me sir. Dr. Howarth will do. You liked him?"

"Yes. Yes, I did."

Dr. Howarth had lowered his eyes again and was turning over the pages of the file.

"Odd, I shouldn't have thought that he would have appealed to women, or women to him."

Brenda said resolutely:

"It wasn't like that."

"What wasn't it like? Do you mean he didn't think of you as a woman?"

"I don't know. I mean, I didn't think that he was trying to . . ."

Her voice broke off. Dr. Howarth turned a page. He said:

"To seduce you?"

Brenda took courage, helped by a spurt of anger. She said:

"Well, he couldn't could he? Not here in the lab. And I never saw him anywhere else. And if you'd known anything about him at all, you wouldn't talk like that."

She was appalled at her own temerity. But the Director only said, rather sadly, she thought:

"I expect you're right. I never knew him at all."

She struggled to explain.

"He explained to me what science is about."

"And what is science about?"

"He explained that scientists formulate theories about how the physical world works, and then test them out by experiments. As long as the experiments succeed, then the theories hold. If they fail, the scientists have to find another theory to explain the facts. He says that, with science, there's this exciting paradox, that disillusionment needn't be defeat. It's a step forward."

"Didn't you do science at school? I thought you'd taken physics and chemistry at O-level."

"No one ever explained it like that before."

"No. I suppose they bored you with experiments about magnetism and the properties of carbon dioxide. By the way, Miss Foley has typed a paper on the ratio of staffing to workloads. I want the figures checked—Mrs. Mallett will do it with you—and the paper circulated to all directors before next week's meeting. She'll give you the list of addresses."

"Yes, sir. Yes, Dr. Howarth."

"And I'd like you to take this file to Miss Easterbrook in the Biology Lab."

He looked up at her, and she thought for the first time that he looked kind. He said, very gently:

"I know how you feel. I felt the same. But there's only a white outline on the floor, just a smudge of chalk. That's all."

He handed her the file. It was a dismissal. At the door Brenda paused. The Director said:

"Well?"

"I was just thinking that detection must be like science. The detective formulates a theory, then tests it. If the facts he discovers fit, then the theory holds. If they don't, then he has to find another theory, another suspect."

Dr. Howarth said dryly:

"It's a reasonable analogy. But the temptation to select the right facts is probably greater. And the detective is experimenting with human beings. Their properties are complex and not susceptible to accurate analysis."

An hour later Brenda took her third set of files into Sergeant Underhill in the Director's office. The pleasant-looking detective-constable leaped forward to relieve her of her burden. The telephone rang on Dr. Howarth's desk, and Sergeant Underhill went over to answer it. He replaced the receiver and looked across at his companion.

"That's the Met Lab. They've given me the result of the blood analysis. The mallet was the weapon all right. There's Lorrimer's blood on it. And they've analyzed the vomit."

He looked up, suddenly remembering that Brenda was still in the room, and waited until she had left and the door was closed. The detective-constable said:

"Well?"

"It's what we thought. Think it out for yourself. A forensic scientist would know that the lab can't determine a blood group from vomit. The stomach acids destroy the antibodies. What they can hope to say is what was in the food. So all you need to do, if it's your vomit and you're a suspect, is to lie about what you ate for supper. Who could disprove it?"

His companion said:

"Unless . . ."

Sergeant Underhill reached again for the phone.

"Exactly. As I said, think it out for yourself."

# III

After the last few days of intermittent rain and fitful autumn sunlight, the morning was cold but bright, the sun unexpectedly warm against their necks. But even in the mellow light, the Old Rectory, with its bricks the color of raw liver under the encroaching ivy, and its ponderous porch and carved overhanging eaves, was a depressing house. The open iron gate to the drive, half off its hinges, was embedded in a straggling hedge which bordered the garden. The gravel path needed weeding. The grass of the lawn was pulled and flattened where someone had made an inexpert attempt at mowing it, obviously with a blunt machine, and the two herbaceous borders were a tangle of overgrown chrysanthemums and stunted dahlias half choked with weeds. A child's wooden horse on wheels lay on its side at the edge of the lawn, but this was the only sign of human life.

As they approached the house, however, a girl and a small boy emerged from the porch and stood regarding them. They must, of course, be Kerrison's children, and as Dalgliesh and Massingham approached the likeness became apparent. The girl must, he supposed, be over school age, but she looked barely sixteen except for a certain adult wariness about the eyes. She had straight, dark hair drawn back from a high, spotty forehead into short, disheveled pigtails bound with elastic bands. She wore the ubiquitous faded blue jeans of her generation, topped with a fawn sweater, loose-fitting enough to be her father's. Around her neck Dalgliesh could glimpse what looked like a leather thong. Her grubby feet were bare and palely striped with the pattern of summer sandals.

The child, who moved closer to her at the sight of strangers, was about three or four years old, a stocky, round-faced boy with a wide nose and a gentle, delicate mouth. His face was a softer miniature model of his father's, the brows straight and dark above the heavily lidded eyes. He was wearing a pair of tight blue shorts and an inexpertly knitted striped sweater against which he was clasping a large ball. His sturdy legs were planted in short red wellington boots. He tightened his hold on his ball and fixed on Dalgliesh an unblinking, disconcertingly judgmental gaze.

Dalgliesh suddenly realized that he knew virtually nothing about children. Most of his friends were childless: those who were not had learned to invite him when their demanding, peace-disturbing, egotistical offspring were away at school. His only son had died, with his mother, just twenty-four hours after birth. Although he could now hardly recall his wife's face except in dreams, the picture of those waxen, doll-like features above the tiny swathed body, the gummed eyelids, the secret look of self-absorbed peace was so clear and immediate that he sometimes wondered whether the image was really that of his child, so briefly but intently regarded, or whether he had taken into himself a prototype of dead childhood. His son would now be older than this child, would be entering the traumatic years of adolescence. He had convinced himself long ago that he was glad to have been spared them.

But now it suddenly occurred to him that there was a whole territory of human experience on which, once repulsed, he had turned his back, and that this rejection somehow diminished him as a man. This transitory ache of loss surprised him by its intensity. He forced himself to consider a sensation so unfamiliar and unwelcome.

Suddenly the child smiled at him and held out the ball. The effect was as disconcertingly flattering as when a stray cat would stalk toward him, tail erect, and condescend to be stroked. They gazed at each other. Dalgliesh smiled back. Then Massingham sprang forward and whipped the ball from the chubby hands.

"Come on. Football!"

He began dribbling the blue and yellow ball across the lawn. Immediately the sturdy legs followed. The two of them disappeared around the side of the house and Dalgliesh could hear the boy's high, cracked laughter. The girl gazed after them, her face suddenly pinched with loving anxiety. She turned to Dalgliesh.

"I hope he knows not to kick it into the bonfire. It's almost out, but the embers are still very hot. I've been burning rubbish."

"Don't worry. He's a careful chap. And he's got younger brothers."

She regarded him carefully for the first time.

"You're Commander Dalgliesh, aren't you? We're Nell and William Kerrison. I'm afraid my father isn't here."

"I know. We've come to see your housekeeper. Miss Willard, isn't it? Is she in?"

"I shouldn't take any notice of anything she says if I were you.

She's a dreadful liar. And she steals Daddy's drink. Don't you want to question William and me?"

"A policewoman will be coming with us to talk to you both, sometime, when your father's at home."

"I won't see her. I don't mind talking to you, but I won't see a policewoman. I don't like social workers."

"A policewoman isn't a social worker."

"She's the same. She makes judgments on people, doesn't she? We had a social worker here after my mother left, before the custody case, and she looked at William and me as if we were a public nuisance which someone had left on her doorstep. She went around the house, too, poking into things, pretending to admire, making out it was just a social visit."

"Policewomen—and policemen—never pretend that they're just paying a social visit. No one would believe us, would they?"

They turned and walked together toward the house. The girl said:

"Are you going to discover who killed Dr. Lorrimer?"

"I hope so. I expect so."

"And then what will happen to him, the murderer, I mean?"

"He'll appear before the magistrates. Then, if they think that the evidence is sufficient, they'll commit him to the Crown Court for trial."

"And then?"

"If he's found guilty of murder, the judge will pass the statutory penalty, imprisonment for life. That means that he'll be in prison for a long time, perhaps ten years or more."

"But that's silly. That won't put things right. It won't bring Dr. Lorrimer back."

"It won't put anything right, but it isn't silly. Life is precious to nearly all of us. Even people who have little more than life still want to live it to the last natural moment. No one has a right to take it away from them."

"You talk as if life were like William's ball. If that's taken away he knows what he's lost. Dr. Lorrimer doesn't know that he's lost anything."

"He's lost the years he might have had."

"That's like taking away the ball that William might have had. It doesn't mean anything. It's just words. Suppose he was going to die next week anyway. Then he'd only have lost seven days. You don't put someone in prison for ten years to repay seven lost days. They might not even have been happy days."

"Even if he were a very old man with one day left to him, the law says that he has a right to live it. Willful killing would still be murder."

The girl said thoughtfully:

"I suppose it was different when people believed in God. Then the murdered person might have died in mortal sin and gone to hell. The seven days could have made a difference then. He might have repented and had time for absolution."

Dalgliesh said:

"All these problems are easier for people who believe in God. Those of us who don't or can't have to do the best we can. That's what the law is, the best we can do. Human justice is imperfect, but it's the only justice we have."

"Are you sure you don't want to question me? I know that Daddy didn't kill him. He isn't a murderer. He was at home with William and me when Dr. Lorrimer died. We put William to bed together at half past seven and then we stayed with him for twenty minutes and Daddy read Paddington Bear to him. Then I went to bed because I'd got a headache and wasn't feeling well, and Daddy brought me up a mug of cocoa which he'd made specially for me. He sat by me reading poetry from my school anthology until he thought I'd gone to sleep. But I hadn't really. I was just pretending. He crept away just before nine, but I was still awake then. Shall I tell you how I know?"

"If you want to."

"Because I heard the church clock strike. Then Daddy left me and I lay there in the dark, just thinking. He came back to look in at me again about half an hour later, but I still pretended to be asleep. So that lets Daddy out, doesn't it?"

"We don't know exactly when Dr. Lorrimer died but, yes, I think it probably does."

"Unless I'm telling you a lie."

"People very often do lie to the police. Are you?"

"No. But I expect I would if I thought it would save Daddy. I don't care about Dr. Lorrimer, you see. I'm glad he's dead. He wasn't a nice man. The day before he died William and I went to the lab to see Daddy. He was lecturing in the morning to the detective training course and we thought we'd call for him before lunch. Inspector Blakelock let us sit in the hall, and that girl who helps him at the desk, the pretty one, smiled at William and offered him an apple from her lunch box. And then Dr. Lorrimer came down the stairs and saw us. I know it was he because the Inspector spoke to him by his name and he said: 'What are those children doing in here? A lab isn't a place for children.' I said: 'I'm not a child. I'm Miss Eleanor Kerrison and this is my brother, William, and we're waiting for our father.' He stared at us as if he hated us, his face white and twitching. He said: 'Well, you can't wait here.' Then he spoke very unkindly to Inspector Blakelock. After Dr. Lorrimer had gone, he said we'd better go but he told William not to mind and took a sweet out of his left ear. Did you know that the Inspector was a conjurer?"

"No. I didn't know that."

"Would you like to see around the house before I take you to Miss Willard? Do you like seeing houses?"

"Very much, but I think perhaps not now."

"See the drawing room anyway. It's much the best room. There now, isn't it lovely?"

The drawing room was in no sense lovely. It was a somber, oak-paneled, overfurnished room which looked as if little had changed since the days when the bombazine-clad wife and daughters of the Victorian rector sat there piously occupied with their parish sewing. The mullioned windows, framed by dark red, dirt-encrusted curtains, effectively excluded most of the daylight so that Dalgliesh stepped into a somber chilliness which the sluggish fire did nothing to dispel. An immense mahogany table, bearing a jam jar of chrysanthemums, stood against the far wall, and the fireplace, an ornate edifice of marble, was almost hidden by two immense, saggy armchairs and a dilapidated sofa. Eleanor said with unexpected formality, as if the room had recalled her to her duty as a hostess:

"I try to keep at least one room nice in case we have visitors. The flowers are pretty, aren't they? William arranged them. Please sit down. Can I get you some coffee?"

"That would be pleasant, but I don't think we ought to wait. We're really here to see Miss Willard."

Massingham and William appeared in the doorway, flushed with their exercise, William with the ball tucked under his left arm. Eleanor led the way through a brass-studded green baize door and down a stone passage to the back of the house. William, deserting Massingham, trotted behind her, his plump hand clutching ineffectively at the skin-tight jeans. Pausing outside a door of unpolished oak, she said:

"She's in here. She doesn't like William and me to go in. Anyway, she smells, so we don't."

And taking William by the hand, she left them.

Dalgliesh knocked. There was a rapid scrabbling noise inside the room, like an animal disturbed in its lair, and then the door was opened slightly and a dark and suspicious eye looked out at them through the narrow aperture. Dalgliesh said:

"Miss Willard? Commander Galgliesh and Inspector Massingham from the Metropolitan Police. We're investigating Dr. Lorrimer's murder. May we come in?"

The eye softened. She gave a short, embarrassed gasp, rather like a snort, and opened the door wide.

"Of course. Of course. What must you think of me? I'm afraid I'm still in what my dear old nurse used to call my disabilly. But I wasn't expecting you, and I usually have a quiet moment to myself about this time of the morning."

Eleanor was right, the room did smell. A smell, Massingham diagnosed after a cautious sniff, composed of sweet sherry, unfresh body linen, and cheap scent. It was very hot. A small blue flame licked the red-hot ovals of coal briquettes banked high in the Victorian grate. The window, which gave a view of the garage and the wilderness that was the back garden, was open for only an inch at the top despite the mildness of the day, and the air in the room pressed down on them, furred and heavy as a soiled blanket. The room itself had a dreadful and perverse femininity. Everything looked moistly soft, the cretonne-covered seats of the two armchairs, the plump row of cushions along the back of a Victorian chaise longue, the imitation fur rug before the fire. The mantelshelf was cluttered with photographs in silver frames, mostly of a cassocked clergyman and his wife, whom Dalgliesh took to be Miss Willard's parents, standing side by side but oddly dissociated outside a variety of rather dull churches. Pride of place was held by a studio photograph of Miss Willard herself, young, toothily coy, the thick hair in corrugated waves. On a wall shelf to the right of the door was a small woodcarving of an armless Madonna with the laughing Child perched on her shoulder. A night-light in a saucer was burning at her feet, casting a soft glow over the tender drooping head and the sightless eye. Dalgliesh thought that it was probably a copy, and a good one, of a medieval museum piece. Its gentle beauty emphasized the tawdriness of the room, yet dignified it, seeming to say that there was more than one kind of human loneliness, human pain, and that the same mercy embraced them all.

Miss Willard waved them to the chaise longue.

"My own little den," she said gaily. "I like to be private, you know. I explained to Dr. Kerrison that I could only consider coming if I had my privacy. It's a rare and beautiful thing, don't you think? The human spirit wilts without it."

Looking at her hands, Dalgliesh thought that she was probably in her middle forties, although her face looked older. The dark hair, dry and coarse and tightly curled, was at odds with her faded complexion. Two sausages of curls over the brow suggested that she had hurriedly snatched out the rollers when she heard their knock. But her face was already made up. There was a circle of rouge under each eye and the lipstick had seeped into the creases pursing her mouth.

Her small, square, bony jaw was loose as a marionette's. She was not yet fully dressed and a padded dressing gown of flowered nylon, stained with tea and what looked like egg, was corded over a nylon nightdress in bright blue with a grubby frill around the neck. Massingham was fascinated by a bulbous fold of limp cotton just above her shoes, from which he found it difficult to avert his eyes, until he realized that she had put on her stockings back to front.

She said:

"You want to talk to me about Dr. Kerrison's alibi, I expect. Of course, it's quite ridiculous that he should have to provide one, a man so gentle, totally incapable of violence. But I can help you, as it happens. He was certainly at home until after nine, and I saw him again less than an hour later. But all this is just a waste of time. You bring a great reputation with you, Commander, but this is one crime that science can't solve. Not for nothing are they called the black fens. All through the centuries, evil has come out of this dank soil. We can fight evil, Commander, but not with your weapons."

Massingham said:

"Well, suppose we begin by giving our weapons a chance."

She looked at him and smiled pityingly.

"But all the doors were locked. All your clever scientific aids were intact. No one broke in, and no one could have got out. And yet he was struck down. That was no human hand, Inspector."

Dalgliesh said:

"It was almost certainly a blunt weapon, Miss Willard, and I've no doubt there was a human hand at the end of it. It's our job to find out whose, and I hope that you may be able to help us. You housekeep for Dr. Kerrison and his daughter, I believe?"

Miss Willard disposed on him a glance in which pity at such ignorance was mixed with gentle reproof.

"I'm not a housekeeper, Commander. Certainly not a housekeeper. Shall we say that I'm a working house guest. Dr. Kerrison needed someone to live in so that the children weren't left alone when he was called out to a murder scene. They're children of a broken marriage, I'm afraid. The old, sad story. You are not married, Commander?"

"No."

"How wise." She sighed, conveying in the sibilant release of breath infinite yearning, infinite regret. Dalgliesh persevered:

"So you live completely separately?"

"My own little quarters. This sitting room and a bedroom next door. My own small kitchenette through this door here. I won't show it to you now because it's not quite as I should like it to be."

"What precisely are the domestic arrangements, Miss Willard?"

"They get their own breakfast. The doctor usually lunches at the hospital, of course; Nell and William have something on a tray when she bothers to prepare it, and I look after myself. Then I cook a little something for everyone in the evenings, quite simple, we're none of us large eaters. We eat very early because of William. It's more a high tea really. Nell and her father do all the cooking during the weekend. It really works out quite well."

Quite well for you, thought Massingham. Certainly William had seemed sturdy and well-nourished enough, but the girl looked as if she ought to be at school, not struggling, almost unaided, with this isolated and cheerless monstrosity of a house. He wondered how she got on with Miss Willard. As if reading his thoughts, Miss Willard said:

"William is a sweet little boy. Absolutely no trouble. I hardly see him really. But Nell is difficult, very difficult. Girls of her age usually are. She needs a mother's firm hand. You know, of course, that Mrs. Kerrison walked out on her husband a year ago? She ran away with one of his colleagues at the hospital. It broke him up completely. Now she's trying to get the High Court to reverse the custody order and give her the children when the divorce is heard in a month's time, and I'm sure it'll be a good thing if they do. Children ought to be with their mother. Not that Nell's really a child any longer. It's the boy they're fighting over, not Nell. If you ask me, neither of them cares about her. She gives her father a terrible time of it. Nightmares, screaming attacks, asthma. He's going to London next Monday for a three-day conference on forensic pathology. I'm afraid she'll make him pay for that little jaunt when he gets back. Neurotic, you know. Punishing him for loving her brother more, although, of course, he can't see that."

Dalgliesh wondered by what mental process she had arrived at that glib psychological assessment. Not, he thought, that it was necessarily wrong. He felt profoundly sorry for Kerrison.

Suddenly Massingham felt sick. The warmth and feculent smell of the room overpowered him. A blob of cold sweat dropped on his notebook. Muttering an apology, he strode over to the window and tugged at the frame. It resisted for a moment, then slammed down. Great drafts of cool, reviving air poured in. The frail light before the carved Madonna flickered and went out.

When he got back to his notebook, Dalgliesh was already asking about the previous evening. Miss Willard said that she had cooked a meal of minced beef, potatoes, and frozen peas for supper, with a blancmange to follow. She had washed up alone and had then gone to say good night to the family before returning to her sitting room. They were then in the drawing room, but Dr. Kerrison and Nell were about to take William up to bed. She had seen and heard nothing else of the family until just after nine o'clock when she had gone to check that the front door was bolted. Dr. Kerrison was sometimes careless about locking up and didn't always appreciate how nervous she felt, sleeping alone and on the ground floor. One read such terrible stories. She had passed the study door, which was ajar, and had heard Dr. Kerrison speaking on the telephone. She had returned to her sitting room and had switched on the television.

Dr. Kerrison had looked in shortly before ten o'clock to talk to her about a small increase in her salary, but they had been interrupted by a telephone call. He had returned ten minutes or so later and they had been together for about half an hour. It had been pleasant to have the opportunity of a private chat without the children butting in. Then he had said good night and left her. She had switched on the television again and had watched it until nearly midnight, when she had gone to bed. If Dr. Kerrison had taken out the car, she felt fairly sure that she would have heard it since her sitting-room window looked out at the garage which was built at the side of the house. Well, they could see that for themselves.

She had overslept the next morning and hadn't breakfasted until after nine. She had been woken by the telephone ringing, but it hadn't been until Dr. Kerrison returned from the laboratory that she knew about Dr. Lorrimer's murder. Dr. Kerrison had returned briefly to the house shortly after nine o'clock to tell her and Nell what had happened and to ring the hospital to say that any calls for him should be transferred to the reception desk at the laboratory.

Dalgliesh said:

"I believe Dr. Lorrimer used to drive you to eleven o'clock service at St. Mary's at Guy's Marsh. He seems to have been a solitary and not a very happy man. No one seems to have known him well. I was wondering whether he found in you the companionship and friendship he seems to have lacked in his working life."

Massingham looked up, curious to see her response to this blatant invitation to self-revelation. She hooded her eyes like a bird, while a red blotch spread like a contagion over her throat. She said, with an attempt at archness:

"Now I'm afraid you're teasing me, Commander. It is Commander, isn't it? It seems so odd, just like a naval rank. My late brother-in-law was in the navy, so I know a little of these matters. But you were talking of friendship. That implies confidence. I should like to have helped him, but he wasn't easy to know. And there was the age difference. I'm not so very much older, less than five years, I suppose. But it's a great deal to a comparatively young man. No, I'm afraid we were just two reprobate High Anglicans in this Evangelical swampland. We didn't even sit together in church. I've always sat in the third pew down from the pulpit and he liked to be right at the back."

Dalgliesh persisted:

"But he must have enjoyed your company. He called for you every Sunday, didn't he?"

"Only because Father Gregory asked him. There is a bus to Guy's Marsh, but I have to wait half an hour and, as Dr. Lorrimer drove past the Old Rectory, Father Gregory suggested that it would be a sensible arrangement if we traveled together. He never came in. I was always ready and waiting for him outside the drive. If his father were ill or he himself was out on a case, he'd telephone. Sometimes he wasn't able to let me know, which was inconvenient. But I knew that if he didn't drive up at twenty to eleven he wouldn't be coming, and then I'd set off for the bus. Usually, of course, he came, except during the first six months of this year when he gave up Mass. But he rang early in September to say that he would be stopping for me as he used to. Naturally I never questioned him about the break. One does go through these dark nights of the soul."

So he had stopped going to Mass when the affair with Domenica Schofield began and had resumed his churchgoing after the break. Dalgliesh asked:

"Did he take the Sacrament?"

She was unsurprised by the question.

"Not since he started coming to Mass again in mid-September. It worried me a little, I confess. I did wonder whether to suggest to him that if anything was troubling him he should have a talk with Father Gregory. But one is on very delicate ground. And it really wasn't any concern of mine."

And she wouldn't want to offend him, thought Massingham. Those lifts in the car must have been very convenient. Dalgliesh asked:

"So he did very occasionally telephone you. Have you ever rung him?"

She turned away and fussed, plumping up a cushion.

"Dear me, no! Why should I? I don't even know his number."

Massingham said:

"It seems odd that he went to church at Guy's Marsh instead of in the village."

Miss Willard looked at him severely.

"Not at all. Mr. Swaffield is a very worthy man, but he's Low, very Low. The fens have always been strongly Evangelical. When my dear father was rector here, he had constant fights with the Parochical Church Council over Reservation. And then I think that Dr. Lorrimer didn't want to get drawn into church and village activities. It's so difficult not to once you're known as a regular member of the congregation. Father Gregory didn't expect that; he realized that Dr. Lorrimer had his own father to care for and a very demanding job. Incidentally, I was very distressed that the police didn't call for Father Gregory. Someone should have called a priest to the body."

Dalgliesh said gently:

"He had been dead some hours when the body was discovered, Miss Willard."

"Even so, he should have had a priest."

She stood up as if signifying that the interview was at an end. Dalgliesh was glad enough to go. He said his formal thanks and asked Miss Willard to get in touch with him immediately if anything of interest occurred to her. He and Massingham were at the door when she suddenly called out imperiously:

"Young man!"

The two detectives turned to look at her. She spoke directly to Massingham, like an old-fashioned nurse admonishing a child:

"Would you please shut the window which you so inconsiderately opened, and relight the candle."

Meekly, as if in obedience to long-forgotten nursery commands, Massingham did so. They were left to find their own way out of the house and saw no one. When they were in the car fastening their seat belts, Massingham exploded:

"Good God, you'd think Kerrison could find someone more suitable than that old hag to care for his children. She's a slut, a dipsomaniac, and she's half-mad."

"It's not so simple for Kerrison. A remote village, a large, cold house, and a daughter who can't be easy to cope with. Faced with the choice of that kind of job and the dole, most women today would probably opt for the dole. Did you take a look at the bonfire?"

"Nothing there. It looks as if they're periodically burning a lot of old furniture and garden rubbish which they've got stacked in one of the coach houses. William said that Nell made a bonfire early this morning."

"William can talk, then?" Dalgliesh asked.

"Oh, William can talk. But I'm not sure that you'd be able to understand him, sir. Did you believe Miss Willard when she gave that alibi for Kerrison?"

"I'm as ready to believe her as I am Mrs. Bradley or Mrs. Blakelock when they confirmed Bradley's and Blakelock's alibis. Who can tell? We know that Kerrison did ring Dr. Collingwood at nine and was here to receive his return call at about ten. If Miss Willard sticks to her story, he's in the clear for that hour, and I've a feeling that it's the crucial hour. But how did he know that? And if he did, why suppose that we should be able to pin down the time of death so precisely? Sitting with his daughter until nine and then calling on Miss Willard just before ten looks very like an attempt to establish that he was at home during the whole of that hour."

Massingham said:

"He must have been, to take that ten o'clock call. And I don't see how he could have got to Hoggatt's, killed Lorrimer, and returned home in less than sixty minutes, not if he went on foot. And Miss Willard seems confident that he didn't take the car. I suppose it would just be possible if he took a shortcut through the new laboratory, but it would be a close thing."

Just then the car radio beeped. Dalgliesh took the call. It was from the Guy's Marsh control room to say that Sergeant Reynolds at the lab wanted to contact them. The Met Lab report had been received.

## IV

They opened the door together. Mrs. Bradley held a sleeping child in her arms. Bradley said:

"Come in. It's about the vomit, isn't it? I've been expecting you."

They moved into the sitting room. He gestured Dalgliesh and

Massingham to the two chairs and sat down on the sofa opposite them. His wife moved close to him, shifting the baby's weight against her shoulder. Dalgliesh asked:

"Do you want a solicitor?"

"No. Not yet, anyway. I'm ready to tell the whole truth and it can't hurt me. At least, I suppose it can lose me my job. But that's the worst it can do. And I think I'm almost beyond caring."

Massingham opened his notebook. Dalgliesh said to Susan Bradley:

"Wouldn't you like to put the baby in her pram, Mrs. Bradley?"

She gazed at Dalgliesh with blazing eyes and shook her head vehemently, holding the child more tightly, as if she expected them to tear her from her arms. Massingham was grateful that at least the child was asleep. But he wished that neither she nor her mother were there. He looked at the baby, bunched in her pink sleeping suit against her mother's shoulder, the fringe of longer hair above the tender hollowed neck, the round bare patch at the back of the head, the close-shut eyes and ridiculous snubbed nose. The frail mother with her milky bundle was more inhibiting than a whole firm of recalcitrant anti-police lawyers.

There was a lot to be said for bundling a suspect into the back of a police car and taking him off to the station to make his statement in the functional anonymity of the interrogation room. Even the Bradleys' sitting room provoked in him a mixture of irritation and pity. It still smelled new and unfinished. There was no fireplace, and the television held pride of place above the wall-mounted electric heater with, above it, a popular print of waves dashing against a rocky shore. The wall opposite had been prepared to match the flowered curtains, but the other three were bare, the plaster already beginning to crack. There was a metal baby's high chair and, underneath it, a spread of plastic sheeting to protect the carpet. Everything looked new, as if they had brought to their marriage no accumulation of small personal impedimenta, had come spiritually naked into possession of this small, characterless room. Dalgliesh said:

"We'll take it that your previous account of your movements

on Wednesday night wasn't true, or was incomplete. So what did happen?"

Massingham wondered for a moment why Dalgliesh wasn't cautioning Bradley; then he thought he knew. Bradley might have had the guts to kill if provoked beyond endurance, but he'd never have had the nerve to drop from that third-floor window. And if he didn't, how did he get out of the laboratory? Lorrimer's killer had either used the keys or he had made that climb. All their investigations, all their careful and repeated examinations of the building, had confirmed that hypothesis. There was no other way.

Bradley looked at his wife. She gave him a brief, transforming smile and held out her free hand. He clasped it and they edged closer. He moistened his lips and then began speaking as if the speech had been long rehearsed.

"On Tuesday Dr. Lorrimer finished writing my annual confidential report. He told me he wanted to talk to me about it the next day before he passed it to Dr. Howarth, and he called me into his private room soon after he arrived in the lab. He'd given me an adverse report and, according to the rules, he had to explain why. I wanted to defend myself, but I couldn't. And there wasn't any real privacy. I felt that the whole laboratory knew what was happening and was listening and waiting. Besides, I was so frightened of him. I don't know why exactly. I can't explain it. He had such an effect on me that he'd only have to be working close to me in the laboratory and I'd start shaking. When he was away at a scene of crime it was like heaven. I could work perfectly well then. The annual confidential report wasn't unjust. I knew that my work had deteriorated. But he was partly the reason why. He seemed to take my inadequacy as a personal denigration of himself. Poor work was just intolerable to him. He was obsessed by my mistakes. And because I was so terrified, I made them all the more."

He paused for a moment. No one spoke. Then he went on:

"We weren't going to the village concert because we couldn't get a babysitter, and anyway, Sue's mother was coming for supper. I got home just before six. After the meal—the curry and rice and peas—I saw her off on the seven-forty-five bus. I came straight back here. But I kept thinking of the adverse report, what Dr. Howarth would say, what I was going to do if he recommended a move, how we could possibly sell this house. We had to buy when prices were at their peak, and it's almost impossible to find buyers now, except at a loss. Besides, I didn't think another lab would want me. After a time I thought I'd go back to the laboratory and confront him. I think I had some idea that we might be able to communicate, that I could speak to him as another human being and make him understand how I felt. Anyway, I felt that I would go mad if I stayed indoors. I had to walk somewhere, and I walked toward Hoggatt's. I didn't tell Sue what I was going to do, and she tried to persuade me not to go out. But I went."

He looked up at Dalgliesh and said:

"Can I have a drink of water?"

Without a word, Massingham got up and went to find the kitchen. He couldn't see the glasses, but there were two washed cups on the drain board. He filled one with cold water and brought it back to Bradley. Bradley drained it. He drew his hand over his moist mouth and went on:

"I didn't see anyone on the way to the laboratory. People don't walk out in this village much after dark, and I suppose most of them were at the concert. There was a light on in the hall of the laboratory. I rang the bell and Lorrimer came. He seemed surprised to see me but I said I wanted to speak to him. He looked at his watch and said he could only spare me five minutes. I followed him up to the Biology Lab."

He looked across directly at Dalgliesh. He said:

"It was a strange sort of interview. I sensed that he was impatient and wanted to get rid of me, and part of the time I thought that he hardly listened to what I was saying, or even knew that I was there. I didn't make a good job of it. I tried to explain that I wasn't being careless on purpose, that I really liked the work and wanted to make a success of it and be a credit to the department. I tried to explain the effect he had on me. I don't know whether he was listening. He stood there with his eyes fixed on the floor.

"And then he looked up and began speaking. He didn't really look at me, he was looking through me, almost as if I weren't there. And he was saying things, terrible things, as if they were words in a play, nothing to do with me. I kept hearing the same words over and over again. Failure. Useless. Hopeless. Inadequate. He even said something about marriage, as if I were a sexual failure too. I think he was mad. I can't explain what it was like, all this hate pouring out, hate and misery and despair. I stood there shaking with this stream of words pouring over me as if . . . as if it were filth. And then his eyes focused on me and I knew that he was seeing me, me, Clifford Bradley. His voice sounded quite different. He said:

" 'You're a third-rate biologist and a fourth-rate forensic scientist. That's what you were when you came into this department and you'll never change. I have two alternatives, to check every one of your results or to risk the Service and this laboratory being discredited in court. Neither is tolerable. So I suggest that you look for another job. And now I've things to do so please leave.'

"He turned his back on me and I went out. I knew that it was impossible. It would have been better not to have come. He'd never told me before exactly what he thought of me, not in those words, anyway. I felt sick and miserable, and I knew I was crying. That made me despise myself the more. I stumbled upstairs to the men's cloakroom and was just able to reach the first basin before I vomited. I don't remember how long I stood there, leaning over the basin, half crying and half vomiting. I suppose it could have been three or four minutes. After a time I put on the cold tap and swilled my face. Then I tried to pull myself together. But I was still shaking, and I felt sick. I went and sat on one of the lavatory seats and sank my head in my hands.

"I don't know how long I was there. Ten minutes perhaps, but it could have been longer. I knew I could never change his opinion of me, never make him understand. He wasn't like a human being. I realized that he hated me. But now I began to hate him and in a different way. I'd have to leave; I knew he'd see to that. But at least I could tell him what I thought of him. I could behave like a man. So I went down the stairs and into the Biology Laboratory."

Again he paused. The child stirred in her mother's arms and gave a little cry in her sleep. Susan Bradley began an automatic jogging and crooning, but kept her eyes on her husband. Then Bradley went on:

"He was lying between the two middle examination tables, face downward. I didn't wait to see whether he was dead. I know that I ought to feel dreadful about that, about the fact that I left him without getting help. But I don't. I can't make myself feel sorry. But at the time I wasn't glad that he was dead. I wasn't aware of any feeling except terror. I hurled myself downstairs and out of the laboratory as if his murderer were after me. The door was still on the Yale and I know that I must have drawn back the bottom bolt, but I can't remember. I raced down the drive. I think there was a bus passing, but it had started up before I reached the gate. When I got into the road it was disappearing. Then I saw a car approaching and instinctively, I stood back in the shadows of the walls. The car slowed down and turned into the laboratory drive. Then I made myself walk slowly and normally. And the next thing I remember was being home."

Susan Bradley spoke for the first time:

"Clifford told me all about it. But, of course, he had to. He looked so terrible that I knew something awful must have happened. We decided together what we'd better do. We knew that he'd had nothing to do with what had happened to Dr. Lorrimer. But who would believe Cliff? Everyone in the department knew what Dr. Lorrimer thought of him. He would be bound to be suspected anyway, and if you found out that he was there, in the laboratory, and at the very moment it happened, than how could he hope to persuade you that he wasn't guilty? So we decided to say that we'd been together the whole evening. My mother did ring about nine o'clock to say that she'd got safely home, and I told her that Cliff was having a bath. She'd never really liked my marriage and I didn't want to admit to her that he was out. She'd only start criticizing him for leaving me and the baby. So we knew that she could confirm what I'd said, and that might be some help, even though she hadn't spoken to him. And then Cliff remembered about the vomit."

Her husband went on, almost eagerly now, as if willing them to understand and believe:

"I knew I'd swilled cold water over my face, but I couldn't be certain that the bowl was clean. The more I thought about it, the more sure I was that it was stained with vomit. And I knew how much you could learn from that. I'm a secreter, but that didn't worry me. I knew that stomach acids would destroy the antibodies and that the lab wouldn't be able to determine my blood group. But there was the curry powder, the dye in the peas. They'd be able to say enough about that last meal to identify me. And I couldn't lie about what we'd had for supper because Sue's mother had been here sharing it with us.

"So we had this idea of trying to stop Mrs. Bidwell going early to the laboratory. I always get to work before nine, so I would be first on the scene quite naturally. If I went straight to the washroom as I normally would, and cleaned the bowl, then the only evidence that I was in the lab the previous evening would be gone forever. No one would ever know."

Susan Bradley said:

"It was my idea to phone Mrs. Bidwell, and I was the one who spoke to her husband. We knew that she wouldn't answer the phone. She never did. But Cliff hadn't realized that old Mr. Lorrimer wasn't entering hospital the previous day. He was out of the department when old Mr. Lorrimer rang. So the plan went all wrong. Mr. Lorrimer telephoned Inspector Blakelock, and everyone arrived at the lab almost as soon as Cliff. After that, there was nothing we could do but wait."

Dalgliesh could imagine how terrible that time of waiting had been. No wonder that Bradley hadn't been able to face going into the lab. He asked:

"When you rang the bell at the laboratory, how long was it before Dr. Lorrimer answered?"

"Almost immediately. He couldn't have come down from the Biology Department. He must have been somewhere on the ground floor."

"Did he say anything at all about expecting a visitor?"

The temptation was obvious. But Bradley said:

"No. He talked about having things to do, but I took it that he meant the analysis he was working on."

"And when you found the body, you saw and heard nothing of the murderer?"

"No. I didn't wait to look, of course. But I'm sure he was there and very close. I don't know why."

"Did you notice the position of the mallet, the fact that there was a page missing from Lorrimer's notebook?"

"No. Nothing. All I can remember is Lorrimer, the body, and the thin stream of blood."

"When you were in the washroom, did you hear the doorbell?"

"No, but I don't think I could have heard it, not above the first floor. And I'm sure I wouldn't have heard it while I was being sick."

"When Dr. Lorrimer opened the door to you, did anything strike you as unusual, apart from the fact that he came so promptly?"

"Nothing, except that he was carrying his notebook."

"Are you quite sure?"

"Yes, I'm sure. It was folded back."

So Bradley's arrival had interrupted what it was that Lorrimer had been doing. And he had been on the ground floor, the floor with the Director's office, the Records Department, the Exhibits Store.

Dalgliesh said:

"The car that turned into the drive as you left—what sort of car?"

"I didn't see. All I can remember are the headlights. We don't have a car and I'm not clever at recognizing the different models unless I get a clear look."

"Can you remember how it was driven? Did the driver turn into the drive confidently as if he knew where he was going? Or did he hesitate as if he were looking for a convenient spot to stop and happened to see the open driveway?"

"He just slowed down a little and drove straight in. I think it was someone who knew the place. But I didn't wait to see if he drove up to the lab. Next day, of course, I knew that it couldn't have been the police from Guy's Marsh or anyone with a key, or the body would have been discovered earlier."

He looked at Dalgliesh with his anxious eyes.

"What will happen to me now? I can't face them at the lab."

"Inspector Massingham will drive you to Guy's Marsh police station so that you can make a formal statement and sign it. I'll explain to Dr. Howarth what has happened. Whether you go back to the lab and when must be for him and your Establishment Department to say. I imagine they may decide to give you special leave until this affair is settled."

If it ever were settled. If Bradley were telling the truth, they now knew that Lorrimer had died between eight-forty-five, when his father had telephoned him, and just before nine-eleven, when the Guy's Marsh bus had moved away from the Chevisham stop. The clue of the vomit had fixed for them the time of death, had solved the mystery of the call to Mrs. Bidwell. But it hadn't pointed them to a murderer. And if Bradley were innocent, what sort of life would he have, inside or outside the Forensic Science Service, unless the case were solved? He watched Massingham and Bradley on their way, then set out to walk the half-mile back to Hoggatt's, not relishing the prospect of his interview with Howarth. Glancing back, he saw that Susan Bradley was still standing at the doorway looking after him, her baby in her arms.

## V

Howarth said:

"I'm not going to trot out the usual platitude about blaming myself. I don't believe in that spurious acceptance of vicarious liability. All the same, I ought to have known that Bradley was near breaking point. I suspect that old Dr. MacIntyre wouldn't have let this happen. And now I'd better telephone the Establishment Department. I expect they'll want him to stay at home for the present. It's particularly inconvenient from the point of view of the work. They need every pair of hands they can get in the Biology Department. Claire Easterbrook is taking on as much of Lorrimer's work as she can manage, but there's a limit to what she can do. At the moment she's busy with the clunch pit analysis. She's insisting on starting the electrophoresis again. I don't blame her; she's the one who'll have to give evidence. She can only speak for her own results."

Dalgliesh asked what was likely to happen about Clifford Bradley.

"Oh, there'll be a regulation to cover the circumstances somewhere. There always is. He'll be dealt with by the usual compromise between expediency and humanity; unless, of course, you propose to arrest him for murder, in which case, administratively speaking, the problem will solve itself. By the way, the Public Relations Branch has rung. You probably haven't had time to see today's press. Some of the papers are getting rather agitated about the lab security. 'Are our blood samples safe?' And one of the Sundays has commissioned an article on science in the service of crime. They're sending someone to see me at three o'clock. Public Relations would like a word with you, incidentally. They're hoping to lay on another press conference later this afternoon."

When Howarth had left, Dalgliesh joined Sergeant Underhill and occupied himself with the four large bundles of files which Brenda Pridmore had provided. It was extraordinary how many of six thousand cases and nearly twenty-five thousand exhibits which the laboratory dealt with each year had the numbers 18, 40, or 1840 in their registration. The cases came from all the departments: Biology, Toxicology, Criminalistics, Document Examination, Blood Alcohol Analysis, Vehicle Examination. Nearly every scientist in the laboratory above the level of Higher Scientific Officer had been concerned in them. All of them seemed perfectly in order. He was still convinced that the mysterious telephone message to Lorrimer held the clue to the mystery of his death. But it seemed increasingly unlikely that the numbers, if old Mr. Lorrimer had remembered them correctly, bore any reference to a file registration.

By three o'clock he had decided to put the task on one side and see if physical exercise would stimulate his brain. It was time, he thought, to walk through the grounds and take a look at the Wren chapel. He was reaching for his coat when the telephone rang. It was Massingham from Guy's Marsh station. The car that had parked in Hoggatt's drive on Wednesday night had at last been traced. It was a gray Cortina belonging to a Mrs. Maureen Doyle. Mrs. Doyle was at present staying with her parents in Ilford in Essex, but she had confirmed that the car was hers and that on the night of the murder it had been driven by her husband, Detective-Inspector Doyle.

# VI

The interview room at Guy's Marsh police station was small, stuffy, and overcrowded. Superintendent Mercer, with his great bulk, was taking up more than his share of space and, it seemed to Massingham, breathing more than his share of the air. Of the five men present, including the shorthand writer, Doyle himself appeared both the most comfortable and the least concerned. Dalgliesh was questioning him. Mercer stood against the mullioned windows.

"You were at Hoggatt's last night. There are fresh tire marks in the earth under the trees to the right of the entrance, your tire marks. If you want to waste time for both of us, you can look at the casts."

"I admit that they're my tire marks. I parked there, briefly, on Monday night."

"Why?"

The question was so quiet, so reasonable, he might have had a genuine, human interest to know.

"I was with someone." He paused and then added, "Sir."

"I hope, for your sake, that you were with someone last night. Even an embarrassing alibi is better than none. You quarreled with Lorrimer. You're one of the few people he would have let into the lab. And you parked your car under the trees. If you didn't murder him, why are you trying to persuade us that you did?"

"You don't really believe I killed him. Probably you already suspect or know who did. You can't frighten me, because I know you haven't any evidence. There isn't any to get. I was driving the Cortina because the clutch had gone on the Renault, not because I didn't want to be recognized. I was with Sergeant Beale until eight o'clock. We'd been to interview a man called Barry Taylor at Muddington, and then we went on to see one or two other people who'd been at the dance last Tuesday. From eight o'clock I was driving alone, and where I went was my own business."

"Not when it's a case of murder. Isn't that what you tell your suspects when they come out with that good old bromide about the sanctity of their private lives? You can do better than that, Doyle."

"I wasn't at the lab on Wednesday night. Those tire marks were made when I parked there last Monday."

"The Dunlop on the left-hand back wheel is new. It was fitted on Monday afternoon by Gorringe's garage, and your wife didn't collect the Cortina until ten o'clock on Wednesday morning. If you didn't drive to Hoggatt's to see Lorrimer, then what were you doing there? And if your business was legitimate, then why park just inside the entrance and under the trees?"

"If I'd been there to murder Lorrimer, I'd have parked in one of the garages at the back. That would have been safer than leaving the Cortina in the drive. And I didn't get to Hoggatt's until after nine. I knew that Lorrimer would be working late on the clunch pit case, but not that late. The lab was in darkness. The truth, if you must know, is that I'd picked up a woman at the crossroads just outside Manea. I wasn't in any hurry to get home, and I wanted somewhere quiet and secluded to stop. The lab seemed as good a place as any. We were there from about nine-fifteen until nine-fifty-five. No one left during that time."

He had taken his time over what was presumably intended to be a quick one-night lay, thought Massingham. Dalgliesh asked:

"Did you trouble to find out who she was, exchanging names?"

"I told her that I was Ronny McDowell. It seemed as good a name as any. She said she was Dora Meakin. I don't suppose that more than one of us was lying."

"And that's all, not where she lived or worked?"

"She said she worked at the sugar-beet factory and lived in a cottage near the ruined engine house on Hunter's Fen. That's about three miles from Manea. She said she was a widow. Like a little gentleman, I dropped her at the bottom of the lane leading to Hunter's Fen. If she wasn't telling me a yarn, that should be enough to find her."

Chief Superintendent Mercer said grimly:

"I hope for your sake that it is. You know what this means for you, of course?"

Doyle laughed. It was a surprisingly light-hearted sound.

"Oh I know, all right. But don't let that worry you. I'm handing in my resignation, and from now."

Dalgliesh asked:

"Are you sure about the lights? The lab was in darkness?"

"I shouldn't have stopped there if it hadn't been. There wasn't a light to be seen. And although I admit I was somewhat preoccupied for a minute or two, I could swear that no one came down that drive while we were there."

"Or out of the front door?"

"That would be possible, I suppose. But the drive isn't more than forty yards long, I'd say. I think I'd have noticed, unless he slipped out very quickly. I doubt whether anyone would have risked it, not if he'd seen my headlights and knew that the car was there."

Dalgliesh looked at Mercer. He said:

"We've got to get back to Chevisham. We'll take in Hunter's Fen on the way."

# VII

Leaning over the back of the Victorian chaise longue, Angela Foley was massaging her friend's neck. The coarse hairs tickled the back of her hands as, firmly and gently, she kneaded the taut muscles, feeling for each separate vertebra under the hot, tense skin. Stella sat, head slumped forward in her hands. Neither spoke. Outside, a light, scavenging wind was blowing fitfully over the fens, stirring the fallen leaves on the patio and gusting the thin, white wood smoke from the cottage chimney. But inside the sitting room all was quiet, except for the crackling of the fire, the ticking of the grandfather clock, and the sound of their breathing. The cottage was full of the pungent, resinous aroma of burning apple wood, overlaid with the savory smell from the kitchen of beef casserole reheated from yesterday's dinner.

After a few minutes Angela Foley said:

"Better? Would you like a cold compress on your forehead?"

"No, that's lovely. Almost gone in fact. Odd that I only get a headache on those days when the book has gone particularly well."

"Another two minutes, then I'd better see about dinner."

Angela flexed her fingers and bent again to her task. Stella's voice, muffled in her sweater, suddenly said:

"What was it like as a child, being in local authority care?"

"I'm not sure that I know. I mean, I wasn't in a Home or anything like that. They fostered me most of the time."

"Well, what was that like? You've never really told me."

"It was all right. No, that's not true. It was like living in a second-rate boarding house where they don't want you and you know that you won't be able to pay the bill. Until I met you and came here I felt like that all the time, not really at home in the world. I suppose my foster parents were kind. They meant to be. But I wasn't pretty, and I wasn't grateful. It can't be much fun fostering other people's children, and I suppose one does rather look for gratitude. Looking back, I can see that I wasn't much joy for them, plain and surly. I once heard a neighbor say to my third foster mother that I looked just like a fetus with my bulging forehead and tiny features. I resented the other children because they had mothers and I hadn't. I've never really outgrown that. It's despicable, but I even dislike Brenda Pridmore, the new girl on our reception desk, because she's so obviously a loved child, she's got a proper home."

"So have you now. But I know what you mean. By the age of five you've either learned that the world is good, and everything and everyone in it stretches out toward you with love. Or you know that you're a reject. No one ever unlearns that first lesson."

"I have, because of you. Star, don't you think we ought to start looking for another cottage, perhaps nearer Cambridge? There's bound to be a job there for a qualified secretary."

"We're not going to need another cottage. I telephoned my publishers this afternoon, and I think it's going to be all right."

"Hearne and Collingwood? But how can it be all right? I thought you said . . ."

"It's going to be all right."

Suddenly Stella shook herself free of the ministering hands and stood up. She went into the passage and came back, her duffle coat over her shoulder, her boots in hand. She moved over to the fireside chair and began to pull them on. Angela Foley watched her without speaking. Then Stella took from her jacket pocket a brown opened envelope and tossed it across. It fell on the velvet of the chaise longue.

"Oh, I meant to show you this."

Puzzled, Angela took out the single folded sheet. She said:

"Where did you find this?"

"I took it from Edwin's desk when I was rummaging about for the will. I thought at the time that I might have a use for it. Now I've decided that I haven't."

"But, Star, you should have left it for the police to find! It's a clue. They'll have to know. This was probably what Edwin was doing that night, checking up. It's important. We can't keep it to ourselves."

"Then you'd better go back to Postmill Cottage and pretend to find it, otherwise it's going to be a bit embarrassing explaining how we came by it."

"But the police aren't going to believe that; they wouldn't have missed it. I wonder when it arrived at the lab. It's odd that he took it home with him and didn't even lock it up."

"Why should he? There was only the one locked drawer in his desk. And I don't suppose anyone, even his father, ever went into that room."

"But Star, this could explain why he was killed! This could be a motive for murder."

"Oh, I don't think so. It's just a gratuitous bit of spite, anonymous, proving nothing. Edwin's death was both simpler and more complicated than that. Murder usually is. But the police might see it as a motive, and I agree that would be convenient for us. I'm beginning to think I should have left it where it was."

She had pulled on her boots and was ready to go. Angela Foley said:

"You know who killed him, don't you?"

"Does that shock you, that I haven't rushed to confide in that extraordinarily personable Commander?"

Angela whispered:

"What are you going to do?"

"Nothing. I've no proof. Let the police do the work they're paid for. I might have had more public spirit when we had the death penalty. I'm not afraid of the ghosts of hanged men. They can stand at the four corners of my bed and howl all night if it pleases them. But I couldn't go on living—I couldn't go on working, which amounts to the same thing for me—knowing that I'd put another human being in prison, and for life."

"Not really for life. About ten years."

"I couldn't stand it for ten days. I'm going out now. I shan't be long."

"But, Star, it's nearly seven! We were going to eat."

"The casserole won't spoil."

Angela Foley watched silently as her friend went to the door. Then she said:

"Star, how did you know about Edwin practicing his evidence the night before he had to go into the box?"

"If you didn't tell me, and you say that you didn't, then I must have invented it. I couldn't have learned it from anyone else. You'd better put it down to creative imagination."

Her hand was on the door. Angela cried out:

"Star, don't go out tonight! Stay with me. I'm afraid."

"For yourself, or for me?"

"For both of us. Please don't go. Not tonight."

Stella turned. She smiled and spread her hands in what could have been a gesture of resignation or a farewell. There was a howl of wind, a rush of cold air as the front door opened. Then the sound of its closing echoed through the cottage, and Stella was gone.

# VIII

"My God, this is a dreary place!"

Massingham slammed the car door and gazed about in disbelief at the prospect before them. The lane, down which they had bumped in the fading light, had at last ended at a narrow iron bridge over a sluice, running gray and sluggish as oil, between high dikes. On the other bank was a derelict Victorian engine house, the bricks tumbled in a disorderly heap beside the stagnant stream, the great wheel half visible through the ruined wall. Beside it were two cottages lying below water level. Behind them the scarred and sullen acres of the hedgeless fields stretched to the red and purple of the evening sky. The carcass of a petrified tree, a bog oak, struck by the plow and dredged from the depths of the peat, had been dumped beside the track to dry. It looked like some mutilated prehistoric creature raising its stumps to the uncomprehending sky. Although the last two days had been dry with some sun, the landscape looked saturated by the weeks of rain, the front gardens sour and waterlogged, the trunks of the few stunted trees sodden as pulp. It looked a country on which the sun could never shine. As their feet rang on the iron bridge a solitary duck rose with an agitated squawking, but otherwise the silence was absolute.

There was a light behind the drawn curtains of only one of the cottages, and they walked between windblown clumps of faded Michaelmas daisies to the front door. The paint was peeling, the iron knocker so stiff that Dalgliesh raised it with difficulty. For a few minutes after the dull, peremptory thud there was silence. Then the door was opened.

They saw a drab, sallow-faced woman, aged about forty, with pale, anxious eyes and untidy straw-colored hair strained back under two combs. She was wearing a brown checked dress topped with a bulky cardigan in a harsh shade of blue. As soon as he saw her, Massingham instinctively drew back with an apology, but Dalgliesh said:

"Mrs. Meakin? We're police officers. May we come in?"

She didn't trouble to look at his proffered identity card. She hardly seemed surprised even. Without speaking she pressed herself against the wall of the passage and they passed before her into the sitting room. It was small and very plainly furnished, drearily tidy and uncluttered. The air smelled damp and chill. There was an electric reflector fire with one bar burning, and the single pendant bulb gave a harsh but inadequate light. A plain wooden table stood in the middle of the room, with four chairs. She was obviously about to start her supper. On a tray there was a plate of three fish fingers, a mound of mashed potato, and peas. Beside it was an unopened carton containing an apple tart.

Dalgliesh said:

"I'm sorry that we're interrupting your meal. Would you like to take it into the kitchen to keep it warm?" She shook her head and motioned them to sit down. They settled themselves around the table like three card players, the tray of food between them. The peas were exuding a greenish liquid in which the fish fingers were slowly congealing. It was hard to believe that so small a meal could produce so strong a smell. After a few seconds, as if conscious of it, she pushed the tray to one side. Dalgliesh took out Doyle's photograph and passed it across to her. He said:

"I believe you spent some time yesterday evening with this man."

"Mr. McDowell. He's not in any trouble, is he? You're not private detectives? He was kind, a real gentleman. I wouldn't like to get him into trouble."

Her voice was low and rather toneless, not, Dalgliesh thought, a countrywoman's voice. He said:

"No, we're not private detectives. He is in some trouble, but not because of you. We're police officers. You can help him best by telling the truth. What we're really interested in is when you first met him and how long you were together."

She looked across at him.

"You mean, a sort of alibi?"

"That's right. A sort of alibi."

"He picked me up where I usually stand, at the crossroads, about half a mile from Manea. That must have been about seven. Then we drove to a pub. They nearly always start off by buying me a drink. That's the part I like, having someone to sit with in the pub, watching the people, hearing the voices and the noise. I usually have a sherry, or a port, maybe. If they ask me, I have a second. I never have more than two drinks. Sometimes they're in a hurry to get away so I only get offered the one."

Dalgliesh asked quietly:

"Where did he take you?"

"I don't know where it was, but it was about thirty minutes' drive. I could see him thinking where to go before he drove off. That's how I know he lives locally. They like to get clear of the district where they're known. I've noticed that, that and the quick look around they give before we go into the pub. The pub was called the Plough. I saw that from the illuminated sign outside. We were in the saloon bar, of course, quite nice really. They had a peat fire and there was a high shelf with a lot of different colored plates around it and two vases of artificial roses behind the bar, and a black cat in front of the fire. The barman was called Joe. He was ginger-haired."

"How long did you stay there?"

"Not long. I had two ports and he had two doubles of whisky. Then he said we ought to be going."

"Where did he take you next, Mrs. Meakin?"

"I think it was Chevisham. I glimpsed the signpost at the crossroads just before we got there. We turned into the drive of this big house and parked under the trees. I asked who lived there, and he said no one, it was just used for government offices. Then he put out the lights."

Dalgliesh said gently:

"And you made love in the car. Did you get into the back seat, Mrs. Meakin?"

She was neither surprised nor distressed at the question.

"No, we stayed in the front."

"Mrs. Meakin, this is very important. Can you remember how long you were there?"

"Oh yes, I could see the clock on the dashboard. It was nearly a quarter past nine when we arrived and we stayed there until just before ten. I know because I was a bit worried wondering whether he'd drop me at the end of the lane. That's all I expected. I wouldn't have wanted him to come to the door. But it can be awkward if I'm just left, miles from home. Sometimes it isn't easy to get back."

She spoke, thought Massingham, as if she were complaining about the local bus service. Dalgliesh said:

"Did anyone leave the house and come down the drive while you were in the car? Would you have noticed if they had?"

"Oh yes, I think so. I should have seen if they'd gone out through the space where the gate used to be. There's a street light opposite and it shines on the drive."

Massingham asked bluntly:

"But would you have noticed? Weren't you a bit occupied?"

Suddenly she laughed, a hoarse, discordant sound which startled them both.

"Do you think I was enjoying myself? Do you suppose I like it?" Then her voice again became toneless, almost subservient. She said obdurately:

"I should have noticed."

Dalgliesh asked:

"What did you talk about, Mrs. Meakin?"

The question brightened her. She turned to Dalgliesh almost eagerly.

"Oh, he's got his troubles. Everyone has, haven't they? Sometimes it helps to talk to a stranger, someone you know you won't ever see again. They never do ask to see me again. He didn't. But he was kind, not in a rush to get away. Sometimes they almost push me out of the car. That isn't gentlemanly; it's hurtful. But he seemed glad to talk. It was about his wife really. Not wanting to live in the country. She's a London girl and keeps nagging him to get back there. She wants him to leave his job and go and work for her father. She's at home with her parents now and he doesn't know whether she'll come back."

"He didn't tell you he was a police officer?"

"Oh no! He said he was a dealer in antiques. He seemed to know quite a lot about them. But I don't take much notice when they tell me about their jobs. Mostly they pretend."

Dalgliesh said gently:

"Mrs. Meakin, what you are doing is terribly risky. You know that, don't you? Some day a man will stop who wants more than an hour or so of your time, someone dangerous."

"I know. Sometimes when the car slows down and I'm standing there waiting at the side of the road, wondering what he'll be like, I can hear my heart thudding. I know then that I'm afraid. But at least I'm feeling something. It's better to be afraid than alone."

Massingham said:

"It's better to be alone than dead."

She looked at him.

"You think so, sir? But then you don't know anything about it, do you?"

Five minutes later they left, having explained to Mrs. Meakin that a police officer would call for her next day so that she could be taken to make a statement at Guy's Marsh station. She seemed perfectly happy about this, only asking whether anyone at the factory need know. Dalgliesh reassured her.

When they had crossed the bridge, Massingham turned to look back at the cottage. She was still standing at the door, a thin figure silhouetted against the light. He said angrily:

"God, it's all so hopeless. Why doesn't she get out of here, move to a town, Ely or Cambridge, see some life?"

"You sound like one of those professionals whose advice to the lonely is always the same: 'Get out and meet people, join a club.' Which, come to think of it, is precisely what she's doing."

"It would help if she got away from this place, found herself a different job."

"What job? She probably thinks that she's lucky to be employed. And this is at least a home. It takes youth, energy, and money to change your whole life. She hasn't any of those. All she can do is to keep sane in the only way she knows."

"But for what? To end up another corpse dumped in a clunch pit?"

"Perhaps. That's probably what she's subconsciously looking for. There's more than one way of courting death. She would argue that her way at least gives her the consolation of a warm, brightly lit bar and, always, the hope that, next time, it may be different. She isn't going to stop because a couple of intruding policemen tell her that it's dangerous. She knows about that. For God's sake let's get out of here."

As they buckled their seat belts, Massingham said:

"Who'd have thought that Doyle would have bothered with her. I can imagine him picking her up. As Lord Chesterfield said, all cats are gray in the dark. But to spend the best part of an hour telling her his troubles."

"They each wanted something from the other. Let's hope they got it."

"Doyle got something: an alibi. And we haven't done too badly out of their encounter. We know now who killed Lorrimer."

Dalgliesh said:

"We think we know who and how. We may even think we know why. But we haven't a scintilla of proof and without evidence we can't move another step. At present, we haven't even enough facts to justify applying for a search warrant."

"What now, sir?"

"Back to Guy's Marsh. When this Doyle affair is settled I want to hear Underhill's report and speak to the Chief Constable. Then back to Hoggatt's. We'll park where Doyle parked. I'd like to check whether it would be possible for someone to sneak down that drive without being seen."

# IX

By seven o'clock the work was at last up to date, the last court report had been checked, the last completed exhibit packed for the police to collect, the figures of cases and exhibits received had been calculated and checked. Brenda thought how tired Inspector Blakelock seemed. He had hardly spoken an unnecessary word during the last hour. She didn't feel that he was displeased with her, merely that he hardly knew she was there. She had talked little herself, and then in whispers, afraid to break the silence, eerie and almost palpable, of the empty hall. To her right the great staircase curved upward into darkness. All day it had echoed to the feet of scientists, policemen, scene of crime officers arriving for their lecture. Now it had become as portentous and threatening as the staircase of a haunted house. She tried not to look at it, but it drew her eyes irresistibly. With every fleeting upward glance she half imagined that she could see Lorrimer's white face forming out of the amorphous shadows to hang imprinted on the still air, Lorrimer's black eyes gazing down at her in entreaty or despair.

At seven o'clock Inspector Blakelock said:

"Well, that's about all then. Your mum won't be best pleased that you've been kept late tonight."

Brenda said with more confidence than she felt:

"Oh, Mum won't mind. She knew I was late starting. I rang her earlier and said not to expect me until half past."

They went their separate ways to collect their coats. Then Brenda waited by the door until Inspector Blakelock had set and checked the internal alarm. All the doors of the separate laboratories had been closed and checked earlier in the evening. Lastly they went out by the front door and he turned the two final keys. Brenda's bicycle was kept in a shed by the side of the old stables, where the cars were garaged. Still together, they went around to the back. Inspector Blakelock waited to start his car until she had mounted, then followed her very slowly down the drive. At the gate he gave a valedictory hoot and turned to the left. Brenda waved and set off briskly, pedaling in the opposite direction. She thought she knew why the Inspector had waited so carefully until she was safely off the premises, and she felt grateful. Perhaps, she thought, I remind him of his dead daughter and that's why he's so kind to me.

And then, almost immediately, it happened. The sudden bump and the scrape of metal against tarmac were unmistakable. The bicycle lurched, almost throwing her into the ditch. Squeezing on both brakes she dismounted and examined the tires by the light of the heavy flashlight which she always kept in her bicycle saddlebag. Both were flat. Her immediate reaction was one of intense irritation. This would happen on a late night! She swept the flashlight beam over the road behind her, trying to identify the source of the mishap. There must be glass or something sharp on the road somewhere. But she could see nothing and realized that it wouldn't help if she did. There was no hope of repairing the punctures. The next bus home was the one due to pass the laboratory just after nine o'clock, and there was no one left at the lab to give her a lift. She spent very little time in thinking. The best plan was obviously to return the bicycle to its rack and then make her way home through the new laboratory. It would cut off nearly a couple of miles and, if she walked fast, she could be home just after seven-thirty.

Anger, and ineffective railing against bad luck, is a powerful antidote to fear. So is hunger and the healthy tiredness that longs for its own fireside. Brenda had jerked the bicycle, now reduced to a ridiculously antiquated encumbrance, back into its stand and had walked briskly through the grounds of Hoggatt's and unbolted the wooden gate that led to the new site before she began to feel afraid. But now, alone in the darkness, the half-superstitious dread, which it had seemed safe to stimulate in the laboratory with Inspector Blakelock so reassuringly by her side, began to prick at her nerves. Before her the black bulk of the half-completed laboratory loomed like some prehistoric monument, its great slabs bloodstained with ancient sacrifices, rearing upward toward the implacable gods. The night was fitfully dark with a low ceiling of cloud obscuring the faint stars.

As she hesitated, the clouds parted like ponderous hands to unveil the full moon, frail and transparent as a Communion wafer. Gazing at it she could almost taste the remembered transitory dough, melting against the roof of her mouth. Then the clouds formed again and the darkness closed about her. And the wind was rising.

She held the flashlight more firmly. It was solidly reassuring and heavy in her hand. Resolutely she picked out her way between the tarpaulin-shrouded piles of bricks, the great girders laid in rows, the two neat huts on stilts which served as the contractor's office, toward the gap in the brickwork that marked the entrance to the main site. Then once again she hesitated. The gap seemed to narrow before her eyes, to become almost symbolically ominous and frightening, an entrance to darkness and the unknown. The fears of a childhood not so far distant reasserted themselves. She was tempted to turn back.

Then she admonished herself sternly not to be stupid. There was nothing strange or sinister about a half-completed building, an artifact of brick, concrete, and steel, holding no memories of the past, concealing no secret miseries between ancient walls. Besides, she knew the site quite well. The laboratory staff weren't supposed to take a shortcut through the new buildings—Dr. Howarth had pinned up a notice on the staff notice board pointing out the dangers—but everyone knew that it was done. Before the building had been started there had been a footpath across Hoggatt's field. It was natural for people to behave as if it were still there. And she was tired and hungry. It was ridiculous to hesitate now.

Then she remembered her parents. No one at home could know about the punctures and her mother would soon begin worrying. She or her father would probably ring the laboratory and, getting no reply, would know that everyone had left. They would imagine her dead or injured on the road, being lifted unconscious into an ambulance. Worse, they would see her lying crumpled on the floor of the laboratory, a second victim. It had been difficult enough to persuade her parents to let her stay on in the job, and this final anxiety, growing with every minute she was overdue and culminating in the relief and reactive anger of her late appearance, might easily tip them into an unreasoned but obstinate insistence that she should leave. It really was the worst possible time to be late home. She shone her flashlight steadily on the entrance gap and moved resolutely into the darkness.

She tried to picture the model of the new laboratory set up in the library. This large vestibule, still unroofed, must be the reception area from which the two main wings diverged. She must bear to the left through what would be the Biology Department for the quickest cut to the Guy's Marsh road. She swept the beam over the brick walls, then picked her way carefully across the uneven ground toward the left-hand aperture. The pool of light found another doorway, and then another. The darkness seemed to increase, heavy with the smell of brick dust and pressed earth. And now the pale haze of the night sky was extinguished and she was in the roofed area of the laboratory. The silence was absolute.

She found herself creeping forward, breath held, eyes fixed in a stare on the small pool of light at her feet. And suddenly there was nothing, no sky above, no doorway, nothing but black darkness. She swept the light over the walls. They were menacingly close. This room was surely far too small even for an office. She seemed to have stumbled into some kind of cupboard or storeroom. Somewhere, she knew, there must be a gap, the one by which she had entered. But, disoriented in the claustrophobic darkness, she could no longer distinguish the ceiling from the walls. With every sweep of the torch the crude bricks seemed to be closing in on her, the ceiling to descend inexorably like the slowly closing lid of a tomb. Fighting for control, she inched gradually along one wall, telling herself that, soon, she must strike the open doorway.

Suddenly the flashlight jerked in her hand and the pool of light spilled over the floor. She stopped dead, appalled at her peril. In the middle of the room was a square protected only by two planks thrown across it. One step in panic and she might have kicked them away, stumbled, and dropped into inky nothingness. In her imagination the well was fathomless; her body would never be found. She would lie there in the mud and darkness, too weak to make herself heard. And all she would hear would be the distant voices of the workmen as, brick on brick, they walled her up alive in her black tomb. And then another and more rational horror struck.

She thought about the punctured tires. Could that really have been an accident? The tires had been sound when she had parked the bicycle that morning. Perhaps it hadn't been glass on the road after all. Perhaps someone had done it purposely, someone who knew that she would be late leaving the lab, that there would be no one left to give her a lift, that she would be bound to walk through the new building. She pictured him in the darkness of the early evening, slipping soundlessly into the bicycle shed, knife in hand, crouching down to the tires, listening for the hiss of escaping air, calculating how big a rent would cause the tires to collapse before she had cycled too far on her journey. And now he was waiting for her, knife in hand, somewhere in the darkness. He had smiled, fingering the blade, listening for her every step, watching for the beam of her flashlight. He, too, would have a flashlight, of course. Soon it would blaze into her face, blinding her eyes, so that she couldn't see the cruel, triumphant mouth, the flashing knife. Instinctively she switched off the light and listened, her heart pounding with such a thunder of blood that she felt that even the brick walls must shake.

And then she heard the noise, gentle as a single footfall, soft as the brush of a coat sleeve against wood. He was coming. He was here.

And now there was only panic. Sobbing, she threw herself from side to side against the walls, thudding her bruised palms against the gritty, unyielding brick. Suddenly there was a space. She fell through, tripped, and the flashlight spun out of her hands. Moaning, she lay and waited for death. Then terror swooped with a wild screech of exultation and a thrashing of wings which lifted the hair from her scalp. She screamed, a thin wail of sound that was lost in the bird's cry as the owl found the paneless window and soared into the night.

She didn't know how long she lay there, her sore hands clutching the earth, her mouth choked with dust. But after a while she controlled her sobbing and lifted her head. She saw the window plainly, an immense square of luminous light, pricked with stars. And to the right of it gleamed the doorway. She scrambled to her feet. She didn't wait to search for the flashlight but made straight for that blessed aperture of light. Beyond it was another. And, suddenly, there were no more walls, only the spangled dome of the sky swinging above her.

Still sobbing, but now with relief, she ran unthinkingly in the moonlight, her hair streaming behind her, her feet hardly seeming to touch the earth. And now there was a belt of trees before her and, gleaming through the autumn branches, the Wren chapel, lit from within, beckoning and holy, shining like a picture on a Christmas card. She ran toward it, palms outstretched, as hundreds of her forebears in the dark fens must have rushed to their altars for sanctuary. The door was ajar and a shaft of light lay like an arrow on the path. She threw herself against the oak, and the great door swung inward into a glory of light.

At first her mind, shocked into stupor, refused to recognize what her dazzled eyes so clearly saw. Uncomprehending, she put up a tentative hand and stroked the soft corduroy of the slacks, the limp, moist hand. Slowly, as if by an act of will, her eyes traveled upward and she both saw and understood. Stella Mawson's face, dreadful in death, drooped above her, the eyes half open, the palms disposed outward as if in a mute appeal for pity or for help. Circling her neck was a double cord of blue silk, its tasseled end tied high to a hook on the wall. Beside it, wound on a second hook, was the single bell rope. There was a low wooden chair upended close to the dangling feet. Brenda seized it. Moaning, she grasped at the rope and swung on it three times before it slipped from her loosening hands, and she fainted.

## X

Less than a mile away across the field and the grounds of Hoggatt's, Massingham drove the Rover into the laboratory drive and backed into the bushes. He switched off the car lights. The street lamp opposite the entrance cast a soft glow over the path, and the door of the laboratory was plainly visible in the moonlight. He said:

"I'd forgotten, sir, that tonight is the night of the full moon. He'd have had to wait until it moved behind a cloud. Even so, he could surely get out of the house and down the drive unseen if he chose a lucky moment. After all, Doyle had his mind—and not only his mind—on other things."

"But the murderer wasn't to know that. If he saw the car arriving, I doubt whether he would have risked it. Well, we can at least find out if it's possible even without the cooperation of Mrs. Meakin. This reminds me of a childhood game, Grandmother's Footsteps. Will you try first, or shall I?"

But the experiment was destined never to take place. It was at that moment that they heard, faint but unmistakable, the three clear peals of the chapel bell.

# XI

Massingham drove the car fast onto the grass verge and braked within inches of the hedge. Beyond them the road curved gently between a tattered fringe of windswept bushes, past what looked like a dilapidated barn of blackened wood, and on through the naked fens to Guy's Marsh. To the right was the black bulk of the new laboratory. Massingham's flashlight picked out a stile and, beyond it, a footpath leading across the field to the distant circle of trees, now no more than a dark smudge against the night sky. He said:

"Odd how remote from the house it is, and how secluded. You wouldn't know it was there. Anyone would think that the original family built it for some secret, necromantic rite."

"More probably as a family mausoleum. They didn't plan for extinction."

Neither of them spoke again. They had instinctively driven the mile and a half to the nearest access to the chapel from the Guy's Marsh road. Although less direct, this was quicker and easier than finding their way by foot through the laboratory grounds and the new building. Their feet quickened and they found they were almost running, driven by some unacknowledged fear, toward the distant trees.

And now they were in the circle of closely planted beeches, dipping their heads under the low branches, their feet scuffling noisily through the crackling drifts of fallen leaves, and could see at last the faintly gleaming windows of the chapel. At the half-open door Massingham instinctively turned as if to hurl his shoulder against it, then drew back with a grin.

"Sorry, I'm forgetting. No sense in precipitating myself in. It's probably only Miss Willard polishing the brass or the rector saying an obligatory prayer to keep the place sanctified."

Gently, and with a slight flourish, he pushed open the door and stood aside; and Dalgliesh stepped before him into the lighted antechapel.

After that there was no speech, no conscious thought, only instinctive action. They moved as one. Massingham grasped and lifted the dangling legs and Dalgliesh, seizing the chair upturned by Brenda's slumping body, slipped the double loop of cord from Stella Mawson's neck and lowered her to the floor. Massingham tore at the fastenings of her duffle jacket, forced back her head, and, flinging himself beside her, closed his mouth over hers. The bundle huddled against the wall stirred and moaned, and Dalgliesh knelt beside her. At the touch of his arms on her shoulders she struggled madly for a moment, squealing like a kitten, then opened her eyes and recognized him. Her body relaxed against his. She said faintly:

"The murderer. In the new lab. He was waiting for me. Has he gone?"

There was a panel of light switches to the left of the door. Dalgliesh clicked them on with a single gesture, and the inner chapel blazed into light. He stepped through the carved organ screen into the chancel. It was empty. The door to the organ loft was ajar. He clattered up the narrow, winding stairway into the gallery. It, too, was empty. Then he stood looking down at the quiet emptiness of the chancel, his eyes moving from the exquisite plaster ceiling, the checkered marble floor, the double row of elegantly carved stalls with their high-arched backs set against the north and south walls, the oak table, stripped of its altar cloth, which stood before the reredos under the eastern window. All it now held were two silver candlesticks, the tall white candles burned half down, the wicks blackened. And on the wall to the left of the altar, hanging incongruously and a little crookedly above the first stall, was a wooden hymn board. It was showing four numbers:

29
10
18
40

He recalled old Mr. Lorrimer's voice:

"She said something about the can being burned and that she'd got the numbers." The last two numbers had been 18 and 40. And what had been burned was not a can, not cannabis, but two altar candles.

# XII

Forty minutes later, Dalgliesh was alone in the chapel. Dr. Greene had been sent for, had briefly pronounced Stella Mawson dead, and had departed. Massingham had left with him to take Brenda Pridmore home and explain to her parents what had happened, to call at Sprogg's Cottage, and to summon Dr. Howarth. Dr. Greene had given Brenda a sedative by injection, but had held out no hope that she would be fit to be questioned before morning. The forensic pathologist had been summoned and was on his way. The voices, the questions, the ringing footsteps, all for the moment were stilled.

Dalgliesh felt extraordinarily alone in the silence of the chapel, more alone because her body lay there, and he had the sense that someone—or something—had recently left, leaving bereft the unencumbered air. This isolation of the spirit was not new to him; he had felt it before in the company of the recently dead. Now he knelt and gazed intently at the dead woman. In life only her eyes had lent distinction to that haggard face. Now they were glazed and gummy as sticky sweetmeats forced under the half-opened lids. It was not a peaceful face. Her features, not yet settled in death, still bore the strain of life's unquietude. He had seen so many dead faces. He had become adept at reading the stigmata of violence. Sometimes they could tell him how, or where, or when. But essentially, as now, they told him nothing.

He lifted the end of the cord still looped loosely around her neck. It was made of woven silk in royal blue, long enough to drape a heavy curtain, and was finished with an ornate silver and blue tassel. There was a five-foot paneled chest against the wall and, putting on his gloves, he lifted the heavy lid. The smell of mothballs came up to him, pungent as an anesthetic. Inside the chest was a folded pair of faded blue velvet curtains, a starched but crumpled surplice, the black and white of an M.A. hood, and, lying on top of this assorted bundle, a second tasseled cord. Whoever had put that cord around her neck—herself or another—had known in advance where it could be found.

He began to explore the chapel. He walked softly, yet his feet fell with portentous heaviness on the marble floor. Slowly, he paced between the two rows of splendidly carved stalls toward the altar. In design and furnishing the building reminded him of his college chapel. Even the smell was the same, a scholastic smell, cold, austere, only faintly ecclesiastical. Now that the altar had been denuded of all its furnishing except the two candlesticks, the chapel looked purely secular, unconsecrated. Perhaps it always had. Its formal classicism rejected emotion. It enshrined man, not God; reason, not mystery. This was a place where certain reassuring rituals had been enacted, reaffirming its proprietor's view of the proper order of the universe and his own place in that order. He looked for some memento of that original owner and found it. To the right of the altar was the chapel's only memorial, a carved bust, half draped with a looped marble curtain, of a bewigged eighteenth-century gentleman, with the inscription:

*Dieu aye merci de son ame.*

This simple petition, unadorned, so out of period, was singularly inapposite to the formal confidence of the memorial, the proud tilt of the head, the self-satisfied smirk on the opulent marble lips. He had built his chapel and set it in a triple circle of trees, and death had not stayed its hand even long enough to give him time to make his carriage drive.

On either side of the organ screen and facing the east window were two ornate stalls under carved canopies, each shielded from drafts by a blue velvet curtain similar to those in the chest. The seats were fitted with matching cushions; soft cushions with silver tassels at each corner lay on the book rests. He climbed into the right-hand stall. On the cushion was a heavy black leather Book of Common Prayer which looked unused. The pages opened stiffly and the bold black and red lettering shone from the page.

> For I am a stranger with thee: and a sojourner, as all my fathers were. O spare me a little, that I may recover my strength: before I go hence, and be no more seen.

He held the book by its spine and shook it. No paper fluttered from its rigid leaves. But where it had lain, four hairs, one fair and three dark, had adhered to the velvet pile. He took an envelope from his pocket and stuck them to the gummed flap. He knew how little the forensic scientists could hope to do with only four hairs, but it was possible that something could be learned.

The chapel, he thought, must have been ideal for them. Shielded by its trees, isolated, secure, warm even. The fen villagers kept indoors once darkness fell and, even in the evening light, would have a half-superstitious dread of visiting this empty and alien shrine. Even without a key they need fear no casual intruder. She need only watch that she was unobserved when she drove the red Jaguar into Hoggatt's drive to park it out of sight in one of the garages in the stable block. And then what? Wait for the light in the Biology Department to go out at last, for the advancing gleam of light from Lorrimer's flashlight as he joined her for that walk through the lab grounds and into the trees. He wondered whether she had dragged the velvet cushions to the sanctuary, whether it had added to the excitement to make love to Lorrimer in front of that denuded altar, the new passion triumphing over the old.

Massingham's flame of hair appeared in the doorway. He said:

"The girl's all right. Her mother got her straight to bed and she's asleep. I called next at Sprogg's Cottage. The door was open and the sitting-room light on, but there's no one there. Howarth was at home when I rang, but not Mrs. Schofield. He said he'd be along. Dr. Kerrison is at the hospital at a medical committee meeting. His housekeeper said that he left just after seven. I didn't ring the hospital. If he is there, he'll be able to produce plenty of witnesses."

"And Middlemass?"

"No answer. Out to dinner, or at the local perhaps. No answer either from the Blakelocks' number. Anything here, sir?"

"Nothing, except what we'd expect to find. You've got a man posted to direct Blain-Thompson when he arrives?"

"Yes, sir. And I think he's arriving now."

# XIII

Dr. Reginald Blain-Thompson had a curious habit, before beginning his examination, of mincing around the body, eyes fixed on it with wary intensity as if half afraid that the corpse might spring into life and seize him by the throat. He minced now, immaculate in his gray pinstriped suit, the inevitable rose in its silver holder looking as fresh in his lapel as if it were a June blossom, newly plucked. He was a tall, lean-faced, aristocratic-looking bachelor with a skin as freshly pink and soft as that of a girl. He was never known to put on protective clothing before examining a body, and he reminded Dalgliesh of one of those television cooks who prepare a four-course dinner in full evening dress for the pleasure of demonstrating the essential refinement of their craft. It was even rumored, unjustly, that Blain-Thompson performed his autopsies in a lounge suit.

But, despite these personal idiosyncrasies, he was an excellent forensic pathologist. Juries loved him. When he stood in the box and recited, with slightly world-weary formality and in his actor's voice, the details of his formidable qualifications and experience, they gazed at him with the respectful admiration of men who know a distinguished consultant when they see one and have no intention of being so disobliging as to disbelieve what he might choose to tell them.

Now he squatted by the body, listened, smelled, and touched. Then he switched off his examination light and got to his feet. He said:

"Yes, well. Obviously she's dead and it's very recent. Within the last two hours, if you press me. But you must have reached that conclusion yourselves or you wouldn't have cut her down. When did you say you found her? Three minutes after eight. Dead one and a half hours then, say. It's possible. You're going to ask me whether it's suicide or murder. All I can say at the moment is that there's only the double mark encircling the neck and the cord fits. But you can see that for yourselves. There's no sign of manual throttling, and it doesn't look as if the cord were superimposed on a finer ligature. She's a frail woman, little more than seven stone, I'd estimate, so it wouldn't take strength to overpower her. But there's no sign of a struggle and the nails look perfectly clean, so she probably didn't get the chance to scratch. If it is murder, he must have come up behind her very swiftly, dropped the looped cord over her head, and strung her up almost as soon as unconsciousness supervened. As for the cause of death—whether it's strangulation, broken neck, or vagal inhibition—well, you'll have to wait until I get her on the table. I can take her away now if you're ready."

"How soon can you do the P.M.?"

"Well, it had better be at once, hadn't it? You're keeping me busy, Commander. No questions about my report on Lorrimer, I suppose?"

Dalgliesh answered:

"None, thank you. I did try to get you on the phone."

"I'm sorry I've been elusive. I've been incarcerated in committees practically all day. When's the Lorrimer inquest?"

"Tomorrow, at two o'clock."

"I'll be there. They'll adjourn it, I suppose. And I'll give you a ring and a preliminary report as soon as I've got her sewn up."

He drew on his gloves carefully, finger by finger, then left. They could hear him exchanging a few words with the constable who was waiting outside to light him across the field to his car. One of them laughed. Then the voices faded.

Massingham put his head outside the door. The two dark-uniformed attendants from the mortuary van, anonymous bureaucrats of death, maneuvered their trolley through the door with nonchalant skill. Stella Mawson's body was lifted with impersonal gentleness. The men turned to trundle the trolley out through the door. But suddenly the way was blocked by two dark shadows, and Howarth and his sister stepped quietly and simultaneously into the light of the chapel. The figures with the trolley paused, stock-still like ancient helots, unseeing, unhearing.

Massingham thought that their entrance seemed as dramatically contrived as that of a couple of film stars arriving at a première. They were dressed identically in slacks and fawn leather jackets, lined with shaggy fur, the collars upturned. And for the first time he was struck by their essential likeness. The impression of a film was reinforced. Gazing at the two pale, arrogant heads framed with fur, he thought that they looked like decadent twins, their fair, handsome profiles theatrically posed against the dark oak paneling. Again simultaneously, their eyes moved to the shrouded lump on the trolley, then fixed on Dalgliesh. He said to Howarth:

"You took your time coming."

"My sister was out driving and I waited for her to return. You said you wanted both of us. I wasn't given to understand that it was of immediate urgency. What has happened? Inspector Massingham wasn't exactly forthcoming when he so peremptorily summoned us."

"Stella Mawson is dead by hanging."

He had no doubt that Howarth appreciated the significance of his careful use of words. Their eyes moved from the two hooks on the chapel wall, one with the bell rope hitched over it, to the blue cord with its dangling tassel held lightly in Dalgliesh's hand. Howarth said:

"I wonder how she knew how to find the cord. And why choose here?"

"You recognize the cord?"

"Isn't it from the chest? There should be two identical cords. We had an idea of hanging the curtains at the entrance to the chancel when we held our concert on the twenty-sixth of August. As it happens, we decided against it. The evening was too hot to worry about drafts. There were two tasseled cords in the chest then."

"Who could have seen them?"

"Almost anyone who was helping with the preparations: myself, my sister, Miss Foley, Martin, Blakelock. Middlemass gave a hand arranging the hired chairs, and so did a number of people from the lab. Some of the women helped with the refreshments after the concert and they were fussing about here during the afternoon. The chest isn't locked. Anyone who felt curious could have looked inside. But I don't see how Miss Mawson could have known about the cord. She was at the concert, but she had no hand in the preparations."

Dalgliesh nodded to the men with the trolley. They pushed it gently forward, and Howarth and Mrs. Schofield stood aside to let it pass. Then Dalgliesh asked:

"How many keys are there to this place?"

"I told you yesterday. I know of one only. It's kept on a board in the Chief Liaison Officer's room."

"And that's the one at present in the lock?" Howarth did not turn his head. He said:

"If it's got the laboratory plastic tab—yes."

"Do you know if it was handed out to anyone today?"

"No. That's hardly the kind of detail Blakelock would worry me with."

Dalgliesh turned to Domenica Schofield:

"And that's the one, presumably, that you borrowed to get extra keys cut when you decided to use the chapel for your meetings with Lorrimer. How many keys?"

She said calmly:

"Two. One you found on his body. This is the second."

She took it from her jacket pocket and held it out in the palm of her hand in a gesture of dismissive contempt. For a moment it appeared that she was about to tilt her palm and let it clatter on the floor.

"You don't deny that you came here?"

"Why should I? It's not illegal. We were both of age, in our right minds, and free. Not even adultery; merely fornication. You seem fascinated by my sex life, Commander, even in the middle of your more normal preoccupations. Aren't you afraid it's becoming rather an obsession?"

Dalgliesh's voice didn't change. He went on:

"And you didn't ask for the key back when you broke with Lorrimer?"

"Again, why should I? I didn't need it. It wasn't an engagement ring."

Howarth hadn't looked at his half sister during this exchange. Suddenly he said harshly:

"Who found her?"

"Brenda Pridmore. She's been taken home. Dr. Greene is with her now."

Domenica Schofield's voice was surprisingly gentle:

"Poor child. She seems to be making a habit of finding bodies, doesn't she? Now that we've explained to you about the keys, is there anything else you want us for tonight?"

"Only to ask you both where you've been since six o'clock."

Howarth said:

"I left Hoggatt's at about a quarter to six and I've been at home ever since. My sister's been out driving alone since seven o'clock. She likes to do that occasionally."

Domenica Schofield said:

"I'm not sure if I can give you the precise route, but I did stop at an agreeable pub at Whittlesford for a drink and a meal shortly before eight o'clock. They'll probably remember me. I'm fairly well-known there. Why? Are you telling us that this is murder?"

"It's an unexplained death."

"And a suspicious one, presumably. But haven't you considered that she might have murdered Lorrimer and then taken her own life?"

"Can you give me one good reason why she should have?"

She laughed softly.

"Murdered Edwin? For the best and commonest of reasons, or so I've always read. Because she was once married to him. Hadn't you discovered that for yourself, Commander?"

"How did you know?"

"Because he told me. I'm probably the only person in the world he ever did tell. He said the marriage wasn't consummated and they got an annulment within two years. I suppose that's why he never brought his bride home. It's an embarrassing business, showing off one's new wife to one's parents and the village, particularly when she isn't a wife at all and one suspects that she never will be. I don't think his parents ever did know, so it's really not so surprising if you didn't. But then, one expects you to ferret out everything about people's private concerns."

Before Dalgliesh could reply, their ears caught, simultaneously, the hurried footfall on the stone step, and Angela Foley stood inside the door. She was flushed with running. Looking wildly from face to face, her body heaving, she gasped:

"Where is she? Where's Star?"

Dalgliesh moved forward, but she backed away as if terrified that he might touch her. She said:

"Those men. Under the trees. Men with a flashlight. They're wheeling something. What is it? What have you done with Star?"

Without looking at her half brother, Domenica Schofield put out her hand. His reached out to meet it. They didn't move closer together, but stood, distanced, rigidly linked by those clasped hands. Dalgliesh said:

"I'm sorry, Miss Foley. Your friend is dead."

Four pairs of eyes watched as her own eyes turned, first to the blue loops of cord dangling from Dalgliesh's hand, then to the twin hooks, lastly to the wooden chair now tidily placed against the wall. She whispered:

"Oh no! Oh no!"

Massingham moved to take her arm, but she shook free. She threw back her head like a howling animal and wailed:

"Star! Star!" Before Massingham could restrain her she had run from the chapel and they could hear her wild, despairing cry borne back to them on the light wind.

Massingham ran after her. She was silent now, weaving through the trees, running fast. But he caught up with her easily before she reached the two distant figures with their dreadful burden. At first she fought madly; but, suddenly, she collapsed in his arms and he was able to lift her and carry her to the car.

When he got back to the chapel, thirty minutes later, Dalgliesh was sitting quietly in one of the stalls, apparently engrossed with the Book of Common Prayer. He put it down and said:

"How is she?"

"Dr. Greene's given her a sedative. He's arranged for the district nurse to stay the night. There's no one else he could think of. It looks as if neither she nor Brenda Pridmore will be fit to be questioned before morning."

He looked at the small heap of numbered cards on the seat beside Dalgliesh. His chief said:

"I found them at the bottom of the chest. I suppose we can test these and the numbers in the board for fingerprints. But we know what we shall find."

Massingham asked:

"Did you believe Mrs. Schofield's story that Lorrimer and Stella Mawson were married?"

"Oh yes, I think so. Why lie when the facts can be so easily checked? And it explains so much; that extraordinary change of will; even the outburst when he was talking to Bradley. That first sexual failure must have gone deep. Even after all these years he couldn't bear to think that she might benefit even indirectly from his will. Or was it the thought that unlike him, she had found happiness—and found it with a woman—that he found so insupportable?"

Massingham said:

"So she and Angela Foley get nothing. But that's not a reason for killing herself. And why here, of all places?"

Dalgliesh got to his feet.

"I don't think she did kill herself. This was murder."

# BOOK FIVE

•

# The Clunch Pit

# I

They were at Bowlem's Farm before first light. Mrs. Pridmore had begun her baking early. Already two large earthenware bowls covered with humped linen stood on the kitchen table, and the whole cottage was redolent with the warm, fecund smell of yeast. When Dalgliesh and Massingham arrived, Dr. Greene, a squat, broad-shouldered man with the face of a benevolent toad, was folding his stethoscope into the depths of an old-fashioned Gladstone bag. It was less than twelve hours since Dalgliesh and he had last met, since, as police surgeon, he had been the first doctor to be called to Stella Mawson's body. He had examined it briefly and had then pronounced:

"Is she dead? Answer: yes. Cause of death? Answer: hanging. Time of death? about one hour ago. Now you'd better call in the expert and he'll explain to you why the first question is the only one he's at present competent to answer."

Now he wasted no time on civilities or questions but nodded briefly to the two detectives and continued talking to Mrs. Pridmore.

"The lass is fine. She's had a nasty shock but nothing that a good night's sleep hasn't put right. She's young and healthy, and it'll take more than a couple of corpses to turn her into a neurotic wreck, if that's what you're frightened of. My family has been doctoring yours for three generations and there's none of you gone off your heads yet." He nodded to Dalgliesh. "You can go up now."

Arthur Pridmore was standing beside his wife, his hand gripping her shoulder. No one had introduced him to Dalgliesh; nor was there need. He said:

"She hasn't faced the worst yet, has she? This is the second body. What do you think life in this village will be like for her if these two deaths aren't solved?"

Dr. Greene was impatient. He snapped shut his bag.

"Good grief, man, no one's going to suspect Brenda! She's lived here all her life. I brought her into the world."

"That's no protection against slander, though, is it? I'm not saying they'll accuse her. But you know the fens. Folk here can be superstitious, unforgetting, and unforgiving. There's such a thing as being tainted with bad luck."

"Not for your pretty Brenda, there isn't. She'll be the local heroine, most likely. Shake off this morbid nonsense, Arthur, and come out to the car with me. I want a word about that business at the Parochial Church Council." They went out together. Mrs. Pridmore looked up at Dalgliesh. He thought that she had been crying. She said:

"And now you're going to question her, make her talk about it, raking it all up again."

"Don't worry," said Dalgliesh gently, "talking about it will help."

She made no move to accompany them upstairs, a tact for which Dalgliesh was grateful. He could hardly have objected, particularly as there hadn't been time to get a policewoman, but he had an idea that Brenda would be both more relaxed and more communicative in her mother's absence. She called out happily to his knock. The little bedroom with its low beams and its curtains drawn against the morning darkness was full of light and color, and she was sitting up in bed fresh and bright-eyed, her aureole of hair tumbling around her shoulders. Dalgliesh wondered anew at the resilience of youth. Massingham, halting suddenly in the doorway, thought that she ought to be in the Uffizi, her feet floating above a meadow of spring flowers, the whole sunlit landscape of Italy stretching behind her into infinity.

It was still very much a schoolgirl's room. There were two shelves of schoolbooks, another with a collection of dolls in national costumes, and a cork board with cutouts from the Sunday supplements and photographs of her friends. There was a wicker chair beside the bed holding a large teddy bear. Dalgliesh removed it and placed it on the bed beside her, then sat down. He said:

"How are you feeling? Better?"

She leaned impulsively toward him. The sleeve of her cream dressing jacket fell over the freckled arm. She said:

"I'm so glad you've come. No one wants to talk about it. They can't realize that I've got to talk about it sometime and it's much better now while it's fresh in my mind. It was you who found me, wasn't it? I remember being picked up—rather like Marianne Dashwood in *Sense and Sensibility*—and the nice tweedy smell of your jacket. But I can't remember anything after that. I do remember ringing the bell, though."

"That was clever of you. We were parked in Hoggatt's drive and heard it, otherwise it might have been hours before the body was found."

"It wasn't clever, really. It was just panic. I suppose you realize what happened? I got a puncture in my bike and decided to walk home through the new lab. Then I rather got lost and panicked. I started thinking about Dr. Lorrimer's murderer and imagining that he was lying in wait for me. I even imagined that he might have punctured the tires on purpose. It seems silly now, but it didn't then."

Dalgliesh said:

"We've examined the bicycle. There was a truckload of grit passing the lab during the afternoon and some of the load was shed. You had a sharp flint in each tire. But it was a perfectly natural fear. Can you remember whether there really was someone in the building?"

"Not really. I didn't see anyone and I think I imagined most of the sounds I heard. What really frightened me was an owl. Then I got out of the building and rushed in panic across a field straight toward the chapel."

"Did you get the impression that anyone might be there alive in the chapel?"

"Well, there aren't any pillars to hide behind. It's a funny chapel, isn't it? Not really a holy place. Perhaps it hasn't been prayed in enough. I've only been there once before when Dr. Howarth and three of the staff from the lab gave a concert, so I know what it's like. Do you mean he could have been crouched down in one of the stalls watching me? It's a horrid idea."

"It is rather. But now that you're safe, could you bear to think about it?"

"I can now you're here." She paused. "I don't think he was. I didn't see anyone, and I don't think I heard anyone. But I was so terrified that I probably wouldn't have noticed. All I could see was this bundle of clothes strung up on the wall, and then the face drooping down at me."

He didn't need to warn her of the importance of his next question.

"Can you remember where you found the chair, its exact position?"

"It was lying overturned just to the right of the body as if she had kicked it away. I think it had fallen backwards, but it might have been on its side."

"But you're quite sure that it had fallen?"

"Quite sure. I remember turning it upright so that I could stand on it to reach the bell rope." She looked at him, bright-eyed.

"I shouldn't have done that, should I? Now you won't be able to tell whether any marks or soil on the seat came from my shoes or hers. Was that why Inspector Massingham took away my shoes last night? Mummy told me."

"Yes, that's why."

The chair would be tested for prints, then sent for examination to the Metropolitan Laboratory. But this murder, if it were murder, had been premeditated. Dalgliesh doubted whether, this time, the killer would have made any mistakes.

Brenda said:

"One thing has struck me, though. It's odd, isn't it, that the light was on?"

"That's another thing that I wanted to ask you. You're quite sure that the chapel was lit? You didn't switch on the light yourself?"

"I'm quite sure I didn't. I saw thc lights gleaming through the trees, rather like the City of God, you know. It would have been more sensible to have run for the road once I'd got clear of the new building. But suddenly I saw the shape of the chapel and the light shining faintly through the windows, and I ran toward it almost by instinct."

"I expect it was by instinct. Your ancestors did the same. Only they would have run for sanctuary to St. Nicholas's."

"I've been thinking about the lights ever since I woke up. It looks like suicide, doesn't it? I don't suppose people kill themselves in the dark. I know I wouldn't. I can't imagine killing myself at all unless I was desperately ill and lonely and in terrible pain, or someone was torturing me to make me give them vital information. But if I did, I wouldn't switch the lights off. I'd want to see my last of the light before I went into the darkness, wouldn't you? But murderers always want to delay discovery of the body, don't they? So why didn't he turn off the light and lock the door?"

She spoke with happy unconcern. The illness, the loneliness, and the pain were as unreal and remote as was the torture. Dalgliesh said:

"Perhaps because he wanted it to look like suicide. Was that your first thought when you found the body, that she'd killed herself?"

"Not at the time. I was too frightened to think at all. But since I've woken up and started considering it all—yes, I suppose I do think it was suicide."

"But you're not sure why you think that?"

"Perhaps because hanging is such a strange way of killing someone. But suicides often do hang themselves, don't they? Mr. Bowlem's previous pigman did—in the tithe barn. And old Annie Makepeace. I've noticed that, in the fens, people usually shoot themselves or hang themselves. You see, on a farm, there's always a gun or a rope."

She spoke simply and without fear. She had lived on a farm all her life. There was always birth and death, the birth and death of animals and of humans, too. And the long, dark nights of the fen winters would bring their own miasma of madness or despair. But not to her. He said:

"You appall me. It sounds like a holocaust."

"It doesn't happen often, but one remembers when it does. I just associate hanging with suicide. Do you think this time I'm wrong?"

"I think you could be. But we shall find out. You've been very helpful."

He spent another five minutes talking to her, but there was nothing that she could add. She hadn't gone with Inspector Blakelock to Chief Inspector Martin's office when he set the night alarms, so couldn't say whether or not the key to the chapel was still on its hook. She had only met Stella Mawson once before, at the concert in the chapel, when she had sat in the same row as Angela Foley, Stella Mawson, Mrs. Schofield, and Dr. Kerrison and his children.

As Dalgliesh and Massingham were leaving, she said:

"I don't think Mum and Dad will let me go back to the lab now. In fact I'm sure they won't. They want me to marry Gerald Bowlem. I think I would like to marry Gerald, at least, I've never thought of marrying anyone else, but not just yet. It would be nice to be a scientist and have a proper career first. But Mum won't have an easy moment if I stay at the lab. She loves me, and I'm all she's got. You can't hurt people when they love you."

Dalgliesh recognized an appeal for help. He went back and sat again in the chair. Massingham, pretending to look out the window, was intrigued. He wondered what they would think at the Yard if they could see the old man taking time from a murder investigation to advise on the moral ambiguities of Women's Lib. But he rather wished that she had asked him. Since they had come into the room she had looked only at Dalgliesh. Now he heard him say:

"I suppose a scientific job isn't easy to combine with being a farmer's wife."

"I don't think it would be very fair to Gerald."

"I used to think that we can have almost anything we want from life, that it's just a question of organization. But now I'm beginning to think that we have to make a choice more often than we'd like. The important thing is to make sure that it's our choice, no one else's, and that we make it honestly. But one thing I'm sure of is that it's never a good thing to make a decision when you're not absolutely well. Why not wait a little time, until we've solved Dr. Lorrimer's murder anyway. Your mother may feel differently then."

She said:

"I suppose this is what murder does, changes people's lives and spoils them."

"Changes, yes. But it needn't spoil. You're young and intelligent and brave, so you won't let it spoil yours."

Downstairs, in the farmhouse kitchen, Mrs. Pridmore was sandwiching fried rashers of bacon between generous slices of crusty bread. She said gruffly:

"You both look as if you could do with some breakfast. Up all night, I daresay. It won't hurt you to sit down and take a couple of minutes to eat these. And I've made fresh tea."

Supper the previous night had been a couple of sandwiches fetched by a constable from the Moonraker and eaten in the antechapel. Not until he smelled the bacon did Massingham realize how hungry he was. He bit gratefully into the warm bread to the oozing saltiness of home-cured bacon and washed it down with strong, hot tea. He felt cosseted by the warmth and friendliness of the kitchen, this cozy, womblike shelter from the dark fens. Then the telephone rang. Mrs. Pridmore went to answer it. She said:

"That was Dr. Greene ringing from Sprogg's Cottage. He says to tell you that Angela Foley is well enough to speak to you now."

# II

Angela Foley came slowly into the room. She was fully dressed and perfectly calm, but both men were shocked by the change in her. She walked stiffly, and her face looked aged and bruised as if she had suffered all night a physical assault of grief. Her small eyes were pale and sunken behind the jutting bones, her cheeks were unhealthily mottled, the delicate mouth was swollen, and there was a herpes on the upper lip. Only her voice was unchanged; the childish, unemphatic voice with which she had answered their first questions.

The district nurse, who had spent the night at Sprogg's Cottage, had lit the fire. Angela looked at the crackling wood and said:

"Stella never lit the fire until late in the afternoon. I used to lay it in the morning before I went to the lab, and she'd put a match to it about half an hour before I was due home."

Dalgliesh said:

"We found Miss Mawson's house keys on her body. I'm afraid we had to unlock her desk to examine her papers. You were asleep, so we weren't able to ask you."

She said, dully:

"It wouldn't have made any difference, would it? You would have looked just the same. You had to."

"Did you know that your friend once went through a form of marriage with Edwin Lorrimer? There wasn't a divorce; the marriage was annulled after two years because of nonconsummation. Did she tell you?"

She turned to look at him, but it was impossible to gauge the expression in those small, piglike eyes. If her voice held any emotion, it was closer to wry amusement than to surprise.

"Married? She and Edwin? So that's how she knew . . ." She broke off. "No, she didn't tell me. When I came to live here it was a new beginning for both of us. I didn't want to talk about the past and I don't think she did either. She did sometimes tell me things, about her life at the university, her job, odd people she knew. But that was one thing she didn't tell me."

Dalgliesh asked gently:

"Do you feel able to tell me what happened last night?"

"She said that she was going for a walk. She often did, but usually after supper. That's when she thought about her books, worked out the plot and dialogue, striding along in the darkness on her own."

"What time did she go?"

"Just before seven."

"Did she have the key of the chapel with her?"

"She asked me for it yesterday, after lunch, just before I went back to the lab. She said she wanted to describe a seventeenth-century family chapel for the book, but I didn't know that she meant to visit it so soon. When she hadn't come home at half-past ten, I got worried and went to look for her. I walked for nearly an hour before I thought of looking in the chapel."

Then she spoke directly to Dalgliesh, patiently, as if explaining something to an obtuse child:

"She did it for me. She killed herself so that I could have the money from her life insurance. She told me that I was her only legatee. You see, the owner wants to sell this cottage in a hurry; he needs the cash. We wanted to buy it, but we hadn't enough money for the deposit. Just before she went out, she asked me what it was like to be in local authority care, what it meant to have no real home. When Edwin was killed, we thought that there might be something for me in his will. But there wasn't. That's why she asked me for the key. It wasn't true that she needed to include a description of the chapel in her book, not this book anyway. It's set in London, and it's nearly finished. I know. I've been typing it. I thought at the time that it was odd that she wanted the key, but I learned never to ask Stella questions.

"But now I understand. She wanted to make life safe for me here, where we'd been happy, safe forever. She knew what she was going to do. She knew she'd never come back. When I was massaging her neck to make her headache better, she knew that I should never touch her again."

Dalgliesh asked:

"Would any writer, any writer who wasn't mentally ill, choose to kill herself just before a book was finished?"

She said dully:

"I don't know. I don't understand how a writer feels."

Dalgliesh said:

"Well, I do. And she wouldn't."

She didn't reply. He went on gently:

"Was she happy, living here with you?"

She looked up at him eagerly, and, for the first time, her voice became animated, as if she were willing him to understand.

"She said that she had never been as happy in all her life. She said that was what love is, knowing that you can make just one other person happy, and be made happy by them in return."

"So why should she kill herself? Could she really have believed that you'd rather have her money than herself? Why should she think that?"

"Stella always underrated herself. She may have thought that I'd forget her in time, but the money and the security would go on forever. She may even have thought that it was bad for me to be living with her—that the money would somehow set me free. She once said something very like that."

Dalgliesh looked across at the slim, upright figure, sitting, hands folded in her lap, opposite him in the high winged chair. He fixed his eyes on her face. Then he said quietly:

"But there isn't going to be any money. The life insurance policy had a suicide clause. If Miss Mawson did kill herself, then you get nothing."

She hadn't known. He could be certain of that at least. The news surprised her, but it didn't shock. This was no murderess balked of her spoils.

She smiled and said gently:

"It doesn't matter."

"It matters to this investigation. I've read one of your friend's novels. Miss Mawson was a highly intelligent writer, which means that she was an intelligent woman. Her heart wasn't strong and her life insurance premiums weren't cheap. It can't have been easy to meet them. Do you really think that she didn't know the terms of her policy?"

"What are you trying to tell me?"

"Miss Mawson knew, or thought she knew, who had killed Dr. Lorrimer, didn't she?"

"Yes. She said so. But she didn't tell me who it was."

"Not even whether it was a man or a woman?"

She thought:

"No, nothing. Only that she knew. I'm not sure that she said that, not in so many words. But when I asked her, she didn't deny it."

She paused, and then went on with more animation:

"You're thinking that she went out to meet the murderer, aren't you? That she tried to blackmail him? But Stella wouldn't do that! Only a fool would run into that kind of danger, and she wasn't a fool. You said so yourself. She wouldn't voluntarily have gone alone to face a killer, not for any money. No sane woman would."

"Even if the murderer were a woman?"

"Not alone and at night. Star was so small and fragile, and her heart wasn't strong. When I put my arms around her it was like holding a bird." She looked into the fire and said, almost wonderingly:

"I shall never see her again. Never. She sat in this chair and pulled on her boots, just as she always did. I never offered to go with her in the evenings. I knew that she needed to be alone. It was all so ordinary, until she got to the door. And then I was frightened. I begged her not to go. And I shall never see her again. She won't ever speak again, not to me, not to anyone. She'll never write another word. I don't believe it yet. I know that it must be true or you wouldn't be here, but I still don't believe it. How shall I bear it when I do?"

Dalgliesh said:

"Miss Foley, we have to know if she went out on the night Dr. Lorrimer was killed."

She looked up at him.

"I know what you're trying to make me do. If I say that she did go out, then the case is finished for you, isn't it? It's all nicely tied up; means, motive, opportunity. He was her ex-husband and she hated him because of the will. She went to try and persuade him to help us with some money. When he refused, she seized the first weapon to hand and struck him down."

Dalgliesh said:

"He may have let her into the laboratory, although it's unlikely. But how did she get out?"

"You'll say that I took the keys from Dr. Howarth's security safe and lent them to her. Then I put them back next morning."

"Did you?"

She shook her head.

"You could only have done that if you and Inspector Blakelock were in this together. And what reason has he for wishing Dr. Lorrimer dead? When his only child was killed by a hit-and-run driver, the evidence of the forensic scientist helped secure an acquittal. But that was ten years ago, and the scientist wasn't Dr. Lorrimer. When Miss Pridmore told me about the child we checked. That evidence was to do with paint particles, the job of a forensic chemist, not a biologist. Are you telling me that Inspector Blakelock lied when he said that the keys were in the security cupboard?"

"He didn't lie. The keys were there."

"Then any case we might seek to build against Miss Mawson weakens, doesn't it? Could anyone really believe that she climbed out of a third-floor window? You must believe that we're here to find the truth, not to fabricate an easy solution."

But she was right, thought Massingham. Once Angela Foley had admitted that her friend had left Sprogg's Cottage that night, it would be difficult to bring home the crime to anyone else. The solution she had propounded was neat enough and, whoever was brought to trial for Lorrimer's murder, the defense would make the most of it. He watched his chief's face. Dalgliesh said:

"I agree that no sane woman would go out alone at night to meet a murderer. That's why I don't think she did. She thought she knew who had killed Edwin Lorrimer, and if she did have an assignation last night, it wasn't with him. Miss Foley, please look at me. You must trust me. I don't know yet whether your friend killed herself or was killed. But if I'm to discover the truth, I'll have to know whether she went out on the night Dr. Lorrimer died."

She said dully:

"We were together all evening. We told you."

There was a silence. It seemed to Massingham to last for minutes. Then the wood fire flared and there was a crack like a pistol shot. A log rolled out on the hearth. Dalgliesh knelt and with the tongs eased it back into place. The silence went on. Then she said:

"Please tell me the truth first. Do you think Star was murdered?"

"I can't be sure. I may never be able to prove it. But, yes, I do."

She said:

"Star did go out that night. She was out from half past eight until about half past nine. She didn't tell me where she'd been, and she was perfectly ordinary, perfectly composed, when she got home. She said nothing; but she did go out." She said at last:

"I'd like you to go now, please."

"I think you should have someone with you."

"I'm not a child. I don't want Mrs. Swaffield or the district nurse or any of the village do-gooders. And I don't need a policewoman. I haven't committed a crime, so you've no right to force yourselves on me. I've told you everything I know. You've locked her desk, so no one can get at Stella's things. I shan't do anything foolish—that's the expression people use when they're trying to ask tactfully if you're planning to kill yourself, isn't it? Well, I'm not. I'm all right now. I just want to be left alone."

Dalgliesh said:

"I'm afraid we shall need to force ourselves on you again later."

"Later is better than now."

She wasn't trying to be offensive. It was a simple statement of fact. She got up stiffly and walked toward the door, her head held rigidly high as if only the body's discipline could hold intact the fragile integrity of the mind. Dalgliesh and Massingham exchanged glances. She was right. They couldn't force comfort or company where neither was wanted. They had no legal authority either to stay or to compel her to leave. And there were things to do.

She went over to the window and watched from behind the curtains as the car rounded Sprogg's Green and accelerated toward the village. Then she ran into the hall and dragged out the telephone directory from its shelf. It took only a few seconds of feverish leafing to find the number she wanted. She dialed, waited, and then spoke. Replacing the receiver, she went back into the sitting room. Slowly, with ceremony, she lifted the French sword from the wall and stood very still, holding out her arms, the weapon resting across her palms. After a few seconds she curled her left hand around the scabbard, and with her right slowly and deliberately withdrew the blade. Then she took her stand just inside the sitting-room door, naked sword in her hand, and measured the room with her eyes, regarding the disposition of furniture and objects, intent as a stranger calculating her chances in some coming trial.

After a few minutes she moved into the study, and again stood silently surveying the room. There was a Victorian button-backed chair beside the fireplace. She dragged it to the study door and hid the naked sword behind it, the tip resting against the floor, then slid the scabbard under the chair. Satisfied that neither could be seen, she returned to the sitting room. She took her seat beside the fire and sat motionless, waiting for the sound of the approaching car.

## III

If Claire Easterbrook was surprised, on her arrival at the laboratory just before nine o'clock, to be asked by Inspector Blakelock to see Commander Dalgliesh immediately, she concealed it. She changed first into her white coat, but otherwise did not delay in obeying the summons more than was strictly necessary to assert her independence. When she went into the Director's office, she saw the two detectives, the dark head and the red, quietly conferring together at the window, almost, she thought, as if their business were ordinary, their presence unremarkable. There was an alien file on Dr. Howarth's desk, and a plan of the laboratory and an Ordnance Survey map of the village laid open on the conference table, but otherwise the room seemed unchanged. Dalgliesh moved to the desk and said:

"Good morning, Miss Easterbrook. You heard what happened last night?"

"No. Should I have? I was at the theater after dinner, so people couldn't reach me, and I've spoken to no one but Inspector Blakelock. He hasn't told me anything."

"Stella Mawson, Miss Foley's friend, was found hanged in the chapel."

She frowned as if the news were personally offensive and said with no more than polite interest:

"I see. I don't think I've met her. Oh yes, I remember. She was at the concert in the chapel. Gray-haired, with remarkable eyes. What happened? Did she kill herself?"

"That's one of two possibilities. It's unlikely to have been an accident."

"Who found her?"

"Miss Pridmore."

She said with surprising gentleness:

"Poor child."

Dalgliesh opened the file, picked up two transparent exhibit envelopes, and said:

"I'd like you to have a look at these four hairs for me. It's urgent and there's no time to get them to the Met Lab. I want to know, if possible, if the dark hairs came from the same head."

"It's easier to say whether they don't. I can have a look under the microscope but I doubt whether I can help you. Hair identification is never easy, and I can't hope to do much with only three samples. Apart from microscopic examination, we'd normally use mass spectrometry to try to identify differences in the trace elements, but even that isn't possible with three hairs. If these were submitted to me, I'd have to say that I couldn't give an opinion."

Dalgliesh said:

"I'd be grateful, all the same, if you'd take a look. It's just a hunch and I want to know whether it's worth following up."

Massingham said:

"I'd like to watch, if you don't mind."

She gazed at him.

"Would it make any difference if I did?"

Ten minutes later she lifted her head from the comparison microscope and said:

"If we're talking of hunches, mine, for what it's worth, is that they came from different heads. The cuticle, cortex, and medulla are all significantly different. But I think they're both male. Look for yourself."

Massingham bent his head to the eyepiece. He saw what looked like the sections of two logs, patterned and grained. And beside them were two other logs, their barks shredded. But he could see that they were different logs, and that they came from different trees. He said:

"Thank you. I'll let Mr. Dalgliesh know."

# IV

There was nothing he could put between himself and that shining, razor-sharp blade. He thought wryly that a bullet would have been worse; but then he wondered. To use a gun at least required some skill, a preliminary aim. A bullet could go anywhere, and if her first shot was wide he could at least have ensured that she got no second chance. But she had three feet of cold steel in her hand and, in this confined space, she had only to lunge or slash and he would be cut to the bone. He knew now why she had shown him into the study. There was no room here to maneuver; no object within his range of sight that he could seize and hurl. And he knew that he mustn't look around, must keep his eyes firmly and without fear on her face. He tried to keep his voice calm, reasonable; one nervous smile, one hint of hostility or provocation, and it might be too late to argue. He said:

"Look, don't you think we ought to talk about this? You've got the wrong man, believe me."

She said:

"Read that note. The one on the desk behind you. Read it out loud."

He didn't dare turn his head, but reached back and fumbled on the desk. His hand encountered a single sheet of paper. He read:

"You'd better check on the cannabis exhibits when Detective-Inspector Doyle's around. How do you think he managed to afford his house?"

"Well?"

"Where did you get this?"

"From Edwin Lorrimer's desk. Stella found it and gave it to me. You killed her because she knew, because she tried to blackmail you. She arranged to meet you last night in the Wren chapel and you strangled her."

He could have laughed at the irony of it, but he knew that laughter would be fatal. And at least they were talking. The longer she waited, the greater his chances.

"Are you saying that your friend thought that I killed Edwin Lorrimer?"

"She knew that you didn't. She was out walking the night he died and I think she saw someone she recognized leaving the laboratory. She knew that it wasn't you. She wouldn't have risked meeting you alone if she'd thought that you were a murderer. Mr. Dalgliesh explained that to me. She went to the chapel thinking that she was safe, that she could come to some arrangement with you. But you killed her. That's why I'm going to kill you. Stella hated the thought of shutting people away in prison. I can't bear the thought of her murderer ever being free. Ten years in exchange for Stella's life. Why should you be alive when she's dead?"

He had no doubt that she meant what she said. He had dealt before with people pushed over the brink of endurance into madness, had seen before that look of dedicated fanaticism. He stood very still, poised on the soles of his feet, his arms held loosely, his eyes watching her eyes, waiting for the first instinctive tightening of the muscles before she struck. He tried to keep his voice low, calm, but with no trace of facetiousness.

"That's a reasonable point of view. Don't think that I'm against it. I've never understood why people are squeamish about killing a convicted murderer instantaneously and resigned to killing him slowly over twenty years. But at least they have been convicted. There's the little matter of a trial. No execution without due process. And believe me, Miss Foley, you've got the wrong man. I didn't kill Lorrimer, and luckily for me I can prove it."

"I don't care about Edwin Lorrimer. I only care about Stella. And you killed her."

"I didn't even know that she was dead. But if she was killed yesterday any time between half past three and half past seven, then I'm in the clear. I've got the best possible alibi. I was at Guy's Marsh police station most of the time being interrogated by the Yard. And when Dalgliesh and Massingham left, I was there for another two hours. Ring them. Ask anyone. Look, you can lock me away in a cupboard—somewhere where I can't escape—while you telephone Guy's Marsh. For God's sake, you don't want to make a mistake, do you? You know me. Do you want to kill me, messily, horribly, while the real murderer escapes? An unofficial execution is one thing; murder's another."

He thought that the hand holding the sword lost some of its tension. But there was no change in the taut, white face. She said:

"And the note."

"I know who sent the note—my wife. She wanted me to leave the Force, and she knew that there'd be nothing like a little official harassment to push me into resigning. I had a spot of trouble with the Force about two years ago. The disciplinary committee exonerated me, but I damn nearly resigned then. Can't you recognize feminine spite when you see it? That note proves nothing except that she wanted me disgraced and out of the Force."

"But you have been stealing cannabis, substituting an inert substance?"

"Ah, that's a different question. But you're not killing me for that. You won't be able to prove it, you know. The last batch of cannabis exhibits I was concerned with had a destruction authorization from the court. I helped burn them myself. Just in time, luckily; the incinerator broke down immediately afterwards."

"And the court exhibits you burned, were they cannabis?"

"Some of them were. But you'll never prove I made the substitution, even if you decide to make use of that note; not now. But what does it matter? I'm out of the Force. Look, you know that I've been working on the clunch pit murder. Do you really suppose that I'd have been sitting at home at this time of day, free to drive over here as soon as you rang me merely to satisfy my curiosity, if I were on a murder case, if I hadn't been suspended or resigned? I may not be a shining example of probity to the Force, but I'm not a murderer, and I can prove it. Ring Dalgliesh and ask him."

There was no doubt about it now, her grip on the sword had relaxed. She stood there, very still, no longer looking at him, but with her gaze fixed out of the window. Her face didn't change, but he saw that she was crying. The tears were streaming out of the tight little eyes to roll unimpeded down her cheeks. He moved quietly forward and took the sword from her unresisting hand. He placed an arm on her shoulders. She didn't flinch. He said:

"Look, you've had a shock. You shouldn't have been left here on your own. Isn't it time we had a cup of tea? Show me where the kitchen is and I'll make it. Or better still, have you anything stronger?"

She said dully:

"There's whisky, but we keep that for Stella. I don't drink it."

"Well, you're going to drink it now. It'll do you good. And, by God, I need it. And then you'd better sit down quietly and tell me all about it."

She said:

"But if it wasn't you, who did kill Stella?"

"My guess is, the same person who killed Lorrimer. A couple of murderers loose in one small community is too much of a coincidence. But look, you've got to let the police know about that note. It can't hurt me now, and it might help them. If your friend found one incriminating piece of information in Lorrimer's desk, then she may have found another. She didn't use that note. She probably knew how little it was worth. But what about the information she did use?"

She said dully:

"You tell them, if you want to. It doesn't matter now."

But he waited until he had made the tea. The tidiness and good order of the kitchen pleased him, and he took trouble over the tray, setting it in front of her on a low table which he drew up before the fire. He replaced the sword above the fireplace, standing back to make sure that it hung correctly. Then he made up the fire. She had shaken her head when he had offered her the whisky, but he poured himself a generous measure and sat opposite her on the other side of the fire. She didn't attract him. Even in their brief encounters at the laboratory he had given her no more than a passing dismissive glance. It was unusual for him to put himself out for a woman from whom he wanted nothing, and the sensation of disinterested kindness was unfamiliar but agreeable. Sitting opposite her in silence, the traumas of the day faded, and he felt a curious peace. They had some quite decent stuff in the cottage, he decided, looking around at the cozy, cluttered sitting room. He wondered whether it was all coming to her.

It was ten minutes before he went out to telephone. When he returned the sight of his face roused her from her benumbed misery. She said:

"What is it? What did he say?"

He moved into the room frowning, puzzled. He said:

"He wasn't there. He and Massingham weren't at Guy's Marsh or at the lab. They're at Muddington. They've gone to the clunch pit."

## V

They drove again over the route they had followed the previous night when they had heard those three clangs from the chapel bell the mile and a half to the junction of Guy's Marsh Road and then right through the main street of the village. Neither spoke. Massingham had taken one look at his chief's face and had decided that silence would be prudent. And it was certainly no time for self-congratulation. They still lacked proof, the one clinching fact that would break the case open. And Massingham wondered if they would ever get it. They were dealing with intelligent men and women who must know that they had only to keep their mouths shut and nothing could be proved.

In the village street, the first Saturday morning shoppers were making their appearance. The gossiping groups of women turned their heads to glance briefly at the car as it passed. And now the houses were thinning and Hoggatt's field, with the new building, was on their right. Massingham had changed down to turn into the drive of the Old Rectory when it happened. The blue and yellow ball bounced out into the road in front of them, and after it, red wellingtons flashing, ran William. They were driving too slowly for danger, but Massingham cursed as he swerved and braked. And then came two seconds of horror.

Afterward it seemed to Dalgliesh that time was suspended so that he saw in memory the whole accident like a film run slowly. The red Jaguar leaping and held suspended in the air; a blaze of blue from the terrified eyes; the mouth gaping in a soundless scream; the white knuckles wrenching at the wheel. Instinctively he cradled his head and braced himself for the impact. The Jaguar crashed the rear bumper of the Rover, ripping it away in a scream of torn metal. The car rocked wildly and spun around. There was a second of absolute silence. Then he and Massingham were out of their seat belts and rushing across to the opposite verge to that small, motionless body. One boot lay in the road, and the ball trickled slowly toward the grass verge.

William had been tossed into a heap of hay left on the verge after the late summer scything. He lay spread-eagled, so relaxed in his perfect stillness that Massingham's first horrified thought was that his neck was broken. In the couple of seconds in which he was resisting the impulse to sweep the boy into his arms, and turning instead to telephone from the car for an ambulance, William recovered his wind and began struggling against the prickling dampness of the straw. Bereft of both dignity and his ball, he began to cry. Domenica Schofield, hair streaming across her bleached, distraught face, rushed up to them.

"Is he all right?"

Massingham ran his hands over William's body, then took the boy in his arms.

"I think so. He sounds all right."

They had reached the drive of the Old Rectory when Eleanor Kerrison came rushing down the path toward them. She had obviously been washing her hair. It lay now in dank, dripping swatches across her shoulders. William, seeing her, redoubled his crying. As Massingham strode toward the house she ran clumsily beside him, clutching his arm. Drops of water sprayed from her hair to lie like pearls on William's face.

"Daddy's been called to a body. He said he'd take William and me to lunch at Cambridge when he got back. We were going to buy a grown-up bed for William. I was washing my hair specially. I left William with Miss Willard. He's all right, isn't he? Are you sure he's all right? Oughtn't we take him to the hospital? What happened?"

"We didn't see. I think he was caught and tossed by the front bumper of the Jaguar. Luckily he landed on a heap of straw."

"He could have been killed. I warned her about the road. He isn't supposed to play in the garden on his own. Are you sure we oughtn't to get Dr. Greene?"

Massingham went straight through the house to the drawing room and laid William on the sofa. He said:

"It might be as well, but I'm sure he's all right. Just listen to him."

William, as if he understood, cut off his bawling instantaneously and struggled upright on the couch. He began hiccuping loudly but, apparently undistressed by the paroxysms that were jerking his body, he regarded the company with interest, then fixed his stare consideringly on his bootless left foot. Looking up at Dalgliesh he asked sternly:

"Where's Willum's ball?"

"At the edge of the road, presumably," said Massingham. "I'll fetch it. And you'll have to do something about fixing a gate for that drive."

They heard footsteps in the hall, and Miss Willard stood, fluttering uneasily, in the doorway. Eleanor had been sitting beside her brother on the sofa. Now she stood up and confronted the woman with a silent contempt so unmistakable that Miss Willard blushed. She glanced around the watching faces and said defensively:

"Quite a little party. I thought I heard voices."

Then the girl spoke. The voice, thought Massingham, was as arrogant and cruel as that of a Victorian matron dismissing a kitchen maid. The confrontation would have been almost comic if it hadn't been at once pathetic and horrible.

"You can pack up your bags and get out. You're dismissed. I only asked you to watch William while I washed my hair. You couldn't even do that. He might have been killed. You're a useless, ugly, stupid old woman. You drink and you smell and we all hate you. We don't need you any more. So get out. Pack your beastly, horrible things and go. I can look after William and Daddy. He doesn't need anyone but me."

The silly, ingratiating smile faded on Miss Willard's face. Two red weals appeared across her cheeks and forehead as if the words had been a physical whiplash. Then she was suddenly pale, her whole body shaking. She reached for the back of a chair for support and said, her voice high and distorted with pain:

"You! Do you think he needs you? I may be middle-aged and past my best but at least I'm not half-mad. And if I'm ugly, look at yourself! He only puts up with you because of William. You could leave tomorrow and he wouldn't care. He'd be glad. It's William he loves, not you. I've seen his face, I've heard him, and I know. He's thinking of letting you go to your mother. You didn't know that, did you? And there's something else you don't know. What do you think your precious daddy gets up to when he's drugged you into sleep? He sneaks off to the Wren chapel and makes love to her."

Eleanor turned and looked at Domenica Schofield. Then she spun around and spoke directly to Dalgliesh.

"She's lying! Tell me she's lying! It isn't true."

There was a silence. It could only have lasted a couple of seconds while Dalgliesh's mind phrased the careful answer. Then, as if impatient to forestall him, not looking at his chief's face, Massingham said clearly:

"Yes, it's true."

She looked from Dalgliesh to Domenica Schofield. Then she swayed as if she were about to faint. Dalgliesh went toward her, but she backed away. She said in a voice of dull calm:

"I thought he did it for me. I didn't drink the cocoa he made for me. I wasn't asleep when he came back. I went out and watched him in the garden, burning the white coat on the bonfire. I knew that there was blood on it. I thought he'd been to see Dr. Lorrimer because he was unkind to William and me. I thought he did it for me, because he loves me."

Suddenly she gave a high despairing wail like an animal in torment, and yet so human and so adult that Dalgliesh felt his blood run cold.

"Daddy! Daddy! Oh no!"

She put her hands to her throat and, pulling the leather thong from beneath her sweater, struggled with it, twisting like a creature in a trap. And then the knot broke. Over the dark carpet they scattered and rolled, six newly polished brass buttons, bright as crested jewels.

Massingham stooped and carefully gathered them up into his handkerchief. Still no one spoke. William propelled himself off the sofa, trotted over to his sister, and fastened his arms around her leg. His lip trembled. Domenica Schofield spoke directly to Dalgliesh.

"My God, yours is a filthy trade."

Dalgliesh ignored her. He said to Massingham:

"Look after the children. I'll ring for a W.P.C. and we'd better get Mrs. Swaffield. There's no one else I can think of. Don't leave her until they both arrive. I'll see to things here."

Massingham turned to Domenica Schofield.

"Not a trade. Just a job. And are you saying that it's one you don't want done?"

He went up to the girl. She was trembling violently. Dalgliesh thought that she would cringe away from him. But she stood perfectly still. With three words he had destroyed her. But who else had she to turn to? Massingham took off his tweed coat and wrapped it around her. He said gently without touching her:

"Come with me. You show me where we can make some tea. And then you'll have a lie-down and William and I will stay with you. I'll read to William."

She went with him as meekly as a prisoner with a jailer, without looking at him, the long coat trailing on the floor. Massingham took William's hand. The door closed after them. Dalgliesh wished never to see Massingham again. But he would see him again and, in time, without even caring or remembering. He never wanted to work with him again; but he knew that he would. He wasn't the man to destroy a subordinate's career simply because he had outraged susceptibilities to which he, Dalgliesh, had no right. What Massingham had done seemed to him now unforgivable. But life had taught him that the unforgivable was usually the most easily forgiven. It was possible to do police work honestly; there was, indeed, no other safe way to do it. But it wasn't possible to do it without giving pain.

Miss Willard had groped her way to the sofa. She muttered, as if trying to explain it to herself.

"I didn't mean it. She made me say it. I didn't mean it. I didn't want to hurt him."

Domenica Schofield turned to go.

"No, one seldom does." She said to Dalgliesh:

"If you want me, you know where I'll be."

"We shall want a statement."

"Of course. Don't you always? Longing and loneliness, terror and despair, all the human muddle, neatly documented, on one and a half sheets of official paper."

"No, just the facts."

He didn't ask her when it had begun. That wasn't really important; and he thought that he didn't need to ask. Brenda Pridmore had told him that she had sat in the same row as Mrs. Schofield and Dr.

Kerrison and his children at the concert in the chapel. That had been held on Thursday the twenty-sixth of August. And early in September, Domenica had broken with Edwin Lorrimer.

At the door she hesitated and turned. Dalgliesh asked:

"Did he telephone you the morning after the murder to let you know that he'd replaced the key on Lorrimer's body?"

"He never telephoned me. Neither of them did, ever. That was our arrangement. And I never rang him." She paused and then said gruffly:

"I didn't know. I may have suspected, but I didn't know. We weren't—what's your expression?—in it together. I am not responsible. It wasn't because of me."

"No," said Dalgliesh. "I didn't suppose it was. A motive for murder is seldom so unimportant."

She fixed on him her unforgettable eyes. She said:

"Why do you dislike me?"

The egotism that could ask such a question, and at such a time, astounded him. But it was his own self-knowledge that disgusted him more. He understood only too well what had driven those two men to creep guiltily like randy schoolboys to that rendezvous, to make themselves partners in her erotic, esoteric game. Given the opportunity, he would, he thought bitterly, have done the same.

She was gone. He went over to Miss Willard.

"Did you telephone Dr. Lorrimer to tell him about the burned candles, the numbers on the hymn board?"

"I chatted to him when he drove me to Mass the Sunday before last. I had to talk about something on the journey; he never did. And I was worried about the altar candles. I first noticed that someone had lit them when I went to the chapel at the end of September. On my last visit they were burned even lower. I thought that the chapel might be being used by devil worshippers. I know it's been deconsecrated, but it's still a holy place. And it's so secluded. No one goes there. The fen people don't like to walk out after dark. I wondered if I ought to talk to the rector or consult Father Gregory. Dr. Lorrimer asked me to go to the chapel again next day and let him know the numbers on the hymn board. I thought it was an odd thing to ask, but he seemed to think that it was important. I hadn't even noticed that they'd been altered. I could ask for the key, you see. He didn't like to."

But he could have taken it without signing for it, thought Dalgliesh. So why hadn't he? Because of the risk that he might be seen? Because it was repugnant to his obsessional, conformist personality to break a laboratory rule? Or, more likely, because he couldn't bear to enter the chapel again, to see with his own eyes the evidence of betrayal? She hadn't even bothered to change their meeting place. She had still used the same ingenious code to fix the date of the next assignation. Even the key she had handed to Kerrison had been Lorrimer's key. And none better than he had known the significance of those four numbers. The twenty-ninth day of the tenth month at six-forty. He said:

"And you waited together last Friday in the shelter of the trees?"

"That was his idea. He needed a witness, you see. Oh, he was quite right to be worried. A woman like that, quite unsuitable to be a stepmother to William. One man after another, Dr. Lorrimer said. That's why she had to leave London. She couldn't leave men alone. Any man would do. He knew about her, you see. He said the whole lab knew. She'd even made advances to him once. Horrible. He was going to write to Mrs. Kerrison and put a stop to it. I couldn't tell him the address. Dr. Kerrison's so secretive about his letters, and I'm not sure that even he knows exactly where his wife is. But we knew that she'd run away with a doctor, and we knew his name. It's quite a common name, but Dr. Lorrimer said he could trace them from the Medical Directory."

The Medical Directory. So that was why he had wanted to consult it, why he had opened the door so quickly when Bradley rang. He had only had to come from the Director's office on the ground floor. And he had been carrying his notebook. What was it that Howarth had said? He hated scraps of paper. He used the book to note down anything of importance. And this had been important. The names and addresses of Mrs. Kerrison's possible lovers.

Miss Willard looked up at him. Dalgliesh saw that she was crying, the tears streaking her face and dropping unimpeded over the twisting hands. She said:

"What will happen to him? What will you do to him?"

The telephone rang. Dalgliesh strode across the hall and into the study and lifted the receiver. It was Clifford Bradley. His voice sounded as high and excited as a young girl's. He said:

"Commander Dalgliesh? They said at the police station you might be there. I have to tell you at once. It's important. I've just remembered how I knew that the murderer was still in the lab. I heard a sound as I got to the lab door. I heard the same sound again two minutes ago coming downstairs from the bathroom. Sue had just finished telephoning her mother. What I heard was someone replacing the telephone receiver."

It was no more than confirmation of what he had long ago suspected. He returned to the drawing room and said to Miss Willard:

"Why did you tell us that you overheard Dr. Kerrison making that nine o'clock call from his study? Did he ask you to lie for him?"

The blotched face, the tear-drained eyes looked up at him.

"Oh no, he'd never do that! All he asked was whether I'd happened to hear him. It was when he came back to the house after he'd been called to the body. I wanted to help him, to make him pleased with me. It was such a little, unimportant lie. And it wasn't really a lie. I thought that perhaps I did hear him. You might have suspected him, and I knew that he couldn't have done it. He's kind, and good, and gentle. It seems such a venial sin to protect the innocent. That woman had got him into her clutches, but I knew he could never kill."

He had probably always intended to telephone the hospital from the laboratory if he wasn't back home in time. But, with Lorrimer lying dead, it must have taken nerve. He could barely have put down the receiver before he heard the approaching footsteps. And what then? Into the darkroom to watch and wait? That must have been one of his worst moments, standing there rigidly in the darkness, breath held, his heart thudding, wondering who could be arriving at this late hour, how they could have got in. And it could have been Blakelock;

Blakelock who would have rung at once for the police, who would have made an immediate search of the lab.

But it had only been a terrified Bradley. There had been no telephone call, no summons for help, only the echo of panicking feet down the corridor. And now all he had to do was to follow, make his way quietly out of the lab and home through the new lab the way he had come. He had put out the light and reached the front door. And then he had seen the headlights of Doyle's car swinging into the drive and backing to park among the bushes. He no longer dared leave by the door. That way was barred. And he couldn't wait for them to drive off. There was Nell at home who might wake and ask for him. There was the return telephone call at ten o'clock. He had to get back.

But he had still kept his head. It had been a clever move to take Lorrimer's keys and lock the laboratory. The police investigation would inevitably concentrate on the four sets of keys and the limited number of people who had access to them. And he knew the one way he could get out and had the skill and nerve to do it. He had put on Middlemass's jacket to protect his clothes; he knew how fatal a torn thread of cloth could be. But there had been no tear. And in the early hours of the morning a light rain had washed away any evidence on walls or windows which could have betrayed him.

He had reached home safely and made an excuse to call in on Miss Willard, establishing his alibi more firmly. No one had telephoned for him; no one had called. And he knew that, the next day, he would be among the first to examine the body. Howarth had said that he had stood by the door while Kerrison made his examination. It must have been then that he had slipped the key into Lorrimer's pocket. But that had been one of his mistakes. Lorrimer carried his personal keys in a leather pouch, not loose in his pocket.

There was the crunch of tires on the gravel of the drive. He looked out the window and saw the police car with Detective-Sergeant Reynolds and two women police constables in the back. The case had broken; except that it was never the case that broke, only the people. And now he and Massingham were free for the last interview, the most difficult of all.

At the edge of the clunch field a boy was flying a red kite. Tugged by the freshening wind it soared and dipped, weaving its convoluted tail against an azure sky as clear and bright as on a summer day. The clunch field was alive with voices and laughter. Even the discarded beer cans glinted like bright toys and the wastepaper bowled along merrily in the wind. The air was keen and smelled of the sea. It was possible to believe that the Saturday shoppers trailing with their children across the scrubland were carrying their picnics to the beach, that the clunch field led on to dunes and marram grass, to the child-loud fringes of the sea. Even the screen, which the police were fighting to erect against the wind, looked no more frightening than a Punch-and-Judy stand with a little group of curious people standing patiently at a distance, waiting for the show to begin.

It was Superintendent Mercer who came first up the slope of the clunch pit toward them. He said:

"It's a messy business; the husband of the girl who was found here on Wednesday. He's a butcher's assistant. Yesterday he took home one of the knives and came here last night to cut his throat. He left a note confessing to her murder, poor devil. It wouldn't have happened if we'd been able to arrest him yesterday. But Lorrimer's death and Doyle's suspension held us up. We only got the blood result late last night. Who is it you want to see?"

"Dr. Kerrison."

Mercer looked at Dalgliesh keenly, but said only:

"He's finished here now. I'll let him know."

Three minutes later Kerrison's figure appeared over the rim of the clunch pit and he walked toward them. He said:

"It was Nell, wasn't it?"

"Yes."

He didn't ask how or when. He listened intently as Dalgliesh spoke the words of the caution, as if he hadn't heard them before and wanted to commit them to memory. Then he said, looking at Dalgliesh:

"I'd rather not go to Guy's Marsh police station, not yet. I want to tell you about it now, just you, no one else. There won't be any difficulty. I'll make a full confession. Whatever happens, I don't want Nell to have to give evidence. Can you promise me that?"

"You must know that I can't. But there's no reason why the Crown should call her if you intend to plead guilty."

Dalgliesh opened the door of the car, but Kerrison shook his head. He said without a trace of self-pity:

"I'd rather stay outside. There'll be so many years of sitting when I shan't be able to walk under the sky. Perhaps for the rest of my life. If it were only Lorrimer's death, I might have hoped for a verdict of manslaughter. His killing wasn't premeditated. But the other was murder."

Massingham stayed by the car while Dalgliesh and Kerrison walked together around the clunch pit. Kerrison said:

"It started here, at this very spot, only four days ago. It feels like an eternity. Another life, another time. We'd both been called to the clunch pit murder, and afterwards he drew me to one side and told me to meet him that evening at eight-thirty at the laboratory. Not asked; told. And he told me, too, what he wanted to talk about. Domenica."

Dalgliesh asked:

"Did you know that he was her lover before you?"

"Not until I met him that night. She had never talked about him to me, never mentioned his name. But when he poured out his stream of hate and envy and jealousy, then, of course, I knew. I didn't ask him how he'd found out about me. I think he was mad. Perhaps we were both mad."

"And he threatened to write to your wife and prevent your getting custody of the children unless you gave her up."

"He was going to write anyway. He wanted her back, and I think, poor devil, that he actually believed that it might be possible. But he still wanted to punish me. I've only once before known such hate. He was standing there, white-faced, railing at me, taunting me, telling me that I'd lose the children, that I wasn't fit to be a father, that I'd never see them again. And suddenly it wasn't Lorrimer speaking. You see, I'd heard it all before from my wife. It was his voice, but her words.

And I knew that I couldn't take any more. I'd been up for most of the night; I'd had a terrible scene with Nell when I got home; and I'd spent the day worrying what Lorrimer might have to tell me.

"It was then that the telephone rang. It was his father complaining about the television. He only spoke briefly, then he put down the receiver. But when he was speaking I saw the mallet. And I knew that I had gloves in my coat pocket. The call to his father seemed to have sobered him. He told me there was nothing else he wanted to say. It was when he turned his back on me dismissively that I seized the mallet and struck. He fell without a sound. I put the mallet back on the table, and it was then I saw the open notebook with the names and addresses of three doctors. One of them was my wife's lover. I tore out the page and crumpled it in my pocket. Then I went to the telephone and made my call. It was just nine o'clock. The rest, I think, you know."

They had circled the clunch pit, pacing together, their eyes fixed on the bright grass. Now they turned and retraced their steps. Dalgliesh said:

"I think you'd better tell me."

But there was nothing new to learn. It had happened just as Dalgliesh had reasoned. When Kerrison had finished describing the burning of the coat and the letter, Dalgliesh asked:

"And Stella Mawson?"

"She rang me at the hospital and asked me to meet her in the chapel at half past seven yesterday. She gave me an idea what it was about. She said that she had a draft letter which she wanted to discuss with me, one she'd found in a certain desk. I knew what it would say."

She must have taken it with her to the chapel, thought Dalgliesh. It hadn't been found in her desk, neither the original nor the copy. It seemed to him extraordinary that she had actually risked letting Kerrison know that she had the letter on her. How could he be sure, when he killed her, that she hadn't left a copy? And how could she be sure that he wouldn't overpower her and take it?

Almost as if he knew what was going through Dalgliesh's mind, Kerrison said:

"It wasn't what you're thinking. She wasn't trying to sell me the letter. She wasn't selling anything. She told me that she'd taken it from Lorrimer's desk almost on impulse because she didn't want the police to find it. For some reason which she didn't explain, she hated Lorrimer, and she bore me no ill will. What she said was: 'He caused enough misery in his life. Why should he cause misery after his death?' She said another extraordinary thing. 'I was his victim once. I don't see why you should be his victim now.' She saw herself as on my side, someone who'd done me a service. And now she was asking me for something in return, something quite simple and ordinary. Something she knew that I'd be able to afford."

Dalgliesh said:

"The cash to buy Sprogg's Cottage, security for herself and Angela Foley."

"Not even a gift, merely a loan. She wanted four thousand pounds over five years at a rate of interest she could afford. She needed the money desperately, and she had to find it quickly. She explained to me that there was no one else she could ask. She was perfectly ready to have a legal agreement drawn up. She was the gentlest, most reasonable of blackmailers."

And she had thought that she was dealing with the gentlest, most reasonable of men. She had been totally without fear, until that last hideous moment when he had drawn the cord from his coat pocket and she had realized that she was facing, not a fellow victim, but her murderer. Dalgliesh said:

"You must have had the cord ready. When did you decide she had to die?"

"Even that, like Lorrimer's death, was almost chance. She had got the key from Angela Foley and she arrived at the chapel first. She was sitting in the chancel, in one of the stalls. She had left the door open, and when I went into the antechapel I saw the chest. I knew the cord was inside it. I'd had plenty of time to explore the chapel when I'd been waiting for Domenica. So I took it out and put it in my pocket. Then I went through to her, and we talked. She had the letter with her, in her pocket. She took it out and showed it to me without the least fear. It wasn't the finished letter; just a draft that he'd been working on. He must have enjoyed writing it, must have taken a lot of trouble getting it right.

"She was an extraordinary woman. I said that I'd lend her the money, that I'd have a proper agreement drawn up by my solicitor. There was a Prayer Book in the chapel, and she made me put my hand on it and swear that I'd never tell anyone what had happened between us. I think she was terrified that Angela Foley would get to know. It was when I realized that she, and only she, held this dangerous knowledge, that I decided that she must die."

He stopped walking. He turned to Dalgliesh and said:

"You see, I couldn't take a chance on her. I'm not trying to justify myself. I'm not even trying to make you understand. You aren't a father, so you never could understand. I couldn't risk giving my wife such a weapon against me when the custody case comes before the High Court. They probably wouldn't worry overmuch that I had a mistress; that wouldn't make me unfit to care for my children. If it did, what chance would most parents have of getting custody? But a secret affair that I'd concealed from the police with a woman whose previous lover was murdered, a murder for which I had only a weak alibi and a strong motive. Wouldn't that tip the balance? My wife is attractive and plausible, outwardly perfectly sane. That's what makes it so impossible. Madness isn't so very difficult to diagnose; neurosis is less dramatic but just as lethal if you have to live with it. She tore us apart, Nell and me. I couldn't let her have William and Nell. When I stood in the chapel and faced Stella Mawson, I knew it was their lives against hers.

"And it was so easy. I slipped the double cord around her neck and pulled tight. She must have died at once. Then I carried her into the antechapel and strung her up on the hook. I remembered to scrape her boots on the chair seat and leave the chair overturned. I walked back across the field to where I'd left my car. I'd parked it where Domenica parks hers when we meet, in the shadow of an old barn on the edge of Guy's Marsh Road. Even the timing was right for me. I was due at the hospital for a medical committee meeting, but I'd planned to go into my laboratory first and do some work. Even if someone at the hospital noted the time when I arrived, there were only about twenty minutes unaccounted for. And I could easily have spent an extra twenty minutes on the drive."

They walked on in silence toward the car. Then Kerrison began speaking again:

"I still don't understand it. She's so beautiful. And it isn't only her beauty. She could have had any man she wanted. It was amazing that, for some extraordinary reason, she wanted me. When we were together, lying by candlelight in the quietness of the chapel, after we'd made love, all the anxieties, all the tensions, all the responsibilities were forgotten. It was easy for us, because of the dark evenings. She could park her car by the barn in safety. No one walks on Guy's Marsh Road at night, and there are only a few cars. I knew it would be more difficult in the spring with the long, light evenings. But then, I didn't expect she would want me that long. It was a miracle that she wanted me at all. I never thought beyond the next meeting, the next date on the hymn board. She wouldn't let me telephone her. I never saw or spoke to her except when we were alone in the chapel. I knew that she didn't love me, but that wasn't important. She gave what she could, and it was enough for me."

They were back at the car now. Massingham was holding open the door. Kerrison turned to Dalgliesh and said:

"It wasn't love, but it was in its own way a kind of loving. And it was such peace. This is peace, too, knowing that there's nothing else I need do. There's an end of responsibility, an end of worry. A murderer sets himself aside from the whole of humanity forever. It's a kind of death. I'm like a dying man now, the problems are still there, but I'm moving away from them into a new dimension. I forfeited so many rights when I killed Stella Mawson, even the right to feel pain."

He got into the back of the car without another word. Dalgliesh closed the door. Then his heart lurched. The blue and yellow ball came bounding across the clunch field toward him and, after it, shouting with laughter, his mother calling after him, ran the child. For one dreadful second, Dalgliesh thought that it was William, William's dark fringe of hair, William's laugh, William's red wellingtons flashing in the sun.

# The Skull Beneath the Skin

# CONTENTS

Webster was much possessed by death
And saw the skull beneath the skin;
And breastless creatures under ground
Leaned backward with a lipless grin.

Daffodil bulbs instead of balls
Stared from the sockets of the eyes!
He knew that thought clings round dead limbs
Tightening its lusts and luxuries.

—From "Whispers of Immortality"
T. S. Eliot

# BOOK ONE

·

# Call to an Offshore Island

# I

There could be no doubt about it; the new nameplate was crooked. Cordelia had no need to adopt Bevis's expedient of dodging through the mid-morning traffic which cluttered Kingly Street and squinting at the plaque through a dazzle of grinding delivery vans and taxis to recognize stark mathematical fact: the neat bronze oblong, so carefully designed and so expensive, was half an inch out of true. Lopsided as it was, it looked, she thought, despite the simplicity of its wording, both pretentious and ridiculous, a fitting advertisement of irrational hope and ill-advised enterprise.

PRYDE'S DETECTIVE AGENCY
(Third Floor)
PROP.: CORDELIA GRAY

Had she been superstitious, she might have believed that Bernie's unquiet spirit was protesting against the new plaque with the deletion of his name. And, indeed, it had seemed at the time symbolic, the final obliteration of Bernie at her hands. She had never considered changing the name of the agency; while it remained in being it would always be Pryde's. But it had become increasingly irksome to be asked by her clients, disconcerted as much by her sex as by her youth, "But I thought I would be seeing Mr. Pryde." They might as well know from the start that there was now only one proprietor and she a female.

Bevis rejoined her at the door, his pretty, mobile face a parody of desolation, and said, "I measured it carefully from the ground, honestly, Miss Gray."

"I know. The pavement must be uneven. It's my fault. We should have bought a spirit level."

But she had been trying to limit expenditure from petty cash, ten pounds a week kept in the battered cigarette tin inherited from Bernie with its picture of the battle of Jutland, from which money seemed to drain away by a mysterious process unrelated to actual expenditure. It had been only too easy for her to accept the assurance of Bevis, leaping from his typewriter, that he was handy with a screwdriver, forgetting that, for Bevis, any job was preferable to the one he was actually supposed to be doing.

He said, "If I close my left eye and hold my head like this, it looks all right."

"But we can't rely on a succession of one-eyed, wry-necked clients, Bevis."

Glancing at Bevis's face, which had now fallen into an extreme of despair which would not have been inappropriate to the announcement of an atomic attack, Cordelia felt an obscure desire to comfort him for his own incompetence. One of the disconcerting aspects of being an employer of staff, a role for which she increasingly felt herself almost wholly unsuited, was this oversensitivity to their feelings coupled with a vague sense of guilt. This was the more irrational because, strictly speaking, she didn't directly employ either Bevis or Miss Maudsley. Both were hired from Miss Feeley's employment agency on a weekly basis when the agency's case load warranted it. There was seldom competition for their services; both were invariably and suspiciously available when asked for. Both gave her honesty, conscientious timekeeping, and a fierce loyalty; both would, no doubt, have also given her efficient secretarial service if that had lain in their power. Both added to her anxieties, since she knew that the failure of the agency would be almost as traumatic for them as for her.

Miss Maudsley would suffer the more. She was a gentle, sixty-two-year-old rector's sister, eking out her pension in a bed-sitting-room in South Kensington, whose gentility, age, incompetence, and virginity had made her the butt of the countless typing pools through which she had drifted since her brother's death. Bevis, with his facile, slightly venial charm, was better equipped to survive in the London jungle. He was supposed to be a dancer working as a temporary typist while resting, an inappropriate euphemism when applied to such a restless boy, perpetually fidgeting in his chair or pirouetting on tiptoe, fingers splayed, eyes widened and alarmed, as if poised for flight. He was certificated to type thirty words a minute by an obscure secretarial school long since defunct, but Cordelia reminded herself that even they hadn't guaranteed his proficiency to undertake minor jobs as a handyman.

He and Miss Maudsley were unexpectedly compatible, and a great deal more chat went on in the outer office between the bouts of inexpert typing than Cordelia would have expected from two such discordant personalities, denizens she would have thought of such alien worlds. Bevis poured out his domestic and professional tribulations, liberally laced with inaccurate and occasionally scurrilous theatrical gossip. Miss Maudsley applied to this bewildering world her own mixture of innocence, High Anglican theology, rectory morality, and common sense. Life in the outer office became very cozy at times, but Miss Maudsley had old-fashioned views on the proper distinction to be made between employer and employed and the inner room where Cordelia worked was sacrosanct.

Suddenly Bevis cried out, "Oh, God, it's Tomkins!"

A small black-and-white kitten had appeared at the doorway, shaken one exploratory paw with deceptive insouciance, stretched its tail rigid, then shivered with ecstatic apprehension and darted under a post-office van and out of sight. Bevis, wailing, fled in pursuit. Tomkins was one of the agency's failures, having been repudiated by a spinster of that name who had employed Cordelia to find her missing black kitten with a white eye patch, two white paws, and a striped tail. Tomkins precisely fulfilled the specifications, but his putative mistress had immediately known him for an impostor. Having rescued him from imminent starvation on a building site behind Victoria Station, they could hardly abandon him, and he now lived in the outer office with a dirt tray, a cushioned basket, and access to the roof via a partly opened window for his nightly excursions. He was a drain on resources, not so much because of the rising cost of cat food—although it was a pity that Miss Maudsley had encouraged an addiction to tastes beyond their means by providing the most expensive tin on the market for his first meal and that Tomkins, although in general a stupid cat, could apparently read labels—but because Bevis wasted too much time playing with him, tossing a Ping-Pong ball or drawing a rabbit's foot on string across the office floor with cries of "Oh, look, Miss Gray! Isn't he a clever leaping beastie?"

The clever leaping beastie, having caused chaos among the traffic in Kingly Street, now streaked into the rear entrance of a pharmacy with Bevis in noisy pursuit. Cordelia guessed that neither kitten nor boy was likely to reappear for some time. Bevis picked up new friends as obsessively as others pick up litter, and Tomkins would be a great introducer. Oppressed by the realization that Bevis's morning was now fated to be almost entirely unproductive, Cordelia was aware of a lethargic disinclination to any further effort herself. She stood against the jamb of the doorway, closed her eyes, and lifted her face to the unseasonable warmth of the late-September sun. Distancing herself by an effort of will from the grind and clamor of the street, the pervading smell of petrol, the clatter of passing feet, she played with the temptation, which she knew she would resist, to walk away from it all, leaving the lopsided plaque as a memorial to her efforts to keep faith with the dead Bernie and his impossible dream.

She supposed that she ought to be relieved that the agency was beginning to make a reputation for something, even if it was only for finding lost pets. Undoubtedly there was a need for such a service, and one in which she suspected they had a monopoly; and the clients, tearful, desperate, outraged by what they saw as the callous indifference of the local C.I.D., never haggled at the size of the bill and paid more promptly than Cordelia suspected they might have done for the return of a relative. Even when the agency's efforts had been unsuccessful and Cordelia had to present her account with apologies, the bill was invariably paid without demur. Perhaps the owners were motivated by the natural human need at a time of bereavement to feel that something had been done, however unlikely that something, to achieve success. But frequently there were successes. Miss Maudsley, in particular, had a persistence in door-to-door inquiries, coupled with an almost uncanny empathy with the feline mind, that had restored at least half a dozen cats, damp, half starved, and feebly mewing, to their ecstatic owners, while occasionally exposing the perfidy of those animals which had been living a double life and had transferred more or less permanently to their second home. She managed to conquer her timidity when in pursuit of cat thieves and on Saturday mornings walked purposefully through the rowdy exuberance and half-submerged terrors of London's street markets as if under divine protection, which no doubt she felt herself to be. But Cordelia wondered from time to time what poor, ambitious, pathetic Bernie would have thought about the debasement of his dream child. Lulled into a trancelike peace by the warmth and the sun, Cordelia recalled with startling clarity that confident, overloud voice: "We've got a gold mine here, partner, if once we get started." She was glad that he couldn't know how small the nuggets and how thin the seam.

A voice, quiet, masculine, and authoritative, broke into her reverie.

"That nameplate's crooked."

"I know."

Cordelia opened her eyes. The voice was deceptive: he was older than she had expected, she guessed a little over sixty. Despite the heat of the day he was wearing a tweed jacket, well tailored but old, with leather patches on the elbows. He wasn't tall, perhaps no more than five feet ten inches, but he stood very upright with an easy, confident stance, almost an elegance, which she sensed concealed an inner wariness as if he were tensed for a word of command. She wondered if he had once been a soldier. His head was held high and fixed, the gray and somewhat sparse hair brushed smoothly back from a high, creased forehead. The face was long and bony, with a dominant nose jutting from cheeks reddened and crossed by broken veins, and a wide, well-shaped mouth. The eyes which scrutinized her, not, she felt, unbenignly, were keen under the bushy eyebrows. The left brow was held higher than the right, and she saw that he had a habit of twitching his brows and working the corners of the wide mouth; it gave his face a restlessness which was singularly at variance with the stillness of his body and which made it slightly embarrassing for her to meet his eyes.

He said, "Better get the job done properly."

She watched without speaking while he put down the briefcase he was carrying, took from a pocket a pen and his wallet, found a card, and wrote on the back of it in an upright, rather school-boyish hand.

Taking the card, Cordelia noted the single name, Morgan, and the telephone number, then turned it over. She read: Sir George Ralston, Bt., D.S.O., M.C.

So she was right. He had been a soldier. She asked, "Will he be expensive, this Mr. Morgan?"

"Less expensive than making a nonsense. Tell him I gave you his number. He'll charge what the job's worth, no more."

Cordelia's heart lifted. The lopsided name plaque, gravely surveyed by the critical eye of this unexpected and eccentric knight errant, suddenly seemed to her irresistibly funny, no longer a calamity but a joke. Even Kingly Street was transformed with her mood and became a glittering, sunlit bazaar, pulsating with optimism and life. She almost laughed aloud.

Controlling her trembling mouth, she said gravely, "It's very kind of you. Are you a connoisseur of nameplates or just a public benefactor?"

"Some people think I'm a public menace. Actually, I'm a client; that is, if you're Cordelia Gray. Don't people ever tell you . . ."

Cordelia, unreasonably, was disappointed. Why should she have supposed that he was different from other male clients? She finished the sentence for him: "That it's an unsuitable job for a woman? They do, and it isn't."

He said mildly, "I was going to say, 'Don't they ever tell you that your office is difficult to find?' This street's a mess. Half the buildings aren't properly numbered. Too much change of use, I suppose. But the new plate should help when it's properly fixed. Better get it done. Gives a poor impression."

At that moment Bevis panted up beside them, his curls damp with exertion, the telltale screwdriver protruding from his shirt pocket. Holding the richly purring Tomkins against one flushed cheek, he presented his charming delinquency to the newcomer. He was rewarded by a curt "A botched job, that" and a look which instantly rejected him as officer material. Sir George turned to Cordelia.

"Shall we go up, then?"

Cordelia avoided Bevis's eyes, which she guessed were rolling heavenward, and they climbed the narrow, linoleum-covered stairs in single file, Cordelia leading, past the single lavatory and washroom which served all the tenants in the building (she hoped that Sir George wouldn't need to use it), and into the outer office on the third floor. Miss Maudsley's anxious eyes looked up at them over her typewriter. Bevis deposited Tomkins in his basket (where he at once began washing away the contamination of Kingly Street), gave Miss Maudsley a wide-eyed admonitory look, and mouthed the word *client* at her. Miss Maudsley flushed, half rose from her chair, then subsided and applied herself to painting out an error with a shaking hand. Cordelia led the way into her inner sanctum.

When they were seated, she asked, "Would you like some coffee?"

"Real coffee or ersatz?"

"Well, I suppose you'd call it ersatz. But best-quality ersatz."

"Tea, then, if you have it, preferably Indian. Milk, please. No sugar. No biscuits."

The form of the request was not meant to be offensive. He was used to ascertaining the facts and then asking for what he wanted.

Cordelia put her head outside the door and said, "Tea, please" to Miss Maudsley. The tea, when it arrived, would be served in the delicate Rockingham cups which Miss Maudsley had inherited from her mother and had lent to the agency for the use of special clients only. She had no doubt that Sir George would qualify for the Rockingham.

They faced each other across Bernie's desk. His eyes, gray and keen, inspected her face as if he were an examiner and she a candidate, which in a way she supposed she was. Their sudden, direct, and glittering stare, in contrast to the spasmodically grimacing mouth, was disconcerting.

He said, "Why do you call yourself Pryde's?"

"Because the agency was set up by an ex-Metropolitan policeman,

Bernie Pryde. I worked for him for a time as his assistant, and then he made me his partner. When he died he left the agency to me."

"How did he die?"

The question, sharp as an accusation, struck her as odd, but she answered calmly. "He cut his wrists."

She didn't need to close her eyes to see again that remembered scene, garish and sharply outlined as a cinema still. Bernie had lain slumped in the chair in which she now sat, his half-clenched right hand close to the open cutthroat razor, his shrunken left hand, with its scored and gaping wrist, resting palm upwards in the bowl like some exotic sea anemone glimpsed in a rock pool, curling in death its pale and wrinkled tentacles. But no rock pool had ever been so brightly pink. She could smell again the sickly sweet, insistent odor of freshly spilled blood.

"Killed himself, did he?"

His tone lightened. He might have been a golfing partner congratulating Bernie on a well-placed putt, while his quick glance around the office suggested that the action had been in all the circumstances entirely reasonable.

She had no need to see the room through his eyes. What she saw through her own was depressing enough. She and Miss Maudsley had redecorated her office together, painting the walls pale yellow to give an impression of greater light and cleaning the faded carpet with a proprietary liquid; it had dried patchily so that the final impression reminded her of diseased skin. With its newly washed curtains, the room at least looked clean and tidy, too tidy since the absence of clutter suggested no great pressure of work. Every surface was crammed with plants. Miss Maudsley had green fingers, and the cuttings she had taken from her own plants and lovingly tended in a variety of oddly shaped receptacles picked up during her forays into the street markets had flourished despite the poor light. The resulting rampant greenery suggested that it had been cunningly deployed to conceal some sinister defect in the structure or decor. Cordelia still used Bernie's old oak desk, still imagined that she could trace the outline of the bowl in which he had bled away his life, could still identify one particular stain of spilled blood and water. But then there were so many rings, so many stains. His hat, with its upturned brim and grubby ribbon, still hung on the curved wooden coat stand. No jumble sale would take it, and she found herself unable to throw it away. Twice she had taken it as far as the dustbin in the backyard but had been unable to drop it in, finding this final symbolic rejection of Bernie even more personal and traumatic than the exclusion of his name from the brass plaque. If the agency did finally fail—and she tried not to think what the new rent would be when the present lease came up for renewal in three years' time—she supposed that she would still leave the hat hanging there in its pathetic decrepitude for unknown hands to toss with fastidious distaste into the wastepaper basket.

The tea arrived. Sir George waited until Miss Maudsley left. Then, measuring milk carefully into his cup, drop by drop, he said, "The job I'm offering is a mixture of functions. You'd be part bodyguard, part private secretary, part investigator, and part—well, nursemaid. A bit of everything. Not everyone's cup of tea. No knowing how it may turn out."

"I'm supposed to be a private investigator."

"No doubt. Shouldn't be too purist in these times. A job's a job. And you could find yourself involved in detection, even in violence, although it doesn't seem likely. Unpleasant but not dangerous. If I thought there was any real risk to my wife or to you I wouldn't be employing an amateur."

Cordelia said, "Perhaps you could explain what exactly you want me to do."

He frowned into his tea as if reluctant to begin. But when he did his account was lucid, concise, and unhesitating.

"My wife is the actress Clarissa Lisle. You may have heard of her. Most people seem to know of her, although she hasn't worked much recently. I am her third husband; we married in June 1978. In July 1980 she was employed to play Lady Macbeth at the Duke of Clarence's Theater. On the third night of the advertised six-month run she received what she saw as a death threat. These threats have continued intermittently ever since."

He began sipping his tea. Cordelia found herself gazing at him with the anxiety of a child hoping that her offering is acceptable. The pause seemed very long. She asked, "You said that she saw the first note as threatening. Are you implying that its meaning was ambiguous? What form exactly do these threats take?"

"Typewritten notes. Variety of machines by the look of it. Each communication surmounted by a small drawing of a coffin or a skull. All are quotations from plays in which my wife has appeared. All the quotations deal with death or dying: the fear of death, the judgment of death, the inevitability of death."

The reiteration of that numinous word was oppressive. But surely it was her imagination that he twisted it on his lips with mordant satisfaction. She said, "But they don't specifically threaten her?"

"She sees this harping on death as threatening. She's sensitive. Actresses have to be, I suppose. They need to be liked. This isn't friendly. I have the notes here, the ones she kept. The first ones were thrown away. You'll need the evidence."

He clicked open the briefcase and took out a stout manila envelope. From it he spilled a heap of small sheets of paper and began spreading them over the desk. She recognized the type of paper at once; it was a popular, medium-quality white writing paper sold over thousands of stationery counters in three sizes with envelopes to match. The sender had been economical and had selected the smallest size. Each sheet bore a typed quotation surmounted by a small drawing about one inch high, of either an up-ended coffin with the initials *R.I.P.* on the lid or a skull with crossbones. Neither had required much skill; they were emblems rather than accurate representations. On the other hand they were drawn with a certain sureness of line and decorative sense which suggested some facility with the pen or, in this case, with a black-tipped ballpoint. Under Sir George's bony fingers the white slips of paper with their stark black emblems shifted and rearranged themselves like the cards for some sinister game, hunt the quotation, murderer's snap.

Most of the quotations were familiar, words which would readily come to the mind of anyone reasonably well read in Shakespeare and the Jacobeans who chose to ponder references in English drama to death and the terror of dying. Even reading them now, truncated and childishly embellished as they were, Cordelia felt their nostalgic power. The majority of them were from Shakespeare and the obvious choices were there. The longest by far—and how could the sender have resisted it?—was Claudio's anguished cry from *Measure for Measure*:

> Ay, but to die, and go we know not where,
> To lie in cold obstruction and to rot,
> This sensible warm motion to become
> A kneaded clod and the delighted spirit
> To bathe in fiery floods, or to reside
> In thrilling region of thick-ribbèd ice—
> To be imprisoned in the viewless winds,
> And blown with restless violence round about
> The pendent world
> . . . . . . . . . . . . . . . . . . . . . . .
> The weariest and most loathèd worldly life
> That age, ache, penury, and imprisonment
> Can lay on nature is a paradise
> To what we fear of death.

It was difficult to interpret that familiar passage as a personal threat, but most of the other quotations could be seen as more directly intimidating, hinting, she thought, at some retribution for real or imagined wrongs.

> He that dies pays all debts.
> Oh, thou weed!
> Who are so lovely fair and smell'st so sweet
> That the sense aches at thee, would thou hadst
>         ne'er been born!

Some care had been taken in the choice of illustration. The skull adorned the lines from *Hamlet*—

Now get thee to my lady's chamber, and tell her, let
her paint an inch thick, to this favour she must come

—as it did a passage which Cordelia thought might be from John Webster, although she couldn't identify the play:

Being heretofore drown'd in security,
You know not how to live, nor how to die;
But I have an object that shall startle you,
And make you know whither you are going.

But, even allowing for the sensitivity of an actress, it would take a fairly robust egotism to wrench these familiar words from their contexts and apply them to oneself; that, or a fear of dying so strong as to be morbid. She took a new notebook from her desk drawer and asked, "How do they arrive?"

"Most come by post in the same sort of envelope as the paper and with the address typed. My wife didn't think to keep any of the envelopes. A few were delivered by hand either at the theater or at our London flat. One was pushed under the dressing-room door during the run of *Macbeth*. The first half dozen or so were destroyed—best thing to do with them all in my view. These twenty-three are all we now have. I've numbered them in pencil on the back in the order of receipt as far as my wife can remember and with information about when and how each was delivered."

"Thank you. That should be helpful. Your wife has played a great deal of Shakespeare?"

"She was a member of the Malvern Repertory Company for three years after she left drama school and played a fair amount then. Less in recent years."

"And the first of these—which she threw away—came when she was playing Lady Macbeth. What happened?"

"The first one was upsetting, but she told no one about it. Thought it was an isolated bit of malice. She says she can't remember what it said, only that it had the drawing of a coffin. Then a second came, and a third, and fourth. During the third week of the season my wife kept breaking down and had to be continually prompted. On the Saturday she ran off the stage during the second act and her understudy had to take over. It's all a matter of confidence. If you think you're going to dry up—drying is the theatrical jargon, I believe—then you dry. She was able to return to the part after a week, but it was a struggle to get through the six weeks. After that she was due to appear at Brighton in a revival of one of those thirties murder mysteries, the sort where the ingenue is called Bunty, the hero is Clive, and all the men wear long tennis flannels and keep dashing in and out of french windows. Curious affair. Not exactly her kind of part—she's a classical actress—but there aren't a lot of opportunities for middle-aged women. Too many good actresses chasing too few parts, so they tell me. Same thing happened. The first quotation appeared on the morning the play opened, and they came at regular intervals thereafter. The play came off after four weeks, and my wife's performance may have had something to do with it. She thought so. I'm not so sure. It was a stupid plot; couldn't make sense of it myself. Clarissa didn't act again until she accepted a part in Webster's *The White Devil at Nottingham,* Victoria something or other."

"Vittoria Corombona."

"Was that it? I was in New York for ten days and didn't see it. But the same thing happened. The first note arrived again on the day the play opened. This time my wife went to the police. Not much joy. They took the notes away, thought about them, and brought them back. Sympathetic but not very effective. Made it obvious that they didn't take the death threat seriously. Pointed out that if people are serious about killing, they do it, they don't just threaten. Must say, that was rather my view. They did discover one thing, though. The note which arrived while I was in New York was typed on my old Remington."

Cordelia said, "You still haven't explained how you think I can help."

"Coming to that. This weekend my wife is to play the leading role in an amateur production of *The Duchess of Malfi.* The play is to be given in Victorian dress and will take place on Courcy Island about two miles off the Dorset coast. The owner of the island, Ambrose Gorringe, has restored the small Victorian theater which was first built by his great-grandfather. I understand that the original Gorringe, who rebuilt the ruined medieval castle, used to entertain the Prince of Wales and his mistress, the actress Lillie Langtry, and the guests used to amuse themselves with amateur theatricals. I suppose the present owner is trying to restore past glories. There was an article in one of the Sunday papers about a year ago describing the island, the restoration of the castle, and theater. You may have seen it."

Cordelia couldn't recall it. She said, "And you want me to go to the island and be with Lady Ralston?"

"I hoped to be there myself, but that won't now be possible. I have a meeting in the west country which I can't miss. I propose to motor down to Speymouth with my wife early Friday morning and take leave of her at the launch. But she needs someone with her. This performance is important to her. There's to be a revival of the play at Chichester in the spring, and if she can regain her confidence she might feel that she can do it. But there's more to it than that. She thinks that the threats may come to a head this weekend, that someone will try to kill her on Courcy Island."

"She must have some reason for thinking that."

"Nothing that she can explain. Nothing that would impress the police. Not rational, perhaps. But that's what she feels. She asked me to get you."

And he had come to get her. Did he always procure for his wife whatever she wanted? She asked again, "What precisely am I being employed to do, Sir George?"

"Protect her from nuisance. Take any telephone calls which come for her. Open any letters. Check the set before the performance if you get the chance. Be on call at night; that's when she's most nervous. And bring a fresh mind to the question of the messages. Find out, if you can in just three days, who is responsible."

Before Cordelia could respond to these concise instructions, there came again that disconcerting pierce of gray frown under the discordant brows.

"D'you like birds?"

Cordelia was temporarily nonplussed. She supposed that few people, except those afflicted with a phobia, would admit to not liking birds. They are, after all, one of the most graceful of life's fragile diversions. But she supposed that Sir George was covertly inquiring whether she could recognize a marsh harrier at fifty yards. She said cautiously, "I'm not very good at identifying the less common species."

"Pity. The island's one of the most interesting natural bird sanctuaries in Great Britain, probably the most remarkable of those in private hands, almost as interesting as Brownsea Island in Poole Harbor. Very similar, come to think of it. Courcy has as many rare birds, the blue-eared and Swinhold pheasants as well as Canada geese, black godwits, and oyster catchers. Pity you're not interested. Any questions—about the case, I mean?"

Cordelia said tentatively, "If I'm to spend three days with your wife, ought she not to interview me before any decision is made? It's important that she feel she can trust me. She doesn't know me. We haven't even met."

"Yes, you have. That's how she knows she can trust you. She was having tea with a Mrs. Fortescue last week when you returned the Fortescue cat—Solomon, I think the brute's called. Apparently you found him within thirty minutes of beginning the search, so your bill was correspondingly small. Mrs. Fortescue is devoted to the animal. You could have charged treble. She wouldn't have queried it. That impressed my wife."

Cordelia said, "We're rather expensive. We have to be. But we are honest."

She remembered the drawing room in Eaton Square, a feminine room if femininity implies softness and luxury; a cluttered, cozy repository of silver-framed photographs, an overlavish tea on a low table in front of the Adam fireplace, too many flowers conventionally arranged.

Mrs. Fortescue, incoherent with relief and joy, had introduced her guest to Cordelia as a matter of form, but her voice, muffled in Solomon's fur, had been indistinct and Cordelia hadn't caught the name. But the impression had been definite. The visitor had sat very still in her armchair beside the fireplace, one thin leg thrown over the other, heavily ringed hands resting on the arms. Cordelia recalled yellow hair intricately piled and wound above a tall forehead, a small, bee-stung mouth, and immense eyes, deep-set but with heavy, almost swollen lids. She had seemed to impose on the lush conformity of the room a hieratic and angular grace, a distinction which, despite the plainness of the formal suede suit, hinted at some histrionic or eccentric individuality. She had gravely bent her head and watched her friend's effusions with a half-mocking smile. Despite her stillness there had been no impression of peace.

Cordelia said, "I didn't recognize your wife but I remember her very well."

"And you'll take the job?"

"Yes, I'll take it."

He said without embarrassment, "Rather different from finding lost cats. Mrs. Fortescue told my wife what you charge per day. This will be higher, I suppose."

Cordelia said, "The daily rate is the same whatever the job. The final bill depends on the time taken, whether I have to use either of my staff, and the level of expenses. These can sometimes be high. But as I'll be a guest on the island, there will be no hotel bills. When do you want me to arrive?"

"The launch from Courcy—it's called *Shearwater*—will be at Speymouth jetty to meet the nine-thirty-two from Waterloo. Your ticket's in this envelope. My wife has telephoned to let Mr. Gorringe know that she's bringing a secretary-companion to help her with various odd jobs during the weekend. You'll be expected."

So Clarissa Lisle had been confident that she would take the job. And why not? She had taken it. And she was apparently equally confident of being able to get her way with Ambrose Gorringe. Her excuse for including a secretary in the party was surely rather thin, and Cordelia wondered how far it had been believed. To arrive for a country-house weekend accompanied by one's private detective was permissible for royalty, but from any less elevated guest showed a lack of confidence in one's host, while to bring one incognito might reasonably be regarded as a breach of etiquette. It wasn't going to be easy to protect Miss Lisle without betraying that she was there under false pretenses, a discovery which would hardly be agreeable for either her host or fellow guests. She said, "I need to know who else will be on the island and anything you can tell me about them."

"There's not much I can tell. There'll be about one hundred people on the island by Saturday afternoon when the cast and invited audience arrive. But the house party is small. My wife, of course, with Tolly—Miss Tolgarth—her dresser. Then my wife's stepson, Simon Lessing, will be there. He's a seventeen-year-old schoolboy, the son of Clarissa's second husband, who drowned in August 1977. He wasn't happy with the relatives who were his guardians, so my wife decided to take him on. I'm not sure why he's invited; music's his interest. Clarissa probably thought it was time he met more people. He's a shy boy. Then there's her cousin, Roma Lisle. Used to be a schoolmistress but now keeps a bookshop somewhere in north London. Unmarried, aged about forty-five. I've only met her twice. I think she may be bringing her partner with her, but if so, I can't tell you who he is. And you'll meet the drama critic Ivo Whittingham. He's an old friend of my wife's. He's supposed to be doing a piece about the theater and the performance for one of the color magazines. Ambrose Gorringe will be there, of course. And there are three servants, the butler, Munter, his wife, and Oldfield, who is the boatman and general factotum. I think that's all."

"Tell me about Mr. Gorringe."

"Gorringe has known my wife since childhood. Both their fathers were in the diplomatic. He inherited the island from his uncle in 1977 when he was spending a year abroad. Something to do with tax avoidance. He came back to the UK in 1978 and has spent the last three years restoring the castle and looking after the island. Middle-aged. Unmarried. Read history at Cambridge, I believe. Authority on the Victorians. I know no harm of him."

Cordelia said, "There's one last question I have to ask. Your wife apparently fears for her life, so much so that she is reluctant to be on Courcy Island without protection. Is there any one of that company whom she has reason to fear, reason to suspect?"

She could see at once that the question was unwelcome, perhaps because it forced him to acknowledge what he had implied but never stated, that his wife's fear for her life was hysterical and unreal. She had demanded protection and he was providing it. But he didn't think it was necessary; he believed neither in the danger nor in the means he was employing to reassure her. And now some part of his mind was repelled by the thought that his wife's host and her fellow guests were to be under secret surveillance. He had done what his wife had asked of him, but he didn't like himself any the better for it.

He said curtly, "I think you can put that idea out of your head. My wife has no reason to suspect any of the house party of wishing to harm her, no reason in the world."

## II

Nothing more of importance was said. Sir George looked at his watch and got to his feet. Two minutes later he said a curt good-bye at the street door, neither mentioning nor glancing at the offending nameplate. As she climbed the stairs, Cordelia wondered whether she could have managed the interview better. It was a pity that it had ended so abruptly. There were questions which she wished she had thought to ask, in particular whether any of the people she was to meet on Courcy Island knew of the threatening messages. She would now have to wait until she met Miss Lisle.

As she opened the office door, Miss Maudsley and Bevis looked up over their typewriters with avid eyes. It would have been heartless to deny them a share in the news. They had sensed that Sir George was no ordinary client, and curiosity and excitement had virtually paralyzed them. There had been a suspicious absence of clacking typewriters from the outer office during his visit. Now Cordelia told them as little as was compatible with telling them anything worth hearing, emphasizing that Miss Lisle was looking for a companion-secretary who would protect her from an irritating but unimportant poison-pen nuisance. She said nothing about the nature of the threatening messages or of the actress's conviction that her life was seriously threatened. She warned them that this assignment, like all other jobs, even the most trivial, was to be treated as confidential.

Miss Maudsley said, "Of course, Miss Gray. Bevis understands that perfectly well."

Bevis was passionate in his assurances. "I'm more reliable than I look. I won't utter, honestly. I never do, not about the agency. But I'll be no good if anyone tortures me for information. I can't stand pain."

Cordelia said, "No one's going to torture you, Bevis."

By general consent they took an early lunch hour. Bevis fetched sandwiches from the Carnaby Street delicatessen and Miss Maudsley made coffee. Sitting cozily in the outer office, they gave themselves over to happy speculation about where this interesting new assignment might lead. And the hour wasn't wasted. Unexpectedly, both Miss Maudsley and Bevis had helpful information to give about Courcy Island and its owner, pouring out a spate of antiphonal chat. It wasn't the first time this had happened. Their more orthodox skills might be suspect, but they not infrequently provided a bonus in the way of useful gossip.

"You'll enjoy the castle, Miss Gray, if you're interested in Victorian architecture. My brother took the Mothers' Union to the island for their summer outing the month before he died. Of course, I'm not a full member; I couldn't be. But I usually went on the outings, and this one was so interesting. I particularly enjoyed the pictures and the porcelain. And there's one delightful bedroom which is almost a museum to the Victorian Arts and Crafts Movement: De Morgan tiles, Ruskin drawings, Mackmurdo furniture. It was quite an expensive outing, I remember. Mr. Gorringe—he's the owner—allows parties only once a week during the season, and he restricts the numbers to twelve at a time, so I suppose he has to charge rather a lot to make it worthwhile. But no one grumbled, not even Mrs. Baggot, who was always, I'm afraid, rather inclined to complain at the end of the day. And the island itself—so beautiful and varied, and such peace. Low cliffs, woods, fields, and marshes. It's like England in miniature."

"Darlings, I was actually in the theater when she dried, Clarissa Lisle, I mean. It was ghastly. It wasn't just that she forgot the lines, though I don't see how anyone can forget Lady Macbeth; the part practically speaks itself. She dried completely. We could hear the prompter positively shrieking at her from where Peter—he was my friend—and I were sitting. And then she gave a kind of gasp and ran offstage."

Bevis's outraged voice recalled Miss Maudsley from her happy recollection of Orpen portraits and William Morris tapestries.

"Poor woman! How terrible for her, Bevis."

"Terrible for the rest of the cast. For us, too. Altogether shame-making. After all, she is a professional actress with something of a reputation. You don't expect her to behave like a hysterical schoolgirl who's lost her nerve at her first amateur performance. I was amazed when Metzler offered her Vittoria after that *Macbeth*. She started all right and the notices weren't that bad, but they say that things got pretty dodgy before it folded."

Bevis spoke as one who had been privy to all the negotiations. Cordelia had often wondered at the assurance which he assumed whenever they spoke of the theater, that exotic world of fantasy and desire, his promised land, his native air. He said, "I'd love to see the Victorian theater on Courcy Island. It's very small—only a hundred seats—but they say it's perfect. The original owner built it for Lillie Langtry when she was mistress to the Prince of Wales. He used to visit the island and the house party would amuse themselves with amateur theatricals."

"How do you get to know these things, Bevis?"

"There was an article about the castle in one of the Sundays soon after Mr. Gorringe completed the restoration. My friend showed it to me. He knows I'm interested. The auditorium looked charming. It even has a royal box decorated with the Prince of Wales feathers. I wish I could see it. I'm madly envious."

Cordelia said, "Sir George told me about the theater. The present owner must be rich. It can't have been cheap, restoring the theater and the castle and collecting the Victoriana."

Surprisingly, it was Miss Maudsley who replied. "Oh, but he is! He made a fortune out of that best-seller he wrote. *Autopsy*. He's A. K. Ambrose. Didn't you know?"

Cordelia hadn't known. She had bought the paperback, as had thousands of others, because she had got tired of seeing its dramatic cover confronting her in every bookshop and supermarket and had felt curious to know what it was about, a first novel that could earn a reputed half a million before publication. It was fashionably long and equally fashionably violent, and she remembered that she had indeed, as the blurb promised, found it difficult to put down, without now being able to remember clearly either the plot or the characters. The idea had been neat enough. The novel dealt with an autopsy on a murder victim and had told at length the stories of all the people involved: forensic pathologist, police officer, mortuary attendant, family of the victim, victim, and, finally, the murderer. You could, she supposed, call it a crime novel with a difference, the difference being that there had been more sex, normal and abnormal, than detection and that the book had attempted with some success to combine the popular family saga with mystery. The writing style had been nicely judged for the mass market, neither good enough to jeopardize popular appeal nor bad enough to make people ashamed of being seen reading it in public. At the end she had been left dissatisfied, but whether that was because she had felt manipulated or because of a conviction that the pseudonymous A. K. Ambrose could have written a better book had he chosen, it was hard to say. But the sexual interludes, cunningly spaced, all written with undertones of irony and self-disgust, and the detailed description of the dissection of a female body certainly had a salacious power. Here at least the writer had been himself.

Miss Maudsley was anxious to disclaim any implied criticism in her question. "It's not surprising that you didn't know. I wouldn't have known myself, only one of the members on the summer outing had a husband who keeps a bookshop and she told us. Mr. Ambrose doesn't really like it to be known. It's the only book he's written, I believe."

Cordelia began to feel a lively curiosity to see the egregiously talented Ambrose Gorringe and his offshore island. She sat musing on the oddities of this new assignment while Bevis collected the coffee cups, it being his turn to wash up.

Miss Maudsley had fallen into a pensive silence, hands folded in her lap. Suddenly she looked up and said, "I do hope you won't be in any danger, Miss Gray. There's something wicked, one might say evil, about poison-pen letters. We had a spate of them once in the parish and it ended very tragically. They're so frighteningly malevolent."

Cordelia said, "Malevolent, but not dangerous. I'm more likely to be bored by the case than frightened. And I can't imagine anything very terrible happening on Courcy Island."

Bevis, precariously balancing the three mugs, turned around at the door. "But terrible things have happened there! I don't know what exactly. The article I read didn't say. But the present castle is built on the site of an old medieval castle which used to guard that part of the Channel, so it's probably inherited a ghost or two. And the writer did mention the island's violent and blood-stained history."

Cordelia said, "That's just a journalistic platitude. All the past is bloodstained. That doesn't mean that its ghosts still walk."

She spoke entirely without premonition, glad of the chance of a real job at last, happy at the thought of getting out of London while the warm autumnal weather still lasted, seeing already in her mind the soaring turrets, the gull-loud marshes, the gentle uplands and woods of that miniature England, so mysterious and beautiful, lying waiting for her in the sun.

# III

Ambrose Gorringe now visited London so rarely that he was beginning to wonder whether the subscription to his town club was really justified. There were parts of the capital in which he still felt at home, but too many others in which he had previously walked with pleasure now seemed to him grubby, despoiled, and alien. When business with his stockbroker, agent, or publisher made a visit desirable, he would plan a program of what he described to himself as treats, an adult reenactment of school holidays, leaving no portion of a day so unprovided for that he had time to ponder on his stupidity in being where he was. A visit to Saul Gaskin's small antique shop near Notting Hill Gate was invariably in his program. He bought most of his Victorian pictures and furniture at the London auction houses, but Gaskin knew and partially shared his passion for Victoriana and he could be confident that there would be, awaiting his inspection, a small collection of the trivia which were often so much more redolent of the spirit of the age than his more important acquisitions.

In the unseasonable September heat, the cluttered and ill-ventilated office at the back of the shop smelled like a lair in which Gaskin, with his white, pinched face, precise little hands, and grubby moleskin waistcoat, scurried around like a tenacious rodent. Now he unlocked his desk drawer and reverently laid before this favored customer the scavengings of the last four months. The Bristol blue decanter engraved with a design of grapes and vine leaves was attractive, but there were only five glasses and Gorringe liked his sets complete; and one of a pair of Wedgwood vases designed by Walter Crane was slightly chipped. He was surprised that Gaskin, knowing that he demanded perfection, had bothered to keep them for him. But the ornately trimmed menu for the banquet given by the Queen at Windsor Castle on October 10, 1844, to celebrate the appointment of King Louis Philippe of France as a Knight of the Garter was a happy find. He played with the idea that it would be amusing to serve the same meal at Courcy Castle on the anniversary, but reminded himself that there were limits both to Mrs. Munter's culinary skills and to the capacity of his guests.

Gaskin had saved the best until last. He now brought out, with his customary grave air of serving at some secular mass, two heavy mourning brooches, beautifully wrought in black enamel and gold, each with a lock of hair intricately twisted into whorls and petals; a widow's black peaked bonnet, still in the hatbox in which it was delivered; and a marble carving of a baby's plump truncated arm reposing on a purple velvet cushion. Gorringe took the cap in his hands and stroked the coffered satin, the streamers of ostentatious woe. He wondered what had happened to its owner. Had she followed her husband to an untimely grave, desolated by grief? Or had the bonnet, an expensive contraption, merely failed to please? Both it and the brooches would be an addition to the bedroom in Courcy Castle which he called Memento Mori and where he kept his collection of Victorian necrophilia: the death masks of Carlyle, Ruskin, and Matthew Arnold; the black-edged memorial cards with their weeping angels and sentimental verses; the commemorative cups, medals, and mugs; the wardrobe of heavy mourning garments, black, gray, and mauve. It was a room Clarissa had entered with a shudder, only once, and now pretended didn't exist. But he had noted with pleasure that those of his guests who were lovers, acknowledged or furtive, liked occasionally to sleep there, rather, he thought, as eighteenth-century whores had copulated with their clients on the flat tops of tombs in London's East End graveyards. He watched with a sardonic and slightly contemptuous eye this symbiosis of eroticism and morbidity, as he did all those human foibles which he happened not to share.

He said, "I'll take these. And probably the marble too. Where did you find it?"

"A private sale. I don't think it's a memorial piece. The owner claimed that it was a duplicate of one of the marble limbs of the royal children at Osborne, carved for Queen Victoria. This one is probably the arm of the infant Princess Royal."

"Poor Viccy! What with her formidable mother, her son, and Bismarck, not the happiest of princesses. It's almost irresistible, but not at that price."

"The cushion is the original. And if it is the arm of the princess, it's probably unique. There's no record as far as I know of any duplicates of the Osborne pieces."

They entered into their usual amicable pattern of bargaining, but Gorringe sensed that Gaskin's heart wasn't in it. He was a superstitious man, and it was apparent to Gorringe that the marble, which he seemed unable to bring himself to touch, both fascinated and repelled him. He wanted it out of his shop.

Hardly had the business concluded when there was a ring on the locked street door. As Gaskin left to answer it, Gorringe asked if he might use the telephone. It had occurred to him that with some slight hurry he could catch an earlier train. As usual, it was Munter who answered the ring.

"Courcy Castle."

"Gorringe, Munter. I'm ringing from London. I find that I shall, after all, be able to catch the two-thirty train. I should be at the quay by four-forty."

"Very good, sir. I will instruct Oldfield."

"Is all well, Munter?"

"Quite well, sir. Tuesday's dress rehearsal was hardly a success, but I understand that this is considered propitious for the actual performance."

"The lighting rehearsal was satisfactory?"

"Yes, sir. If I may say so, the company is more fortunate in the talent of its amateur electricians than in its actors."

"And Mrs. Munter? Have you been able to get all the help she needs for Saturday?"

"Not quite all. Two of the girls from the town have defaulted, but Mrs. Chambers is bringing her granddaughter. I have interviewed the girl and she seems well intentioned if untrained. If the Courcy play is to be an annual event, we may have to reconsider our staffing needs, at least for this one week of the year."

Gorringe said calmly, "I don't think that either you or Mrs. Munter need assume that the play will be an annual event. If you feel the need to plan for twelve months ahead, it would be safer to assume that this is the last performance which Lady Ralston will give on Courcy."

"Thank you, sir. I should tell you that Lady Ralston telephoned. Sir George has an unexpected meeting to attend and is unlikely to arrive before Saturday afternoon and, possibly, not until after the performance. Lady Ralston proposes to solace marital deprivation by inviting a secretary-companion, a Miss Cordelia Gray. She will arrive with the rest of the party on Friday morning. Lady Ralston appeared to think that she need not speak to you personally about this arrangement."

Munter's disapproval came over the line as clearly as his carefully controlled irony. He was adept at judging just how far he could safely go, and since his veiled insolence was never directed against his employer, Gorringe was indulgent. A man, particularly a servant, was entitled to his small recalcitrant bolsterings of self-respect. Gorringe had noted early in their relationship how Munter's persona, modeled as it was on Jeeves and his near namesake Bunter, became markedly closer to parody when any of his carefully contrived domestic arrangements was upset. During Clarissa's visits to the castle he became almost intolerably Bunterish. Relishing his manservant's eccentricities, the contrast between his bizarre appearance and his manner, and totally uncurious about his past, Gorringe now hardly bothered to wonder whether a real Munter existed and, if so, what manner of man he might be.

He heard him say, "I thought that Miss Gray could be companionable in the De Morgan room, subject to your agreement."

"That would seem suitable. And if Sir George does arrive for Saturday night he can have Memento Mori. A soldier should be inured to death. Do we know anything about Miss Gray?"

"A young lady, I understand. I take it that she will eat in the dining room."

"Of course."

Whatever Clarissa thought she was up to, it would at least even the numbers at his dinner table. But the thought of Clarissa with a secretary-companion, and a woman at that, was intriguing. He hoped that her addition to the party wouldn't make the weekend more complicated than it already promised to be.

"Good-bye, Munter."

"Good-bye, sir."

When Gaskin returned to the office, he found his customer sitting contemplatively holding the marble arm. He gave an involuntary shiver. Gorringe replaced the marble on its cushion and watched while Gaskin busied himself finding a small cardboard box and lining it with tissue paper.

He said, "You don't like it?"

Gaskin could afford to be frank. The limb was sold, and Mr. Gorringe had never yet rejected a piece once the price was agreed. He lowered the arm into its box, taking care to touch only the cushion.

"I can't say I'm sorry to see it go. I usually do very well with those porcelain models of the human hand which the Victorians were so fond of, ring stands and so on. I had a nice one in last week but the wrist frill was chipped. It wouldn't have interested you. But a child's arm! And cut off like that! I call it brutal, almost morbid. It's just a feel I have about the piece. You know how I am. It reminds me of death."

Gorringe took a final look at the brooches before they were wrapped and boxed.

"Less rationally, surely, than should the jewelry and the widow's cap. I agree with you; I doubt whether this is a memorial marble."

Gaskin said firmly, "They're different. They don't worry me; memorials never have. But this is different. To tell you the truth, I took against it as soon as it came into the shop. Whenever I look at it, I keep imagining that it's oozing blood."

Gorringe smiled. "I must try it on my houseguests and watch their reactions. The Courcy play this weekend is *The Duchess of Malfi*. If this were a full-size male hand we could use it for one of the props. But even the duchess in her extremity could hardly mistake this for the dead hand of Antonio."

The allusion was lost on Gaskin, who had never read Webster. He murmured, "No indeed, sir," and smiled his sly, sycophantic smile.

Five minutes later, he saw his customer and his parcels formally off the premises, congratulating himself with premature satisfaction—for despite his carefully nurtured sensitivity he had never claimed to be a clairvoyant—that he had seen and heard the last of the arm of the dead princess.

# IV

Less than two miles away in a Harley Street consulting room, Ivo Whittingham slipped his legs over the edge of the examination couch and watched Dr. Crantley-Mathers shuffle back to his desk. The doctor, as always, was wearing his old but well-tailored pin-stripe suit. Nothing so clinical as a white coat ever intruded into his consulting room, and the room itself, with its patterned Axminster carpet, its Edwardian carved desk holding the silver-framed photographs of Sir James's grandchildren and distinguished patients, its sporting prints, and the portrait of some solidly prosperous ancestor holding pride of place above the carved marble mantel shelf, looked more like a private study than a consulting room. No apparent effort was made to keep infection at bay; but, then, thought Whittingham, germs would know better than to lurk in the well-upholstered armchair in which Sir James's patients awaited his advice. Even the examination couch looked unclinical, being covered with brown leather and mounted by way of elegant eighteenth-century library steps. The assumption was that, although a number of Sir James's guests might wish for some private whim to take off their clothes, that eccentricity could have nothing to do with the state of their health.

Now he looked up from his prescription pad and asked, "That spleen troubling you?"

"As it must weigh twenty pounds and I look and feel like a lop-sided pregnant woman, yes, you could say that it's troubling me."

"The time may come when it's better out. No hurry, though. We'll have another think in a month's time."

Whittingham went behind the painted oriental screen where his clothes were folded over a chair and began to dress, drawing his trousers up over the heavy belly. It was, he thought, like carrying one's own death, feeling it drag at the muscles, a fetus-like incubus which never stirred, reminding him with its dead weight, by the deformity which he saw in his mirror every time he bathed, what it was he bore within him. Looking over the screen, he said, his voice muffled by his shirt, "I thought you explained that the spleen is enlarged because it's taken over the manufacture of the red blood corpuscles, which my blood's no longer producing."

Sir James didn't look up. He said with careful unconcern, "That's more or less what's happening, yes. When one organ ceases to function, another tends to take over."

"So would it be tactless to inquire which organ will obligingly take over the job when you've whipped out the spleen?"

Sir James guffawed at this witticism. "Let's cross that bridge when we come to it, shall we?"

He had never, thought Whittingham, been a man for originality of speech.

For the first time since his illness had begun, Whittingham would have liked to ask his doctor directly how much time remained for him. It wasn't that there were affairs that he needed to put in order. He was divorced from his wife, alienated from his children, and living now alone; his affairs, like his obsessively tidy flat, had been depressingly in order for the last five years. The need to know was now little more than a mild curiosity. He would be glad to learn that he was to be spared another Christmas, his most disliked time of the year. But he realized that the question would be in the worst of taste. The room itself had been designed to make it unsayable; Sir James was adept at training his patients not to ask questions which they knew it would distress him to have to answer. His philosophy—and Whittingham wasn't altogether in disagreement with it—was that patients would realize in their own good time that they were dying and that, by then, physical weakness would ensure that the realization would be less painful than a sentence of death pronounced when the blood still ran strong. He had never believed that the loss of hope did anyone any good; and besides, doctors could be wrong. This last assertion was a conventional gesture to modesty. Sir James did not privately believe that he personally could be wrong, and indeed he was a superb diagnostician. It was hardly his fault, thought Whittingham, that the ability of the medical profession to diagnose is so far in advance of its ability to cure. Slipping his arms through his jacket sleeves, he spoke aloud Brachiano's words from *The White Devil*: " 'On pain of death, let no man name death to me: / It is a word infinitely terrible.' "

It was a view Sir James obviously shared. It was surprising, supposing he knew the words, that he hadn't carved them over his door lintel.

"I'm sorry, Mr. Whittingham. I didn't quite catch what you said."

"Nothing, Sir James. I was merely quoting Webster."

Escorting his patient to the consulting-room door at which an exceedingly pretty nurse was waiting to see him finally on his way, the doctor asked, "Are you going out of London this weekend? It's a pity to waste this weather."

"To Dorset, actually. To Courcy Island, off Speymouth. An amateur company with some professional support is putting on *The Duchess of Malfi*, and I'm doing a piece for one of the color supplements." He added, "It's chiefly about the restoration of the Victorian theater on the island and its history."

Immediately he despised himself for the explanation. What was it but a way of saying that dying he might be, but he wasn't yet reduced to reviewing amateurs.

"Good. Good." Sir James boomed out a note of approval which might have sounded excessive even for God on the seventh day.

When the imposing front door had closed behind him, Whittingham was tempted to hire the taxi which had just drawn up, presumably to deposit another patient. But he decided he might manage a mile of the walk to his Russell Square flat. And there was a new coffeehouse in Marylebone High Street where the young couple who owned it ground the beans freshly and made their own cakes, and where a few chairs under umbrellas gave the locals the illusion that the English summer was suitable for eating outdoors. He might rest there for ten minutes. It was extraordinary how important these trivial self-indulgences had become. As he resigned himself to the accidiae of mortal illness, he was beginning to acquire some of the foibles of old age: a liking for small treats, a fussiness about routine, a reluctance to bother with even his oldest acquaintances, an indolence which made even dressing and bathing a burden, a preoccupation with his bodily functions. He despised the half-man he had become, but even this self-disgust had some of the querulous resentment of senility. Sir James was right. It was difficult to feel regret about losing a life so diminished; by the time this sickness had finished with him, death would be no more than the final disintegration of a body from which the spirit had already seeped away, worn out by pain, by weariness, and by a malaise which went deeper than physical weakness, some brittle-armed traitor of the heart which had never mustered the will to fight.

As he made his way down Wimpole Street through the mellow autumn sunlight he thought of the great performances he had seen and reviewed and mentally spoke the names like a roll call: Olivier's Richard the Third, Wolfit playing Malvolio, Gielgud's Hamlet, Richardson's Falstaff, Peggy Ashcroft's Portia. He could recall them, could remember the theaters, the directors, even some of the most quoted extracts from his reviews. It was interesting that after thirty years of playgoing, it was the classics which had lasted longest for him. But he knew that even if he were this night to take his accustomed seat in the third row of the stalls, formally dressed as he always was for a first night, listening to that anticipatory hum which is unlike any other sound in the world, nothing that happened when the curtain rose would move or excite him beyond a mild, detached interest. The glory and the wonder had departed. Never again would he feel that tingle between the shoulder blades, that almost physical surge of the blood which, for all his youth, had been his response to great acting. It was ironic that now, all passion spent, he was about to review his last play, and that an amateur production. But somehow he would find the energy for what he had to do on Courcy Island.

The island was reputed to be beautiful and the castle an interesting example of high Victorian panache. Seeing them would probably be worth the effort of the journey, which was as close as he could now get to enthusiasm. But he was less sure about the company. Clarissa had mentioned that her cousin Roma Lisle was to be there with a friend. He hadn't met Roma, but had had to listen to Clarissa's caustic disparagement of her for too many years to relish being under the same roof as them both, and the careful omission of the friend's name hadn't been reassuring. And the boy was to be with them, apparently. Clarissa's decision to take on the son of her drowned husband, Martin Lessing, had been one of her more spectacular impulses; he wondered who was regretting it more, benefactress or victim. On the three occasions on which he had met Simon Lessing, two at the theater and one at a party at Clarissa's Bayswater flat, he had been struck by the boy's gaucherie and by a sense of deep personal wretchedness which he thought had less to do with adolescence than with Clarissa. There had been something doglike in his servility, a desperate need to win her approval without the least idea what it was she wanted of him. Whittingham had seen that same look in his father's eyes; the prick of memory hadn't been comfortable. Simon was supposed to be a talented pianist. Probably Clarissa had seen herself splendidly cantilevered in one of the front boxes at the Royal Festival Hall while her prodigy, adoring eyes glancing upwards, took his triumphant bow. It must be disconcerting for her to be faced instead with the moodiness and the physical gracelessness of adolescence. He found himself possessed of a slight interest in seeing how the two of them were doing. And there would be other minor satisfactions; not the least would be watching how Clarissa Lisle was coping with her own neurosis. If this were to be his last performance, there was some satisfaction in knowing that it might well be hers. She would know that he was dying. She had the use of her eyes. But he wouldn't grudge her any pleasure she could get from observing the process of his physical disintegration. There were subtler pleasures than that; watching mental disintegration might, he suspected, be among them. He was discovering that even hatred died a little at the end. But it still lasted longer than desire, longer even than love. Walking slowly in the sunshine and thinking of the weekend ahead, he smiled at the realization that what was most alive in him now was the capacity for mischief.

# V

In the basement of a small shop in a passageway of the north end of Tottenham Court Road, Roma Lisle was on her knees unpacking and sorting a box of secondhand books. The room, which had originally been a kitchen and which still contained an old porcelain sink, a row of wall-mounted cupboards, and a disconnected gas stove so heavy that the combined efforts of Colin and herself had been unable to shift it, was oppressively hot despite the tiled floor. Outside, the accumulated heat of the dying summer seemed to have concentrated in the area beneath the iron railings, pressing against the one small window like a sweaty, fume-soaked blanket, cutting off air as well as light. Above her the single pendant light threw shadows rather than illumination; it was ridiculous to have to be using expensive electricity on such a day. She must have been mad ever to have thought that this hole could be transformed into an intimate, invitingly cozy secondhand books department, a browser's delight.

The books, she now saw, were a poor lot. She had bid for them and bought them cheaply at a country-house sale. Now the first real inspection revealed that it hadn't been cheap enough. The best had been on the top. The rest were a motley collection of Victorian sermons, reminiscences of retired generals, biographies of minor politicians as undistinguished in death as they had been in life, novels which provoked no interest except a wonder that anyone should have chosen to publish them.

Her knees were numb against the tiles, her nostrils choked with the smell of dust, of moldering cardboard and rotting paper. In her imagination it was to have been so different: Colin kneeling beside her, the happy rummaging, the exclamations of pleasure as each treasure came to light, the laughter, the planning, the fun. She remembered their last day at Pottergate Comprehensive: the farewell party with its cheap sherry and inevitable crisps and cheese savories; the barely concealed envy of their colleagues that she and Colin were getting out, setting up business together, saying good-bye to timetables, mark sheets, examinations, the daily dispiriting struggle to impose order on a class of forty in an inner-city comprehensive where teaching had always to be subordinated to the struggle to maintain some semblance of discipline.

And that was only nine months ago! Nine months in which everything they had bought, everything they needed, had become more expensive, in which the shop had been as dead as if boarded up and bankrupt. Nine months of overwork and dwindling returns, of fading hope and half-acknowledged panic. Nine months—could it be?—of the slow death of desire. She almost cried out in protest, shoving her strong hands against the box as if the thought and its pain could be physically pushed from her mind. And then she heard his step on the stairs. She turned her face to his, making herself smile. He had hardly spoken over luncheon. But that was three hours ago. Sometimes his moods didn't last. His first words destroyed hope.

"My God, this place stinks."

"It won't, once we get it cleaned up."

"And how long will that take? It needs an army of cleaners and decorators. And even then it'll still look what it is, a basement slum."

He slumped down on an unopened box of books and began turning over the pile she had unpacked, letting them drop with careful disdain in an untidy heap. In the dim light his handsome, petulant face looked lined with weariness. Why? she wondered. It was she who had been doing the work. She held out her hand, and after a moment he took it in a limp grasp.

She thought, Oh, God, I love you! We love each other. Don't take that away from me.

He slid his hand from hers almost furtively and began to pretend an interest in one of the books. As he opened it, a small sheet of thick and faded paper fluttered out.

She said, "What's that?"

"Some kind of old woodcut by the look of it. I shouldn't think it has any value."

"We could ask Ambrose Gorringe when we get to Courcy Island. He knows about these things even if they aren't his period."

They peered at it together. It was certainly old, early seventeenth century she guessed from the antiquated spelling, and it was in remarkably good condition. The paper was headed with a crude woodcut of a skeleton holding in its right hand an arrow and in its left an hourglass. Beneath was the title, "The Gt Me*ff*enger of Mortality," followed by the verse. She read the first four lines aloud.

> Fair lady lay your costly robe aside,
> No longer may you glory in your pride,
> Take leave of all yr carnal vain delight,
> I'm come to summon you away tonight.

The undated subscription gave the printer's name as John Evans of Long Lane, London.

Roma said, "It reminds me of Clarissa."

"Of Clarissa? Why?"

"I don't know. I don't know why."

He pressed her, sounding irritably insistent, as if it mattered, as if she had intended something.

"It's just something I said, something that came into my mind. It didn't mean anything. Put the paper by the sink, on the draining board. We'll show it to Ambrose Gorringe." He did so and returned moodily to his box. He said, "It was a mistake, buying this junk. We should have stuck to the new stock. London seems to have a surfeit of bookshops. And God knows why I let you talk me into buying all that left-wing stuff upstairs. No one wants it. The left wing already have enough cozy haunts in this neighborhood and it only repels the other buyers. Those pamphlets are just gathering dust. I must have been mad."

She knew that he wasn't referring only to the left-wing literature. The injustice stung her into anger. She knew even as she spoke that it was folly. He needed to be cajoled, humored, comforted. The quarrels which he seemed increasingly to provoke only left him sulky and resentful and herself exhausted. But she had had enough.

"Look, you didn't take on this place to oblige me. You were just as keen to get out of Pottergate. You loathed teaching. Remember? I was fed up with it, I admit, but I wouldn't have resigned if you hadn't made the first move."

"You mean it's all my fault."

"All! What all? It isn't anyone's fault. We both did what we wanted."

"Then what are you complaining about?"

"It's just that I'm tired of being made to feel as if I'm some kind of encumbrance, worse than a wife, as if you're keeping on the shop only because of me."

"I'm keeping it—we're keeping it on—because there's no alternative. Pottergate wouldn't take us back even if we apply."

And where else could they apply? He didn't need her to tell him about the unemployment in the teaching profession, the expenditure cuts, the desperate search for jobs even by the best qualified.

She said, knowing even as she spoke that argument was folly, that it would only fuel his irritation, "If you do chuck it, it'll please Stella. I suppose that's what she's been waiting for. She can say, 'I told you so' and hand you over, neatly trussed, a sacrificial victim to dear Daddy and the family business. My God, she must be praying for our bankruptcy! It's a wonder she doesn't lurk outside counting the customers."

His protest was sulky rather than vehement. It was, after all, an argument they had had before.

"She knows I'm worried, obviously. She's worried herself. She has a right to be. Half the money I put in here was hers."

As if that needed saying. As if Roma didn't know exactly how much cash from Daddy's generous allowance Stella had graciously handed over. And that it was generous of her, generous or stupid or cunning. Or all three. Because she must have known that Colin was going into partnership with his mistress; she wasn't that blind. Oh, she'd known all right! Stella couldn't understand what he saw in Roma—she wasn't unique in that—but she'd known the score. And had this been her revenge, the money to set up a partnership which was bound to fail, given their inexperience, their small capital, their self-delusions, a failure that would draw him back, suitably chastened, to the place where he belonged—the place, come to think of it, that he'd never really left? And then what would there be for him but Daddy's business, the store in Kilburn which sold cheap plywood furniture on the installment plan to customers too ignorant to know when they were being cheated or too proud in their poverty to rummage around the street markets and buy good solid oak, secondhand? The stuff he dazzled them with—cocktail cabinets, room dividers, ornate suites—would fall or be kicked to pieces long before they'd finished paying for it. Was that what Colin wanted to do with his life? Had he left teaching for that? And had Stella thought all this out for herself, or had Daddy had a hand in it? The money she had lent them, hadn't it been carefully calculated, enough to make the enterprise possible but not enough to enable them to succeed? She was sharp enough. She had a shrewd little mind to go with those sharp painted nails, those white childlike teeth. And she had other weapons, Justin and Joanna. Possessiveness and acquisitiveness had been sanctified by maternity. She had the twins. And, by God, she knew how to use them! With every childhood infection, every school speech day, every dental appointment, every family holiday, every Christmas demanding his presence at home, it was as if she were saying, "He may sleep with you, play at keeping shop with you, imagine that he's in love with you, confide in you. But he'll never give you children. And he'll never divorce me to marry you."

Appalled at her thoughts, at what was happening to them, she cried, "Look, darling, don't let's quarrel. We're tired, we're hot, and it's a bloody day. On Friday we shut the door on the whole scene and take off for Courcy Island. Three days of peace, sunshine, good wines, first-class food, and the sea. The island's only three miles by two and a half, so Clarissa says, but there are marvelous walks. We can get away from the rest of the party. Clarissa will be busy with the play. I don't suppose Ambrose Gorringe will care a damn what we do. No creditors, no people, just peace. And, my God, don't I need it."

She was going to add, "And I need you, my darling. More and more. Always." But then she looked up and saw his face.

It wasn't an unfamiliar look, that mixture of shame, irritation, embarrassment. She had seen it before. This, after all, had been the pattern of their lives, the plans so confidently, so happily, made, the last-minute cancellations. But never before had it mattered so desperately. Tears scalded her eyes. She told herself that she had to stay calm, that she mustn't break down; but when she could speak, the note of angry recrimination was unmistakable even to her own ears and she saw the look of shame harden into defiance.

"You can't do this to me! You can't! You promised! And I've told Clarissa I'm bringing my partner. It's all arranged."

"I know and I'm sorry. But Stella's father telephoned at breakfast to say that he's coming for the weekend. I've got to be there. I've told you what he's like. He was pretty fed up about my leaving teaching. We've never got on. He thinks I don't appreciate her enough; you know how it is with an only child. He's not going to be pleased if he finds I'm away for a long weekend, leaving her to cope with the kids. And he won't believe the story about attending a book sale. I don't think even Stella does."

So that was it. Daddy was arriving. Daddy, who paid the twins' school fees, provided the car, the annual holiday, the luxuries which had become necessities. Daddy, who had his own ideas about his son-in-law's future.

She said in a voice that was almost a wail, "What is Clarissa going to think?"

"Well, isn't it rather what she'd think if I did come? She knows I'm married. I mean, you must have let that drop. Wouldn't it look rather odd, the two of us arriving together? And it's not as if we could have shared a room or anything like that."

"By 'anything like that' I suppose you mean that we couldn't have slept together. Why not? Clarissa isn't exactly a model of purity, and I don't suppose Ambrose Gorringe creeps down his corridors at night checking that his guests are in their own rooms."

He muttered, "It's not that. I explained. It's Stella's father."

"But this weekend might have freed you from him and her. I thought we could have spoken to Clarissa, told her about the shop, asked if she couldn't help. That's why I wangled the invitation. After all, a third of her money comes to me if she dies without a child. It's all in Uncle's will. It wouldn't harm her to part with some when it's most needed. We'd only be asking for a loan."

She tried not to see the hope brightening in his face. Then it faded. He said sulkily, "I couldn't ask a woman for money."

"You wouldn't have to. I'd do the asking. What I thought was that she'd meet you, like you. She'd be seeing you under the best possible conditions. Then I could speak to her when the time seemed right. It's worth a try, darling. Even twenty thousand would mean all the difference."

"What would you get if she died?"

"I'm not sure. About eighty thousand, I think. It could be more."

He turned away. "And that's about what we'd need if I were to leave Stella, get a divorce. But Clarissa isn't going to die just to convenience us. Twenty thousand might just save the shop. But that's about all it would do. And why should she part with it? Anyone with an ounce of financial sense would see that it would be throwing good money after bad. It's no use. I can't come this weekend."

Above them the floor creaked. Someone had come into the shop. He said quickly, gratefully, "Sounds like a customer. Look, I'll close promptly at five if there's nothing doing and give you a hand down here. We'll get this room together somehow."

When he had gone, she went over and stared out the window, standing rigidly, grasping the edges of the sink so tightly that her knuckles were white. Her eyes were unfocused, staring beyond the railings, the crumbling stucco on the basement wall, to where the brightly patterned reds, greens, and yellows of the fruit stall on the opposite pavement fused and shivered. From time to time feet passed, voices called, the narrow street broke momentarily into life. And still that silent figure at the window stood unmoving. Then she gave a little sigh. The taut shoulders relaxed, the fingers loosened their grip. She took up the woodcut from the draining board and studied it as if she hadn't seen it before. Then she opened her shoulder bag and folded it carefully away.

# VI

Simon Lessing stood at the open window of his study at Melhurst and gazed out over the wide lawns to where the river cut its slow stream between the horse chestnuts and the limes. In his hand he held Clarissa's still-unopened letter. It had arrived by the morning post, but there had been an excuse for not opening it then. He had had an early practice period. And that had been followed by the sixth-form seminar. He had told himself that he would wait until break. But the morning had passed and now it was the lunch hour. In less than five minutes the bell would sound. He couldn't delay indefinitely. It was ridiculous and humiliating to be so afraid, to stand like a first-former holding a dreaded school report, knowing that however long and cunningly deferred, the moment of truth must come at last.

He would wait until the bell actually sounded, and then he would read it, quickly, uncaring, and with his mind on luncheon. And at least he could do so in peace. From the middle school upwards, every boy at Melhurst had his own study. The importance of a daily period of silence and privacy was one of the more enlightened precepts of the school's pious seventeenth-century founder, and, largely because it had been incorporated into the almost monastic architecture, it had endured through three hundred years of changing educational fashion. It was one of the things about Melhurst which Simon most valued, one of the privileges which Clarissa's patronage, Clarissa's money, had procured for him. Neither she nor Sir George had ever considered another choice of school, and Melhurst had made no difficulty about finding a place for the stepson of one of its more distinguished alumni. Its motto, in Greek rather than in the more usual Latin, extolled the virtues of moderation, and for three hundred years, in obedience to Theognis's dictum, the school had been moderately famous, moderately expensive, and moderately successful.

No other school could have suited Simon better. He recognized that its traditions and occasionally bizarre rituals, which he quickly learned and sedulously observed, were designed as much to discourage too personal a commitment as to promote a corporate identity. He was tolerated but left alone, and he asked nothing more. Even his talents were acceptable to the ethos of the school, which, perhaps because of a strong personal antipathy between a nineteenth-century headmaster and Dr. Arnold of Rugby, by tradition eschewed muscular Christianity and almost all manifestations of the team spirit and espoused High Anglicanism and the cult of the eccentric. But music was well taught; the school's two orchestras had a national reputation. And swimming, the only physical skill at which he excelled, was one of the more acceptable sports. Compared with the Norman Pagworth Comprehensive, Melhurst seemed to him a haven of civilized order. At Pagworth he had felt like an alien set down without a phrase book in a lawless, ill-governed, and alien country whose language and customs, crudely harsh as the playground in which they were born, were terrifyingly incomprehensible. The prospect of having to leave Melhurst and return to his old school had been one of his worst terrors since he began to sense that things were going wrong between himself and Clarissa.

It was strange that fear and gratitude should be so mixed. The gratitude was genuine enough. He only wished that he could experience it as it surely ought to be experienced, as a graciousness, a reciprocal benison, free of this dragging load of obligation and guilt. The guilt was the worse to bear. When its weight became almost too much for him, he tried to exorcise it by rational thought. It was ridiculous to feel guilty, ridiculous and unnecessary even to feel too oppressive an obligation. Clarissa owed him something after all. It was she who had destroyed his parents' marriage, enticed away his father, helped kill his mother through grief, left him an orphan to endure the discomforts, the vulgarities, the suffocating boredom of his uncle's house. It was Clarissa, not he, who should feel guilt.

But even to let this thought creep traitorously into his mind only increased his burden of obligation. He owed her so much. The trouble was that everyone knew just how much. Sir George was seldom there, but when he was, he presented himself to Simon as a silent, accusing personification of all those masculine qualities which he knew were alien to his own personality. He sometimes sensed in Clarissa's husband an inarticulate goodwill which he would have liked to put to the test if only he could summon the courage. But most of the time he imagined that Sir George had never really approved of Clarissa's taking him on and that their secret marital conversations were punctuated with the phrases "I told you so. I warned you." Miss Tolgarth knew; Tolly, whose eyes he dared not meet for fear of encountering one of those judgmental gazes in which he thought he detected dislike, resentment, and contempt. Clarissa knew it, probably to the last penny. Increasingly he had come to feel that Clarissa repented of a generosity which at first had held all the charm of novelty, the magnificent gesture, superbly theatrical at the time in all its eccentricity, but which she now saw had lumbered her with a spotty, inarticulate adolescent, ill at ease with her friends; with school bills, holiday arrangements, dental appointments; with all the minor irritations of motherhood and none of its essential compensations. He sensed that there was something she required of him which he could neither identify nor give, some return, unspecified but substantial, which would one day be demanded of him with all the brutal insistence of a tax collector.

She seldom wrote to him now, and when he did see in his cubbyhole that tall, curved hand—she disapproved of personal letters being typed—he had to steel himself to open the envelope. But the apprehension had never before been as bad as this. The letter seemed to have stuck to his hand, to have grown heavy with menace. And then the one o'clock bell clanged out. With sudden vehemence he tore at the corner of the envelope. The pale blue linen-based paper which she always used was tough. He wrenched in his thumb and tore a jagged slit through envelope and letter, as roughly as a lover who cannot wait to know his fate. He saw that the letter was short, and his immediate reaction was a moan of relief. If she was throwing him out, if there was to be no last term at Melhurst, no chance of a place at the Royal College of Music, no more allowance, surely the excuse, the justification, would require more than half a page. The first sentence did away with his worst fears.

> This is to let you know the arrangements for next weekend. George will drive Tolly and me down to Speymouth before breakfast on Friday but it will be best if you arrive with the rest of the house party in time for lunch. The launch will meet the nine-thirty-two from Waterloo. Be at the harbor at Speymouth by eleven-forty. Ivo Whittingham and my cousin Roma will be on the train and you'll also meet a girl, Cordelia Gray. I shall need some extra help during the weekend and she is a kind of temporary secretary, so

there will be someone young on the island for you to practice talking to. You should also be able to get some swimming so you won't need to be bored. Bring your dinner jacket. Mr. Gorringe likes to dress in the evenings. And he knows something about music so you may as well select some of your best pieces, the ones you know, nothing too heavy. I've written to your housemaster about the extra days' leave. Did Matron give you that acne lotion I sent last month? I hope you've been using it.

Love,
*Clarissa*

It was odd how soon relief could change to a new and different anxiety, even to resentment. Reading the letter for the second time, he wondered why he should have been invited to the island. It was Clarissa's doing, of course. Ambrose Gorringe didn't know him and would hardly be likely to include him among his guests if he did. He remembered vaguely having heard about the island, the restored Victorian theater, the plans to stage the Webster tragedy, and he sensed that the performance was important to Clarissa, amateur production though it was. But why should he be there? He was expected to keep out of her way, not to make a nuisance of himself; that much was evident. He could disport himself in the sea or the pool. He supposed that there would be a pool and pictured Clarissa, pale and golden, stretched out in the sun, and beside her this new girl, this Cordelia Gray, with whom he was supposed to practice making conversation. And what else did Clarissa want him to practice? Making himself agreeable? Paying compliments? Knowing what jokes women like and when to make them? Flirting? Showing himself to be a susceptible heterosexual male? The prospect made his mouth dry with terror.

It wasn't that he disliked the idea of a girl. He had already created in his mind the girl he would like to be with on Courcy Island, on any island: sensitive, beautiful, intelligent, kind, and yet wanting him, wanting him to do to her those terrifyingly exciting and shameful things which would no longer be shameful because they loved each other, acts which would reconcile for him in sweet responsive flesh, finally and forever, that dichotomy between romanticism and desire which so occupied his daydreaming hours. He didn't expect to meet this girl, on Courcy or anywhere else. The only girl with whom he had so far had anything to do had been his cousin Susie. He hated Susie, hated her bold, contemptuous eyes, her perpetually chewing mouth, her voice which alternately whined and yelled, her dyed hair, her grubby beringed fingers.

But even if this girl were different, even if he liked her, how could he get to know her when Clarissa would be watching them, marking him for articulacy, attraction, wit, checking up on his social performance, as she and this Ambrose Gorringe would be checking up on his musicianship? The reference to his music made his cheeks burn. He was insecure enough about his talent without having it diminished by this coy reference to his pieces as if he were a child showing off to the neighbors at a suburban tea party. But the instruction was clear enough. He was to bring with him something showy or popular or both, something he could play with practiced bravado so that she wouldn't be disgraced by any nervous misfingerings, and she and Ambrose Gorringe would together decide whether he had enough tal ent to justify a final year at school, a chance to try for a place at the Royal College or the Academy.

And suppose the verdict went against him? He couldn't return to Mornington Avenue, to his aunt and uncle. Clarissa couldn't do that to him. After all, it was she who had brought the order of release. She had arrived unannounced on a warm afternoon during the summer holidays, when he had been in the house alone as usual, reading at the sitting-room table. He couldn't remember how she had announced herself, whether he had been told that the silent, upright man with her was her new husband. But he remembered how she had looked, golden and effulgent, a cool, sweet-smelling, miraculous vision who had immediately taken hold of his heart and his life as a rescuer might pluck a drowning child from the water and set him firmly on a sunlit rock. It had been too good to last, of course. But how marvelous in memory shone that long-dead summer afternoon.

"Are you happy here?"

"No."

"I don't see how you could be, actually. This room's pretty gruesome. I've read somewhere that a million copies of that print have been sold, but I didn't realize people actually hung it on their walls. Your father told me that you're musical. Do you still play?"

"I can't. There isn't a piano here. And they only teach percussion at school. They have a West Indian steel band. They're only interested in music where everyone can join in."

"Things which everyone can join in usually aren't worth doing. They shouldn't have put two different papers on the walls. Three or four might have been bizarre enough to be fun. Two are just vulgar. How old are you? Fourteen, isn't it? How would you like to come and live with us?"

"For always?"

"Nothing is for always. But perhaps. Until you grow up, anyway."

Without waiting for his reply, without even looking into his face to watch his initial response, she turned to the silent man at her side. "I think we can do better than this for Martin's boy."

"If you are sure, my dear. Not a thing to decide quickly. Shouldn't make an impulse buy of a child."

"Darling, where would you be if I hadn't made an impulse buy? And he's the only son I'm ever likely to give you."

Simon's eyes were turning from one face to the other. He remembered how Sir George had looked, the features stiffening as if the muscles were bracing themselves against pain, against vulgarity. But Simon had seen the hurt, visible, unmistakable, before Sir George had turned silently away.

She had turned to him. "Will your aunt and uncle mind?"

The misery, the grievances, had spilled out. He had had to prevent himself from clutching at her dress.

"They won't care! They'll be glad! I take up the spare room and

I haven't any money. They're always telling me how much it costs to feed me. And they don't like me. They won't mind, honestly."

And then, on impulse, he had done the right thing. It was the only time he had done exactly the right thing where Clarissa was concerned. There had been a pink geranium in a pot on the window ledge; his uncle was a keen gardener and grew cuttings in the lean-to greenhouse at the side of the kitchen. One of the flower heads was small and as delicate as a rose. He had broken it off and handed it to her, looking up into her face. She had laughed aloud and taken it from him and slipped it into the belt of her dress. Then she had looked at her husband and had laughed again, a peal of happy triumph.

"Well, that seems to have decided itself. We'd better stay until they come home. I can't wait to see the owners of this wallpaper. And then we'll take you to buy some clothes."

And so, with such promise, in such an exhilaration of surprised joy, it had all begun. He tried now to recall when the dream had faded, when things had first started to go wrong. But, apart from that first meeting, had they ever really gone right? He sensed that he was worse than a failure, that he was the last of a series of failures, that earlier disappointments had reinforced her present discontent. He was beginning to dread the holidays, although he saw little either of Clarissa or of Sir George. Their official life together, such as it was, was lived in the London flat overlooking Hyde Park. But they were seldom there together. Clarissa had a flat in Regency Square in Brighton, her husband a remote flint cottage on the marshes of the east coast. It was there that their real lives were lived, she in the company of her theatrical friends, he in bird-watching and, if rumor were correct, in right-wing conspiracy. Simon had never been invited to either place, although he often pictured them in those other secret worlds: Clarissa in a whirl of gaiety, Sir George conferring with his mysterious, hard-faced, and nameless confederates. For some unexplainable reason, these imaginings, which occupied a disproportionate part of his holiday hours, were in the guise of old films. Clarissa and her friends, dressed in the waistless shifts of the twenties, hair shingled, and flourishing long cigarette holders, flung out their legs in a hectic

Charleston, while Sir George's friends arrived at their rendezvous in veteran cars, trench-coated, their wide-brimmed trilbys pulled down over secretive eyes. Excluded from both these worlds, Simon spent the holidays in the Bayswater flat, looked after occasionally by an almost silent Tolly or coping on his own, eating his dinner each night, by arrangement, in a local restaurant. Recently the meals had become poorer; dishes he chose were no longer available although they were served to others; he was shown to the worst table and kept waiting. Some of the waiters were almost openly offensive. He knew that Clarissa was no longer getting value for money, but he dared not complain. Who was he, so expensively bought and maintained, to talk about value for money?

It was time to go if he wanted any luncheon. He crumpled the letter in his hand and stuffed it into his pocket. Shutting his eyes against the brightness of grass and trees and shimmering water, he found himself praying, petitioning the God in whom he no longer believed, with all the desperate urgency, all the artless importunity, of a child.

"Please let the weekend be a success. Don't let me make a fool of myself. Please don't let the girl despise me. Please let Clarissa be in a good mood. Please don't let Clarissa throw me out. Oh, God, please don't let anything terrible happen on Courcy Island."

# VII

It was ten o'clock on Thursday night, and in her top-floor flat off Thames Street in the City, Cordelia was completing her preparations for the weekend ahead. The long, uncurtained windows were fitted with wooden slatted blinds, but these were still up and as she moved from the single large sitting room to her bedroom she could see spread below her the glittering streets, the dark alleyways, the towers and steeples of the city, could glimpse beyond them the necklace of light slung along the Embankment and the smooth, light-dazzled curve of the river. The view, in daylight or after dark, was a continual marvel to her, the flat itself a source of astonished delight.

It had only been after Bernie's death and at the end of her own first traumatic case that she had learned that her father's small estate had at last been wound up. She had expected nothing but debts, and it had been a surprise to discover that he had owned a small house in Paris. It had, she imagined, been purchased years before when he had been comparatively well off to provide a safe house and occasional refuge for the comrades and himself; such a dedicated revolutionary would surely otherwise have despised the acquisition of even so dilapidated and insalubrious a piece of real estate. But the area had been zoned for development and it had sold surprisingly well. There had been enough money, when the debts were paid, for her to finance the agency for another six months and to begin her search for a London flat cheap enough to buy. No building society had been interested in a sixth-floor apartment at the top of a Victorian warehouse with no lift and the barest amenities, or in an applicant with an income as uncertain as it was erratic. But her bank manager, apparently to his surprise as much as hers, had been sympathetic and had authorized a five-year loan.

She had paid for the installation of a shower and for the fitting out of the small kitchen, narrow as a galley. She had done the rest of the work herself and had furnished the flat from junk shops and suburban auctions. The immense sitting room was in white with one wall covered by a bookcase made from painted planks resting on columns of bricks. The dining and working table was scrubbed oak, and the heating was provided by an ornate wrought-iron stove. Only the bedroom was luxurious, an intriguing contrast to the spartan bareness of the sitting room. As it was only eight feet by five, Cordelia had felt justified in extravagance and had chosen an expensive and exotic hand-printed paper with which she had covered the ceiling and cupboard door as well as the walls. At night, with the window which occupied almost all of one wall wide open to the sky, she would lie, warmly cocooned in eccentric luxury, feeling that she was drawn up in her bright capsule to float under the stars.

She guarded her privacy. None of her friends and no one from the agency had ever been in the flat. Adventures occurred elsewhere. She knew that if any man shared that narrow bed, for her it would mean commitment. There was only one man she ever pictured there, and he was a commander of New Scotland Yard. She knew that he, too, lived in the City; they shared the same river. But she told herself that the brief madness was over, that at a time of stress and frightening insecurity she had only been seeking her lost father. There was this to be said for a smattering of amateur psychology: it enabled one to exorcise memories which might otherwise be embarrassing.

A narrow ledge with a parapet ran outside all the windows, wide enough for rows of potted herbs and geraniums and for a single deck chair in summer. Underneath were warehouses and offices, mysterious businesses symbolized rather than identified by a double row of ancient nameplates. By day the building had a secretive, many-tongued, and sometimes raucous life. But by five o'clock this began to seep away, and at night it held a vast, almost unbroken silence. One of the tenant firms imported spices. To Cordelia, climbing up to her flat at the end of the day, that pungent, alien smell permeating the stairs represented security, comfort, her first real home.

The most onerous part of the preparation for this new case was deciding which clothes to pack. In her more puritanical moments Cordelia despised women who spent an inordinate amount of time and money on their appearance. Such a total preoccupation with externals must, she felt, argue a need to compensate for some deficiency at the heart of personality. But she was quick to recognize that her own interest in clothes and makeup, although spasmodic, was intense while it lasted and that she had never known the state of not caring how she looked. In this, as in all other matters, she preferred to travel light, and the whole of her wardrobe could be comfortably accommodated within one cupboard and three drawers which were fitted along a wall of her bedroom.

She opened them now and considered what would be necessary

for a weekend which, apart from detection, might offer anything from sailing and rock climbing to amateur theatricals. The creamy fawn pleated skirt in fine wool and the matching cashmere two-piece, both bought at Harrod's in the July sale, should, she felt, take care of most occasions; the cashmere's understated extravagance might, with luck, inspire confidence in the agency's prosperity. If the warm weather held, her brown corduroy knickerbockers might be warm for sleuthing or walking, but they were tough and she liked the jerkin and jacket, either of which looked good with them. Jeans and a couple of cotton tops were an obvious choice, as was her guernsey. The evenings were more difficult. Few people now dressed for dinner; but this was a castle, Ambrose Gorringe might well be an eccentric, and anything was possible. She would need something cool and reasonably formal. In the end she packed her only long dress, in Indian cotton in subtle shades of pink, red, and brown, and a pleated cotton skirt with matching top.

She turned with relief to the more straightforward business of checking her scene-of-crime kit. It was Bernie who had first devised it, basing it, she knew, on the kit issued to the Murder Squad of New Scotland Yard. His had been less comprehensive, but all the essentials had been there: envelopes and tweezers for the collection of specimens, dusting powder to detect fingerprints, a Polaroid camera, a pocket torch, fine rubber gloves, a magnifying glass, scissors and a sturdy penknife, a tin of Plasticine for taking impressions of keys, test tubes with stoppers for the collection of blood samples. Bernie had pointed out that, ideally, these should hold a preservative and an anticlotting agent. Neither had ever been necessary, then or now. Rescuing lost cats, shadowing errant husbands, tracing runaway teenagers, had required persistence, good feet, comfortable footwear, and infinite tact rather than the esoteric lore which Bernie had so enjoyed teaching her, compensating in those long summer sessions in Epping Forest of stalking, tracking, physical combat, and even gun lore for his own professional failure, trying to re-create through Pryde's Agency the lost hierarchical and fascinating world of the Metropolitan C.I.D.

She had made only a few alterations to the kit since Bernie's death, dispensing with the original case and using instead a canvas shoulder bag fitted with inner pockets which she had bought in a store which sold ex-army equipment. And since her first case she had included an additional item, a long leather belt with a buckle, the belt with which that first victim had been hanged. She had no wish to dwell on the case which had promised so much and had ended so tragically, one which had left her with its own legacy of guilt. But the belt had once saved her life, and she recognized an almost superstitious attachment to it, justifying its inclusion with the thought that a length of strong leather always came in useful.

Last she took a manila envelope file and wrote the name CLARISSA LISLE in capitals on the cover, taking care to make the letters neat and even. She had often thought that this was the most satisfying part of a new investigation, a moment of hope spiced with anticipatory excitement, the pristine folder and crisp lettering themselves symbolic of a fresh beginning. She glanced through her notebook before adding it to the folder. Except for Sir George and his briefly seen wife, her companions on the island were still only names, a roll call of putative suspects—Simon Lessing, Roma Lisle, Rose Tolgarth, Ambrose Gorringe, Ivo Whittingham—sounds written on paper but holding the promise of discovery, of challenge, of the fascinating variety of human personality. Like planets they circled the golden figure of Clarissa Lisle: her stepson, her cousin, her dresser, her host, her friend.

She spread out the twenty-three quotations on the table to study them before filing them in the case folder in the order of their receipt by Miss Lisle. Then she took from her shelf her two volumes of quotations, the paperback *Penguin Dictionary of Quotations* and the second edition of the *Oxford Dictionary*. As she had expected, all the passages appeared in one or the other, all but three in the paperback. Almost certainly that had been the dictionary used; it could be bought in almost any bookshop and its size would make it easy to conceal and light to carry about. To select the quotations would take no great trouble or time, merely a look at the index under *death* or *dying* or a quick read through the forty-five pages devoted to the plays of Shakespeare, the two which covered Marlowe and Webster. And it would not be too difficult to discover which plays Clarissa Lisle had appeared in. She had been a member of the Malvern Repertory Company for three years, and Shakespeare and the Jacobean dramatists were their forte. Any program note covering her career, then or later, would list her main appearances. But it was a safe bet that, given the exigencies of a Shakespearean production with the resources of a medium-sized repertory company, she would have had at least a walk-on part in all the plays.

Only two of the quotations which she had tentatively identified as Webster were not in the Penguin dictionary. But these could be found by studying the texts. All the quotations were familiar; she herself had had no difficulty in recognizing most of them even if she wasn't always sure of the play. But typing them accurately from memory was another matter. In each passage the lines were set out correctly and the punctuation was faultless, another reason for concluding that the typist had worked with the Penguin dictionary at his or her elbow.

Next she studied them under her magnifying glass, wondering as she did so how much attention the Metropolitan police had thought it worthwhile to give them. As far as she could judge, only three were typed on the same machine. The quality as well as the size of the letters varied; some were uneven, others faint or partly broken. The typing wasn't particularly expert, the work of someone who was used to a machine perhaps for his own correspondence but didn't type professionally. She thought that none had been typed on an electric typewriter. And who would have access to twenty-one different machines? Obviously someone who dealt in secondhand typewriters or someone who owned or worked in a secretarial school. It was unlikely to be a secretarial agency; the quality of the machines wasn't good enough. And it needn't necessarily be a secretarial school. Probably most modern comprehensives taught shorthand and typing; what was to prevent any member of the staff, whatever his or her subject, from staying after school hours and making private use of the machines?

And there was another way in which the messages could have been produced and one which she thought the most likely. She had bought cheap secondhand machines for her own agency, visiting the shops and showrooms where they were chained on display and trying them out, moving unhindered and unregarded from machine to machine. Anyone armed with a pad of paper and the dictionary of quotations could have provided himself—or herself—with a sufficient supply to keep the menace going, making a series of short visits to a variety of shops in districts where he was unlikely to be recognized. A reference to the yellow pages of the telephone directory would show him where to find them.

Before filing the messages in the folder she looked closely at the one which Sir George had told her had been typed on his machine. Was it her imagination that the skull and crossbones had been drawn by a different, a more careful, less assured, hand? Certainly the heads of the two crossing bones were differently shaped and slightly larger than in the other examples, the skull broader. The differences were small but, she thought, significant. The drawings of the other skulls and the coffin were practically identical. And the quotation itself, typed with erratic spacing of the letters, had no venom in its admonition:

> On pain of death let no man name death to me:
> It is a word infinitely terrible.

It wasn't a quotation known to her, and she couldn't find it in the Penguin dictionary. Webster, she thought, rather than Shakespeare; perhaps *The White Devil* or *The Devil's Law Case*. The punctuation looked accurate enough, although she would have expected a comma after the first word *death*. Perhaps this quotation had been remembered, not looked up; certainly it had been typed by a different and less expert hand. And she thought she knew whose.

The remaining quotations varied in the degree of their menace. Christopher Marlowe's bleak despair—

Hell hath no limits, nor is circumscribed
In one self place; for where we are is hell,
And where hell is, must we ever be

—could only doubtfully be described as a death threat, although its stark contemporary nihilism might well be unwelcome to a nervous recipient. The only other Marlowe quotation, received six weeks earlier—

Now hast thou but one bare hour to live,
And then thou must be damned perpetually!

—was direct enough, but the threat had proved baseless; Clarissa had lived out more than her hour. But it seemed to Cordelia that since these earlier messages, the quotations had increased in menace, had been selected to build up to some kind of climax, from the sinister threat typed underneath a coffin—

I wish you joy o' the worm

—to the brutally explicit lines from *Henry VI:*

Down, down to hell; and say I sent thee thither.

Seen together the sonorous reiteration of death and hatred was oppressive, the silly childish drawings limned with menace. She began to understand what this carefully organized program of intimidation might do to a sensitive and vulnerable woman, to any woman come to that, darkening the mornings, making terrible such ordinary events as the arrival of the post, a letter on the hall salver, a note pushed under the door. It was easy to advise the victim of a poison pen to flush the messages down the lavatory like the rubbish they were. But in all societies there was an atavistic fear of the malevolent power of a secret adversary, working for evil, willing one to failure, perhaps to death.

There was a horrible and rather frightening intelligence at work here, and it wasn't pleasant to think that the person responsible might be one of that small group who would be with her on Courcy Island, that the eyes which would meet hers over the dining table could be hiding such malignancy. For the first time she wondered whether Clarissa Lisle could be right, whether there really was a threat to her life. Then she put the thought aside, telling herself that the messages were beginning to exercise their malevolence even on her. A murderer did not advertise his intention over a period of months. But was that necessarily true? To a mind consumed with hatred, might not the act of killing be too swift, too momentary in its satisfaction? Could Clarissa Lisle have an enemy so bitter that he needed to watch her suffer, to destroy her slowly with terror and failure before he moved in for the kill?

She shivered. The warmth of the day was already dissipating; the night air drifting through the open window, even in this city aerie, held the taste and tang of autumn. She put away the last message and closed the folder. Her own instructions had been clear: to safeguard Clarissa Lisle from any worry or distress before Saturday's performance of *The Duchess of Malfi* and, if possible, to discover who was sending her the messages. And that, to the best of her ability, she would do.

# BOOK TWO

# Dress Rehearsal

# I

Victorian Speymouth, which to the surprise of its citizens had converted its street lamps to gas without explosion or other disaster, had seen no reason to reject the new railway or, while accepting its inevitability, to banish it as had Cambridge to an inconvenient distance from the town. The charming little station was only a quarter of a mile from the statue of Queen Victoria which marks the center of the promenade, and when Cordelia stepped out into the sunlight, bag in one hand and portable typewriter in the other, she found herself gazing down over a jumble of brightly painted houses to a stone-enclosed harbor, tiny as a pool, and beyond it to the stunted pier and the shimmering sea. She was almost sorry to leave the station. With its gleaming white paint and its curved roof of wrought iron, delicate as lace, it reminded her of the summer issues of her weekly childhood comic where the sea had been always blue, the sand a bright yellow, the sun a golden ball, and the railway a highly colored toy-town welcome to these imagined joys. Mrs. Wilkins, the poorest of all her foster mothers, had been the only one to buy her a comic, the only one whom Cordelia remembered with affection. Perhaps it was a happy augury that she should think of her now.

There was already a small queue waiting for the taxis, but she saw no reason to join it. The road was downhill and the quay clearly in sight. She stepped out, almost oblivious of the weight of her luggage in the pleasure of the day. The little town was bathed in sunshine, and the rows of Georgian terraced houses, simple, unpretentious, and dignified with elegant façades and wrought-iron balconies, looked as charmingly artificial and as brightly lit as a stage set. In the bay the gray shape of a small warship rested stiffly immobile as a child's cutout toy. She could almost imagine putting out her hand and plucking it from the water. As she made her way down a steep cobbled street, terraces of fawn, pink, and blue houses curved upwards toward a glimpse of distant hills, while below the brightly painted statue of Queen Victoria, majestically robed, pointed her scepter imperiously toward the public lavatories.

And everywhere there were people, jostling on the pavements, spilling from the esplanade onto the beach, laid in sunburned rows on the gritty sand, lumped in sagging deck chairs, queuing at the ice-cream kiosk, peering from the windows of cars in search of a parking place. She wondered where they had all come from on this mid-September weekday when the holiday season was surely over, the children back at school. Were they all truants from work or schoolroom, drawn out from autumn's hibernation by this resurgence of summer, with their mottled red faces above white necks, their glistening chests and arms, recently covered against September's chills revealing again the unlovely evidence of harsher suns? The day itself smelled of high summer, of seaweed, hot bodies, and blistering paint.

The busy little harbor was a confusion of rocking dinghies and furled sails, but the launch with *Shearwater* painted on its bow was soon identified. It was about thirty feet long with a central low-roofed cabin and a slatted seat in the stern. One wizened seaman seemed to be in charge. He was squatting on a bollard, his thin legs clamped, wearing sea boots and a blue jumper with *Courcy Island* emblazoned across the chest. He looked so like Popeye that Cordelia suspected that the pipe, which he slowly took from his apparently toothless gums on seeing her approach, was sucked for effect rather than solace. He touched his hat and grinned when she gave her name but he didn't speak. He took the typewriter and her bag and stowed them in the cabin, then turned to offer her his hand. But Cordelia had already jumped on board and had seated herself in the rear. He resumed his seat on the bollard and together they waited.

Three minutes later a taxi drew up at the mouth of the quay, and a boy and a woman got out. The woman paid the fare—not, it seemed, without some argument—while the boy stood uneasily to one side, then loitered to the edge of the quay to stare down at the water. She joined him and they moved together to the launch, he a little behind her like a reluctant child. This, thought Cordelia, must be Roma Lisle with Simon Lessing in tow, neither apparently pleased with the chance that had forced them into sharing a taxi.

Cordelia observed her as she allowed herself to be handed aboard. Superficially, she had nothing in common with her cousin except the shape of the lower lip. She was too fair, but it was an ordinary Anglo-Saxon blondness in which the strong sun already revealed a glint of gray. Her hair was short and expensively shaped to her head. She was taller than her cousin and moved with a certain assurance. But her face with its lines scored across the forehead and from nose to mouth had a look of brooding discontent, and there was no peace in the eyes. She was dressed in an extremely well-tailored fawn trouser suit with blue braid facing the collar and a high-necked sweater striped in fawn and pale blue, an outfit which seemed to Cordelia to combine superficial suitability for a holiday weekend with an inappropriate smartness, perhaps because she was wearing it with high-heeled shoes which made the descent into the launch less than graceful. The color, too, was unflattering to her skin. It was impossible not to recognize that here was a woman who cared about clothes without having any clear idea what suited either her or the occasion. About the young man there was less chance to make a judgment, sartorial or otherwise. He glimpsed Cordelia in the stern, blushed, and scuttled into the cabin with an alacrity which suggested that he was unlikely to add to the gaiety of the weekend. Miss Lisle seated herself in the bow while the boatman again took his seat on the bollard. They waited in silence while the launch gently rocked against the fender of old tires slung against the stones of the quay and small boats gently edged past them on the way to the open sea.

After a few minutes Miss Lisle called out, "Oughtn't we to be moving off? We're expected for lunch."

"One more a-comin'. Mr. Whittingham."

"Well, he couldn't have been on the nine-thirty-two. He'd have been here by now. And I didn't recognize him at the station. Perhaps he's driving down and has been delayed."

"Mr. Ambrose said he'd be a-comin' by train. Said to wait for him."

Miss Lisle frowned and gazed fixedly out to sea. Two more minutes passed.

Then the boatman called out, "Here he be. He's a-comin' now. That'll be Mr. Whittingham." The triple assurance given, he rose and began making ready to move off. Cordelia looked up and saw through a distorting dazzle of sun what seemed at first like a death's head on stilts jerking across the quay toward her, its skeleton fingers grasping a canvas holdall. She blinked and the picture composed itself, moved into focus, became human. The skull clothed itself in flesh, stretched and gray over the fineness of the bones, but still human flesh. The sockets moistened into eyes, keen and a little amused. The figure was still the thinnest and most desperately sick man she had ever seen moving on his own feet, but the voice was firm, and the words were easy and comfortable.

"Sorry to hold you up. I'm Ivo Whittingham. The quay looked deceptively close. And having started walking, I couldn't, of course, find a taxi."

He brushed aside Oldfield's proffered arm but without impatience and lowered himself into a seat in the bow, wedging his bag between his legs. No one spoke. The final end of rope spilled free from the bollard and was wound aboard. The engine shuddered into life. Almost imperceptibly the launch crept away from the quay and made for the harbor mouth.

Ten minutes later they seemed no closer to the island toward which, crabwise, they were edging, although the shore was visibly receding. The fishermen on the end of the pier shrank into matchstick men with fairy wands; the bustle of the town was swallowed up in the noise of the engine and finally shaken off; the royal statue became a colored blur. The horizon was a pale purple curdling into low clouds from which there separated great islands of creamy whiteness which rose to float almost motionless against a clear azure blue. The small waves seemed to be leaping with light, absorbing it from the bright air and reflecting it back to the paler blue of the sky. Cordelia thought that the sea and the distant shore were like a Monet painting, bright color laid in streaks against bright color, light itself made visible. She leaned over the edge of the boat and plunged her hand into the leaping wake. The cold made her gasp, but she held her arm under the water, spreading her fingers so that three small wakes spouted into the sunlight, watching the hairs on her forearm catch and hold the shining drops.

Suddenly her mood was broken by a woman's voice. Roma Lisle had made her way around the cabin and come up beside her. She said, "It's typical of Ambrose Gorringe just to send Oldfield and leave his guests to introduce themselves. I'm Roma Lisle, Clarissa's cousin."

They shook hands. Her fingers were firm and pleasantly cool.

Cordelia gave her name. She said, "But I'm not a guest. I'm going to the island to work."

Miss Lisle's glance went to the typewriter. She said, "Good Lord, Ambrose isn't writing another blockbuster, is he?"

"Not as far as I know. I'm employed by Lady Ralston." It might, thought Cordelia, have been more accurate to say that she was employed by Sir George, but she sensed that this might only lead to complications. But sooner or later some explanation of her presence would have to be given. It might as well be now. She prepared for the inevitable questions.

"By Clarissa! Doing what, for God's sake?"

"Dealing with her correspondence. Making telephone calls. Generally easing things along while she concentrates on the play."

"She's got Tolly to ease things along. What does she think of this—Tolly, I mean?"

"I haven't the least idea. I haven't met her yet."

"I can't see her liking it." She gave Cordelia a look in which suspicion mingled with puzzlement.

"I've read of those stagestruck oddballs, without talent themselves, who try to buy themselves into the club by attaching themselves to one of their idols, cooking, shopping, running errands, acting as a kind of poodle. They either die of overwork or end up with nervous breakdowns. You're not one of that pathetic breed, are you? No, I can see that you aren't. But don't you find your job, well . . . odd?"

"What do you do? And is your job any less odd?"

"I'm sorry. I was being offensive. Put it down to the fact that I'm a failed schoolteacher. At present I work in a bookshop. It may sound pretty orthodox, but I assure you it has its moments. You'd better meet Clarissa's stepson, Simon Lessing. He's probably nearer your age than anyone else on this benighted weekend."

Hearing his name, the boy came out of the cabin and blinked in the sun. Perhaps, thought Cordelia, he preferred a voluntary appearance to being dragged out by Miss Lisle. He held out his hand and she shook it, surprised that his clasp should be so firm. They murmured a conventional greeting. He was better-looking than a first glimpse had suggested, with a long, sensitive face and widely spaced gray eyes. But his skin was pitted with the scars of old acne, with a fresh outcrop along the forehead, and his mouth was weak. Cordelia knew that with her wide brow, high cheekbones, and catlike face she looked younger than her age, but she couldn't imagine any time when she wouldn't have felt older than this shy boy.

And then there was a fresh voice. The last passenger was making his way astern to join them. He said, "When the Prince of Wales came to Courcy Island in the eighteen-nineties, puffing across the bay in a steam launch, old Gorringe used to have his private band waiting on the quay to play him ashore. They were dressed, for some reason not recorded, in Tyrolean costume. Do you suppose that Ambrose's love affair with the past extends to laying on a similar welcome for us?"

But before anyone had a chance to respond, the launch had turned, and the eastern edge of the island and the castle itself came suddenly into sight.

## II

Although Cordelia wasn't aware that she had consciously thought about the architecture of Courcy Castle, it had, nevertheless, formed itself in her mind as a gray-stoned, massive, crenellated sham, overornate in its Victorian solidity, an unsatisfactory compromise between domesticity and grandeur. The reality, suddenly presented to her in the clarity of the morning sunlight, made her catch her breath with wonder. It stood on the edge of the sea, almost as if it had risen from the waves, a castle of rose-red brick, its only stonework the pale flush lines and the tall curved windows which now coruscated in the sun. To the west soared a slender round tower topped with a cupola, solid yet ethereal. Every detail of the mat-surfaced walls, the patterned buttresses, and the battlements was distinct, unfussy, confident. The whole was compact, even massive, yet the high, sloping roofs and the slender tower gave an impression of lightness and repose which she hadn't associated with High Victorian architecture. The southern façade overlooked a wide terrace—surely wave-swept in winter—from which two flights of steps led down to a narrow beach of sand and shingle. The proportions of the castle seemed to her exactly right for its site. Larger and it could have looked pretentious; smaller and there would have been a suggestion of facile charm. But this building, compromise though it might be between castle and family house, seemed to her brilliantly successful. She almost laughed aloud at the pleasure of it.

She was unaware that Ivo Whittingham had come up beside her until he spoke. "This is your first visit, isn't it? What do you think of it?"

"It's remarkable. And unexpected."

"You're interested in Victorian architecture."

"Interested, but not at all knowledgeable."

"I shouldn't tell Ambrose that. He'll devote the whole weekend to educating you in his passions and prejudices. I've done my homework, so I'll forestall him by telling you now that the architect was E. W. Godwin, who worked for Whistler and Oscar Wilde and was associated with the aesthetes. What he aimed for—so he tells us—was the careful adjustment of solids and voids. Well, he's achieved that here. He did some perfectly awful town halls, including one at Northampton—not that Ambrose would admit to its awfulness—but I think that he and I will agree about this achievement. Are you taking part in the play?"

"No, I'm here to work. I'm Miss Lisle's secretary, her temporary secretary."

His quick glance was surprised. Then his lips curved in a smile. "So I should imagine. Clarissa's relationships tend to be temporary."

Cordelia said quickly, "Do you know anything about the play? I mean, which company is acting in it?"

"Didn't Clarissa explain? They're the Cottringham Players, said to be the oldest amateur company in England. They were started in 1834 by the then Sir Charles Cottringham, and the family have more or less kept them going ever since. The Cottringhams have been mad about acting for over three generations, their enthusiasm invariably in inverse proportion to their talent. The present Charles Cottringham is playing Antonio. His great-grandfather used to take part in the revels here until he was imprudent enough to cast a lascivious eye on Lillie Langtry. The Prince of Wales made his displeasure known, and no Cottringham has spent the night under the castle roof since. It's a convenient tradition for Ambrose. He need only entertain the leading lady and a few private guests. Judith Cottringham has a house party for the producer and the rest of the cast. They'll all come over tomorrow by launch."

"Where did they act before Mr. Gorringe offered the castle?"

"It was offered, I imagine, by Clarissa rather than Gorringe. They gave an annual performance in the old assembly rooms at Speymouth, an occasion more social than cultural. But tomorrow shouldn't be too discouraging. A Speymouth butcher, appropriately enough, is playing Bosola, and he's reputed to be good. Ferdinand is taken by Cottringham's agent. Hardly Gielgud, but Clarissa tells me that he knows how to speak verse."

The sound of the engine died to a gentle shudder and the launch slowly edged toward the jetty. The stone quay curved from the terrace in two arms to form a miniature harbor. At intervals, steep steps festooned with seaweed led down to the water. At the end of the eastern and longer arm was a charming folly, a circular bandstand of delicate wrought iron, painted white and pale blue with slender pillars supporting a curved canopy. Beneath this stood the welcoming party, a group of two men and two women, as immobile and carefully positioned as a tableau. Clarissa Lisle was a little to the front, her host attendant at her left shoulder. Behind them, waiting with the impassive, careful noninvolvement of servants, stood a dark-clad man and woman, the man outtopping the group in height.

But the dominant figure was Clarissa. The immediate impression, whether by chance or by design, was of a goddess of classical mythology with her attendants. As the launch drew alongside the quay, Cordelia saw that she was wearing what looked like shorts and a sleeveless top in closely pleated cream muslin with over it a loose-fitting, almost transparent shift of the same material, wide-sleeved and corded at the waist. Beside this deceptively simple, cool, flowing elegance Roma Lisle in her trouser suit seemed to exude a sweaty and eye-dazzling discomfort. The waiting group, as if under instruction, held their pose until the launch gently bumped the landing steps. Then Clarissa fluted a small cry of welcome, spread bat wings of fluttering cotton, and ran forward. The pattern was broken.

During the chatter which followed the formal introductions and while Ambrose Gorringe was supervising the unloading of luggage and the humping ashore of boxes of supplies from a locker in the stern, Cordelia studied her host. Ambrose Gorringe was of middle height with smooth black hair and delicate hands and feet. He gave an impression of spry plumpness, not because he carried excess fat but because of the feminine softness and roundness of his arms and face. His skin gleamed pink and white; the circular flush on each cheekbone looked almost artificial. His eyes were his most striking feature. They were large and sparkling, bright as black sea-washed pebbles, the surrounding whites clear and translucent. Above them the brows curved in a strong arch as tidily as if they had been plucked. The ends of the mouth curved upwards in a fixed smile so that the whole face held the shining, humorous animation of a man enjoying a perpetual internal joke. He was wearing brown cotton trousers and a black short-sleeved singlet. Both were highly suitable for the weather and the occasion, yet to Cordelia they seemed incongruous. Something more formal was needed to define and control the latent strength of what she guessed was a complex and, perhaps, a formidable personality.

In his way the manservant, now supervising the loading of the luggage and crates of supplies onto a small motorized truck, was equally remarkable. He must, thought Cordelia, be well over six feet in height, and with his dark suit and heavy white lugubrious face he had the spurious gloom of a Victorian undertaker's mute. His long, rather pointed head sloped to a high and shiny forehead topped with a wig of coarse black hair, which made absolutely no pretensions to realism. It was parted in the middle and had been inexpertly hacked rather than trimmed. Cordelia thought that such a bizarre appearance could hardly be inadvertent, and she wondered what perversity or secret compulsion had led him to contrive and present to his world a persona so uncompromisingly eccentric. Could it be revulsion against the tedium, the conformity, or the deference demanded of his job? It seemed unlikely. Servants who found their duties frustrating or uncongenial nowadays had a simple remedy. They could leave.

Intrigued by the man's appearance, she scarcely noticed his wife: a short, round-faced woman who stood always at her husband's side and didn't speak during the whole course of the disembarkation.

Clarissa Lisle had taken absolutely no notice of Cordelia since their arrival, but Ambrose Gorringe came forward, smiled, and said, "You must be Miss Gray. Welcome to Courcy Island. Mrs. Munter will look after you. We've put you next to Miss Lisle."

Cordelia waited until the Munters had finished unloading the launch. As the three of them walked together behind the main party, Munter handed his wife a small canvas bag with the words "Not much post this morning. The parcel from the London Library hasn't come. That means Mr. Gorringe probably won't get his books until Monday."

The woman spoke for the first time. "He'll have plenty to do this weekend without new library books."

At that moment Ambrose Gorringe turned and called to Munter. The man moved forward, changing his quick steps to a stately, unhurried walk which was probably part of his act. As soon as he was out of earshot Cordelia said, "If there's any post for Miss Lisle, it comes first to me. I'm her new secretary. And I'll take any telephone calls for her. Perhaps I'd better take a look at the post. We're expecting a letter."

Rather to her surprise, Mrs. Munter handed over the bag without demur. There were only eight letters in all, held together in a rubber band. Two were for Clarissa Lisle. One, in a stout envelope, was obviously an invitation to a dress show. The name, but not the address, of the prestigious designer was engraved on the flap. The second, an ordinary white envelope, was addressed in typing to:

The Duchess of Malfi
c/o Miss Clarissa Lisle
Courcy Island
Speymouth
Dorset

She walked a few steps ahead. She knew that it would be wise to wait until she reached the privacy of her room, but restraint was impossible. Controlling her excitement and curiosity, she slipped her finger under the flap. It was loosely gummed and came apart easily. She guessed the communication would be short and it was. Inside, on a small sheet of the same paper was a neatly drawn skull and crossbones, and typed underneath just two lines which she instinctively knew rather than recognized were from the play:

Call upon our dame aloud,
And bid her quickly don her shroud!

She put the message back into the envelope and slipped it quickly into her jacket pocket, then lingered until Mrs. Munter had caught her up.

Cordelia saw that the main rooms opened onto the terrace with a wide view of the Channel, but that the entrance to the castle was on the sheltered eastern side away from the sea. They passed through a stone archway which led to a formal walled garden, then turned down a wide path between lawns and finally through a high arched porch and into the great hall. Pausing at the doorway, Cordelia could picture those first nineteenth-century guests, the crinolined ladies with their furled parasols, followed by their maids, the leather round-topped trunks, the hatboxes and gun cases, the distant beat of the welcoming band as that heavy Germanic prince carried his imposing paunch before him under Mr. Gorringe's privileged portals. But then the great hall would have been ostentatiously overfurnished, a lush repository of sofas, chairs, and occasional tables, rich carpets, and huge pots of palms. Here the house party would congregate at the end of the day before slowly processing in strict hierarchical order through the double doors to the dining room. But now the hall was furnished only with a long refectory table and two chairs, one on each side of the stone fireplace. On the opposite wall was a six-foot tapestry which she thought was almost certainly by William Morris: Flora, rose-crowned, with her maidens, her feet shining among the lilies and the hollyhocks. A wide staircase, branching to left and right, led to a gallery which ran around three sides of the hall. The eastern wall was almost entirely taken up by a stained-glass window showing the travels of Ulysses. Motes of colored light danced in the air, giving the great hall something of the quiet solemnity of a church. She followed Mrs. Munter up the staircase.

The main bedrooms opened out of the gallery. The room into which Cordelia was shown was charming with a lightness and delicacy which she hadn't expected. The two windows, high and curved, had curtains of a lily-patterned chintz which was used also for the bed cover and the fitted cushion of the mahogany cane-backed bedside chair. The simple stone fireplace had a paneled frieze of six-inch tiles, their patterns of flowers and foliage echoed in the larger tiles which surrounded the grate. Above the bed was a row of delicate watercolors, iris, wild strawberry, tulip, and lily. This, she thought, must be the De Morgan room of which Miss Maudsley had spoken. She glanced around with pleasure and Mrs. Munter, noting her interest, assumed the role of guide. But she recited the information without enthusiasm as if she had learned the facts by rote.

"The furniture here is not as old as the castle, miss. The bed and chair were designed by A. H. Mackmurdo in 1883. The tiles here and in the bathroom are by William De Morgan. Most of the tiles in the castle are by him. The original Mr. Herbert Gorringe, who rebuilt the castle in the eighteen-sixties, saw a house that he'd done in Kensington and had all the original tiles here ripped out and replaced by De Morgan. That mahogany and pine cabinet was painted by William Morris and the paintings are by John Ruskin. What time would you like your early tea, miss?"

"At half past seven, please."

After she left, Cordelia went through to the bathroom. Both rooms faced west, and any broad view of the island was blocked by the tower which rose immediately to her right, a phallic symbol in patterned brick, soaring to pierce the blue of the sky. Gazing up at its smooth roundness, she felt her head swim and the tower itself reeled dizzily in the sun. To her left she could just glimpse the end of the southern terrace and, beyond it, a wide sweep of sea. Beneath the bathroom window a wrought-iron fire escape led down to the rocks, from which, presumably, it was possible to reach the terrace. Even so, the escape route seemed to her precarious. In a high storm one would surely feel trapped between fire and sea.

Cordelia had started to unpack when the communicating door between her room and the adjoining one opened and Clarissa Lisle appeared.

"Oh, here you are. Come next door, will you? Tolly will see to your unpacking for you."

"Thank you, but I'd rather do my own."

Apart from the fact that the few clothes she had brought could be hung up in minutes and she preferred to do these things for herself, Cordelia had no intention of letting other eyes see the scene-of-crime kit. She had already noticed with relief that the bottom drawer of the cabinet had a key.

She followed Clarissa into her bedroom. It was twice as large as her own and very different in style; here opulence and extravagance replaced lightness and simplicity. The room was dominated by the bed, a mahogany half-tester with canopy, cover, and side curtains of crimson damask. The head and footboard were elaborately carved with cherubs and swags of flowers, the whole surmounted by a countess's coronet. Cordelia wondered whether the original owner, thrusting his way upwards through the Victorian social hierarchy, had commissioned it to honor a particularly important guest. On either side of the bed was a small bow-fronted chest and, across its foot, a carved and buttoned chaise longue. The dressing table was set between the two tall windows from which, between the looped curtains, Cordelia saw only an expanse of blue untroubled sea. Two ponderous wardrobes covered the opposite wall. There were low chairs and a screen of Berlin woolwork before the marble fireplace in which a small pile of sticks had already been laid. Ambrose Gorringe's chief guest was to have the luxury of a real fire. She wondered whether some housemaid would creep in during the early hours to light it, as had her Victorian counterpart when the long-dead countess stirred in her magnificent bed.

The room was very untidy. Clothes, wraps, tissue paper, and plastic bags were flung across the chaise longue and the bed, and the top of the dressing table was a jumble of bottles and jars. A woman was walking about, calmly and uncensoriously gathering up the clothes over her arm.

Clarissa Lisle said, "This is my dresser, Miss Tolgarth. Tolly, meet Miss Cordelia Gray. She's come to help with my correspondence. Just an experiment. She won't be in anyone's way. If she wants anything done, look after her, will you?"

It wasn't, thought Cordelia, an auspicious introduction. The woman neither smiled nor spoke, but Cordelia didn't feel that the steady gaze which met her own held any resentment. It didn't even hold curiosity. She was a heavily busted, rather sturdy woman with a face that looked older than her body and with remarkably elegant legs. Their shape was enhanced by very fine stockings and high-heeled court shoes, an incongruous touch of vanity which emphasized the plainness of the high-necked black dress, its only ornament a gold cross on a chain. Her dark hair, parted in the middle and drawn back into a bun at the nape of the neck, was already streaked with gray, and there were lines as deep as clefts across the forehead and at the ends of the wide mouth. It was a strong, secretive face, not, Cordelia thought, the face of a woman willingly subservient.

When she had disappeared into the bathroom, Clarissa said, "I suppose we'll have to talk, but it can't be now. Munter has set lunch in the dining room. It's ridiculous on a day like this. We ought to be in the sun. I've told him that we shall eat on the terrace, but that means he'll see that we don't get it until one-thirty, so we may as well make a quick tour of the castle. Is your room comfortable?"

"Very, thank you."

"I suppose I'd better give you some letters to type just to allay suspicion. There are one or two that need answering. You may as well do some work while you're here. You can type, I suppose."

"Yes, I can type. But that's not why I'm here."

"I know why you're here. I was the one who wanted you. And I still want you. But we'll talk about that tonight. There won't be a chance until then. Charles Cottringham and the other principals are coming across after lunch for a run-through of one or two scenes, and they won't be gone until after tea. You've met my stepson, haven't you, Simon Lessing?"

"Yes, we were introduced on the boat."

"Find him, will you, and tell him there's time for him to have a swim before lunch. There's no point in his trailing round the castle with us. You'll probably find him hiding in his room. It's two down from your own."

Cordelia thought that the message could more suitably have come from Clarissa. But she reminded herself that she was supposed to be a secretary-companion, whatever that meant, and that the job probably included running errands. She knocked on Simon's door. He didn't call out, but after what seemed an inordinate delay, the door slowly opened and his apprehensive face appeared. He blushed when he saw who it was. She gave him Clarissa's message, suitably edited, and he managed a smile and a whispered "Thank you" before quickly reclosing the door. Cordelia felt rather sorry for him. It couldn't be altogether easy, having Clarissa as a stepmother. She wasn't sure that it would be any easier having her as a client. For the first time she felt some of her euphoria drain away. The castle and the island were even lovelier than she had pictured. The weather was glorious and no change threatened in this balmy resurgence of summer. It promised to be a weekend of comfort, even of luxury. And, above all, the envelope in her pocket confirmed that the job was real, that she would pit her brain and her wits against a human adversary at last. Why, then, should she have to struggle against a sudden and overwhelming conviction that her task was doomed to disaster?

## III

"And now," announced Clarissa, leading the way down the staircase and across the great hall, "we'll end with a visit to Ambrose's private chamber of horrors."

The tour of the castle had been hurried and incomplete. Cordelia sensed that the sun-warmed terrace beckoned and that the thoughts of the party were less on Ambrose's treasures than on their pre-luncheon sherry. But there were treasures, and she promised herself that if she had the chance, she would enjoy later and at leisure what was a small but comprehensive museum of the artistic achievements and spirit of Victoria's long reign. The tour had been too rushed. Her mind was a confusion of form and color; porcelain, pictures, glass, and silver jostled for place: pottery exhibited at the Great Exhibition of 1851, jasper, Grecian ware, terra-cotta, majolica; cabinets of painted Wedgwood dishes and delicate pâte-sur-pâte made by M. L. Solon for

Minton; part of a Coalport dinner service presented by Queen Victoria to the Emperor of Russia and decorated with English and Russian Orders surrounding the Russian royal crown and eagles.

Clarissa had floated on ahead, waving her arms and producing a stream of doubtfully accurate information. Ivo had lingered when he was allowed to and had said little. Roma stumped behind them with an expression of careful uninterest and from time to time made an acid comment about the misery and exploitation of the poor represented by these glittering monuments to wealth and privilege. Cordelia felt some sympathy with her. Sister Magdalen, who had taught nineteenth-century history at the convent, hadn't shared the view of some of the sisters that since the pleasures of the world were to be rejected, so might some of its vicarious sorrows, and had attempted to instill a social sense into her privileged pupils. Cordelia couldn't see a picture of that pudding-faced queen with her plain, discontented-looking children around her without seeing also the wan, aching-eyed seamstresses working their eighteen-hour day, the factory children half asleep at their looms, the bobbin-lace makers bent double over their cushions, and the steaming tenements of the East End.

Cordelia had found more to interest her than to admire in Ambrose's collection of pictures. Everything that she most disliked in High Victorian art was here: the strained eroticism, the careful naturalism which had nothing to do with nature, the vapid anecdotal pictures, and the debased religiosity. But he did have a Sickert and a Whistler.

As they passed along the gallery, Roma said to her, "There's a William Dyce in my room called *The Shell Gatherers.* Not badly painted; rather good, in fact. A crinolined group of ladies examining their finds on a Kentish beach. But what's the reality? A group of overfed, overclad, bored, and sexually frustrated upper-class females with nothing to do with their time but collect shells to make their useless shell boxes, paint insipid watercolors, entertain the gentlemen after dinner at the pianoforte, and wait for a man to give status and purpose to their lives."

It was while Cordelia and Roma were standing in front of a Holman Hunt, neither of them finding anything to say, that Ambrose had come up to them.

"Not, perhaps, one of his best. The Victorians may have got their money from the dark satanic mills, but they had a passionate craving for beauty. It was their tragedy that, unlike us, they understood only too well how far they fell short of achieving it."

The tour was now almost at an end. Clarissa led them down a tiled passageway to Ambrose's business room. Here, apparently, was the promised Chamber of Horrors.

It was a smaller room than most in the castle and looked out over the lawn which faced the eastern entrance. One wall was hung with a framed collection of Victorian popular gallows literature, the crudely printed and illustrated broadsheets which were sold to the mob after a notable trial or execution. Roma seemed particularly interested in them. Murderers, looking remarkably slim and elegant in their breeches, sat penning their last confessions under the high barred window of the condemned cell, listened in the chapel at Newgate to their last sermon with their coffins placed at hand, or drooped from the rope end as the robed chaplain stood, his book in hand. Cordelia disliked the pictures of hanging and moved to join Ambrose and Ivo, who were examining a wall shelf of Staffordshire figures. Ambrose identified his favorites.

"Meet my Victorian murderers and murderesses. That pair are the notorious Maria and Frederick Manning, hanged in November 1847 in front of Horsemongers Lane Gaol before a riotous crowd of fifty thousand. Charles Dickens saw the execution, and he wrote afterward that the behavior of the crowd was so indescribable that he thought he was living in a city of devils. Maria wore black satin for her part in the entertainment, a choice which did absolutely nothing for its subsequent fashionable appeal. The gentleman appropriately clad in a shooting jacket is William Corder, aiming his pistol at poor Maria Marten. Notice the red barn in the background. He might have got away with it if her mother hadn't repeatedly dreamed that her daughter's body was buried there. He was hanged at Bury St. Edmunds in 1828, also in front of a large and appreciative audience. The lady next to him in the bonnet and carrying a black bag is Kate Webster. The bag contains the head of her mistress, whom she beat to death, cut into pieces, and boiled in the kitchen boiler. She is said to have gone round the local shops offering cheap dripping for sale. She was turned off, as they used to say, in July 1879."

Leaving the business room, they paused at two elegant rosewood display cases which stood on each side of the door. The left-hand one contained a clutter of small objects which were all neatly labeled: a doll and a solitaire set with small colored marbles, both of which had belonged to the Queen as a child; a fan; early Christmas cards; scent bottles of crystal, silver gilt, and enamel; and a collection of small silver objects, waist hook, chatelaine, prayer book, and posy holder. But it was the right-hand case which drew their eyes. Here were less agreeable mementos, an extension of Ambrose's museum of crime.

He explained: "That tag end of rope is part of the executioner's rope which hanged Dr. Thomas Neill Cream, the Lambeth poisoner, in November 1892. The stained linen nightdress with the *broderie anglaise* frills was worn by Constance Kent. It's not the nightdress she had on when she slit the throat of her small stepbrother, but it has a certain interest all the same. That pair of handcuffs with the key were used on young Courvoisier who murdered his master, Lord William Russell, in 1840. The spectacles are a pair which belonged to Dr. Crippen. As he was hanged in November 1910 he's really nine years out of my period, but I couldn't resist them."

Ivo asked, "And the marble of a baby's arm?"

"That hasn't any criminal interest as far as I know. It should be in Memento Mori or in the other cabinet, but I hadn't time to rearrange the exhibits. But it doesn't look out of place among the props of murder. The man who sold it to me would approve. He told me that he kept imagining that the limb was oozing blood."

Clarissa hadn't spoken, and glancing at her, Cordelia saw that her eyes were fixed on the marble with a mixture of fear and repulsion which none of the other exhibits had evoked. The arm, a chubby replica in white marble, lay on a purple cushion bound with cord. Cordelia herself thought it an unpleasant object, sentimental and morbid, useless and undecorative, and to that extent not untypical of the minor art of its age.

Clarissa said, "But it's perfectly hateful! It's disgusting! Where on earth did you pick it up, Ambrose?"

"In London. A man I know. It may be the only extant copy of one of the limbs of the royal children made for Queen Victoria at Osborne House, said to be by Mary Thornycroft. This one could be poor Vicky, the Princess Royal. It's either that or a memorial piece. And if you dislike it, Clarissa, you should see the Osborne collection. They look like the remnants of a holocaust, as if the Prince Consort had descended on the royal nursery with a machete, as he may well have been tempted to do, poor man."

Clarissa said, "It's repulsive! What on earth possessed you, Ambrose? Get rid of it."

"Certainly not. It may be unique. I regard it as an interesting addition to my minor Victoriana."

Roma said, "I've seen the Osborne pieces. I find them repulsive too. But they throw an interesting light on the Victorian mind, the Queen's in particular."

"Well, this throws an interesting light on Ambrose's mind," Ivo said quietly. "As a piece of marble, it's rather well done. It's the association you find unpleasant, perhaps. The death or mutilation of a child is always distressing, don't you think, Clarissa?"

But Clarissa appeared not to have heard. She turned away and said, "For God's sake, don't start arguing about it. Just get rid of it, Ambrose. And now I need a drink and my lunch."

# IV

Half a mile from the shore, Simon Lessing stopped his slow and regular crawl stroke, turned on his back, and let his eyes rest on the horizon. The sea was empty. Faced with that shuddering waste of water, he found it possible to imagine that there was emptiness also behind him, that the island and its castle had gently subsided under the waves, silently and without turbulence, and that he floated alone in a blue infinity of sea. This self-induced sense of isolation excited but didn't frighten him. Nothing about the sea ever did. Here was the element in which he felt most at peace; guilt, anxiety, failure, washed away in a gentle and perpetual baptism of redemption.

He was glad that Clarissa hadn't wanted him tagging along behind her on the tour of the castle. There were rooms he would be interested to see, but there would be time enough to explore on his own. And it would give him another excuse to keep out of her way. He couldn't swim more than twice a day at most without its seeming odd and deliberately unsociable, but it would seem perfectly natural to ask if he might wander off to explore the castle. Perhaps the weekend might not be so terrifying after all.

He had only to thrust himself upright to feel the bite of the cold undercurrent. But now he floated, spread-eagled under the sun, feeling the sea creep over his chest and arms as softly warm as a bath. From time to time he let his face submerge, opening his eyes on the thin film of green, letting it wash lightly over his eyeballs. And deep down there was the knowledge, unfrightening and almost comforting, that he only had to let himself go, to give himself up to the power and gentleness of the sea, and there need never again be guilt or anxiety or failure. He knew that he wouldn't do it; the thought was a small self-indulgence which, like a drug, could be safely experimented with as long as the doses were small and one stayed in control. And he was in control. In a few minutes it would be time to turn and strike for the shore, to think about luncheon and Clarissa and getting through the next two days without embarrassment or disaster. But now there was this peace, this emptiness, this wholeness.

It was only at moments like this that he could think without pain of his father. This was how he must have died, swimming alone in the Aegean on that summer morning, finding the tide too strong for him, letting himself go at last without a struggle, without fear, giving himself up to the sea he loved, embracing its majesty and its peace. He had imagined that death so often on his solitary swims that the old nightmares were almost exorcised. He no longer awoke in the darkness of the early hours as he had in those first months after he had learned of his father's death, sweating with terror, desperately tearing at the blankets as they dragged him down, living every second of those last dreadful minutes, the stinging eyes, the agony as he glimpsed through the waves the lost, receding, unattainable shore. But it hadn't been like that. It couldn't have been like that. His father had died secure in his great love, unresisting and at peace.

It was time to turn back. He twisted under the water and began again his steady, powerful crawl. Now his feet found the shingle and he pulled himself ashore, colder and more tired than he had expected. Looking up, he saw with surprise that there was someone waiting for him, a dark-clad still figure standing like a guardian beside his pile of clothes. He shook the water from his eyes and saw it was Tolly.

He came up to her. At first she didn't speak but bent and picked up his towel and handed it to him. Panting and shivering, he began patting dry his arms and neck, embarrassed by her steady gaze, wondering why she was there.

Then she said, "Why don't you leave?"

She must have seen his incomprehension. She said again, "Why don't you leave, leave this place, leave her?" Her voice, as always, was low but harsh, almost expressionless. He stared at her, wild-eyed under the dripping hair.

"Leave Clarissa! Why should I? What do you mean?"

"She doesn't want you. Haven't you noticed that? You aren't happy. Why go on pretending?"

He cried out in protest. "But I am happy! And where can I go? My aunt wouldn't want me back. I haven't any money."

She said, "There's a spare room in my flat. You could have that for a start. It isn't much, a child's room. But you could stay there until you found something better."

A child's room. He remembered hearing that she had once had a child, a girl who had died. No one ever spoke about her now. He didn't want to think about her. He had thought enough about dying and death. He said, "But how could I find somewhere? What would I live on?"

"You're seventeen, aren't you? You're not a child. You've got five 'O' levels. You could find something to do. I was working at fifteen. Most children in the world start younger."

"But doing what? I'm going to be a pianist. I need Clarissa's money."

"Ah, yes," she said, "you need Clarissa's money."

And so, he thought, do you. That's what this is all about. He felt a surge of confidence, of adult cunning. He wasn't a child to be so easily fooled. Hadn't he always sensed her dislike of him, caught that contemptuous glance as she set down his breakfast on those days when she and he were alone in the flat, watched the silent resentment with which she gathered up his laundry, cleaned his room? If he weren't there, she wouldn't need to come in except twice a week to check that all was well. Of course she wanted him out of the way. Probably she expected to be left something in Clarissa's will; she must be ten years younger even if she didn't look it. And she was only a servant after all. What right had she to upset him, to criticize Clarissa, to patronize him, offering her sordid little room as if it were a favor? It would be as bad as Mornington Avenue; worse. The small seductive devil at the back of his mind whispered its enticement. However difficult things might be at times, he would be crazy to give up the patronage of Clarissa, who was rich, to put himself at the mercy of Tolly, who was poor.

Perhaps something of this reached her. She said, almost humbly but with no trace of solicitation, "You'd be under no obligation. It's just a room."

He wished she would go. Yet he couldn't walk away, couldn't start dressing while that dark, oppressive figure stood there, seeming to block the whole beach. He drew himself up and said as stiffly as his shivering body would permit, "Thank you, but I'm perfectly happy as I am."

"Suppose she gets tired of you like she did your father."

He gaped at her, clutching his towel. Above them a gull shrieked, shrill as a tormented child. He whispered, "What do you mean? She loved my father! They loved each other! He explained to me before he left us, mother and me. It was the most marvelous thing that had ever happened to him. He had no choice."

"There's always a choice."

"But they adored each other! He was so happy."

"Then why did he drown himself?"

He cried, "It isn't true! I don't believe you!"

"You don't have to if you don't want to. Just remember it when your turn comes."

"But why should he do it? Why?"

"To make her feel sorry, I suppose. Isn't that usually why people kill themselves? But he should have known. Clarissa doesn't understand about guilt."

"But they told me that there was an inquest. They found that it was accidental death. And he didn't leave a note."

"If he did they didn't see it. It was Clarissa who found his clothes on the beach."

Her eyes fell to where his own trousers and jacket were jumbled under a stone. A picture came unbidden into his mind, so clear that it might have been memory. The gritty sand, hot as cinders, an alien sea layered in purple and blue to the horizon, Clarissa standing with the wind billowing her sleeves, the note in her hand. And then the tattered scraps of white, fluttering down like petals, briefly littering the sea before floating and dissolving in the surf. It had been three weeks before his father's body, what was left of it, was washed up. But bones and flesh, even when the fish have finished with it, last longer than a scrap of paper. It wasn't true. None of it was true. As she had told him, there is always a choice. He would choose not to believe.

He looked down so that he need not meet her eyes, that compelling stare which was much more convincing than any words she could speak. There was a swath of seaweed wound around his calf, brown as a gash on which the blood has dried. He bent and plucked at it. It tightened, a slimy ligature. He knew that she was watching him.

Then she said, "Suppose she died. What would you do then?"

"Why should she die? She isn't sick, is she? She never said anything to me about being sick. What's wrong with her?"

"Nothing. Nothing's wrong with her."

"Then why are you talking about dying?"

"She thinks she's going to die. Sometimes when people think that strongly enough they do die."

His heart surged with relief. But that was ridiculous! She was trying to frighten him. Everything was plain to him now. She had always been jealous of him, just as she had been jealous of his father. He picked up his jacket and tried to sound dignified through the chattering of his teeth.

"If she does die I'm sure you'll be remembered. I shouldn't worry if I were you. And now perhaps you'll let me get dressed. I'm cold and it's time for luncheon."

As soon as the words were out he felt ashamed. She turned away without another word. And then she looked back and their eyes met for the last time. He knew what she must see in his: the shame, the fear. He was prepared to encounter anger and resentment. But what he hadn't expected to see was pity.

# V

A long arcade, brick-built but with columns and arches of patterned stonework, led from from the west side of the castle, past a rose garden and formal pool to the theater. Making his solitary way, rather late, to watch part of the final run-through, Ivo could picture the slow after-dinner procession of Victorian guests passing under the arches, pale arms and necks above the richness of satin and velvet, jewels sparkling on bosoms and in the intricately piled hair, the white shirt fronts of the men gleaming in the moonlight.

The theater itself surprised him, less by the perfection of its proportions, which he had expected, than by its contrast to the rest of the castle. He wondered whether it was the work of a different architect; he would have to ask Ambrose. But if Godwin had been responsible, it was apparent that his client's insistence on opulence and ostentation had prevailed over any inclination he himself might have had for lightness or restraint. Even now, with only half the house lights lit, the theater glowed with richness. The deep red velvet of the curtains and seats had faded but was still remarkably well preserved. The candle lighting had been replaced by electricity—the conversion must have given Ambrose a pang—but the delicate convolvulus light shades were still in use and the original crystal chandelier still glittered from the domed ceiling. Everywhere there was ornament, sumptuous, florid, occasionally charming, but always splendid in its craftsmanship. Across the front of the boxes gilded plump-buttocked cherubs held swags of flowers or lifted trumpets to pouting mouths, and the richly carved royal box with its Prince of Wales feathers and twin seats, regal as thrones, must have satisfied even the most ardent monarchist's view of what was owing to the heir apparent.

Ivo had settled himself at the end of the fourth row of the stalls with no intention of staying for more than an hour. He was eager to disabuse the cast of any idea they might have that he was on the island primarily to review their performance, and this casual appearance to watch the final rehearsal would remind them that he was less interested in what they managed to make of Webster's tragedy than in the glories, scandals, and legends of the theater itself. He was glad that the seats, designed for broad Victorian rumps, were so luxuriously comfortable. The afternoon was always the worst time for him when his luncheon, however frugal, lay heavily on his distorted stomach and the monstrous spleen seemed to grow and harden under his supporting hands. He twisted himself more comfortably into the velvet plush, aware of Cordelia sitting silent and upright farther along the row, and tried to fix his attention on the stage.

The cast had obviously decided, or been instructed by DeVille, to concentrate on the sense and let the verse look after itself, a ploy which would have been disastrous with Shakespeare but which succeeded well enough with Webster's rougher meter. And at least it made for pace. Ivo had always believed that there was only one way to direct Webster: as a highly stylized drama of manners, the characters mere ritual personifications of lust, decadence, and sexual rapacity, moving in a pavane toward the inevitable orgiastic triumph of madness and death. But DeVille, half sunk in lugubrious disgust at finding himself actually directing amateurs, was obviously aiming at some semblance of realism. It would be interesting to see how he dealt with the more gratuitous horrors. He would be lucky to get away with the proffered severed hand and the gaggle of madmen without a suppressed giggle or two. Revenge tragedy was hardly a genre for the inexperienced; but, then, what classic was? Certainly this charnelhouse poet, heaping horror on horror until the appetite sickened and then suddenly piercing the heart with lines of redeeming beauty, demanded more than the present enthusiastic bunch of playactors. Still, DeVille had to get only one performance out of them. It wasn't what you could raise yourself to on one night, but what you could continue to do, night after night and two matinees a week, for three months or more, that distinguished the professional from the amateur. He had known that the play was to be done in Victorian costume. The idea had seemed to him an eccentric, slightly ludicrous conceit. But he could see that it had its uses. The stage and the small auditorium fused into one claustrophobic cockpit of evil; the high-necked dresses and the bustles hinted at a sexuality which was the more lascivious because covert, overlaid with Victorian respectability. And there was some wit in the decision to dress Bosola as a kilted Highlander, although it was hard to imagine Victoria's good old Brown in this complex creature of nihilism and thwarted nobility.

The four principals had been rehearsing now for nearly fifty-five minutes. DeVille had been leaving them pretty much to themselves, his heavy froglike face expressing nothing but a settled gloom. Probably he had resented being dragged away from his postprandial nap and subjected to yet another sea trip merely to indulge Clarissa's wish for a final run-through in costume of her more important scenes. Ivo glanced at his watch. Boredom was taking hold of him as he had known it would, but the effort of moving seemed too great. He glanced along the row and watched Cordelia's face, upturned to the stage, the firm yet delicate chin, the sweet curve of the throat. He thought, Two years ago I should have been mildly agonizing over her, scheming how I might get into her bed before the weekend was out, fretting at the possibility of failure. He recalled his past exploits, less with disgust than with a detached wonder that so much time and thought and energy should have been expended on such petty expedients against boredom. The trouble had been so disproportionate to the satisfaction, the desire less urgent than the need to prove himself still desirable. What, after all, would getting into bed with her have meant but a small fillip to the ego, ranking only a little higher than the quality of the food and wine and the wit of the after-dinner conversation as an index of the success of the weekend? Always he had aimed to conduct his affairs on the level of a civilized, uncommitted exchange of pleasure. And always they had ended in rows, recriminations, in messiness and disgust. It had been no different with Clarissa except the rows had been more bitter, the disgust more lasting. But, then, with Clarissa he had made the mistake of letting himself become involved. With Clarissa, at least for those first six months when he had been cuckolding Simon's father, he had known again the agonies, the ecstasies, the uncertainties of love.

He made himself look again at the stage. They were playing the second scene of act three. Clarissa, dressed in a voluminous lace-trimmed dressing gown, was seated at her looking glass with Cariola in attendance, hairbrush in hand. The dressing table, like all the other props, was authentic, borrowed, he supposed, from the castle. There was more than one advantage in staging the play in the 1890s. The scene was being played to the accompaniment of a music box which had been placed on the dressing table and which tinkled out a medley of Scottish airs. That too was probably another of Ambrose's pieces of Victoriana, but he suspected that the idea was Clarissa's.

The scene began well enough. He had forgotten how Clarissa could take on an almost luminous beauty, the power of that high, slightly cracked voice, the grace with which she used her arms and body. She wasn't a Suzman or a Mirren, but she did manage to convey something of the high erotic excitement, the vulnerability, and the rashness of a woman deeply in love. That wasn't surprising; it was a part she had played often enough in real life. But to produce such conviction with a leading man who obviously saw Antonio as an English country gentleman sinning above his station was something of an achievement. But Cariola was a disaster, nervous and skittish, tripping across the stage in her goffered cap like a soubrette in a French farce. When she had stumbled for the third time over her lines, DeVille called out impatiently, "You've only to remember three lines, God help you. And cut out the coyness. You're not playing *No, No, Nanette*. All right. Take it from the beginning of the scene."

Clarissa protested, "But it needs pace, lightness. I lose the impetus if I have to keep going back."

He reiterated, "Take it from the beginning."

She hesitated, shrugged, then sat silent. The cast glanced at each other furtively, shuffled, waited. Ivo's interest suddenly rekindled. He thought, She's losing her temper. With her, that's halfway to losing her nerve.

Suddenly she took the music box and slammed down the lid. The crack was as sharp as a gunshot. The tinkling little tune stopped. It was followed by absolute silence as the cast seemed to hold their breath. Then Clarissa came forward to the footlights.

"That bloody box is getting on my nerves. If we have to have background music in this scene, surely Ambrose can find something more suitable than those damn Scottish tunes. They're driving me mad, so God knows what they'll do to the audience."

Ambrose called quietly from the back of the auditorium. Ivo was surprised to hear him and wondered how long he had been silently sitting there.

"It was your idea, as I remember."

"I wanted a music box but not a bloody Scottish medley. And do we have to have an audience? Cordelia, can't you find something useful to do? God knows, we're paying you enough. Tolly could do with some help ironing costumes, unless you propose to sit on your ass all afternoon."

The girl got to her feet. Even in the half-light, Ivo could detect the flush rising on her throat, could see her mouth half open in protest, then close resolutely. Despite those candid, almost judgmental eyes, the disconcerting honesty, the impression of controlled competence, she was at heart a sensitive child. Anger rose in him, satisfyingly strong and uncomplicated. He rejoiced that he could feel it. With difficulty he pulled himself erect. He was aware that all eyes had turned toward him. He said calmly, "Miss Gray and I will take a walk. The performance hasn't been exactly riveting so far and the air outside will be fresher."

When they were outside, their going silently watched by the cast, she said, "Thank you, Mr. Knightley."

He smiled. Suddenly he felt well, extraordinarily well, his whole body mysteriously lighter. "I'm afraid I'd make a poor dancer in my present state, and if I had to cast you as any character in *Emma* it certainly wouldn't be poor Harriet. You must excuse Clarissa. When she's nervous, she's apt to become rude."

"That may be her misfortune, but I don't find it particularly excusable."

He added, "And public rudeness provokes in me the kind of childish retort which is only satisfying for the second after it's spoken. She'll apologize very prettily when she next sees you alone."

"I'm sure she will." Suddenly she turned to him and smiled. "Actually, I should like a walk if you won't find it too exhausting."

She was, he thought, the only person on the island who could say that to him without making him feel either irritated or embarrassed. He said, "What about the beach?"

"I'd like that."

"It'll be slow going, I'm afraid."

"That doesn't matter."

How very sweet she was, with that gentle, self-contained dignity. He smiled and held out his hand to her. " 'Upon such sacrifices, my Cordelia, / The Gods themselves throw incense.' Well, shall we go?"

# VI

They trudged slowly side by side along the very edge of the tide where the firmer sand made the going easiest. The beach was narrow, cut by rotting breakwaters and bounded by a low stone wall beyond which rose the tree-covered, friable cliffs. Much of the bank must once have been planted. Between the beeches and the oaks were clumps of laurel, old rosebushes twined among the thicker foliage of rhododendrons, woody geraniums distorted by the wind, hydrangeas in their autumn shades of bronze, lime yellow, and purple, so much more subtle and interesting, thought Cordelia, than the gaudy heads of high summer. She felt at peace with her companion and wished, for a moment, that she could confide in him, that her job needn't impose such a weight of deception.

For ten minutes they walked in undemanding silence. Then he said, "This may be a stupid question. Gray isn't an uncommon name. But you're not by any chance related to Redvers Gray?"

"He was my father."

"There's something about the eyes. I only met him once, but his was a face one didn't forget. He had a great influence on my generation at Cambridge. He had the gift of making rhetoric sound sincere. Now that the rhetoric and the dream are not only discredited, which is discouraging, but unfashionable, which is fatal, I suppose he is almost forgotten. But I should like to have known him."

Cordelia said, "So should I."

He glanced down at her. "It was like that, was it? The revolutionary idealist dedicated to mankind in the abstract but not much good at caring for his own child. Not that I can criticize. I haven't done too well with mine. Children need you to talk to them, play with them, give time to them when they're young. If you can't be bothered, it isn't surprising if, when they're adolescents, you find that you don't much like each other. But, then, by the time mine were adolescents I didn't much like their mother either."

Cordelia said, "I think I could have liked him if we'd had time. I did spend six months with him and the comrades in Germany and Italy. But then he died."

"You make death sound like a betrayal. And so, of course, it is."

Cordelia thought of those six months. Half a year of cooking for the comrades, shopping for the comrades, carrying messages, sometimes not without danger, finding rooms, propitiating landladies and shopkeepers, sewing for the comrades. They and her father believed implicitly in equality for women without troubling to acquire the basic domestic skills which would have made that equality possible. And it was for that precarious nomadic existence that he had taken her from the convent, made it impossible for her to take up her place at Cambridge. She no longer felt any particular resentment. That period of her life was passed, finished. And she hoped that they had given something to each other, if only trust. She had early dropped Redvers from her name, telling herself that it was an unnecessary piece of cabin luggage. She had been reading Browning at the time. Now she wondered if it had been a more significant rejection, even a small revenge. The thought was unwelcome and she thrust it away.

She heard Ivo say, "And what about your education? One was always seeing pictures of him being dragged off by the police. That's all very admirable in youth, no doubt. In middle age it begins to look embarrassing and ridiculous. I don't remember hearing about a daughter, or of a wife for that matter."

"My mother died when I was born."

"And who looked after you?"

"I was placed with foster parents for most of the time. Then, when I was eleven, I won a scholarship to the Convent of the Holy Child. That was a mistake, not the scholarship but the choice of school. They muddled my name with another C. Gray, who was a Roman Catholic. I don't think Father much liked it, but by the time he bothered to reply to the education officer's letter I was settled and they didn't like to move me. And I wanted to stay."

He laughed. "Redvers Gray with a convent-educated daughter! And they didn't succeed in converting you? That would have taught Papa, dedicated atheist, to answer his letters more promptly."

"No, they didn't convert me. But, then, they didn't try. I didn't believe, but I was happy in my invincible ignorance. It's rather an enviable state. And I liked the convent. I suppose it was the first time I felt secure. Life wasn't messy anymore."

She had never before spoken so freely of her time at the convent, she who was so slow to confide. She wondered whether this unusual frankness was possible only because she knew he must be dying. The thought seemed to her ignoble and she tried to put it from her.

He said, "You agree with Yeats. 'How but in custom and in ceremony are innocence and beauty born?' I can see that it must have been reassuring, even having one's sins neatly categorized into venal and mortal. Mortal sin. I like the expression even if I reject the dogma. It has a note of splendid finality. It dignifies wrongdoing, almost gives it form and substance. One can imagine oneself saying, 'What have I done with my mortal sin? I must have put it down somewhere.' One could carry it around, neatly packaged."

Suddenly he stumbled. Cordelia put out her hand to steady him. His palm in hers was cold, the dry skin sliding over the bones. She saw that he looked very tired. The walk over the shingle had not, after all, been easy.

She said, "Let's sit for a while."

There was a kind of grotto above them, cut out of the cliff, with a mosaic terrace, now fractured and almost overgrown, and a curved marble seat. She helped pull him up the slope, watching as his feet found convenient clumps of grass and half-hidden stone steps. The back of the seat, warmed by the sun, still struck a little chill through her thin shirt. They sat side by side, untouching, and lifted their faces to the sun. Above them hung a beech tree. Its trunk and boughs had the tender luminosity of a girl's arm; its leaves, just beginning to burn with their autumn gold, were veined marvels of reflected light. The air was very still and quiet, the silence pierced only by the occasional cry of a gull, while below them the sea hissed and withdrew in its everlasting restlessness.

After a few minutes, his eyes still closed, he said, "I suppose a mortal sin has to be something special, something more original and momentous than the expedients, the meannesses, the small delinquencies which make up everyday living for most of us."

Cordelia said, "It's a grievous offense against the law of God, which puts the soul at risk of eternal damnation. There has to be full knowledge and consent. It's all laid down. Any R.C. will explain it to you."

He said, "Something evil, if the word means anything to you, if you believe in the existence of evil."

Cordelia thought of the convent chapel, altar candles flickering fitfully, her own bowed lace-covered head among the ranks of muttering conformists. "And deliver us from evil." For six years she had repeated those words at least twice a day long before she had ever asked herself what it was from which she craved deliverance. It had taken her first case, after Bernie's death, to teach her that. She could still recall, in sleeping and waking dreams, the horror which she had not in fact actually seen: a white, elongated neck, a boy's disfigured face drooping from the noose, the twisting feet pointing to the floor. It was when she had finally stared into the face of his murderer that she had known about evil.

She said, "Yes, I believe in the existence of evil."

"Then Clarissa once did something which you might dignify as evil. I don't know whether the good sisters would designate it as mortal sin. But there was knowledge and consent. And I've a feeling that, for Clarissa, it could prove mortal."

She didn't speak. She wouldn't make it easy for him. But there was no self-control in her silence. She knew he would go on.

"It happened during the run of *Macbeth* in July 1980. Tolly—Miss Tolgarth—had had an illegitimate daughter four years earlier. There was no particular secret about it; most of us in Clarissa's set knew about Viccy. She was a sweet child. Grave-faced, rather silent, intelligent I think, as far as one can judge at that age. Sometimes, but only rarely, Tolly would bring her to the theater, but most of the time she kept her private and her working life separate. She paid a child-minder to look after Viccy while she was working, and it must have been convenient having mainly an evening job. She wouldn't take any money from the father. I think she was too possessive about Viccy to want to share even the cost of her food. Then two days before Clarissa opened in *Macbeth* it happened. Clarissa was at the theater—there was a final rehearsal—and the minder was in charge of Viccy. The child had slipped out into the street and was playing with something in the gutter behind a parked lorry. It was the usual tragedy. The driver didn't see her and reversed. She was horribly injured. They rushed her to hospital and operated, and she stood that very well. We thought that she'd make it. But on the first night of *Macbeth* the hospital telephoned at nine-forty-five to say that there had been a relapse and to ask Tolly to go at once. Clarissa took the call. She had just come offstage for her costume change before the third act. She was appalled at the thought of losing her dresser at that moment. She took the message and put down the receiver. Then she told Tolly that the hospital wanted her to visit but that there was no hurry, after the performance would be all right. When Tolly wanted to ring back she wouldn't let her. And shortly after the performance ended, the hospital rang again to say that the child was dead."

"How do you know this?"

"Because I took the trouble to get in touch with the hospital and ask about that first message. And because I was there in Clarissa's dressing room when it came. You could say I was in something of a privileged position at the time. I wasn't with them when Clarissa finally told Tolly that she couldn't leave. I'd have stopped that; at least I hope I would. But I was there when the call came through. Then I went back to my seat. When the play ended and I went backstage to take Clarissa out to supper, Tolly was still there. And fifteen minutes later the hospital telephoned to say the child was dead."

"And when you learned what had happened, was that when you stopped being a privileged person?"

"I should like to be able to tell you that it was. The truth is less flattering. She became my mistress for two reasons: first because I'd gained some reputation and Clarissa has always found power an aphrodisiac, and second because she imagined that a lay a week would ensure her good notices. When she discovered her mistake—like most other men I'm capable of betrayal but not of that particular betrayal—the privileges ceased. There are some favors it is unwise to pay for in advance."

"Why are you telling me this?"

"Because I like you. Because I don't want to have this weekend spoiled by watching yet another person I respect being seduced by her charm. She has charm even if she hasn't bothered yet to exercise it on you. I don't want to see you behaving like all the others. I suspect that you may be possessed of that divine common sense which is impervious to the blandishments of egotism, whether sexual or other, but who can be sure? So I am committing one more small act of betrayal to strengthen you against temptation."

"Who was the child's father?"

"No one knows, except presumably Tolly, and she isn't saying. The question is who did Clarissa think he was."

Cordelia glanced at him. "Not her husband?"

"Poor besotted Lessing? Possible, I suppose, but hardly probable. He and Clarissa had been married only a year. Admittedly, she was already giving him hell, but I can't see him choosing that way of revenge. My guess is that it was DeVille. His only requirements are that the woman be comely and willing and not an actress. He's reputed to be impotent with anyone who holds an equity card, but that may be only his device for keeping his professional and private lives separate."

"The man who is directing the Webster? The one who's here now? Do you think that Clarissa was in love with him?"

"I don't know what Clarissa means by that word. She may have wanted him if only to prove that she could get him. One thing's certain: if he wouldn't play, she wouldn't easily forget an affair with her own dresser."

"Why do you think he's here? He's famous; he doesn't have to bother with an amateur production, particularly out of London."

"Why are any of us here? He may see the island as a future dramatic Glyndebourne, a world-famous center for experimental drama. This may just be a way of getting his foot in the door. After all, he's not exactly sought after now. His tricks were much admired in their day, but there are some clever young dogs coming along now. And Ambrose, if he's prepared to spend money, could make something of his Courcy Festival. Not commercially, of course; a theater which seats only a hundred comfortably can hardly be that, particularly when it could always be cut off by a storm on the first night. But he could have some fun with it once he's got rid of Clarissa."

"And does he want to get rid of Clarissa?"

"Oh, yes," said Ivo easily. "Hadn't you noticed that? She's trying to take him over, him and his theater and his island. He likes his private kingdom. Clarissa is a particularly persistent invader."

Cordelia thought of the child, lying alone on her high aseptic hospital bed behind the drawn curtains. Had she been conscious? Had she known that she was dying? Had she perhaps cried out for her mother? Had she gone frightened and alone into that last good night? She said, "I don't see how Clarissa can live with that memory."

"I'm not sure that she can. When people are terrified of dying, it could be because with one part of their minds they feel that they deserve it."

"How do you know she's terrified?"

"Because there are some emotions which even an actress as experienced as Clarissa can't altogether hide."

He turned to her, saw the expression on her face, upturned to the glitter of shuddering green and gold, and said quietly, "There are, perhaps, excuses one should make for her. And if not excuses, explanations. She was about to make an important costume change. She couldn't have managed it herself, and there wasn't another dresser available."

"Did she even try to find one?"

"I don't suppose so. You see, from her point of view, she wasn't in the world of hospitals and sick children. She was Lady Macbeth. She was at Dunsinane Castle. I doubt whether she would have left the theater to go to her own dying child, not at that moment. It didn't occur to her that someone else might want to."

Cordelia cried, "But you can't excuse it! You can't explain it. You don't really believe that a play, any play, any performance, is more important than a dying child."

"I don't suppose for one moment that she really believed the child to be dying, assuming that she gave the matter thought."

"But is that what you believe? That a performance, any performance, could be more important?"

He smiled. "Now we're edging toward that old philosophical mine field. If the building's on fire and you can rescue only a syphilitic old tramp or a Velázquez, which, or who, gets incinerated?"

"No, we aren't. We're talking about a dying child wanting her mother, balancing that need against a performance of *Macbeth*. And I get tired of that old burning-building analogy. I should throw the Velázquez out the window and start lugging the tramp to safety. The real moral choice is when you find that he's too heavy. Do you escape alone or keep trying and risk getting incinerated with him?"

"Oh, that's easy. Obviously you escape alone and without leaving the decision too conscientiously to the last possible moment. About the child: no, I don't believe that any performance could be more important, certainly none that Clarissa is capable of giving. Does that satisfy you?"

"I don't understand how Miss Tolgarth can go on working for her. I couldn't."

"But you will. I confess I'm intrigued about your precise function here. But presumably you won't throw in your hand."

"But that's different; at least I shall persuade myself that it is. I'm just a temporary employee. But Tolly believed Clarissa when she was told that there was no immediate danger; she trusted her. How can she stay with her now?"

"They've been together almost all their lives. Tolly's mother was Clarissa's nurse. The family with a small *f* served the Family with a large *F* for three generations. They're born to be served; she was born to serve them. Perhaps, given the habit of subservience, a dead child here or there doesn't make any difference."

"But that's horrible! It's ridiculous and degrading. It's Victorian!"

"Don't you believe it! The instinct for worship is remarkably persistent. What else is religious belief? Tolly's lucky to have her god walking the earth with shoes that need cleaning, clothes that need folding, hair that needs brushing."

"But she can't want to go on serving. She can't like Clarissa."

"What has liking to do with it? 'Though she slay me yet shall I trust her.' It's a perfectly common phenomenon. But I admit I do sometimes wonder what would happen if she faced the truth about her own feelings. If any of us did, come to that. It's getting colder, isn't it? Don't you feel it? Perhaps it's time we were getting back."

# VII

They hardly spoke on the way back to the castle. For Cordelia, the sunlight had drained out of the day. The beauty of sea and shore passed unregarded by her desolated heart. Ivo was obviously very tired by the time they reached the terrace and said that he would rest in his room; he wouldn't bother with tea. Cordelia told herself that it was her job to stay close to Clarissa, however unwelcome that might be to both of them. But it took an effort of will before she could make her way back to the theater, and it was a relief to find that the rehearsal still wasn't over. She stood for a minute at the back of the auditorium, then made her way to her own room. The communicating door was open and she could see Tolly moving from bathroom to bedroom. But the thought of having to speak to her was intolerable and Cordelia made her escape.

Almost on impulse she opened the door next to her own, which gave access to the tower. A circular staircase of elaborately decorated wrought iron curved upwards into semidarkness lit only by occasional slit windows less than a brick in width. She could see there was a light switch, but preferred to climb steadily upwards in the gloom in what seemed an endless spiral. But at last she reached the top and found herself in a small, light-filled, circular room with six tall windows. The room was unfurnished except for one cane armchair with a curved back and was obviously used to store acquisitions for which Ambrose hadn't yet found a place or which he had inherited from the previous owner, chiefly a collection of Victorian toys. There was a wooden horse on wheels, a Noah's ark with carved animals, three china dolls with bland faces and stuffed limbs, a table of mechanical toys including an organ grinder with his monkey, a set of cat musicians on a revolving platform, gaudily dressed in satin, each with an instrument, a toy grenadier soldier with a drum, a wooden music box.

The view was spectacular. The whole island, seen as if from an aircraft, was a neatly patterned colored map precisely placed in a crinkled sea. To the east was a smudge which must be the Isle of Wight. To the north the Dorset coast looked surprisingly close; she could almost make out the stunted pier and the colored terraces. She gazed down over the island, at the northern marshes fringed with white gulls, the central uplands, the fields, small patches of green amid the many-hued curdle of autumnal trees, the brown cliffs sliding down to the shore, the spire of the church rising amid the beeches, the roof of the arcade leading to a toy theater. From his cottage in the stable block the foreshortened figure of Oldfield crept, a bucket in either hand, and as she watched, Roma emerged from the corpse of beech trees which lined the lawn and made her way, hands hunched in her pockets, toward the castle. Across the grass a peacock stalked, dragging its tattered tail.

Here, slung between earth and sky in a brick-enclosed aerie, the sound of the sea was a low moan almost indistinguishable from the sighing of the wind. Suddenly Cordelia felt immensely lonely. The job which had promised so much seemed now a humiliating waste of time and effort. She no longer cared who was sending the messages or why. She felt that she hardly cared whether Clarissa lived or died. She wondered what was happening at Kingly Street, how Miss Maudsley was coping, whether Mr. Morgan had come to see to the nameplate. And thinking of him reminded her of Sir George. He had paid her to do a job. She was here to protect Clarissa, not to judge her. And there were only two more days to be got through. By Sunday it would all be over and she would be free to get back to London, need never hear Clarissa's name again. She recalled Bernie's words when he had once rebuked her for being overfastidious: "You can't make moral judgments about your clients in this job, mate. Start that and you may as well shut up shop."

She turned from the window and, on impulse, opened the music box. The cylinder slowly revolved and the delicate metal filaments plucked out the tune "Greensleeves." Then one by one she set the other mechanical toys in motion. The grenadier thumped his drum; the cats revolved, mouths grinning, jerking their satined arms; cymbals clashed; the plaintive "Greensleeves" was lost in the discordant din. And thus, in a gentle cacophony of childish sounds, which couldn't entirely shut out from her mind the image of a dying child but which helped to release some tension in her, Cordelia stared down over Ambrose's colored kingdom.

# VIII

Ivo had been wrong. Clarissa didn't apologize for her behavior at the rehearsal, but she did exert herself to be particularly charming to Cordelia over tea. It was a boisterous and protracted feast of sandwiches and overrich cake, and it was after six before the launch bearing DeVille and the other principals back to Speymouth finally drew away from the quay. Clarissa spent the hour before it was time to dress for dinner playing Scrabble in the library with Ambrose. She played noisily and badly, constantly calling out to Cordelia to look up challenged words in the dictionary or to support her against Ambrose's allegations that she was cheating. Cordelia, happily engrossed in old copies of *The Illustrated London News* and *The Strand* magazine, in which she could read the Sherlock Holmes stories as they had originally appeared, wished that she could have been left in peace. Simon was apparently to entertain them with music after dinner, and the distant sound of Chopin from the drawing room where he was practicing was pleasantly restful and evocative of her school days. Ivo was still in his room, and Roma sat in silence with the weekly journals and *Private Eye.*

The library, with its barrel roof and carved brass-fronted bookcases set between the four tall windows, was one of the most beautifully proportioned in the castle. The whole of the southern wall was taken up with one immense window decorated with round panes of colored glass. In the daytime the window framed nothing but a view of sea and sky. But now the library was in darkness except for the three pools of light from the desk lamps, and the great window rose like a sheet of rain-washed marble, blue-black and smudged with a few high stars. It was a pity, thought Cordelia, that, even here, Clarissa was incapable of occupying herself in peaceable silence.

When it was time to dress they went up together, and Cordelia unlocked both rooms and made a check on Clarissa's bedroom before she went in. All was well. She dressed quickly, put out the light, and then sat quietly at her window, looking out at the distant clumps of trees, black against the night sky, and the faint shimmer of the sea. Suddenly a light flashed from the south. She watched. In three seconds it flashed again and then for a third and last time. She thought that it must be some kind of signal, perhaps in answer to one from the island. But why and from whom? But then she told herself that the thought was childish and melodramatic. It was probably some solitary sailor on his way back to Speymouth harbor casually flashing a light over the quay. But there remained something discomforting and almost sinister about that threefold flash, as if someone were signaling that the cast was assembled, the leading lady ensconced in splendor under the castle roof, that the drawbridge could be drawn up and the play begin. But this was a castle without a drawbridge, its moat the sea. For the first time since her arrival, Cordelia was touched by a sense of claustrophobic unease. Here their only lifelines were the telephone and the launch, both easily put out of commission. She had been drawn to the mystery and loneliness of the island; now she missed the solid reassurance of the mainland, of towns and fields and hills ranged at her back. It was then that she heard Clarissa's door close and Tolly's departing footsteps. Clarissa must be ready. Cordelia went through the communicating door and they made their way together to the hall.

The dinner was excellent, artichokes followed by poussins and spinach au gratin. The south-facing room still held the warmth of the day, and the wood fire had been lit more for its sweet-smelling and comforting glow than because it was needed. The three tall candlesticks threw a steady light on the epergne of colored glass and Parian, the rich gold, green, and rose of the Davenport dinner service, and the engraved table glasses. Above the fireplace was an oil painting of the two daughters of Herbert Gorringe. Their poses were awkward, almost angular, and the faces with their bright exophthalmic eyes under the strong Gorringe brows and the moist half-open mouths looked flushed and feverish, while the reds and deep blues of the evening dresses shone as brightly as if the paint had recently dried. Cordelia found it difficult to keep her eyes from the picture, which so far from being tranquil or domestic seemed to her charged with a hectic sexual energy. Watching her gaze, Ambrose said, "It's by Millais, one of the comparatively few social portraits which he did. The dinner service we're using was a wedding gift to the elder daughter from the Prince and Princess of Wales. Clarissa insisted that I bring it out for tonight."

It seemed to Cordelia that there was a great deal which Clarissa insisted on at Courcy Castle. She wondered if she also proposed to supervise the washing up.

It should have been a festive meal, but the pleasure didn't match the food or the excellence of the wines. Beneath the glittering surface and the easy social chat flowed a current of unease, which from time to time spurted into antagonism. No one but Simon and herself with their youthful appetites did justice to the food, and he shoved it in furtively, watching Clarissa from the corners of his eye like a child allowed up for his first diningroom meal and expecting any minute to be banished to the nursery. Clarissa, elegant in her high-necked dress of blue-green chiffon, began by teasing her cousin about the absence of her partner, who had apparently been expected for the weekend, a topic which she seemed reluctant to let go.

"But it's so odd of him, darling. Surely we didn't frighten him away? Who are you ashamed of, us or him?"

Roma's face was an unbecoming pink above the harsh blue of her taffeta dress.

"We're expecting an American customer to drop into the shop this Saturday. And Colin has got behind with the accounts. He's hoping to get them finished before Monday."

"On a weekend? How conscientious of him. But I'm relieved to hear that you have some accounts worth doing. Congratulations."

Cordelia, finding that she could make little headway with Simon, who seemed afraid to speak, withdrew her interest from her fellow guests and concentrated on her meal. When she next took notice it was to hear Roma's belligerent voice. She was addressing Ambrose across the table, clutching her fork as if it were a weapon.

"But you can't opt out of all responsibility for what's happening in your own country! You can't just say that you're not concerned, not even interested!"

"But I can. I didn't collude in the depreciation of its currency, the spoliation of its countryside, the desecration of its towns, the destruction of its grammar schools, or even the mutilation of the liturgy of its church. For what am I personally expected to feel a responsibility?"

"I was thinking of aspects which some of us see as more important. The growth of fascism, the fact that our society is more violent, less compassionate, and more unequal than it has been since the nineteenth century. And then there's the National Front. You can't ignore the Front!"

"Indeed I can, together with Militant Tendency, the Trots, and the rest of the rabble. You'd be surprised at my capacity for ignoring the ignorable."

"But you can't just decide to live in another age!"

"But I can. I can live in any century I wish. I don't have to choose the dark ages, old or new."

Ivo said quietly, "I'm grateful that you don't reject modern amenities or modern technology. If I should enter into the final process of dying during the next few days and need a little medical help to ease the way, I take it you won't object to using the telephone."

Ambrose smiled around at them and raised his glass. "If any of you decides to die in the next few days, all necessary measures will be taken to ease you on your way."

There was a short, slightly embarrassed silence. Cordelia looked across at Clarissa, but the actress's eyes were on her plate. For a second, the long fingers trembled and were still.

Roma said, "And what happens to Eden when Adam, solaced with no Eve, finally returns to dust?"

"It would be pleasant to have a son to follow one here, I admit, almost worth marrying and breeding for. But sons, even supposing they came to order and if the process of getting them, deceptively simple physiologically, weren't so fraught with practical and emotional complications, are notoriously unreliable. Ivo, you're the only one here with experience of children."

Ivo said, "It's unwise, certainly, to look to them for vicarious immortality."

"Or anything else, wouldn't you say? A son might easily convert the castle into a casino, lay down a nine-hole golf course, make the air hideous with speedboats and waterskiing, and hold pretentious Saturday hops for the locals, eight-fifty a head, three-course dinner included, evening dress obligatory, no extras guaranteed."

Clarissa looked across at Ivo. "Talking of children, what's the news of your two, Ivo? Is Matthew still living in that Kensington squat?"

Cordelia saw that Ivo's chicken had been pushed almost untouched to the side of his plate and that although he was forking his spinach into shreds, little of it was reaching his mouth. But he had been drinking steadily. The claret decanter was on his right hand and he reached for it again, adding to a glass which he seemed not to realize was already three-quarters full. He looked across at Clarissa's eyes, bright in the candlelight.

"Matthew? I suppose he's still with the Children of the Sun or whatever they call themselves. As we don't communicate, I'm not in a position to say. Angela, on the other hand, writes a filial letter at boring length every month. I have two granddaughters now, she informs me. Since Angela and her husband refuse to visit a country where they might find themselves sharing a dining table with a black and I have a distaste for sharing a table with my son-in-law, I am unlikely to make their acquaintance. My ex-wife, in case you meant to inquire, is with them in Johannesburg, which she calls Jo'burg, and is said to be enchanted with the country, the climate, the company, and the kidney-shaped swimming pool."

Clarissa laughed, a small bell note of triumph. "Darling, I wasn't asking for a family history."

"Weren't you?" he said easily. "Oh, I rather thought you were."

The table fell into a silence which, to Cordelia's relief, lasted with few interruptions until the meal was at last over and Munter opened the door for the women to follow Clarissa into the drawing room.

# IX

Ivo wanted neither coffee nor liqueur, but he carried the decanter of claret and his glass with him into the drawing room and settled himself in an armchair between the fire and the open french windows. He felt no particular social responsibility for the rest of the evening. The dinner had been sufficiently grim, and he had every intention of getting quietly but thoroughly drunk. He had listened too much to his doctors. Throw physic to the dogs; he'd have none of it. Obviously, what he needed was to drink more, not less; and if it could be wine of this quality and at Ambrose's expense, so much the better. Already his self-disgust at allowing Clarissa to provoke him into that spurt of angry revelation was fading under the influence of the wine. What was taking its place was a gentle euphoria in which his mind became supernaturally clear, while the faces and words of his companions moved into a different dimension, so that he watched their antics with bright sardonic eyes as he might actors on a stage.

Simon was preparing to play for them, arranging his music on the stand with uncertain hands. Ivo thought, Oh, God, not Chopin followed by Rachmaninoff. And why, he wondered, was Clarissa draping herself over the boy, ready to turn the pages? It wasn't as if she could read music. If this was to be the start of her usual system of alternate kindness and brutality, she would end by driving the boy out of his wits as she had his father. Roma, in the taffeta dress which would have looked too young on an ingenue of eighteen, was sitting rigidly on the edge of her chair like a parent at a school concert. Why should she care how the boy performed? Why should any of them care? Already his nervousness was communicating itself to his audience. But he played better than Ivo expected, only occasionally attempting to disguise the misfingerings by too fast a tempo and the overuse of the loud pedal. Even so, it was too like a public performance to be enjoyable, the pieces chosen to show off his technique, the occasion made more important than anyone wanted. And it went on too long.

At the end Ambrose said, "Thank you, Simon. What are a few

wrong notes among friends? And now, where are the songs of yesteryear?"

The decanter was now less than a quarter full. Ivo stretched himself more deeply in the chair and let the voices come to him from an immense distance. They were all around the piano now, roaring out sentimental Victorian drawing-room ballads. He could hear Roma's contralto, invariably late and slightly off-key, and Cordelia's clear soprano, a convent-trained voice, a little unsure but clear and sweet. He watched Simon's flushed face as he bent over the keys, the look of intense, exultant concentration. He was playing with more assurance and sensitivity now than he had alone. For once, the boy was enjoying himself.

After about half an hour Roma drifted away from the piano and walked over to look at two oils by Frith, crowded anecdotal canvases showing rail travelers going to the Derby by first class and third class. Roma walked from one to the other, studying them intently as if to check that no detail of social or sartorial contrast had been neglected by the artist. Then Clarissa suddenly dropped her hand from Simon's shoulder, swept past Ivo, her chiffon floating against his knee, and went out onto the terrace alone. Cordelia and Ambrose were left singing together. The three of them at the piano were linked by their enjoyment, seemingly unaware of their audience, transposing and consulting, choosing and comparing and collapsing into laughter when a piece proved beyond their range or competence. Ivo recognized only a few of the songs: Peter Warlock's Elizabethan pastiches, Vaughan Williams's "Bright Is the Ring of Words." He was listening now with the nearest he had come to happiness since his illness had been diagnosed. Nietzsche was wrong; it wasn't action but pleasure which bound one to existence. And he had become afraid of pleasure; to admit even the possibility of joy to his shriveled senses was to open the mind to anguish and regret. But now, listening to that sweet voice blending with Ambrose's baritone and floating past him out and over the sea, he lay back, weightless, in a dreamy contentment which was without bitterness and without pain. And gradually his senses began to tingle into life. He was aware of thc cool stream of air from the window on his face, nothing as inconvenient as a draft, but a barely perceptible sensation like a stroking finger; of the sharp red of the wine glowing in the decanter and its softness against his tongue; of the smell of the wood fire, evocative of lost boyhood autumns.

And then his mood was broken. Clarissa stormed into the room from the terrace. Simon heard her and stopped playing in midbar. The two voices sang on for a few notes, then broke off.

Clarissa said, "I'll have enough of amateurs before the weekend's finished without you three adding to the boredom. I'm going to bed. Simon, it's time you called it a day. We'll go together; I want to see to your room. Cordelia, ring for Tolly, will you, and tell her I'm ready for her, then come up in fifteen minutes; I want to discuss arrangements for tomorrow. Ivo, you're drunk."

She waited with a shiver of impatience until Ambrose had opened the door for her, then swept out, merely pausing briefly to offer him her cheek to kiss. He bent forward but was too late, and his pursed lips pecked ludicrously at the air. Simon bundled up his music with shaking hands, looked around as if for help, and ran after her. Cordelia went across to where the embroidered rope hung by the side of the fireplace.

Roma said, "Black marks all round. We should have realized that we're here to applaud Clarissa's talent, not to demonstrate our own. If you plan to make a career as secretary-companion, Cordelia, you'll have to learn more tact."

Ivo was aware of Ambrose bending over him, of his flushed face and the black eyes bright and malicious under the strong half circles.

"Are you drunk, Ivo? You're remarkably quiet."

"I thought I was, but I seem not to be. Sobriety has overtaken me. But if you would open another bottle I could begin the agreeable process again. Good wine is a good familiar creature, if it be well used."

"But shouldn't you keep your mind clear for the task of tomorrow?"

Ivo held out the empty decanter. He was surprised to see that his hand was perfectly steady. He said, "Don't worry. I shall be sober enough for what I have to do tomorrow."

# X

Cordelia waited exactly fifteen minutes, refused Ambrose's offer of a nightcap, then made her way upstairs. The communicating door between her room and Clarissa's was ajar, and she went through without knocking. Clarissa, in her cream satin dressing gown, was sitting at the dressing table. Her hair was tugged back from her face and tied with a ribbon at the nape of the neck; her hairline was bound with a crepe band. She was scrutinizing her face in the glass and didn't look around.

The room was lit by only one bright light on the dressing table and the softer glow of the bedside lamp. A thin wood fire crackled in the grate and threw leaping shadows over the richness of damask and mahogany. The air smelled of wood smoke and perfume, and the room, dim and mysterious, struck Cordelia as smaller and more luxurious than it had been in its daytime brightness. But the bed was more than ever dominant, glowing under its scarlet canopy, sinister and portentous as a catafalque. Cordelia saw that Tolly must have been there before her. The sheets were turned back and Clarissa's nightdress had been laid out, its waist pinched. It looked like a shroud. In the shadowed half-light it was easy to imagine that she stood in the doorway of a bedroom in Amalfi with Webster's doomed duchess bright-haired at her toilet while horror and corruption stalked in the shadows and, beyond the half-open window, a tideless Mediterranean lay open to the moon.

Clarissa's voice broke into her mood. "Oh, here you are. I've sent Tolly away so that we can talk. Don't just stand there. Find yourself a chair."

On each side of the fireplace was a low spoon-backed chair with carved arms and feet. Cordelia slid one forward on its casters and seated herself to the left of the dressing table. Clarissa peered at herself in the glass, then unscrewed a jar of cleansing pads and began wiping off her eye shadow and mascara. Thin, black-stained scraps of tissue crept over the polished mahogany. The left eye, wiped clean of makeup, looked diminished, almost lifeless, giving her suddenly the mask of a lopsided clown. She peered at the denuded lid, frowned, then said, "You seem to have enjoyed yourself this evening. Perhaps I should remind you that you were hired as a detective, not an after-dinner entertainer."

It had been a long day and Cordelia couldn't summon the energy for anger. "Perhaps if you were honest with them and told them why I'm here they'd be less likely to treat me as a fellow guest. Private detectives aren't expected to sing, at least I wouldn't think so. They probably wouldn't even want to eat with me. A private eye is hardly a comfortable dining companion."

"What good would that do? If you don't mix with them, how can you watch them? Besides, the men like you. I've seen Ivo and Simon looking at you. Don't pretend that you don't know it. I hate that kind of sexual coyness."

"I wasn't going to pretend anything."

Clarissa was busy now with an immense jar of cleansing cream, smearing dollops of the cream over face and neck and wiping them off with strong upward sweeps of cotton wool. The discarded greasy balls were added to the mess on the dressing table. Cordelia found herself studying Clarissa's face with as much intensity as did its owner. The eyes were a little too far apart; the skin was thick, unluminous, but almost without lines; the cheeks were flat and wide; the mouth with its pouting lower lip too small for beauty. But it was a face that could take on loveliness at Clarissa's will, and even now, bandaged, unenhanced, and sunk in repose, it held the assurance of its latent, eccentric beauty.

Suddenly, she asked, "What do you think of Simon's playing?"

"I'm not really qualified to judge. Obviously, he has talent." She was about to add that he might make a more successful accompanist than solo performer, then thought better of it. It was perfectly true: she wasn't competent to judge. And she had the feeling that ignorant though she was, some kind of decision might depend on her answer.

"Oh, talent! That's common enough. One doesn't invest six thousand pounds or so in mere talent. The thing is, has he the guts to succeed? George thinks not, but he may as well be given his chance."

"Sir George knows him better than I do."

Clarissa said sharply, "But it isn't George's money, is it? I'll consult Ambrose, but not until after the play. I can't worry about anything until then. He'll probably damn the poor boy. Ambrose is such a perfectionist. But he does know something about music. He'd be a better judge than poor George. If only Simon had taken up a stringed instrument, he might eventually try for a place in an orchestra. But the piano! Still, I suppose he could always work as an accompanist."

Cordelia wondered whether she should point out that the job of a professional accompanist, so far from being an easy option, required a formidable combination of technical ability and musicality, but she reminded herself that she hadn't been employed to advise on Simon's career. And this talk of Simon was wasting time. She said, "I think we should discuss the messages and our plans for the weekend, especially tomorrow. We ought to have spoken earlier."

"I know, but there hasn't really been time what with the rehearsal and Ambrose showing off his castle. Anyway, you know what you're here for. If there are any more messages, I don't want to receive them. I don't want to be shown them. I don't want to be told about them. It's vital that I get through tomorrow. If I can only get back my confidence as an actress, I can face almost anything."

"Even the knowledge of who is doing this to you?"

"Even that."

Cordelia asked, "How many of the people here know about the messages?"

Clarissa had finished cleaning her face and now began removing the varnish from her nails. The smell of acetone overlaid the smell of scent and makeup.

"Tolly knows. I haven't any secrets from Tolly. Anyway, she was with me in my dressing room when some of them were brought in by the doorman, the ones sent by post to the theater. I expect Ivo knows; there's nothing happens in the West End that he doesn't get to hear about. And Ambrose. He was with me in my dressing room at the Duke of Clarence when one was pushed under the door. By the time he'd picked it up for me and I'd opened it, whoever it was had gone. The corridor was empty. But anyone could have got in. Backstage at the Clarence is like a warren, and Albert Betts used to drink and wasn't always on the door when he should have been. They've sacked him now, but he was still working there when the note was delivered. And my husband knows, of course. Simon doesn't, unless Tolly has told him. I can't think why she should."

"And your cousin?"

"Roma doesn't know, and if she did, she wouldn't care."

"Tell me about Miss Lisle."

"There's not much to tell and what there is, is boring. We're first cousins, but George has told you that. It's quite a common story. My father made a sensible marriage and his younger brother ran off with a barmaid, left the army, drank, and made a general mess of his life, then expected Daddy to help out. And he did, at least as far as Roma was concerned. She was always staying with us when I was a child, particularly after Uncle died. Poor Little Orphan Annie. Glum, badly dressed, and perpetually miserable. Even Daddy couldn't stand her for long. He was the most marvelous person; I adored him. But she was such a bore, and so plain, worse than she is now. Daddy was one of those people who really couldn't bear ugliness, particularly in women. He loved gaiety, wit, beauty. He just couldn't make himself look at a plain face."

Cordelia thought that Daddy, who sounded like a self-satisfied humbug, must have spent most of his life with his eyes shut, depending, of course, on his standard of ugliness.

Clarissa added, "And she wasn't a bit grateful."

"Should she have been?"

Clarissa seemed to feel that the question deserved serious thought, or as much as she could spare from the business of filing her nails. "Oh, I think so. He didn't have to take her in. And she could hardly expect him to treat her the same as me, his own child."

"He could have tried."

"But that's not reasonable, and you know it. You wouldn't behave like that, so why expect him to? You really must guard against becoming just a bit of a prig. Men don't like it."

Cordelia said, "I don't much like it myself. Someone once told me that it's the result of having an atheist father, a convent education, and a nonconformist conscience."

There was silence between them, not uncompanionable. Then Cordelia said on impulse, "These notes—could Miss Tolgarth have anything to do with them?"

"Tolly! Of course not. Whatever put that idea into your head? She's devoted to me. You mustn't be put off by her manner. She's always been like that. But we've been together since I was a child. Tolly adores me. If you can't see that, you're not much of a detective. Besides, she can't type. The messages are typed, in case you hadn't noticed."

Cordelia said gravely, "You should have told me about her child. If I'm to help I need to know anything that might be relevant." She waited, apprehensive, for Clarissa's response. But the hands, busy with their self-ministrations, didn't falter.

"But that isn't relevant. It was all a mistake. Tolly knows that. Everyone knows it. I suppose Ivo told you. That's typical of his malice and disloyalty. Can't you see that he's sick? He's dying! And he's eaten up with jealousy. He always has been. Jealousy and malice."

Cordelia wondered whether she could have asked the question more tactfully, whether it had been wise to ask it at all. Ivo hadn't asked her not to betray their conversation, but presumably he had hoped for discretion. And the weekend promised to be difficult enough without setting two of the guests at each other's throats. Direct lying had never been easy for her. She said cautiously, "No one has been disloyal. Obviously I did some tactful research before I arrived here. These things do get talked about. I have a friend in the theater." Well, that was true enough anyway, even if poor Bevis was more often out than in. But Clarissa was uninterested in putative theatrical friends.

"I'd like to know what right Ivo has to criticize me. Do you realize how many careers he's ruined by his cruelty? Yes, cruelty! I've seen actors—actors, mind you—in tears after one of his reviews. If he could have resisted the impulse to be clever, he might have been one of the great British critics. He could have been a second Agate or a Tynan. And what is he now? Dying on his feet. He's no right to come here looking as he does. It's like having a death's head at table. It's indecent."

It was interesting, thought Cordelia, the way in which death had replaced sex as the great unmentionable, to be denied in prospect, endured in decent privacy, preferably behind the drawn curtains of a hospital bed, and followed by discreet, embarrassed, uncomforted mourning. There was this to be said about the Convent of the Holy Child: the views of the sisters on death had been explicit, firmly held, and not altogether reassuring; but at least they hadn't regarded it as in poor taste.

She said, "Those first messages, the ones that came when you were playing Lady Macbeth, the ones you threw away. Were they the same as the later ones, typed and on white paper?"

"Yes, I suppose so. It was a long time ago."

"But you can't have forgotten!"

"They must have been the same, mustn't they? What does it matter? I don't want to talk about it now."

"It's the only chance we may get. I haven't been able to see you alone today, and tomorrow isn't going to be any easier."

Clarissa was on her feet now, pacing between the dressing table and the bed. "It wasn't my fault. I didn't kill her. She wasn't properly cared for. If she had been she wouldn't have had the accident. What's the point of having a child—a bastard, too—if you don't look after it?"

"But wasn't Tolly at work, looking after you?"

"The hospital had no right to phone like that, upsetting people. They must have known that it was a theater that they were calling, that West End curtains rise at eight, that we'd be in the middle of a performance. She couldn't have done anything if I had let her go. The child was unconscious; she wouldn't have known her. It's sentimental and morbid, this sitting by the bedside waiting for people to die. What good does it do? And I had three changes in the third act. Kalenski designed the banquet costume himself: barbaric jewelry, a crown set with great dollops of red stones like blood, a skirt so stiff I could hardly move. He meant me to be weighed down, to walk stiffly like an overencumbered child. 'Think of yourself as a seventeenth-century princess,' he said, 'wonderingly loaded with inappropriate majesty.' Those were his words, and he made me keep moving my hands down the side of the skirt as if I couldn't believe that I was actually wearing so much richness. And of course it made a marvelous contrast with the plain cream shift in the sleepwalking scene. It wasn't a nightgown; they used to sleep naked apparently. I used it to wipe my hands. Kalenski said, 'Hands, darling, hands, hands; that's what this part is all about.' It was a new interpretation, of course. I wasn't the usual kind of Lady Macbeth, tall, domineering, ruthless. I played her like a sex kitten but a kitten with hidden claws."

It was, thought Cordelia, a novel interpretation of the part, surely not altogether consonant with the text. But perhaps Kalenski, like other Shakespearean directors whose names came to mind, didn't let that bother him. She said, "But was it true to the text?"

"Oh, my dear, who cares about the text? I don't mean that exactly, but Shakespeare's like the Bible: you can make it mean anything. That's why directors love him."

"Tell me about the child."

"Macduff's son? Desmond Willoughby played him, an intolerable child. A vulgar Cockney accent. You can't find a child actor now who knows how to speak English. Too old for the part too. Thank God I never had to appear with him."

One biblical text came into Cordelia's mind, brutally explicit in its meaning, but she didn't speak it aloud:

"Whoso shall offend one of these little ones which believe in me, it were better that a millstone were hanged about his neck, and that he were drowned in the depth of the sea."

Clarissa turned and looked at her. Something in Cordelia's face must have pierced even her egotism. She cried, "I'm not paying you to judge me! What are you looking like that for?"

"I'm not judging you. I want to help. But you have to be honest with me."

"I am being honest, as honest as I know how. When I first saw you, that day at Nettie Fortescue's, I knew I could trust you, that you were someone I could talk to. It's degrading to be so afraid. George doesn't understand; how could he? He's never been afraid of anything in his life. He thinks I'm neurotic to care. He went to see you only because I made him."

"Why didn't you come yourself?"

"I thought you might be more likely to accept the job if he asked you. And I don't enjoy asking people for favors. Besides, I had a fitting for one of my costumes."

"There wasn't any question of a favor. I needed the job. I probably would have taken almost anything if it wasn't illegal and didn't disgust me."

"Yes, George said that your office was pretty squalid. Well, pathetic rather than squalid. But you aren't. There's nothing squalid or pathetic about you. I couldn't have put up with the usual kind of female private eye."

Cordelia said gently, "What is it that you're really afraid of?"

Clarissa turned on Cordelia, her softly gleaming, cleansed, uncolored face looking for the first time, in its nakedness, vulnerable to age and grief, and gave a sad, rather rueful smile. Then she lifted her hands in an eloquent gesture of despair.

"Oh, don't you know? I thought George had told you. Death. That's what I'm afraid of. Just death. Stupid, isn't it? I always have been, even when I was a child. I don't remember when it began, but I knew the facts of death before I knew the facts of life. There never was a time when I didn't see the skull beneath the skin. Nothing traumatic happened to start it off. They didn't force me to look at my nanny, dead in her coffin; nothing like that. And I was at school when Mummy died and it didn't mean anything. It isn't the death of other people. It isn't the fact of death. It's my death I'm afraid of. Not all the time. Not every moment. Sometimes I can go for weeks without thinking about it. And then it comes, usually at night, the dread and the horror and the knowledge that the fear is real. I mean, no one can say, 'Don't worry, it may never happen.' They can't say, 'It's all your imagination, darling, it doesn't really exist.' I can't really describe the fear, what it's like, how terrible it is. It comes in a rhythm, wave after wave of panic sweeping over me, a kind of pain. It must be like giving birth, except that I'm not delivering life; it's death I have between my thighs. Sometimes I hold up my hand, like this, and look at it and think, Here it is, part of me. I can feel it with my other hand, and move it and warm it and smell it and paint its nails. And one day it will hang white and cold and unfeeling and useless, and so shall I be all those things. And then it will rot. And I shall rot. I can't even drink to forget. Other people do. It's how they get through their lives. But drink makes me ill. It isn't fair that I should have this terror and not be able to drink! Now I've told you, and you can explain that I'm stupid and morbid and a coward. You can despise me."

Cordelia said, "I don't despise you."

"And it's no good saying that I ought to believe in God. I can't. And even if I could, it wouldn't help. Tolly got converted after Viccy died, so I suppose she believes. But if someone told Tolly that she was going to die tomorrow, she'd be just as unwilling to go. I've noticed that about the God people. They're just as frightened as the rest of us. They cling on just as long. They're supposed to have a heaven waiting but they're in no hurry to get there. Perhaps it's worse for them: judgment and hell and damnation. At least I'm only afraid of death. Isn't everyone? Aren't you?"

Was she? Cordelia wondered. Sometimes, perhaps. But the fear of dying was less obtrusive than more mundane worries: what would happen when the Kingly Street lease ran out, whether the Mini would pass inspection, how she would face Miss Maudsley if the agency no longer had a job for her. Perhaps only the rich and successful could indulge the morbid fear of dying. Most of the world needed its energies to cope with living.

She said cautiously, knowing that she had no comfort to offer, "It doesn't seem reasonable to be afraid of something which is inevitable and universal and which I shan't be able to experience, anyway."

"Oh, those are just words! All they mean is that you're young and healthy and don't have to think about dying. 'To lie in cold obstruction and to rot.' That was in one of the messages."

"I know."

"And there's another for you to add to the collection. I've been keeping it for you. It came by post to the London flat yesterday morning. You'll find it at the bottom of my jewel case. It's on the bedside table, the left-hand side."

The instruction as to the side was unnecessary; even in the subdued light and amid the clutter of Clarissa's bedside table, the softly gleaming casket was an object that caught the eye. Cordelia took it in her hands. It was about eight inches by five, with delicately wrought clawed feet, the lid and sides embossed with a representation of the judgment of Paris. She turned the key and saw that the inside was lined with cream quilted silk.

Clarissa called, "Ambrose gave it to me when I arrived this morning, a good-luck present for the performance tomorrow. I took a fancy to it when I saw it six months ago but it took a time before he got the message. He has so many Victorian baubles that one less can't make any difference. The casket we're using in act three is his; well, most of the props are. But this is prettier. More valuable too. But not as valuable as the thing I'm keeping in it. You'll find the letter in the secret drawer. Not so very secret, actually. You just press the center of one of the leaves. You can see the line if you look carefully. Better bring it here. I'll show you."

The box was surprisingly heavy. Clarissa pulled out a tangle of necklaces and bracelets as if they were cheap costume jewelry. Cordelia thought that some of the pieces probably were, bright beads of colored stone and glass intertwined with the sparkle of real diamonds, the glow of sapphires, the softness of milk-white pearls. Clarissa pressed the center of one of the leaves which decorated the side of the box and a drawer in the base slid slowly open. Inside Cordelia saw first a folded cutting of newsprint. Clarissa took it out.

"I played Hester in a revival of Rattigan's *The Deep Blue Sea,* at the Speymouth Playhouse. That was in 1977, Jubilee Year, when Ambrose was abroad on his year's tax exile. The theater's closed now, alas. But they seemed to like me. Actually, that's probably the most important notice I ever had."

She unfolded it. Cordelia glimpsed the headline. "Clarissa Lisle Triumphs in Rattigan Revival." Her mind busied itself for only a second on the oddity of Clarissa's attaching so much importance to the review of a revival in a small provincial town, and she noticed, almost subconsciously, that the cutting was oddly shaped and larger than the space taken by the notice. But her interest fastened on the letter. The envelope matched the one handed to her by Mrs. Munter from the morning post bag, but the address had been typed on a different and obviously older machine. The postmark was London, the date two days earlier, and like the other it was addressed to the Duchess of Malfi but at Clarissa's Bayswater flat. Inside was the usual sheet of white paper, the neat black drawing of a coffin, the letters *R.I.P.* Underneath was typed a quotation from the play:

> Who must despatch me?
> I account this world a tedious theatre
> For I must play a part in 't 'gainst my will.

Cordelia said, "Not very appropriate. He must be getting to the end of suitable quotations."

Clarissa tugged off her hair band. In the glass her reflection gazed back at them both, a ghost face, hung about with pale, disheveled hair, the huge eyes troubled under their heavy lids.

"Perhaps he knows that he won't need many more. There's only tomorrow. Perhaps he knows—who better?—that tomorrow will be the end."

# BOOK THREE

·

# Blood Flies Upwards

# I

Cordelia slept more deeply and for longer than she had expected. She was awakened by a quiet knock at the door. Instantly she was fully conscious and throwing her dressing gown around her shoulders as she went to open it. It was Mrs. Munter with early-morning tea. Cordelia had meant to be up well before she arrived. It was embarrassing to be discovered sleeping behind a locked door as if she were confusing Courcy Castle with a hotel. If Mrs. Munter was surprised at this eccentricity she gave no sign, but placed the tray on the bedside table with a quiet "Good morning, miss," and left as unobtrusively as she had arrived.

It was half past seven. The room was filled with the smudged half-light of dawn. Going to the window, Cordelia saw that the eastern sky was just beginning to streak into brightness and that a low mist hung over the lawn and curled like smoke between the treetops. It was going to be another lovely day. There was no sign of any bonfire, yet the air held the smoky wood-fire smell of autumn, and the great mass of the sea heaved, gray and silver, as if it exuded its own mysterious light.

She crept to the communicating door and opened it very gently. It was heavy, but it swung open without a creak. The curtains were drawn across the windows, but there was enough light from her own room to show her Clarissa, still sleeping, one white arm curved around her pillow. Cordelia tiptoed up to the bed and stood very still, listening to the quiet breathing. She felt a sense of relief without knowing exactly why. She had never believed that there was a real threat to Clarissa's life. And their precautions against mischief had been thorough. Both the doors to the corridor had been locked and the keys left in the locks. Even if someone had a duplicate there was no way in which he could have got in. But it was only after this reassurance that she felt free to drink her tea in comfort.

And then she saw the paper, a pale oblong gleaming against the carpet. Another message had been delivered, pushed under the door. So whoever was responsible was here, on the island. She felt her heart jolt. Then she took hold of herself, angry that she hadn't thought of the possibility of a missive under the door, resenting her own fear. She crept across to pick up the paper and took it into her own room, shutting the door behind her.

It was another passage from *The Duchess of Malfi*, eleven short words surmounted by a skull:

> Thus it lightens into action,
> I am come to kill thee.

The form was the same, but the paper was different. This message was typed on the back of an old woodcut headed "The Gt Meſſenger of Mortality." Beneath the title was the crude figure of death bearing an hourglass and an arrow, followed by four stanzas of verse.

She gulped down her tea, pulled on her trousers and shirt, and went in search of Ambrose. She had hardly hoped to find him so early, but he was already in the breakfast room, coffee cup in hand, gazing out over the lawn. It was one of the rooms which she had seen on Friday's quick tour of the castle, the furniture and fittings all designed by Godwin. There was a simple refectory table with a set of fretwork-backed chairs, and one long wall was entirely covered by a set of cupboards and open shelves, charmingly carved in light wood and surmounted by a tiled frieze in which orange trees in bright blue pots alternated with highly romanticized scenes from the legend of King Arthur and the Round Table. At the time Cordelia had thought it an interesting example of the architect's move toward the simplicities of the Aesthetic Movement, but now its self-conscious charm was lost on her.

Ambrose turned at her entrance and smiled. "Good morning. It looks as if we're going to be lucky in the weather. The guests should arrive in sunshine and get back without risk of parting with their supper. The crossing can be treacherous in bad weather. Is our leading lady awake?"

"Not yet."

Cordelia made a sudden resolution. It could do no harm to tell him. The woodcut almost certainly came from his house. Clarissa had told her that he already knew about the poison-pen messages. And Clarissa was his guest. Above all, she wanted to see his reaction to the paper. She held it out and said, "I found this pushed under Clarissa's door this morning. Does it belong to you? If so, someone has mutilated it for you. Look on the back."

He studied it briefly, then turned it over. For a moment he was silent. Then he said, "So the messages are still coming. I did wonder. Has she seen this?"

There was no need to ask whom he meant. "No. And she won't."

"Very wise of you. I take it that weeding out this kind of nuisance is one of your duties as secretary-companion?"

"One of them. But does it belong to you?"

"No. It's interesting, but not my period."

"But this is your house. And Miss Lisle is your guest."

He smiled and wandered over to the sideboard. "Will you have coffee?"

She watched while he went over to the hot plate, poured her cup, and refilled his own. Then he said, "I accept the implied criticism. One's guests certainly have the right not to be harassed or menaced while under one's roof. But what do you suggest I can do? I'm not a policeman. I can hardly interrogate my other houseguests. That, apart from its certain lack of success, would only result in six aggrieved persons instead of one. I doubt whether Clarissa would thank me. And, forgive me, aren't you taking this a little too seriously? I admit that it's a practical joke in poor taste. But is it any more than a joke? And surely the best response to this kind of nonsense is a dignified silence, even a certain amused contempt. Clarissa is an actress. She should be able to simulate one response or the other. If there is someone on the island who is trying to spoil her performance, he—or more likely she—will soon give up if Clarissa demonstrates total unconcern."

"That's what she will do, at least until after the play. She won't see this. I can trust you not to tell her?"

"Of course. I have a strong interest in Clarissa's success, remember. You didn't put the thing there yourself by any chance."

"No."

"I thought not. Forgive my asking, but you see my difficulty. If it wasn't you, it was presumably her husband—except that he isn't here at the moment—her stepson, her cousin, her faithful dresser, or one of her oldest friends. Who am I to start probing these family and long-standing relationships? Incidentally, that woodcut belongs to Roma."

"To Roma! How do you know?"

"You do sound fierce, quite like a schoolmistress. Roma used to teach, you know. Geography and games, Clarissa tells me. A strange combination. I can't quite picture Roma, whistle at the lip, panting down the hockey field exhorting the girls to greater efforts, or plunging into the deep end of the swimming pool. Well, perhaps I can believe that. She has aggressively muscular shoulders."

Cordelia said, "But the woodcut?"

"She told me that she found it in a secondhand book and thought I might be interested in seeing it. She showed it to me yesterday, just before the rehearsal, and I left it on the blotter on my desk in the business room."

"Where anyone could have seen and taken it?"

"You sound like a detective. As you say, where anyone could have seen and taken it. It looks, incidentally, as if the message was typed on my machine. That, too, is kept in the business room."

The typing, at least, would be easy enough to check. She might as well do it now. But before she could make the suggestion Ambrose said, "And there's another thing. Forgive me if I find it rather more annoying than Clarissa's poison pen. Someone has broken the lock of the display cabinet outside the business room and taken the marble arm. If during your duties as secretary-companion you should happen to learn who it is, I'd be grateful if you would suggest that he or she put it back. I admit that the marble's not to everyone's taste, but I have a fondness for it."

Cordelia said, "The arm of the Princess Royal? When did you notice that it had gone?"

"Munter tells me that it was in the display case when he locked up last night. That was at ten minutes past midnight. He unlocked this morning shortly after six but didn't look at the display case, although he thinks that he might have noticed if the arm had gone. But he can't be sure. I myself saw that it was missing and that the lock had been forced when I went to the kitchen to make tea just before seven."

Cordelia said, "It couldn't have been Clarissa. She was asleep when I got up this morning. And I doubt whether she'd have the strength to break a lock."

"Not much strength was required. A strong paper knife would have done the trick. And, conveniently enough, there was a strong paper knife on the desk in the business room."

Cordelia asked, "What are you going to do?"

"Nothing, at least until after the play. I can't see how it affects Clarissa. It's my loss, not hers. But I take it you would prefer her not to know?"

"I think it's vital that she doesn't find out. The least thing could upset her. We'll just have to hope no one else notices that the arm has gone."

He said, "If they do, I suppose I can say that I've removed it since Clarissa found it so displeasing. It's humiliating to have to lie when there's no need, but if you think it important that Clarissa isn't told . . ."

"I do. Very important. I'd be grateful if you'd say and do nothing until after the play."

It was then that they heard the footsteps, firm, quick, clanging on the tiled floor. Both turned simultaneously and gazed at the door. Sir George Ralston appeared, tweed-coated and holding a grip. He said, "I got through the meeting late yesterday. Drove most of the night and slept in a turnoff. Thought Clarissa would like me to put in an appearance if I could make it."

Ambrose said, "But how did you get to the island? I didn't hear a launch."

"Found a couple of early fishermen. They put me ashore in the small bay. Got my feet wet but nothing worse. I've been on the island a couple of hours. Didn't like to disturb you. Is that coffee?"

A jumble of thoughts ran through Cordelia's mind. Was she still wanted? She could hardly ask Sir George directly with Ambrose present. She was supposed to be on the island as Clarissa's secretary, a job that was unlikely to be affected by his sudden appearance. And what about her room? Presumably he would wish to move next door to his wife. She was uncomfortably aware that she must look less than pleased to see him and that Ambrose was glancing at her with a sardonic, wryly amused look which recognized her discomfiture. Murmuring an excuse, she slipped away.

Clarissa was stirring, although Tolly hadn't yet brought in the early tray. Cordelia drew back the curtains and unlocked the door. She stood by the bed until Clarissa opened her eyes, then said, "Your husband has just arrived. Apparently the meeting ended sooner than he expected."

Clarissa heaved herself up from her pillows. "George? But that's ridiculous! He isn't expected until late tonight at the earliest."

"Well, he's here."

Cordelia thought that it was as well that she had warned Clarissa. Sir George could hardly have been gratified at her reception of the news. She sat up and stared straight ahead, her face expressionless. Then she said, "Tug on that bell rope, will you? The one by the fireplace. It's time Tolly brought in my tea."

Cordelia said, "I wondered whether you'll still want me."

Clarissa's voice was sharp, almost frightened. "Of course I still want you! What possible difference does this make? You know what you're here to do. If someone's out to get me, he isn't going to stop because George has arrived."

"I could move out of the next-door room if you like."

Clarissa swung her legs out of bed and made for the bathroom.

"Oh, don't be so bloody naive, Cordelia! Stay where you are. And tell George I'm awake if he wants to see me."

She disappeared. Cordelia decided to wait in the bedroom until Tolly arrived with the tea. If she could help it, there would be no time between now and the rise of the curtain when Clarissa would be left unguarded.

Clarissa returned from the bathroom and climbed back into bed.

Cordelia said, "Before Miss Tolgarth arrives, could you tell me what the program is today?"

"Oh, don't you know? I thought I'd explained it all. The curtain is due to rise at three-thirty. Ambrose is arranging an early lunch, about midday, and I shall rest up here alone from one until two-forty-five. I don't want to spend too long in my dressing room before a performance. You can call me at two-forty-five and we'll decide what, if anything, I want you to do during the play. The launch will fetch the Cottringham party from Speymouth. They should arrive at two-thirty or shortly afterward. There is a larger hired launch for the guests and that is due at three. We have tea in the interval at four-thirty, set out under the arcade if it's warm enough, and supper at seven-thirty in the great hall. The launches are ordered for nine."

Cordelia said, "And this morning? What is planned for the three hours between breakfast and luncheon? I think we should try to stay together."

"We shall all stay together. Ambrose has suggested that we might like a trip round the island in *Shearwater*, but I've told him that we're not a party of his five-pounds-a-day summer trippers. I've thought of a better plan. There are sights on Courcy that he hasn't shown us yet. I don't think you need worry about being bored. We'll start with a visit to the skulls of Courcy."

Cordelia said, "The skulls of Courcy? Do you mean real skulls, here in the castle?"

Clarissa laughed. "Oh, they're real enough. In the crypt of the church. Ambrose will recite the famous legend. They should put us all nicely in the mood for the horrors of Amalfi."

Tolly with the tea tray and Sir George arrived simultaneously. He was received very prettily. Clarissa held out a languid arm. He raised her hand to his lips, then bent with a stiff, graceless movement and briefly laid his face against hers.

She cried, her voice high and brittle, "Darling, how lovely! And how clever of you to find someone to bring you across."

He didn't look at Cordelia. He said gruffly, "You're all right?"

"Darling, of course. Did you think I wasn't? How touching! But, as you see, here I am, Duchess of Malfi still."

Cordelia left them. She wondered whether Sir George would find an opportunity of speaking to her privately and, if so, whether she should tell him about the woodcut pushed under the door. It was, after all, he who had employed her. But it was Clarissa who had sent for her, Clarissa who was her client, Clarissa she was paid to protect. Some instinct urged her to keep her counsel, at least until after the play. And then she remembered the missing marble. In the surprise of Sir George's arrival it had slipped from the front of her mind. But now its pale image gleamed in her imagination with all the sinister force of an omen. Ought she at least to warn Sir George that it was missing? But warn him against what? It was only the carved replica of a baby's limb, the limb of a long-dead princess. How could it harm anyone? Why should it hold in its chubby fingers such a weight of portentous power? She couldn't even explain to herself why she thought it so important that Clarissa not be told about the loss, except that the marble had repelled her and that any mention of it would be upsetting. Surely she had been right in asking Ambrose to say nothing, at least until after the play. So why tell Sir George? He hadn't even seen the limb. It would be time enough for them all to be told when Ambrose started inquiring and looking for it after the play. And that would be this evening. There was only today to be got through.

She was aware that she wasn't thinking very clearly. And one thought in particular surprised and fretted her. Surely the presence of Clarissa's husband on Courcy Island ought to make her job easier. She should be feeling relieved at a sharing of responsibility. Why, then, should she see this unexpected arrival as a new and unwelcome complication? Why should she feel for the first time that she was caught in a charade in which she stumbled blindfold, while unseen hands spun her around, pushed and pulled at her, in which an unknown intelligence watched, waited, and directed the play?

# II

Breakfast was a long-drawn-out meal to which the members of the house party came singly, ate at leisure, and seemed reluctant to finish. The dishes would have done justice to Herbert Gorringe's Victorian notions of a proper start to the day. As the lids of the silver dishes were raised, the discordant smells of eggs and bacon, sausages, kidneys, and haddock filled the breakfast room, stifling appetite. Despite the early promise of another warm day, Cordelia sensed that the party was ill at ease and that she wasn't the only one present who was mentally counting the hours to nightfall. There seemed to be an unspoken conspiracy not to upset Clarissa, and when she announced her plan to visit the church and the crypt the murmur of agreement was suspiciously unanimous. If anyone would have preferred a trip around the island or a solitary walk, no one admitted it. Probably they were well aware how precarious was her control before a performance, and no one wanted to risk being held responsible if that control broke. As they walked in a group along the arcade, past the theater and under the shadow of the trees which led to the church, it seemed to Cordelia that Clarissa was surrounded by the solicitous care afforded to an invalid or—and the thought was disagreeable—to a predestined victim.

Sir George was the one most at ease. When they entered the church and the rest of the party gazed around with the air of people resolved to find something positive to say, his reaction was immediate and uncompromising. He obviously found its nineteenth-century fusion of religious enthusiasm with medieval romanticism unsympathetic and viewed the richly decorated apse with its mosaic of Christ in glory, the colored tiles, and the polychromatic arches with a prejudiced eye.

"It looks more like a Victorian London club—or a Turkish bath come to that—than a church. I'm sorry, Gorringe, but I can't admire it. Who'd you say the architect was?"

"George Frederick Bodley. My great-grandfather had quarreled with Godwin by the time he came to rebuild the church. His relationships with his architects were always stormy. I'm sorry you don't like it. The paintings on the reredos are by Lord Leighton, by the way, and the glass is by William Morris's firm, which specialized in these lighter hues. Bodley was one of the first architects to use the firm. The east window is considered rather fine."

"I don't see how anyone could actually pray in the place. Is that the war memorial?"

"Yes. Put up by my uncle from whom I inherited. It's the only architectural addition he ever made to the island."

The memorial was a plain stone slab set in the wall to the south of the altar which read:

In memory of the men of Courcy Island
who fell on the battlefields of two world wars
and whose bones lie in foreign soil.
1914–1918
1939–1945

This at least met with Sir George's approval.

"I like that. Plain and dignified. Wonder who put the wreath there. Been there some time by the look of it."

Ambrose had come up behind them. He said, "There'll be a fresh one on the eleventh of November. Munter makes them from our own laurels and hangs one up each year. His father was killed in the war, in the navy I think. Anyway, he was drowned. He told me that much."

Roma asked, "And do you assist at this charade?"

"No, he hasn't asked me. It's a purely private ceremony. I'm not sure that I'm even supposed to know that it happens."

Roma turned away and said, "It throws a new light on Munter though. Who would suspect him of that streak of romanticism? But I wouldn't have thought that the memorial was particularly appropriate. His father didn't live or work on the island, did he?"

"Not to my knowledge."

"And if he drowned, his bones won't be buried in any soil, foreign or otherwise. It all seems rather pointless. But, then, Remembrance Day is pointless. No one seems to know any longer what it's supposed to be for."

Sir George said, "It's for remembering the good chaps who've gone. Once a year. For two minutes. You wouldn't think that was too much to ask. And why degrade it into a sentimental mass love-in? At our last Parade the padre preached a sermon about the Third World and the World Council of Churches. I could see that some of the older chaps in the Legion were getting restless."

Roma said, "I suppose he thought his sermon had something to do with world peace."

"Armistice Day isn't to do with peace. It's to do with war and remembering one's dead. A nation that can't remember its dead will soon cease to be worth dying for. And what's so peaceful about the Third World?"

He turned quickly away, and for a moment Cordelia thought that his eyes were moist. But then she saw that it was just a trick of the light and was embarrassed at her naiveté. He might be remembering his own good chaps and the lost, forgotten, and discredited causes for which they had died. But he was remembering without tears. He had seen so many bodies, so many deaths. Could any death now, she wondered, be more to him than a single statistic?

A door in the vestry led down to the crypt. To make their way down narrow stone steps lit by Ambrose's pocket torch was to descend into a different world, a different time. Here alone was there any trace of the original Norman building. The roof was so low that Ivo, the tallest of them, could hardly stand upright, and the heavy, squat pillars strained as if bearing on their capitals the weight of nine centuries. Ambrose put out his hand to a wall switch and the claustrophobic chamber sprang into harsh, unflattering light. They saw the skulls at once. One whole wall was patterned with them, a grinning parade of death. They had been ranged on rough oak shelves and were so tightly wedged that Cordelia judged that it would be impossible to separate them except by hacking them apart. Little care had been taken in the arrangement. In some places cement had been poured over them, fixing mouth to mouth in the parody of a kiss. In others, the grit of the years had seeped between them, binding them into cohesion, blocking the nasal cavities, collecting in the eye sockets, and laying over the smooth domes a patina of dust like a shroud.

Ambrose said, "There's a legend about them, of course; there always is. In the seventeenth century the island was held by the de Courcy family; they had, in fact, been here since the fourteen-hundreds. The de Courcy at that time was a particularly unpleasant representative of his breed. Someone must have told him about Tiberius's little doings on Capri—I don't suppose he could himself read—and he started to emulate them here. You can imagine the kind of thing: local maidens from the mainland abducted, *droit du seigneur* exercised on a scale which even the most complaint tenants found unreasonable, mutilated bodies brought in on the tide to the general disapproval of the locals. Speymouth was a small fishing village then. The town only reached any size or importance in the Regency—a sort of West Country Brighton. But the word got around. No one did anything, of course. The story is that the father of one of the abducted girls, whose tortured body floated ashore three weeks later, laid information against him with the local magistrate. De Courcy was subsequently tried at the assizes but acquitted. One supposes it was managed in the usual way: a venal judge, perjured witnesses, bribed jurymen, a mixture of subservience and fear. And, of course, there was no direct evidence. At the end of the trial the father—he was an immensely powerful man according to the legend—rose up in court and cursed de Courcy and all his clan in the customary dramatic terms of dead firstborn, revolting diseases, the castle falling into ruins, the line extinct. Everyone must have enjoyed that part immensely. And then in 1665 came the plague."

Cordelia thought that Ambrose's pause, if intended for dramatic effect, was unnecessary. The little group ranged around him were gazing at him with the rapt attention of foreign tourists whose guide, for once, is giving value for money. Ambrose went on.

"The plague raged particularly fiercely on this coast. It was said to have been brought here by a family from Cheapside who had relations in the village and fled here for safety. One by one the local families fell victim. The parson and his family died early, and there was no one to say the rites over the dead. Soon there was only one old man willing to bury them. Anarchy reigned. The island felt itself to be safe and de Courcy threatened death to anyone who landed. The story is that a boatload of women and children with one adult male to manage the boat did try. But if they were hoping to arouse de Courcy's compassion they were disappointed. He was behaving perfectly reasonably in this instance, of course. The only way to escape the pestilence was quarantine. It wasn't quite as reasonable to drive holes in the planks in the bottom of the boat before forcing it out to sea so that the human cargo drowned before they could reach shore, but that may be only a gloss on the story. About those seventeenth-century boat people, I think we ought to give him the benefit of the doubt. And now for the climax."

Ivo murmured, "This story has everything but costumes by Motley and background music by Menotti." But Cordelia saw that he was as interested as any of them.

"I don't know whether you know about the bubonic plague, the symptoms, I mean. The victims would first have the sensation that they could smell rotting apples. After that came the dreaded pink rash on the forehead. The day came when the father of the murdered girl smelled the smell, saw in his glass the mark of death. It was a summer night but unruly, the sea turbulent. He knew that he hadn't long to live; the plague killed swiftly. He launched his boat and set sail for the island.

"De Courcy and his private court were at dinner when the door of the great hall opened and he appeared, this great shambling sea-drenched figure, stumbling toward his enemy, eyes blazing. There was a moment when they were all too astounded for action. And in that moment he reached de Courcy, flung his great arms around him, and kissed him full on the mouth."

No one spoke. Cordelia wondered whether they would break into polite applause. The story had been well told and it had, in its simplicity, its terror, its almost symbolic confrontation of innocence with evil, a remarkable power.

Ivo said, "That story would make an opera. You've got the libretto. All you need is a Verdi or a second Benjamin Britten."

Roma Lisle, gazing at the skulls in fascinated distaste, asked, "And did the curse come true?"

"Oh, yes. De Courcy and all his people here caught the plague and were wiped out. The line is now extinct. It was four years before anyone came here to bury them. By then a kind of superstitious awe surrounded the island. The landsfolk averted their eyes from it. Fishermen, remembering the old religion, crossed themselves when they sailed in its shadow. The castle crumbled. It remained a ruin until my great-grandfather bought the place in 1864, built himself a castle in the modern style, reclaimed the land, cleared the undergrowth. Only the ruins of the old church remained standing. De Courcy and his islanders hadn't been buried in the churchyard. The locals hadn't thought that they merited Christian burial. As a result Herbert Gorringe kept turning up the skeletons when planting his pleasure garden. His men collected the skulls and arranged them here, a nice compromise between Christian disposal and tossing them on the bonfire."

Roma said, "There's something carved about the top shelf, words and numbers. The carving's a bit crude. It could be a biblical reference."

"Ah, that's a personal comment by one of the Victorian workmen who thought that the setting up of this row of Yoricks might be an opportunity to point a moral and adorn a tale. No, I shan't identify it for you. Look it up for yourselves."

Cordelia didn't need to look it up. A convent-born knowledge of the Old Testament and a lucky guess led her unerringly to the text. "Judgement is mine saith the Lord. I will repay." It was, she thought, an inappropriate comment on a vengeance which, if Ambrose's story was true, had been so singularly, so satisfyingly, human.

It was very cold in the crypt. Conversation had died. They stood in a ring looking at the row of skulls as if those smooth domes of bone, the ragged nasal orifices, the gaping sockets, could be made to yield the secret of their deaths. How unfrightening they were, thought Cordelia, those age-long symbols of mortality, set up like a row of grinning devils to frighten children at a fairground and, in their denuded anonymity, stripping human pretensions to the risible evidence that what lasted longest in man were his teeth.

From time to time during Ambrose's story she had glanced at Clarissa, wondering what effect this recital of horrors might have on her. It seemed to her strange that the crudely drawn caricature of a skull could produce such fear while the reality provoked no more than an exaggerated frisson of distaste. But Clarissa's refined sensibilities were apparently capable of sustaining any amount of assault, provided the horrors were anesthetized by time and there were no threats to herself. Even in the harsh, draining glare of the crypt her face looked flushed and the immense eyes shone more brightly. Cordelia doubted whether she would be happy to visit the crypt alone, but now, feeling herself the center of the company, she was enjoying a thrill of vicarious dread like a child at a horror movie who knows that none of the terror is real, that outside is the familiar street, the ordinary faces, the comfortable world of home. Whatever Clarissa feared, and Cordelia couldn't believe that the fear was faked, she had no sympathy with these long-dead tormented souls, no dread of a supernatural visitation in the small hours. She was expecting that, when her fate came and in whatever guise, it would still wear a human face.

But now excitement had made her euphoric. She said to Ambrose,

"Darling, your island's a repository of horrors, charming on the surface and seething underneath. But isn't there something closer in time, a murder which really did happen? Tell us about the Devil's Kettle."

Ambrose avoided looking at her. One of the skulls was unaligned with its fellows. He took the white ball between his hands and tried to grind it back into place. But it couldn't be shifted and, suddenly, the jawbone came apart into his hands. He shoved it back, wiped his hands on his handkerchief, and said, "There's nothing to see. And the story is rather beastly. Only interesting really to those who relish in imagination the contemplation of another's pain."

But the warning and the implied criticism were wasted on her. She cried, "Darling, don't be so stuffy! The story's forty years old at least and I know about it anyway. George told me. But I want to see where it happened. And I've got a personal interest. George was here on the island at the time. Did you know that George was here?"

Ambrose said shortly, "Yes, I know."

Roma said, "Whatever it is, you may as well show us. Clarissa won't give you any peace until you do, and the rest of us are entitled to have our curiosity satisfied. It can hardly be worse than this place."

No one else spoke. Cordelia thought that Clarissa and her cousin were unlikely allies even in persuasion and wondered whether Roma was genuinely interested or merely hoped to get the story over with so that she could get out of the crypt.

Clarissa's voice assumed the wheedling note of an importunate child. "Please, Ambrose. You promised that you would some time or other. Why not now? After all, we're here."

Ambrose looked at George Ralston. The look seemed to invite consent, or at least comment. But if he was hoping for support in resisting Clarissa, he was disappointed. Sir George's face was impassive, its restlessness for once stilled.

Ambrose said, "All right, if you insist."

He led them to a low door at the west end of the crypt. It was made of oak, almost black with age and with strong bands of iron and a double bolt. Beside it on a nail hung a key. Ambrose shot back the bolts, then inserted the key in the lock. It turned easily enough, but he needed all his strength to pull open the door. Inside he reached up and switched on a light. They saw before them a narrow vaulted passage only wide enough for two to walk abreast. Ambrose led the way with Clarissa at his shoulder. Roma walked alone, followed by Cordelia and Simon with Sir George and Ivo at the rear.

After less than twenty feet, the passage gave way to a flight of steep stone steps which curved to the left. At the bottom it widened, but the roof was still so low that Ivo had to stoop. The passage was lit by unshaded but protected light bulbs hung from a cable, and the air, although fusty, was fresh enough to breathe without discomfort. It was very quiet and their footsteps echoed on the stone floor. Cordelia estimated that they must have covered about two hundred yards when they came to a turn in the passage and then a second flight of steps, steeper than the first and rougher as if hewn out of the rock. And it was then that the light failed.

The shock of instantaneous and total blackness after the artificial brightness of the tunnel made them gasp, and one of the women—Cordelia thought that it was Clarissa—gave a cry. She fought against a moment of panic, calming by an act of will her suddenly pounding heart. Instinctively she stretched out her hand into the darkness and encountered a firm warm arm under thin cotton, Simon's arm. She let go but almost immediately felt her hand grasped by his. Then she heard Ambrose's voice.

"Sorry, everyone. I'd forgotten that the lights are on a time switch. I'll find the button in a second."

But Cordelia judged that it must have been fifteen seconds before the light came on. They blinked at each other in the sudden glare, smiling a little sheepishly. Simon's hand was immediately withdrawn as if scalded, and he turned his face from her.

Clarissa said crossly, "I wish you'd warn us before playing silly tricks."

Ambrose looked amused. "No trick, I assure you. And it won't happen again. The chamber above the Devil's Kettle has an ordinary light system. Only another forty yards to go. And you did insist on this excursion, remember."

They went down the steps with the aid of a looped rope which had been threaded through rings bolted into the rock. After another thirty yards the passage widened to form a low roofed cave.

Ivo said, his voice sounding unnaturally loud, "We must be forty feet below ground. How is it ventilated?"

"By shafts. One of them comes up into the concrete bunker built in the war to guard the southern approach to the island. And there are a number of others. The first of them is believed to have been installed by de Courcy. The Devil's Kettle must have had its uses for him."

In the middle of the floor was an oak trapdoor furnished with two strong bolts. Ambrose drew them back and pulled open the flap. They crowded around and six heads bent to peer down. They saw an iron ladder leading down to a cave. Below them heaved seawater. It was difficult to tell which way the tide was running, but they could see the light streaming in from an aperture shaped like a half-moon, and they heard for the first time the faint susurration of the sea and smelled the familiar salty seaweed tang. With each wave the water gushed almost silently into the cave and swirled around the rungs of the ladder. Cordelia shivered. There was something remorseless, almost uncanny, about that quiet, regular spouting.

Clarissa said, "Now tell!"

Ambrose was silent for a minute. Then he said, "It happened in 1940. The island and the castle were taken over by the government and used as a reception and interrogation center for foreign nationals of the Axis powers trapped in the United Kingdom by the war, and others, including a number of British citizens who were suspected, at worst, of being enemy agents or at best of being Nazi sympathizers. My uncle was living in the castle with only his one manservant, and they were moved out to the cottage in the stable block now occupied by Oldfield. What went on in the castle was, of course, top secret. The internees were kept here for only a relatively short time, and I've no reason to suppose that their stay was particularly uncomfortable. A number were released after interrogation and clearance; some went on to internment on the Isle of Man; some, I suppose, eventually came to less agreeable ends. But George knows more about the place than I do. As Clarissa says, he was stationed here as a young officer for a few months in 1940."

He paused, but again there was no response. He had spoken as if Sir George were no longer with them. Cordelia saw Roma glance at Ralston, surprised, a little wary. She half opened her mouth, then thought better of it. But she kept her gaze on him with a stubborn intensity, rather as if she were seeing him for the first time.

Ambrose went on, "I don't know any of the details. Someone does, I suppose, or as much of the truth as came out. There must be an official record of the incident somewhere, although it was never published. All I know is what my uncle told me on one of my rare visits, and that was mostly rumor."

Clarissa permitted herself a display of nicely judged impatience. It was, thought Cordelia, as artificial as the simulated moue of distaste with which she had first regarded the shelf of skulls. Clarissa had no need of impatience; Clarissa knew exactly what was coming.

Ambrose spread plump hands and shrugged, as if resigned to a recital he would have preferred to avoid. But he could have avoided it, thought Cordelia, if he had really tried. And for the first time she wondered whether the conversation, even the visit to the crypt, had been the result of collusion.

He said, "In March 1940 there were about fifty internees on Courcy and, among them, a hard core of dedicated Nazis, most of whom were Germans trapped in Britain at the outbreak of war. They suspected one of their number, a boy of twenty-two, of having betrayed their secrets to the British authorities during interrogation. Perhaps he did. On the other hand, he may have been a British undercover agent who had infiltrated their group. All I know are rumors, and secondhand rumors at that. What does seem beyond dispute is that the group of Nazis convened a secret court in the crypt of the church, convicted their comrade of treason, and condemned him to death. Then they gagged him, bound his arms, and brought him down the passageway to this cave. It's called the Devil's Kettle. As you can see, it has a narrow opening which leads to the east cove, but the cave is always flooded at high tide. They bound their victim to that iron ladder and left him to drown. He was a very tall young man. He died slowly in the darkness, and he died hard. Later one of them crept back to untie him and let the body float out to sea. When it was washed up only two days later, the wrists were cut through almost to the bone. One of his fellow internees told a story of the young man's mounting depression, and it was suggested that he had bound his wrists to prevent himself from swimming and had leaped into the sea. None of his judges or executioners ever spoke."

Roma asked, "Then how was the story ever known?"

"Someone talked eventually, I suppose, but not until after the war. Oldfield was living in Speymouth at the time and was employed here by the army. He may have heard rumors. He doesn't admit it now, but someone on the island must have suspected. Someone may even have condoned what happened, or at least closed his eyes. After all, the army were in charge here. Yet the gang got their hands on the keys to the crypt and the secret passage and managed to return them undetected. That suggests, well, let's say a certain degree of official carelessness on someone's part."

Clarissa turned to her husband. "What was he called, darling, the boy who died?"

"His name was Carl Blythe."

Clarissa turned to the company. Her voice was as out of key as a hysteric's: "And the most extraordinary thing is that he was English—well, his father was anyway; his mother was German—and George was at school with him, weren't you, darling? They were both at Melhurst. He was three years older and rather a horrid boy, cruel really, one of those bullies who make other boys' lives a torment to them, so he and George weren't exactly friends. In fact George hated him. And then to find him here and at his mercy. Wasn't it odd?"

Ivo said easily, "Not particularly. The British public schools produced their share of Nazi sympathizers, and this is where you'd expect to find them in 1940."

Cordelia stared down at the iron ladder. The light in the passage, fierce and garish, did nothing to mitigate the horror; rather it intensified it. In the old days, the cruelty of man to man was decently shrouded in darkness; the mind dwelt on airless, unlit dungeons, on light filtering through the slits of narrow windows. But the modern interrogation rooms and torture chambers were ablaze with light. The technocrats of pain needed to see what they were at. Suddenly the place became intolerable to her. The chill of the passageway intensified. She had to tauten her arms and clench her fists to prevent herself visibly shaking. In her imagination the tunnel behind them stretched to infinity and they were doomed to rush down its contracting brightness like terrified rats. She felt a bead of sweat roll down her forehead and sting her eyes and knew that it had nothing to do with the cold. She made herself speak, hoping that her voice didn't betray her.

"Can't we get out of here? I feel like a voyeuse."

Ivo said, "And I feel cold."

Taking her cue promptly, Clarissa shivered. Then Sir George spoke for the first time. Cordelia wondered whether it was her confused senses or the echo from the low roof which made his voice sound so different.

"If my wife has satisfied her curiosity, perhaps we might go." Then he made a sudden jerk forward. Before they could guess what was coming, he put his foot behind the open trapdoor and pushed. It crashed down. The walls seemed to crack and the passage shook under their feet. They must all have cried out, their voices thin screams in the echoing, reverberating roar. When it had faded no one spoke. Sir George had already turned on his heel and was making his way toward the entrance.

Cordelia found herself a little ahead of the others. Fear, and a deadening sense of misery which was stronger than fear and which added to her claustrophobia, urged her forward. Even the crypt with its neatly disposed ossuary was preferable to this horrible place. She stooped to pick up the neatly folded oblong of paper almost instinctively and without curiosity, without even turning it over to see if it was addressed. In the harsh light of the single bulb the neatly drawn skull and the typed quotation were starkly clear, and she realized that she had known from the first what it must be.

> Thy death is plotted; here's the consequence of murder,
> We value not desert nor Christian breath
> When we know black deeds must be cured with death.

It was not, she thought, completely accurate. Surely the first word should be *My,* not *Thy*. But the message was plain enough. She slipped it into her trouser pocket and turned to wait for the rest of the party. She tried to recall where they had all been standing when the lights went out. Surely it had been at about this spot where the tunnel curved. It would have taken only a few seconds for one of them to dart back under cover of the darkness, someone who had the message ready, someone who didn't care, might even have been pleased, that Clarissa would know that her enemy was one of this small party. And if anyone other than she had seen it first, or if the group had been together, it would have been placed in Clarissa's hands. It was addressed to her in the same typed letters. Ambrose was perhaps the most likely culprit. That light had failed very conveniently. But any of the others could have done it, any except Simon. She had felt his hand firmly in hers.

And then they came into view. She stood under the light and scanned their faces. But none betrayed anxiety, none showed any surprise, no eyes dropped to the ground. Joining them, she felt that she fully understood for the first time why it was that Clarissa was so afraid. Until now the messages had seemed little more than a childish persecution which no intelligent woman would think worth more than a moment's real anxiety. But they were a manifestation of hatred, and hatred, whatever else it was, could never be petty. They were childish, but there was an adult and sophisticated malice behind the childishness, and the danger they threatened might, after all, be real and imminent. She wondered whether she was right in keeping this message and the earlier ones from Clarissa, whether it might not be safer to put her on increased guard. But her instructions had been clear: to save Clarissa from any anxiety or annoyance before the performance. There would be time enough after the play to decide what else should be done. And there were less than four hours now before the curtain rose.

While they were passing the row of skulls, this time without a glance, Cordelia found herself walking with Ivo. His speed, whether by necessity or by design, was slower than that of the others and she kept pace with him. He said, "That was an instructive episode, don't you think? Poor Ralston! I take it that the whole episode and his subsequent moral scruples were an offering of conjugal unreserve. What did you think of it all, O wise Cordelia?"

"I thought that it was horrible." And both of them knew that she wasn't thinking only of that poor renegade's last agony, his lonely and terrible death.

Roma came alongside them. Cordelia saw that, for once, she looked animated, her eyes brightly malicious. She said, "Well, that was an unedifying performance. For those of us fortunate enough to be unmarried it makes holy matrimony seem a pretty unholy estate. Almost terrifying."

Ivo said, "Marriage is terrifying. At least I've found it so."

Roma was unwilling to let the matter rest. "Does she always need to psych herself up with an exhibition of cruelty before a performance?"

"She's nervous certainly. It takes people different ways."

"But this is only an amateur performance, for God's sake! The theater can't hold more than eighty or so. And she's supposed to be a professional. What do you think George Ralston was feeling back there?"

The note of satisfaction was unmistakable. Cordelia wanted to say that one had only to have looked at his face to see what Sir George was thinking. But she didn't speak.

Ivo said, "Like most professional soldiers, Ralston is a sentimentalist. He takes the great absolutes, honor, justice, loyalty, and binds them to his heart with hoops of steel. I find it rather appealing. But it does make for a certain . . . rigidity."

Roma shrugged. "If you mean that he's abnormally controlled, I agree. It will be interesting to see what happens if ever the control snaps."

Clarissa turned and called to them, her voice happily imperious, "Come on, you three. Ambrose wants to lock the crypt. And I want lunch."

# III

The contrast between the sun-warmed terrace, where, once again, luncheon was set out on a linen-covered trestle table, and the dark, rank-smelling pit of the Devil's Kettle was so great that Cordelia felt disoriented. That brief descent into the hell of the past could have happened in a different place and time. Looking out across the light-flecked sea to where the canvases of the Saturday sailors curved to catch the breeze, she found it possible to imagine that it hadn't happened at all, that de Courcy's plague-ridden court, Carl Blythe's agony as he struggled against the horror of his long dying, were the remnants of a nightmare which had no more reality than the crude caricatures of a horror comic.

It was a light meal, a watercress-and-avocado salad followed by salmon soufflé, chosen, perhaps, to soothe a nervous digestion. But, even so, no one ate with appetite or evident enjoyment. Cordelia took one glass of the cool Riesling and forced down the salmon, knowing, rather than tasting, that it was delicious. Clarissa's brittle euphoria had given way to a silent preoccupation which no one liked to disturb. Roma crouched on the step at the end of the terrace, her unregarded plate in her lap, and gazed moodily out to sea. Sir George and Ivo stood together but neither spoke. But all of them, except Clarissa and herself, drank steadily. Ambrose said little but moved among them, refilling the glasses, his bright eyes amused and indulgent as if they were children behaving predictably under stress.

Unexpectedly, Simon was the liveliest of the party. He was drinking heavily, apparently unnoticed by Clarissa, swilling the wine down as if it were beer, his hand a little unsteady, his eyes bright. At about ten to one, he suddenly announced loudly that he would go for a swim, looking around at them rather as if he expected them to take an interest in this news. No one did, but Clarissa said, "Not so soon after a meal, darling. Take a walk first."

The endearment was so unexpected that they all looked up. The boy blushed, gave them a stiff little bow, and disappeared. Shortly afterward, Clarissa put down her plate, looked at her watch, and said, "Time to rest. No coffee, thank you, Ambrose. I never take it before a performance. I thought you knew that. Will you ask Tolly to bring up the tea tray at once? China tea. She knows the kind I have. George, would you come up in five minutes? I'll see you later, Cordelia. Better make it ten past one."

She made her slow way across the terrace with the graceful deliberation of a stage exit. For the first time, she seemed to Cordelia to be vulnerable, almost pathetic, in her lonely, self-absorbed fear. She felt an impulse to follow, but knew that it would only arouse Clarissa's fury. And she had no fear of Clarissa's finding another message thrust under her door. Cordelia had checked the room immediately before coming down to lunch. She knew now that the person responsible had been one of the small party who had visited the Devil's Kettle, and all of them had been under her eye throughout the meal. Only Simon had left early. And she did not believe for one moment that the culprit was Simon.

Suddenly Roma struggled to her feet and hurried out after her cousin, almost running from the terrace. The eyes of Ambrose and Ivo met but neither spoke, inhibited, perhaps, by the presence of Sir George. He walked to the end of the terrace, his back to them, coffee cup in hand. He seemed to be counting the minutes. Then he glanced at his watch, replaced his cup on the table, and made for the french windows. Looking around, foot on the step, he asked, "What time does the curtain rise, Gorringe?"

"At three-thirty."

"And we change before then?"

"That's what Clarissa expects. There won't be time afterward, anyway. Supper is at seven-thirty."

Sir George nodded and was gone.

Ivo said, "Clarissa organizes her helots with the brutal precision of a military commander. Ten minutes before you need report for duty, Cordelia. Time surely for a second cup of coffee."

When Cordelia unlocked her bedroom and went through the communicating door, Sir George was with his wife, standing by the window looking out over the sea. The round silver tea tray with its single cup and saucer, its elegant matching pot, was on the bedside chest, as yet untouched. Clarissa, still in her Bermuda shorts and shirt, was pacing up and down, her color high.

"She asked me for twenty-five thousand, came out with it, red-faced, as if she were a child asking for an increase in pocket money. And now of all times! She couldn't even wait until after the performance. Talk about crass stupidity! Is she deliberately trying to upset me or something?"

Sir George spoke without turning. "Important to her, I expect. Couldn't bear the suspense of waiting. Had to know. It's not easy to get you alone."

"She never had any sense of timing, even as a child. If there was a wrong moment for anything, trust Roma to pick it. Part of her general insensitivity. By God, she's chosen the wrong moment now!"

The voice from the window said quietly, "Would there have been a right one?"

Clarissa seemed not to have heard. "I told her that I wasn't prepared to hand over capital to support a lover who hadn't even the guts or decency to come and ask for it himself. I gave her some advice. If you have to buy yourself a man, he's not worth having. And if you can't get sex without buying it, buy cheaper. She's madly in love with him, of course. That's what this shop of theirs is all about, a ploy to get him away from his wife. Roma in love! I could almost feel sorry for him if he wasn't such a fool. When a plain virgin of forty-five falls in love for the first time and gets her first taste of sex, God help the man."

"My dear, is that our concern?"

She said sharply, "The money's my concern. Apart from anything else, they haven't a chance of making a go of it. No capital, no experience, no sense. Why should I throw good money after bad?" She turned to Cordelia. "You'd better go and get yourself dressed. Then lock your room and come out this way. I don't want you fussing about next door while I'm resting. I suppose you'll be wearing that Indian thing again. It shouldn't take long to get into that."

Cordelia said, "None of my clothes take long to get into."

"Nor to get out of, no doubt."

Sir George swung around, his voice low. "Clarissa!"

She smiled, gratified, went up to him, and gently tapped his cheek. "Dear George. Always so gallant." She might have been patting a dog.

Cordelia said, "I wondered whether you'd like me to stay next door while you rest. The communicating door could be open or locked as you like. I wouldn't make any noise."

"I've told you! I don't want you next door, or anywhere near me for that matter. I might want to speak some of the verse and I can't do that when I know someone's listening. With the three doors locked and no telephone in the room I suppose I can hope to be left in peace." Suddenly she called out, "Tolly."

Tolly came out of the bathroom, dark-clad, expressionless as ever. Cordelia wondered how much, if anything, she had heard. Without being asked, she went to the wardrobe and brought out Clarissa's satin robe and folded it over her arm. Then she went and waited silently beside her mistress. Clarissa unbuttoned her shirt and let it fall. Tolly made no move to pick it up but unhooked the back of Clarissa's brassiere. That too fell away and was plucked off by Clarissa, held out, and let drop. Last Clarissa unbuttoned the front of her shorts and eased them off, together with her pants, letting them fall together over her knees to the floor. She stood there for a moment immobile, her pale body dappled in the sunlight, the full, almost heavy breasts, the narrow waist, the jutting angular hips, and the smudge of corn-gold hair. Without haste Tolly unfolded the dressing gown and held it out for Clarissa's arms. Then she knelt, collected the bundle of discarded clothes, and returned to the bathroom. Cordelia thought that it had been a ritualistic display of almost innocent sensuality, less vulgar than she would have expected, narcissistic rather than provocative. A conviction came to her, as certain as it was irrational, that this was the image of Clarissa that she would remember all her life. And, whatever its motive, Clarissa's moment of frank exultation in her beauty seemed to have calmed her. She said, "Don't take any notice of me, darlings. You know what it is before a performance." She turned to Cordelia. "Just get anything you want from your room and let me have both the keys. I'll set the alarm for two-forty-five, so come up about then and I'll let you know if there's anything I want you to do during the performance. And don't rely on being able to watch up front. I may want you backstage."

Cordelia left them still together and went into her room by the communicating door. As she substituted her long cotton dress for shirt and jeans, she thought about Roma's extraordinary request. Why hadn't she done the obvious thing and waited until after the performance when she might have hoped to catch her cousin in the euphoria of success? But perhaps she had seen this as the most propitious, perhaps the only possible, time. If the performance were a fiasco, Clarissa would be unapproachable; it was possible that she might even leave the island without waiting for a celebratory party. But surely Roma must have known her cousin well enough to see that whatever moment she chose, hers was a hopeless cause. What was she hoping for; that Clarissa would once again indulge in the grand generous gesture as she obviously had with Simon Lessing, that she wouldn't be able to resist the insidiously gratifying role of patron and deliverer? Cordelia thought that two things were certain: Roma must be in desperate need of the money; and Roma, for one, wasn't betting on Clarissa's success.

She brushed her hair vigorously, gave a final look at herself in the glass without enthusiasm, and locked her bedroom door, leaving the key in the lock. Then she knocked at the communicating door and went through. The key to that door was in the lock on Clarissa's side. Sir George and Tolly had left, and Clarissa was seated at the dressing table, brushing her hair with long, firm strokes. Without looking around she said, "What have you done with your key?"

"Turned it and left it in the lock. Shall I lock the communicating door now?"

"No. I'll see to it. I want to check that you've locked your outside door."

Cordelia said, "I'll stay within call. If you want me I'll be at the end of the corridor. I can perfectly well get a chair from my room and sit there with a book."

Clarissa's anger flared. "Can't you understand English? What are you trying to do, spy on me? I've told you! I don't want you next door and I don't want you pussyfooting up and down the corridor. I don't want you, or anyone, near me. What I want now is to be left in peace!"

The note of hysteria was new and unmistakable. Cordelia said, "Then will you roll up one of your towels tightly and wedge it against the door? I don't want any notes delivered to you by hand."

Clarissa's voice was sharp. "What do you mean? Nothing has happened since I arrived, nothing!"

Cordelia said soothingly, "I just want to ensure that it stays that way. If whoever is responsible should land on Courcy Island, he might make one last attempt to get a message to you. I don't in the least think that it will happen. I'm sure it won't. The notes have probably stopped for good. But I don't want to take any risks."

Clarissa said ungraciously, "All right. It's not a bad idea. I'll block the bottom of the door."

There seemed nothing else to say. As Cordelia went out, Clarissa followed her, firmly closed the door on her, and turned the key. The scrape of metal, the small click, were faint, but Cordelia's keen ears heard them distinctly. Clarissa was locked in. There was nothing more that she could do until two-forty-five. She looked at her watch. It was just one-twenty.

## IV

There was only an hour and a half to be got through, but Cordelia found herself possessed of an irritable restlessness which made the slow minutes stretch interminably. It was a nuisance that her room was barred to her and that before locking it she had forgotten to pick up her book. She went to the library, hoping to pass an hour with old bound copies of *The Strand* magazine. But Roma was there, not reading but sitting upright, close to the telephone, and the look she gave Cordelia was so unwelcoming that it was obvious that she was expecting or hoping for a call and wanted to take it in private. Closing the door, Cordelia thought with envy of Simon, probably even now enjoying his solitary swim, and of Sir George, striding out with his binoculars at the ready. She wished that she could be with him, but her long skirt was unsuitable for walking, and in any case she felt that she shouldn't leave the castle.

She made her way to the theater. The house lights were already on and the crimson-and-gold auditorium with its rows of empty seats seemed to be waiting in a hushed, portentous, nostalgic calm. Backstage, Tolly was checking the main women's dressing room, setting out boxes of tissues and a supply of hand towels. Cordelia asked if she needed any help and received a polite but definite refusal. Then she remembered that there was something she could do. Sir George, when he was at Kingly Street, had mentioned checking the set. She wasn't sure what he had had in mind. Even if the poison pen managed to secrete a missive on the set or among the props, Clarissa would hardly open and read it in the middle of a performance. But Sir George had been right. It was a sensible precaution to check the set and the props and she was glad to have something definite to do.

All was well. The set for the first scene, a Victorian garden outside the palace, was simple: a blue back cloth, bay trees and geraniums in stone urns, a highly sentimental statue of a woman with a lute, and two ornate cane armchairs with cushions and footrests. At the side of the stage stood the props table. She checked over the assortment of Ambrose's Victoriana assembled for the indoor scenes: vases, pictures, fans, glasses, even a child's rocking horse. A suede glove stuffed with cotton wool was placed ready for the prison scene and did, indeed, look unpleasantly like a severed hand. The music box was there, as was the silver-bound jewel chest for the second act. Cordelia opened it, but no missive lurked in its rosewood depths.

There was nothing else she could usefully do. There was still an hour before she was due to wake Clarissa. She walked for a time in the rose garden, but the sun was less warm here on the westerly side of the castle, and in the end she returned to the terrace and sat in the corner of the bottom step leading to the beach. It was a small sun trap; even the stones struck warm to her thighs. She closed her eyes and lifted her face to the sun, relishing the soft air on her eyelids, the smell of pines and seaweed, and soothed by the gentle hiss of the waves on the shingle.

She must have dozed briefly, but was roused by the arrival of the launch. Ambrose and both the Munters were there to receive the cast, Ambrose already changed and wearing a voluminous silk cloak over his dinner jacket, which gave him the appearance of a Victorian music-hall conjurer. There was a great deal of excited chatter as the cast, some of the men already in Victorian costume, jumped ashore and disappeared through the archway which led to the eastern lawn and the main entrance to the castle. Cordelia looked at her watch. It was two-twenty; the launch was early. She settled down again but didn't dare risk closing her eyes. And twenty minutes later, she set off through the french windows to call Clarissa.

She paused outside the bedroom door and glanced at her watch.

It was two-forty-two. Clarissa had asked to be called at two-forty-five but a few minutes could hardly matter. She knocked, quietly at first, and then more loudly. There was no reply. Perhaps Clarissa was already up and in the bathroom. She tried the door; to her surprise it opened, and looking down, she saw that the key was in the lock. The door opened easily with no obstructing wedge of towel. So Clarissa must have finished her rest.

For some reason which she was never able afterward to understand, she felt no premonition, no unease. She moved into the dimness of the room calling gently, "Miss Lisle, Miss Lisle. It's nearly two-forty-five."

The lined and heavy brocade curtains were drawn across the windows, but brightness pierced the paper-thin slit between them, and even their heavy folds couldn't entirely exclude the afternoon sun which seeped through as a gentle diffusion of pinkish light. Clarissa lay, ghostlike, on her crimson bed, both arms gently curved at her sides, the palms upwards, her hair a bright stream over the pillow. The bedclothes had been folded down, and she was lying on her back, uncovered, the pale satin dressing gown drawn up almost to her knees. Lifting her arms to draw back the curtains, Cordelia thought that the subdued light in the room played odd tricks; Clarissa's shadowed face looked almost as dark as the canopy of the bed, as if her skin had absorbed the rich crimson.

As the folds of the second curtain swung back and the room sprang into light, she turned and saw clearly for the first time what it was on the bed. For a second of incredulous time her imagination whirled crazily out of control, spinning its fantastic images: Clarissa had applied a face mask, a darkening, sticky mess which had even seeped into the two eye pads; the canopy was disintegrating, dripping its crimson fibers, obliterating her face with its richness. And then the ridiculous fancies faded and her mind accepted the stark reality of what her eyes had seen. Clarissa no longer had a face. This was no beauty mask. This pulp was Clarissa's flesh, Clarissa's blood, darkening and clotting and oozing serum, spiked with the brittle fragments of smashed bones.

She stood at the side of the bed, shaking. The room was full of noise, a regular drumming which filled her ears and pounded against her ribs. She thought, I must get someone; I must get help. But there was no help. Clarissa was dead. And she found that her limbs were rooted; only her eyes could move. But they saw things clearly, too clearly. Slowly she turned them from the horror on the bed and fixed them on the bedside chest. Something was missing, the silver jewel casket. But the small round tray of tea was still there. She saw the shallow cup, delicately painted with roses, the pale dregs of tea with two floating leaves, the smear of lipstick on the rim. And beside the tray there was something new: the marble limb, thick with blood, resting on top of a sheet of white paper, the chubby blood-stained fingers seeming to pin it to the polished wood. The blood had seeped over the paper, almost obliterating the familiar skull and crossbones, but the typed message had escaped that insidious stream and she could read it clearly:

> Other sins only speak; murder shrieks out:
> The element of water moistens the earth,
> But blood flies upwards and bedews the heavens.

And then it happened. The alarm clock on the other bedside cabinet rang, making her leap with terror. Her limbs were galvanized into life. She dashed around the bed and tried to silence it, grabbing it with hands so shaking that the clock clattered on the polished wood. Oh, God! Oh, God! Would nothing stop it? Then her fingers found the button. The room was silent again, and in the echo of that dreadful ringing she could hear once again the thudding of her heart. She found herself looking at the thing on the bed as if terrified that the din had waked it, that Clarissa would suddenly jerk up stiff as a marionette and confront her with that faceless horror.

She was calmer now. There were things she must do. She must tell Ambrose. Ambrose would have to ring the police. And nothing must be touched until the police arrived. She found herself looking around the room, noticing all the details with great intensity: the balls of cotton wool smeared with makeup on the dressing table, the bottle of eye lotion still unstoppered, Clarissa's embroidered slippers neatly placed on the hearth rug, her makeup box open on a fireside chair, her copy of the script fallen by the bed.

As she turned to the door it opened, and she saw Ambrose with Sir George behind him, his binoculars still around his neck. They stared at each other. No one spoke. Then Sir George pushed past Ambrose and moved up to the bed. Still without a word he stood gazing down at his wife, his back rigid. Then he turned. His face was taut, all its restlessness stilled, the skin almost green. Then he swallowed and put his hand to his throat as if he were about to retch. Cordelia made an instinctive movement toward him and cried, "I'm sorry. I'm so very sorry!"

The words in all their futile banality appalled her as soon as she had uttered them. And then she saw his face, a mask of astonished horror. She thought, Oh, God, he thinks I'm confessing! He thinks I killed her.

She cried, "You employed me to look after her. I was here to keep her safe. I should never have left her."

She watched the horror drain from his face. He said calmly, almost crisply, "You couldn't have known. I didn't believe she was in any danger; no one did. And she wouldn't have let you stay with her, you or anyone. Don't blame yourself."

"But I knew that the marble had been taken! I should have warned her."

"Against what? You couldn't have expected this." He said again, sharply as if he were giving a command, "Don't blame yourself, Cordelia."

It was the first time he had used her Christian name.

Ambrose was still at the door. He said, "Is she dead?"

"See for yourself."

He moved up to the bed and looked down at the body. His face flushed a deep red. Watching him, Cordelia thought that he looked more embarrassed than shocked. Then he turned away. He said, "But this is incredible!" Then he whispered, "Horrible! Horrible!"

Suddenly he darted to the communicating door and turned the knob. It was unlocked. They followed him into Cordelia's room and through into the bathroom. The window to the fire escape was open as she had left it.

Sir George said, "He could have got out this way and down the fire escape. We'd better organize a search of the island. The castle too, of course. How many men can we muster, including those in the play?"

Ambrose made a rapid calculation. "About twenty-five of the players and six of us, including Oldfield. I don't know whether Whittingham will be much use."

"That's enough for four search parties, one for the castle, three to cover the island. It needs to be systematic. You'd better ring the police at once. I'll get the men organized."

Cordelia could imagine the disruption that thirty or more people tramping over the house and island would cause. She said, "We mustn't touch anything. Both these rooms must be locked. It's a pity that you handled the doorknob. And we'd better prevent the audience from landing. About the search; mightn't it be better to wait for the police?"

Ambrose looked uncertain. Sir George said, "I'm not prepared to wait. That's not possible. It's not possible, Gorringe!" His voice was fierce. His eyes looked almost wild.

Ambrose said soothingly, "No, of course not."

Sir George asked, "Where's Oldfield?"

"In his cottage, I imagine. The stable block."

"I'll get him to take out the launch and patrol the channel between here and Speymouth. That'll block any escape by sea. And then I'll join you in the theater. Better warn the men that I'll be wanting them."

He was gone.

Ambrose said, "It's best that he should have something to keep him busy. And I don't suppose they'll do any harm."

Cordelia wondered what Oldfield was supposed to do if he did intercept a boat leaving the island. Board it and tackle a murderer single-handed? And did either Ambrose or Sir George seriously expect to find an intruder on Courcy? Surely the significance of that bloody arm couldn't have escaped them.

Together they checked the door in Cordelia's room leading to the corridor. It was locked from the inside with the key still in place. So the murderer couldn't have left by that route. Next they closed and locked the communicating door. Finally they locked Clarissa's room behind them and Ambrose pocketed the key.

Cordelia said, "Are there any duplicate keys?"

"No, none. The spare bedroom keys were missing when I inherited and I've never bothered to have others made. It wouldn't have been easy, anyway. The locks are complicated; these are the original keys."

As they turned from the door they heard footsteps, and Tolly appeared around the corner of the gallery. Acknowledging them with only a nod, she went up to Clarissa's door and knocked. Cordelia's heart thumped. She looked at Ambrose, but he seemed bereft of speech. Tolly knocked again, this time more loudly. Then she turned to Cordelia.

"I thought you were supposed to call her at two-forty-five. She should have left it to me."

Cordelia said, through lips which were so dry and swollen that she thought they would crack, "You can't go in. She's dead. Murdered."

Tolly turned and knocked again.

"She's going to be late. I have to go to her. She always needs me before a performance."

Ambrose took a step forward. For a moment Cordelia thought that he was going to lay a hand on Tolly's shoulder. Then his arm dropped. He said in a voice which seemed unnaturally harsh, "There isn't going to be a performance. Miss Lisle is dead. She's been murdered. I'm just about to ring the police. Until they arrive no one can go into that room."

This time she understood. She turned and faced him, her face expressionless but so white that Cordelia, thinking she would faint, put out a hand and grasped her arm. She felt Tolly shudder, a small spasm of rejection, almost of revulsion, which was unmistakable, as shocking as a blow in the face. Quickly she withdrew her hand.

Tolly said, "The boy. Does the boy know?"

"Simon? Not yet. No one knows except Sir George. We've only just discovered the body."

His voice held a trace of aggrieved impatience, like that of an overworked servant. Cordelia almost expected him to protest that he couldn't see to everything at once.

Tolly still fixed her eyes on him. She said, "You'll break it gently, sir. It will be a shock to him."

Ambrose said curtly, "It's a shock for us all."

"Not for one of us, sir."

She turned and left them without another word.

Ambrose said, "Extraordinary woman! I've never understood her. I doubt whether Clarissa did. And why this sudden concern for Simon? She's never shown any particular interest in the boy. Oh, well, we'd better get on with telephoning the police."

They made their way down the stairs and through the great hall. There preparations for the buffet supper was already under way. The long refectory table was covered with a cloth and rows of wineglasses were ranked at one end. The door to the dining room was open, and Cordelia could see Munter pulling the chairs from the table and putting them in line, presumably before carrying them into the hall.

Ambrose said, "Wait here a moment, will you?"

A minute later he was back. He said, "I've told Munter. He'll get down to the quay and prevent the launches from tying up."

They went together into the business room. Ambrose said, "If Cottringham were here, he'd probably insist on speaking to the chief constable personally. But I suppose the Speymouth police are the ones to ring. Ought I to ask for the C.I.D.?"

"I should just ring the Speymouth station and leave it to them. They'll know the procedure."

She looked up the number for him and waited while he got through. He gave the facts succinctly and without emotion, mentioning that Lady Ralston's jewel box was missing. Cordelia was interested that he had noticed its absence; nothing had been said about it while they were in the bedroom. There was a certain amount of delay from the other end of the line and then the crackle of a voice. She heard Ambrose say, "Yes, we've already done that," and, later, "That is what I propose doing as soon as I get off the line." Shortly afterward he put down the receiver and said, "Much as you expected. Lock the rooms. Don't touch anything. Keep people together. Don't let anyone land. They're sending a Chief Inspector Grogan."

In the theater the house lights were already on. A door to the left of the proscenium led backstage. From the open doors of the two main dressing rooms came laughter and a confusion of voices. Most of the cast had already changed and were now making up with a great deal of giggling advice from their friends. The atmosphere was reminiscent of an end-of-term frolic. Ambrose knocked on the closed doors of the two rooms reserved for the principals, then called out loudly, "Will you all come on stage please, immediately."

They tumbled out in an unruly bunch, some clutching their clothes around them. But one glance at his face silenced them, and they trooped onto the stage, subdued and expectant. Partly costumed and half made up as they were, their faces white except for the garish patches of rouge, they looked, thought Cordelia, like the clients and inmates of some Victorian bawdy house pulled out by the police for interrogation.

Ambrose said, "I'm afraid I have some very shocking news for you. Miss Lisle is dead. It looks very much like murder. I've telephoned the police and they'll be here shortly. In the meantime, they've asked that you all stay together here in the theater. Munter and his wife will bring you all some tea and coffee and anything else you need. Perhaps, Cottringham, you'd take charge here. There are still people I have to tell."

One of the women, a blonde, pert-faced girl dressed as a parlor maid in a frilled apron and goffered cap with long streamers, said, "But what about the play?"

It was a question born of shock which Cordelia thought she would probably remember with shame all her life. Someone gasped, and she blushed scarlet.

Ambrose said curtly, "The performance is canceled."

Then he turned on his heel and left.

Cordelia followed. She said, "What about the search parties?"

"I'll leave that to Ralston and Cottringham to sort out. I've told the cast to stay together. I can't cope with trying to enforce police instructions against the determination of the bereaved husband to demonstrate his competence. Where do you suppose are the rest of the party?" He sounded almost peevish.

Cordelia said, "I suppose Simon is swimming. Roma was in the library, but she's probably dressing by now. I imagine that Ivo is in his room, resting."

"See them, will you, and break the news. I'll go and find Simon. Then we'd better stay together until the police arrive. I suppose it would be courteous if I kept company with my guests in the theater, but I'm not in the mood to cope with a gaggle of agitated women all hurling questions at me."

Cordelia said, "The less they're told until the police arrive, the better."

He glanced at her with his sharp bright eyes. "I see. You mean we should keep quiet about the actual cause of death?"

"We don't know the actual cause of death. But, yes, I think we should say as little as possible to anyone."

"But surely the cause of death was obvious. Her face had been battered in."

"That may have been done after death. There was less blood than one would expect."

"There was more than enough blood for me. You're remarkably knowledgeable for a secretary-companion."

"I'm not a secretary-companion. I'm a private detective. There's no point in carrying on the charade any longer. Anyway, I know that you'd already guessed. And if you're going to say that I've been useless, I know that too."

"My dear Cordelia, what more could you have done? No one

could have expected murder. Stop blaming yourself. We're going to be stuck here together at least until the inquest, and it will be boring enough being grilled by the police without having you sunk in lugubrious self-reproach. It doesn't suit you."

They had reached the door which led from the arcade into the castle. Glancing around, they saw Simon in the distance, towel slung around his shoulders, making his way down the long grass slope which led upwards from the rose garden between the avenue of beeches to the crown of the island. Without speaking, Ambrose went to meet him. Cordelia stood in the shadow of the doorway and watched. Ambrose didn't hurry; his walk was little more than a leisurely stroll. The two figures came together and stood in the sun, their heads bent, their shadows staining the bright grass. They didn't touch. After a moment, still distanced, they began walking slowly toward the castle. Cordelia passed into the great hall. Coming down the staircase was Ivo with Roma at his side. He was in his dinner jacket; Roma was still wearing her trouser suit.

She called down to Cordelia, "Where is everyone? The place is dead as a morgue. I've just been telling Ivo I've no intention of changing and I'm not coming to the play. You two can do what you like, but I'm damned if I'll climb into an evening dress in the middle of a warm afternoon just to watch a bunch of amateurs make fools of themselves and pander to Clarissa's megalomania. You all indulge her nonsense as if you're terrified of her. Someone should put a stop to Clarissa."

Cordelia said, "Someone has."

They froze on the stairway, gazing down at her.

She said, "Clarissa's dead. Murdered."

And then her control broke. She gave a gasp and felt the hot tears coursing down her face. Ivo ran down to her and she felt his arms, thin and strong as steel rods, pulling her toward him. It was the first human contact, the first sympathetic gesture, which anyone had made since the shock of finding Clarissa's body, and the temptation to give way and cry like a child against his shoulder was almost irresistible.

But she gulped back her tears, fighting for control, while he held her gently without speaking. Looking up over his shoulder, she saw, through her tears, Roma's face hanging above her, a streaked amorphous pattern of white and pink. Then she blinked and the features came into focus: the mouth, so like Clarissa's, hanging loose; the eyes staring wide; the whole face blazing with an emotion which could have been terror or triumph.

She wasn't sure how long they stayed there, she locked in Ivo's arms, Roma staring down at them. Then she heard footsteps behind her. She broke free, murmuring over and over again, "I'm sorry. I'm sorry. I'm sorry."

Ambrose spoke: "Simon's gone to his room. He's very shocked and he wants to be alone. He'll be down as soon as he feels ready."

Ivo asked, "What happened? How did she die?"

Ambrose hesitated and Roma cried out, "You've got to tell us! I insist that you tell us!"

Ambrose looked at Cordelia. He gave a shrug of resigned apology. "Sorry, but I'm not prepared to do the work of the police. They have a right to know." He looked up at Roma. "She was battered to death. Her face has been smashed to pulp. It looks as if the weapon used was the limb of the dead princess. I haven't told Simon how she was killed and I think it better that he shouldn't know."

Roma sank down on the stairs and grasped the banister. She said, "Your marble? The killer took your marble? But why? How did he know it was there?"

Ambrose said, "He, or she, took it from the display cabinet some time before seven o'clock this morning. And I'm afraid that the police are only too likely to take the view that he knew it was there, because, yesterday before luncheon, I myself showed it to him."

# V

Ten minutes later Roma, Ivo, and Cordelia stood at the drawing-room window and looked down over the terrace to the landing stage. All three of them were now outwardly calm. The first shock had been replaced by a restlessness, almost an unhealthy prurient excitement, which they recognized in themselves and each other and which was as shaming as it was unexpected. They had all resisted the temptation to take alcohol, perhaps feeling that it would be unwise to face the police with its smell on their breath. But Munter had served strong coffee in the drawing room and it had been almost as effective.

Now they watched as the two heavily loaded launches rocked dangerously at the quayside, the passengers in their evening clothes crowding to one side like a gaudily clad cargo of aristocratic refugees fleeing from some republican holocaust. Ambrose was talking to them, with Munter standing at his shoulder like a second line of defense. There was a great deal of gesticulating. Even at this distance, Ambrose's pose, the slightly bent head, the spread hands, conveyed regret, distress, and some embarrassment. But he was standing firm. The sound of chattering came to them, faint but high like the squeaking of distant starlings. Cordelia said to Ivo, "They look restless. I expect they want to stretch their legs."

"Want to pee I expect, poor dears."

"There's someone standing up on the gunwale taking photographs. If he's not careful, he'll go overboard."

"That's Marcus Fleming. He's supposed to be taking the pictures to illustrate my article. Oh, well, he'll be able to phone a scoop of sorts to London if they don't capsize with excitement before they reach shore."

"The fat lady seems very determined, the one in mauve."

"That's Lady Cottringham, the formidable dowager. Ambrose had better watch her. If she gets one foot on the quay there'll be no holding her. She'll dash in to give poor Clarissa the once-over, subject us all to third degree, and solve the crime before the police get here. Ah, victory for Ambrose! The launches are pulling away."

Roma said quietly, "And here come the police."

Around the corner of the island came four bright wings of spray. Two sleek dark blue launches were approaching, their long wakes feathering the paler blue of the sea.

Roma said, "Odd that one feels so apprehensive. Stupid, too. It's like being a schoolgirl again. One always felt and looked most guilty when one was totally innocent."

Ivo said, "Totally? That's an enviable state. I've never managed to achieve it. But I shouldn't worry. The police have a formula for these occasions. The suspects are ranked in strict order of priority: first the husband, then the heirs, then the family, then close friends and acquaintances."

Roma said dryly, "As I'm both an heir and a relation, I can hardly find that reassuring."

They watched in silence as the two brightly laden launches drew clumsily away and those sleek blue hulls came rapidly closer.

# BOOK FOUR

•

# The Professionals

# I

Sergeant Robert Buckley was young, good-looking, and intelligent and well aware of these advantages. He was also, less commonly, aware of their limitations. He had gained three A-level subjects with respectable grades at the end of his two years in the sixth, an achievement which would have justified going on to university in company with friends similarly qualified. But it wouldn't have been the university of his choice. He suspected that his intelligence, although keen, was superficial, that he couldn't compete with real scholars, and he had no intention of joining the overeducated unemployed at the end of another three years of mildly boring academic grind. He judged that success would come quickest in a job for which he was over- rather than under-qualified and where he would be competing with men who were less rather than better educated than himself. He recognized in himself a streak of sadism which found a certain mild satisfaction in the pain of others without necessarily needing actively to inflict it.

Buckley was an only child of elderly parents who had begun by doting on him, moved on to admiring him, and had ended by being a little afraid of him. That too he found agreeable. His choice of career had been natural and easy, the final decision made while he was loping with long, easy strides over the Purbeck hills, watching the earth move in streaks of fawn and green. There had been only two possibilities, the army or the police, and he had quickly rejected the first. He was aware of some social insecurity; there were traditions, mores, a public-school ethos, about the army for which he felt a wary distrust. This was an alien world which might expose him, even reject him, before he had had a chance to master it. The police, on the other hand, given what he had to offer, ought to be pleased to have him. And to do them justice, they had been pleased.

Sitting now in the bow of the launch, he felt particularly pleased with the world and with himself. He made a practice of concealing his enthusiasm as he did his imagination. Both were like fascinating but wayward friends, to be enjoyed rarely and with caution since they had about them the taint of treachery. But as he watched Courcy Island steadily taking form and color across a dazzle of sea, he was aware of a heady mixture of exultation and fear. He exulted at the promise that here, at last, was the murder case of which he had dreamed since he had gained his sergeant's stripes. He feared that it might yet collapse, that they would be met at the jetty with those depressingly familiar words: "He's waiting for you upstairs. We've got someone watching him. He's in a terrible state. He says he doesn't know what came over him."

They never did know what came over them, those self-confessed murderers, as pathetic in defeat as they were incompetent in their killing. Murder, the unique and ultimate crime, was seldom the most interesting forensically or the most difficult to solve. But when you did get a good one there was no excitement like it: the heady combination of a manhunt with a puzzle; the smell of fear in the air, strong as the metallic smell of blood; the sense of randy well-being; the fascinating way in which confidence, personality, morale, subtly changed and deteriorated under its contaminating impact. A good murder was what police work was about. And this promised to be a good one.

He glanced across to where his chief sat, his red hair glinting in the sun. Grogan looked as he always did before a case, silent and withdrawn, the eyes hooded but wary, the muscles tensed under the well-cut tweed, the whole of that powerful body gathering its energies for action like the predator he was. When Buckley had been introduced to him three years earlier, he had been at once reminded of pictures in his boyhood comics of an Indian brave and had mentally crowned that carved and ruddy head with ceremonial feathers. But the comparison had in some subtle way been inaccurate. Grogan was too large a man, too English, and too complicated for so uncompromisingly simple an image. Buckley had only once been invited briefly into he stone cottage outside Speymouth where, separated from his wife, gan lived alone. It was rumored that he had a son and that there was some trouble with the boy; what exactly no one seemed to know. The cottage had revealed nothing. There were no pictures, no mementos of old cases, no photographs of family or colleagues, few books apart from what looked like a complete set of the Famous Trials series, little but bare stone walls and a bank of expensive stereo equipment. Grogan could have packed his bags and been out of it in half an hour, leaving nothing of himself behind. Buckley still didn't understand him, although after two years of working under him he knew what to expect: the alternate taciturnity and volubility during which he would use his sergeant as a sounding board, the occasional sarcasm, the ruthlessness, and the impatience. He only partly resented being used as a combination of clerk, shorthand writer, pupil, and audience. Grogan did too much of the work himself. But you could learn from him, he got results, he wasn't tainted with failure, and he was fair. And he was nearing retirement; only two years to go. Buckley took what he wanted from him and bided his time.

There were three figures waiting for them on the jetty, motionless as statues. Buckley guessed who two of them must be before the launches had chugged to a stop: Sir George Ralston, standing almost at attention in his old-fashioned shooting jacket; Ambrose Gorringe, more relaxed but incongruously formal in his dinner jacket. Both of them watched the arrivals disembark with wary formality like the commanders of a besieged castle awaiting the armistice negotiators and watching with undeluded eyes for the first hint of treachery. The third man, dark-clad and taller than the other two, was obviously some kind of servant. He stood a little behind them and gazed stolidly past them out to sea. His stance conveyed that certain guests were welcome on Courcy but that the police were not among them.

Grogan and Gorringe made the introductions. Buckley noticed that his chief expressed no sympathy, spoke no words of formal regret to the widower. But, then, he never did. He had once explained why: "It's offensively insincere, and they know it. There's enough duplicity in police work without adding to it. Some lies are insulting." And if Ralston or Gorringe noticed the omission, neither made a sign.

Ambrose Gorringe did all the talking. As they moved between

wide lawns toward the castle entrance, he said, "Sir George has organized a search of the castle and the island. The castle has been searched but the three groups covering the island aren't back yet."

"My men will take that over now, sir."

"So I supposed. The rest of the cast are in the theater. Sir Charles Cottringham would be glad of a word with you."

"Did he say what about?"

"No. Merely a matter, I imagine, of letting you know that he's here."

"I know that already. I'll see the body now, and then I'd be grateful for the use of a small and quiet room for the rest of the day and, possibly, until Monday."

"I thought that my business room would be the most suitable. If you will ring from Miss Lisle's room when you're ready, I'll show you where it is. And Munter will get you anything you need. My guests and I will be in the library when you want us."

They moved through a large hall and up the staircase. Buckley noticed nothing of his surroundings. He walked with Sir George immediately behind Grogan and Ambrose Gorringe and listened while Gorringe gave his chief a succinct but remarkably comprehensive account of the events leading up to Miss Lisle's death: how she came to be on the island; brief particulars of the rest of the house party; the threatening letters; the fact that she had thought it necessary to bring her own private detective with her, a Miss Cordelia Gray; the loss of the marble limb; the discovery of the body. It was an impressive performance, as carefully impersonal and factual as if it had been rehearsed. But, then, thought Buckley, it probably had.

Outside the door the party paused. Gorringe handed over three keys. He said, "I locked all three doors after the discovery of the body. These are the only keys. I take it you don't want us to come in."

Sir George spoke for the first time: "When you need me, Chief Inspector, I'll be with my wife's stepson in his room. Boy's upset. Natural in the circumstances. Munter knows where to find me." He turned abruptly and left them.

Grogan answered Gorringe's question. "You've been very helpful, sir. But I think we can manage here on our own."

She was an actress even in death. The scene in the bedroom was extraordinarily dramatic. Even the set had been cleverly designed for melodrama in the grand manner, the props glittering and ostentatious, the dominant color red. And there she lay, sprawled under the crimson canopy, one white leg carefully raised to show an expanse of thigh, her face plastered with artificial blood, while director and cameraman stepped around her, contemplating the best angles, careful not to touch or disturb that artfully provocative pose. Grogan stood at the right of the bed and looked down at her, frowning as if wondering whether the casting director had been right in choosing her for the role. Then he leaned down and sniffed at the skin of her arm. The moment was bizarre. Buckley thought: Is thy servant a dog that he should do this thing? Almost he expected her to shudder with outrage, sit up and stretch out groping hands, demand a towel to wipe the mess from her face.

The room was overcrowded but the experts in death—investigating officers, fingerprint officers, photographer, and scene-of-crime searchers—were adept at keeping out of each other's way. Grogan, as Buckley knew, had never reconciled himself to the use of civilian scene-of-crime officers, which was odd when you considered that he had come from the Met where the employment and training of civilians had gone about as far as it could go. But these two knew what they were about. They moved as delicately and confidently as a couple of cats prowling their familiar habitat. He had worked with both of them before, but he doubted whether he would recognize them in the street or the pub. He stood back out of the way and watched the senior of them. It was always their hands that he watched, hands sheathed in gloves so fine that they looked like a second glistening skin. Now those hands poured the remnants of the tea into a collecting flask; stoppered, sealed, and labeled it; gently eased the cup and saucer into a plastic bag; scraped a sample of blood from the marble limb and placed it in a specially prepared tube; took up the limb itself, touching it only with the tips of the fingers, and lowered it into a sterile box; delicately picked up a note with tweezers and insinuated that gently into its transparent envelope. At the bed his colleague was busy with magnifying glass and tweezers, collecting hairs from the pillow, seemingly oblivious of that shattered face. When the Home Office pathologist had completed his examination, the bedclothes would be bundled into a plastic bag, sealed, and added to the other exhibits.

Grogan said, "Doc Ellis-Jones is visiting his mother-in-law at Wareham, conveniently for us. They've sent an escort. He should be here within the next half hour. Not that there's much he can tell us that we can't see for ourselves. And the time of death is fixed within pretty tight limits anyway. If you reckon the loss of body heat on this kind of day at about one and a half degrees an hour for the first six hours, he's unlikely to be able to put it any closer than we already know, sometime between twenty past one when the girl left her alive, so Ambrose Gorringe tells us, and two-forty-three when the same girl found her dead. To be the last one to see the victim and the one to find the body suggests that Miss Cordelia Gray is either careless or unfortunate. We may be able to judge which when we see her."

Buckley said, "From the appearance of the blood, sir, I'd say that she died sooner rather than later."

"Yes. My guess would be within about thirty minutes of being left. That quotation under the marble limb. You recognized it, Sergeant?"

"No, sir."

"I'm relieved to hear it. From *The Duchess of Malfi,* so Ambrose Gorringe informs us, the play in which Miss Lisle was cast in the title role. 'Blood flies upwards and bedews the heavens.' I applaud the sentiment even if I couldn't identify the source. But it isn't particularly apposite. The blood didn't fly upwards, or not to any great extent. This systematic destruction of the face was done after death. And we know the possible reasons for that."

It was rather like a viva-voce examination, thought Buckley. But this question was an easy one.

"To conceal identity. To obscure the real cause of death. To make absolutely sure. An explosion of anger, hatred, or fear."

"And then, after that brainstorm of violence, our literary-minded murderer calmly replaces the eye pads. He has a sense of humor, Sergeant."

They moved together into the bathroom. Here was a compromise between period opulence and modern functionalism. The great bath was marble and encased in a mahogany surround. The seat of the lavatory was mahogany, too, with a high flush. The walls were tiled, each tile painted in blue with a different posy of wild flowers, and there was a cheval glass, its frame decorated with cherubs. But the towel rail was heated, there was a bidet, a shower had been installed above the bath, and a shelf over the handbasin held a formidable assortment of bath essences, powder, and expensive wrapped soaps.

Four white towels were untidily hung over the rail. Grogan sniffed each of them and rumpled them in his huge hands. He said, "It's a pity about that heated rail. They're completely dry. And so are the bath and handbasin. There's no way of telling whether she had time to bath before she was killed, not unless Doc Ellis-Jones can isolate traces of powder or bath essence from her skin, and even that wouldn't be conclusive. But the towels look as if they've been recently used and they're slightly scented. So is the body, and it's the same smell. My guess is that she did have time. She drank her tea, took off her makeup, and bathed. If Miss Gray left her at twenty past one, that would bring us to about twenty minutes to two."

The senior scene-of-crime officer was waiting at the door. Grogan stood aside for him, then went back into the bedroom and stood at the window, looking out to where a hairline of purple separated the darkening sea from the sky. He said, "Have you heard of the Birdhurst Rise Poisonings?"

"In Croydon, wasn't it, sir? Arsenic."

"Three members of the same middle-class family murdered with arsenic between April 1928 and March 1929, Edmund Duff, a retired colonial civil servant, his sister-in-law, and her widowed mother. In each case the poison must have been administered in food or medicine. It could only have been a member of the family or the household, but the police never made an arrest. It's a fallacy to suppose that a small circle of suspects, all known to each other, makes a case easier to solve. It doesn't; it only makes failure indefensible."

*Failure* wasn't a word which Buckley could remember having heard before on Grogan's lips. His euphoria gave way to a small weight of anxiety. He thought of Sir Charles Cottringham, even now cooling his heels in the theater, of the chief constable, of Monday's publicity. "Baronet's Wife Battered to Death in Island Castle." "Well-known Actress Slain." This wasn't a case which any officer ambitious for his future could afford to lose. He wondered what it had been about this room, this victim, this weapon, perhaps the air of Courcy Island itself, which had evoked that depressing note of caution.

For a moment neither of them spoke. Then there was a sudden roar and a speedboat rounded the eastern tip of the island and swept a wide, curving wake toward the quay.

Grogan said, "Doc Ellis-Jones is making his usual dramatic appearance. Once he's told us what we already know, that she's a female and she's dead, and has explained what we can work out for ourselves, that it wasn't accident or suicide and it happened between one-twenty and two-forty-three, we can get down to the business of finding out what our suspects have to say for themselves, beginning with the baronet."

## II

It was nearly half past four, and Ambrose, Ivo, Roma, and Cordelia were standing together on the jetty looking out to sea as *Shearwater*, taking the cast back to Speymouth, moved beyond the eastern tip of the island and out of sight.

Ambrose said, "Well, they may have been done out of their moment in the spotlight, but they can't complain that the day has been dull. Clarissa's murder will be all over the county by dinner time. That means we can expect a press invasion by dawn."

Ivo said, "What will you do?"

"Prevent anyone from landing, although not with the brutal effectiveness of de Courcy at the time of the plague. But the island is private property. And I'll instruct Munter to refer all telephone inquiries to the police at Speymouth. They've presumably got a public-relations department. Let them cope."

Cordelia, still in her cotton dress, shivered. The bright day was beginning to fade. Soon would come that transitory and lovely moment when the setting sun shines with its last and brightest rays, intensifying the color of grass and trees so that the air itself is stained with greenness. Now the shadows lay long and heavy over the terrace. The Saturday sailors had turned for home and the sea stretched in an empty calm. Only the two police launches rocked gently against the quay, and the smooth bricks of the castle walls and turrets, which for a moment had glowed with a richer red, darkened and reared above them, ponderous and forbidding.

As they passed through the great hall, the castle received them in an unnatural silence. Somewhere upstairs the police were busy with their secret expertise of death. Sir George was either being questioned or was with Simon in his room. No one seemed to know and no one liked to ask. The four of them, still awaiting their formal questioning, turned by common consent into the library. It might be less comfortable than the drawing room, but at least it offered plenty of material for those who chose to pretend that they wanted to read. Ivo took the only easy chair and lay back with his eyes turned to the ceiling, his long legs stretched. Cordelia sat at the chart table and slowly turned the pages of an 1876 bound copy of *The Illustrated London News*. Ambrose stood with his back to them, looking out over the lawn. Roma was the most restless, regularly pacing between the bookshelves like a prisoner under compulsory exercise. It was a relief when Munter and his wife brought in the tea, the heavy silver teapot, the brass kettle with the wick burning under it, the Minton tea service.

Munter drew the curtains across the tall windows and put a match to the fire. It crackled into life. Paradoxically, the library became at once cozier but more oppressive, enclosed in its shadowed hermetic calm. They were all thirsty. No one had much appetite, but ever since the finding of the body they had craved the comfort and stimulus of strong tea or coffee, and busying themselves with cups and saucers at least gave them something to do.

Ambrose settled himself beside Cordelia. Stirring his tea, he said, "Ivo, you have all the London gossip. Tell us about this man Grogan. I confess that, on first acquaintance, I don't take to him."

"No one has all the London gossip. London, as you very well know, is a collection of villages, socially, occupationally, as well as geographically. But theatrical gossip and police gossip do occasionally overlap. There's an affinity between detectives and actors as there is between surgeons and actors."

"Spare us the dissertation. What do you know about him? You've spoken to someone, I suppose?"

"I admit I did telephone a contact; from this room actually, while you were busy receiving Grogan and his minions. The story is that he resigned from the Met because he was disgusted with the corruption in the C.I.D. That, of course, was before the latest purge. He is, apparently, a proper William Morris man: 'No more now my knight, or God's knight any longer, you / Being than they so much more white, so much more pure and good and true.' That should reassure you, Roma."

"Nothing about the police reassures me."

Ambrose said, "I suppose I'd better be careful about offering him a drink. It could be construed as an attempt to bribe or corrupt. I wonder if the chief constable, or whoever it is who decides these things, sent him here to fail."

Roma said sharply, "Why should anyone do that?"

"Better the incomer than one of your own men. And he could very easily fail. This is a storybook killing: a close circle of suspects, isolated scene of crime conveniently cut off from the mainland, known *terminus a quo* and *terminus ad quem*. It should be perfectly possible to tie it up—that's the jargon, isn't it?—within a week. Everyone will expect it to be solved quickly. But if the killer keeps his head clear and his mouth shut, I very much doubt whether he or she is in real danger. All he needs to do—let's be chivalrous and assume it's a man—is to stick to his story; never excuse, never embellish, never explain. It isn't what the police know or suspect; it's what they can prove."

Roma said, "You sound as though you don't want it solved."

"Without having strong feelings on the matter, I should prefer to have it solved. It would be tedious to spend the rest of one's life as a suspected murderer."

"It'll bring in the summer tourists, though, won't it? People love blood and horror. You'll be able to show the scene of the crime—for an extra twenty pence, of course."

Ambrose said easily, "I don't pander to sensationalism. That's why summer visitors don't get shown the crypt. And this is a murder in poor taste."

"But aren't all murders in poor taste?"

"Not necessarily. It would make a good parlor game, classifying the classical murder cases according to their degree of tastelessness. But this one strikes me as particularly bizarre, extravagant, theatrical."

Roma had drained her first cup of tea and was pouring a second. "Well, that's appropriate enough." She added, "It's odd that we've been left here alone, isn't it? I thought that there'd be a plainclothes underling sitting in and taking a note of all our indiscretions."

"The police know the limit of their territory and of their powers. I've given them the use of the business room and, naturally, they've locked the two guest rooms. But this is still my house and my library and they come in here by invitation. Until they decide to charge someone, we're all entitled to be treated as innocent. Even Ralston, presumably, although as husband he has to be elevated to chief suspect. Poor George! If he really loved her, this must be hell for him."

Roma said, "He stopped loving her six months after the wedding. He must have known by then that she wasn't capable of fidelity."

Ambrose asked, "He never showed the least sign, did he?"

"Not to me, but then I hardly ever saw them. And what could he do, faced with that particular insubordination? You can hardly deal with an unfaithful wife as if she were a recalcitrant subaltern. I don't suppose he liked it. But if he didn't kill her, and I don't for one moment believe that he did, he's probably not entirely ungrateful to whoever did. The money will come in useful to subsidize that fascist organization he runs. The Union of British Patriots, U.B.P. Wouldn't you know from the name that it's a fascist front?"

Ambrose smiled. "Well, I wouldn't expect it to be full of Trots and international socialists certainly. It's harmless enough. A *Boys' Own Paper* mentality and a geriatric army."

Roma slammed down her cup and began again her restless pacing.

"My God, you're good at deceiving yourselves, aren't you? It's nasty, it's embarrassing, and most unforgivable of all, the people concerned actually take themselves seriously. They really believe in their dangerous nonsense. So let's all laugh at it, and perhaps it will go away. When the chips are down, who do you think this geriatric army are going to be defending? The poor bloody proles? Not likely!"

"I rather hope they'll be defending me."

"Oh, they will, Ambrose, they will! You and the multinational corporations, the establishment, the press barons. Clarissa's money will do its bit toward keeping the rich man in his castle, the poor man at his gate."

Ambrose said mischievously, "But don't you get some of the money? And won't it come in useful to you?"

"Of course; money always does. But it isn't important. I'll be glad enough of it, I suppose, when it actually comes, but I don't need it. It certainly isn't important enough to kill for. Come to that, I don't know what is."

"Oh, come on, Roma, don't be naive! A cursory read of the daily papers will tell you what people find important enough to kill for. Dangerous and destructive emotions, to begin with. Love, for example."

Munter was at the door, He coughed, rather, thought Cordelia, like a stock butler in a play, and said, "The Home Office pathologist, Dr. Ellis-Jones, has arrived, sir."

Ambrose looked for a moment distracted as if wondering whether he was expected to greet the newcomer formally. He said, "I'd better come, I suppose. Do the police know he's here?"

"Not yet, sir. I thought it right to inform you first."

"Where is he, the pathologist?"

"In the great hall, sir."

"Well, we can't keep him waiting. You'd better take him to Chief Inspector Grogan. I suppose there are things he may need. Hot water, for example." He looked vaguely around as if expecting a jug and basin to materialize from the air. Munter disappeared.

Ivo murmured, "You make it sound like a childbirth."

Roma swung around; her tone was a mixture of the peevish and appalled. "But surely he's not going to do the postmortem here!"

They all looked at Cordelia. She thought that Ambrose must surely know the procedure, but he too gazed at her with a look of bland, almost amused inquiry.

She said, "No. He'll just do a preliminary examination at what they call the scene of the crime. He'll take the temperature of the body, try to estimate the time of death. Then they'll take her away. They don't like to move the body until the forensic pathologist has seen it and certified that life is extinct."

Roma Lisle said, "What a lot of curious information you have acquired for a girl who calls herself a secretary-companion. But of course, I forgot. You're not a secretary-companion. Ambrose tells us that you're a private eye. So perhaps you'll explain why we've all had to have our fingerprints taken. I found it particularly offensive, the way they take hold of your fingers and press them down on the pad. It wouldn't be so repulsive if you were allowed to do it yourself."

Cordelia said, "Didn't the police explain the reason? If they find any prints in Clarissa's room, they want to be able to eliminate ours."

"Or identify them. And what else are they doing, apart from grilling George? God knows they've brought enough men with them."

"Some of them are probably scientific officers from the forensic science laboratory. Or they may be what are called scene-of-crime officers. They'll collect the scientific evidence, samples of blood and body fluids. They'll take away the bedclothes and the cup and saucer. And they'll analyze the dregs of tea to find out if she was poisoned. She could have been drugged before she was killed. She was lying very peaceably on her back."

Roma said, "It didn't need a drug for Clarissa to lie peaceably on her back." Then she saw their faces. Her own went scarlet and she cried, "I'm sorry! I shouldn't have said that. It's just that I can't really believe it; I can't picture her lying there, battered to death. I haven't that kind of imagination. She was alive. Now she's dead. I didn't like her and she didn't like me. Death can't alter that for either of us." She almost stumbled to the door. "I'm going for a walk. I've got to get out of this place. If Grogan wants me, he can come and find me."

Ambrose refilled the teapot and poured himself another cup, then seated himself leisurely next to Cordelia.

"That's what surprises me about political commitment. Her cousin, the woman she was practically brought up with, is messily done to death and will shortly be carted off to be scientifically carved up by a Home Office pathologist. She's shocked, obviously. But basically she cares as little as if she'd been told that Clarissa is inconvenienced by a mild attack of fibrositis. But one mention of poor Ralston's Union of British Patriots and she's hysterical with outrage."

Ivo said, "She's frightened."

"That's obvious, but what of? Not that pathetic bunch of amateur warriors."

"They frighten me occasionally. I suppose she was right about the money and Ralston will get most of it. How much is that?"

"My dear Ivo, I don't know. Clarissa never confided the details of her personal finances; we weren't that close."

"I rather thought you were."

"And even if we had been, I doubt whether she would have told. That's one surprising fact about Clarissa. You won't believe this but it's true. She loved to gossip, but she could keep a secret when she wanted to. Clarissa liked hoarding, and that included nuggets of useful information."

Ivo said lightly, "How unexpected, and how very dangerous."

Cordelia looked at them, at Ambrose's bright malicious eyes, at Ivo's barely covered skeleton angularly disposed in his chair, at the long bony hands drooping from wrists which looked too thin and brittle to hold them, at the putty-colored face with its jutting bones turned upward to the stuccoed ceiling. She was seized with a confusion of feelings: anger, a deep unfocused pity, and a less familiar emotion which she recognized as envy. They were so secure in their sardonic, half-humorous detachment. Could anything really touch their hearts or nerves except the possibility of their own pain? And even physical pain, that universal leveler, they would meet with wry disgust or derisive contempt. Wasn't that how Ivo was facing his own death? Why should she expect them to grieve because a woman neither of them had greatly liked was lying upstairs with her face smashed in? And yet it wasn't necessary to affirm Donne's overworked aphorism to feel that something was owed to a death, that something in their relationships, in the castle itself, in the very air they breathed, had been touched and subtly altered.

Suddenly she felt very alone and very young. She was aware of Ambrose looking at her. As if he had read her thoughts he said, "Part of the horror of murder is that it does the dead out of their rights. I don't suppose anyone in this room is personally desolated by Clarissa's death. But if she'd died a natural death, at least we'd be mourning her in the sense that we'd be thinking of her with that confused mixture of regret, sentimentality, and sympathetic interest which is the normal tribute to the recently dead. As it is, all we're thinking of is ourselves. Well, aren't we? Aren't we?"

Ivo said, "I don't think Cordelia is."

The library enclosed them again in its silence. But their ears were abnormally alert to every creak, and three heads jerked upwards simultaneously at the sound of muffled footfalls across the hall and the distant thud, faint but unmistakable, of a closing door.

Ivo said quietly, "I think they're taking her away."

He moved silently behind one of the curtains and Cordelia followed. Between the wide lawns, frosted by moonlight, four dark and elongated figures, shadowless as phantoms, bent to their task. Behind them paced Sir George, stiff-legged and erect, as if his sword clanked at his side. The small procession looked like a group of mourners surreptitiously burying their dead according to some esoteric and prohibited rite. Cordelia, drained by shock and tiredness, wished she could feel some personal and appropriate response of pity. But there came into her mind instead a whisper of atavistic horror, images of plague and secret murder, de Courcy's men disposing of his victims under the cloak of night. It seemed to her that Ivo had stopped breathing. He didn't speak, but she sensed through the contact of his rigid shoulder the intensity of his gaze.

Then the curtains parted and Ambrose stood behind them. He said, "She arrived in the morning sun and leaves by moonlight. But I should be out there. Grogan should have told me they were ready to take her away. Really, that man's behavior is becoming intolerable!"

And so it was, thought Cordelia, that Clarissa left on her final journey from Courcy Island, on that note of slightly peevish complaint.

An hour later the door opened and Sir George came in. He must have been aware of their inquiring looks, of the question which no one cared to ask. He said, "Grogan was perfectly civil, but I don't think he's formed any theories. I suppose he knows his business. That red hair must be a disadvantage—disguise, you know."

Ambrose said gravely, controlling the twitching of his mouth, "I think detection at his level is chiefly desk work. I don't suppose he does much lurking in the undergrowth."

"Must do some fieldwork, keep his hand in. He could dye it, I suppose."

He picked up *The Spectator* and settled himself at the chart table, as much at ease as if he were in his London club. The others stood and regarded him in baffled silence. Cordelia thought, We're behaving like candidates at an oral examination who'd rather like to know what questions to expect but feel that it would be taking an unfair advantage actually to ask.

The same thought must have struck Ivo. He said, "The police aren't running a competition for their favorite suspect of the year. I confess to some curiosity about their strategy and technique. Reviewing Agatha Christie at the Vaudeville is poor preparation for the real thing. So how did it go, Ralston?"

Sir George looked up from his journal and appeared to give the question serious thought. "Much as you'd expect. Where exactly was I and what was I doing this afternoon? I told them I was bird-watching on the west cliffs. Told them, too, that I'd seen Simon coming ashore through my binoculars on the way home. Seemed to think that was important. Asked about Clarissa's money. How much? Who gets it? Grogan wasted twenty minutes asking me about bird life on Courcy. Trying to put me at my ease, I suppose. A bit odd, I thought."

Ivo said, "Trying to catch you out more likely with cunning traps about the nesting habits of nonexistent species. What about this morning? Are we expected to detail every waking moment of the day?" His voice was carefully casual, but all four of them knew what it was he was asking and the importance of the reply.

Sir George took up his journal again. Without looking up he said, "Didn't say more than I needed. Told them about the visit to the church and the Devil's Kettle. Mentioned the drowning but didn't give names. No point in confusing the investigation with old history. Not their concern."

Ivo said, "You reassure me. That's rather the line I propose to take. I'll have a word with Roma when the opportunity arises, and you, Ambrose, might speak to the boy. As Ralston says, there's no point in confusing them with old, unhappy, far-off things and battles long ago."

No one replied, but Sir George suddenly looked up over his journal. "Sorry, I forgot. They want to see you now, Cordelia."

# III

Cordelia could understand why Ambrose had offered the business room for the use of the police. It was appropriately furnished as an office, it wasn't too large, and it kept them well out of his way. But as she seated herself in the mahogany-and-cane chair and faced Chief Inspector Grogan across the desk, she wished that Ambrose had chosen any room other than this private museum of murder. The Staffordshire figures on the wall shelf behind Grogan's head seemed to have grown, no longer quaintly fashioned antiques but real people, their bland painted faces glowing and twisting into life. And the framed Victorian broadsheets with their crudely drawn scaffolds and death cells were intrusive in their horror, stark celebrations of the cruelty of man to man. The room itself was smaller than she remembered, and she felt herself closeted with her interrogators in frightening and claustrophobic proximity. She was only half aware that there was a uniformed woman police officer sitting almost motionless in the corner by the window, watchful as a chaperone. Did they think that she would faint or accuse Grogan of assaulting her? She wondered briefly whether it was the same anonymous officer who had helped move her clothes and belongings from the De Morgan room to her new bedroom. She had no doubt that they had been thoroughly examined before being neatly arranged on the bed.

She found herself studying Grogan for the first time. He seemed even larger than the tall, broad figure she had first watched alighting from the police launch. The strong red-gold hair was longer than one would expect on a police officer; one swath fell across his forehead and from time to time he would sweep it back with a huge hand. Despite its size, his face with its jutting cheekbones and deep-set eyes gave an impression of gauntness. Under each cheekbone a brush of hair increased the sense of rough animality, an impression oddly at variance with the excellent cut of his formal tweed suit. His skin was ruddy so that his whole appearance was of redness; even the whites of his eyes seemed bloodshot. When he moved his head, Cordelia could glimpse, under his immaculate collar, the clear dividing line between the sunburned face and his white neck. It was so marked that he looked like a man who has been decapitated and joined together again. She tried to imagine him, red-bearded, as an Elizabethan adventurer, but the image was subtly wrong. For all his strength, he wouldn't have been found among the men of action but secretly scheming in the closets of power. Might he perhaps have been discovered in that dreaded room at the Tower, working the levers of the rack? But that was unfair. She thrust the morbid images out of her mind and made herself remember what he in fact was: a twentieth-century senior police officer, bound by force regulations, restricted by Judges' Rules, doing a vital if disagreeable job, and entitled to her cooperation. Yet she wished that she weren't so frightened. She had expected to feel anxiety, but not this rush of humiliating terror. She managed to master it but was miserably aware that Grogan, experienced as he was, had recognized it and that it wasn't unwelcome to him.

He listened in silence while, at his request, she recounted the sequence of events between the arrival of Sir George at Kingly Street and her discovery of Clarissa's body. She had handed over the collection of messages and they were spread out on the desk before him. From time to time, as her quiet voice rose and fell, he shifted them about as if searching for some meaningful pattern. She was glad that she wasn't wired up to a lie detector. Surely the needle must have leaped as she came to those moments when, although she told no direct untruth, she carefully omitted the facts which she had decided not to tell: the death of Tolly's child, Clarissa's disclosure in the Devil's Kettle, Roma's unsuccessful appeal to her cousin for money. She didn't try to justify these suppressions by pretending that they wouldn't be of interest to him. She was too tired now to make up her mind about the morality of her decision. She only knew that, even when recalling Clarissa's battered face, there were things that she couldn't bring herself to tell.

He made her go over her story again and again, particularly pressing her about the locking of the bedroom doors. Was she absolutely certain that she had heard Clarissa turn her key? How could she be so sure that she had, in fact, locked her own door? Sometimes she wondered whether he were deliberately trying to confuse her as a counsel for the defense might, pretending to be obtuse, pretending that he hadn't quite understood. She was increasingly aware of her own tiredness, of his strong hand lying in the pool of light from the desk lamp, the ruddy hair gleaming on the back of his fingers, of the soft rustle as Sergeant Buckley turned the page. She must have been speaking for well over an hour before he finished the long interrogation and both their voices fell silent.

Then he said suddenly, as if rousing himself from boredom, "So you call yourself a detective, Miss Gray?"

"I don't call myself anything. I own and run a detective agency."

"That's a nice distinction. But we haven't time to go into it now. You tell me that Sir George Ralston employed you as a detective. That's why you were here when his wife died. Suppose you tell me what you've detected so far."

"I was employed to look after his wife. I let her be killed."

"Now, let's get this straight. Are you telling me that you stood by and let someone kill her?"

"No."

"Or killed her yourself?"

"No."

"Or encouraged, or helped, or paid anyone else to kill her?"

"No."

"Then stop feeling sorry for yourself. Presumably you didn't think she was in any real danger. Nor did her husband. Nor did the Metropolitan Police apparently."

Cordelia said, "I thought that they might have had a reason for skepticism."

His eyes were suddenly sharp. "You did?"

"I wondered whether Miss Lisle sent one of the notes herself, the one typed on her husband's typewriter. He was in America at the time, so he couldn't have posted it to her himself."

"And why should she do that?"

"To try to exonerate Sir George. I think she was afraid that the police might suspect him. Don't they usually think of the husband first? She wanted to make sure that he was in the clear, perhaps because she didn't want the police to waste their time on him, perhaps because she genuinely knew that he wasn't guilty. I think the Metropolitan Police might have suspected that she sent the message herself."

Grogan said, "They did more than suspect it. They tested the saliva on the flap of the envelope. It belonged to a secretor with the same blood group as Miss Lisle, and that group is rare. They asked her to type an innocuous note for them, a message which had some of the same letters and in the same order as the quotation. On that evidence they suggested, tactfully, that she might have sent the note. She denied it. But you could hardly expect them to take the death threats very seriously after that."

So she had been right. Clarissa had sent that one message. But she might be wrong about the reason. It had, after all, been clumsily done, and had it really exonerated Sir George? But it had ensured that the police took no further interest in what they must have seen as the time-wasting mischief of an attention-seeking and probably neurotic woman. And that would have suited the real culprit very well. Had anyone suggested to Clarissa that she should send that one note herself? And had it been the only one for which she had been responsible? Could the whole sequence of quotations be an elaborate conspiracy between herself and one other person? Cordelia rejected that theory almost as soon as it came into her mind. Of one thing she was sure: Clarissa had dreaded the arrival of the messages. No actress could have simulated that fear. She had been convinced that she would die. And she had died.

Cordelia was aware that the two men were looking at her intently. She had been sitting silently, hands curved in her lap, eyes lowered, occupied with thought. She waited for them to break the silence, and when the chief inspector spoke she thought she could detect a different note in his voice which could have been respect.

"Did you deduce anything else about these notes?"

"I thought that they might have been sent by two different people, apart from Miss Lisle, I mean. I wasn't shown the first half dozen which she received. I thought it possible that they might have been different from the later communications. And most of the ones I saw, the ones I've handed over to you, can be found in the *Penguin Dictionary of Quotations.* I think that whoever typed them had that book in front of him and typed them from the text."

"On different machines?"

"That wouldn't be difficult. They aren't new machines and the makes are different. There are numerous shops in London and the suburbs which sell new and reconditioned typewriters and which put out a machine or two for people to try. It would be almost impossible to trace a machine if one went from shop to shop and typed a few lines in each."

"And who do you suggest did?"

"I don't know."

"And what about the original anonymous correspondent, the one you might say who had the bright idea in the first place?"

"I don't know that either."

That was as far as she was willing to go. She had told them enough, perhaps too much. If they wanted motives, let them grub around for themselves. And there was one motive for the poison pen that she would never divulge. If Ivo Whittingham had kept silent about Tolly's tragedy, so would she.

And then Grogan was speaking again, leaning over the desk toward her so that the powerful body, the strong coarse voice, surged toward her, palpable as a force.

"Let's get one thing straight, shall we? Miss Lisle was battered to death. You know what happened to her. You saw the body. Now, she may not have been a good or likable woman. That has nothing to do with it. She had as much right to live her life to the last natural moment as you or I or any creature under the Queen's peace."

"Of course. I don't see why that needs saying." Why did her own voice sound so small, almost peevish?

"You'd be surprised what needs saying in a murder investigation.

It's the most powerful mutual protection society in the world, the trade union of the living. It's the living you'll be thinking about, wanting to protect, yourself most of all, of course. My job is to think of her."

"You can't bring her back." The words, torn out of her, fell between them in all their sad banality.

"No, but I can stop someone else from going the same way. No one is more dangerous than a successful murderer. I'm boring you with platitudes because I want you to get one thing straight. You may be too bright for your own good, Miss Gray. You're not here to solve this crime. That's my job. You're not here to protect the living. Leave that to their lawyers. You're not even here to protect the dead. They're beyond needing your condescension. *On doit des égards aux vivants; on ne doit aux morts que la vérité*. You're an educated young woman. You know what that means."

" 'We owe respect to the living; to the dead we owe only the truth.' It's Voltaire, isn't it? But I was taught a different pronunciation."

As soon as the words were out she was ashamed. But to her surprise his only response was a bellow of laughter. "I bet you were, Miss Gray. I bet you were. I taught myself with a primer and a key to phonetics. But think about it. There's no better motto for a detective, and that includes female private eyes who would like to help the police but still be able to lie abed with a good conscience. It can't be done, Miss Gray. It can't be done."

She didn't reply. After a moment Grogan said, "What surprises me a little, Miss Gray, is how much you noticed and how carefully when you found the body. Most people, and not only young women, would have been in a state of shock."

Cordelia thought that he was entitled to the truth, or as much as she herself understood of it. "I know. That has surprised me too. I think what happened was that I couldn't bear to feel too much emotion. It was so horrible that it was almost unreal. My intellect took over and made it into a kind of detective puzzle because, if I hadn't concentrated on detaching myself from the horror, examining the room, noticing little things like the lipstick smear on the cup, it would have been unbearable. Perhaps that's how doctors feel at the scene of an accident. You have to keep your mind on procedures and techniques because, otherwise, you might realize that what you have lying there is a human being."

Sergeant Buckley said quietly, "It's how a policeman trains himself to behave at the scene of an accident. Or a murder."

Without taking his eyes from Cordelia, Grogan said, "You find that credible, then, do you, Sergeant?"

"Yes, sir."

Fear sharpens perception as well as the senses. Glancing at Sergeant Buckley's handsome, rather heavy face, at the controlled, self-satisfied smile, Cordelia doubted whether he had ever in his life needed such an expedient against pain and wondered whether he was trying to signal his sympathy or was colluding with his superior in some prearranged interrogatory ploy.

The chief inspector said, "And what exactly did your intellect deduce when it had so conveniently taken over from your emotions?"

"The obvious things: that the curtains had been drawn although they weren't when I left, that the jewel box was missing, that the tea had been drunk. And I thought it odd that Miss Lisle had cleaned the makeup from her face but that there was a lipstick stain on the cup. That surprised me. I think she has—she had—sensitive lips and used a creamy lipstick which smears easily. So why hadn't it come off when she ate her lunch? It looked as if she must have made up her lips again before she drank her tea. But if so, why had she taken off the rest of her makeup? The balls of stained cotton wool were all over the dressing-table top. And I noticed that there wasn't as much blood as one would expect from a head wound. I thought it possible that she might have been killed some other way and the injuries to her face made afterward. And I was puzzled about the pads over her eyes. They must have been put there after death. I mean, it wouldn't be possible for them to stay so neatly in place while her face was being destroyed."

After she finished there was a long silence. Then Grogan said, his voice expressionless, "You're sitting on the wrong side of the desk, Miss Gray."

Cordelia waited. Then she said, hoping that she wasn't doing more harm than good, "There's one thing more I ought to tell you. I know that Sir George can't have killed his wife. I'm sure that you wouldn't suspect him, anyway, but there is something you should know. When he first arrived in the bedroom and I blurted out how sorry I was, he looked at me with a kind of amazed horror. I realized that he thought for a moment that I'd killed her, that I was confessing."

"And you weren't?"

"Not to murder. Only to failure to do what I was here for."

He changed the tack of his questioning again. "Let's go back to the Friday night, the time when you were with Miss Lisle in her room and she showed you the secret drawer in her jewel box. That review of the Rattigan play. Are you sure that that is what it in fact was?"

"Quite sure."

"The paper wasn't a document or a letter?"

"It was a newspaper cutting. And I read the headline."

"And at no time did your client—and she was your client, remember—ever give you the least indication that she knew or suspected who it was who was threatening her?"

"No, never."

"And she had no enemies as far as you know?"

"None that she told me of."

"And you yourself can throw no light on why and by whom she was killed?"

"No."

It must, she thought, feel like this to be in the witness box: the careful questions, the even more careful answers, the longing to be released.

He said, "Thank you, Miss Gray. You've been helpful. Not, perhaps, as helpful as I'd hoped. But helpful. And it's early days yet. We shall be talking again."

# IV

After Cordelia left, Grogan relaxed in his chair.

"Well, what do you think of her?"

Buckley hesitated, uncertain whether his chief wanted assessment of the last interviewee as a woman or as a suspect. He said cautiously, "She's attractive. Like a cat." Since this evoked no immediate response, he added, "Self-contained and dignified."

He was rather pleased with the description. It had, he thought, a certain cleverness while committing him to nothing. Grogan began doodling on the blank sheet in front of him, a complicated mathematical design of triangles, squares, and precisely interlacing circles spread over the page and reminding Buckley of the more obscure of his school geometry problems. He found it difficult not to fix his eyes obsessively on isosceles triangles and bisecting arcs. He said, "Do you think she did it, sir?"

Grogan began filling in his design. "If she did, it was during those fifty-odd minutes when she claims she was taking the sun on the bottom step of the terrace, conveniently out of sight and sound. She had time and opportunity. We've only her word that she locked her bedroom door or that Miss Lisle actually locked hers. And even if both doors and the communicating one were locked, Gray is probably the only person Lisle would have let in. She knew where the marble was kept. She was up and about early this morning when Gorringe first discovered that it was missing. She had a locked cabinet in her room where she could have kept it safely hidden. And we know that the final message, like the one typed on the back of the woodcut, was typed on Gorringe's machine. Gray can type and she had access to the business room where it's kept. She's intelligent, and she can keep her head even when I'm trying to needle her into losing it. If she did have a hand in it, my guess is that it was as Ralston's accomplice. His explanation of why she was called in sounded contrived. Did you notice how she and Ralston gave almost identical accounts of his visit to

Kingly Street, what he said, what she said? It was so neat it could have been rehearsed. It probably was."

But Buckley could think of an objection and he voiced it. "Sir George was a soldier. He's used to getting his facts right. And she has a good memory, particularly for important events. And that visit was important. He probably paid well, and it could have led to other jobs. The fact that they gave the same account, got the details right, speaks as much for innocence as guilt."

"According to both of them, that's the first time they met. If they are conspirators, they must have got together before then. Whatever there is between them, it shouldn't be too difficult to grub it out."

"They're an unlikely couple. I mean, it's difficult to see what they have in common."

"Politics rather than bed, I imagine. Although, when it comes to sex, nothing is too bizarre to be ruled out. Police work teaches you that if nothing else. She could have taken a fancy to being Lady Ralston. There must be easier ways of getting money than running a detective agency. And Ralston will have money, remember. His wife's, to be specific. And I don't suppose that will come before it's needed. He must be spending a packet on that organization of his—the U.B.P. or whatever they call it. And that's an odd business if you like. I suppose you can argue a case for an amateur force trained and ready to support the civil power in an emergency, but isn't that what General Walker has in hand? So what exactly do George Ralston and his geriatric conspirators think they're up to?"

As Buckley didn't know the answer and had, in fact, hardly heard of the Union of British Patriots, he wisely kept silent. Then he said, "Did you believe Gray when she said that Sir George thought that she was confessing?"

"What Miss Gray thought she saw in Sir George's face isn't evidence. And no doubt he did look amazed if he thought he heard her confessing to a murder he'd done himself."

Buckley thought about the girl who had just left them, saw again that gentle, uplifted face, the immense and resolute eyes, the delicate hands folded like a child's in her lap. She was keeping something back, of course; but didn't they all? That didn't make her a murderess. And the idea of her and Ralston together was ludicrous and disgusting. Surely the chief hadn't yet reached the age when he needed to start believing that pathetic old lie with which the middle-aged and the elderly deceive themselves, that the young find them physically attractive. What they can do, the old goats, he told himself, is to buy youth and sex with money and power and prestige. But he didn't believe that Sir George Ralston was in that market or that Cordelia Gray could be bought. He said stolidly, "I can't see Miss Gray as a murderess."

"It takes an effort of the imagination, I grant you. But that's probably what Mr. Blady thought of Miss Blady. Or L'Angelier of Miss Madeleine Smith, come to that, before she so unkindly handed him his cocoa and arsenic through the basement railings."

"Wasn't there a verdict of not proven in that case, sir?"

"A fainthearted Glasgow jury who should have known better and probably did. But we're theorizing in advance of facts. We need the postmortem result, and we need to know what, if anything, was in that tea. Doc Ellis-Jones will probably get her on the slab tomorrow, Sunday or no Sunday. Once he's got his hands on the body he's quick enough at his butchering, I'll say that for him."

"And the lab, sir. How long are they likely to take?"

"God knows. It's not as if we've any idea what they're supposed to be looking for. There isn't an unlimited number of drugs which can put you out, or kill you, within a short time and with no obvious signs on the body. But there are enough to keep them busy for the next few days if this is the only murder on the stocks. We may get a clue from the p.m., of course. Meanwhile we get on with the London end. How well did any of these people know each other before they arrived on the island this weekend? What, if anything, do the Met know about Cordelia Gray and her agency? What did Simon Lessing really feel about his benefactress, and how, exactly, did his father die? Is Miss Tolgarth quite the devoted dresser-*cum*-family retainer that we're supposed to believe? What sort of money is Sir George spending on his toy soldiers? How much exactly is Roma Lisle going to get under the will and how badly does she need it? And that's just for starters."

And none of it, thought Buckley, was the kind of information people came running to give you with happy smiles. It meant talking to bank managers, lawyers, friends, acquaintances, and colleagues of the suspects, most of whom would know to a word just how far they needed to go. In theory everyone wanted murderers caught, just as in theory they all approved of hostels for the mentally ill in the community, provided they weren't built at the bottom of their garden. It would be simpler for the police as well as reassuring to the house party at the castle if they did discover those convenient young burglars hiding terrified somewhere on the island. But he didn't believe that they existed; nor, he suspected, did anyone else. And it would be a tamely disappointing ending to the case. What glory would there be in pulling in a couple of terrified local villains who'd killed on impulse and wouldn't have the sense even to keep their mouths shut until they got a lawyer? There was an intelligence at work here. The case was exactly the kind of challenge he enjoyed and which police work so seldom provided.

"There are facts. There are suppositions. There are beliefs. Learn to keep them separate, Sergeant. All men die. Fact. Death may not be the end. Supposition. There's pie in the sky when you die. Belief. Lisle was murdered. Fact. She received anonymous communications. Fact; other people were there when they arrived. They threatened her life. Supposition; they were a bloody sight more likely to put her off her stroke as an actress. They terrified her. Supposition; that's what her husband tells us and what she told Miss Gray. But she was an actress, remember. The thing about actresses is that they act. Suppose she and her husband concocted the whole scheme, threatening messages, apparent terror and distress, breakdown in the middle of a play, calling in a private eye, the lot."

"I don't see why, sir."

"Nor do I, yet. Would any actress willingly humiliate herself onstage? God knows. Actors are an alien breed to me."

"If she knew that she was finished as an actress, could she and her husband have concocted the messages to provide a public excuse for failure?"

"Overingenious and unnecessary. Why not just pretend that her health has failed? And she didn't make the messages public. On the contrary, she seems to have taken care to prevent the news getting out. Would any actress wish her public to know that someone hated her that much? Don't they crave to be loved by all the world? No, I was thinking of something rather more subtle. Ralston somehow persuades her into pretending that her life is threatened, and then kills her, having, as it were, seduced her into conniving at her own murder. My God, that would be neat. Too neat, perhaps."

"But why take the risk of calling in Miss Gray?"

"What risk? She could hardly discover that the letters were faked, not in one short weekend. A very short weekend as far as Lisle was concerned. Employing Gray gave the final artistic touch to the whole plan."

"I still think he'd have been taking a risk."

"That's because we've seen the girl. She's intelligent and she knows her job. But Ralston wasn't to know that. Who is she, after all? The proprietor of a one-woman detective agency, apparently. After Lisle first met her at the house of that friend of hers—Mrs. Fortescue, wasn't it?—she probably suggested to Ralston that they call her in. That's why she never bothered to interview the girl herself. Why trouble when the whole thing was a ploy."

"It's ingenious, sir, but it still begs the question why Lisle should have connived it at all. I mean, what possible reason could Ralston give to persuade her to pretend that her life was threatened?"

"What, indeed, Sergeant? Like Miss Gray, I'm in danger of being too clever for my own good. But one thing I'm sure of. The murderer spent last night under this roof. And I've a choice bunch of suspects. Sir George Ralston, baronet, something of a war hero and darling of the geriatric Right. A distinguished theater critic, one even I have actually heard of. Seriously ill, too, by the look of him, which means that he'll probably die on me under the gentlest interrogation. Interrogation. Odd how one dislikes that word. Too many echoes of the Gestapo and K.G.B., I suppose. A best-selling novelist who not only owns the island but happens to be friendly with the Cottringhams, who have the ear of the lord lieutenant, the chief constable, the M.P., and anyone else who matters in the county. A respectable bookseller, ex-schoolteacher, who's probably a member of the civil rights and women's lib lobbies and who will protest to her M.P. about police harassment if I raise my voice to her. And a school kid—and sensitive with it. I suppose I should be grateful that he's not a juvenile."

"And a butler, sir."

"Thank you for reminding me, Sergeant. We mustn't forget the butler. I regard the butler as a gratuitous insult on the part of fate. So let's give the gentry in the library a respite and hear what Munter has to tell us."

## V

Buckley noted with irritation that Munter, invited by Grogan to sit, managed in the mere act of lowering his buttocks onto the chair to suggest both that it was unseemly for him to seat himself in the business room and that Grogan had committed a social solecism in inviting him to do so. He couldn't remember ever having seen the man in Speymouth; his was certainly not an appearance one was likely to forget. Watching Munter's strong and lugubrious face on which the unease proper to his present situation was noticeably absent, he found himself prepared to disbelieve everything he heard. It seemed to him suspicious that a man should want to make himself more grotesque than nature had intended, and if this was Munter's way of thumbing his nose at the world he had better not try it on with the police.

Basically conforming and ambitious, Buckley had no resentment of those wealthier than himself; he had every intention of eventually joining them. But he despised and distrusted those who chose to earn their living by pandering to the rich and suspected that Grogan shared this prejudice. He watched them both with a wary and critical eye and wished that he were taking a more active part in the interrogation. Never had his chief's insistence that he sit silently unless invited to speak, watch carefully, and take unobtrusive shorthand notes seemed more restrictive and demeaning. Morbidly sensitive to any nuance of condescension, he felt that the glance Munter casually gave him conveyed slight surprise that he should have been allowed into the house.

Grogan, seated at the desk, leaned back in his chair so strongly that its back creaked, twirled around to face Munter, and spread his legs wide as if to assert his right to feel perfectly at home. He said, "Suppose you begin by telling us who you are, where you came from, and what precisely is your job here."

"My duties, sir, have never been precisely defined. This is not altogether an orthodox household. But I am in charge of all the domestic arrangements and supervise the two other members of staff, my wife and Oldfield, who is the gardener, handyman, and boatman. Any additional help necessary when Mr. Gorringe is entertaining or has houseguests is obtained on a temporary basis from the mainland. I look after the silver and the wine and wait at table. The cooking is generally shared. My wife is the pastry cook and Mr. Ambrose himself occasionally cooks a meal. He is fond of preparing savories."

"Very tasty, I'm sure. And how long have you been part of this unorthodox household?"

"My wife and I came into Mr. Gorringe's service in July 1979, three months after his return from a year abroad. He had inherited the castle from his uncle in 1977. Perhaps you would wish for a brief curriculum vitae. I was born in London in 1940 and educated at Pimlico primary and secondary schools. I then took a course in hotel catering and for seven years worked in hotels here and abroad. But I decided that institutional life was unsuited to my temperament and entered private service, first with an American business gentleman living in London and then, when he returned home, here in Dorset with his lordship at Bossington House. I am sure my previous gentlemen will speak for me if necessary."

"No doubt. If I were looking for a manservant you'd do very nicely. But I'll be consulting a more objective character reference source, the criminal records office. Does that worry you?"

"It offends me, sir. It doesn't worry me."

Buckley wondered when Grogan would stop this needling and get down to the main inquiry, what Munter had been doing between the ending of lunch and the finding of the body. If these preliminaries were meant to provoke the witness, they weren't succeeding. But Grogan knew his business; at least the Met had appeared to think so. He had come to Dorset burdened with something of a reputation. Now he stopped looking at Munter; his voice became conversational.

"This play. It was to be a regular event, was it? An annual drama festival perhaps?"

"I have no means of knowing. Mr. Gorringe did not confide his plans to me."

"Once was enough, I should think. It must have made a lot of extra work for you and your wife."

Munter's slow and disapproving glance around the business room was an inventory of unwelcome change: the slight rearrangement of the furniture, Buckley's jacket slung over the back of his chair, the coffee tray with the two stained cups, its surface crumbled with half-eaten biscuits. He said, "The domestic inconvenience occasioned by Lady Ralston living was nugatory compared with the inconvenience of Lady Ralston murdered."

Grogan held his pen in front of his face and peered at its tip, moving it backward and forward as if testing his eyesight. "You found her a pleasant, likable guest, easy to get on with?"

"That was not a question to which I addressed myself."

"Address yourself to it now."

"Lady Ralston seemed a very agreeable lady."

"No trouble? No disagreements? No rows as far as you knew?"

"None, sir. A great loss to the English stage." He paused and added woodenly, "And, of course, to Sir George Ralston."

It was impossible to judge whether the statement was ironic, but Buckley wondered whether Grogan, too, had caught the clear bite of contempt. Grogan rocked back in his chair, legs stretched, and stared consideringly at his witness. Munter gazed ahead with a look of patient resignation and, after a minute of silence, permitted himself a glance at his watch.

"Right! Let's get on with it. You know what we want, a full account of where you were, what you were doing, and whom you saw between one o'clock when lunch was over and two-forty-three when Miss Gray found the body."

According to Munter's account, he had spent the whole of that time on the ground floor of the castle, chiefly moving between the dining room, his pantry, and the theater. As he had been continually busy with preparations for the play and the supper party, it wasn't always possible to say where he had been or with whom at any particular moment, although he doubted whether he had ever been alone for more than a few minutes. He said in a voice which held no trace of regret that he very much regretted not being able to be more precise, but he could not, of course, have known so detailed an account would subsequently be required. At first he had helped his wife clear away the luncheon and had then gone to check on the wine. There had been three telephone calls to answer, one from a guest who was prevented by illness from attending the performance, a second inquiring about the time the launch would leave Speymouth, a call from Lady Cottringham's housekeeper wanting to know whether they needed any extra glasses. He had been checking on the men's dressing room when his wife had appeared backstage to ask him to look at one of the tea urns which she thought might not be working. It was unfortunate that they had to hire urns; Mr. Gorringe had a strong dislike of them and complained that they made the great hall look like a meeting of the Women's Institute, but with an audience of eighty people and the cast to provide for, the use of the urns had been necessary.

At some time, he couldn't remember precisely when, he had remembered that Mr. Gorringe had asked him to find a second music box for use in the third act of the play, Miss Lisle having expressed dissatisfaction with the one provided at the dress rehearsal. He had come here into the business room to fetch it from the walnut chiffonier. At this stage his eyes indicated what Buckley sourly thought could very well have been described as a cupboard. His Aunt Sadie had one like it, not as fancily carved on the doors or at the end of the shelves, but pretty much the same. She claimed it had been in the family for generations, kept it in the back parlor, and called it a dresser. She used it for the bits and pieces her kids brought back from holiday for her, cheap souvenirs from the Costa del Sol, Malta, and, now, from Miami. He'd have to tell her that what she'd got was a chiffonier, and she'd reply that he made it sound like a bloody ice cream.

He turned the page of his notebook. Munter's resigned voice droned on. He had taken the second music box and placed it with the first one on the props table. Shortly afterward, it could have been as late as two-fifteen, Mr. Gorringe had appeared and they had checked over the props together. By then it was time to go to the quay to meet the launch bringing the rest of the cast from Speymouth. He had gone with Mr. Gorringe to receive them and had helped with the disembarkation. Mr. Gorringe and he had escorted the gentlemen to their dressing rooms, and his wife and Miss Tolgarth had looked after the ladies. He had stayed backstage for about ten minutes and had then gone to his pantry, where Mrs. Chambers and her granddaughter were polishing glasses. He had had occasion to complain to the girl, Debbie, about a smeared glass and had supervised the arrangements to rewash them all. After that he had gone to the dining room to collect the chairs for the supper party, which was to be held in the great hall. He had been there when Mr. Gorringe put his head in to inform him of Miss Lisle's murder.

Grogan sat with his great head lowered, as if bowed with the weight of assimilating this succinct account. Then he said quietly, "You are, of course, devoted to Mr. Gorringe."

"A man is well advised to be devoted to something or to someone."

"A man is well advised to take murder seriously."

"Yes, indeed, sir. When Mr. Gorringe broke the news to me I said, 'What, in our house?' "

"Quite Shakespearean. The Macbeth touch. And no doubt Mr. Gorringe could riposte with 'Too awful anywhere'?"

"No doubt he could have, sir. Actually, what he said was that I should go to the landing stage and prevent the guests from landing. He would follow as soon as possible and explain the lamentable circumstance which necessitated the cancellation of the performance."

"The launches were then at the quay?"

"Not at that time. I judged that they were three-quarters of a mile away."

"So there was no particular hurry to warn them?"

"It was not a matter to be left to chance. Mr. Gorringe was anxious that the police investigation should not be hampered by the presence on the island of another eighty people in a state of confusion or distress."

Grogan said, "In a state of highly enjoyable excitement, more likely. Nothing like a good murder for a thrill. Or wouldn't you know?"

"I wouldn't know, sir."

"Still, it was considerate of your master—I suppose that's what you call him—to have as his first thought the convenience of the police. Highly commendable. What was he doing, do you know, while you were wasting a certain amount of time at the quay?"

"I suppose that he was telephoning the police and acquainting his guests and the cast of the play of the fact of Lady Ralston's death. I have no doubt he will inform you if asked."

"And how exactly did he acquaint you with the fact of Lady Ralston's death?"

"He told me that she had been battered to death. He instructed me to inform the guests when they arrived that she had been killed by a blow to the head. There was no need to harrow them unnecessarily. In the event I was not required to tell them anything, as Mr. Gorringe had joined me by the time the launches arrived."

"A blow to the head. You have seen the body?"

"No, sir. Mr. Gorringe locked the door of Lady Ralston's room after the discovery. There was no occasion for any of the staff to see the body."

"But you have, no doubt, formed some opinion as to how this blow to the head was inflicted? You permitted yourself a theory, a little natural curiosity? You went so far, perhaps, as to discuss it with your wife?"

"It did occur to me to wonder whether the assault was connected with the missing marble arm. Mr. Gorringe will have told you that the display case was forced in the early hours of this morning."

"So suppose you tell us what you know about that."

"The object was brought back to the castle by Mr. Gorringe on his return from London on Thursday night and placed by him in the showcase. The showcase is kept locked, since groups of visitors are shown around the castle during the summer months on days which are announced in advance, and Mr. Gorringe's insurance company has insisted on this degree of security. Mr. Gorringe himself placed the arm in position, watched by me, and we had some conversation on its possible provenance. He then locked the showcase. The keys to the display cabinets are not, of course, kept on the key board with the house keys but in the bottom left locked drawer of the desk at which you are now sitting. The showcase was undamaged and the marble arm in place when I saw it shortly after midnight. Mr. Gorringe found it in its present state when he was on his way to the kitchen just before seven o'clock. He is an early riser and prefers to make his own morning tea and carry the tray either onto the terrace or into the library, depending on the state of the weather. We inspected the damage together."

"You saw no one, heard nothing?"

"No, sir. I was busy in the kitchen preparing the early-morning tea trays."

"And they were all there when you took up the early tea trays?"

"The gentlemen were. I understand from my wife that the ladies were also in bed. Lady Ralston's early tea was taken up later by her maid, Miss Tolgarth. At about seven-thirty Mr. Gorringe came to tell me that Sir George had arrived unexpectedly, put ashore in the small bay west of the headland by a local fishing boat. I did not myself see him until I set breakfast on the hot plate in the small breakfast room at eight o'clock."

"But anyone could have got into the house at any time after six-five when you opened up the castle?"

"The back door leading to the great hall was unlocked by me at six-fifteen. At the time I looked out over the lawn and the path leading to the beach and the coastal walk. I saw no one. But anyone could have entered and done the damage between six-fifteen and seven o'clock."

The rest of the interview was unfruitful. Munter appeared to repent of his loquacity and his answers became shorter. He had no idea that Lady Ralston was receiving poison-pen communications and had no suggestions to offer as to their origin. Shown one of the messages, he fingered the paper with fastidious distaste and said that it was the kind he and his wife commonly bought but in cream, not white. The castle writing paper had an engraved address and was of a different quality, as the chief inspector would be able to check by opening the top left-hand drawer of the desk. He had not known that Mr. Gorringe had given Lady Ralston one of his Victorian jewel caskets, nor had he been told that it was missing. He could, however, describe the casket in question since there were only two in the castle. It had been made by a silversmith of Hunt and Rosken in 1850 and was thought to have been among their pieces shown at the Great Exhibition of 1851. It had been considered for use as a prop in the third act of the play, but the larger and less valuable if more showy casket had been thought the better choice.

Grogan frowned, irritated by this display of irrelevant knowledge. He said, "There's been murder done here, bloody murder of a defenseless woman. If there's anything you know, anything you suspect, anything that later occurs to you bearing on this crime, I expect to be told it. The police are here, and here to stay. We may not always be physically present, but we'll be around; we'll be concerned with this island, concerned with what happens here, and that means concerned with you, until the murderer is brought to justice. Have I made myself clear?"

Munter got to his feet. His face was still impassive. He said, "Perfectly, sir. May I say that Courcy Island is used to murder. And the murderers commonly haven't been brought to justice. Perhaps you and your colleagues will have better luck."

After he left, there was a long silence which Buckley knew better than to interrupt. Then Grogan said, "He thinks the husband did it, or he wants us to think that the husband did it. No marks for originality. It's what we're bound to think anyway. D'you know the Wallace case?"

"No, sir." Buckley told himself that if he were to continue working with Grogan, it would be as well to get hold of a copy of the murderers' who's who.

"Liverpool, January 1931. Wallace, William Herbert. Inoffensive little insurance agent trotting round door to door and collecting the odd bob weekly from poor sods terrified they wouldn't be able to pay for their own funerals. Taste for chess and the violin. Married a bit above himself. He and his wife, Julia, lived in genteel poverty, which is the worst poverty of the lot, in case you didn't know, and kept themselves to themselves. Then on nineteenth January, when he's out looking for the address of a prospective customer who may or may not exist, Julia gets her head savagely bashed in, in her own front sitting room. Wallace stood trial for the murder and a sturdy Liverpool jury, who probably weren't entirely unbiased, convicted. The Court of Criminal Appeal subsequently made legal history by quashing the verdict on the grounds that it was unsafe having regard to the evidence. So they let him go and he died of kidney disease two years later, a bloody sight more slowly and painfully than he would have done at the end of a rope. It's a fascinating case. Every piece of evidence can point either way, depending on how you choose to look at it. I can lie awake at night thinking about it. It ought to be compulsory study for every detective constable, a warning of how a case can go wrong if the police get it fixed in their minds that it has to be the husband."

Which was all very well, thought Buckley, but in these cases, if the criminal statistics were to be believed, it usually was the husband. Grogan might be keeping an open mind, but he had no doubt whose name featured at the head of his list. He said, "They've got a cozy little setup here, the Munters."

"Haven't they just? Nothing to do but fuss around Gorringe while he concocts his little delicacies, polish the antique silver, and wait on each other. But he lied about at least one thing. Look back to that interview with Mrs. Chambers."

Buckley thumbed back through his notebook. Mrs. Chambers and her granddaughter had been two of the first interviewed, since the woman had demanded that she be returned to the mainland in time to cook her husband's supper. She had been voluble, aggrieved, and pugnacious, viewing the tragedy as one more trick of fate designed to cause domestic inconvenience. What chiefly concerned her was the waste of food; who, she had demanded, was going to eat a supper prepared for over a hundred? Buckley had been interested, thirty minutes later, to watch her waddling down to the launch with her granddaughter, both lugging a couple of covered baskets. Some of the food, at least, would find its way down the gullets of the Chambers family. She and her granddaughter, a cheerful seventeen-year-old apt to giggle in moments of emotion, had been busy, for the most part together or with Mrs. Munter, for the whole of the critical time. Buckley privately thought that Grogan had wasted too much time on them and had resented having to record the woman's spate of irrelevancies. He found the page at last and began to read, wondering if the old man was checking up on the accuracy of his shorthand.

" 'It's disgusting, that's what it is! I always say there's nothing worse than being killed away from home and by strangers. There never was anything like this when I was a girl. It's them mods on their motorcycles, that's who it is. Great crowd of them came roaring into Speymouth last Saturday with their noisy, smelly machines. Why don't the police do something about it? That's what I want to know. Why don't you take their machines away and chuck them off the end of the pier, and their trousers too? That'd put a stop to it fast enough.

Don't you waste time interviewing decent law-abiding women. Go after them motorcycling mods.' "

Buckley broke off. "That's where you pointed out that even mods could hardly motorcycle to Courcy Island, and she replied darkly that they had their little ways, they were that cunning."

Grogan said, "Not that part. A little earlier when she was rabbiting on about the domestic arrangements."

Buckley flipped back a couple of pages. " 'I'm always happy to oblige Mr. Munter. I don't mind coming to the island for the odd day and bringing Debbie if wanted. And it wasn't the girl's fault if the glasses were smeary. They've no right to send them out like that. And Mr. Munter had no call to go on at Debbie like he did. It's always the same when Lady Ralston's here. He gets his knickers in a twist when she's about, no mistake. We were here last Tuesday for the dress rehearsal and you never heard such goings-on. Asking for this, asking for the other, nothing quite to her ladyship's liking. And forty of the cast for lunch and tea, if you please. Everything had to be just so even if Mr. Gorringe wasn't here. Took himself off to London, Mr. Munter said, and I don't know as I blame him. Anyone would think she was mistress here. I said to Mr. Munter, I don't mind helping out this time, but if you're going to be stuck with this palaver next year you can count me out. That's what I said. Count me out. And he said not to worry. He reckoned that this would be the last play Lady Ralston would appear in on Courcy Island.' "

Buckley stopped reading and looked at Grogan. He told himself that he should have remembered that piece of evidence. He must have taken it down in a fugue of boredom. Black mark. His chief said quietly, "Yes, that's it. That's the passage I wanted. I'll be asking Munter for an explanation of that remark when the time's right, but not yet. It's as well to keep a few unpleasant shocks in hand. I've no doubt that Mrs. Munter will be equally discreet when she obligingly confirms her husband's story. But we'll let the lady wait. I think it's time to hear what Miss Lisle's host has to say for himself. You're a local man, Sergeant. What do you know of him?"

"Very little, sir. He opens the castle to visitors in the summer, but

I imagine it's a ploy to get tax relief on the maintenance. He keeps himself to himself, discourages publicity."

"Does he now? He'll get a bellyful of it before this case is finished. Put your head outside and ask Rogers to summon him, with, of course, the usual compliments."

# VI

Buckley thought that he had never seen a murder suspect as much at ease under questioning as Ambrose Gorringe. He sat back in the chair opposite Grogan, immaculate in his dinner jacket, and gazed across the desk with bright, interested eyes in which Buckley, occasionally glancing up from his notetaking, thought he could detect a gleam of amused contempt. Admittedly Gorringe was on his own ground, sitting, in fact, in his own chair. Buckley thought it rather a pity that the chief hadn't deprived him of this psychological advantage by bundling the lot of them off to Speymouth station. But Gorringe was too calm for his own good. If the husband didn't kill her, here for his money was a close runner-up.

Now being formally questioned for the first time, he repeated without discrepancies the facts he had first briefly told them when they arrived on the island. He had known Miss Lisle from childhood—both their fathers had been in the diplomatic service and had been stationed for a time at the same embassies—but they had lost touch in recent years and had seen very little of each other until he had inherited the island from his uncle in 1977. The next year they had met at a theatrical first night and she had been invited to the island. He couldn't now remember whether the suggestion had come from him or from Miss Lisle. From that visit and her enthusiasm for the Victorian theater flowed the decision to stage a play. He had known about the threatening messages since he had been with her when one of them was delivered, but she hadn't confided that they were still arriving, nor had she told him that Miss Gray was a private detective, although he had suspected that she might be when she had confronted him with the woodcut pushed under Miss Lisle's door. It had been their joint decision not to worry Miss Lisle either with that or with the news that the marble limb had been stolen. He admitted without apparent concern that he had no alibi for the crucial ninety-odd minutes between one-twenty and the discovery of the body. He had lingered over his coffee with Mr. Whittingham, gone to his room about one-thirty, leaving Whittingham on the terrace, had rested for about fifteen minutes until it was time to change, and had left his room to go to the theater shortly after two. Munter had been backstage and they had checked over the props together and discussed one or two matters relating to the after-show supper party. At about two-twenty they had gone together to meet the launch bringing the cast from Speymouth, and he had been backstage in the male dressing room until about two-forty-five.

Grogan said, "And the marble limb? That was last seen by you when?"

"Didn't I tell you, Chief Inspector? By me at about eleven-thirty last night when I went to check the tide timetable. I was interested to estimate how long the launches would take on Saturday afternoon and returning to Speymouth that night. The water can run strongly between here and the mainland. Munter saw the marble in place just after midnight. I found that it was missing and the lock forced when I went to the kitchen at six-fifty-five this morning."

"And all the members of the house party had seen it and knew where it was kept?"

"All except Simon Lessing. He was swimming when the rest of the party were shown round the castle. As far as I know, he has never been near the business room."

Grogan asked, "What is the boy doing here, anyway? Shouldn't he be at school? I take it that Miss Lisle—Lady Ralston—was buying him a privileged education, that he isn't a day boy at the local comprehensive." The question could have sounded offensive, thought

Buckley, if the carefully controlled voice had held a trace of emotion.

Gorringe replied, equally calmly, "He's at Melhurst. Miss Lisle wrote for special weekend leave. She may have thought that Webster's play would be educational. Unfortunately, the weekend has proved educational for the boy in ways she could hardly have foreseen."

"A proper little mother to him, was she?"

"Hardly that. Miss Lisle's maternal sense was, I should have thought, undeveloped. But within her capacity she genuinely cared for the boy. What you must understand about the victim in this case was that she enjoyed being kind, as indeed most of us do, provided it doesn't cost us too much."

"And how much did Mr. Lessing cost her?"

"His school fees primarily. About four thousand pounds a year I suppose. She could afford it. It all began, I imagine, because she had a conscience about breaking up his parents' marriage. If she did, it was quite unnecessary. The man had a choice presumably."

"Simon Lessing must have resented the marriage, on his mother's account if not his own. Unless, of course, he thought a rich stepmama a good exchange."

"It was six years ago. He was barely eleven when his father walked out on him. And if you're suggesting, without much subtlety I may say, that he resented it enough to bash in stepmama's face, then he waited long enough to do it and he chose a singularly inappropriate time. Does Sir George Ralston know that you suspect Simon? He probably considers himself the boy's stepfather. He'll want to take steps to see that the boy's interests are safeguarded if you're going on with that somewhat ridiculous idea."

"I never said that we suspected him. And, in view of the boy's youth, I have agreed with Sir George that he shall be present when I speak to the boy. But Mr. Lessing is seventeen. He's no longer a juvenile in law. I find these concerted measures to protect him interesting."

"As long as you don't find them sinister. He was extremely shocked when I broke the news to him. His own parents are dead. He was devoted to Clarissa. It's natural that we should wish to minimize his pain. After all, you're hardly here in the capacity of child-care officers."

Grogan had scarcely glanced at his witness during this exchange. The unlined note pad which he preferred to the normal police issue was on the desk blotter in front of him, and he was sketching with his fountain pen. A careful oblong shape with two doors and two windows took shape under the huge speckled hand. Buckley saw that it was a representation of Clarissa Lisle's bedroom, something between a plan and a drawing. The proportions of the room were drawn carefully to scale, but small objects were being inserted, overlarge and carefully detailed, as a child might draw them: the jars of cosmetics, a box of cotton-wool balls, the tea tray, the alarm clock.

Suddenly and still without looking up, he asked, "What made you go to her room, sir?"

"Just after Miss Gray went to call her? Merely a chivalrous impulse. I thought that, as her host, it would be seemly if I escorted her to her dressing room. And there were things to be carried. Her makeup case for one. As we haven't much dressing-room accommodation and she was having to share with Miss Collingwood, who plays Cariola, Miss Collingwood had undertaken to be dressed and out before the star wanted the room, but Miss Lisle wasn't going to risk anyone borrowing her greasepaint. So I went to carry the box and escort the lady."

"In the absence of her husband, who would normally perform that service?"

"Sir George had just come in to change. We met at the top of the stairs as I've already explained."

"You seem to have taken a lot of trouble for Miss Lisle." He paused and added, "One way or another."

"Walking her two hundred yards from her room to the theater hardly counts as trouble."

"But putting on the play for her, restoring the theater, entertaining her guests. It must have been an expensive business."

"I'm not a poor man, happily. And I thought that you were here to investigate a murder, not to inquire into my finances. The theater, incidentally, was restored for my satisfaction, not Miss Lisle's."

"She wasn't hoping that you might partly finance her next professional appearance? What's the theatrical jargon, be her angel?"

"I'm afraid you've been gossiping with the wrong people. That particular angelic role has never attracted me. There are more amusing ways of losing money. But if you're trying tactfully to suggest that I may have owed Miss Lisle a favor, you're perfectly right. It was she who gave me the idea for *Autopsy*, my best-seller, in case you're one of the half dozen who haven't heard of it."

"She didn't write it for you, by any chance?"

"No, she didn't write it. Miss Lisle's talents were varied and egregious but they didn't extend to the written word. The book was fabricated rather than written by an unholy triumvirate of my publisher, my agent, and myself. It was then suitably packaged, promoted, and marketed. No doubt there are sins to be laid to Clarissa's charge, but *Autopsy* isn't one of them."

Grogan let his pen drop from his hand. He leaned back in his chair and looked at Gorringe full in the face. He said quietly, "You knew Miss Lisle from childhood. For the last six months or so you've been intimately concerned with this play. She came here as your guest. She was killed under your roof. However she died—and we shan't know until after the postmortem—the killer almost certainly used your marble to bash in her face. Are you sure that there is nothing you know, nothing you suspect, nothing she ever said to you, that can throw any light on how she died?"

Put it any plainer, thought Buckley, and you'd have to be administering an official caution. He half expected Gorringe to reply that he would say nothing until he had seen his lawyer. But he spoke with the calm unconcern of a disinterested party who has been asked for his considered opinion and has no objection to giving it.

"My first thought—and it remains my theory—was that a trespasser had somehow gained access to the island, knowing that my staff and I would be busy with preparations for the play and that the castle would be, as it were, undefended. He climbed up the fire escape, perhaps out of mischief or devilment and with no clear idea of what he meant to do. It could have been a young man."

"The young usually hunt in gangs."

"Several young men, then. Or a couple if you prefer it. One of them gets in with the general idea of a prowl round while the house is quiet. That supposes a local boy, one who knew about the play. He creeps into Miss Lisle's room—she had forgotten to lock the communicating door or had thought the precaution unnecessary—and sees her apparently asleep on the bed. He is about to make his exit, with or without the jewel case, when she takes the pads off her eyes and sees him. In a panic he kills her, seizes the box, and makes his escape the same way as he came in."

Grogan said, "Having thoughtfully provided himself in advance with the marble hand, which according to your evidence must have been taken from the display case between midnight and six-fifty-five this morning."

"No, I don't think he came provided with anything except a general intention of mischief. My theory is that he found the weapon ready to hand—forgive the atrocious pun—on the bedside table, together, of course, with the quotation from the play."

"And who are you suggesting put them there? The door to that room was locked, remember."

"I don't think there's much mystery about that, surely. Miss Lisle did."

Grogan said, "With the object of frightening herself into hysteria, or merely of providing any potential murderer who might drop in with a convenient weapon?"

"With the object of providing herself with an excuse if she failed in the play. As I'm afraid she almost certainly would. Or she may have had more devious reasons. Miss Lisle's complex personality was something of a mystery to me, as it was, I suspect, to her husband."

"And are you suggesting that this young, impulsive, unpremeditating killer then replaced the pads over his victim's eyes? That argues we have two complex personalities to elucidate."

"He could have done. You're the expert on murder, not I. But I could think of a reason if pushed. Perhaps she seemed to be staring up at him and his nerve broke. He had to cover those dead, accusing eyes. The suggestion is a little overimaginative, perhaps, but not impossible. Murderers do behave oddly. Remember the Gutteridge case, Chief Inspector."

Buckley's hand jerked on his shorthand pad. He thought, My God, is he doing it on purpose? The small audacity must surely have been deliberate. But how could Gorringe have learned of the chief's habit of referring to old cases? He glanced up, not at Grogan, but at Gorringe, and met only a look of bland innocence. And it was to him that Gorringe spoke.

"Long before your time, Sergeant. Gutteridge was the police constable shot by two car thieves in an Essex country lane in 1927. An ex-convict, Frederick Browne, and his accomplice, William Kennedy, were hanged for the crime. After killing the man, one of the thugs shot out both his eyes. It is thought that they were superstitious. They believed that the dead eyes of a murdered man, fixed on the killer's face, will bear his visage imprinted on the pupils. I doubt whether any murderer willingly looks into his victim's eyes. An interesting feature of an otherwise dull and sordid case."

Grogan had finished his drawing. The plan of the room was complete. Now, while they watched him in silence, he drew on the great bed a small sprawled matchbox figure with wisps of hair over the pillow. Last and with care, he blocked in the face. Then he put his great hand over the drawing and ripped out the page, crumpling it in his fist. The gesture was unexpectedly violent, but his voice was quiet, almost gentle.

"Thank you, sir. You've been very helpful. And now, if you've nothing else to tell us, no doubt you'll be wanting to go back to your guests."

# VII

When Ivo Whittingham came into the room, Buckley, embarrassed, looked quickly down and began flipping back the pages of his notebook, hoping that Whittingham hadn't caught his first look of horror and surprise. Only once before had he seen so gaunt a figure, and that was his Uncle Gerry in those last weeks before the cancer finally got him. He had felt as much affection for his uncle as he was capable of feeling, and the protracted agony of his dying had left him with one resolution: if that was what the body could do to a man, it owed something in return. From now on he would take his pleasures without guilt. He might have become a cheerful hedonist if ambition and the caution which went with it hadn't been stronger. But he hadn't forgotten either the bitterness or the pain. And Ivo Whittingham reminded him in another way. His uncle had looked at him with just such glittering eyes as if they burned with all that remained of life and intelligence. He glanced up as Whittingham seated himself, stiffly grasping the chair sides with skeletal hands. But when he spoke his voice was surprisingly strong and relaxed.

"This is unpleasantly reminiscent of a summons to one's housemaster. Good seldom came of it."

It was an irreverent beginning which Grogan was unlikely to encourage. He said curtly, "In that case I suggest that we make it as brief as possible. I take it that you knew Miss Lisle well."

"You may take it that I knew her intimately."

"Are you telling me, sir, that she was your mistress?"

"That hardly seems the right word for so spasmodic a liaison. *Mistress* suggests a certain permanence, even a measure of respectability. One is reminded of dear Mrs. Keppel and her king. It would be more accurate to say that we were lovers for a period of about six years as opportunity and her whim dictated."

"And did her husband know?"

"Husbands. Our relationship outlasted more than one marital

episode. But I imagine that you're interested only in George Ralston. I never told him. I don't know whether she did. And if you're wondering whether he took his revenge, the idea is ludicrous. Why should he wait until a higher power, or fate or luck, whatever you choose to believe in, is about to rid him of me permanently? Ralston isn't a fool. And if you would like to ask whether I sent the lady on before me, the answer is no. Clarissa Lisle and I had exhausted each other's possibilities on this bank and shoal of time. But I could have killed her. I had the opportunity; I was alone in my room conveniently close all afternoon. In case you haven't already inquired, it's on the same floor as Clarissa's, a mere fifty feet away, overlooking the eastern front of the castle. I had access to the means since I had been shown the marble limb. I suppose I could have found the strength. And I think she might have opened her door to me. But I didn't kill her and I don't know who did. You'll have to take my word for it. I can't prove my innocence."

"Tell me what she was like." It was the first time Grogan had asked that question. And yet, thought Buckley, it was at the heart of every murder investigation. If it were possible to find the answer, most other questions would become superfluous.

Whittingham said, "I was going to say that you've seen her face, but, of course, you haven't. A pity. One needed to know the physical Clarissa to get any clue to what else there might have been to know. She lived intensely in and through her body. The rest is a list of words. She was egocentric, insecure, clever but not intelligent, kind of cruel as the mood took her, restless, unhappy. But she had certain skills which a gentlemanly reticence inhibits me from discussing but which weren't unimportant. She probably gave more joy than she caused misery. Since that can't be said of many of us, it's unbecoming of me to criticize her. I remember that I once sent to her the words Sir Thomas Malory has Lancelot speak to Guinevere: 'Lady, I take record of God, in thee I have had my earthly joy.' I don't take them back, whatever she may have done."

"Whatever she may have done, sir?"

"A form of words merely, Chief Inspector."

"So you mourn her?"

"No. But I shan't forget her."

There was a pause. Then Grogan asked quietly, "Why are you here, sir?"

"She asked me to come. But there was another reason. One of the Sunday papers commissioned me to do a piece on the island and the theater. What was wanted was period charm, nostalgia, and salacious legend. They should have sent a crime reporter."

"And that was enough to tempt a reviewer of your eminence?"

"It must have been, mustn't it, since here I am."

When Grogan asked him, as he had the other suspects, to describe the events of the day, Whittingham showed signs of tiredness for the first time. The body sagged in its chair like a puppet jerked from its string.

"There isn't much to tell. We had a late breakfast and then Miss Lisle suggested we see the church. There's a crypt with some ancient skulls and a secret passage to the sea. We explored both and Gorringe entertained us with old legends about the skulls and a reputed drowning of a wartime internee in the cave at the end of the passage. I was tired and didn't listen very closely. Then back to luncheon at twelve. Miss Lisle went to rest immediately afterward. I was in my room by quarter past one and stayed there, resting and reading, until it was time to dress. Miss Lisle had insisted that we change before the play. I met Roma Lisle at the head of the staircase as she came down from her room, and we were together when Gorringe appeared with Miss Gray and told us that Clarissa was dead."

"And during the morning, the visit to the church and the cave, how did Miss Lisle seem to you?"

"I think I would say, Chief Inspector, that Miss Lisle was her usual self."

Last Grogan spilled out from the folder the sheaf of messages. One of them fluttered to the floor. He bent and picked it up, then handed it to Whittingham.

"What can you tell us about these, sir?"

"Only that I knew she was getting them. She didn't tell me, but one does tend to pick up bits of theater gossip. Still, I don't think it was generally known. And here, again, I seem to be the natural suspect. Whoever sent these knew Miss Lisle and knew his Shakespeare. But I don't think I would have added the coffin and the skull. An unnecessarily crude touch, don't you think?"

"And that is all that you want to tell us, sir?"

"It's all that I can tell you, Chief Inspector."

# VIII

It was nearly seven o'clock before they got around to seeing the boy. He had changed into a formal suit and looked, thought Buckley, as if he were on the way to his stepmother's funeral instead of an interview with the police. He guessed that there was no more than eight years' difference between his age and the boy's, but it could have been twenty. Lessing looked as neatly pressed and nervous as a child. But he had himself well under control. Buckley felt that there was something vaguely familiar about his entrance, the care with which he seated himself, the serious, expectant gaze which he fixed on Grogan's face. And then he remembered. This was how he himself had looked and behaved at his final interview to join the police. He had been advised by his headmaster: "Wear your best suit, but no fountain pen or fancy handkerchief peeping coyly out of the jacket pocket. Look them straight in the eye, but not so fixedly that you embarrass them. Be slightly more deferential than you feel; they're the ones with the job on offer. If you don't know an answer, say so, don't waffle. And don't worry if you're nervous, they prefer that to overconfidence, but show that you've got the guts to cope with nervousness. Call them 'sir' or 'madam' and thank them briefly before you leave. And for God's sake, boy, sit up straight."

And as the interview progressed beyond the first easy questions, designed, Buckley could almost believe, to put the candidate at his ease, he sensed something else, that Lessing was beginning to feel as he had done: if you follow the advice, the ordeal isn't so bad after all. Only his hands betrayed him. They were broad and unpleasantly white with thick, stubbed fingers but narrow, almost girlish nails cut very short and so pink that they looked painted. He held his hands in his lap, and from time to time he would stretch and pull at the fingers as if he were routinely performing some prescribed strengthening exercise.

Sir George Ralston remained standing with his back to them, looking out the window through the partly drawn curtains. Buckley wondered whether the intention was to demonstrate that he wasn't influencing the boy by word or glance. But the pose looked perverse, the more so as there was nothing in that still darkness which he could possibly see. Buckley had never known such silence. It had a positive quality; not the absence of noise but a silence which sharpened perception and gave importance and dignity to every word and action. He wished, not for the first time, that they were at headquarters with the sound of passing feet, of doors closing, of distant voices calling, all the comfortable background noises of ordinary life. Here it wasn't only the suspects who were under judgment.

This time Grogan's doodle looked innocuous, even charming. He seemed to be redesigning his kitchen garden. Neat rows of chubby cabbages, climbing runner beans, and fern-topped carrots grew under his hand. He said, "So after your mother died you went to live with her brother and his family, and you were there when Lady Ralston came to visit you in the summer of 1978 and decided to adopt you?"

"There was no formal adoption. My uncle was my guardian and he agreed that Clarissa would be . . . well, a kind of foster mother, I suppose. She took over the whole responsibility for me."

"And you welcomed that arrangement?"

"Very much, sir. Life with my uncle and aunt wasn't really congenial to me."

That was an odd word for the boy to use, thought Buckley. It made it sound as if they'd taken the *Mirror* instead of the *Times* and he hadn't been able to get his after-dinner port.

"And you were happy with Sir George and his wife?" Grogan couldn't resist the small note of sarcasm. He added, "Life was congenial to you?"

"Very, sir."

"Your stepmother—is that how you thought of her, as a stepmother?"

The boy blushed and glanced sideways at the silent figure of Sir George. He moistened his lips and said, "Yes, sir. I suppose so."

"Your stepmother has been receiving some rather unpleasant communications during the last year or so. What do you know about that?"

"Nothing, sir. She didn't tell me." He added, "We don't . . . we didn't see a great deal of each other. I'm at school and she was often at the Brighton flat during the holidays."

Grogan pulled one of the messages from his file and pushed it over the desk.

"That's a sample. Recognize it?"

"No, sir. It's a quotation, isn't it? Is it Shakespeare?"

"You tell me, lad. You're the one at Melhurst. But you've never seen one of these before?"

"No, never."

"Right, then. Suppose you tell us exactly what you did between one o'clock today and two-forty-five."

Lessing looked down at his hands, seemed to become aware of his nervous methodical stretching, and grasped both sides of his chair as if to prevent himself from springing to his feet. But he gave his account lucidly and with growing confidence. He had decided to swim before the play and had gone straight to his room after lunch, where he had put on his swimming trunks under his jeans and shirt. He had taken his jersey and towel and made his way across the lawn to the shore. He had walked on the beach for about an hour because Clarissa had warned him not to swim too soon after his meal. He had then returned to the small cove just beyond the terrace and had entered the water at about two o'clock or shortly after, leaving his clothes, towel, and wristwatch on the shore. He had seen no one during either his walk or his swim, but Sir George had told him that he had watched him coming ashore through his binoculars when he himself was returning to the castle after his bird-watching. Here he again glanced around at his stepfather as if inviting corroboration and again got no response.

Grogan said, "So Sir George Ralston has told us. And what then?"

"Well, nothing really, sir. I was on my way back to the castle when Mr. Gorringe saw me and came to meet me. He told me about Clarissa." The last few words were almost a whisper.

Grogan bent his ruddy head forward and asked softly, "And what exactly did he tell you?"

"That she was dead, sir. Murdered."

"And did he explain how?"

Again the whisper. "No, sir."

"But you asked, presumably? You betrayed some natural curiosity?"

"I asked him what had happened, how she had died. He said that no one could be sure until after the postmortem."

"He's right. There's nothing you need to know except the fact that she is dead, and that it must have been homicide. And now, Mr. Lessing, what can you tell us about the arm of the dead princess?"

Buckley thought that Sir George gave an exclamation of protest; but he still didn't interrupt.

The boy looked from face to face as if the police had gone mad. No one spoke. Then he said, "You mean in the church? We visited the crypt to see the skulls this morning. But Mr. Gorringe didn't say anything about a dead princess."

"It wasn't in the church."

"You mean it's a mummified arm? I don't understand."

"It's a marble arm, a limb to be accurate. A baby's limb. Someone has taken it from Mr. Gorringe's display case, the one outside this door, and we'd rather like to know who and when."

"I don't think I've seen it, sir. I'm sorry."

Grogan had completed his kitchen garden and was separating it from the lawn by a trellis and archway. He looked up at Lessing and said, "My officers and I will be back here tomorrow. We'll probably be around for a day or two. If there's anything that occurs to you, anything that you remember which is the least unusual or likely to help, however small and unimportant it seems, I want you to get in touch. Understand?"

"Yes, sir. Thank you, sir."

Grogan nodded and the boy got to his feet, glanced for the last time at the still back of Sir George, and went out. Buckley almost expected him to turn at the door and ask whether he'd got the job.

Sir George turned at last.

"He's due back at school on Monday morning before midday. Special leave. I take it he can go."

Grogan said, "It would be helpful to us, sir, if he could stay until Tuesday morning. It's just a question of convenience. If anything does occur to him or to us, it would be helpful to be able to clear it up quickly. But obviously he can go early on Monday if you think it important."

Sir George hesitated. "Don't suppose a day will make much odds. Better for him, though, to be away from here, back at work. I'll get in touch with the school tomorrow or Monday. He'll need leave later for the funeral, but I suppose it's too early yet to think about that."

"I'm afraid so, sir."

Sir George was almost at the door when Grogan called softly, "There's one other thing, sir, which I have to ask. Your relationship with your wife. Would you say that yours was a happy marriage?"

The slim, upright figure paused for a second, hand on the doorknob. Then Sir George turned to face them. His face was twitching violently, like that of a man afflicted with a nervous spasm. Then he controlled himself.

"I find that question offensive, Chief Inspector."

Grogan's voice was still gentle, dangerously gentle. "In a murder investigation, we sometimes have to ask questions which people find offensive."

"It's meaningless unless you ask both parties. Too late for that now. Not sure that my wife had the capacity for happiness."

"And you, sir?"

He answered with great simplicity. "I loved her."

# IX

After he had gone, Grogan said with sudden vehemence, "Let's pack up and get out of this place. It's getting claustrophobic. What time is the launch expected with Roper and Badgett?"

Buckley looked at his watch. "It should be here within fifteen minutes."

Detective Constables Roper and Badgett were to be on duty in the business room but for one night only. Their presence was almost a formality. No one at the castle had asked for police protection, nor did Grogan believe that they were in need of it. He had few enough officers without wasting manpower. The whole of the island including the secret passage to the Devil's Kettle had been searched; if the theory of the casual intruder were true, it was apparent that he wasn't now on Courcy. Tomorrow the police inquiries on the island would be complete and the investigation moved to an incident room at the Speymouth station. It was likely, thought Buckley, to be a tedious and less than comfortable vigil for Roper and Badgett. Ambrose Gorringe had offered a bedroom and had said that the two officers should ring Munter for anything they needed. But Grogan's instructions had been clear.

"You'll bring your own flasks and sandwiches, lads, and ring for no one. You'll be beholden to Mr. Gorringe for nothing but his light and heating and the water that flushes his bog."

He pulled the bell cord. It seemed to Buckley that Munter took his time in coming.

Grogan said, "Will you tell Mr. Gorringe that we're now leaving?"

"Yes, sir. The police launch isn't yet sighted, sir."

"I'm aware of that. We shall wait for it on the quay."

When the man had gone, he said irritably, "What does he think we propose to do? Walk on water?" Ambrose Gorringe arrived within minutes to see them off the premises with formal courtesy. They might, thought Buckley, have been a couple of dinner guests, if not particularly welcome or agreeable ones. He said nothing about the event that had brought them to Courcy and made no inquiries about the progress of the investigation. Clarissa Lisle's murder might have been an embarrassing mishap in an otherwise not unsuccessful day.

It was good to be in the air again. The night was extraordinarily balmy for mid-September, and there still seemed to rise from the stones of the terrace a genial warmth like the last breath of a summer day. Briefcases in hand, they strolled together along the eastern arm of the quay. Turning to retrace their steps, they could see in the distance a stream of light from the dining-room windows and dark figures moving to and fro on the terrace, joining and then parting, pausing and then walking on as if taking part in a pavane. It looked to Buckley as if they had plates in their hands. Probably making do with the cold leftover party food, he thought, and some irrelevant quotation about baked funeral meats came into his mind. He didn't blame them for not wanting to sit together around a table, faced with one empty chair.

He and Grogan settled themselves under the canopy of the bandstand to wait for the first lights of the launch. The peace of the night was seductive. Here on the southern shore where the mainland couldn't be seen, it was easy to imagine that the island was totally isolated in a waste of sea, that they were waiting and watching for the masts of some overdue relief ship, and that the figures gliding on the terrace were the ghosts of long-dead settlers, that the castle itself was a shell, hall and library and drawing room open to the sky, the great staircase rising into nothingness, ferns and weeds pushing their way between the broken tiles. He wasn't normally imaginative, but now he deliberately indulged his tiredness by letting his mind elaborate the fantasy while he sat gently massaging his right wrist.

Grogan's voice broke harshly into the reverie. Neither the peace nor the beauty had touched him. His thoughts were still on the case. Buckley told himself that he should have known there would be no respite. He remembered the overheard comment of a detective inspector: "Red Rufus treats a murder investigation like a love affair. Gets obsessed with his suspects. Moves into their lives. Lives and breathes with the case, edgy and restless and frustrated, until it climaxes at the arrest." Buckley wondered if that was one of the reasons for his failed marriage. It must be disconcerting to live with a man who, for most of the night as well as the day, simply wasn't there.

When Grogan spoke his voice was as vigorous as if the inquiry had just begun.

"Miss Roma Lisle, cousin of the deceased, aged forty-five, shopkeeper, ex-schoolmistress, unmarried. What struck you most about the lady, Sergeant?"

Buckley dragged his mind back to the interview with Roma Lisle.

"That she was frightened, sir."

"Frightened, defensive, embarrassed, and unconvincing. Consider her story. She admits that the woodcut is hers and says that she brought it to Courcy because she thought that Ambrose Gorringe would be interested in it and would be able to advise her about its age and value. As he doesn't claim to be an authority on early seventeenth-century manuscripts, the hope was optimistic. Still, we needn't read too much into that. She found the thing, she thought it was interesting, and she brought it with her. And now for today. She tells us that she left her cousin's bedroom at about five minutes past one, went straight to the library, and stayed there until half past two when she went up to her room. It's on the floor immediately above the gallery and she didn't have to pass Miss Lisle's room to get to it. She saw and heard no one. During the hour and twenty minutes when she was in the library she was alone. Miss Gray briefly put her head round the door at about twenty past one but didn't stay. Miss Lisle remained in the library, expecting a private business call from her partner, which didn't, in fact, come through. She tells us that she also wrote a letter. Asked to produce it as a small indication of verisimilitude—not that it greatly matters—she blushes with embarrassement and says that she decided not to send it after all and tore it up. When we gently point out that there are no fragments in the library wastepaper basket she becomes even redder and confides that she took the scraps with her when she went to her room and flushed them down the W.C. All very curious. But consider something even odder. She was one of the last people to see her cousin alive; not the last, but one of the last. And she tells us that she followed Miss Lisle up to her room because she wanted to wish her good luck in the play. All very proper and cousinly. But when we point out that she'd left it rather late to get changed, she tells us that she'd decided to give the performance a miss. Would you care to propound a theory which would explain these intriguing eccentricities of behavior?"

"She was expecting a telephone call from her lover, sir, not necessarily her partner. When it didn't come, she decided to write to him. Then she thought better of it and tore up the letter. She retrieved the fragments from the wastepaper basket because she didn't want us piecing them together and reading her private correspondence, however innocuous."

"Ingenious, Sergeant. But you see where it leaves us. At the time when, according to her, she took those scraps upstairs she couldn't have known that the police would be here to poke their inquisitive noses into anyone's private correspondence, not unless she also knew by then that her cousin was dead."

"And that last visit to Miss Lisle?"

Grogan said, "My guess is that it was less friendly than she makes out."

"But why tell us about the letter, sir? She didn't have to. Why not just say that she spent the time in the library, reading?"

"Because she's a woman who normally tells the truth. She made no pretense, for example, of liking her cousin or being particularly grieved by her death. If she is going to lie to the police, she prefers to lie as little as possible. That way she has fewer untruths to remember and is able to persuade herself that, essentially, she isn't really lying at all. It's a sound enough principle as far as it goes. But we shouldn't read too much into that torn-up letter. She may merely have wanted to save the servants trouble, or have been afraid that they might have been curious enough to piece it together. And if Miss Roma Lisle's story is less than convincing, it's not the only one. Consider the curious reticence of the lady's maid. It sounds like the chapter heading for one of those snobbish thirties thrillers."

Buckley thought back over the interview with Rose Tolgarth. Before she had come in, Grogan had said to him, "You question the lady, Sergeant. She may prefer youth to experience. Give her a treat."

Surprised, Buckley had asked, "At the desk, sir?"

"That would seem the obvious place, unless you intend to prowl round her like a predator."

Grogan himself had greeted her and invited her to sit with more courtesy than he had shown Cordelia Gray or Roma Lisle. If she was surprised to find herself facing the younger of the two officers, she hadn't shown it. But, then, she hadn't shown anything. She had gazed at him with her remarkable eyes, with their smudgy black irises, as if she were looking into . . . what? he wondered. Not his soul, since he didn't believe that he had one, but certainly into some part of his mind which wasn't intended to be public property. All his questions had been answered politely but with the minimum of words. She had admitted that she knew about the threatening messages but refused to speculate about who might have sent them. That job, she implied, was the responsibility of the police. It was she who had made and taken up Miss Lisle's tea before she settled for her usual preperformance rest. The routine was always the same. Miss Lisle drank Lapsang Souchong tea with no milk or sugar but with two thick slices of lemon put into the teapot before the boiling water was poured in. She had made the tea in the usual way in Mr. Munter's pantry, and Mrs. Chambers and Debbie had been with her at the time. She had taken up the tray immediately and at no time had the teapot been out of her sight. Sir George had been in the bedroom with his wife. She had placed the tea tray on the bedside cabinet and had then gone into the bathroom where there was a certain amount of tidying to be done before Miss Lisle took her bath. She had returned to the bedroom to help her mistress undress and had found Miss Gray there. After Miss Gray had returned to her own room, Sir George had left his wife and she herself had followed almost immediately afterward. She had spent the afternoon preparing the ladies' dressing room backstage and helping Mrs. Munter with the arrangements for the party. At two-forty-five she had become concerned in case Miss Gray had forgotten to call Miss Lisle and had gone herself. She had met Sir George, Mr. Gorringe, and Miss Gray outside the bedroom and had then learned of Miss Lisle's death.

They had taken her up to the bedroom and asked her to look around carefully, but without touching anything, and say whether the room was as she would expect to find it, whether there was anything which struck her as unusual. She had shaken her head. Before leaving she had stood for a moment gazing over the chaise longue, the stripped and empty bed, with a look which Buckley couldn't fathom. Sadness? Speculation? Resignation? The right word eluded him. Her eyes were open but he thought he saw her lips moving. For a moment he had the extraordinary idea that she might be praying.

Back in the business room he had asked, "You were happy working for Miss Lisle? You liked each other?" That was as tactful a way as he knew of asking whether she had hated her employer enough to bash in her skull.

She had replied quietly, "We were used to each other. My mother was her nurse. She asked me to look after her."

"And you can't think of a reason why anyone should want to kill her? All one big happy family, were they?"

The attempt at Grogan-like sarcasm had been unsuccessful. She had met it with a brand of her own.

"There's never a good reason for people to kill each other, even in happy families."

He had had little more success with Mrs. Munter. She, too, had been a polite but unrewarding witness, saying as little as possible, resisting all his blandishments to entice her into volubility or indiscretion. Ambrose Gorringe had concealed his secrets, if any, with a spate of apparently artless conjecture. Miss Tolgarth and Mrs. Munter had concealed theirs with a silence and obstinacy which just avoided being overtly uncooperative. Buckley thought that Grogan could hardly have selected two more difficult witnesses for him to practice interrogation on. Perhaps that had been the idea. The impression they apparently wanted to convey was that murder, like most of the world's violence, was a male concern from which, as women, they were only too happy to be excluded. From time to time he had found himself staring at them with what he was uncomfortably aware must have been obvious frustration. But human beings weren't like school geometry problems. If you stared at them long enough, they didn't suddenly make sense.

He said, "Miss Tolgarth admits that she didn't leave Miss Lisle until after Sir George had gone, and that accords with his evidence. Miss Gray was in her own room, so nobody saw Miss Tolgarth leave. She could have returned to the bathroom, pretended to busy herself with preparations for the bath, come back into the bedroom when Gray left, and killed her mistress then."

"The timing would be very tight. Mrs. Munter saw her downstairs in the pantry at one-twenty."

"So she says. I got the feeling, sir, that those two are standing together. I got precious little out of either of them, Rose Tolgarth in particular."

"Except one highly interesting lie. Unless, of course, the lady is less sharp-eyed than I give her credit for."

"Sir?"

"In the bedroom, Sergeant. Think. You asked her if everything looked as she would expect to find it. Her answer was a nod. But visualize that dressing table. What among all that female clutter was missing, something which we would have expected to see, given the things which, in fact, we did see?"

But the launch bringing Roper and Badgett had actually touched the quay before Buckley was able to work out the answer to the conundrum.

# X

And now, at last, the dreadful day was over. Soon after ten o'clock struck, one by one and with brief "Good nights," they had crept silently to their beds. The casual nighttime commonplaces had become unsayable. "I'm terribly tired. It's been a long day. Sleep well. See you all in the morning"—all bore a weight of innuendo, tactlessness, or bad taste. Two women police officers had moved Cordelia's things from the De Morgan room, a touch of delicacy which would have amused her had she been capable of being amused. The new bedroom was on the same gallery floor but on the other side of Simon's and overlooking the rose garden and the pool. As she turned the key in the lock and breathed the stuffy, scented air, Cordelia thought that it might not often be used. It was small, dim, and cluttered and looked as if Ambrose had furnished it strictly in period for the edification of his summer visitors. The lightness and delicacy which he had achieved in so much of the castle was absent. Every square inch of the walls was covered with pictures and ornaments, and the ornate furniture, papier-mâché lined with mahogany, seemed to press in on her, dark and threatening. The room felt musty, but when she opened wide the window the sound of the sea burst in, no longer soporific and comforting but a steady menacing roar. She lay wondering whether she could summon up the energy to get out of bed and half close the window. But that was her last conscious thought before weariness took over and she felt herself drifting unresistingly down the long stream of tiredness into sleep.

# BOOK FIVE

·

# Terror by Moonlight

# I

At nine-fifteen Cordelia went into the business room to ring Miss Maudsley, wondering as she lifted the receiver whether the police would be listening in. But monitoring private telephone calls, even from the scene of a murder, counted as phone tapping and for that the consent of the Home Secretary was surely necessary. It was strange how little she knew about a real police investigation despite Bernie's tutelage. It had already struck her that their legal powers were a great deal less extensive than a reading of detective fiction might suggest. On the other hand, their physical presence was far more frightening and oppressive than she would have believed possible. It was like having mice in the house. They might for a time be both silent and invisible, but once they were known to be there, it was impossible to ignore their secret and polluting presence. Even here in the business room the force of Inspector Grogan's rebarbative personality still lingered, although all trace of his brief occupation had been cleared away. It seemed to her that the police had left the room tidier than they had found it, and this in itself was sinister. As she dialed the London number it was difficult to believe that the call wound go unrecorded.

It was a nuisance that Miss Maudsley in her cheap bed-sitting-room had no private telephone. The single instrument was in the darkest and most inaccessible corner of the hall at Mancroft Mansions, and Cordelia knew that she might have to wait for minutes until one of the other residents, driven mad by the insistent ring, came out to silence it. She would then be lucky if he understood English and luckier still if he were willing to trudge up four flights to call Miss Maudsley. But this morning her call was answered almost immediately. Miss Maudsley confided that she had bought her usual Sunday paper on the way home from eight o'clock mass and had been crouching on the bottom step of the stairs wondering whether to ring the castle or to wait for Cordelia's call. She was almost incoherent with anxiety and distress, and the brevity of the press report hadn't helped. Cordelia thought how chagrined Clarissa would be to learn that her fame, even after a violent death, didn't justify top billing on a day when a spectacular parliamentary scandal, the death of a pop star from a drug overdose, and a particularly brutal terrorist attack in northern Italy had presented the editor with a surplus of candidates for the front page.

Miss Maudsley, her voice breaking, said, "It says that she was . . . well . . . battered to death. I can't believe it. And it's so horrible for you. Her husband, too, of course. That poor woman. But naturally one thinks of the living. I suppose it was some kind of intruder. The paper does say that her jewelry is missing. I do hope that the police won't get any wrong ideas."

And that, thought Cordelia, was as tactful a way as any of saying that she hoped that Cordelia herself wasn't under suspicion.

Cordelia gave her instructions slowly, and Miss Maudsley made audible attempts to calm herself and listen.

"The police will be sure to check up on me and on the agency. I don't know the procedure, whether someone will call from the Dorset C.I.D. or whether they'll get the Met to do it for them. But don't worry. Just answer their questions."

"Oh, dear, yes, I suppose we must. But it's all so dreadful. Am I to show them everything? Suppose they ask to see the accounts? I did balance the petty cash on Friday afternoon, at least it didn't balance exactly, I'm afraid. Mr. Morgan, a delightful man, came to fix the name plaque. He said that he'd leave the bill until you got back, but I sent Bevis for some biscuits for him to have with his coffee and he forgot how much they cost, and we threw away the packet with the price on it."

"They're more likely to ask about Sir George Ralston's visit. I don't think the police will be interested in the petty cash. But let them see anything they ask for, except, of course, the clients' files. They're confidential. And Miss Maudsley, tell Bevis not to try to be clever."

Miss Maudsley promised in a voice which had become calmer; she was obviously making efforts to convey her total reliability to deal with whatever crises Monday might bring. Cordelia wondered which would be the more damaging, Bevis's playacting or Miss Maudsley's passionate protestations that in no possible circumstances could dear Miss Gray be capable of murder. Probably Bevis would be intimidated by the physical presence of the law from the worst excesses of his histrionic talents, unless by some ill chance he had happened recently to have viewed one of those television documentaries devoted to exposing the corruption, brutality, and racism of the police, in which case anything was possible. But at least she could be certain that whoever visited Kingly Street, it wouldn't be Adam Dalgliesh. From the rarefied and mysterious heights of hierarchy which he now inhabited, any such chore was unthinkable. She wondered whether he would read about the crime, whether he would learn that she was involved.

Nothing could have prepared Cordelia for the singularity of the rest of Sunday morning. Ambrose, as he was helping himself to his breakfast scrambled eggs, suddenly paused, spoon in hand.

"My God, I've forgotten to cancel Father Hancock! It's too late now. Oldfield will be on his way to fetch him."

He turned to explain. "He's an elderly Anglican priest who has retired to Speymouth. I usually invite him to take Sunday-morning service when I have guests. People nowadays seem to feel the need of these ministrations. Clarissa liked him to come when she was here for a weekend. He amused her."

"Clarissa!" Ivo gave a hoarse burst of laughter which shuddered his gaunt frame. "He'll probably arrive at the same time as the police. So we explain to Grogan that we aren't at his disposal for an hour or so because we'll all be at Divine Service. I can't wait to see his face. Admit it was on purpose that you didn't cancel, Ambrose."

"No, I assure you. It entirely slipped my mind."

Roma said, "He probably won't come. He'll have heard of the murder by now—it'll be all over Speymouth—and he'll assume that you don't expect him."

"Don't you believe it. If we were reduced by mass homicide to two, and Oldfield was available to fetch him, he'd come. He's nearly ninety and has his own priorities. Besides, he enjoys his sherry and luncheon. I'd better remind Munter."

He went out, smiling his secretive, complacent smile.

Cordelia said, "I wonder if I ought to change out of trousers."

Ivo seemed suddenly to have found an appetite. He spooned out a generous helping of egg. "Unnecessary, surely. I don't suppose you've brought gloves and a prayer book. Never mind; even if the props are missing we can still proceed to church in the approved Victorian fashion. I wonder whether the Munters and Oldfield will come to make a showing in the servants' pew. And what on earth will the old man find to preach about?"

Ambrose reappeared.

"Well, that's settled. Munter hadn't forgotten. Will you all be coming or have we any conscientious objectors?"

Roma said, "I disapprove, but I don't mind putting in an appearance if the object is to irritate Grogan. We aren't expected to sing, are we?"

"Of course. There is the *Te Deum* and the responses and we have one hymn. Would anyone like to choose it?"

No one volunteered.

"Then I suggest 'God Moves in a Mysterious Way.' We meet the launch at ten-forty."

And so the astonishing morning got under way. *Shearwater* beat the police launch to the jetty by five minutes, and Ambrose received a frail figure in cloak and biretta, who alighted with remarkable sprightliness and gazed on them benignly from moist and faded blue eyes. Before Ambrose could make the introductions the priest turned to him and said, "I was sorry to hear of your wife's death."

Ambrose said gravely, "Yes, it was unexpected. But we weren't married, Father."

"Were you not? Dear me! Forgive me, I hadn't realized. Drowned, I think they said. These waters can be very treacherous."

"Not drowned, Father. She suffered a severe concussion."

"I thought that my housekeeper said drowned. But perhaps I'm thinking of someone else. The war, perhaps. A long time ago, anyway. I'm afraid my memory is not what it was."

The police launch shuddered to the quay, and they watched while Grogan, Buckley, and two other plainclothes officers alighted.

Ambrose said formally, "May I introduce Father Hancock, who is here to take Morning Service according to the rite of the Church of England. It usually lasts an hour and a quarter. You and your officers are, of course, very welcome to attend."

Grogan said curtly, "Thank you, but I am not a member of your church and my men make their own arrangements in their off-duty time. I should be glad if we could again have access to all parts of the castle."

"Of course. Munter will look after you. And I shall, of course, be available myself after luncheon."

The church received them into its archaic, multicolored silence. Simon was persuaded to seat himself at the organ, and the rest of the party filed decorously into the high pew originally built for Herbert Gorringe. The organ was old, requiring to be pumped, and Oldfield was already there, hand at the ready. With the appearance of Father Hancock in surplice the service got under way.

Ambrose obviously took the view that his guests were dissenters, if not worse, who required a strong lead in the responses, and Ivo retained throughout an attentive gravity and showed a familiarity with the liturgy which suggested that this was his normal Sunday-morning activity. Simon managed the organ competently enough, although Oldfield let it almost run out of wind at the end of the *Te Deum* and it produced a late, noisy, and discordant amen. Roma forgot her resolve to remain silent and sang in a rich contralto only slightly out of tune. Father Hancock used the 1662 Book of Common Prayer without deletions or substitutions, and his congregation proclaimed themselves miserable offenders who had followed too much the devices and desires of their own hearts and in a slightly ragged but resolute chorus promised amendment of life. It was only at the end of the petitions, when unexpectedly he inserted a prayer for the souls of the departed, that Cordelia heard a small concerted intake of breath and the air of the church grew for a moment colder. The sermon lasted fifteen minutes and was a learned dissertation on the Pauline theology of the redemption.

As they rose to sing the hymn, Ivo whispered to Cordelia, "That's all one asks of a sermon. No possible relevance to anything but itself."

Before luncheon, Munter served sherry, dry and chilled, on the terrace. Father Hancock managed three glasses without apparent effect and talked happily to Sir George about birdwatching and to Ivo about liturgical reform, on which Ivo showed himself surprisingly well informed. No one mentioned Clarissa, and it seemed to Cordelia that for the first time since her murder, her restless, menacing spirit was subdued. For a few precious moments the weight of guilt and misery lifted from her heart. It was possible to believe, innocently talking in the sun, that life was as well ordered, as certain, as austerely decent and reasonable, as the great Anglican compromise in which they had taken part. And when they went in to their roast ribs of beef and rhubarb tart—a conventional and rather heavy Sunday luncheon, provided, she suspected, primarily for the benefit of Father Hancock—it was a relief to have him there, to hear the thin but beautiful voice discussing such a harmless interest as the nesting habits of the song thrush, and to watch his frank enjoyment of the food and wine. Only Simon, his face flushed, drank as steadily, downing the claret as if it were water, reaching for the decanter with a shaking hand. Father Hancock seemed as spry as ever after a meal which would have reduced many a younger man to stupor, and he took his leave of them with the same serene contentment with which he had greeted them four hours earlier.

As *Shearwater* drew away, Roma turned to Cordelia and said with gruff embarrassment, "I'm going for a walk for half an hour. Would you care to come? I'd like to have a word with you."

"All right. If Grogan wants us he can send for us."

They walked together, without speaking, up the long greensward beyond the rose garden, then under the shadow of the beeches, crunching their way through the bright drifts of fallen leaves tnd hearing above the scuffle of their tramping feet the strengthening pulse of the sea. After five minutes they emerged from the trees and found themselves on the edge of the cliff. To their right was a concrete bunker, part of the 1939 defenses of the island, its low entrance almost blocked with leaves. They moved around it and settled their backs against its rough-textured wall, looking down through a green-and-gold pattern of beech leaves to the narrow strip of beach and the glitter of the sea-washed shingle.

Cordelia didn't speak. The walk had been at Roma's request. It was for her to say what was on her mind. But she felt curiously peaceful and at ease with her companion, as if none of their differences could weigh against the fact of their common femininity. She watched as Roma picked up a beech twig and began methodically shredding it of leaves.

Without looking at Cordelia, she said, "You're supposed to be an expert in these things. When do you suppose we can get away? I've got a shop to look after; my partner can't manage indefinitely on his own. The police can't keep us here, surely. The investigation could take months."

Cordelia said, "They can't legally hold us at all unless they arrest us. Some of us will have to attend the inquest. But I should think you could leave tomorrow if you wanted to."

"And what about George? He'll need some help. Is he going to sort out her things, jewelry, clothes, makeup, or does he expect me to?"

"Hadn't you better ask him?"

"We can't even get into her bedroom. The police still have it sealed. And she's brought drawers of stuff with her. She always did, even for a weekend. And then there'll be all the clothes in the Bayswater flat and at Brighton, suits, dresses, her furs. He can hardly dump it all on Oxfam."

Cordelia said, "They'd be surprised, certainly. But I expect they'd find a good use for it all. They could sell the clothes in their gift shops." She would have found this female chat about Clarissa's wardrobe bizarre if she hadn't realized that Roma's concern about her cousin's clothes masked a deeper concern—Clarissa's money. Again there was a silence.

Then Roma said gruffly, "Did you know that I'd asked Clarissa for a loan just before she was killed and that she'd turned me down?"

"Yes. I was there when she told Sir George."

"And you haven't told the police?"

"No."

"That was decent of you, considering that I haven't been particularly pleasant to you."

"What has that to do with it? If they want that kind of information, they can get it from the person concerned: you."

"Well, they haven't got it so far. I lied. I'm not proud of it and I'm not even sure why. Panic, I suppose, and a feeling that it would suit them to pin the murder on me rather than on George or Ambrose. One's a baronet and war hero and the other's rich."

"I don't think they want to pin it on anyone except the guilty person. I don't take to either of them, Grogan or Buckley. But I think they're honest."

Roma said, "It's odd. I've never much liked or trusted the police, but I always took it for granted that, faced with a crime as serious as murder, I'd cooperate with them up to the hilt. I want Clarissa's murderer caught, of course I do. So why do I feel so defensive? Why do I act as if Grogan and Buckley are in league against me? And it's humiliating to find oneself lying, lying and terrified, and ashamed."

"I know. I feel the same."

"It looks as if George hasn't told them about our quarrel either. Nor has Tolly, apparently. Clarissa sent her out while we were talking, but she must have guessed. What do you think she has in mind, blackmail?"

Cordelia said, "I'm sure not. But I think she knows. She was in the bathroom while I was there, and she probably overheard. Clarissa was pretty vehement."

"She was vehement with me, vehement and offensive. If I were capable of killing her, I'd have done it then."

They were silent for a moment; then she said, "What I can't get used to is the way we all carefully avoid discussing who it was who killed her. We don't even confide what we've told Grogan. Since the murder, we've behaved to each other like strangers, telling nothing, asking nothing. Don't you find it strange?"

"Not really. We're stuck here together. Life will be intolerable if we start hurling accusations or recriminations at each other or divide into cliques."

"I suppose so. But I don't think I can go on, not knowing, not even talking about it, pretending to make polite conversation, when we're all thinking the same thing, avoiding each other's eyes, wondering, locking our doors at night. Did you lock yours?"

"Yes. I wasn't sure why. I don't think for one moment that there's a homicidal maniac on the island. Clarissa was always the intended victim. She wasn't killed by mistake. But I did lock my door."

"Against whom? Who do you think did it?"

Cordelia said, "One of us who slept in the castle on Friday night."

"I know that. But which one?"

"I don't know. Do you?"

Roma's twig was a thin, denuded wand. She threw it away, found another, and began again the work of methodical destruction.

"I should like it to be Ambrose if anyone, but I can't believe it. Wasn't it George Orwell who wrote that murder, the unique crime, should arise only from strong emotions? Ambrose never felt a strong emotion in his life. And he hasn't the courage or the ruthlessness. He isn't capable of that much hatred. He likes to play with the toys of violence: a tag end of executioner's rope, a bloodstained nightdress, a pair of Victorian handcuffs. With Ambrose, even the horror comes secondhand, disinfected by time and charm and quaintness. And it can't be Simon. He never even saw the marble limb, and, anyway, he'd have confessed by now. He's a weakling like his father. He wouldn't have the psychological strength to stand up to Grogan for five minutes if the going got rough. And Ivo? Well, Ivo's dying. He's nearly served his life sentence. He may feel that he's out of the reach of the law. But where's his motive? I suppose George is the main suspect, but I don't believe that either. He's a professional soldier, a professional killer if you like. But he wouldn't do it in that way, not to a woman. It could be the Munters, singly or together, or even Tolly, but I can't think why. That leaves you and me. And it wasn't me. And, if it's any comfort to you, I don't think it was you either."

Cordelia said, "Tell me about Clarissa. You spent a lot of your holidays with her as a child, didn't you?"

"Oh, God, those awful Augusts! They had a house on the river at Maidenhead and spent most of the summer there. Her mother thought that Clarissa ought to have young company, and my parents were glad to have me fed and boarded free. Oddly enough, we got on quite well together then, united I suppose by our fear of her father. When he came down from London she lived in terror."

"I thought that she adored him, that he was an overindulgent devoted papa."

"Is that what she told you? How typical of Clarissa! She couldn't even be honest about her own childhood. No, he was a brute. I don't mean he physically ill-treated us. In some ways that would have been more endurable than sarcasm, a cold adult anger, contempt. I didn't understand him then, of course. Now I think I do. He didn't really like women. He married to get himself a son—he had the egotism that can't imagine a world in which he hasn't at least a vicarious immortality—and he found himself with a daughter, an invalid wife who'd no intention of breeding again, and a job in which divorce wasn't an option. And Clarissa wasn't even pretty when she was a child. His coolness and her fear killed any spontaneity, any affection, even any intelligence which she might have shown. No wonder she spent the rest of her life obsessively looking for love. But, then, don't we all?"

Cordelia said, "After I was told something about her, something she'd done, I thought that she was a monster. But perhaps no one is, not entirely, not when you know the truth about them."

"She was a monster all right. But when I think of Uncle Roderick, I can understand why. Hadn't we better be getting back? Grogan will suspect us of conspiracy. We can probably scramble down to the beach from here and walk back by the sea."

They trudged back along the edge of the surf. Roma, her hands sunk in her jacket pockets, walked ahead, splashing through the small receding waves, seeming oblivious of the wet trouser bottoms flapping against her ankles, of her sodden shoes. The way back was longer and slower than the walk through the copse, but at last they turned the headland of a small bay and the castle was suddenly before them. They stopped and watched. A young man in bathing trunks and carrying a rough wooden box was climbing down the fire escape from the window of Cordelia's first bedroom. He climbed carefully, hooking his arms around the rungs, being careful not to touch them with his hands. Then he glanced around, walked to the edge of the rocks, and with a sudden violent gesture flung the box out to sea. Then he stood poised for a moment, arms raised, and dived. About thirty yards from the end of the terrace rocked a boat, a different boat from the police launch. A diver, sleek and glittering in his black suit, rested on the gunwale. As soon as the box hit the water he twisted his body and dropped backward out of sight.

Roma said, "So that's what the police are thinking."

"Yes. That's what they're thinking."

"They're after the jewel casket. And suppose they do manage to dredge it up."

Cordelia said, "It will be bad news for someone on this island. I think that they'll find that it still holds Clarissa's jewels."

But what else might it hold? Would the notice of Clarissa's performance in *The Deep Blue Sea* still be in the secret drawer? The police had taken very little interest in that single square of newsprint, but suddenly it seemed to Cordelia that it must have had some significance. Wasn't there just a possibility that it had a bearing on Clarissa's death? The thought at first seemed absurd, but it persisted. She knew that she wouldn't be satisfied until she had seen a duplicate. The obvious first step was to call at the newspaper office in Speymouth and examine the morgue. She knew the year, Jubilee Year, 1977. It shouldn't be too difficult. And at least it would give her something positive to do.

She was aware that Roma was standing absolutely still, her eyes fixed on the lone swimmer. Her face was expressionless. Then she shook herself and said, "We'd better go in and face another round of what, with Chief Inspector Grogan, passes for the third degree. If he were openly impertinent, or even brutal, I'd find it less offensive than his veiled masculine insolence."

But when they passed through the hall and were drawn by the sound of voices into the library, they were told by Ambrose that Grogan and Buckley had left the island. They were said to be meeting Dr. Ellis-Jones at the Speymouth mortuary. There would be no more questioning until Monday morning. The rest of the day was their own to get through as best they could.

## II

Buckley thought that Sunday afternoon was a hell of a time for an autopsy. He didn't exactly enjoy them whenever he had to attend, but Sunday, even when he was on duty, had about it a lethargic postprandial calm which called for a comfortable chair in the sergeants' mess and a desultory reading over of reports rather than an hour spent on his feet while Doc Ellis-Jones sliced, sawed, cut, weighed, and demonstrated with his gloved and bloody hands. It wasn't that Buckley felt squeamish. He didn't in the least care what indignities would be practiced on his own body once he was dead, and he couldn't see why anyone should be more perturbed by the ritual dismemberment of a corpse than he had been as a lad watching his Uncle Charlie in that exciting shed behind his butcher's shop. Come to think of it, Doc Ellis-Jones and Uncle Charlie shared the same expertise and went about their business in much the same way. This had surprised him when, as a newly appointed constable fresh out of regional training school, he had attended his first postmortem. He had expected that it would be more scientific, less brutal, and far less messy than it had, in fact, proved to be. It had occurred to him then that the main differences between Doc Ellis-Jones and Uncle Charlie were that Uncle Charlie worried less about infection, used a smaller variety of somewhat cruder instruments, and treated his meat with more respect. But that wasn't surprising when you considered what he charged for it.

He was glad to get out at last into the fresh air. It wasn't that the p.m. room stank. It would have been less objectionable to him if it had. Buckley strongly disliked the smell of disinfectant which overlaid rather than masked the smell of putrefaction. The smell was elusive but persistent and tended to linger in his nose.

The mortuary was a modern building on upper ground to the west of the little town, and as they made their way to their Rover they could see the lights coming on like glow worms along the curving streets and the dark form of Courcy Island lying supine like a half-submerged and sleeping animal, far out to sea. It was odd, thought Buckley, how the island seemed to draw closer or recede, depending on the light and the time of day. In the mellow autumnal sunshine it had lain in a blue haze, looking so near that he could imagine it possible to swim to that multicolored and tranquil shore. Now it had drawn far into the Channel, remote and sinister, an island of mystery and horror. The castle was on its southern shore and no lights beckoned. He wondered what the small company of suspects was doing at this moment, how they would face the long night ahead. It was his guess that all but one of them would sleep behind locked doors.

Grogan came up to him. Nodding toward the island, he said, "So now we know what one of them knew already, how she died. Stripped of Doc Ellis-Jones's technical chat about the mechanics of force and the local absorption of kinetic energy in injuries to the head, not to mention the interesting and characteristic pattern in which the skull disintegrates under the weight of impact, what have we? Much as we expected. She died from a depressed fracture of the front of the skull made with our old friend, a blunt instrument. She was probably lying on her back at the time, much as Miss Gray found her. The bleeding was steady but almost entirely internal, and the effect of the blow was intensified by the fact that the bones of her skull are thinner than normal. Unconsciousness supervened almost immediately and she died within five to fifteen minutes. The subsequent damage was done after death; how long after, he can't unfortunately say. So we have a murderer who sits and waits while his victim dies and then . . . what? Decides to make sure? Decides that he didn't much like the lady and may as well make that fact plain? Decides to cover up how she died by giving her more of the same thing? You aren't going to tell me that he waited for ten minutes or so before deciding to panic?"

Buckley said, "He could have spent the time searching for something and been enraged when he didn't find it. So he took out his frustration on the corpse."

"But searching for what? We haven't found it either, unless it's still there in the room and we've missed its significance. And there's no sign of a search. If the room was searched, it was done with care and by someone who knew what he was about. And if he was looking for something, my guess is that he found it."

"There's still the lab report to come, sir. And they'll have the viscera within the hour."

"I doubt whether they'll find anything. Doc Ellis-Jones saw no sign of poison. She may have been drugged—we mustn't theorize too far ahead of the facts—but my guess is that she was awake when she died and that she saw the face of her killer."

It was extraordinary, thought Buckley, how cold the day became once the sun had gone. It was like moving from summer to winter in a couple of hours. He shivered and held open the car door for his chief. They moved slowly out of the parking lot and turned toward the town. At first Grogan spoke only in laconic spurts.

"You've heard from the coroner's officer?"

"Yes, sir. The inquest's fixed for two o'clock on Tuesday."

"And the London end? Burroughs is getting on with those inquiries?"

"He's going up first thing in the morning. And I've told the divers we'll be needing them for the rest of the week."

"What about that bloody press conference?"

"Tomorrow afternoon, sir. Four-thirty."

Again there was silence. Changing gear to negotiate the steep and twisting hill which ran down to Speymouth, Grogan suddenly said,

"The name Commander Adam Dalgliesh mean anything to you, Sergeant?"

There was no need to ask, "Commander of what force?" Only the Met had commanders. Buckley said, "I've heard of him, sir."

"Who hasn't? The commissioner's blue-eyed boy, darling of the establishment. When the Met, or the Home Office come to that, want to show that the police know how to hold their forks and what bottle to order with the *canard à l'orange* and how to talk to a Minister on terms level with his Permanent Secretary, they wheel out Dalgliesh. If he didn't exist, the force would have to invent him."

The gibes might be unoriginal, but there was nothing second-hand about the dislike. Buckley said, "It's a bit old-fashioned, isn't it, sir, all that stuff?"

"Don't be naive, Sergeant. It's only unfashionable to talk like that anymore, but that doesn't mean that they've changed their thinking or their actions. He could have had his own force by now—probably be chairing the Association of Chief Police Officers—if he hadn't wanted to stick to detection. That and personal conceit. The rest of you can struggle in the muck for the prizes. I'm the cat who walks alone and all places are alike to me. Kipling."

"Yes, sir." Buckley paused and then asked, "What about the commander?"

"He knows the girl, Cordelia Gray. They tangled together in a previous case. Cambridge, apparently. No details offered and none asked for. But he's given her and that agency a clean bill. Like him or not, he's a good copper, one of the best. If he says that Gray isn't a murderess, I'm prepared to take that as evidence of a sort. But he didn't say that she's incapable of lying, and I wouldn't have believed him if he had."

He drove on in a moody silence. But his mind must have been mulling over yesterday's interviews. After a space of ten minutes in which neither of them spoke, he said, "There's one thing which struck me as intriguing. You probably noticed it yourself. They all described the visit on Saturday morning to the church and the crypt. They all mentioned that story about the drowned internee. But it was done a little too casually; the mere mention of an unimportant trifle; just a short excursion we happened to fancy before lunch. As soon as I invited them to dwell on the incident they reacted like a bunch of virgins who'd had an interesting experience in the Marabar Caves. I suppose the allusion is wasted on you, Sergeant?"

"Yes, sir."

"Don't worry. I'm not degenerating into one of those literary cops. I'll leave that to Dalgliesh. We did *A Passage to India* as a set book when I was at school. I used to think it overrated. But no knowledge is wasted in police work, as they used to tell me at training school, not even E. M. Forster apparently. Something happened in the Devil's Kettle which none of them is prepared to talk about and I'd like to know what."

"Miss Gray found one of the messages."

"So she says. But I wasn't thinking of that. It's probably a long shot, but we'd better find out more about that 1940 drowning. I suppose Southern Command would be the starting point."

Buckley's thoughts went back to that white, scientifically butchered body, to a nakedness which had been totally unerotic. And more than that. For a moment, watching those gloved and probing fingers, he had felt that no woman's body would ever excite him again. He said, "There was no rape and no recent intercourse."

"That hardly surprised us. Her husband hadn't the inclination and Ivo Whittingham hadn't the strength. And her murderer had other things on his mind. We'll call it a day, Sergeant. The chief constable wants a word with me first thing tomorrow. No doubt that means that Sir Charles Cottringham has been having a word or two with him. That man's a nuisance. I wish he'd stick to amateur theatricals and leave real-life drama to the experts. And then we'll get back to Courcy Island and see if a night's sleep has refreshed their memories."

# III

At last the interminable hours dragged to dinner time. Cordelia came in from a last and solitary walk with barely time to shower and change. By the time she went down, Ambrose, Sir George, and Ivo were already in the dining room. They were all seated before Simon appeared. He was wearing a dark suit. He looked at the others, flushed, and said, "I'm sorry. I didn't realize that we were going to change. I won't be long." He turned to the door.

Ambrose said with a touch of impatience, "What does it matter? You can dine in your swimming trunks if it makes you feel more comfortable. No one here cares what you wear."

Cordelia thought that it wasn't the happiest way of putting it. The unspoken words hung on the air. Clarissa would have cared; but Clarissa wasn't there. Simon's eyes slewed to the empty chair at the top of the table. Then he sidled to a chair beside Cordelia.

Ivo said, "Where's Roma?"

"She asked for soup and chicken sandwiches in her room. She says she has a headache."

It seemed to Cordelia that everyone was simultaneously doubting the reality of the headache while mentally congratulating Roma on having hit on so simple an expedient for avoiding this, their first formal dinner together since Clarissa's death. The table had been rearranged, perhaps in an attempt to minimize the trauma of that empty chair. The two end places hadn't been laid, and Cordelia and Simon sat facing Ambrose, Ivo, and Sir George, almost, it seemed, eyeball to eyeball, while an expanse of mahogany stretched gleaming on either side. Cordelia thought that the arrangement made them look like a couple of vive-voce candidates facing a not particularly intimidating panel of examiners, an impression which was strengthened by Simon's suit in which, paradoxically, he looked less cool and more formally overdressed than did the other three in their frills and dinner jackets.

Neither Munter nor his wife was present. Bowls of vichyssoise were already set at each place, and the second course was under covers on the sideboard hot plates. There was a faint smell of fish, an unlikely choice for a Sunday. It was obviously to be a convalescent's dinner, blandly inoffensive, unexciting to the palate or the digestion. It was, thought Cordelia, a nice point of culinary etiquette, the choice of menu for a house party of murder suspects dining together the day after the crime.

Ivo's thoughts must have been running with hers, for he said, "I wonder what Mrs. Beeton would reject as the most inappropriate meal for this kind of occasion. My choice would be borscht followed by steak tartare. I can't decide on the pudding. Nothing too crude, but it needs to be richly indigestible."

Cordelia said in a low voice, "Don't you care at all?"

He paused before replying as if her question merited careful thought. "I don't like to think that she suffered or was in terror even for a moment. But, if you mean do I care that she's no longer alive, then no, I don't really care."

Ambrose had finished pouring the Graves. He said, "We'll have to serve ourselves. I told Mrs. Munter to take the evening off and get some rest, and Munter hasn't shown himself since luncheon. If the police want to interview him again tomorrow they'll be unlucky. It happens about every four months, and invariably if I've had a house party. I'm not sure whether it's a reaction to the excitement, or just his way of discouraging me from too much entertaining. As he's usually considerate enough to wait until my guests have left, I can't really complain. He has compensating qualities."

Sir George said, "Drunk, is he? I thought he might take to the bottle."

"I fear so. It usually lasts three days. I did wonder whether the violent death of one of my guests would break the pattern, but apparently not. I suppose it's his release from some intolerable internal boredom. The island isn't really congenial to him. He has an almost pathological dislike of water. He can't even swim."

Ambrose, Ivo, and Cordelia had moved to the sideboard. Ambrose lifted a silver lid to reveal thin fillets of sole in a cream sauce.

Ivo asked, "Why, then, does he stay?"

"I've never asked him for fear that the same question might occur to him. Money, I suppose. And he likes solitude even if he would prefer it not to be guaranteed by two miles of sea. He has only me to please. An easy job on the whole."

"And easier now that Clarissa's dead. I take it you won't be going ahead with the drama festival?"

"Not even, my dear Ivo, as a memorial to her."

They then seemed to realize that the exchange, even though Sir George was seated too far away to overhear, was in poor taste. Both of them glanced at Cordelia. She felt a little angry with Ambrose.

Helping herself to *haricots verts*, she said on impulse, "I was wondering whether he might have found a way to augment his wage, perhaps a little smuggling on the side. The Devil's Kettle would be a useful unloading point. I noticed that he keeps the trapdoor bolt well oiled, and he'd hardly need to do that if you don't show the place to summer visitors. And on Friday night I saw a light flashing at sea. I thought that it might be acknowledging a signal."

Ambrose laughed as he carried back his plate, but when he spoke the thin note of spite was unmistakable. "Clever Cordelia! You're wasted as an amateur. Grogan would be glad to enroll you in the ranks of official snoopers. Munter may have his private arrangements, but he doesn't confide in me and I certainly have no intention of inquiring. Courcy is traditionally a smuggler's haven and most sailors in these parts do a little amateur smuggling. It wouldn't amount to much—a few casks of brandy, an occasional bottle of scent. Nothing as spectacularly naughty as drugs, if that's what you have in mind. Most people like a little tax-free income, and a touch of risk adds to the fun. But I don't advise you to confide your suspicions to Grogan. Let him get on with the investigation he has in hand."

Ivo said, "What about the lights Cordelia saw?"

"Warning off his pals, I expect. He'd hardly want the stuff landed with the island swarming with police."

Ivo said evenly, "Except that Cordelia saw the signal on Friday. How could he know that the police would be here next day?"

Ambrose shrugged, unworried. "Then it couldn't have been the police he feared. Perhaps he knew or guessed that we were being favored with the company of a private eye. Don't ask me how he knew. Clarissa didn't confide in me and I shouldn't have told Munter even if she had. But it's my experience that little goes on under any roof that a good servant doesn't learn first."

They rejoined Sir George. He had already helped himself to sole and was eating with a stolid determination but with no evident enjoyment. Cordelia pondered on Munter. She thought it unlikely that he had guessed her secret or that he would have altered his plans if he had. It was more possible that with the castle full of guests he had felt the time unpropitious for the reception of his loot: too many people about, too much extra work, the possibility that he would find it difficult to slip away unnoticed. Perhaps he hadn't been able to get a message to his confederates or the message had gone astray. Or had there been an unexpected arrival on the island, someone he feared particularly, or someone who might have known of the Devil's Kettle, might even have visited it? There was only one person who fitted that bill: Sir George.

The meal seemed endless. Cordelia sensed that they all wished it over but that no one wanted to appear to hurry or to be the first to leave. Perhaps that was why they appeared to be eating with deliberate slowness. She wondered whether it was the absence of staff that made the occasion so portentous; they might be the remnants of some deserted and soon to be beleaguered garrison stoically eating their last meal with traditional ceremony, ears tuned for the first distant shouts of the barbarians. They ate and drank but were silent. The six candles in their branched entwined stems seemed to burn less brightly than on their first evening so that their features, half shadowed, were sharpened into caricatures of their daytime selves. Pale etiolated hands reached out to the fruit bowl, to furred and flushed peaches, the curved shininess of bananas, apples burnished so that they looked as artificial as Ambrose's candlelit skin.

The french windows had been shut against the chill of the autumn night and a thin wood fire crackled in the immense grate. But surely those fitfully leaping flames couldn't account for the oppressive heat of the room. It seemed to Cordelia that it was getting hotter by the minute, that the heat of the day had been trapped and thickened, making it difficult to breathe, intensifying the smell of the food so that she felt faintly nauseated. And in her imagination the room itself changed; the Orpens splurged and spread into amorphous colors, so that the walls appeared to be hung with crude tapestries, and the elegantly stuccoed roof raised smoked hammer beams to a black infinity, open to an everlastingly starless sky. She shivered despite the heat and reached for her wineglass as if the physical feel of cool glass could strengthen her hold on reality. Perhaps only now were the full horror of Clarissa's death and the strain of the police interrogation taking their physical toll.

One candle wavered as if blown by an invisible breath, flickered, and went out. Simon gave a gasp, then a long, terrified moan. Hands, half lifted to mouths, became motionless. They turned in a single movement and stared at the window. Silhouetted against the moonlight reared an immense form, its black arms flailing, hurling itself against the window. Its anger came to them faintly, something between a wail and a bellow. As they gazed in fascinated horror it suddenly ceased its frantic beating and was for a moment still, quietly looking in at their faces. The gaping mouth, raw as a wound, seemed to suck at the window. Two gigantic palms, fingers splayed, imprinted themselves on the glass. The pressed, distorted features dissolved against the window into a mess of slowly draining flesh. Then the creature gathered its strength and heaved. The doors gave, and Munter, wild-eyed, almost fell into the room. The night air rushed cool and sweet over their faces, and the distant sighing of the waves became a surging tide of sound as if the swaying figure had been borne in on them by the force of a violent storm, bringing the sea with him.

No one spoke. Ambrose got to his feet and moved forward. Munter brushed him aside and shambled up to Sir George until their faces almost touched. Sir George stayed in his seat. Not a muscle moved. Then Munter spoke, throwing back his head and almost howling the words, "Murderer! Murderer! Murderer!"

Cordelia wondered when Sir George would move, whether he

would wait until Munter's fingers were actually at his throat. But Ambrose had moved behind and had seized the shuddering arms. At first the contact seemed to calm Munter. Then he gave a violent wrench.

Ambrose said breathlessly, "Could one of you help?"

Ivo had begun peeling a peach. He seemed totally unconcerned. He said, "I'd be no use in this particular emergency, I'm afraid."

Simon got up and grasped the man's other arm. At his touch Munter's belligerency left him. His knees buckled and Ambrose and Simon moved closer, supporting his sagging weight between them. He tried to focus his eyes on the boy, then slurred out a few words, guttural, unintelligible, sounding hardly English. But his final words were clear enough: "Poor sod. God, but she was a bitch, that one."

No one else spoke. Together Ambrose and Simon urged him to the door. He gave no further trouble but went as obediently as a disciplined child.

After they left, the two men and Cordelia sat in silence for a minute. Then Sir George got up and closed the french windows. The noise of the sea became muted, and the wildly flickering candles steadied and burned with a clear flame. He returned to the table, selected an apple, and said, "Extraordinary fellow! I was at Sandhurst with a chap who drank like that. Sober for months at a time, then paralytic for a week. Torpedoed in the Med in the winter of 'forty-two. Foul weather. Picked up from a raft three days later. Only one of the party to survive. He said that it was because he was pickled in whiskey. D'you suppose Gorringe lets Munter have the key to his cellar?"

"I shouldn't think so." Ivo sounded amused.

Sir George said, "Extraordinary arrangement, a butler who can't be trusted with the keys. Still, I suppose he has other uses. Devoted to Gorringe obviously."

Ivo asked, "What happened to him, your friend I mean?"

"Fell in his own swimming pool and drowned. The shallow end. Drunk at the time, of course."

It seemed a long time before Ambrose and Simon reappeared.

Cordelia was struck with the boy's pallor. Surely coping with a drunken man couldn't have been so horrifying an experience.

Ambrose said, "We've put him to bed. Let's hope he stays there. I must apologize for the performance. I've never known Munter to behave before in such a spectacular way. Will someone please pass the fruit bowl?"

After dinner they gathered in the drawing room. Mrs. Munter had not appeared and they poured their own coffee from the glass percolator on the sideboard. Ambrose opened the french windows and one by one, as if drawn by the sea, the guests walked out onto the terrace. The moon was full, silvering a wide swath to the horizon, and a few high stars pinpricked the blue-black of the night sky. The tide was running strongly. They could hear it slapping against the stones of the quay and the distant whisper of the spent waves hissing on the shingle beach. The only other sound was the muted footfalls of their walking feet. Here in this peace, thought Cordelia, it would be easy to believe that nothing mattered, not death, nor life, nor human violence, nor any pain. The mental picture of that splotch of battered flesh and congealed blood which had been Clarissa's face, scored as she thought forever on her mind, became unreal, something she had imagined in a different dimension of time. The disorientation was so strong that she had to fight against it, to tell herself why she was here and what it was she had to do. She came out of her trance to hear Ambrose's voice. He was speaking to Simon.

"You may as well play if you want to. I don't suppose a half hour of music would offend anyone's susceptibilities. There must be something appropriate, somewhere between a music-hall medley and the Dead March from *Saul.*"

Without replying, Simon went over to the piano. Cordelia followed him into the drawing room and watched while he sat, head bowed, silently contemplating the keys. Then, suddenly hunching his shoulders, he brought down his hands and began playing with quiet intensity, and she recognized the slow movement of Beethoven's "Moonlight Sonata."

Ambrose called from the terrace, "Trite but appropriate."

He played well. The notes sang into the silent air. Cordelia thought it interesting that he should play so much better with Clarissa dead than he had when she was alive.

When he had finished the movement she asked, "What's going to happen, about your music I mean?"

"Sir George has told me not to worry, that I can stay on at Melhurst for a final year and then go to the Royal College of the Academy if I can get in."

"When did he tell you this?"

"When he came to my room after Clarissa was found."

That was a remarkably quick decision, thought Cordelia, given the circumstances. She would have expected Sir George to have other things on his mind just then than Simon's career.

The boy must have guessed her thoughts. He looked up and said quickly, "I asked him what would happen to me now and he said that I wasn't to worry, that nothing would change, that I could go back to school and then on to the Royal College. I was frightened and shocked and I think he was trying to reassure me."

But not so shocked that he hadn't thought first of himself. She told herself that the criticism was unworthy and tried to put it out of her mind. It had, after all, been a natural childish reaction to tragedy. What will happen to me? How will this affect my life? Wasn't that what everyone wanted to know? He had at least been honest in asking it aloud.

She said, "I'm glad, if that's what you want."

"I want it. I don't think she did. I'm not sure I ought to do something she wouldn't have approved of."

"You can't live your life on that basis. You have to make your own decisions. She couldn't make them for you even when she was alive. It's silly to expect her to make them now that she's dead."

"But it's her money."

"I suppose it will be Sir George's money now. If it doesn't worry him I don't see why it need worry you."

Watching the avid eyes desperately gazing into hers, Cordelia felt that she was failing him, that he was looking to her for sympathy, for some reassurance that he could take what he wanted from life and take it without guilt. But wasn't that what everyone craved? Part of her wanted to respond to his need; but part of her was tempted to say, "You've taken so much. Why jib at taking this?"

She said, "I suppose if you want to salve your conscience about the money more than you want to be a professional pianist, you'd better give up now."

His voice was suddenly humble. "I'm not all that good, you know. She knew that. She wasn't a musician, but she knew. Clarissa could smell failure."

"Oh, well, that's a different issue, whether you're good enough or not. I think you play very well, but I can't really judge. I don't suppose that Clarissa could either. But the people at the colleges of music can. If they think you're worth accepting, they must think you have at least a chance of making a career in music. After all, they know what the competition's like."

He looked quickly around the room and then said, his voice low, "Do you mind if I talk to you? There are three things I must ask you."

"We are talking."

"But not here. Somewhere private."

"This is private. The others don't seem likely to come in. Is it going to take long?"

"I want you to tell me what happened to her, how she looked when you found her. I didn't see her, and I keep lying awake and imagining. If I knew, it wouldn't be so awful. Nothing is as awful as the things I imagine."

"Didn't the police tell you? Or Sir George?"

"No one told me. I did ask Ambrose but he wouldn't say."

And the police would, of course, have had their own reasons for keeping silent about the details of the murder. But they had interviewed him by now. She didn't see that it mattered anymore whether he knew or not. And she could understand the horror of those nightly imaginings. But there was no way in which she could make the brutal truth sound gentle. She said, "Her face was battered in."

He was silent. He didn't ask how or with what.

She said, "She was lying quite peacefully on the bed, almost as if she were asleep. I'm sure she didn't suffer. If it were done by someone she knew, someone she trusted, she probably didn't even have time to feel afraid."

"Could you recognize her face at all?"

"No."

"The police asked me if I'd taken anything from a display cabinet, a marble arm. Does that mean they think it was the weapon?"

"Yes." It was too late now to wish that she'd kept quiet. She said, "It was found by the bed. It was . . . it looked as if it had been used."

He whispered, "Thank you," but so quietly that she had difficulty in hearing him.

After a moment she said, "You said there were three things."

He looked up eagerly as if glad that his mood had been broken. "Yes, it's Tolly. On Friday when I went swimming while the rest of you toured the castle, she waited for me on the shore. She wanted to persuade me to leave Clarissa and live with her. She said that I could go straightaway and that she had a room in her flat I could have until I'd found myself a job. She said that Clarissa might die."

"Did she say how or why?"

"No. Only that Clarissa thought she was going to die and that people who thought that often did die." He looked straight at her. "And next day, Clarissa did die. I don't know whether I ought to tell the police what happened, about waiting for me, what she said."

"If Tolly was actually planning to murder Clarissa, she'd hardly warn you in advance. She was probably trying to tell you that you couldn't rely on Clarissa, that she might change her mind about you, that she might not always be there."

"I think she did know. I think she guessed. Ought I to tell the chief inspector? I mean, it is evidence, isn't it? Suppose he found out that I'd been keeping something back?"

"Have you told anyone?"

"No. Only you."

"You must do what you think is right."

"But I don't know what's right! What would you do if you were in my place?"

"I wouldn't tell. But then I have a reason. If you feel that it's right to tell, then tell. If it's any comfort to you, I don't think the police will arrest Tolly on that evidence alone, and they haven't any other, at least as far as I know."

"But she'd know that I must have told them! What would she think of me? I don't think I could face her after that."

"You might not have to. I don't suppose she'll stay on now that Clarissa's dead."

"So you would tell if you were me?"

Cordelia's patience snapped. It had been a long day, ending in the trauma of Munter's dramatic appearance, and she was weary in spirit as well as body. And it was difficult to sympathize with Simon's obsessive self-concern.

"I've told you. I wouldn't tell. But I'm not you. It's your responsibility and you can't force it on anyone else. Surely there's some thing you're capable of deciding for yourself."

She regretted the unkindness almost as soon as the words were out of her mouth. She turned her eyes from his scarlet face and stricken, doglike eyes and said, "I'm sorry. I shouldn't have said that. I suppose we're all on edge. Wasn't there a third thing you wanted to ask?"

He whispered, his mouth trembling, "No. There's nothing else. Thank you." He got up and closed the piano. He added quietly and with some attempt at dignity, "If anyone asks about me, I've gone to bed."

Unexpectedly, Cordelia found that she, too, was close to tears. Torn between irritation and pity and despising her own weakness, she decided to follow Simon's example. The day had gone on long enough. She went out on the terrace to say good night. The three black-clad figures were standing apart, silhouetted against the iridescence of the sea, motionless as bronze statues. At her approach they simultaneously turned, and she could feel the concentrated gaze of three pairs of eyes. No one moved or spoke. The moment of moonlit silence seemed to her portentous, almost ominous, and as she said her good nights the thought that for the past twenty-four hours she had tried to suppress surfaced in all its stark and frightening logic. "We are here together, ten of us on this small and lonely island. And one of us is a murderer."

# IV

Cordelia fell asleep almost as soon as she had closed her book and put out the bedside light. But her awakening was as sudden. She lay for a moment confused and then put out her hand and found the switch. Her wristwatch, curled on the bedside table, showed her that it was just after three-thirty, far too early, surely, for her to have waked naturally. She thought that her sleep had been pierced by some sound, perhaps the shriek of a night bird. The moonlight streamed through the half-drawn curtains, cutting a swath of light over the ceiling and walls. The silence was absolute except for the pulse of the plangent sea, louder now than in the stir of the daylight hours. Her mind, still drugged with sleep, took hold of the tag end of a dream. She had been back in Kingly Street, and Miss Maudsley had been showing her with pride a newly rescued kitten. As is the way of dreams, she found it unsurprising that the kitten should be sleeping in a carved cradle with a red canopy and side curtains, a miniature of Clarissa's bed, or that, when she peered into the cot and pulled aside the shawl, she should see, not a kitten, but a baby, and should know that this was Miss Maudsley's illegitimate child and that she must be very tactful and not betray that she knew. She smiled at the memory, put out the light, and tried to relax into sleep.

But this time it was elusive. Once awake, she was restless. Her mind busied itself again with the mystery and horror of Clarissa's death. Image succeeded image, unsought but insistent, disconnected in time but horribly clear: Clarissa's satin-clad body gleaming palely under the crimson canopy; Clarissa gazing down into the swirl of water at the Devil's Kettle; Clarissa's slim figure passing to and fro on the terrace, pale as a ghost; Clarissa standing on the pier and stretching her arms bat-winged in welcome; Clarissa removing her makeup, turning on Cordelia one naked and diminished eye in a freakish, strange, discordant gaze which seemed now to hold a look of sad reproach.

Her mind held that last picture as if unwilling to let it fade. Something about it was significant, something that she ought to have known or remembered. And then the realization came. She saw again the dressing table, the balls of cotton wool smeared with makeup, the smaller pads shifting across the mahogany, blackened with mascara. Clarissa had used a special lotion to cleanse her eyes. But those pads hadn't been on the dressing table when her body was discovered. Perhaps she hadn't troubled to remove her eye makeup. Was that something which the forensic pathologist would be able to detect even beneath that shattered and swollen flesh? But why should she take off her powder and foundation and leave her eyes under a weight of shadow and mascara, particularly as she proposed to rest them under the moistened pads. But wasn't there another possibility, that she had kept on all her makeup because she was expecting a visitor and that it had been the visitor who had wiped her face clean before smashing it to pulp? And that implied a man. A man was surely the most likely secret visitor. But Clarissa was too obsessed with her appearance to meet even a woman with a naked face. Still, wouldn't a woman be more likely to realize that she must use the special pads to remove the eye makeup? Tolly would have known it certainly. But Roma? Roma's eyes were devoid of mascara, and in the urgency and terror of the moment she would be unlikely to make a close inventory of the bottles on the dressing table. A man was still the most likely to make such a mistake, except perhaps Ivo, with his knowledge of theatrical makeup. The strangest part of it all was surely Tolly's silence. The police must have questioned her about the makeup, must have asked her if everything on the dressing table looked normal. And that meant that Tolly had held her tongue. Why and for whom?

It was impossible now to will herself to sleep. But she must have dozed at last, if only fitfully, for it was nearly four when she next awoke. She was too hot. The bedclothes lay heavily on her like the weight of failure, and she knew that there would be no more sleep that night. The sea was louder than ever, the air itself seeming to throb. She had a vision of the tide rising inexorably over the terrace, sweeping into the dining room, floating the heavy table and the carved chairs, rising to cover the Orpens and the stuccoed ceiling, creeping up the stairs until the whole island was covered except for the slender tower, rising like a lighthouse above the waves. She lay rigidly, longing for the first flush of day. It would be Monday, a working day in Speymouth. She would be able to get away from the island, if only for a few hours, to visit the local newspaper office, to try to trace the cutting about Clarissa's Jubilee performance. She had to have something positive to do, however unlikely to prove successful and significant. It would be good to feel free, free of Ambrose's ironic, half-secret smile, Simon's misery, Ivo's gaunt fortitude; free most of all from the eyes of the police. She had no doubt that they would be back. Yet, short of arresting her, there was nothing they could do to prevent her spending a day on shore.

Now it seemed that the morning would never come. She gave up the attempt at sleeping and got out of bed. She pulled on her jeans and guernsey, went to the window, and drew back the curtains. Below her lay the rose garden, the last overblown heads drooping on their spiky branches, bleached pale by the moon. The water on the pond looked as solid as beaten silver, and she could see clearly the smudge of lily leaves, the gleam of their blossoms. But there was something else on the surface, something black and hairy, an immense spider crawling, half submerged, spreading and waving its innumerable hairy legs under the shimmering water. She gazed in fascinated disbelief. And then she knew what it was and her blood ran cold.

She wasn't aware of her flight down to the gate which led from the passage to the garden. She must have banged on bedroom doors as she ran, indiscriminately, aware only that she might need help, not waiting for a response. But others must have been sleeping lightly. By the time she reached the door into the garden and was straining upwards to shoot back the top bolt, she was aware of muffled footsteps padding down the passageway, a confused murmur of voices. And then she was standing at the edge of the pool with Simon, Sir George, and Roma beside her and viewing clearly for the first time what it was she knew that she had seen: Munter's wig.

It was Simon who threw off his dressing gown and waded into the pool. The water came up to his thrashing arms. He gulped, then dived. The rest of them watched and waited. The water had scarcely steadied after the flurry of his disappearance when his head shot up, sleek as a seal's. He called, "He's here. He's caught on some wire netting where the lilies are rooted. Don't come in. I think I can free him."

He disappeared again. Almost at once they saw two black shapes surfacing. Munter's bald head, face upwards, looked as swollen as if it had been in the water for weeks. Simon pushed the body toward the side of the pool, and Cordelia and Roma bent and tugged at the sodden sleeves. Cordelia knew that it would be easier to take his hands, but the bloated fingers, yellow as udders, repelled her. She bent over his face and shifted her grasp to his shoulders. The eyes were open and glazed, the skin as smooth as latex. It was like pulling a dummy from the water, some discarded manikin with a sawdust-stuffed body, water-logged and inert in its ridiculous formal coat. The clown's mask with its sagging jaw seemed to be gazing into hers with a look of piteous inquiry. She could imagine that she smelled his breath, stinking with drink. She was suddenly ashamed of the repugnance which had rejected the sad remnant of his humanity, and in a spasm of pity she grasped his left hand. It felt like a taut bladder, fleshless and cold. And it was in that moment of touch that she knew he was dead.

They tugged him onto the grass. Simon pulled himself out of the water. He folded his dressing gown under Munter's head, forced back his neck, and felt in the gaping mouth for dentures. There were none. Then he fastened his mouth over the thick lips and began the kiss of life. They watched silently. No one spoke, even when Ambrose and Ivo came up quickly and stood among them. There was no sound but the squelch of sodden clothes as Simon bent to his task and the regular gasp of his intaken breath. Cordelia glanced at Sir George, wondering a little at his silence. He was gazing down at the bloated, inverted face, at the half-shut and unseeing eyes, with a look of great intensity, almost of incredulous recognition. And in that moment, Cordelia's heart jolted. Her eyes met his and she thought they flashed a warning. Neither spoke, but she wondered whether he had shared her revelation. There came into her mind an old incongruous picture: the music room at the convent, Sister Hildegarde stretching wide her mouth and eyes in an anticipatory mime, raising the white baton. "And now, my children, the Schumann. Happy, happy! Mouths wide. *Ein munteres Lied.*"

She dragged her mind back to the present. There was no time to think about her discovery or to explore its implications. She forced herself to look again at the sodden lump of flesh on which Simon was so desperately working. He was close to exhaustion when Ambrose bent and felt for the pulse at Munter's wrist. He said, "It's no good. He's dead. And he's icy cold. He's probably been in the water for hours."

Simon didn't reply. He went on mechanically pumping breath into the inert body as if performing some indecent and esoteric rite.

Roma said, "Ought we to give up? I thought you were supposed to go on for hours."

"Not when the pulse has gone and the body's cold."

But Simon took no notice. The rhythm of his harsh, indrawn breath and the antics of his crouched body seemed to have become more frantic. It was then that they heard Mrs. Munter's voice, low but harsh: "Leave him be. He's dead. Can't you see that he's dead?"

Simon heard her. He stood up and began to shiver violently. Cordelia took his dressing gown from under Munter's head and wrapped it around his shoulders.

Ambrose turned to Mrs. Munter. "I'm so very sorry. When did it happen, do you know?"

"How can I tell?" She paused, then added, "Sir. I don't sleep with him when he's drunk."

"But you must have heard him go out. He can't have walked steadily or quietly."

"He left his room just before three-thirty."

Ambrose said, "I wish you had let me know."

Cordelia thought, he sounds as peevish as if she were proposing to take a week's holiday without consulting him.

"I thought you paid us to protect you from trouble and inconvenience. He'd made enough for one night."

There seemed to be nothing to say. Then Sir George came forward and beckoned to Simon. "Better get him indoors."

There was a new note in Mrs. Munter's voice. She said quickly, "Don't bring him into the servants' flat, sir."

Ambrose said soothingly, "Of course not, if that's how you feel."

"That's how I feel." She turned and walked away.

The rest of the party looked after her. Then Cordelia ran and caught her up.

"Please let me come with you. I don't think you should be alone."

She was surprised that the eyes lifted to hers could hold so much dislike.

"I want to be alone. There's nothing the likes of you can do. Don't worry, I'm not going to kill myself." She nodded toward Ambrose. "You can tell him that."

Cordelia returned to the group. She said, "She doesn't want anyone with her. She says to tell you that she'll be all right."

No one answered. They were still standing in a circle, looking down on the body. Dressing-gowned as they were, their feet muffled by slippers, they loomed over the corpse like a group of oddly clad mourners: Sir George in shabby checked wool, Ivo's dark green silk through which his shoulders stuck like wire hangers, Ambrose's somber blue faced with satin, Roma's padded and flowered nylon, Simon's brown bathrobe. Watching the circle of bent heads, Cordelia half expected them to raise in concert and wail a threnody in the thin air.

Then Sir George roused himself and turned to Simon. "Shall we get on with it?"

Ivo had wandered a little way along the edge of the pool and was contemplating the remnants of the water lilies as if they were some rare marine vegetation in which he had a scientific interest. He looked up and said, "But ought you to move him? Isn't it usual not to disturb the body until the police arrive?"

Roma cried, "But that's only in a case of murder! This is an accident. He was drunk, he staggered, and he fell in. Ambrose told us that Munter couldn't swim."

"Did I? I can't remember. But it's perfectly true. He couldn't swim."

Ivo said, "You told us so at dinner. But Roma wasn't there."

Roma cried, "Someone told me, Mrs. Munter perhaps. What does it matter? He was drunk, he fell in, and he drowned. It's perfectly obvious what happened."

Ivo resumed his contemplation of the water lilies. "I don't think anything is ever perfectly obvious to the police. But I daresay you're right. There's enough mystery without making more. Are there any marks of violence on the body?"

Cordelia said, "Not that I can see."

Roma said obstinately, "We can't leave him here. I think we should take him indoors." She looked at Cordelia as if inviting her support.

Cordelia said, "I don't think it matters if we move him. It isn't as if we had found him like this."

They all looked at Ambrose as if waiting for instructions. He said, "Before we move him, please come with me, all of you. There's something we have to decide."

# V

They followed him toward the castle. Only Simon glanced behind him at the ungainly lump of cold flesh, still spreadeagled, which had been Munter. His glance conveyed an embarrassed regret, almost a look of apology, that they should have to desert him, leave him so uncomfortably circumstanced.

Ambrose led them into the business room and switched on the desk lamp. The atmosphere was at once conspiratorial; they were like a gang of dressing-gowned schoolchildren planning a midnight prank.

He said, "We have a decision to make. Do we tell Grogan what happened at dinner? I think we ought to agree about that before I telephone the police."

Ivo said, "If you mean do we tell the police that Munter accused Ralston of murder, why not say so plainly?"

Simon's hair, plastered over his brow and dripping water into his eyes, looked unnaturally black. He was shivering under the dressing gown. He looked from face to face, astounded. "But he didn't accuse Sir George of . . . well, of any particular murder. And he was drunk! He didn't know what he was saying. You all saw him. He was drunk!" His voice was getting dangerously close to hysteria.

Ambrose spoke with a trace of impatience. "No one here thinks it of any importance. But the police may. And anything that Munter did or said during the last hours of his life will obviously interest them. There's a lot to be said for saying nothing, for not complicating the investigation. But we have to give roughly the same account. If some tell and the others don't, those who opt for reticence will obviously be placed in an invidious position."

Simon said, "Do you mean that we pretend that he didn't come in through the dining-room windows, that we didn't see him?"

"Of course not. He was drunk and we all saw him in that state. We tell the police the truth. The only question is, how much of the truth?"

Cordelia said quietly, "It isn't only Munter's shouted accusation at Sir George. After you and Simon took Munter out, Sir George told us about an army friend of his who had drunk in just that compulsive way . . ."

Ivo finished the sentence for her, "And had been drowned in just that way. The police will find that an interesting coincidence. So unless Sir George told you both the same story on a different occasion—which I take it he didn't—Cordelia and I are already in what you might call an invidious position."

Ambrose took in this information in silence. It seemed to give him some satisfaction. Then he pronounced, "In that case the choice would seem to be: do we all give a truthful account of the evening's proceedings, or do we omit Munter's shout of 'Murderer' and the story about Ralston's unfortunate friend?"

Cordelia said, "I think we should tell the truth. Lying to the police isn't as easy as it sounds."

Roma said, "You speak from experience, perhaps."

Cordelia ignored the note of malice and went on, "They'll question us closely. What did Munter say when he burst in? What did the rest of us talk about when Ambrose and Simon were helping him to bed? It isn't only a question of omitting embarrassing facts. We have to agree on the same lies. That's apart from any moral considerations."

Ambrose said easily, "I don't think we need complicate the decision with moral considerations. Doing evil that good may come is a perfectly valid option whatever the theologians tell you. Besides, I imagine that we all did a little judicious editing in our interviews with Grogan. I did. He seemed to feel that my staging the play for Clarissa required explaining, so I told him that she gave me the idea for *Autopsy.* An ingenious but quite unnecessary lie. So our first decision is easy. We tell the truth, or we agree on a story. I suggest we take a secret ballot."

Ivo said quietly, "Here, or do we all repair to the crypt?"

Ambrose ignored him. He turned first to where Simon stood, his chattering mouth half open, his washed face pale under the feverish eyes, and thought better of it. He said to Cordelia with formal courtesy, "Would you be good enough to bring me two cups from the kitchen? I think you know the way."

The short journey, the incongruous errand, seemed to her of immense significance. She walked down the empty passages and into the kitchen and took down two breakfast cups from the dresser with grave deliberateness as if an unseen audience were watching the grace of every movement. When she got back to the business room it seemed to her that no one had moved.

Ambrose thanked her gravely and placed the cups side by side on the desk. Then he went out to the display cabinet and returned, carrying the round board with its colored marbles, Princess Victoria's solitaire board. He said, "We each take a marble. Then we close our eyes—no peeping, I implore you—and drop it into one of the cups. We'll make it easy to remember. The left cup for the more sinister option, the right for righteousness. You'll see that I've even aligned the handles appropriately so there's no excuse for confusion. When we've heard the five marbles drop we open our eyes. It's convenient that Roma wasn't at dinner. There's no possibility of a tie."

Sir George spoke for the first time. He said, "You're wasting time, Gorringe. You'd better ring for the police now. Obviously we tell Grogan the truth."

Ambrose took his marble, selecting it with some care and examining its veining as if he were a connoisseur of such trifles. "If that's what you want, that's what you vote for."

Ivo said, "Do you then intend to take a second ballot to decide whether we tell the police about the first ballot?"

But he took a marble. Sir George, Simon, and Cordelia followed. She closed her eyes. There was a second's silence, and then she heard the first marble tinkle into a cup. The second followed almost immediately, then a third. She stretched out her hands. They were briefly brushed by ice-cold fingers. She felt for the cups and placed a hand on each so that there could be no mistake. Then she dropped the marble into the right-hand cup. A second later she heard the last marble fall. The sound was unexpectedly loud; it must have been dropped from a height. She opened her eyes. Her companions were all blinking as if the period of darkness had lasted for hours, not seconds. Together they looked into the cups. The right-hand one held three marbles.

Ambrose said, "Well, that simplifies matters. We tell the truth, apart, of course, from mentioning this little divertissement. We came together into the business room and you all sat here together, appropriately subdued, while I rang the police. We've only spent a few minutes, so there will be no embarrassing hiatus of time to account for."

He replaced the marbles, after carefully scrutinizing each one, handed the two cups to Cordelia, and took up the telephone receiver. As she was returning the cups to the kitchen, two thoughts chiefly occupied her. Why had Sir George waited until the ballot was inevitable before announcing that he favored the truth, and which of the two of them had dropped a marble into the left-hand cup? She did briefly wonder whether anyone could have transferred someone else's marble in addition to dropping his own, but decided that this would have required some sleight of hand even if done with open eyes. Her own ears were exceptionally sharp, and they had detected only the four clear tinkles as the other marbles fell.

Ambrose was apparently practicing a policy of togetherness. He waited until she returned before ringing the Speymouth police station. He said, "It's Ambrose Gorringe speaking from Courcy Island. Will you tell Chief Inspector Grogan that my butler, Munter, is dead? He was found in the pool here, apparently drowned."

Cordelia thought that the statement was notable for being brief, accurate, and carefully noncommittal. Ambrose for once was keeping an open mind on the cause of Munter's death. The rest of the conversation was monosyllabic. Ambrose eventually replaced the receiver. He said, "That was the duty sergeant. He'll let Grogan know. He says not to move the body. The less interference the better until the police arrive."

There was silence in which it seemed to Cordelia that they all simultaneously recognized that they were cold. It wasn't yet half past six, and while it might appear unfeeling to express a wish to return to bed and hopeless to expect sleep once there, it was unreasonably early to get dressed and face the day.

Ambrose said, "Would anyone care for tea or coffee? I don't know what's likely to happen about breakfast. You may get none unless I cook it, but I assure you I'm perfectly competent. Is anyone hungry?"

No one admitted to being hungry. Roma shivered and hunched herself deeper into her padded nylon dressing gown. She said, "Tea would be welcome, the stronger the better. And then I, for one, am going back to bed."

There was a general murmur of acquiescence.

Then Simon spoke. "There's something I forgot. There's some kind of box down there. I felt it when I released the body. Ought I to bring it up?"

"The jewel casket!" Roma turned, reanimated, the desire for bed apparently forgotten. "So he had it after all!"

Simon said eagerly, "I don't think it's the casket. It felt larger, smoother. He must have dropped it as he fell."

Ambrose hesitated. "I suppose we ought to wait until the police arrive. On the other hand, I have a curiosity to see what it is, if Simon has no objection to a second immersion."

So far from objecting, the boy, shivering as he was with cold, seemed impatient to get back to the pool. Cordelia wondered if he had temporarily forgotten that sprawled body. She had never seen him so animated, almost frantic. Perhaps it was the result of being, for once, the center of the action.

Ivo said, "I think I can contain my curiosity. I'm going back to bed. If anyone is making tea later, I'd be grateful if you'd bring up a cup."

He left on his own. Roma was apparently cured of both her headache and her tiredness. They returned to the pool. The fading moon was tissue thin and the sky was streaked with the first light of day. The air rose in a thin mist from the water and struck them with a damp autumnal chill. Bereft of the moonlight's bleak enchantment and the sense of unreality which moonlight bestows, the body looked at once more human and more grotesque. The flesh of the left cheek, resting against the stones, was pressed upwards to distort the eye so that it seemed to be leering at them, ironic and knowing. From the drooling mouth a trickle of bloodstained saliva had hung and dried on the stubble of the chin. The sodden clothes looked as if they had already shrunk, and a thin stream of water still ran from the trouser legs and dripped slowly into the pool. In the uncertain light of the first dawn it seemed to Cordelia that his life blood was seeping away, unregarded and unstanched. She said, "Can't we at least cover him up?"

"Of course." Ambrose was at once solicitous. "Could you fetch something from the house, Cordelia? A tablecloth, a sheet, a towel, or even a coat would do. I'm sure you'll find something suitable."

Roma turned on him, her voice harsh. "Why send Cordelia? Why should she be expected to run all the errands round here? She's not paid to take your orders. Cordelia isn't your servant. Munter was."

Ambrose looked at her as if she were an unintelligent child who had for once succeeded in making a sensible remark. He said calmly, "You're perfectly right. I'll go myself."

But Roma, in angry spate, was beyond appeasement. "Munter was your servant and you can't even bring yourself to say you're sorry he's dead. You don't care, do you? You didn't care about Clarissa and you don't care about him. Nothing touches you as long as you're comfortable and saved from boredom. You haven't said a word of regret since we found his body. And who are you, for God's sake? Your grandfather made his money out of liver pills and gripe water. You haven't even the excuse of caste for not behaving like a human being."

For a second Ambrose's body froze, and two moons of red appeared on the smooth cheeks, then as quickly faded, leaving him very pale. But his voice hardly altered. "The only human being I know how to behave like is myself. I shall grieve for Munter in my own time and place. This hardly seems an appropriate moment for a valediction. But if its absence offends you I can always emulate Prince Hal. 'What! old acquaintance! could not all this flesh / Keep in a little life? Poor Jack, farewell, / I could have better spared a better man.' And if it's any comfort to you, I would rather see all of you, with one possible exception, dead at the bottom of my pool than lose Carl Munter. But you're right about Cordelia. One is too ready to take advantage of competence and kindness."

After he left there was an embarrassed silence. Roma, her face blotched, her chin creased with stubborn anger, stood a little apart. She had the truculent, slightly defensive air of a child who knows that she has said something indefensible but who is not altogether ungratified by the result.

Suddenly she swung round and said gruffly, "Well, at least I managed to provoke a human reaction from our host. So now we know where we stand. I take it that Cordelia is the privileged one among us whom Ambrose would be reluctant to see dead at the bottom of his pool. Even he isn't entirely immune to a pretty face, apparently."

Sir George stared down at the water lilies. "He's upset. Natural, after all. Hardly the time to quarrel among ourselves."

Cordelia felt that she ought to make some comment but, unable to think of anything appropriate, remained silent. She was puzzled by Roma's outburst, which she hardly felt was the result of concern or affection for herself. It could, she supposed, have been a gesture of feminine solidarity or a blast against male arrogance. But she suspected that it was more likely a spontaneous release of pent-up terror and shock. Whatever the cause, the result had been interesting. And Ambrose had been remarkably apt with his quotation from *Henry IV*. Was that because he was a natural lover of Shakespeare, or because he had recently been spending some time looking through the Shakespearean section of the *Penguin Dictionary of Quotations*?

They heard Ambrose's returning footsteps on the stones. He was carrying a folded red-checked tablecloth. While they watched he shook it out, then let it fall gently over the body. Cordelia thought that, as a temporary shroud, it was hardly the most appropriate covering he could have found. He knelt and tucked it solicitously around the body as if making it comfortable. Still no one spoke.

Then Sir George turned to Simon and barked out his order. "Right, boy. Let's get on with it."

Simon had already judged the depth of the pool, and this time he dived. His body cleft the water in a neat curve, parting the water lilies. There was a flurry and a brief commotion. And then his sleek head broke the surface and he raised both his arms high. Between them he held a dark wooden box about twelve inches by nine. A few seconds later he pushed his burden into Ambrose's waiting hands and was drawing himself up over the side of the pool. He gasped, "It was caught under the netting. What is it?"

For reply Ambrose opened the lid. The music box, watertight, had emerged a little scratched but otherwise undamaged. The cylinder slowly turned, and a tinkle of sweet disjointed notes plucked out a familiar tune, one which Cordelia had last heard during the final rehearsal, "The Blue Bells of Scotland."

They listened silently until the tune was at an end. Then there was a pause and the next tinkle began, soon to be identified as "My Bonnie Lies Over the Ocean."

Ambrose closed the box. He said, "The last time I saw this it was with the other music box on the props table. He must have been taking it back to the tower room. This would be the direct route from the theater to the tower."

"But why? What was the hurry?" Roma frowned at the box as if its appearance had disappointed her expectations.

Ambrose said, "There was no hurry. But he was drunk and I suppose he was acting irrationally. Munter shared my slight obsession with order, and he strongly disliked any of the things in the castle being used as theatrical props. I suppose his muddled brain thought that this was as good a time as any to start putting things to right."

Cordelia thought that Sir George had been remarkably silent. Now he spoke for the first time. "What else has he moved? What about the other box?"

"That was kept in the cupboard in the business room. As far as I can remember, one box was there, the second with the clutter in the tower room."

Sir George turned to Simon. "Better get dressed, boy. You're shivering. There's nothing else to do here."

It was a dismissal, almost brutal in its peremptoriness. Simon seemed to realize for the first time that he was cold. His teeth began to chatter. He hesitated, nodded, then shambled off.

Roma said, "That boy has more talents than I gave him credit for. And how, incidentally, did he know what Clarissa's jewel box was like? I thought you only gave it to her when she arrived on Friday morning."

Cordelia said, "I suppose he knows in the same way as you and I know: because we've been to her room and been shown it."

Roma turned to go. "Oh, I realized, of course, that he must have been in her room. I was just wondering when exactly." She added, "And how did he know that Munter was carrying the box when he fell? It could have been lying there on the bottom for months."

"It was a safe assumption, surely, given the position of the body and the fact that it and the box were both caught by the netting." Ambrose's voice held a lightness and a determined incuriosity which Cordelia sensed was a little too controlled, a little too careful. He added, "Why not leave the questions to Grogan? One amateur detective in the house is surely enough. And accusations of murder come more appropriately from the police, don't you feel?"

Roma turned away, hunching her shoulders more deeply into the collar of her dressing gown. "Well, I'll get back to bed. Perhaps I could have some tea in my room, too, when you get around to making it. And when I've had my stint with Grogan I'll relieve you of my presence here. Either the Courcy curse is still operative, or in your paradise death is becoming infectious."

Ambrose watched while she slumped away and disappeared into the shadows of the arches. He said, "That woman could be dangerous."

Sir George was still staring after her departing back. "Only unhappy."

"With a woman that amounts to the same thing. And with those beefy swimmer's shoulders, she shouldn't wear a padded dressing gown. And she shouldn't choose that shade of blue, or any blue for that matter. I suppose that we may as well see whether the second music box is back where it's normally kept."

In the business room he knelt and opened the doors of a walnut chiffonier. Cordelia could see that it contained a number of box files, two carefully wrapped parcels, which could have been ornaments as yet unpacked, and a box of dark wood similar in size to the first. He placed it on the table and raised the lid. The box plucked out the tune "Greensleeves."

Sir George said, "So he did return it. Odd. Probably couldn't rest until he'd started putting things to rights."

Cordelia said, "Except that he's changed them around. This one belonged in the tower room."

Ambrose's voice was unexpectedly sharp. "How can you possibly know?"

"Because I saw it there on Friday afternoon while Clarissa was rehearsing. I went to explore the tower and found the room. I couldn't be mistaken."

"They look very alike."

"But they play different tunes. I opened the box in the tower, this box. It played 'Greensleeves.' The one used at the rehearsal played the Scottish medley. You know. You were there."

Sir George said, "So yesterday afternoon he fetched this one from the tower and not from the business room." He turned to Ambrose. "Did you know that, Gorringe?"

"Naturally not. I knew that we had two boxes and that one was kept here, the other in the tower room. I didn't know which was which. They aren't a particular passion of mine. When Munter told me what he also told the police, that he hadn't left the ground-floor apartments and that he'd fetched a music box from the business room, I saw no reason to doubt him."

Cordelia said, "When Clarissa or the producer first asked for a music box, Munter acted as one would expect. He fetched the nearer and less valuable box. Why trouble to go all the way to the tower room when there was a box easily to hand here in the business room? He wouldn't have gone to the tower room if Clarissa hadn't rejected the first box."

Ambrose said, "The only entrance to the tower is from the gallery.

Munter lied to the police: at about two o'clock yesterday he was within a few feet of Clarissa's door. That means he could have seen someone entering or leaving. The police may feel that he could have gone in to her himself, locked door or no locked door. And that's why he was so obsessive about returning the boxes, each to the room he said he'd taken it from. He needn't have troubled, of course. I don't see how anyone could have known the truth. It was pure chance that you, Cordelia, wandered into the tower and found the second box. Whether the police believe you is, of course, another matter."

Cordelia said, "It wasn't altogether chance. If Clarissa hadn't ordered me out of the theater I should have watched the rehearsal to the end. And I don't see why the police shouldn't believe me. They may find it easier to believe that I was curious to explore the tower room than that you, who are so fond of your Victoriana, didn't know precisely where you kept each of your music boxes." As soon as she had spoken, she wondered whether this frankness had been wise; spoken to her host, it had hardly been courteous.

But Ambrose accepted the comment without offense. He said easily, "You're probably right. I doubt whether they'll believe either of us. After all, they have only our word for it that Munter lied. And it's very convenient for us, isn't it: a dead suspect who can't now deny what any of us chooses to say about him? 'The butler did it.' Even in fiction, so I'm led to believe, that solution is regarded as unsatisfactory."

Sir George lifted his head. "I think the police launches are arriving."

He must, thought Cordelia, have remarkable ears for an aging man. Hers had caught nothing. And then she sensed rather than heard the throb of engines. They looked at one another. For the first time Cordelia saw in their eyes what she knew they must be recognizing in hers, the flicker of fear.

Ambrose said, "I'll meet them at the quay. You two had better get back to the body."

Sir George and Cordelia were alone. If it were to be said, it had to be said now, before the police questioning began. But it was hard to get out the words, and when she did they sounded harsh, accusatory.

"You recognized that drowned face, didn't you? You think he could have been Blythe's son?"

He said, unsurprised, "It did strike me, yes. Never occurred to me before."

"You'd never seen Munter like that before, his face upturned, dead and drowned. That's how you last saw his father."

"What made you think of it?"

"Your face when you looked down at him. The war memorial he decorates every Armistice Day. The words he shouted out at you: 'Murderer, murderer!' It was his father he meant, not Clarissa. And I think he muttered in German to Simon. And his Christian name. Didn't Ambrose say he was Carl? And his height. His father died slowly because he was so tall. But, most of all, his name. *Munter* is German for *Blythe*. It's one of the few German words I know."

She had seen that look of strained endurance on his face before, but all he said was "Could be. Could be."

She asked, "Are you going to tell Grogan?"

"No. None of his business. Not relevant."

"Not even if they arrest you for murder?"

"They won't. I didn't kill my wife." Suddenly he said, quickly as if the words were forced out of him, "I don't believe I deliberately let them kill him. May have done. Difficult to understand one's motives. Used to think it was all so simple."

Cordelia said quickly, "You don't have to explain to me. It's none of my business. And you were a very young officer at the time. You can't have been in command here."

"No, but I was on duty that evening. Should have discovered that something was afoot, should have stopped it. But I hated Blythe so much that I couldn't trust myself to go near him. That's one thing you never forget or forgive, cruelty when you're a child and defenseless. I shut my mind and my eyes to anything that concerned him. May have shut them deliberately. You could call it a dereliction of duty."

"But no one did. There was no court-martial, was there? No one blamed you."

"I blame myself." There was a moment's silence; then he said, "Never knew he was married. No mention of a wife at the inquest. There was talk of a girl in Speymouth but she never showed herself. No talk of a child."

"Munter probably wasn't born. And he could have been illegitimate. I don't suppose we shall ever know. But his mother must have been bitter about what happened. He probably grew up believing that the army had murdered his father. I wonder why he took a job on the island: curiosity, filial duty, the hope of revenge. But he couldn't have expected that you would turn up here."

"He might have hoped for it. He took the job in the summer of 1978. I married Clarissa that year and she has known Ambrose Gorringe nearly all her life. Munter probably kept track of me. I'm not exactly a nonentity."

Cordelia said, "The police have made mistakes before now. If they do arrest you I shall feel free to tell them. I shall have to tell them."

He said quietly, "No, Cordelia. It's my concern, my past, my life."

Cordelia cried, "But you must see how it will look to the police! If they believe me about the music box, they'll know that Munter was in the gallery a few feet from your wife's room at about the time she died. If he didn't kill her himself, he could have seen the person who did. Taken with that shout to you of 'Murderer,' it's damning unless you tell them who Munter was."

He didn't respond but stood as rigid as a sentry, his eyes gazing into nothingness.

She said, "If they arrest the wrong person, it's double injustice. It means that the guilty one goes free. Is that what you want?"

"Would it be the wrong person? If she hadn't married me she'd be alive today."

"You can't know that!"

"I can feel it. Who was it said we owe God a death?"

"I can't remember. Someone in Shakespeare's *Henry the Fourth.* But what has that to do with it?"

"Nothing, I expect. It came into my mind."

She was getting nowhere. Beneath that apparently guileless and inarticulate front of personality he harbored his private undercover agent, a mind more complex and perhaps more ruthless than she had imagined. And he wasn't a fool, this deceptively simple soldier. He knew precisely the extent of his danger. And that could mean that he had his own suspicions, that there was someone he wanted to protect. And she didn't think that it would be either Ambrose or Ivo.

She said helplessly, "I don't know what you want of me. Am I to carry on with the case?"

"No point, is there? Nothing can frighten her ever again. Better leave it to the professionals." He added awkwardly, "I'll pay, of course, for your time so far. I'm not ungrateful."

Ungrateful for what? she wondered.

He turned and looked down at Munter's body. He said, "Extraordinary business, putting that wreath on the war memorial every year. Do you suppose Gorringe will keep up the tradition?"

"I shouldn't think so."

"He should. I'll have a word with him. Oldfield could see to it."

They turned to make their way across the rose garden, then stopped. Coming across the lawn toward them in the pale apricot light, their footfalls absorbed by the soft grass, were Grogan and his coterie of officers. Cordelia was caught unawares. Facing their silent, inexorable advance, their bleak, unsmiling faces, Cordelia resisted the temptation to glance at Sir George. But she wondered whether he shared her sudden and irrational vision of how the two of them must look to the police: as guilty and discomfited as a couple of poachers surprised by the gamekeepers with their dead spoils at their feet.

# BOOK SIX

·

# A Case Concluded

# I

Munter's body was taken away with a speed and efficiency which Cordelia thought almost unseemly. By ten o'clock the metal container with its two long side handles had been slid from the jetty onto the deck of the police launch with as little ceremony as if it had held a dog. But what, after all, had she expected? Munter had been a man. Now he was a weight of latent putrefaction, a case to be given a file and a number, a problem to be solved. She told herself that it was unreasonable to expect that the men—police officers? mortuary attendants? undertaker's staff?—would bear him away with the solemnity appropriate to a funeral. They were doing a familiar job without emotion and without fuss.

With this second death the suspects had been able to watch the police at work. They did it discreetly from the window of Cordelia's bedroom, watching while Grogan and Buckley walked slowly around the body like a couple of marine scientists intrigued by some bedraggled specimen washed up by the tide. They watched while the photographer did his job, hardly seeming to notice or speak to the police, occupying himself with his own expertise. And this time Dr. Ellis-Jones didn't appear. Cordelia wondered whether this was because the cause of death was apparent or he was busy elsewhere with another body. Instead, a police surgeon arrived to certify that life was extinct and to make the preliminary examination. He was a large and jovial man, dressed in sea boots and a knitted jersey, patched on both elbows, who greeted the police like old drinking companions. His cheerful voice rose clearly on the quiet morning air. It was only when he knelt to rummage in his case for his thermometer that the watchers at the window silently withdrew and took refuge in the drawing room, ashamed of what had suddenly seemed an indecent curiosity. And it was from the drawing-room windows, less than ten minutes later, that they saw Munter's body borne through the archway and across the quay to the launch. One of the bearers said something to his mate and they both laughed. He was probably complaining about the weight.

And with this second death even the police questioning didn't take long. There was, after all, not a great deal that anyone could tell, and Cordelia guessed how suspiciously unanimous that little must sound. When it was her turn she went into the business room weighed down by the conviction that nothing she said would be believed. Grogan stared at her across the desk, his pale, unfriendly eyes red-rimmed as if he had gone without sleep. The two music boxes were on the desk in front of him, carefully positioned side by side.

When she had finished her account of Munter's appearance at the dining-room windows, of the finding of his body and the recovery of the music box, there was a long silence. Then he said, "Why exactly did you go up to the tower room on Friday afternoon?"

"Just curiosity. Miss Lisle didn't want me at the rehearsal and Mr. Whittingham and I had finished our walk. He was tired and had gone to rest. I was at a loose end."

"So you amused yourself by exploring the tower?"

"Yes."

"And then you played with the toys?" He made it sound as if she were a tiresome child who hadn't been able to keep her hands off someone else's kiddy car. She realized with a mixture of anger and hopelessness the impossibility of explaining, of making him understand that impulse to set the whole childish menagerie working, to drown wretchedness with a cacophony of sound. And even if she had confided the cause of her distress—Ivo's telling her of the death of Tolly's child—would her story have sounded any more plausible? How did one explain to a policeman, perhaps to a judge, a jury, those small, seemingly irrational compulsions, the pathetic expedients against pain, which hardly made sense to oneself? And if it were difficult for her, so egregiously privileged, how did those others cope—the ignorant, the uneducated, the inarticulate—faced with the esoteric and uncompromising machinery of the law?

She said, "Yes, I played with the toys."

"And you are absolutely certain that the music box you found in the tower room played the tune 'Greensleeves'?" He smacked his great palm down on the lid of the left-hand box, then lifted the lid. The cylinder turned and the delicate teeth of the long comb once more picked out the nostalgic, plaintive tune.

She said, "I'm absolutely sure."

"Externally, they're very alike. The same size, the same shape, the same wood, almost the same pattern on the lids."

"I know. But they play different tunes."

She could understand the frustration and the irritation which he was keeping so tightly under control. Had she liked him better, she might have sympathized. If she were telling the truth, Munter had lied. He had left the ground floor of the castle some time during that critical hour and forty minutes. The only entrance to the tower was from the gallery floor. He had been within feet of Clarissa's door. And Munter was dead. Even if Grogan believed him innocent, even if some other suspect was brought to trial, her evidence about the music box would be a gift for the defense.

He said, "You didn't mention your visit to the tower when you were questioned yesterday."

"You didn't ask me. You were chiefly interested in what I did and saw on Saturday. I didn't think it important."

"There's nothing else that you didn't think important?"

"I've answered all your questions as honestly as I can."

He said, "Perhaps. But that isn't quite the same thing, is it, Miss Gray?"

And the small voice of her own conscience, in collusion with him, indicted her. Have you? Have you?

Suddenly he leaned across the desk and put his face close to hers. She thought she could smell his breath, sour and tainted with beer, and had to force herself not to draw back.

"What exactly happened on Saturday morning in the Devil's Kettle?"

"I've told you. Mr. Gorringe told us the story of the young internee who was left to drown. And I found that quotation from the play."

"And that's all that happened?"

"It seems to me enough."

He sat back and she waited. He didn't speak.

At last she said, "I should like to go to Speymouth this afternoon. I want to get off the island."

"Who doesn't, Miss Gray?"

"That's all right, is it? I don't have to ask permission? I mean, you can't stop me from going where I like unless you arrest me."

He said, "That, no doubt, is what you'd advise your clients if you had any. And you'd be perfectly right. We can't stop you. But you must be in Speymouth tomorrow at two o'clock for the inquest. It won't take long, just a formality. We'll be asking for an adjournment. But you were the one who found the body. You were the last person to see Miss Lisle alive. The coroner will want you there."

She wondered whether it was intended to sound like a threat. She said, "I'll be there."

He looked up and said, so gently that she almost believed him to be sincere, "Enjoy yourself in Speymouth, Miss Gray. Have a good day."

## II

It was after twelve-thirty when she was released. Having strolled out to join the others who were drinking their preluncheon sherry on the terrace, she learned that Oldfield had already gone to the mainland to fetch the post and supplies. Ambrose was expecting a parcel of books from the London Library. Cordelia asked if *Shearwater* could be ordered for her for two o'clock and he agreed without curiosity, merely inquiring when she would like the launch to be at Speymouth quay for the return journey. Cordelia ordered it for six o'clock.

She wasn't hungry for luncheon, nor, apparently, was anyone

else. Mrs. Munter had provided a cold buffet in the dining room, too much food, most of it intended for the party, set out indiscriminately in an appetite-stifling mass. The wonder was, thought Cordelia, that she had bothered at all. No one had spoken of her since the finding of her husband's body. She too had been interviewed by the police but had spent most of the morning secluded in her flat or moving silently and unnoticed from pantry to dining room. Cordelia doubted whether Ambrose was greatly concerned about her, and there was no one else to care. She decided to see if she was all right, to ask, before setting out, whether there was anything she could do for her in Speymouth. She doubted that her intrusion would be welcomed. What was there, after all, that she or anyone could do? But at least she could ask.

She didn't trouble to sit down but cut herself slices of cold beef and put them between bread. Then, making her excuses to Ambrose, she helped herself to an apple and a banana and took her picnic onto the beach. Already her mind was moving away from this claustrophobic island toward the mainland. She felt like a refugee, waiting to be rescued from some plague-ridden and violent colony, watching with desperate eyes for the boat which would bear her away from the smell of rotting corpses, the shouting and tumult, the bodies strewn on the shore, toward the safety and normality of home. The mainland which she had seen recede with such high hopes only three days earlier now shone in the imagination with all the effulgence of a promised land. It seemed to her that two o'clock would never come.

Shortly before one-thirty she made her way along the tiled passage past the business room to the baize door which she knew must lead to the servants' flat. There was no bell or knocker, but while she was wondering how to attract attention, Mrs. Munter came quietly up behind her, carrying on her hip a basket of washing. Without speaking, she held open the door and Cordelia passed before her down a shorter passageway and into a small sitting room to her right. Like all other Victorian architects, Godwin had ensured that from none of their rooms could the servants overlook their betters, whether the family were disporting themselves indoors or out. The single window gave a view only of a wide yard with, beyond it, the stable block with its charming clock tower and weather vane. Across the yard was slung a washing line from which drooped a pair of Munter's huge pajamas. They seemed to Cordelia pathetic and embarrassing, and she averted her eyes as if detected in a morbid curiosity.

The room itself was starkly furnished, not uncomfortable, but, despite the artful simplicity of the Art Nouveau furniture, almost devoid of character. There was a television set in the corner but no books or pictures and no photographs or ornaments on the dresser. It was as if the inhabitants had no past to remember, no present to celebrate. And no third person, apparently, ever sat here. There were only two easy chairs, one on each side of the elegantly carved iron grate, and only two upright chairs set opposite each other at the dining table.

Mrs. Munter didn't invite her to sit down. Cordelia said, "I didn't mean to bother you. I just wanted to see that you are all right. And I'm going into Speymouth shortly. Is there anything I can get or do for you?"

Mrs. Munter swung her basket of washing down on the table and began folding the clothes. "There's nothing. I'll be with you on the boat likely enough. I'm leaving, miss. I'm getting off the island."

"I know how you must feel. But if you're frightened I could share a room with you tonight."

"I'm not frightened. What is there to be frightened of? I'm leaving, that's all. I never liked being here and now that he's gone I don't have to stay."

"Of course not, if that's how you feel. But I'm sure Mr. Gorringe wouldn't want you to do anything in a hurry. He'll want to talk to you. There are bound to be, well . . . arrangements."

"There's nothing to talk about. He's been a good enough master but it was Munter he wanted. I came with Munter. Now we're separate."

Separate, thought Cordelia, finally and forever. There had been no mistaking the note of satisfaction, almost of triumph. And she had come to the flat out of an embarrassed compassion, inexperienced as she might be, to try to give comfort. None, it appeared, was wanted or necessary. But surely there would be wages outstanding, offers of help to be made, funeral arrangements to be discussed. Ambrose would surely want to reassure her that she could stay on at the castle as long as it suited her. And, of course, there would be the police, Grogan and his ubiquitous experts in death, trained in suspicion and mistrust. If Munter had been deliberately pushed to his death, she could have done it. With one undetected murderer already on the island, what better time to get rid of an unwanted husband? Cordelia didn't doubt that Grogan, faced with this ungrieving widow, would place her high on his list of suspects. And the police were bound to see this hurried departure as highly suspicious.

She was wondering whether she ought to say a word of warning when Mrs. Munter spoke. "I've spoken to the police. They've no call to keep me. They know where they can find me. Mr. Gorringe can see to the funeral arrangements. It's no concern of mine."

"But you were his wife!"

"I never was his wife. He wasn't the marrying kind, nor am I. I'll be leaving in the launch as soon as Oldfield is ready."

"Are you all right for money? I'm sure that Mr. Gorringe . . ."

"I don't need his help. Munter had money. He had ways of making a bit on the side and I know where he kept it. I'll take what's due to me. And I'll be all right. Good cooks don't starve."

Cordelia felt totally inadequate. She said, "No indeed. But have you somewhere to go, for tonight I mean?"

"She'll be staying with me."

Tolly came quietly into the room. She was wearing a dark blue fitted coat with padded shoulders and a small hat pierced with one long feather. The outfit was reminiscent of the thirties and gave her a slightly raffish smartness. She was carrying a bulging suitcase bound with a strap. She moved unsmiling to Mrs. Munter's side—it was impossible for Cordelia to think of her by any other name—and the two women faced her together.

Cordelia felt that she was seeing Mrs. Munter clearly for the first time. Until now she had hardly noticed her. The strongest impression she had made was of an unobtrusive competence. She had been an adjunct to Munter, little more. Even her appearance was unmemorable: the coarse hair, neither fair nor dark, with its stiff, corrugated waves; the stolid body; the stumpy, workworn hands. But now the thin mouth which had given so little away was taut with an obstinate triumph. The eyes which had been so deferentially downcast stared boldly into hers with a look of challenging, almost insolent confidence. They seemed to say, "You don't even know my name. And now you never will." Beside her stood Tolly, unchanged in her self-contained serenity.

So they were going away together. Where, she wondered, would they live? Presumably, since she'd offered Simon a room, Tolly had a house or flat somewhere in London where she had made a home for her child. Cordelia had a sudden and disconcertingly clear picture of them, not living there surrounded by memories, but installed in a neat suburban house within convenient distance of the tube and the shopping center, net curtains looped across the bay window, hindering inquisitive eyes, a small front garden railed against unwelcome intruders, against the past. They had thrown off their servitude. But surely that servitude must have been voluntary. Both were adult women. Surely it wasn't the fear of unemployment that had kept them from their freedom. They could have left their jobs whenever it suited them. So why hadn't they? What was the mysterious alchemy that kept people tied together against all reason, against inclination, against their own interests? Well, death had parted them now, one from Clarissa, the other from Munter; parted them very conveniently, the police might think.

Cordelia thought, I'm seeing both of them clearly for the first time and still I know nothing about them. Some words of Henry James fell into her mind. "Never believe that you know the last word about any human heart." But did she know even the first word, she who called herself a detective? Wasn't it one of the commonest of human vanities, this preoccupation with the motives, the compulsions, the fascinating inconsistencies of another personality? Perhaps, she thought, we all enjoy acting the detective, even with those we love; with them most of all. But she had accepted it as her job; she did it for money.

She had never denied its fascination, but now, for the first time, it occurred to her that it might also be presumptuous. And never before had she felt so inadequate for the task, pitting her youth, her inexperience, her meager store of received wisdom against the immense mysteriousness of the human heart.

She turned to Mrs. Munter. "I should like to have a word with Miss Tolgarth alone. May I, please?"

The woman didn't reply but looked at her friend and was given a small nod. Without speaking, she left them.

Tolly waited, patient, unsmiling, her hands folded before her. There was something which Cordelia would have liked to ask first, but she didn't need to. And she was less arrogant now than when she had first taken the case. She told herself that there were questions she had no right to ask, facts she had no right to be told. No human curiosity, no longing to have every piece of the jigsaw neatly fitted into place as if her own busy hands could impose order on the muddle of human lives, could justify asking what she knew in her heart was true, whether Ivo had been the father of Tolly's child. Ivo, who had spoken of Viccy with knowledge and love, who had known that Tolly had refused to accept any help from the father; Ivo, who had taken the trouble to get in touch with the hospital and learn the truth about that telephone call. How strange to think of them together, Ivo and Tolly. What was it, she wondered, that they had wanted of each other? Had Ivo been trying to hurt Clarissa or assuage a deeper hurt of his own? Was Tolly one of those women, desperate for a child, who prefer not to be burdened with a husband? The birth of Viccy, if not the pregnancy, must surely have been deliberate. But none of it was her business. Of all the things that human beings did together, the sexual act was the one with the most various of reasons. Desire might be the commonest, but that didn't mean that it was the simplest. Cordelia couldn't even bring herself to mention Viccy directly. But there was something she had to ask.

She said, "You were with Clarissa when the first of the messages came, during the run of *Macbeth*. Would you tell me what they looked like?"

Tolly's eyes burned into hers with a somber, considering stare, but not, she thought, with resentment or dislike.

Cordelia went on, "You see, I think it was you who sent them, and I think she might have guessed and known why. But she couldn't do without you. It was easier to pretend. And she didn't want to show the messages to anyone else. She knew what she had done to you. She knew that there were things even her friends might not forgive. And then what she hoped would happen did happen. Perhaps there had been some change in your life which had made you feel that what you were doing was wrong. So the messages stopped. They stopped until one of the small number of people who had known about them took over. But then they were different messages. They looked different. Their purpose was different. And their end was different and terrible."

Still there was no reply.

Cordelia said gently, "I know I've no right to ask. Don't answer me directly if you'd rather not. Just tell me what those first messages were like and I think I shall know."

Then Tolly spoke. "They were written by hand in capital letters on lined paper. Paper torn from a child's exercise book."

"And the messages themselves. Were they quotations?"

"It was always the same message. A text from the Bible."

Cordelia knew that she was lucky to have gained so much. And even this confidence wouldn't have been given if Tolly hadn't recognized some sympathy, some empathy, between them. But there was one more question which she thought she might risk.

"Miss Tolgarth, have you any idea who it was who took over?"

But the eyes looking into hers were implacable. Tolly had told all she intended to tell.

"No. I concern myself with my own sins. Let others look to theirs."

Cordelia said, "I shall never pass on to anyone what you've just said to me."

"If I thought that you would, I wouldn't have told you." She paused, and then asked in the same even tone, "What will happen to the boy?"

"To Simon? He told me that Sir George will keep him on at Melhurst for his final year and that he'll then try for a place at one of the colleges of music."

Tolly said, "He'll be all right now she's gone. She wasn't good for the young. And now, if you'll excuse me, miss, I'd like to help my friend finish her packing."

# III

There was nothing more to be said or done. Cordelia left the two friends together and went to her bedroom to get ready for the afternoon's excursion. As her object was to search for the newspaper review, her full scene-of-crime kit was hardly necessary, but she slipped a hand magnifying glass, a pocket torch, and a notebook into her shoulder bag and pulled her guernsey over her shirt. It might be cold on the boat on the return trip. Last she wound the leather belt twice around her waist and buckled it tightly. As always, it felt like a talisman, a girding on of resolution. As she crossed the terrace from the western front of the castle, she saw that Mrs. Munter and Tolly were already making their way toward the launch, both of them carrying a case in either hand. Oldfield must only recently have landed. He was still dragging his crates of wine and groceries onto the jetty, helped rather surprisingly by Simon. Cordelia thought that the boy was probably glad of something to do.

Suddenly Roma appeared from the dining-room windows and hurried down the terrace in front of her. She went up to Oldfield and spoke to him. The canvas post bag was on top of his trolley, and he unbuckled it and took out the bundle of letters. Drawing close to them, Cordelia could sense Roma's impatience. It looked as if she might snatch the bundle from Oldfield's gnarled fingers. But then he found what she was wanting and handed her a letter. She almost ran from him, then slowed to a walk, and, without noticing Cordelia's approach, tore the envelope open and read the letter. For a moment she stood absolutely still. Then she gave a sob, so high that it was almost a wail, and began stumbling along the terrace, pushed past Cordelia, and disappeared down the far steps to the beach.

Cordelia paused for a moment, uncertain whether to follow. Then she called to Oldfield to wait for her, that she wouldn't be long, and ran after Roma. Whatever the news, it had devastated her. There might be something she herself could do to help. Even if not, it was impossible just to board the launch and set off as if the scene had never happened. She tried to silence the small resentful voice which protested that it couldn't have occurred at a more inconvenient time. Was she never to be allowed to get off the island? Why should she always have to be the one to act as universal social worker? But it was impossible to ignore such distress.

Roma was stumbling and reeling along the shore, her hands flung out before her, groping in the air. Cordelia thought that she could hear a high continued scream of pain. But perhaps it was the cry of the gulls. She had almost caught up with the fleeing figure when Roma tripped, fell at full length on the shingle, and lay there, her whole body shaking with sobs. Cordelia came up to her. To see the proud and reserved Roma in such an abandonment of grief was as physically shocking as a blow to the stomach. Cordelia felt the same rush of impotent fear, the same helplessness. All she could do was to kneel in the sand and put her arms around Roma's shoulders, hoping that this human contact might at least help to calm her. She found herself softly cooing as she might to a child or an animal. After a few minutes the dreadful shaking ceased. Roma lay so still that, for a second, Cordelia feared that she had ceased to breathe. Then she heaved herself clumsily upright and threw off Cordelia's arm. Having walked unsteadily into the surf, she bent and began splashing her face. Then she stood upright for a moment, looking out to sea, before turning to face Cordelia.

Her face was grotesque, bloated like a long-drowned visage, the eyes like gummed slits, the nose a bulbous mess. When she spoke her voice was harsh and guttural, the sounds forcing themselves through swollen vocal cords.

"I'm sorry. That was a disgusting exhibition. I'm glad it was you, if that's any comfort."

"I wish I could help."

"You can't. No one can. As you've probably guessed, it's the usual commonplace sordid little tragedy. I've been chucked. He wrote on Friday night. We only saw each other on Thursday. He must have known then what he was going to do."

She pulled the letter from her pocket and held it out.

"Go on, read it! Read it! I wonder how many drafts it took to produce this elegant, self-justifying piece of hypocrisy."

Cordelia didn't take the letter. She said, "If he hadn't the decency and courage to tell you to your face, he isn't worth crying over; he isn't worth loving."

"What has worth to do with love? My God, why couldn't he have waited?"

Waited for what? thought Cordelia. For Clarissa's money? For Clarissa's death?

She said, "But if he had, could you ever have been sure?"

"Of his motive, you mean? Why should I care? I haven't that kind of pride. But it's too late now. He wrote a day too soon. Oh, God, why couldn't he have waited? I told him that I'd get the money. I told him!"

A wave, larger than its fellows, broke at Cordelia's feet and rolled a woman's silver evening sandal among the brighter seawashed stones. She found herself looking at it with an artificial intensity, making herself wonder what sort of woman had worn it, how it had come to be in the sea, from what wild party on what yacht it had been lost overboard. Or was its owner out there somewhere, a slim, half-clad body turning in the waves? Any thought, even that thought, helped to shut out the harsh unnatural voice which might any moment say those fatal words which couldn't be taken back and which neither of them would be able to forget.

"When I was a child I went to a coeducational school. All the children paired off. When the friendship cooled, they used to send each other what they called a chuck note. I never had one. But then I never had a boyfriend. I used to think it would be worth getting the chuck note if only I'd had the friendship first, just for one term. I wish I could feel that now. He was the only man who has ever wanted me. I think I always knew why. You can only deceive yourself so far. His wife doesn't much enjoy sex and I was a free fuck. All right, don't look like that! I don't expect you to understand. You can get love whenever you want it."

Cordelia cried, "That isn't true; not of me, not of anyone!"

"Isn't it? It was true of Clarissa. She only had to look at a man. One look, that's all it ever took. All my life I've watched her using those eyes. But she won't any more. Never again. Never, never, never."

Her anguish was like an infection, strong and feverish and smelling of sweat. Cordelia could feel its contamination in her own blood. She stood on the shingle, afraid to approach Roma since she knew that physical comfort would be unwelcome, reluctant to leave her, miserably aware that Oldfield would be getting impatient.

Then Roma said gruffly, "You'd better go if you want to catch the launch."

"What about you?"

"Don't worry. You can escape with an easy conscience; I shan't do anything stupid. That's the euphemism, isn't it? Isn't that what they always say? Don't do anything stupid. I've been taught my lesson. No more stupidity, Roma! I can tell you what will happen to me, in case you're interested. I'll take Clarissa's money and buy myself a London flat. I'll sell the shop and find myself a part-time job. From time to time I'll take a foreign holiday with a woman friend. We shan't much enjoy each other's company, but it will be better than traveling alone. We'll devise little treats for ourselves, the theater, an art show, dinner at one of those restaurants where they don't treat solitary women as pariahs. And in the autumn I'll enroll for evening classes and pretend an interest in throwing pots or the Georgian architecture of London or comparative religion. And every year I shall get a little more fussy about my comforts, a little more censorious of the young, a little more fretful with my friend, a little more right-wing, a little more bitter, a little more lonely, a little more dead."

Cordelia would have liked to say, "But you'll have enough to eat. You'll have your own roof over your head. You won't die of cold. You'll have your strength and your intelligence. Isn't that more than three-quarters of the world enjoys? You're not a Victorian shell gatherer, waiting for a man to give purpose and status to your life. There doesn't even have to be love." But she knew that the words would be as futile and insulting as telling a blind man that there was always the sunset.

She turned and walked away, leaving Roma still staring out to sea. She felt like a deserter. It seemed discourteous to hurry, and she waited until she reached the terrace before breaking into a run.

## IV

No one spoke during the passage to the mainland. Cordelia sat in the prow of the launch, fixing her eyes on the gradually approaching shore. Mrs. Munter and Tolly settled themselves together in the stern, their bags at their feet. When *Shearwater* finally berthed, Cordelia waited until they had left before herself getting up. She watched while the two women, side by side but still unspeaking, made their slow way up the hill toward the station.

The town was less crowded and less busy than on the Friday morning, but it still held its slightly archaic air of cheerful sunlit domesticity. What she found extraordinary was to be so unnoticed. She had half expected that people would turn to stare at her, that she would hear the whispered word *Courcy* at her back, that she would bear an all-too-visible mark of Cain. How marvelous it was to be free of Grogan and his minions, at least for a few blessed hours, no longer one of that apprehensive, self-regarding coterie of suspects, but an ordinary girl walking an ordinary street, anonymous among the early-afternoon shoppers, the last holiday visitors, the office workers hurrying back to their desks after a belated lunch. She wasted a few minutes in a chemist's shop behind a charming Regency façade buying a lipstick which she didn't need, taking more than usual care over her selection. It was a small gesture of hope and confidence, a salute to normality. The only mention she saw or heard of Clarissa's death was a couple of placards advertising national dailies with the words ACTRESS MURDERED ON COURCY ISLAND written, not printed, under the paper's name. She bought one at a kiosk and found a brief account on the third page. The police had given the minimum of information, and Ambrose's refusal to speak to the press had obviously frustrated them in making much of a story. Cordelia wondered whether, in the end, it would prove to have been wise.

She learned from the newsagent that there was now only one local paper, the *Speymouth Chronicle,* which came out twice a week on Tuesday and Friday. The office was at the northern end of the esplanade. Cordelia found it without difficulty. It was a white converted house with two large windows, one painted with the words *Speymouth Chronicle* and the other filled with a display of newspaper photographs. The front garden had been paved to provide a parking space for half a dozen cars and a delivery van. Inside she found a blond girl of about her own age presiding at a reception desk and simultaneously coping with a small switchboard. At a side table an elderly man was sorting pictures.

Her luck held. She had feared that old copies of the paper might be kept elsewhere or might not be readily available to the public. But when she explained to the girl that she was researching into provincial theater and wanted to look up the reviews of Clarissa Lisle's performance in *The Deep Blue Sea,* no questions were asked and no difficulties made. The girl called out to her companion to keep an eye on the desk, ignored a light on the switchboard, and took Cordelia through a swinging door and down a steep flight of ill-lit stairs to the basement. There she unlocked a small front room from which the exciting musty smell of old newsprint rose to the nostrils like a miasma. Cordelia saw that the back numbers were found in folders filed in chronological order on steel shelves. In the middle of the room was a long trestle table. The girl switched on the light and two fluorescent tubes glowed into harsh brightness.

She said, "They're all here, going back to 1860. You can't take anything away and you mustn't write on the papers. Don't slip off without telling me. I have to come and lock up after you've finished. Okay? See you later then."

Cordelia approached her task methodically. Speymouth was a small town and was unlikely to have a permanent theater company. It was almost certain, therefore, that Clarissa had played with a repertory company during the summer season, most likely between May and September. She would begin her search with those five months. She found no mention of the Rattigan play in May, but she did note that the summer repertory company, based in the old theater, opened with each new offering on a Monday and played for two weeks. The first reviews appeared on a page devoted to the arts in each Tuesday's edition, a commendably quick response for a small provincial paper. Presumably the reviewer telephoned his copy from the theater. The first mention of *The Deep Blue Sea* appeared in an advertisement in early June, which stated that Miss Clarissa Lisle would be guest star for the two weeks beginning July 18. Cordelia calculated that the notice would appear on the arts page, invariably page nine, on July 19. She lugged the heavy bound volume containing the editions from July to September onto the table and found the paper for that date. It was larger than the normal edition, consisting of eighteen pages instead of the usual sixteen. The reason was made apparent on the first page. The Queen and the Duke of Edinburgh had visited the town on the previous Saturday as part of their Jubilee Year provincial tour, and the Tuesday edition had been the first one following the visit. It had been a big day for Speymouth, the first royal visit since 1843, and the *Chronicle* had made the most of it. The account on the first page stated that further pictures were shown on page ten. The words struck a chord of memory. Cordelia was now almost sure that the reverse side of the notice she had seen had been not newsprint but a picture.

But now that success was so close she felt a sudden loss of confidence. All she would discover would be the review by a provincial reporter of a revival which hardly anyone in Speymouth would now remember. Clarissa had said that it was important to her, important enough to keep in the secret drawer of her jewel box. But that, with Clarissa, could have meant anything. Perhaps she had liked the notice, met the reviewer, enjoyed on the occasion a brief but satisfactory love affair. It could have been as sentimentally unimportant as that. And what possible relevance could it have to her death?

And then she saw that the sheet she wanted wasn't there. She checked twice. No careful turning of the newspaper disclosed pages nine and ten. She bent back the thick wedge of newsprint where it was gripped by the binder. Down the margin of page eleven she thought she could detect a thin impression as if the paper had been faintly scored with a knife or razor blade. She got out her magnifying glass and moved it slowly over the bound edges. Now she could see it clearly, the telltale mark, in some places actually cutting the paper, showing where the sheet had been excised. She could detect, too, minute shreds of paper where the edge of page nine was still clasped in the binder. Someone had been here before her.

The girl at the desk was busy with a customer inquiring, but without any visible signs of grief, how she went about inserting a death notice and how much extra a nice bit of verse would cost. She handed over a child's exercise book and pointed out the rounded, laboriously formed letters. Cordelia, always curious about the idiosyncrasies of her fellow human beings and for a moment forgetting her own concerns, edged closer and slewed her eyes to read:

> The pearly walls were shining,
> St. Peter whispered low,
> The golden gate was opened,
> And in walked Joe.

This piece of extremely dubious theology was received by the girl with a lack of interest which suggested that she had read its like before. She spent the next three minutes attempting to explain what the probable cost would be, including the extras if the notice was boxed and surmounted with a wreathed cross, a consultation which was punctuated by long considering silences as they both contemplated samples of the designs on offer. But after ten minutes all was satisfactorily decided and she was then able to turn her attention to Cordelia, who said, "I've found the right edition but the sheet I think I want isn't there. Someone's cut it out."

"They can't have. It isn't allowed. That's the archives."

"Well, they have. Is there another copy?"

"I'll have to tell Mr. Hasking. They can't go cutting the morgue about. Mr. Hasking will be in a rare state about that."

"I'm sure. But I do need to see that page urgently. It's page nine of the edition of July nineteenth, 1977. Haven't you any other back numbers I could look through?"

"Not here. The chairman might have a set up in London. Cutting up the morgue! Mr. Hasking sets great store by those old copies. That's history, that is, he says."

Cordelia asked, "Can you remember who last asked to see them?"

"There was a blond lady from London last month. Writing a book about seaside piers, she said. They blew this one up in 1939 so the Germans couldn't land, then the council hadn't any money to build it again. That's why it's so stumpy. She said they used to have a music hall on the end when she was a girl and artistes used to come down from London in the season. She knew a lot about piers."

Cordelia thought that a better-equipped or more efficient private detective would have come with photographs of the victim and suspects for possible identification. It would have been useful to know whether the blond woman who was so knowledgeable about piers looked like Clarissa or Roma. Tolly, unless she had disguised herself, surely an unnecessarily dramatic ploy, was obviously out. She wondered whether Bernie would have thought of photographing the house party unseen, prepared for just such an eventuality. She hadn't herself felt such a tricky procedure to be possible or useful. But she did, after all, have the Polaroid in her kit on the island. Perhaps it would be worth a try. She could come back tomorrow.

She said, "And is the pier lady the only one who has recently asked to see the archives?"

"While I've been here. But, then, I've only been on the desk a couple of months. Sally could have told you about anyone before that, but she's left to get married. And I'm not always on the desk. I mean someone could've come when I was in the office and Albert was on the desk."

"Is he here?"

The girl looked at her as if astounded at such ignorance. "Albert? Of course he isn't. Albert's never here Mondays." She looked at Cordelia with sudden suspicion. "Why d'you want to know who else has been here? I thought you were just after seeing that review."

"I am. But I was curious who could have cut out that page. As you said, these are important records. And I wouldn't like anyone to think it was I. You're quite sure there isn't a copy anywhere else in the town?"

Without looking around, the elderly man who was still arranging new photographs in the display frame with a deliberation and an eye for artistic effect which suggested that the job could well take the rest of the day made his suggestion. "July nineteenth, 'seventy-seven, did you say? That's three days after the Queen's visit. You could try Lucy Costello. She's kept press cuttings on the royal family for the last fifty years. Isn't likely she'd have missed the royal visit."

"But Lucy Costello's dead, Mr. Lambert! We had an article about her and her press cuttings the day after they buried her. Three months ago, that was."

Mr. Lambert turned around and spread out his arms in a parody of patient resignation. "I know Lucy Costello's dead! We all know she's dead! I never said she wasn't dead. But she's got a sister, hasn't she? Miss Emmeline's still alive as far as I know. She'll have the cuttings books. Isn't likely she'd throw them out. They may have buried Miss Lucy but they haven't buried her press cuttings with her, not that I know of. I said to try her. I didn't say speak to her."

Cordelia asked how she could find Miss Emmeline. Mr. Lambert turned away again to his photographs and spoke gruffly, as if regretting his former loquacity. "Windsor Cottage, Benison Row. Up the High Street, second left. Can't miss it."

"Is it far? I mean, ought I to take a bus?"

"You'd be lucky. Catch yer death, you would, waiting for that number twelve. Ten minutes' walk at most. No trouble for a young 'un."

He selected a picture of a portly gentleman wearing a mayoral chain, whose sideways glance of salacious bonhomie suggested that the official banquet had more than fulfilled expectations, and positioned it carefully beside a photograph of a well-endowed and decidedly underclad bathing beauty, so that his eyes appeared to be gazing down her cleavage. Cordelia thought that here was a man who enjoyed his work. She thanked him and the girl for their help and set out to find Miss Emmeline Costello.

## V

Mr. Lambert had been right about the distance. It was almost exactly ten minutes' brisk walk to Benison Row. Cordelia found herself in a narrow street of Victorian houses curving above the town. Although there was a pleasing unity in the age, architecture, and height of the cottages, they were charmingly individual. Some had bow windows; others had been fitted with wooden window boxes from which a profusion of variegated ivy, geraniums, and aubrietia trailed their bright pattern against the painted stucco; and the two at the end of the row had bay trees in painted tubs set each side of the gleaming front door. Each had a narrow front garden set behind wrought-iron railings which, perhaps because of their delicate ornamentation, had escaped being sacrificed for scrap iron in the last war. Cordelia realized that she had never before seen a row of houses with their railings complete, and they gave to the street, which was outwardly so English in its small-scale prettiness, a touch of charming but alien eccentricity. The little gardens rioted with color, the warm, deep reds of autumn seeming to burst against the railings. Although it was late in the season, the air was a potpourri of lavender and gillyflowers. There were no cars parked at the curb, no throat-catching tang of petrol fumes. After the bustle and hot smells of the High Street, walking into Benison Row was like stepping back into the cozy simplicity of another and legendary age.

Windsor Cottage was the fourth house down on the left-hand side. Its garden was plainer than the rest, a neat square of immaculate lawn bordered with roses. The brass door knocker in the shape of a fish gleamed brightly in every scale. Cordelia rang the bell and waited. There was no sound of hurrying footsteps. Again she rang, this time a longer peal. But there was silence. She realized with a pang of disappointment that the owner was out. It had, perhaps, been stupidly sanguine to expect that Miss Costello would be waiting at home simply because she, Cordelia, wanted to see her. But the disappointment dragged at her spirit and filled her with a restless impatience. She was convinced now that the missing news cutting was vital, and only in this neat little house was there a chance of finding it. The prospect of having to return to the island with this clue unexplored, her curiosity unsatisfied, appalled her. She began pacing up and down outside the railings, wondering how long it might be worth waiting, whether Miss Costello would return, perhaps from shopping, or had shut up the house and gone away for a holiday. And then she noticed that the two upper windows were open at the top, and her spirits rose. A middle-aged woman came out of the next-door house, looked up the road as if expecting someone, and was about to close the door when Cordelia ran forward.

"Excuse me, but I was hoping to see Miss Costello. Do you know if she's likely to be back this afternoon?"

The woman replied pleasantly, "She'll be at the washateria, I expect. She always does her washing on Monday afternoons. She shouldn't be long, unless she decides to have tea in the town."

Cordelia thanked her. The door closed. The little street sank back into silence. She leaned against the railings and tried to wait in patience.

It wasn't long. Less than ten minutes later she saw an extraordinary figure turn the corner into Benison Row and knew at once that this must be Miss Emmeline Costello. She was an elderly woman, trundling after her a canvas-covered shopping trolley from the top of which bulged a plastic-covered bundle. She walked slowly but upright, her thin figure obliterated by a khaki army greatcoat so long that its hem almost scraped the pavement. Her small face was as softly puckered as an old apple and further diminished by a red-and-white-striped scarf bound around her head and tied under her chin. Over it had been pulled a knitted purple cap topped with a bobble. If such a superfluity of clothing was necessary on a warm September day, Cordelia could only wonder how she dressed in winter.

As Miss Costello came up to the gate, Cordelia moved to open it for her and introduced herself. She said, "Mr. Lambert of the *Speymouth Chronicle* suggested that you might be able to help me. I'm looking for a cutting from an old edition of the paper—July nineteenth, 1977. Would it be an awful nuisance if I looked through your sister's collection? I wouldn't trouble you, but it really is important. I've tried the newspaper morgue but the page I want isn't there."

Miss Costello might present to the world an appearance of almost intimidating eccentricity, but the eyes which looked into Cordelia's were sharp, bright as beads, and accustomed to making judgments, and when she spoke it was in a clear, educated, and authoritative voice, which immediately and unmistakably defined her precise place in the complicated hierarchy of the British class system.

"When you're eighty-five, my child, don't live on top of a hill. You'd better come in and have some tea."

In just such a voice had Reverend Mother greeted Cordelia when she had first arrived, tired and frightened, at the Convent of the Holy Child.

She followed Miss Costello into the house. It was apparent that nothing would be done in a hurry, and as a supplicant she could hardly insist that it be. She was shown into the drawing room while her hostess went off to remove several layers of her outer clothing and to make tea. The room was charming. The antique furniture, probably brought from a larger family home, had been selected to suit the room's proportions. The walls were almost covered with small family portraits, watercolors, and miniatures, but the effect was of an ordered domesticity, not of clutter. A mahogany wall cupboard inlaid with a pattern of rosewood held a few choice pieces of porcelain, and on the mantel shelf a carriage clock ticked away the moments. When Miss Costello reappeared, wheeling a trolley before her, Cordelia saw that the tea service was in green decorated Worcester and that the teapot was silver. It was an occasion, she thought, on which Miss Maudsley would have felt perfectly at home.

The tea was Earl Gray. As she sipped it from the elegant shallow cups, Cordelia had a sudden and irresistible impulse to confide. She couldn't, of course, tell Miss Costello who she was or what she was really seeking. But the peace of the room seemed to enclose her with a warm security, a comforting respite from the horror of Clarissa's death, from her own fears, even from loneliness. She wanted to tell Miss Costello that she came from the island, to hear a sympathetic human voice saying how awful it must have been, a comforting elderly voice assuring her in the remembered tones of Reverend Mother that all would be well.

She said, "There's been a murder on Courcy Island. The actress Clarissa Lisle has been killed. But I expect you know. And now Mr. Gorringe's manservant has been drowned."

"I have heard about Miss Lisle. The island has a violent history. I don't suppose these will be the last deaths. But I haven't read the newspaper account, and, as you see, we don't have a television set. As my sister used to say, there's so much ugliness now, so much hatred, but at least we don't have to bring it into our sitting room. And at eighty-five, my dear, one is entitled to reject what one finds unpleasing."

No, there was no comfort to be had here in this seductive but spurious peace. Cordelia was ashamed of the momentary weakness that had sought it. Like Ambrose, Miss Costello had carefully constructed her private citadel, less beautiful, less remote, less extravagantly self-indulgent, but just as self-contained, just as inviolate.

Neither excitement nor impatience had impaired Cordelia's appetite. She would have been grateful for more than the two thin slices of bread and butter provided, particularly as the meagerness of the meal bore no relation to its length. It was surprising that Miss Costello could take so long drinking two cups of tea and nibbling her share of the food. But at last they had finished.

Miss Costello said, “My late sister’s press cuttings are in her room upstairs. She was a dedicated monarchist”—here Cordelia thought she detected a nuance of indulgent contempt—“and there is scarcely a royal occasion during the last fifty years which escaped her attention. But her main interest was, of course, in the House of Saxe-Coburg-Gotha. I shall leave you to search on your own if I may. I am unlikely to be able to help you. But please don’t hesitate to call if you feel that I could.”

It was interesting but not altogether surprising, thought Cordelia, that Miss Costello hadn’t troubled to inquire what she was seeking. Perhaps she regarded such a question as vulgar curiosity or, more likely, feared that it might only provoke one more intrusion of the disagreeable into her ordered life.

She showed Cordelia into the front bedroom. Here Miss Lucy’s obsession was immediately apparent. The walls were almost covered with photographs of royalty, some of them half effaced with scribbled signatures. On a long shelf over the bed was closely ranged a collection of coronation mugs, and a glass-fronted display cabinet was filled with other memorabilia, crested and decorated teapots, cups and saucers, and engraved glass. The whole of the wall facing the window was fitted with shelves holding a collection of scrapbooks. Here was the famous collection.

Each of the books was marked on the spine with the dates covered, and Cordelia was able, without difficulty, to find July 1977. The local press photographers had done justice to Speymouth’s big day. There was hardly an aspect of the royal visit which had gone unrecorded. There were pictures of the royal arrival, the mayor in his chain, the curtseying mayoress, the children with their miniature Union Jacks, the Queen smiling from the royal car, hand raised in the distinctive royal wave, the Duke at her side. But there was no cutting which precisely fitted Cordelia’s memory of the shape and size of the missing piece. She sank back on her heels, the book open before her, and felt for a moment almost sick with disappointment. The microdots of grinning, anticipatory, self-satisfied faces mocked her failure. The chance of success had been slight, but she was chagrined to realize how much hope she had invested in it. And then she saw that hope was not yet lost. On the bottom shelf was stacked a row of stout manila envelopes, each with the year written on it in Miss Lucy's upright hand. Opening the top one, she saw that it also contained press cuttings, perhaps duplicates sent to Miss Lucy by friends eager to help with her collection or cuttings she had rejected as unworthy of inclusion but hadn't liked to throw away. The envelope for 1977 was plumper than its fellows as befitted Jubilee Year. She tipped out the medley of cuttings, most already fading with age, and spread them around her.

Almost immediately she found it: the remembered oblong shape, the heading "Clarissa Lisle Triumphs in Rattigan Revival," the third column cut down the middle. She turned it over. She didn't know what she had expected, but her first reaction was one of disappointment. The whole of the reverse was taken up with a perfectly ordinary press photograph. It had been shot across the esplanade and showed the opposite pavement thronged with smiling faces, a row of children squatting on the curb, their flags at the ready, their more adventurous elders perched on window ledges or clinging to lamp posts. At the back of the crowd two stout women with Union Jacks around their hats stood on the steps of a house, holding up a sagging banner with the words *Welcome to Speymouth.* Royalty hadn't yet arrived, but the picture conveyed the sense of happy expectation. Cordelia's first irrelevant thought was to wonder why Miss Costello had rejected it. But, then, there had been so many pictures to choose from, many in which the Queen was actually shown. But what possible interest could this not particularly distinguished photograph, this record of local patriotism, have for Clarissa Lisle? She looked at it more closely. And then her heart leaped. To the right of the photograph was the slightly blurred figure of a man. He was just stepping out into the road, obviously intent on some private business, oblivious of all the excitement around him, his preoccupied face staring past the camera. And there could be no doubt about it. The man was Ambrose Gorringe.

Ambrose in Speymouth in July 1977. But that had been the year of his tax exile. Surely he had had to stay overseas for the whole of the financial year; she could remember reading somewhere that even to set foot in the United Kingdom would vitiate the nonresident status. But suppose he had sneaked back—and this picture proved that he must have done—wouldn't that make him liable for all the tax he had avoided, all the money he must have spent on restoring the castle, acquiring his pictures and porcelain, beautifying his private island? She would have to find an expert, discover what the legal position was. There would be firms of solicitors in Speymouth. She could consult a lawyer, put a general question on tax law; there would be no need to be specific. But she had to know, and there wasn't much time. She glanced at her watch. Already it was ten minutes to five. The launch would be waiting for her at six o'clock. It was essential to get some kind of confirmation before she returned to the island.

As she gathered up the unwanted cuttings and replaced them in the envelope and went downstairs to find Miss Costello, her mind was busy with this new knowledge. If Clarissa had realized the significance of that press photograph, why hadn't anyone else? But, then, why should they? Ambrose hadn't lived on the island in 1977. He had probably visited it only rarely; it was unlikely that his face would be known locally. Those who knew him best lived in London and were unlikely ever to see the *Speymouth Chronicle*. And he had written his best-seller under a pseudonym. Even if someone living locally did recognize the picture, he was unlikely to realize that this was A. K. Ambrose, the author of *Autopsy*, who was supposed to be spending a year in tax exile. It was hardly the kind of thing one advertised. No, it had been his appallingly bad luck that Clarissa had been playing in Speymouth that week and had wanted to read her notice. And Clarissa had extorted her price for silence. Oh, it would have been subtly managed; there would have been nothing crude or blatant about this blackmail. Clarissa would have laid down her terms with charm, even a tinge of amused regret. But the price would have been demanded, and it had been paid. So much was clear to her now: why Ambrose had tolerated the disruption of his life by the players, why Clarissa made use of the castle as if she were its chatelaine. Cordelia told herself that none of this proved that Ambrose was a murderer, only that he had a motive. And she held the proof of it in her hand.

Afterward it was to strike her as strange that never for one moment did she consider taking the cutting at once to the police. First she must get confirmation; then she must confront Ambrose. It was as if this murder investigation had nothing to do with the police. It was a matter between herself and Sir George who had employed her, or perhaps between herself and the woman she had failed to protect. And Chief Inspector Grogan's arrogant masculine voice rang in her ears: "You may be too bright for your own good, Miss Gray. You're not here to solve this crime. That's my job."

She found Miss Costello in her small back kitchen, folding her linen ready for ironing. She was happy for Cordelia to take away the cutting and said so without bothering to look at it or to take her attention from her pillowcases. Cordelia asked whether she could recommend a firm of local solicitors. This request did evoke a swift upwards glance from the shrewd eyes, but still she asked no questions. Escorting her guest to the door, she merely said, "My own advisers are in London, but I have heard that Blake, Franton, and Fairbrother are considered reliable. You will find them on the esplanade about fifty yards east from the Victoria memorial. You would be wise to hurry. Little useful activity, professional or otherwise, goes on in Speymouth after five o'clock."

# VI

Miss Costello was right. By the time Cordelia arrived, panting, at the polished Georgian door of Messrs. Blake, Franton, and Fairbrother it was shut firmly against any further clients for that day. The lower rooms were in darkness, and although there was a light in the second story, a nameplate on the side of the door showed that this part of the house was a separate flat. Even if it hadn't been, she could hardly disturb a strange solicitor in his private house for advice on what was, after all, on the face of it, hardly an urgent matter. Perhaps there was a firm which remained open until six; but how to find it? There was always the yellow pages, if the post office provided this directory in the provinces. She was ashamed to discover that, Londoner as she was, this was a fact she didn't know. And even if she could find a directory which gave the names of local solicitors, there would be the difficulty of locating the offices without a town map. She seemed to have come on this excursion singularly ill equipped.

As she stood irresolute, a young man came up bearing a carton of vegetables and pressed the bell of the flat. He said, "Closed, are they?"

"Yes, as you see. I wanted a solicitor in a hurry. It's rather urgent."

"Yeah, that's the thing about solicitors. If you have to have 'em it's usually urgent. You could try Beswick. He's got an office in Gentleman's Walk. About thirty yards down the street and turn left. He's about halfway up on the right."

Cordelia thanked him and ran. Gentleman's Walk was easily found, a narrow cobbled street of elegant early eighteenth-century houses. A brass nameplate, polished to the point of being almost indecipherable, identified James Beswick, Solicitor. Cordelia was relieved to see that a light still shone behind the translucent glass and that the door opened to her touch.

Seated at the desk was a fat, rather untidy woman with immense scarlet-rimmed spectacles, wearing a tightly belted suit in a brightly patterned cretonne of overblown roses and intertwined vine leaves which gave her the look of a newly upholstered sofa. She said, "Sorry, we're shut. Call or ring tomorrow, ten o'clock onward."

"But the door was open."

"Literally, but not figuratively. I should have locked it five minutes ago."

"But since I'm here . . . it's very urgent. It won't take more than a few minutes, I promise."

A voice from an upper room called out, "Who is it, Miss Magnus?"

"A client. A girl. She says it's very urgent."

"Is she comely?"

Miss Magnus jerked her spectacles to the end of her nose and looked at Cordelia over the rims. Then she shouted up the stair, "What's that got to do with it? She's clean, she's sober, and she says it's urgent. And she's here."

"Send her up."

The footsteps receded. Cordelia, suddenly assailed by doubts, asked, "He is a lawyer, isn't he? A good one?"

"Oh, yes, he's that all right. Nobody's ever said that he isn't a good lawyer."

The emphasis on the last word was ominous. Miss Magnus nodded at the staircase. "You heard him. First floor to the left. He's feeding his tropical fish."

The man who turned to her from the window was tall and gangling with a lean, creased, humorous face and half spectacles worn low on his long nose. He was sprinkling seed from a packet into an immense fish tank, not shaking it from the packet but pinching small quantities between his fingers and dropping the seed in a careful pattern on the surface of the water. There was a tumble of red and bright blue as the fish swirled together and snapped at the food. He pointed as one of the fish streaked to the surface in a blaze of polished bronze. "Look at him. Isn't he a beauty? That's the dawn tetra, an expensive little fellow from British Guiana. But perhaps you prefer the glowlight tetra. There he is, lurking under the shells."

Cordelia said, "He's very beautiful, but I don't much enjoy tropical fish in tanks."

"Is it the fish or the tanks or the conjunction you object to? They're perfectly happy, I assure you, at least one assumes so. Their small world has been artistically and scientifically devised for their comfort, and they get their food regularly. They sow not, neither do they reap. Ah, there's a beauty! Look at that flash of gold and green."

Cordelia said, "I wanted some information urgently. It isn't about my affairs, it's just a general inquiry. You do give that kind of advice?"

"Well, it isn't usual. I'm not sure that it's wise. Solicitors are rather like doctors. You can't really generalize or deal in hypothesis; each case is unique. You have to know all the circumstances if you're really going to help. That's an interesting analogy, come to think of it; and I'll go further. If your doctor tells you to go abroad at once you can always settle for sunny Torquay instead. If your solicitor suggests you go abroad, you'd be wise to make for Heathrow immediately. I hope you're not in that precarious situation."

"No, but it's about going abroad that I've come to consult you. I want to know about tax avoidance."

"Do you mean tax avoidance, which is legal, or tax evasion, which isn't?"

"The first. Suppose I came into a very large sum of money, all of it in one tax year. Could I avoid paying tax if I went abroad for twelve months?"

"That depends what you mean by 'came into a large sum of money.' Are you talking about an inheritance, a gift, a football-pool win, a sale of property, or shares, or what? You're not contemplating a bank raid, are you?"

"I mean earned income. Money I received by writing a successful play or a novel, or painting a picture or acting in a film."

"Well, if you were sensible you would arrange your contracts so that the money wasn't all received during the one financial year. That would be a matter for your accountant rather than for me."

"But suppose I didn't expect it to be so successful."

"Then you could avoid paying tax on it by becoming nonresident for the whole of the subsequent financial year. Money earned in that way is taxed retrospectively as you probably know."

"Could I come home for a holiday or a weekend?"

"No. Not even for a day."

"Suppose I needed to. I might be homesick."

"I should strongly advise you not to. Tax exiles can't afford the luxury of homesickness."

"But if I did come back?"

He sighed. "If you really want an authoritative answer I would have to do some delving to see if there is any case law. And as I say, it's more a question for a tax accountant than for me. My present view, for what it's worth, is that you would become liable for tax on the income received during the whole of the preceding year."

"And if I concealed the fact of my return from the Inland Revenue?"

"Then you could be prosecuted for attempted fraud. Probably they wouldn't bother with that if the amount wasn't large, but they would see that they got the tax due. I mean, they're in the business of getting their hands on tax properly due."

"How much would that be?"

"Well, the present top rate on earned income is sixty percent."

"And in 1977?"

"Ah, in those unregenerate days it was rather more. Eighty percent or more on an income of over twenty-four thousand of taxable income. Something like that."

"So they might ruin me?"

"Bankrupt you, you mean? Indeed they might, if you were so ill advised as to spend all your previous year's income in advance in the confident expectation that it wouldn't be taxable. Death and taxation catch up with us all."

"Thank you. You've been very kind. Can I pay now? If it's more than two pounds I'm afraid I'll have to give you a check. I have a check card."

"Well, it hasn't taken very long, has it? And I think Miss Magnus has balanced the petty cash and locked away the box. Suppose you have this consultation on me."

"I don't think that would be right. I ought to pay for your time."

"Then put a pound in the doggy box and we'll call it quits. When you've written your best-seller you can come back and I'll give you some proper advice and charge you very high for it."

The doggy box was on his desk, the brightly painted model of a lugubrious spaniel holding between its paws a collecting tin bearing the name of a well-known animal charity. Cordelia folded in a couple of pound notes with the mental promise that she would charge only one to Sir George's account.

And then she remembered. There probably wouldn't be any account. Perhaps she would return to the office poorer than when she had left. Sir George had reassured her that she would be paid, but how could she charge him for so tragic a failure? It would be too like blood money. And how on earth would her bill be worded? It was strange how many small complications the huge complication of murder threw up. She thought, Even in the midst of death we are in life, and the petty concerns of life don't go away.

She reached the harbor with two minutes to spare. She was surprised and a little disconcerted to find that the launch wasn't waiting but told herself that Oldfield must have been kept by some job on the island; she was, after all, a little ahead of time. She sat on the bollard to wait, glad of the chance to rest, although her mind, stimulated by the excitements of the day, soon drove her to action. She got up and began restlessly pacing the harbor wall. Below her a sluggish tide sucked at the verdurous stones and a swag of seaweed spread its gnarled and drowned hands under the darkening surface. Daylight was fading and the warmth died with the light. One by one the houses climbing the hill lit their glowing oblongs behind drawn curtains and the winding streets became festive with sparkling necklaces of light. The late shoppers and holiday makers had gone home, and she heard only the occasional echo of a solitary footfall on the harbor wall. The little town, as if regretting its hours of unseasonable frivolity, was settling into a chill autumnal calm. The smells of summer were forgotten, and a rank watery smell rose from the harbor.

She looked at her watch. She saw that it was six-fifteen, and the time was immediately confirmed by the striking of a distant church clock. She walked to the harbor mouth and gazed toward the island. There was no sign of the launch, and the sea was empty except for two or three late-returning boats gliding with slackened sails toward their moorings.

Still she paced and waited. Seven-fifteen. The evening sky, layered in mauve and purple, had flamed into darkness, and the moon, pale as a tissue, shed a trembling path of light over the sea. In the distance,

Courcy Island crouched like an animal against the paler hue of the sky. Night had distanced it. It was hard now to believe that only two miles of water separated that black and ominous shore from the lights, the gathered domesticity of the town. Looking out at it, she shivered. Ambrose's story came back into her mind with the primitive atavistic force of a childhood nightmare. She could understand why so many local fishermen down the ages had thought the island accursed. Almost she could picture that desperate sailor, fighting the onset of the plague and the fury of the sea, wild-eyed and exultant on his way to his dreadful vengeance.

It was after seven-thirty now. Whether by accident or by design, Oldfield wasn't going to come. But at least she could leave the quay to ring the island and inquire without the fear of missing him. She remembered seeing two telephone boxes near the Victoria statue. Both were free, and when she had shut herself into the first she was glad to find that it hadn't been vandalized. It was irritating that she hadn't made a note of the castle number, and for a moment she feared that Ambrose's obsession with privacy might have caused him to be ex-directory. But the number was listed, although under Courcy Island, not his name. She dialed and could hear the ringing tone. Then the receiver was lifted, but no one replied to her voice. She thought that she could detect the sound of breathing but told herself that this must be imagination. She said again, "It's Cordelia Gray here. I'm ringing from Speymouth. I was expecting the launch at six o'clock." Still there was no reply. She spoke again, more loudly, but there was nothing but silence and the impression, eerie but unmistakable, that there was someone there, someone who had lifted the receiver but who had no intention of speaking. She replaced the hand piece and dialed again. This time she got the engaged signal. The receiver had been taken off the rest.

She made her way back to the harbor, though now with little hope that the launch would be in sight. Then she saw that there were lights and signs of activity on one of the moored vessels. Standing on the edge of the quay, she looked down at a shabby but sturdy wooden boat with a crudely constructed cabin amidships, brown sails, and an outboard motor. The port and starboard lamps were lit, and there was a dragnet heaped in the stern. It looked as if the sailor was preparing for a night's fishing. And he must, she thought, have a small galley. The salty, mouthwatering tang of fried bacon rose from the cabin above the fainter pervasive smell of tar and fish. As she gazed down, a stocky and bearded young man squeezed through the cabin door and looked up, first at the sky and then at her. He was wearing a patched jersey and sea boots and was biting into a thick sandwich. With his cheerful, ruddy face and shock of black hair he looked like an amiable buccaneer.

On impulse she called down to him, "If you're setting out, could you land me on Courcy Island? I'm staying there and the launch hasn't come for me. It's terribly important that I get back tonight."

He moved along the boat, still munching the wedge of greasy bread, and looked up at her with eyes which were shrewd but not unfriendly. He said, "They say there's someone murdered there. A woman, isn't it?"

"Yes, the actress Clarissa Lisle. I was staying there when it happened. I'm still supposed to be staying there. They should have sent the launch for me at six. I must get back tonight."

"A murdered woman. That's nothing new for Courcy Island. I'll be fishing off the southeast point. I'll take you if you're sure you want to go." Neither his voice nor his face betrayed any particular curiosity.

She said quickly, "I'm quite sure. I'll pay for the petrol, of course. That's only fair."

"No need. The wind's free. There'll be enough of it out in the bay. You can crew if you like."

"I'm not sure that I know how. But I'll pull on the right rope when you tell me."

He transferred the sandwich to his left hand, wiped the right on his jersey and held it out to help her aboard.

She said, "How long do you think it will take us?"

"The tide's running against us. Best part of forty minutes. Maybe more."

He disappeared into the cabin and she waited, seated in the bow, willing herself to patience. A minute later he reappeared and handed her a sandwich, two rashers of bacon, greasy and strong-smelling, wedged between thick slices of crusty bread. Until she bit into it, almost dislocating her jaw in the process, Cordelia hadn't realized just how hungry she was. She thanked him. He said with a trace of boyish satisfaction at the evident success of his catering arrangements, "There'll be cocoa once we get under way."

He clambered along the outside of the cabin toward the stern. A minute later the engine shuddered and the small boat began to creep from the quay.

# VII

It was almost impossible to believe that she had first seen Courcy Castle only three days earlier. In that short span of time she seemed to have lived through long, action-packed years, to have become a different person. Surely it had been some excitable expectant child who had gasped in wonder at her first sight of those sunlit walls, those patterned battlements, that high, luminous tower. But now, as the little boat turned the headland, she almost gasped again. The castle was ablaze with light. Every window shone, and from the tower, scored with pencil-slim lines of light, the high window threw a strong beam like a warning beacon over the sea. The castle seemed buoyant with light, lifted above the rocks to float in motionless serenity under an indigo sky, obliterating the nearer stars with brightness. Only the moon held her place, wan as a circle of rice paper, moving behind a thin veil of cloud.

She stood on the quay until the boat had drawn away. For a moment she was tempted to call out to the boy to stay, at least within call. But she told herself that she was being ridiculous and fanciful.

She wouldn't be alone with Ambrose. Even if Ivo was too sick to be much support, Roma, Simon, and Sir George would be there. And even if they weren't, why should she be afraid? She would be facing someone with a motive. But motive alone didn't make a murderer. And she agreed in her heart with Roma. Ambrose hadn't the nerve, the ruthlessness, the capacity for hatred, which drove a man to the ultimate crime.

Light lay across the terrace like a sheet of silver. She trod it as if on air, as if she, too, were buoyant, moving silently toward the open french windows of the drawing room. And then Ambrose appeared and stood watching her approach, a dark figure silhouetted against the light. He was wearing a dinner jacket and holding a glass of red wine in his left hand. The picture had the clarity and distinction of a painting. She found herself admiring the artist's technique: the careful positioning of the body, the artful blob of red in the glass cunningly and deftly painted in to emphasize the dark vertical lines of the figure, the splash of white at the shirt front, the dominant eyes which gave a focus and meaning to the whole composition. This was his kingdom, his castle. He was in command. He had illuminated it as if to celebrate and exult in his mastery. But when she came up to him his voice was light and casual. He might have been welcoming her home after an afternoon's shopping on the mainland. But wasn't that precisely what he thought he was doing?

"Good evening, Cordelia. Have you eaten? I didn't wait dinner, such as it is. I cooked myself some soup and an herb omelet. Would you care for one?"

Cordelia moved into the drawing room. Here only the wall lights and one table lamp were lit, making a cozy circle of light by the fire. The corners of the room were dark, and long shadows moved like fingers over the carpet and the walls. The fire must have been lit for some time. A single large log was burning steadily.

She slipped off her shoulder bag and asked, "Where is everyone?"

"Ivo's in bed, not at all well, I'm afraid. He'll be going home tomorrow if he's fit for the journey. Roma has left. She was anxious to get back to London. Sir George had one of his mysterious calls to a meeting at Southampton and she took the launch with him. They won't be returning, although they'll both be in Speymouth tomorrow for the inquest. Simon said that he wasn't hungry. He's gone to bed."

So they were alone after all, alone except for the sick Ivo and a boy. She asked, hoping that her voice didn't betray her dismay, "Why wasn't the launch at Speymouth? Oldfield was supposed to meet me at six."

"He or I must have misunderstood. He'll be back with *Shearwater,* but not until the morning. He's visiting his daughter in Bournemouth for the night."

"I did ring, but whoever answered put down the receiver."

"I'm afraid that's been my stock response to the telephone today. Too many calls, too many reporters."

They stood together in front of the fire. She took the newspaper photograph from her bag and held it out to him. "I went to Speymouth to find this."

He didn't touch it or even glance at it. "I did wonder. I congratulate you. I didn't think you'd succeed."

"Because you'd already cut it out of the newspaper morgue?"

He said calmly, "Yes, I destroyed it about a year ago. It seemed a sensible precaution."

"I found another."

"So I see." Suddenly he said gently, "You look tired, Cordelia. Hadn't you better sit down? May I get you some claret or brandy?"

"I'd like a glass of claret, please."

She had to keep her mind clear, but the thought of the wine was irresistible. Her mouth was so dry that she could hardly frame her words. He fetched a glass for her from the dining room, poured her wine, and refilled his own glass, then sat with the decanter close at hand. They settled themselves on each side of the fireplace. It seemed to Cordelia that no chair had ever been more welcoming or as comfortable, no wine had ever tasted so good. He began to speak as calmly and unemotionally as if they were sitting together after dinner, discussing the ordinary events of an unremarkable day.

"I came back to visit my uncle. I was his heir and he wanted to see me. I don't think he understood that I couldn't return and still have a tax-free year. That wasn't the way his mind worked. It would never have occurred to him that a man could spend a year of his life doing what he didn't want to do, living where he didn't want to live, because of money. I wish you'd known him. You would have liked each other. It wasn't difficult getting here unnoticed. I flew from Paris to Dublin and took an Aer Lingus flight to Heathrow. Then I traveled by rail to Speymouth and rang the castle for my uncle's servant, William Mogg, to meet me after dark with the launch. They'd lived together here for nearly forty years. I asked Mogg not to tell anyone that he'd seen me, but it wasn't necessary. He never spoke of his master's business. Three months after my uncle died he turned his face to the wall and followed him. So you see, there wasn't really any risk. He asked me to come. I came."

"And if you hadn't, perhaps he would have altered his will."

"Unkind, Cordelia. You probably won't believe me, but I wasn't influenced by that disagreeable possibility. I didn't even believe that it was a possibility. I liked him. I seldom saw him—he didn't encourage visits even from his heir—but when I did pay my annual homage there was something between us which both of us recognized. Not love. I think he loved only William Mogg, and I'm not sure that *I* know what the word means. But whatever it was, I valued it. And I valued him. He had toughness, obstinacy, courage. He was his own man. He lay in that immense bedroom like some ancient chieftain gazing out over the sea and fearing nothing; nothing, nothing. And then he asked me to get for him something he fancied, a last taste of blue Stilton. He can't have tasted it for thirty years. He and William Mogg practically lived off the island, making their own butter and cheese. God knows what put that need into his mind. He could have asked Mogg to get it for him. But he didn't; he asked me."

"So that's why you went to Speymouth?"

"That's why. If I hadn't done that simple act of filial kindness, Clarissa wouldn't have seen that press photograph, wouldn't have forced me into staging *The Duchess of Malfi,* would still be alive. Odd, isn't it? It makes nonsense of any theory of the beneficent governance of human life. But then I learned that lesson when I was eight and my mother died because she was one minute late for the plane home and the one she caught crashed. It was a matter, you see, of whether the Paris traffic lights were red or green. We live by chance and we die by chance. With Clarissa, if you look back far enough, it was a matter of eight ounces of blue Stilton. Evil coming out of good, if those two words mean something to you."

Ivo had asked her much the same question. But this time she wasn't expected to answer.

He went on, "A man should have the courage to live by his beliefs. If you accept, as I do absolutely, that this life is all that we have, that we die as animals, that everything about us is finally lost irrevocably, that we go into the night without hope, then that belief must influence how you live your life."

"Millions of people live with that knowledge and still live good and kindly and useful lives."

"Because goodness and usefulness and kindness are expedient. I have my share of them. It is necessary for comfort to be at least a little liked. And perhaps some of the virtuous unbelievers still retain a vestigial hope or fear that there could be an afterlife, a measure of reward or punishment, a rebirth. There isn't, Cordelia. There isn't. There's nothing but darkness, and we go into it without hope."

Remembering how he had sent Clarissa into her darkness, she gazed, appalled, at the gently smiling face with its look of spurious sorrow, as if the full knowledge of what he had done had only now come home to her.

"You smashed in her face! Not once; time and time again! You could make yourself do that!"

"It wasn't agreeable. And if it's any consolation to you, I had to close my eyes. And it seemed to go on for so long. The sensation was horribly specific, softness cushioning the brittleness of bones. And so many bones. I could feel them splintering like smashing a tin of toffee in childhood. Our old cook used to let me make it. Smashing it when it had cooled was the best part. And when I opened my eyes and made myself gaze, Clarissa wasn't there. Of course, she hadn't been there before, but once her face was gone I couldn't even remember what she had looked like. More than anyone else I know, Clarissa was her face. That demolished, I knew afresh what I'd always known: the ridiculous presumption of supposing that she had a soul."

Cordelia told herself, I won't be sick. I won't. I won't. And I must stay calm. I mustn't panic.

His voice came to her faintly but very clearly. "When I was sixteen and first came to this island as a schoolboy, I knew for the first time what I wanted of life. Not power, not success, not sex, with men or women. That has always been to me an expense of spirit in a waste of shame. It wasn't even money, except as it contributed to my passion. I wanted a place. This place. I wanted a house. This house. I wanted this view, this sea, this island. My uncle wanted to die on it. I wanted to live on it. It's the only real passion I've ever known. And I wasn't going to let a nyphomaniac second-rate actress take it from me."

"And so you killed her?"

He refilled her glass and his own, then looked at her. She had the feeling that he was measuring something: her probable response, his need to confide, perhaps even how much time remained to them. He smiled, and the smile was one of genuine amusement which almost broke into a laugh. "My dear Cordelia! Do you really believe that you're sitting here sipping Château Margaux with a murderer? I congratulate you on your sangfroid. No, I didn't kill her. I thought you understood that. I haven't that brand of courage or ruthlessness. No, she was dead when I battered in her face. Someone had been there before me. She couldn't feel it, you see. Nothing matters, nothing exists, as long as you can't feel it. It wasn't living flesh that I beat to a pulp. It wasn't Clarissa."

But of course. What had made her so blind? She had reasoned all this out before. Clarissa must have been dead when he raised the marble limb and brought it down, the limb of a dead princess who, by chance, had borne the same name as that other child, who more than a century later had died, uncomforted by her mother, in a London hospital bed.

He said, "There was no upwards spurt of blood. How could there be? She was already dead. It isn't so very difficult to strike when the kill has been made. No blood, no pain, no guilt. All I did was to cover up for the murderer. Admittedly my motive was mainly self-interest. I needed to find and destroy that vital scrap of newsprint. I knew that it would be somewhere in the room. That was one of her little tricks, to keep it near her, to take it out of her handbag occasionally and pretend to read the review. But you should credit me with some disinterested concern for the killer. It pleased me to concoct for him a way of escape if he had the guts to take it. After all, I did owe him something."

"She could have taken photocopies of the photograph."

"Perhaps, although it wasn't likely. And what would it matter if she had? They'd be found with her effects at home, trivia to be thrown away with the detritus of her essentially trivial life, the half-used jars of face cream, the dead love letters, the hoarded theater programs. And even if George Ralston had found it and realized its significance—an unlikely eventuality—he wouldn't have done anything. George wouldn't have seen it as his business to do the work of the Inland Revenue. I came back here for one day and one night to be with a dying old man. Would you, or anyone you know, use that knowledge to inform on me?"

"No."

"And will you now?"

"I must. It's different now. I have to tell; not the tax people, the police. I have to."

"Oh, no, you don't, Cordelia! No, you don't! Don't try to fool yourself that you no longer have the responsibility of choice."

She didn't answer.

He leaned forward and refilled her glass. "It wasn't the possibility of other copies that worried me. What I couldn't risk was the police finding that one copy in her room. And I knew that if it were there to find, they'd find it. They'd be looking for a motive. Everything in that room would be collected, docketed, scrutinized, examined. There was a chance, of course, that they'd take the cutting at its face value, a critic's notice kept for purely sentimental reasons. But why that particular notice, a not-very-important play in a provincial theater? It's never safe to rely on the stupidity of the police."

She said with great sadness, "So it was Simon. Poor Simon! Where is he now?"

"In his room. Perfectly safe, I assure you. Don't you want to know what happened?"

"But he couldn't have planned it. Not Simon. He couldn't have meant it."

"Planned it, no. Meant it? Who's to say what he meant? She's just as dead, isn't she, whatever he meant? What he told me was that she invited him to her room. He was to say that he was going for a swim, put on his swimming trunks under his jeans and shirt, wait until thirty minutes after she'd gone to rest, then knock three times at the door. She'd let him in. She said there was something she wanted to talk to him about. There was, of course. Herself. Whatever else did Clarissa ever want to talk about? He, poor deluded fool, thought she was going to tell him that he could go to the Royal College, that she'd pay for his musical education."

"But why send for Simon? Why him?"

"Ah, that I doubt whether we shall ever know. But I can make a guess. Clarissa liked to make love before a performance. Perhaps it gave her confidence; perhaps it was a necessary release of tension; perhaps she knew of only one way to stop herself thinking."

"But Simon! That boy! She couldn't have wanted him!"

"Perhaps not. Perhaps, this time, she only wanted to talk, wanted companionship. And, with all respect to you, my dear Cordelia, she had never looked to a woman for that. But she may have thought that she was doing him a service in more ways than one. Clarissa is totally incapable of believing that a man existed—a normal man anyway—who wouldn't take her if he could get her. To do her justice, my sex hasn't done much to disabuse her of the idea. And what better time for Simon to begin his privileged education than on a warm afternoon after, I pride myself, an excellent luncheon and when she needed a new sensation, a divertissement, to take her mind off the performance ahead? And who else was there? George, poor chivalrous booby, would lie to the death to protect her reputation, but my guess is that he hasn't touched her since he discovered that he was a cuckold. I'm no use to her. And Whittingham? Well, Ivo has had his turn. And can you imagine her wanting him even if he had the strength? It would be like handling the dry skin of death, infecting your tongue with the taste of death, smelling corruption in your nostrils. Given dear Clarissa's peculiar needs, who was there but Simon?"

"But it's horrible!"

"Only because you're young, pretty, and intolerant. It would have done no harm with a different boy and at a different time. He might even have thanked her. But Simon Lessing was looking for a different kind of education. Besides, he's a romantic. What she saw in his face wasn't desire; it was disgust. Of course, I could be wrong. She may not have thought it out very clearly. Clarissa seldom did. But she asked him to come to her. And as with me and my uncle, he came."

She said, "What happened? How did you find out?"

"I lied to Grogan about the time I left my room. I changed at once and quickly so that just after twenty minutes to two I was passing Clarissa's door. At that moment Simon looked out. The encounter was completely fortuitous. We stared at each other. His face was ghastly, ashen white, the eyes glazed. I thought he was going to collapse. I pushed him back into the bedroom and locked the door. He was wearing only his swimming trunks, and I saw his shirt and jeans in a heap on the floor. And Clarissa was lying sprawled on the bed. She was dead."

"How could you be sure? Why didn't you get help?"

"My dear Cordelia, I may have led a sheltered life, but I know death when I see it. I did check. I felt for a pulse. None. I drew the corner of my handkerchief across her eyeball, a disagreeable procedure. No response. He had brought the jewel box crashing down on her head and smashed the skull. The box was actually lying there on her forehead. Oddly enough, there was very little bleeding, a small smudge on his forearm where the blood had spurted upwards, a thin trickle running from her left nostril. It had almost dried when I saw her, and yet she had been dead for only ten minutes. It looked like a crooked gash, a disfigurement above the gaping mouth. That's one last humiliation which none of us can do anything about, looking ridiculous in death. How she would have hated it! But, then, you know. You saw her."

Cordelia said, "You forget. I saw her later. I saw her when you'd finished with her. She didn't look ridiculous then."

"Poor Cordelia! I'm sorry. I would have spared you that if I could. But I thought it would look suspicious if I went up early to call her myself. That's something I've learned from popular fiction. Never be the one to find the body."

"But why? Did he say why?"

"Not very coherently. And I was more concerned to get him away than to discuss the psychological complications of the encounter. But neither of them had got what they wanted. She must have seen the shame and the disgust in his eyes. And he saw the loss of all his hopes in hers. She taunted him with his sexual failure. She told him that he was as useless to her as his father had been. I think it was at that moment when she lay there, half naked on the bed, smiling up at him, mocking him and his dead father together, destroying all his hopes, that his control snapped. He seized the jewel casket, the only weapon to hand, and brought it down."

"And after that?"

"Can't you guess? I told him precisely what he must do. I schooled him in his story to the police. He was to say that he'd gone to swim after lunch as he had told us all that he would. He'd walked along the beach until about an hour after the end of the meal and had then entered the water. He had started off back to the castle at about a quarter to three to dress for the play. I made sure that he had it by heart. I took him into Clarissa's bathroom and washed off the small spot of blood. Then I dried the basin with toilet paper and flushed it down the W.C. I found the newspaper cutting. It didn't take long. Her handbag or the jewel box were the two obvious places. Then I took him next door and instructed him how to get down the fire escape from your bathroom window, being careful not to touch any of the rungs with his hands. He was like a dutiful child, obedient, extraordinarily calm. I watched while he managed the fire escape, carrying the box under his arm, then as he went to the edge of the cliff and hurled it out to sea as I'd instructed him. And if the police do succeed in dredging it up, they'll find that the valuable jewels are missing. I took them out and flung them into another part of the sea. Forgive me if I don't demonstrate my confidence in you by saying precisely where. But it would never have done if all that the police found missing in the casket was one reputed sheet of newsprint. Then he dived and I watched him strike out strongly toward the west cove."

"But someone else was watching, too: Munter from the tower-room window, the only window which overlooks the fire escape."

"I know. He managed to make that plain to us in his drunken ramblings when Simon and I were helping him to his room. It wouldn't have mattered. Munter was absolutely safe. I told Simon not to let it worry him. Munter would have taken any secret of mine to the grave."

Cordelia said, "He took it to the grave conveniently early. And could you really trust a drunkard?"

"I could trust Munter, drunk or sober. And I didn't kill him. Nor, as far as I know, did Simon. That death, at least, was accidental."

"What did you do next?"

"I had to work quickly. But the haste and the risk were remarkably stimulating. My plotting of this real-life mystery was almost as ingenious as it was in *Autopsy.* I cleaned the makeup from Clarissa's face so that the police wouldn't suspect that she'd invited a visitor to her room. Then I set out to destroy the evidence of how precisely she was killed and to substitute a weapon which Simon couldn't have brought with him because he didn't know it existed, a weapon which would deceive the police into thinking that the murder was connected with the threatening quotations. I didn't tell Simon what I proposed and didn't touch the body until he'd left. His ignorance was his greatest safeguard. He didn't have to act or pretend. He knew nothing about the marble. He never saw Clarissa's shattered face."

"And you had the limb with you, I suppose, in the inside pocket of your cloak?"

"I had both of them ready, the marble and the note. I was intending to put them in the casket which Clarissa would open in the second scene of act three. It would have had to be done under cover of the cloak and at the last minute, requiring some sleight of hand. But I think I might have managed it. And I assure you the result would have been spectacular. I doubt whether she would have got through the scene."

"And is that why you took the job of assistant stage manager and occupied yourself with the props?"

"That's why. It was natural enough. People assumed that I wanted to keep an eye on my belongings."

"And after you'd destroyed Clarissa's face, I suppose you took Simon's clothes to the cove, also hiding them under your cloak."

"How well you understand duplicity, Cordelia. I should have liked to leave them farther down the shore, but there wasn't time. The small cove beyond the terrace was as far as I could manage. And then I entered the theater by the arcade and checked the props with Munter. I should mention that I didn't have to worry unduly about fingerprints when I was in Clarissa's room. This is my house. The furniture and the objects, including the marble, belong to me. It was perfectly reasonable that they should bear my prints. But I did wonder about my palm print on the communicating door. That could have shown that I was the last person to touch it. That's why I took good care to open it after we found the body."

"And the threatening quotations, you sent those, too? You took over when Tolly stopped?"

"So you know about Tolly. I think I've underestimated you, Cordelia. Yes, it wasn't difficult. Poor Tolly took to religion as an opiate for grief, and I continued the good work but in a rather more artistic form. It was only then that Clarissa called the police. It wasn't a development I welcomed, so I suggested a little ploy to her that effectively scotched their interest. Clarissa really was an extraordinarily stupid woman. She had instinct but absolutely no intelligence. My success depended on two things about Clarissa: her stupidity and her terror of death. So when Tolly's little notes with their remarkably apt biblical reference to millstones around necks ceased, I initiated my own brand of unpleasantness with the occasional help of Munter. The object was, of course, to destroy her as an actress and give me back my privacy, my peaceable island. It was only as an actress that Clarissa had any power over me. She would never return to Courcy if its theater was the scene of her final humiliation. Once her confidence and her career were effectively and totally destroyed, I should be free. To do her justice, she wasn't a common blackmailer. She didn't need to be. She first saw that newspaper cutting in 1977. Clarissa liked to pamper her ego with discreditable secrets about her friends, and this was one she hugged to herself for three years before she needed to make use of it. It was my bad luck that the restoration of the theater and the crisis in her career should coincide. Suddenly there was something she wanted of me. And she had the means to get it. I assure you that the blackmail was carried out with the greatest delicacy and discretion."

Suddenly he leaned toward her and said, "Look, Cordelia, it isn't going to be possible to shield him for much longer. He's beginning to drink. You must have seen it. And he's making mistakes. That gaffe which Roma noticed, for example. How could he have known what the jewel box was like if he hadn't seen or handled it? And there will be others. I like the boy and he's not without talent. I've done all I can to save him. Clarissa destroyed his father, and I didn't see why she should add the son to her list of victims. But I was wrong about him. He hasn't the guts to see this through. And Grogan is no fool."

"Where is he now?"

"I told you. In his room as far as I know."

She looked into his face, at the smooth, womanish skin burnished by the light of the fire, the eyes like black coals, the perpetually half-smiling mouth. She felt the persuasive force flowing toward her, rooting her into the comfort of her chair. And then, as if the claret had mysteriously cleared her mind, she knew exactly what he was doing. The careful explanations, the wine, the almost companionable chat, the seductive comfort folded like a shawl around her tiredness; what were they but a ploy to waste time, to keep her at his side? Even the place had conspired with him against her: the cheerful domesticity of the fire, the sense of unreality induced by the long restless shadows, the windows wide to the disorienting blackness of the night and the ceaseless sleep-inducing susurration of the sea.

She snatched up her shoulder bag and ran from the room, through the echoing hall, up the wide staircase. She flung open the door of Simon's bedroom and switched on the light. The bed was made, the room empty. She fled like a wild creature from room to empty room. Only in one did she see a human face. In the soft glow of his bedside lamp, Ivo was lying on his back, staring at the ceiling. As she came up to him he must have sensed her desperation. But he smiled sadly and gave a small rueful shake of the head. There was no help here.

There was still the tower to search, that and the theater. But perhaps he wasn't any longer in the castle. The whole island was open to him, cliffs and uplands, meadows and woodlands, the black unsearchable island holding like a shell in its dark intricacies the everlasting murmur of the sea. There was still the business room and the kitchen quarters, unlikely as it was that he had taken refuge there. She sped down the tiled passage and flung herself at the business-room door. And then she stood, arrested. The second display cabinet, the one which held the small mementos of Victorian crime and horror, had been violated. The glass had been smashed. Staring down, she saw that something was missing: the handcuffs. And then she knew where she would find Simon.

# VIII

She flung her shoulder bag on the desk of the business room, taking with her only her pocket torch. There was only one other thing she wished to have, the leather belt. But it was no longer around her waist. Somewhere and somehow during the day's activities she had lost it. She had a memory of hurriedly putting it on in the women's cloakroom of a chain store where she had stopped on her way to Benison Row. In her anxiety to find Miss Costello she must have buckled it insecurely. As she ran across the lawn and into the darkness of the wood, she wished that she still felt the reassuring strength of that private talisman clasped around her waist.

The church loomed before her, numinous and secret in the moonlight. No lights shone from the open door, but the faint gleam from the east window was enough to light her to the crypt even without the aid of her pocket torch. And that door, too, was open with the key in the lock. Ambrose must have told him where it could be found. The strong, dusty smell of the crypt came up to meet her. She didn't pause to find the switch but followed the shifting pool of light from her pocket torch past the rows of domed skulls, the grinning mouths, until it shone on the heavy iron-bound door which led to the secret passage. This too was open.

She dared not run; the passage was too twisting, the ground too uneven. She remembered that the passage lights were on a time switch and pressed each button as she passed, knowing that in a few minutes the lights would go out behind her, that she was moving from brightness into the dark. The way seemed interminable. Surely that small party, only two days earlier, hadn't traveled as far as this. She had a moment of panic, fearing that she might have found and taken a hidden turning and be lost in a maze of tunnels. But then she saw the second flight of steps, and there gleamed before her the low-roofed cavern above the Devil's Kettle. The single bulb suspended in its protective grille was shining steadily. The trapdoor was up, the lid resting against the wall of the cave. Cordelia knelt and gazed down into Simon's face. It strained up at her, the eyes wide and staring, the whites showing, like the eyes of a terrified dog. His left arm was stretched above his head, the wrist handcuffed to the top rail. His hand drooped from the bar of the handcuff, not the strong hand she remembered coming down on the piano keys, but as tender and pale as the hand of a child. And the steadily rising water, flapping like black oil against the cave walls and glazed with light from the cavern above, was already up to his shoulders.

She climbed down beside him. The cold cut her thighs like a knife. She said, "Where's the key?"

"I dropped it."

"Dropped it or threw it? Simon, I have to know where."

"I just dropped it."

Of course. He would have no need to hurl it far. Handcuffed and helpless as he was, he couldn't retrieve it now, however close it lay and however tempted or desperate he might be. She prayed that the bottom of the cave would be rock, not sand. She had to find the key. There was no other way. Her mind had already done its rapid calculation. Five minutes to get back to the castle, another five to return. And where would she find a tool box, a file sufficiently strong to cut through the metal? Even if there were someone in the castle able and willing to help her, there still wasn't time. If she left him now she would be leaving him to drown.

He whispered, "Ambrose told me I'd be in prison for the rest of my life. That or Broadmoor."

"He lied."

"I couldn't stand it, Cordelia! I couldn't stand it!"

"You won't have to. Manslaughter isn't murder. You didn't mean to kill her. And you aren't mad." But how clearly the words of Ambrose fell into her mind. "Who's to say what he meant? She's just as dead, isn't she, whatever he meant?"

Any additional light was welcome. She switched on her torch, resting it on the top rung. Then she gulped in a lungful of air and lowered herself carefully under the gently heaving surface. It was important not to disturb the sea bed more than she could help. The water was icy cold and so black that she could see nothing. But she felt with her hands, scraping them along the bottom, feeling the gritty sand, the spurs of sharp unyielding rock. A swath of seaweed wound itself around her arm like a soft detaining hand. But her slowly creeping fingers found nothing that could have been the key.

She came up for air and gasped, "Show me where exactly you dropped it."

He whispered through his bloodless, chattering lips, "About here. I held my right hand out like this. Then I let it fall."

She cursed her folly. She should have taken more trouble to discover the exact place before disturbing the sand. Now she might have lost it forever. She had to move gently and slowly. She had to stay calm and take her time. But there wasn't any time. Already the water was up to their necks.

She lowered herself again, trying methodically to cover the area he had indicated, letting her fingers creep like crabs over the surface of the sand. Twice she had to come up for air and see briefly the horror and the despair in those staring eyes. But on the third attempt her hand found the stub of metal and she brought up the key.

Her fingers were so cold that they felt lifeless. She could hardly grasp the key and was terrified that she might drop it, that she might not be able to fit it into the lock.

Watching her shaking hands, he said, "I'm not worth it. I killed Munter, too. I couldn't sleep and I was there, in the rose garden. I was there when he fell in. I could have saved him. But I ran away so that I wouldn't have to look. I pretended that I hadn't seen, that I hadn't been near."

"Don't think about that now. We've got to get you out of here, get you warm again."

The key was in the lock at last. She was fearful that it might not work, that it might not even be the right key. But it turned easily enough. The bar of the handcuff loosened. He was free.

And then it happened. The trapdoor crashed down in an explosion of sound as physical as a blow cleaving their skulls. The noise seemed to thunder through the island, shaking the iron ladder under their rigid hands, lifting the water at their throats, and bursting it against the walls of the cave in a tidal wave of concentrated fury. It seemed that the cave itself must split open to let in the roaring sea. The burning flashlight, dislodged from the top rung of the ladder, curved in a shining arc before Cordelia's horrified eyes, gleamed for a second under the swirling water, and then died. The darkness was absolute. And then, even before the echo of that crash had rumbled into silence, Cordelia's ears caught a different sound, the hideous rasp of metal against metal, once and then repeated, a noise so dreadful in its implication that she threw back her sea-drenched head and almost howled her protest into the blackness.

"Oh, no! Please God, no!"

Someone—and she knew who it must be—had kicked down the trapdoor. Someone's hand had shot home the two bolts. The killing ground had been sealed. Above them was unyielding wood, surrounding them the rock face, at their throats the sea.

She raised herself and pressed with all her strength against the wood. She bent her head and strained against it with her shoulders. But it didn't move. She knew that it wouldn't. She was aware of Simon dragging himself up beside her, of his palms beating ineffectually against it. She couldn't see him. The darkness was as thick and heavy as a blanket, an almost palpable weight against her chest. He was aware only of his terrified moans, long drawn out and tremulous as the waiting sea, of the rank smell of his fear, of the harsh indrawing of his breath, of a thudding heart which could have been his or hers. She reached out for him with her hands. They moved in what was meant to be comfort over his wet face, knowing only by their warmth which of the drops were seawater and which were tears. She felt his trembling hands on her face, her eyes, her mouth. He said, "Is this death?"

"Perhaps. But there's still a chance. We can swim for it."

"I'd rather stay here and have you close to me. I don't want to die alone."

"It's better to die trying. And I won't try without you."

He whispered, "I'll try. When?"

"Soon. While there's still air enough. You go first. I'll be behind you."

It was better for him that way. The first one through would have an easier passage, unhampered by the leader's thrusting feet. And if he gave up, there was the hope that she might have the strength to push him through. For a second she wondered how she would cope if the passage narrowed and his inert body blocked her escape. But she put the thought away from her. He was now less strong than she, weakened by cold and terror. He must go first. The water was now so high that only a fragile ribbon of light marked the exit. Its beam lay pale as milk on the dark surface. With the next wave that, too, would go and they would be trapped in utter darkness with nothing to point the way out. She tugged off her waterlogged jersey. They let go of the ladder, joined hands, and paddled to the middle of the cave where the roof was highest, then turned on their backs and gulped in their long last lungfuls of air. The rock face almost scraped Cordelia's forehead. Water, cool and sweet, fell on her tongue like the last taste of life. She whispered, "Now," and he let go of her hand without hesitation and slid under the surface. She took her final gulp of air, twisted, and dived.

She knew that she was swimming for her life, and that was almost all she knew. It had been a moment for action, not for thought, and she was unprepared for the darkness, the icy terror, the strength of the inflowing tide. She could hear nothing but a pounding in her ears, feel nothing but the pain above her heart and the black tide against which she fought like a desperate and cornered beast. The sea was death, and she struggled against it with all she could muster of life and youth and hope. Time had no reality. It could have been minutes, even hours, that passage through hell, yet it must have been counted in seconds. She wasn't aware of the thrashing body in front of her. She had forgotten Simon, forgotten Ambrose, forgotten even the fear of dying in the struggle not to die. And then, when the pain was too great, her lungs bursting, she saw the water above her lighten, become translucent, gentler, warm as blood, and she thrust herself upward to the air, the open sea, and the stars.

So this was what it was like to be born, the pressure, the thrusting, the wet darkness, the terror, and the warm gush of blood. And then there was light. She wondered that the moon could shed so warm a light, gentle and balmy as a summer day. And the sea, too, was warm. She turned on her back and floated, arms widespread, letting it bear her where it would. The stars were companionable. She was glad they were there. She laughed aloud at them in her joy. And it wasn't in the least surprising to see Sister Perpetua there bending over her in her white coif. She said, "Here I am, Sister. Here I am."

How strange that Sister should be shaking her head, gently but firmly, that the coiffed whiteness should fade and that there should be only the moon, the stars, and the wide sea. And then she knew who and where she was. The struggle still wasn't over. She had to find the strength to fight this lassitude, this overwhelming happiness and peace. Death, which had failed to seize her by force, was creeping on her by stealth.

And then she saw the sailing boat gliding toward her on the moonlit stream. At first she thought that it was a sea phantom born of her exhaustion and no more tangible than the white-coiffed face of Sister Perpetua. But it grew in form and solidity, and as she turned toward it she recognized its shape and the tousled head of its owner. It was the boat which had brought her back to the island. She could hear it now, the swish of the waves under the keel, the faint creaking of wood, and the hiss of the air in its sail. And now the stocky figure was standing back against the sky to fold the canvas in his arms and she heard the splutter of the engine. He was maneuvering to draw alongside. He had to drag her aboard. The boat lurched, then steadied. She was aware of a sharp pain dragging at her arms. And then she was lying on the deck and he was kneeling beside her. He seemed unsurprised to see her. He asked no questions, only pulled off his jersey and folded it around her.

When she could speak she gasped, "Lucky for me you were still here."

He nodded toward the mast and she saw, buckled around it like a talisman, the narrow strip of leather.

"I was coming to bring you that."

"You were bringing me back my belt!"

She didn't know why it was so funny, why she had to fight the impulse to break into wild hysterical laughter.

He said easily, "Oh, well, I had a fancy to land on the island by moonlight, and Ambrose Gorringe is none too keen on trespassers. I had it in mind to leave the belt on the quay. I reckoned you'd find it soon enough in the morning."

The moment of incipient hysteria had passed. She struggled upright and gazed back at the island, at the dark mass of the castle, as impregnable as rock, all its lights extinguished. And then the moon arrived from behind a cloud and suddenly it glowed with magic, each separate brick visible yet insubstantial, the tower a silver fantasy. She gazed enchanted at its beauty. And then her numbed brain remembered. Would he be watching for her, there on his citadel, binoculars raised, eyes scanning the sea for her bobbing head? She could picture how it might have been: her exhausted body dragging itself ashore through the squelch of the shingle and the drag of the receding waves, her bleared eyes looking up only to meet his implacable eyes, his strength confronting her weakness. She wondered if he could have brought himself to kill in cold blood. She thought that it would have been difficult for him. Perhaps it would have been impossible. How much easier to kick shut the trapdoor, to shoot back the bolts and leave the sea to do your work for you. She remembered Roma's words: "Even his horror is second-hand." But how could he have let her live, knowing what she did?

She said, "You saved my life."

"Saved you a bit of a swim, that's all. You'd have made it. You're close enough to the shore."

He didn't ask why, almost naked, she should be swimming at such an hour. Nothing seemed to surprise or disconcert him. And it was only then that she remembered Simon. She said urgently, "There are two of us. There was a boy with me. We've got to find him. He'll be here somewhere. He's a very strong swimmer."

But the sea stretched in a calm, moonlit emptiness. She made him wait and search for an hour, tacking slowly up and down the shoreline with the sails furled, the engine gently purring. She lay slumped against the gunwale and stared desperately, watching for any movement on the sea's calm face. But at last she accepted what she had known from the beginning. Simon had been a strong swimmer. But weakened by cold and terror and perhaps by some despair which went beyond them, he hadn't been strong enough. She was too tired now to feel grief. She was hardly aware even of disappointment. And then she saw that they were making slowly for the quay.

She said quickly, "Not to the island, to Speymouth."

"You'll be wanting a doctor, then?"

"Not a doctor, the police."

Still he asked no questions, but put the boat about. After a few minutes with warmth and energy flowing back into her limbs, she tried to get up and give him a hand. But she seemed to have no strength in her arms.

He said, "Better go into the cabin and get some rest."

"I'd rather stay here on deck if that's all right."

"You'll not be in my way."

He fetched a pillow and a heavy coat from the cabin and tucked her up beside the mast. Looking up at the pattern of unregarding stars, hearing the flap of the canvas as the boom swung over, and soothed by the swish of the waves under the slicing hull, Cordelia wished that the journey could go on forever, that this respite of peace and beauty between the horror passed and the trauma to come might never end.

And so in a companionable silence they sailed together toward the harbor, feeling the peace of the night flowing between them. Cordelia must have slept. She was dimly aware of the boat gently bumping the quay, of being carried ashore, of his hands under her breasts, of the strong sea smell of his jersey, of a heart beating strongly against her own.

# IX

The next twelve hours remained in Cordelia's memory only as a confused impression of time passing but disoriented, of a limbo in which individual pictures and people stood out with startling and unnatural clarity as if a clicking camera had spasmodically recorded them, fixing them instantaneously and forever in all their capricious banality.

A huge teddy bear on the desk at the police station, humped against the wall at the end of the counter, squint-eyed, with a tag around its neck. A cup of strong, sweet tea slopping into the saucer. Two sodden biscuits disintegrating into mush. Why should they produce so clear an image? Chief Inspector Grogan in a blue jersey with frayed cuffs wiping egg off his mouth, then looking down at his handkerchief as if sharing her wonder that he should be eating so late. Herself huddled in the back of a police car and feeling the rough tickle of a blanket on her face and arms. The foyer of a small hotel, smelling of lavender furniture polish, with a lurid print of the death of Nelson above the desk. A cheerful-faced woman, whom the police seemed to know, half supporting her up the stairs. A small back bedroom with a brass bedstead and a picture of Mickey Mouse on the lamp shade. Waking in the morning to find her jeans and shirt neatly folded on the bedside chair and turning them over in her hands as if they belonged to someone else; thinking that the police must have gone back to the island the night before and how odd they hadn't taken her with them. One old man silently sharing the breakfast room with her and two women police officers, paper napkin tucked into his collar, a vivid red birthmark covering half his face. The police launch butting its way across the bay against a freshening wind with herself, like a prisoner under escort, wedged between Sergeant Buckley and a policewoman in uniform. A sea gull hovering above them with its strong curved beak, then dropping to settle on the prow like a figurehead. And then a picture which jerked all the unrealities into focus, brought back all the horror of the previous day, and clamped it around her heart like a vise: the solitary figure of Ambrose waiting for them on the quay. And among all these disjointed images there was the memory of questions, endless repetitive questions, of a ring of watching faces, of mouths opening and shutting like automatons. Afterward she could recall every word of the dialogue although the place had slipped forever from her mind, whether it had been the police station, the hotel, the launch, the island. Perhaps it had been all of those places and the questions had been asked by more than one voice. She seemed to be describing events that had happened to someone else, but to someone she knew very well. It was all clear in the mind of that other girl, although it had happened so long ago, years ago, so it seemed when Simon had been alive.

"Are you sure that when you first arrived at the trapdoor it was up?"

"Yes."

"And the door itself resting back against the wall of the passage?"

"It must have been if the trapdoor was open."

"If? But you said it was open. You're sure you didn't open it yourself?"

"Quite sure."

"How long were you with Simon Lessing in the cave before you heard it crash down?"

"I can't remember. Long enough to ask about the key to the handcuffs, to dive and find it, to set him free. Less than eight minutes perhaps."

"Are you sure that the trapdoor was bolted? Did you both try to lift it?"

"Me at first; then he joined me. But I knew it wasn't any good. I heard the scrape of the bolts."

"Is that why you didn't try very hard, because you knew that it wasn't any good?"

"I did try hard. I pressed my shoulders against it. I suppose it was a natural reaction, to try. But I knew it wasn't any use. I heard the bolts being shot home."

"You heard that small sound against the rush of the incoming tide?"

"There wasn't very much noise in the cave. The tide spouted in quietly like water into a kettle. That's what was so frightening."

"You were frightened and you were cold. Are you sure you would have had the strength to push open the door if it had fallen accidentally?"

"It didn't fall accidentally. How could it? And I heard the bolts."

"One or two?"

"Two. The scrape of metal against metal. Twice."

"You realize what that means? You understand the importance of what you're saying?"

"Of course."

They made her go back with them to the Devil's Kettle. It was neither kind nor merciful; but, then, they weren't in the business of being kind or merciful. There were bright lights trained on the trapdoor, a man kneeling and dusting it for prints with the careful delicate strokes of a painter. Then they raised it, not resting it against the rock face but balancing it upright on its hinges. They stood back and, after no more than a couple of seconds, it crashed down. She shivered like a puppy, remembering another such crash. They asked her to raise it. It was heavier than she had expected. Underneath was the iron ladder leading down to death, the ray of bright daylight shining from a crescent exit, the slap of dark, strong-smelling water against the rock. They even made her go down, then shut the trapdoor gently over her. As they had instructed, she pushed her shoulders against it and was able without much strength to force it open. One of the officers climbed down into the cave and they closed the trapdoor and gently shot back the bolts. She knew that they were testing how much she could have heard. Then they asked her to balance the trapdoor on its hinges and she tried but couldn't. They asked her to try again, and when she failed they said nothing. She wondered if they thought that she wasn't trying. And all the time she saw, in her mind's eye, Simon's drowned body with its gaping mouth and glazed eyes, turning and twisting, sucked to and fro like a dead fish in the ebbing tide.

And then she was sitting in a corner of the terrace, alone except for the unspeaking, unsmiling woman police officer, waiting beside the police launch which would take her away from the island forever. Her typewriter and hand baggage were at her feet. There was still a wind but the sun had come out. She could feel its comforting warmth on her back and was grateful. She had thought that, since yesterday, she would never be warm again.

A shadow fell across the stones. Ambrose had come up silently to stand beside her. The waiting policewoman was out of earshot, but he spoke as if she were not there, as if they were totally alone. He said, "I missed you last night. I was worried about you. The police tell me that they found a hotel for you. I hope that it was comfortable."

"Comfortable enough. I can't remember much about it."

"You've told them everything, of course. Well, that's obvious from the mixture of coolness, speculation, and slight embarrassment with which they've regarded me since they made their untimely if not unexpected visit late last night."

"Yes, I've told them."

"I can almost smell their exhilaration. It's understandable. If you aren't lying or mistaken or mad, they're onto a very good thing. Promotion gleams like the Holy Grail. They haven't arrested me, as you see. The situation is unusual, requiring tact and care. They'll take their time. At the moment I imagine that they're still testing the trapdoor, trying to decide whether it could have crashed down accidentally, whether you really could have heard the bolts shot home. After all, when they returned here last night, in a state I might say of some excitement, they found the trapdoor closed but not bolted. And I don't think they'll get any identifiable prints from the bolts, do you?"

Suddenly she felt an immense and overpowering anger, almost cosmic in its intensity as if one fragile female body could hold all the concentrated outrage of the world's pitiable victims robbed of their unvalued lives. She cried, "You killed him, and you tried to kill me. Me! Not even in self-defense. Not even out of hatred. My life counted for less than your comfort, your possessions, your private world. My life!"

He said with perfect calmness, "If that's what you believe, a certain resentment is reasonable. But you see, Cordelia, what I'm saying to the police and to you is that it didn't happen. It isn't true. No one tried to kill you. No one shot back those bolts. When you reached the trapdoor you found it closed. You raised it just wide enough to slide through and climb down to Simon, but you didn't prop it up completely. You closed that door after you; either that or you partly raised it and it accidentally fell. You were terrified, you were cold and you were exhausted. You hadn't the strength to shift it."

"And what about the motive, the photograph in the *Chronicle?*"

"What photograph? It was unwise of you to leave it in your shoulder bag on the business room table. A natural oversight in your anxiety about Simon, but highly convenient for me. Don't tell me you haven't yet discovered that it's missing."

"The police are checking with the woman who gave it to me. They'll know that I did have a press cutting. Then they'll begin searching for a duplicate."

"Which they'll be lucky to find. And even if they do and the copy, after four years, is as clear as the one you so carelessly lost, I shall still have my defense. Obviously I have a double somewhere. Is that so unusual? Finding any real proof that I was in the United Kingdom in 1977 will get more difficult with every month that passes. In a year or so I should have felt safe even from Clarissa. And even if they can prove I was here that doesn't make me a murderer or a murderer's accomplice. Simon Lessing's death was suicide and it was he, not I, who killed Clarissa. He confessed the truth to me before he disappeared. He fractured her skull, beat her face to a pulp in his hatred and disgust, then made his escape through the bathroom window. And last night, unable any longer to face the truth of what he'd done or its consequences, he tried to kill himself. Despite your heroic attempt to save him, he succeeded. It was fortunate that he didn't take you with him. I had no hand in any of it. That, Cordelia, is my story, and nothing you choose to fabricate can disprove it."

"Why should I want to fabricate? Why should I lie?"

"That's what the police asked me. I had to reply that the imagination of young women is notoriously fertile and that you had, after all, been through an appalling experience. I added that you are the proprietress of a detective agency which—forgive me, I'm judging from externals—isn't exactly prospering. You'd have to spend a fortune to get the kind of publicity that this case will bring you if it ever comes to trial."

"Hardly the kind of publicity anyone would want. Failure."

"Oh, I wouldn't be too depressed about that. You showed admirable courage and intelligence. 'Above the call of duty' is how poor George Ralston would put it. I think that George will feel that he's had value for money." He added, "If you persist in going on with this, it will be my word against yours. Simon's dead. Nothing can touch him further. It isn't going to be comfortable for either of us."

Did he think that she hadn't thought of that, of the long months of waiting, the interrogations, the trauma of the trial, the speculative eyes, the verdict which could brand her as a liar, or worse, a publicity-crazed hysteric? She said, "I know. But, then, I'm not much used to comfort."

So he was going to make a fight for it. Even as he watched her rescue last night he must have been planning, scheming, perfecting his lies. He would use every ounce of his skill, his reputation, his knowledge, his intelligence. He would hold onto his private kingdom until his last breath. She glanced up at him, at the half smile, the calm, almost exultant confidence. Already he was rejoicing in the release from boredom, buoyant with the euphoria of success. He would buy the best advice, the most prestigious lawyers. But essentially it would be his fight and he wouldn't yield an inch now or later.

If he succeeded, how would he live with the memory of what he had done? Easily enough. As easily as Clarissa had lived with the memory of Viccy's death, Sir George with his guilt over Carl Blythe. You didn't need to believe in the sacrament of penance to find expedients for coping with guilt. She had hers; he would contrive his. And was it so very remarkable, what had happened to him? Somewhere, every minute of every day, a man or woman is suddenly faced with an overwhelming temptation. It had gone ill with Ambrose Gorringe. But what had he been able to draw upon at the core of his being which could give him the strength to resist? Perhaps if you opted out long enough from human concerns, from human life with all its messiness, you opted out also from human pity.

She said, "Please leave me. I want you to go away."

But he didn't move. After a moment she heard him say, quietly and gently, "I'm sorry, Cordelia. I'm sorry." And then, as if aware for the first time of that silent uniformed watcher, he added, "Your first visit to Courcy Island hasn't been as happy for you as I hoped. I wish it could have been otherwise. Please forgive me."

She knew that this was the only admission that he would ever make. It had no validity in law. It would never be given in evidence. But she believed, almost despite herself, that it had been sincere.

She watched him as he walked briskly toward his castle. At the doorway Chief Inspector Grogan appeared and moved out to meet him. Without speaking they went inside together.

Still she sat and waited. A uniformed officer, painfully young and with the face of a Donatello angel, came across to her. He blushed and said, "There's a telephone call for you, Miss Gray. In the library."

Miss Maudsley was trying hard not to sound fussed, but her voice was close to panic. "Oh, Miss Gray, I do hope it's all right to call you. The young man who answered said that it was. He was so helpful. But I wondered when you'll be coming home. There's a new case just in. It's terribly urgent, a lost Siamese kitten, a seal point. It belongs to a child who is just out of hospital after her leukemia treatment and she's had it only a week. It was a coming-home present. She's dreadfully distressed. Bevis is at another audition. If I go there's no one to look after the office. And Mrs. Sutcliffe has just rung. Her Pekinese, Nanki-Poo, is lost again. She wants someone to go round at once."

Cordelia said, "Put a notice on the door to say that we'll be open at nine o'clock tomorrow. Then lock up and start looking for the kitten. Ring Mrs. Sutcliffe and tell her I'll call round this evening about Nanki-Poo. I'm just on my way to the inquest, but Chief Inspector Grogan will ask for an adjournment. It shouldn't take long. And then I'll catch the mid-afternoon train."

Putting down the receiver, she thought, And why not? The police would know where to find her. She wasn't yet free of Courcy Island. Perhaps she never would be. But she had a job waiting for her. It was a job that needed doing, one that she was good at. She knew that it couldn't satisfy her forever, but she didn't despise its simplicities; almost she welcomed them. Animals didn't torment themselves with the fear of death, or torment you with the horror of their dying.

They didn't burden you with their psychological problems. They didn't whine about their condition. They didn't surround themselves with possessions or live in the past. They didn't scream with pain because of the loss of love. They didn't expect you to lie for them. They didn't try to murder you.

She walked through the drawing room and out to the terrace. Grogan and Buckley were waiting for her, standing motionless, Grogan at the prow of the police launch, Buckley at the stern. In their still intensity they looked like unweaponed knights standing guardian over some fabled vessel, waiting to bear their king to Avalon. She paused and regarded them, feeling the concentrated gaze of their unwavering eyes, aware that the moment held a significance which all three recognized but which none of them would ever put into words. They were struggling with their own dilemma. How far could they rely on her sanity, her honesty, her memory, her nerve? How far dare they trust their reputations to her fortitude when the going got rough? How would she acquit herself if the case ever came to trial and she found herself standing in that loneliest of places, the witness box of the Crown Court? But she felt distanced from their preoccupations as if nothing that they could do or think or plan had any relevance to her. It would all pass as they and she would pass. Time would take their story and fold it with the half-forgotten legends of the island, Carl Blythe's lonely death, Lillie Langtry sweeping down the great staircase, the crumbling skulls of Courcy.

Suddenly she felt inviolate. The police would have to make their own decisions. She had already made hers, without hesitation and without a struggle. She would tell the truth, and she would survive. Nothing could touch her. She hitched her bag more firmly on her shoulder and moved resolutely toward the launch. For one sunlit moment it was as if Courcy Island and all that had happened during that fateful weekend was as unconcerned with her life, her future, her steadily beating heart, as was the blue uncaring sea.